A far...
re...

Bella Lucia

SECRETS REVEALED

A wealthy dynasty
An inheritance at stake
And four beautiful heroines about
to meet their matches!

The story continues in

THE BRIDES OF

Bella Rosa

Beauty and the Reclusive Prince
by Raye Morgan
Coming next month from
Mills & Boon® Romance

BRIDES OF

Bella Lucia

When William Valentine returned from the war, as a testament to his love for his beautiful Italian wife, Lucia, he opened the first Bella Lucia restaurant in London. The future looked bright and William had, he thought, the perfect family.

Now William is nearly ninety and not long for this world, but he has three top London restaurants with prime spots throughout Knightsbridge and the West End. He has two sons, John and Robert, and grown-up grandchildren on both sides of the Atlantic who are poised to take this small gastronomic success story into the twenty-first century.

But when William dies and the family fight to control the destiny of the Bella Lucia business, they discover a multitude of long-buried secrets, scandals, the threat of financial ruin – and ultimately two great loves they hadn't even dreamt of: the love of a lifelong partner – and the love of a family reunited…

BRIDES OF

Bella Lucia

SECRETS REVEALED

LINDA GOODNIGHT

TERESA SOUTHWICK

BARBARA MCMAHON

LIZ FIELDING

M&B™ and M&B™ with the Rose Device
are trademarks of the publisher.
Harlequin Mills & Boon Limited, Eton House,
18-24 Paradise Road, Richmond, Surrey TW9 1SR

BRIDES OF BELLA LUCIA: SECRETS REVEALED
© by Harlequin Books SA 2010

Married under the Mistletoe © Harlequin Books SA 2006
Crazy About the Boss © Harlequin Books SA 2006
The Nanny and The Sheikh © Harlequin Books SA 2006
The Valentine Bride © Harlequin Books SA 2006

Special thanks and acknowledgement are given to Linda Goodnight,
Teresa Ann Southwick, Barbara McMahon and Liz Fielding for their
contribution to the Brides of Bella Lucia series.

ISBN: 978 0 263 87894 3

25-0410

Harlequin Mills & Boon policy is to use papers that are
natural, renewable and recyclable products and made from
wood grown in sustainable forests. The logging and
manufacturing processes conform to the legal environmental
regulations of the country of origin.

Printed and bound in Spain
by Litografia Rosés S.A., Barcelona

MARRIED UNDER
THE MISTLETOE

LINDA GOODNIGHT

Winner of the RITA® Award for excellence in inspirational fiction, **Linda Goodnight** has also won the Booksellers' Best, ACFW Book of the Year and a Reviewers' Choice Award from *Romantic Times* magazine. Linda has appeared on the Christian bestseller list and her romance novels have been translated into more than a dozen languages. Active in orphan ministry, this former nurse and teacher enjoys writing fiction that carries a message of hope and light in a sometimes dark world. She and husband Gene live in Oklahoma. Readers can write to her at linda@lindagoodnight. com

To the children of Gorlovka Hope Orphanage
in Ukraine, who may never read the book
but who will benefit from its proceeds.
My prayers are with you.

CHAPTER ONE

IN HIS wildest fantasies, if he were given to such things, Daniel Stephens had never expected to be here, doing this.

He shifted the heavy canvas duffel bag from his shoulder to the pavement in front of the beautiful, light-washed building, slicked back a damp clutch of hair and gazed up at the Knightsbridge Bella Lucia Restaurant.

London pulsed around him, the genteel hum of the élite, the roar of buses, the swirling, thick moisture of a damp October night, all both familiar and foreign after so many years away.

This was his birth family's restaurant. One of three, if he understood correctly. Fabulously successful. Exclusive. Expensive.

His nostrils flared. Outward façades never impressed him much. To his way of thinking most were lies, like his own childhood, covering a multitude of sins. But he had to admit, the Valentine family had style.

A chic woman stepped out of a taxicab beside him, tucked her designer bag beneath her arm, and sailed past without a glance to enter the glass double-doors of the restaurant. Soft jazz wafted out briefly, then was sucked back inside as the doors vacuumed shut.

Daniel had blood here. Blood that hadn't claimed him or his twin until now when it no longer hurt so much to have no father, no extended family, no one to care. Now his father wanted him. Or so he said. People like John Valentine generally hid ulterior motives. If Daniel waited around awhile, he'd find out what his father was really after.

The notion of claiming John Valentine as father still rankled as much as Mrs Valentine's demand for a DNA test to prove it. He'd refused her request during his brief visit a week and a half ago and, furious, had returned to the familiar call of Africa. But his twin brother Dominic had obliged, proving once and for all that the father who had abandoned them before birth was a rich and respected man.

Now that his troublesome temper had cooled and he'd thought the matter over, Daniel was back. Not that he wanted anything from the family he didn't know or trust. Not at all. But he did want something he couldn't get in Africa. Money. Lots and lots of money.

But first, he needed a place to live. His father—and he used the word loosely—had all but insisted he stay here in the flat above the Knightsbridge restaurant.

Light rain patted against his cheeks. His lips twitched an ironic smile. Water. The most precious commodity on earth. One so abundant here in his native country and so desperately scarce in his adopted one. He'd spent his entire career trying to rectify that problem, but project funds always ran short at the worst possible times. Now he was determined to use his skills and contacts in the UK to change all that. Life's inequities had always bothered him.

He lifted the heavy duffel bag back onto his shoulder. Might as well go up. Introduce himself to the American restaurant manager who had somehow been persuaded to share her lodging with him. He still wondered how John had worked that one out, but the old man had assured him that the woman was not only in agreement but was delighted with the arrangement. After all, the flat was large and roomy and there was some sort of problem in the restaurant that might make a woman alone uneasy. He hadn't added, though Daniel was no fool, that the flat also belonged to the Valentine family and that Miss Stephanie Ellison had no real choice in the matter.

If not for his determination to sink every shilling he had into the new business and ultimately into the Ethiopian water project, he might have felt badly about intruding upon the restaurant manager. He might have. But he didn't.

Obsessing. Stephanie Ellison was obsessing. And she had to get a handle on it fast. She glanced at the stylish pewter clock above the sofa. Five minutes.

"Oh, Lord."

The pressure against her temples intensified.

She paced from one side of her flat to the other, stopping to straighten every piece of framed art, two fresh flower arrangements and a pewter bowl of vanilla potpourri. All useless, obsessive gestures.

The living room, like every other room in the luxury Knightsbridge flat, was immaculate. And why not? She had cleaned, re-cleaned, and triple-cleaned today. Even the cans in the kitchen cupboards were organized into groups according to the alphabet.

And yet the throb in her temple grew louder and her gut knotted as if something was out of order.

Something *was* out of order. Seriously out of order.

"But I can do this." She paced across the white-tiled floor and down the hall to her bedroom to assess her appearance—again. "Oh, why did John put me in this situation?"

Especially now, with the problems in the restaurant. Until the missing money was recovered, Stephanie needed to concentrate her attention there. After all, as manager she was ultimately responsible. But thanks to her employer, she had to deal with an even more dreaded scenario. An unwanted *male* flatmate.

A shudder rippled through her.

John Valentine had no way of knowing that thrusting his son upon her as a temporary roommate had the power to push her over the edge. John, like everyone else, knew nothing of the hidden shame that caused her to keep people at arm's length.

Oh, she was friendly enough. She'd learned from a master to put on a smile, keep her mouth shut, and play the game so that the world at large believed the masquerade instead of the truth.

That was why she'd never taken on a roommate. Brief visits by girlfriends such as Rebecca Valentine, yes. But a roommate? Never. Having someone invade her space for a few days was bad enough. A roommate was sheer terror.

Anyone who got too close might discover the truth. And she couldn't even face that herself.

Since hiring her a year ago as manager of the exclusive Knightsbridge restaurant, the Valentine family had given her carte blanche in remodeling and running the Bella Lucia. They'd even indulged her penchant for contemporary art décor. Her boss seldom interfered. Which was exactly why she hadn't been able to say no when he'd asked her to house the son who'd spent years doing charity work in Africa.

She chewed on that, allowing a seed of hope that Daniel Stephens was as noble as his work implied. From her boss's enthusiastic description, Daniel was one minor step below sainthood.

She laughed, though the sound was as humorless as the hammering in her head.

"A saint. Sure, he is. Like all men."

One other thing worried her. Actually, a lot of other things worried her. But in her flummoxed state, she'd failed to ask how long Daniel would be staying. With all her heart, she hoped not long. There was too much at stake to have him here indefinitely.

She swiveled around backwards, twisting her head to look at the slim, smooth line of her pale green dress. Everything was covered. Nothing showed. But she'd have to be extra careful with a flatmate lurking about. She hated that. Hated worrying that someone would discover the secret she kept hidden away beneath designer labels.

Someone tapped softly at the door.

Stephanie jumped, then gritted her teeth in frustration. She would not, could not, let anxiety take over. The willowy redhead staring back from the mirrored tub enclosure looked in complete control, unruffled, and well groomed. Good. As long as the outside appeared in control, let the inside rage.

She smoothed newly manicured hands down the soft, flowing skirt, realigned the toiletries on the counter for the third time, and went to greet her boss's son.

One look at the big, dark, wild-looking man filling up her foyer and Stephanie's heart slammed against her ribcage. The throbbing in her head intensified. Fight or flight kicked into high gear. Escape lay past him and down the elevator to the restaurant below. She had little choice but to stand and fight.

There had to be a mistake. This could not be Daniel. Mr Valentine had called him a boy, and, even though she had fully expected a grown man, she hadn't expected this… this…barbarian!

"My boy," John had said with an indulgent chuckle. "He's a tad rough around the edges. Too much time abroad living without the amenities of the civilized world."

A *tad* rough around the edges? A *tad*? That understatement was a record even for the British.

This was no boy. This was a motorcycle gang in battered jeans, bomber jacket and rough-out boots. A pirate with piercing blue eyes, stubble darkening his jaw and unruly black hair in need of a cut. She had expected him at the worst to resemble his twin brother, Dominic, who worked for her as a part-time accountant. But this man was nothing like harmless, middle-aged Dominic. There wasn't a bald spot or an ounce of fat anywhere on this guy. And he was anything but harmless.

Surely there was a mistake.

Another equally disturbing concern struck. If this was

Daniel, and she prayed he wasn't, could John have sent him to spy on her, suspicious that *she* was responsible for the money missing from the restaurant accounts?

Fighting panic and forcing a bland expression she didn't feel, Stephanie took a small step back. The stranger was too close, too threatening.

"Are you Daniel?"

One corner of his mouth quirked. "And if I say no?"

If he said no? What kind of introduction was that?

She blinked several times, then drew upon a glib tongue and a sharp mind to gloss over her real feelings. "Then I'll assume you're the plumber, at which rate you're five days late and fired."

He laughed, a quick flash of white teeth in a sun-burnished face. *Oh, my.*

"To save myself that indignity, I'll confess. I'm Daniel Stephens, your new flatmate."

She'd always enjoyed the British male voice with its soft burr in the back of the throat. But this man's voice was half purr, half gravel and all male, a sound that shimmied down her spine to the toes of her new heels.

Heaven help her. What had she agreed to? This could never work. Not even if she wanted it to. And she most decidedly did not. He was too rugged to be handsome and too blatantly male not to be noticed. And Stephanie did not notice men. Not anymore.

She couldn't meet his gaze but she couldn't take her eyes off him either.

Her silence must have gone on a bit too long because he said, "May I come in?"

Stephanie opened the door wider, determined to remain

as composed as possible under the circumstance. "Of course. Please."

She couldn't let him know how much his size and strength and sheer manliness unnerved her. She could handle him. Hadn't she determined long ago that no man would ever get close enough to hurt her again? Hadn't she rid herself of that fear by moving far, far away from Colorado?

"I'm afraid you caught me by surprise." A lie, of course. "The flat is…"

He poked his rather unkempt, and altogether too attractive head inside and finished her sentence. "Fine."

Her flat, like her person, was always ultra-clean and tidy. Outward appearances were everything. And having things out of place distressed her.

Stephanie turned and led the way to the living room. Her stomach jittered and her heart raced, but she was good at the pretense game.

Trouble was, it had been a while since she'd had to pretend quite this much. Or for quite this long. There was that troubling question again. How long would he be here?

Daniel's bulk filled up the large living room as if it were elevator-small. He glanced around with an unconcerned expression. The luxury of a flat that most could only dream of was apparently lost on him.

"Where should I stash my bedroll?" He swung the bag from his wide shoulder as if it contained nothing but packing peanuts. "Any place will do. A room, the floor, the couch. Makes no difference to me."

Well, it certainly made a difference to Stephanie.

"I've put you in the back guest room." She forced a smile. "I assure you, it's more comfortable than the floor."

And as far away from her room as possible.

She led the way down the short hall toward the back of the flat, pointing out the other rooms along the way.

"This is the kitchen here. You're welcome to make use of it anytime." She felt like a Realtor.

"I wouldn't think you'd need much of a kitchen with the restaurant below."

"A person tires quickly of too much rich food."

"I can't imagine."

She paused to look at him. Bad decision. "Are you making fun of me?"

"Am I?" Blue eyes glittered back at her, insolent eyes that challenged. Stephanie glanced away.

Perhaps her statement had been rude. The man *had* spent a lot of years in places where food such as that served in the Bella Lucia was unheard of.

He was the boss's son. She didn't want to get off on the wrong foot with him. "I apologize. I'm really not a snob. But you'll have to understand, I'm accustomed to living on my own." She pushed the door open to the last bedroom. "You have your own bathroom through here."

"Nice," he said, though his tone indicated indifference as he gazed from the sage and toast décor to the queen-sized bed and then to the pristine bathroom beyond. He tossed the duffel bag into a corner next to a white occasional table. "I can see you aren't nearly as happy to have me here as John thought you'd be."

Stephanie wasn't certain what to say to that. She loved her job and couldn't chance upsetting her generous employer.

"I'm sure we'll get on fine." She hovered in the

doorway, eager to have him settled, but equally eager to make her escape.

"I don't think you're sure of that at all."

He moved across the room in her direction. Stephanie resisted the urge to shrink back into the hallway.

"I don't know what you mean."

"Sure you do."

Before she knew what he was about, he touched her forearm. The gesture was harmless, meaning only to convey reassurance. It had just the opposite effect.

Try as she might to stand her ground, Stephanie flinched and pulled away, desperate to rub away the feel of his calloused fingers against her flesh.

Hand in mid-air, Daniel studied her, clearly bewildered by her overreaction.

"I meant no harm, Stephanie. You're quite safe with me here."

Right. As safe as a rabbit in a fox's den.

Forcing a false little laugh, she tried to make light of her jitters. "I'm sure all serial murderers say the same thing."

"Cereal murderers?" He dropped his hand and slouched against the door facing, too close for comfort. "Can't imagine harming an innocent box of cornflakes."

So, he had a sense of humor. She backed one step out into the hallway. "My oatmeal will be relieved to hear that."

"Ah, now, porridge. There's nothing innocent about horse feed cooked to the gooey consistency of wallpaper paste. I might be tempted to do in a few boxes of those, after all."

This time Stephanie laughed. For a barbarian, he displayed a pleasant sense of the ridiculous.

"There's tea in the kitchen if you'd like a cup." She started back down the hall.

"Sounds great. If you're having one too."

She hesitated in the living-room entry, not wanting to appear rude, but certainly not wanting to become friends. Her idea of a male friend was one that lived somewhere else. Preferably Mars.

The gravelly purr moved up behind her, too close again. "We might as well get acquainted, Stephanie. We're going to be living together."

She wasn't overly fond of that term, but it wouldn't do to offend the son of her employer. From the rumors astir in the restaurant, she knew Daniel and Dominic were John's only sons, the result of a fling he'd had as a young man. Though he'd only recently discovered their existence, Mr Valentine was trying hard to make up for lost time.

"All right, then. I have a few minutes." She really should go, get away from him while she could still carry on a lucid conversation. Trouble was he'd be here when she came back.

In the kitchen, she poured tea into two china cups and set them on the small breakfast bar.

Daniel, instead of taking a seat, made himself at home by rummaging about for milk and sugar. In the narrow kitchen, they bumped once. Stephanie shifted away, rounding the bar to sit opposite him. If Daniel noticed her avoidance, he didn't react.

Instead, he slouched into the straight-backed white chair and splashed a generous amount of milk into the cup. Stephanie had never embraced the English penchant for milk in her tea. She did, however, favor sugar. In abundance.

"Tsk. Tsk. Three sugars?" Daniel murmured when she'd doused her cup. "Bad girl."

An unwanted female reaction skittered through her. The words were innocent enough, but his sexy tone gave them new meaning. Either that or she was losing touch with reality.

She inclined her head. "Now you know."

A black eyebrow kicked upward. "Sweet tooth?"

"A decidedly evil one. Grabs me in the middle of the night sometimes." Why was she telling him this?

"You don't look the part." His laser-blue gaze drifted over her slim body, hesitating a millisecond too long.

"I jog. I also have enormous self-control." Like now, when I really want you out of my flat, but I can't say so.

"Don't tell me you never sneak down to the restaurant for cheesecake and chocolate sauce?"

She smiled in spite of herself. "How did you guess?"

Small crinkles appeared around his eyes. The African sun had been kind to him. "Because that's what I'd do if I lived over a restaurant."

"Which you now do." Unfortunately.

"But you hold the keys to the Bella Lucia."

She stirred the spoon round and round in her cup. "There is that."

"Think I can persuade you to make your midnight runs with me in tow?"

Perhaps not, big boy.

Without comment, she lifted her cup and sipped.

Daniel did likewise, eyelids dropping in a soft sigh of appreciation. Stephanie had a hard time not staring. Though she was loath to admit it, Daniel Stephens was a stunningly attractive man.

"Can't get tea like this where I've been," he said, clattering the cup onto the saucer.

"Tell me about Africa." As she'd done countless times, Stephanie slipped into hostess mode, tucking away real feelings to skim the surface of civilized conversation. "Your father's very proud of what you've done there."

His face, so full of pleasure moments before, closed up tight. "My father doesn't know a thing about my work."

And from the stormy look of him, Stephanie figured John might never know. Her boss might want to mend fences with his sons, but this one had some hostility that might not be so easily overcome.

Daniel's anger reminded her of the kids she sometimes worked with in special art classes. There, where she volunteered her time teaching troubled children to paint, she had learned to listen as well as to share simple techniques of line and color.

In the same quiet voice she used to encourage those kids, she said, "Would you tell me about it?"

Forearms on the table edge, he linked his fingers and leaned forward. Too close again. The man had an unpleasant habit of invading her space. Stephanie tilted back a few inches.

"The work is rewarding and equally frustrating," he said.

So he'd chosen to sidestep the issue of his father and move on to the safer ground of Africa. She didn't know why she'd felt compelled to dig into his personal life in the first place. The less she knew about him, the better.

"Is that why you quit?"

"I didn't quit. I'll never quit," he said vehemently. "But

I've finally realized that I can make more of a difference here than I can there."

She frowned, not following. "How?"

"To build sustainable, safe water systems takes money and expertise. I'm a civil engineer. I've spent my whole life dealing with the problem. I have the expertise. What I lack is that vulgar little commodity called money."

"So you're back in England to raise money, then."

"In a manner of speaking. I'm starting my own business, contracting water projects throughout England. The demand is high, especially in the area of flood control. A man who has the right skills and contacts can make a fortune."

Maybe he *was* as giving as John had indicated. "And you're planning to use that money to fund projects in Africa?"

"It's the best way I can think of." He shoved a hand over dark, unruly hair. "That's why I'm grateful to you for sharing this flat, and that's also why I agreed to the arrangement in the first place. I dislike accepting favors, particularly from my father, but the less spent on living expenses, the more I can spare for Ethiopia."

Despite her determination not to get too close, Stephanie's opinion of Daniel rose several notches. He had a caring heart, at least where the needy in Africa were concerned. This knowledge gave her hope that he would not be difficult to room with. If her luck held out, he would keep his distance until the business was started and he could afford his own place to live.

And this brought her to the question that had burned on her mind since that first telephone call from Mr Valentine. Just exactly how long would all that take? How long would she have this disturbing, intriguing, terrifying man living in her flat?

Because, for her own protection and peace of mind, the sooner he was gone, the better.

CHAPTER TWO

SURREPTITIOUSLY, Daniel watched the stunning red-haired woman from behind his teacup. The moment she'd opened the door he'd lost his breath, knocked out by the sheer beauty of her long legs, slim, shapely body, and the long, wavy just-got-out-of-bed hairstyle. Though her dress was mid-calf and modest, his first, very wayward thoughts had been of sex, a natural male reaction that he'd reined in right away. Mostly. He'd once had a penchant for redheads and, if his body's reaction was an accurate indicator, he still did. But he was here on business. And business it would remain.

A few minutes in her company, however, had told him what the old man hadn't. That she wasn't all that thrilled to have him here. But he was here and planned to stick around. And it didn't hurt at all that his flatmate was gorgeous and smelled incredible as well. He could look, but that was the end of it.

Long ago, he'd come to grips with his own shortcomings where women were concerned. He liked them, enjoyed their company, but he'd never been able to fall in love. After too many years, he'd finally faced reality.

Thanks to his mother, he lacked the capacity to love anybody.

"I need to get back down to the restaurant." Stephanie's teacup rattled against the saucer as she set it in place. "There's more tea if you want it."

"Thanks, but no. No time like the present to get started on the telephone contacts."

She reached for his cup and he handed it over.

"You should consider getting a mobile phone."

"Hmm. Possibly later." Right now he was conserving funds.

"I have a computer if you need one." She motioned toward the hall. "Sometimes I work on orders and supplies at night."

"I'll probably take you up on that." He pushed up from the chair and came around the bar to stand beside her at the sink. "Let me help with this."

Wariness flickered across her pretty face. "I have it."

"Okay." He backed off, wondering if his size intimidated her. She wouldn't be the first, though she reached his shoulders. He propped his backside against the blue granite counter several feet away from her. The tension eased.

With a grace that had him watching her hands, she washed the cups, dried them and placed them, handles aligned to the right, inside the cupboard. The orderliness of her flat was almost amusing. His idea of domestic order was keeping the mosquito net untangled around his face at night.

She tidied up, putting everything away until the kitchen looked as if no one lived there. In fact, the entire flat had that look. As if it were a photograph, a perfect, sophisticated, contemporary ad of an apartment. Not a lived-in place.

Folding a snowy tea-towel into a precise rectangle, she hung it neatly over a holder, straightening the edges while she spoke. "Is there anything else I can show you before I go? Anything you need?"

"I'm not a guest, Stephanie. No need for you to fret over me. I can find my way around." Hadn't he fended for himself as long as he could remember?

"Right. Of course." Her hands fidgeted with the edge of the towel. "I'd better go, then. The evening crowd begins soon."

"I may go out this afternoon myself. Do you have an extra key to the flat?"

She clasped the butterfly hands in front of her. "I'm sorry. I never thought of having another key made."

"Give me yours and I'll go to the locksmith."

"I'll get it." She looked none too excited about the prospect of sharing her key with him, but she disappeared down the hall and was back in moments, key extended. "This also fits the doors leading out onto the balcony. In case you didn't notice, there are two entrances to the flat. A staircase up the outside as well as the elevator in back of the restaurant."

"Good to know. Thanks." He pocketed the key, keeping watch on her fidgety movements. She'd relaxed somewhat since his arrival, but Daniel had the strongest feeling her tension was more than the normal discomfort of acquiring an unfamiliar flatmate. Though good breeding or schooling gave her the right words to say, her real feelings lay hidden behind the serenely composed expression. And yet, her hands gave her away.

With an inner shrug, he dismissed the idea. Stephanie's

problems were her own. He wasn't interested in getting past the pretty face and tantalizingly long legs. His business here was exactly that—business.

"You're welcome to come down to the restaurant later and get acquainted if you'd like," she said, heading for the door. "Some of your family may come round. They often do."

The comment brought him up short. He still had trouble thinking of the Valentines as family.

"Is Dominic working today?" He'd had little time with his twin since returning to England. Discovering that Dominic had become a part-time employee of the restaurant below added to the appeal of living here. They'd been apart a very long time.

Stephanie glanced at her watch. "He should be in his office about now. I'm sure he'd enjoy a visit."

And so would Daniel, though he was every bit as eager to begin setting up appointments. The list of contacts in his bag was impressive. With it, his business should be up and running in no time.

His flatmate was halfway out the door when she stopped and turned. "Oh, one more thing, Daniel."

"Yes?"

Cool aqua eyes assessed him. "If you don't mind my asking, how long are you planning to be here?"

"Why, Stephanie—" he playfully placed a hand over his heart "—I'm crushed. Already trying to get rid of me?"

"No, no, of course not. I didn't mean that at all. I was just thinking…"

He knew exactly what she was thinking, but he couldn't accommodate her. "New businesses take a while to get off the ground. A year. Perhaps longer." He watched her, hoping to gauge her true reaction, but she gave nothing away. "That won't be a problem, will it?"

"That will be…fine," she said.

Daniel didn't believe a word of it.

Several hours later, Daniel exited the tube in high spirits, returning to Knightsbridge after a successful afternoon. He'd found a locksmith to cut a new flat key and afterwards had spent an hour chatting up a former university mate about business prospects. All in all, a good beginning.

Above ground, the rain had begun in earnest. Though he'd failed to bring an umbrella, the smell of rain in the air and the feel of it on his skin were a pleasure after years in the African sun. He resisted the childish urge to lift his face and catch the drops on his tongue.

At the back door of the Bella Lucia, he shook himself off to spare the floors a puddle. A kitten, no bigger than his hand, meowed up at him in protest.

"Sorry there, little one." He scooped the ball of fluff into one hand and slid her inside his jacket while he looked about for a dry place. She snuggled close, a warm, damp ball against his shirt, and turned her motor on. Daniel spotted an overhang and withdrew the kitten from his jacket. She meowed again.

"Hungry?" he asked, crouching down to set her beneath the overhang. Her yellow eyes blinked at him. With a final stroke of the small head, he decided to steal a bite for her later, and then went inside the Bella Lucia to find his brother.

To the right of the wide entry were the lift and a door marked "Storage." On his left were the offices. Taking a guess, he tapped at the first one and went inside. Dominic sat at a desk, intently staring at a computer screen.

Daniel stood for a moment, observing his brother at work. Fraternal twins, they had once shared similarities, but now, beyond the blue eyes and tall stature, they bore little resemblance. Domestication and long hours in a high-pressure accounting firm had taken a toll on Dominic's once powerful physique.

"Careful there, brother. You'll be getting eye strain from all that hard work."

The balding head lifted with a smile and a brotherly jab. "No chance of that happening to you, now, is there, mate?"

"Not if I can avoid it," he joked in return. Hard work was all he'd ever known, as Dominic well knew.

A bit wearily, Dominic removed a pair of reading glasses and rubbed at his eyes. "Are you settled in, then? Finding the flat upstairs to your liking?"

Daniel flopped into a chair. "You know I don't care about the flat. Why didn't you warn me about my flatmate?"

"Warn you?" Humor glinted on Dominic's tired face. "About what?"

"That she was young and beautiful. And not nearly as willing to have me move in as John let on."

A slow smile crept up Dominic's cheeks. "You always were a sucker for redheads."

"Getting this business off the ground is my first priority. The flat is just a step in that direction."

"Then why is Stephanie a problem? Did she try to toss you out?"

"No, nothing like that." Quite the opposite, actually. "She was polite, accommodating." She'd put on the pretense of welcome, but her fidgety movements told a different story.

"Then what's the problem?"

He wasn't sure how to answer that one. "I make her nervous."

Dominic guffawed. "Look in the mirror. You make everyone nervous."

Daniel shoved a hand through his unruly hair. He never could figure out why his appearance concerned people. Just because he didn't care about the usual conventions of dress or style, people sometimes shied away. Or maybe it was the darkness. Dark skin, dark hair. Bad attitude.

But this wasn't the feeling he had with Stephanie. "I think the problem is deeper than the way I look."

"Shave. Get a haircut. See if that helps."

He'd skip that advice. Unlike his conservative, by-the-book twin, Daniel had never been a suit-and-tie kind of a man. Perhaps that was why he meshed with Africa so well. That, and the fact that Africa needed and appreciated him.

"Is there a boyfriend lurking around to punch my face for moving in with her?"

"I thought you weren't interested."

"I'm not dead either."

Dominic chuckled. "Good. You were starting to worry me."

"I gave up on love, not on life."

Dominic knew better than anyone about Daniel's empty heart.

"Sometimes they're one and the same."

The profound statement stirred the old restless longing,

the feeling that, no matter how much good he did, life was passing by without him.

"Are you going to annoy me about my nonexistent love-life or tell me about Stephanie Ellison?"

"Well, let's see." Dominic gnawed at the earpiece of his glasses, pretending to think. "She doesn't allow staff to smoke anywhere near the restaurant. Says it projects a bad image to the customers."

"That's not exactly the kind of information I meant."

"None of us know much about her before she came here. She's a mystery really."

A mystery. Hmm. Better steer clear of that. He had enough puzzles to solve with the new business. "What kind of manager is she? Demanding? Difficult to work for?"

Though Dominic had only been in this job just over a week, he was good at gathering information, a knack that also made him a good accountant. Most of the time he knew more about a company than the owner.

"Stephanie's a bit of a workaholic, a real control freak about tidiness," Dominic said, "but she treats employees well. She gives every appearance of being an excellent manager."

Daniel heard the subtle hesitation. "What do you mean by 'gives every appearance'?"

"Nothing really. She's doing a fine job." Dominic glanced away, fidgeted with his glasses. He was holding back.

"I know you, Dominic. What are you not saying?"

"I don't want to spread unsubstantiated rumors."

"I'm your brother. I've just moved in with the woman. If she's trouble, you have to tell me."

"All right, then, between you and me." He sighed and rolled a squeaky chair back from the desk. "You've heard about the money missing from the restaurant accounts?"

Daniel nodded, frowning. John had mentioned the problem. "You think Stephanie's involved?"

"No. I don't. Someone kind enough to take sick waiting staff to her flat, give them an aspirin and take over their shift while they rest isn't a likely thief. Plus, she's meticulous to the point of obsession about every detail of running this place. I can't see her dipping into the till."

"Yet, someone is responsible."

"Right. And she's the newcomer, the outsider."

"Not the only one," Daniel pointed out.

Dominic blinked, clearly shocked at the suggestion. "You think I—"

Daniel laughed. "Not in a million years." His straight-down-the-line brother was so honest, he'd often confessed to childhood mischief before being confronted. "Have you talked to John about it?"

"Actually, the first clue came from him. He asked me to balance the dates when the money disappeared with all the other transactions filtering in and out of the three restaurants. There were some interesting inconsistencies, but nothing definite yet."

"So what's your decision? Is our pretty manager guilty?"

"I'm still watching, but, like I said, I don't want to think Stephanie is involved. She isn't the type."

Daniel didn't think so either, though he barely knew the woman. He'd much rather believe her anxiety around him was personal than an embezzler's guilty conscience.

The idea gave him pause and, before he could stop the words, he asked, "What about her personal life? Does she see anyone?"

Dominic tossed his glasses onto the desk and tilted back, his gaze assessing. Daniel shifted in his chair. Okay, he'd admit it. He wanted to know about his flatmate as a woman, not as a restaurant manager.

"She goes out now and then, though the gossip mill says she never dates seriously."

"Why? Too busy with work?"

"That's my guess. But Rachel thinks she's had her heart broken."

"Rachel?" Daniel frowned. "Employee or relative?" He was having trouble keeping track.

"A cousin. Our uncle Robert's daughter. Her sister, Rebecca, is a close friend of Stephanie's. I think she may know more about your lovely manager than anyone."

"She's not *my* anything," Daniel groused. "I was just asking." And he didn't know why, so he decided to let the subject of his flatmate drop. "So, tell me about you, Dominic. How's the job? The family?"

Dominic's gaze flicked to the computer screen. He picked up a pen and twirled it in his fingers.

"Alice is pregnant again."

Daniel tried not to let the surprise show. Dominic looked stressed enough without being reminded that his other kids were nearly grown. "How many does this make? Four? Five?"

Daniel spent so little time in England that he couldn't keep up. Never fond of his brother's wife, he hadn't tried too hard. Alice's well-to-do family had vigorously protested when she had married a nobody like Dominic, and since then she had maintained an air of superiority that rankled Daniel.

"This makes four." Dominic ran a hand over his face, and Daniel noticed again how much his brother had aged. "Alice is thrilled. She thinks another baby will keep us young. And a new addition also gives her a reason to shop."

As if she needed one. Daniel remembered his sister-in-law's propensity for spending. Luckily, his brother had done so well that his family could afford the best of everything. They lived in a fashionable area of London. His children attended private school, and both Dominic and Alice drove a Mercedes. Holidays in Rome or Madrid or anywhere they fancied were the norm. Daniel was glad for his brother's success.

Dominic had only taken the extra position here at the restaurant as a way to get acquainted with the family he'd never known, and now to help ferret out the thief in the ranks. He certainly didn't need the money.

"What about you? How do you feel about a new baby?"

Dominic drew in a deep breath and let it slowly out. "Stunned. I never expected to be a father again at forty."

"Forty's not too old."

"Easy for you to say," Dominic said with a rueful grin. "You aren't losing your hair."

Daniel returned the grin. "Is Alice all right, then? The pregnancy going well?"

"Sure. Everything's fine. Great. You'll have to come to the house for dinner one night and see for yourself." He gave a self-conscious laugh. "Get that haircut first, though."

In other words, Alice would have a fit if her uncivilized brother-in-law embarrassed her in front of her friends.

"How about one night next week?" Dominic went on. "I'll invite John as well."

"I don't think so."

"Come on, Daniel. Don't be a hard case. We wanted a father all our lives and now we have one. He wants to get to know us."

Tension coiled in Daniel's gut. John Valentine was not his favorite subject. "He has a daughter—he adopted Louise; he wanted her. Why would he want to know us?"

"Because we're blood. You and I have a right to be in this family."

"Not according to Ivy." John's wife had thrown a fit to discover her husband had two sons with a former lover. "And maybe she has a point. Being adopted is better than being illegitimate." The word left a nasty taste in his mouth.

"Louise doesn't think so. She's very upset. She's even started one of those birth-parent searches. Has John worried sick. He says she's not herself at all."

"Do you blame her? This must be a terrible shock to her." It had been to him. And he blamed the parents, not the children. Though he'd only briefly met Louise, she seemed nice enough, a quiet, accommodating woman dedicated to her family. She didn't deserve to be blindsided by two long-lost brothers and the revelation that she had been adopted by John and Ivy Valentine.

"Maybe." Dominic lifted a doubting brow. "Maybe not."

"Meaning?"

"John phoned earlier, fretting over her as usual. Which is very bad for his heart, by the way, and she well knows that. Says Louise is planning to leave for Meridia tomorrow for some nonsense. A make-over, I think he called it, for Emma."

Daniel searched his memory banks but came up empty, sighing in resignation. "Am I supposed to know Emma?"

"Cousin. Yet another of Uncle Robert's numerous offspring. Emma's the chef. Quite a renowned one, I hear. She was commissioned for a king's coronation. That's why she's in Meridia though who knows why Louise thinks she needs a make-over."

"Ah." Not that Daniel comprehended any of this. After living a lifetime with a handful of family to his name, he was now swimming in relatives he didn't know. From Dominic, he knew that their father John and his half-brother Robert were at odds. He also knew that the recent death of their grandfather William had increased the rivalry and battle for control of the restaurants. Beyond that, Daniel was lost. Even if he cared, which he hadn't yet decided if he did or not, sorting out all the Valentines would require time and exposure. "So how does this relate to our sister?"

"Our father thinks Louise is going off the deep end and needs him more than ever." His nostrils flared. "I think she's an attention seeker, drumming up sympathy to keep a wedge between John and his blood children."

"You and me."

"Right. She's on the defensive, trying to hold John's allegiance. After growing up in the wealth and society that actually belonged to us, she's unwilling to share. I, for one, think it's time you and I reaped the benefits she's had all her life."

The answer bothered Daniel. Though he didn't necessarily feel the same, he could understand his brother's emotional need to embrace their birth family. But he and Alice were well set. They didn't need the Valentine "benefits", either social or financial.

Settling back against the plush office chair, he studied his twin. They had always been different, but in the years since they'd spent any real time together the differences had increased tenfold.

Daniel wasn't sure he liked the changes.

CHAPTER THREE

FEET propped on a chair, Daniel slouched in broody silence on the too-small red sofa. His belly growled, but the half-eaten fish and chips on the table had long ago grown cold and greasy. Papers, phone numbers, business cards and other evidence of a budding business venture lay strewn around him in the darkness. He should be satisfied. But he wasn't.

Except for a few, brief conversations Stephanie Ellison had avoided being alone with him since his arrival. She was friendly enough when he went into the restaurant. She even smiled indulgently at his feeble jokes and brought him a drink. But long after the restaurant closed, she remained downstairs.

And he wanted to know why. This was her flat. She should be comfortable here even with him present. Worst of all, he didn't enjoy feeling like an interloper. He'd had enough of that when he was a kid and Mum brought friends to their hotel.

So tonight he'd waited up for little Miss Manager.

When her key turned in the lock and she walked in, Daniel was ready for her.

Light flooded the room.

"Are you avoiding me?"

Stephanie looked up, manicured fingers on the light switch, clearly startled to find him still awake, sitting in the midnight darkness. "I beg your pardon?"

"You heard me."

She didn't answer. Instead, she took one glance at the flat and started her incessant tidying up.

"Leave it," he growled, annoyed that once again she was trying to sidestep him.

She kept working. "My goodness, you're in a mood tonight. What's wrong?"

"You." Actually, she wasn't the only problem, but the one he wanted fixed first. The others could wait.

Her fidgety hands stilled on the fish and chips wrapper. "And just what have I done that's so terrible?"

"You skip out of here at pre-dawn, seldom come up to your own flat throughout the day, and then sneak in long after I've gone to bed."

"Managing a restaurant requires long hours." She tossed his forgotten dinner into the bin and then turned on him, green eyes flashing. "And I do not sneak."

"Have you always worked eighteen-hour days? Or only since taking me on as a flatmate?"

She gathered the papers from the floor and made a perfect stack on the table. "Why are you asking me this?"

"Just answer the question. Are you avoiding me?"

"Of course not. How ridiculous."

"Good. Then stop clearing up my mess and come sit down."

"I've worked all day and I'm very tired."

"You *are* avoiding me. All I'm asking is a few minutes

of your time. We are flatmates, after all. We live together, but one of us is not living here." Daniel didn't care that he sounded like a nagging wife. He wanted to know what her problem was.

She rolled her eyes. "Okay. Fine. I'll sit."

And she did. Like a gorgeous red-plumed bird, she perched on the edge of a chair opposite him ready to fly away at any moment. Her hands twisted restlessly in her lap. He had the strongest urge to reach over and take hold of them.

"I haven't ax-murdered you in your sleep, have I?"

Her lips twitched. "Evidently not."

At last. He was getting somewhere, though why he cared, he couldn't say.

"So stop being so jumpy." It irritated him.

"I am not—" But she didn't bother to finish the denial. "What do you want to talk about? Is there a problem with the flat? A problem with the new business?"

"Do you ever relax? Maybe read a book or watch the telly?"

"When I have time."

Which he doubted was ever.

He pushed. "How much of London have you seen since you've been here?"

"Not nearly as much as I'd like, but I love it. The museums, the history."

"We're steps away from some of the finest museums in the world. Which ones have you seen?"

"The Royal College of Art," she shot back.

No surprise there. He knew from looking at the walls in the flat and in the restaurant that she fancied modern art, the kind he couldn't begin to understand. There wasn't a realistic picture anywhere in the place.

"Where else?"

She shrugged and went silent.

"That's it? You've not done the palace or the Victoria and Albert Museum?" They were right around the corner.

"Not yet. But I will."

"What about Hyde Park?"

"I jog there."

"A picnic is better. What say we have one?"

Her hands stopped fidgeting. "A picnic?"

Was that longing he heard?

"Yep. Tomorrow afternoon. Hyde Park."

She shook her head; waves of red swung around her shoulders. "I'm too busy."

"So am I." Suddenly, he wanted a picnic more than anything. "But real life happens in between the busyness, Stephanie."

Her gaze slid up to his, slid away, then came back again. She wanted to. He was certain of it.

He gave her a half smile. It probably looked sinister but he hoped for charm. "Avoiding me again?"

"No!"

He lifted a doubting brow.

She sighed. "All right, then, a picnic. Tomorrow after the noon rush."

Triumph, way out of proportion to the event, expanded in Daniel's chest. At last. He was getting somewhere with the cool and aloof one. Though why it mattered, he had no idea.

* * *

"You're going on a picnic?" Chef Karl, slim and neat in his burgundy chef's coat, froze with one hand on the parmesan and the other on a giant pan of fresh veal.

"Yes, Karl, a picnic," Stephanie said coolly, though her nerves twitched like a cat's tail. "Not bungee jumping from the London Bridge."

"But—" his wide brow, reddened by heat and concentration, puckered "—you never take time off."

"She is today." Daniel, purring like an oversized pussycat and resembling a pillaging pirate, burst through the metal swinging doors that led into the kitchen from the back of the restaurant.

Stephanie's twitchy nerves went haywire. She had to grab on to the stainless-steel counter to, literally, get a grip.

My goodness, that man takes up a lot of space.

Karl, who hadn't a subtle bone in his body, looked from Stephanie to Daniel. "Oh. I see."

Exactly what he saw, Stephanie didn't know and didn't want to know. The staff had no right to poke into her personal life, although she now realized she and Daniel would become this afternoon's gossip.

Great. She was already struggling with last night's decision. What had she been thinking to agree to such a silly thing? Such a dangerous thing? But the truth was she wanted to go on a picnic. With her new roommate. And she did not want to obsess over the reasons.

When she'd come in last night to find Daniel sitting in the dark surrounded by his usual mess, she'd been tempted to run back down the stairs. He was right. She *had* been avoiding the flat, partly because of him. Partly because she dreaded the nightmares that had begun with his arrival.

She was exhausted both physically and mentally. When he'd goaded her, she'd been too tired to think. And now, here she was, both dreading and longing for a picnic with a pirate.

"Don't worry about it, Karl." She patted the chef's arm. "I'll prepare the lunch myself. This is a restaurant, you know. We're bound to have something picnic-worthy around here. You go ahead with preparations for this evening."

"Anything I can do to help?" Daniel asked, eyes dancing with a devilish gleam that said he didn't give a rip about becoming the latest fodder for gossip.

"You could let me off the hook." But she hoped he wouldn't.

The gleam grew brighter. "Not a chance. Be ready in ten minutes. We're walking."

Then he shouldered his way out of the kitchen, slowing long enough to hold the door for one of the hostesses.

"Bossy man," Stephanie muttered half to herself.

"The macho ones always are," the blonde hostess said. "But they are *so* worth it."

Stifling a groan, Stephanie settled on simple picnic fare, which she packed into a bread basket before going out to check the restaurant one more time.

Only a few stray shoppers sipped lattes or fragrant teas at this hour of the day. The dining room was quiet except for the efficient staff preparing for later when things really got hopping. Everything was well-organized. Stephanie's sense of order was intact—except for the little matter of an afternoon with a most disorderly man.

She passed by the bar, scanning the stock, the glasses, the bartenders. A lone customer sat at the bar sipping one of their special hand-mixed drinks. As was her habit, she stopped to offer a smile and a welcome.

From the corner of her eye she spotted Daniel's dark head. He poked around behind the bar and came out with a bottle of wine. He held it up, arching an eyebrow at her.

She pointed a finger in chastisement, but he only laughed and tapped a wide-strapped watch. "Two minutes. Back door."

As soon as he was out of hearing distance, Sophie, one of the bartenders, leaned toward her. "You and Delicious Dan seem to be hitting it off nicely."

Stephanie frosted her with a look. Grinning, Sophie slunk away to polish glasses.

Two minutes later, basket clenched in chilled fingers, Stephanie joined Daniel in the hallway. Her pulse, already racing, kicked up more when John Valentine walked in the door.

Her boss's portly face lit up. "Daniel. Stephanie. What a delight!"

Beside her, Daniel stiffened. "John."

They exchanged greetings, but Stephanie could feel the tension emanating from Daniel and the disappointment from her boss.

"So," John said, somewhat too jauntily. "Are the two of you off somewhere, then?"

"Hyde Park and the Serpentine. Stephanie hasn't been." Daniel's response was almost a challenge, as if he expected argument.

Guilt suffused Stephanie. She shouldn't be running off to play with the boss's son. "I hope you don't mind, Mr Valentine."

"Mind? Why should I? You hardly ever take an afternoon."

Since his mild heart attack a few weeks back, Stephanie thought John looked tired. With all that was going on, she wondered how his health was holding up. Missing money was bad enough, but the family problems continued to mount. John's wife was still angry about the arrival of the twins, though John longed to get to know them. Then there was his daughter, Louise. She'd had a whirlwind trip to Meridia and then, instead of working through her problems with John, had already jetted off again. This time to Australia to meet a woman who could be her biological sister. And none of that included the lifelong bitterness between him and his brother, Robert. How much more could the poor man handle?

"Are you sure, Mr Valentine?" she asked. "I can stay here if you prefer." In fact, considering the way Daniel got under her skin, working would probably be wiser.

"I'm available if any problems arise in the dining room. Go on. Have a lovely time. I'm going to pop in and say hello to Dominic. He thinks he may have some news for me."

With a fatherly pat to Daniel's shoulder, he left them. Daniel stared at the closing door, expression wary and brooding.

"Are you all right?" Stephanie asked.

His jaw flexed. "Why wouldn't I be?"

Then he took the basket from Stephanie's hands, pushed the back door open, and led her out into the overcast day.

The walk to the park was much more pleasant than Stephanie had anticipated. After the encounter in the hallway, she'd expected dark silence. Instead Daniel provided a wickedly humorous and totally cynical commentary on élite London that had her laughing when they entered the beautiful park.

The laughter of children sailing toy boats along the Serpentine Lake wafted up to them from a hundred yards away. A cool breeze, in line with the glorious autumn day, played tag with the curls around Stephanie's face. Daniel's hair, too, rugged and unruly, was tossed by the wind. His was the kind of hair a woman wanted to touch, to smooth back from his high, intelligent brow, to run her fingers through.

The thoughts bothered her and she forced her attention to the wonders of the historic park, breathing in the scent of green grass and fall flowers. "This is a gorgeous park."

"You can thank Henry VIII. He acquired it from the monks."

"Acquired?"

The corners of his eyes crinkled. "In much the way he *acquired* everything."

"Ah, bad Henry."

"Not all bad. We're here, aren't we?"

Well, there was that.

They passed kite flyers, strolling mothers, moon-eyed lovers, and other picnickers before finding a clear shady area to spread their blanket.

Daniel did the honors, flapped the red and white cloth into the breeze and then collapsed on it as it settled to the grass.

"Here you go, m'lady," he teased. And with one jean-jacketed arm, he exaggerated a flourish. "The finest seat in all of London."

Legs carefully folded beneath her, Stephanie sat on the edge of the blanket as far from her companion as was polite. He puzzled her, did Daniel Stephens, vacillating from broody and cautious to light-hearted in a matter of minutes.

Stretched out upon his elbow like some big cat basking in the sun, he seemed happier in the outdoors, as though the inside of buildings couldn't quite contain all there was of him. His mouth fascinating in motion, Daniel chatted tour-guide style about Rotten Row, famous duels, kings and queens, regaling her with stories of the famous old park while she emptied the contents of her picnic basket.

"I suppose we could have got food here," he said motioning to the eating places sprinkled about.

"I wouldn't have come for that. Only a picnic."

"Woman, you crush my fragile ego. I thought you came for my charming company."

She snorted. To her delight, he fell back, clutching his chest. "And now you laugh at my broken heart."

Relaxed and enjoying herself more than she'd thought possible in the company of a barbarian, she thrust a sandwich toward him. "Here. Try this. Karl's tarragon chicken salad is guaranteed to cure broken hearts as well as crushed egos."

"Yes, the way to a man's heart and all that." He unwrapped the sandwich and took a man-sized bite. "Mmm. Not sheep's blood or lizard's eyes, but it will do."

"You haven't actually eaten that sort of thing?"

He arched a wicked brow. "When in Rome, do as the Romans. When in Africa…"

She lifted a bunch of fat grapes. "Suddenly, these don't look too tasty."

"Very similar to lizard's eyes. Right down to the squish."

She made a stop-sign with her palm. "Hush."

Unrepentant but thankfully silent, he reached for the grapes. With an air of mischief he studied one closely, then met Stephanie's gaze before popping it into his mouth.

Refusing to watch, Stephanie said, "If we have time later, I'd like to walk awhile."

"We'll make the time." He tossed a grape into her lap. "A long walk after a picnic is good for the soul."

She could certainly use that.

"I wouldn't know. I've never been on one." She tossed the grape back to him. It thudded against his chest.

"You've never been on a walk?" Head back, Daniel threw a grape high into the air and caught it in his mouth.

Stephanie tried to look away and failed. "No, silly. A picnic."

Another grape had winged upward. Daniel let it plop onto the blanket uncaught.

"Never? No childhood jaunts to the country? No egg sandwiches in the garden?"

"No. My family was far too stuffy for that. Little girls sat at the dinner table, learned to play hostess, and never, ever got dirty."

"Unbelievable."

"Yes." And I don't want to talk about it. Some things didn't merit conversation at a girl's first picnic. "You, on the other hand, look perfectly comfortable sprawled beneath a spreading chestnut tree with a sandwich and a bunch of grapes."

"Far more my style than your fancy London flat."

"Is that why you're so messy?"

He tapped her shoe. "I'm not messy. You're far too tidy."

"That's been said about me before. I'm just a perfectionist."

"What makes you so obsessive about it?"

She wasn't going down that road either.

"There's nothing wrong with order," she replied, more defensively than she'd intended.

"Never said there was." He levered up to rummage in the basket, coming out with the wine and two glasses swiped from the restaurant. Following another foray into the basket, he extracted a corkscrew. With little effort on his part, the cork slid out with a pop.

Daniel widened his eyes at her. Stephanie giggled. She didn't know why, but a popping cork always made her laugh.

He poured, handed her a glass and waited while she sipped.

"You have good taste in wine," she said, savoring the rich flavor on her tongue.

"I have good *luck* in wine. Don't know a thing about the stuff."

"Really? I thought a son of John Valentine—"

"I wasn't always John's son. Remember? My mum was a club singer. Not the worst, but not the best either. Our upbringing wasn't quite on par with the Valentines." He made the admission easily, but some of his conversational ease had seeped away.

"Did you grow up here in London?"

"All around England. Wherever Mum could get a gig."

"That must have been an interesting life."

"Not really. Hotel staff make good nannies for a day or two but they don't substitute well for parents." Bitterness laced his words, telling Stephanie she'd touched a nerve. His meaning was clear. Two boys left alone to fend for themselves in strange hotels could not be the best situation.

"I'm sorry you were unhappy." And she was. Very sorry.

He shifted his attention from her to a red-dragon kite floating overhead. "Being alone all the time is scary to a little kid. And confusing."

Stephanie's heart squeezed. It couldn't have been easy for him to tell her such a thing, but the peek into his unhappy childhood made him seem less intimidating, more approachable. And she liked him for it.

"What about when you were older?"

"Then we were terrors." The mischief was back. "Pounding on guests' doors at two o'clock in the morning. Dumping ice over the balconies onto unsuspecting passers-by. We got our mum kicked out of more than one fine establishment."

Stephanie chuckled. "I can see you doing that. You bad boy."

He toasted her with his glass and knocked it back in one drink. "All Dom's idea, I assure you."

"It was not." She couldn't imagine easygoing Dominic coming up with any mischief on his own. If ever there was a by-the-book, rule-following man, it was Dominic Stephens.

"You're right. I was the rabble rouser." He sighed, a happy sound, and flopped onto his back. "Poor Dom."

She smiled down at him, trying to imagine him as a child. He was so completely man. But he'd been a little boy once, and he'd been wounded in the process.

Something in that knowledge caused her to relax. She had nothing to fear from Daniel. He knew about heartbreak too.

Daniel reached up and wrapped his fingers around a lock of her hair. He tugged, pulling her down toward the blanket. Slowly, she gave in to the gentle pressure and reclined on the soft flannel, the wineglass discarded in the grass.

He didn't touch her, for which she was grateful. She wasn't ready for that yet.

The thought caught her by surprise. *Yet?* She would never be ready for that. Daniel might have an alluring charisma about him, but so had Brett. Worse yet, so had Randolph.

She shivered and pulled her sweater closer.

Though Daniel didn't move or speak, she felt him there, warm and appealing. After a few seconds, she gave in to the quiet and closed her eyes, relaxed by the wine.

The breeze whispered against her face. In the distance a victory shout went up as one boater bested another. In her imagination, she could hear the clip-clop of royal carriages and envision the elegantly clad ladies from times gone by.

Something tickled her nose. She wiggled it. The tickle came again. She pushed at it and received a purring chuckle for her efforts.

Lazily, slowly, she opened her eyes to see Daniel hovering above her, a blade of grass between thumb and forefinger. Before she could stop the instinctive reaction, she cringed.

He pulled back. "Hey. I didn't mean to startle you."

Her heart hammered crazily. "I must have dozed."

He continued to hover, muscled forearms holding him above her. His eyes darkened in concern. "You're shaking."

She managed a false laugh. "It's nothing. A sudden wake-up."

Daniel brushed a hair from the corner of her lips. He let his fingers linger on her cheek, his gaze searching.

Stephanie froze, breath lodged in her throat. She didn't want him to remove his hand, though common sense said to do so. She lay there, examining the emotions as the therapists had taught her, until she knew—*she knew*—she wasn't afraid of Daniel. At least, not for the usual reasons. If she had fear, it was of herself, because she couldn't start a relationship with this man. She couldn't go there again and face the inevitable rejection. Years of counseling had brought her this far, but she'd long ago decided being alone was easier than risking heartache.

And Daniel could easily be a danger to her fragile heart.

"Let's walk," she said, her voice a breathy murmur.

Though obviously full of curiosity, Daniel helped her to her feet without comment. Shakily, she gathered the remains of their picnic, looking around for a garbage can. She'd hardly touched her chicken salad. No wonder the wine had rushed to her head.

They fell in step, strolling toward the long bridge spanning the lake. Daniel didn't try to take her hand and she was grateful. She knew he wanted to, but he must have known she would pull away.

In silence now, they walked over the bridge, pausing at the top to lean on the rails and look down. On the shore two lovers lay stretched upon the grass. The young man kissed his girlfriend with such tenderness that Stephanie's chest ached. She glanced away. But the view of a young family, doting over an infant in a stroller, was no better.

Today seemed to be the day to stir her latent domestic urges. Perhaps it was the amazing and romantic news that Emma, one of the Valentines and head chef at the Chelsea restaurant, had married a king. Or worse, maybe Daniel was to blame.

She slid a glance in his direction. The brooding Daniel had returned, staring in dark silence at the kissing lovers.

Being with him turned her thoughts in strange directions, down roads she'd closed long ago.

Unintentionally, she sighed. Daniel's dark head slowly swiveled in her direction. She kept her focus trained on the happy little family below.

Once, a long time ago, she'd believed she could break free from the past and embrace the future with a loving husband. She'd even dreamed of having a child to cherish. But Randolph had made sure that could never happen. That no man would ever want her.

Yes. Long ago, she'd come to grips with her inevitable destiny. So why did the thought depress her so much today?

CHAPTER FOUR

IN THE days to follow, Daniel had a hard time getting that picnic out of his mind. Correction. He had a hard time concentrating on business instead of his copper-haired flatmate. He had discovered that he was not only attracted to Stephanie, he also liked her. She was witty, and when she let her guard down, she was warm. It was that guard that puzzled and challenged him, and he reckoned the challenge was the fascination. That was why he couldn't get her out of his mind.

He loved challenges. Why else would he try to single-handedly solve the water-shortage problems of African countries?

He watched her flit around the living area, doing her usual fussy tidying-up thing. The television blabbed in the background and lemon furniture polish fragranced the air.

Daniel was supposed to be working at the desk he'd set up in one end of the large reception room, but he watched her instead.

Tonight, she'd come up from the restaurant early, claiming the flat needed cleaning. Yeah, right. The only mess was his and he couldn't bring himself to feel bad over it.

She'd changed into casual trousers and top and pulled her hair into a loose, sexy knot on top of her head. Wispy tendrils played around her elegant cheekbones, tempting him.

He shifted restlessly and tossed down the pen. He'd been celibate too long.

Last night, he'd heard her in the throes of a nightmare. He'd wanted to go to her but had resisted. What help could he offer? That sort of involvement required emotion, and he didn't have that in him. Besides, he doubtless would not be welcome in Stephanie's bedroom, bad dream or not.

He pushed up from the desk and stretched to relieve the kink in his back. When he turned, Stephanie knelt on the floor, polishing an end table. She looked up, luscious mouth curved in a smile. Daniel experienced another of his wayward, unflatmate-like thoughts.

"You've been working hard," she said. "Any progress?"

"Actually, more than I expected. My father—" he could barely say the word with civility "—has offered his support."

"Daniel, that's awesome." Her eyes glowed with true pleasure. "He has contacts that can give your business a real boost."

Daniel didn't answer. How did he admit that he didn't trust the man who had given him life?

Stephanie stopped polishing to study him. "You don't exactly seem overjoyed."

"I don't understand why he wants to do this."

"Because you're his son."

"He doesn't even know me. He has no idea if I can do the work, or if I have the integrity to carry out these projects in an ethical manner."

"That's right." She aimed the cloth at him. "Yet, he's willing to introduce you to some influential people. He's willing to put his name and reputation on the line."

"Yeah." And Daniel didn't get it. What did the old man expect in return? What was his game? Nobody did something for nothing. "He's set up a lunch meeting with some important investors over at the other restaurant."

"Are you going?"

"I haven't decided." He didn't like favors. They obligated.

Folding the polishing cloth into her usual crisp rectangle, Stephanie stood and faced him. "You didn't ask my advice, but I'm giving it anyway. Go. From all I've observed in a year of working for the man, John's a good guy."

Yeah? Then where was he when I was a kid?

"I'll think about it." He turned his attention to the television, hoping for distraction. All this talk about his father annoyed him. "Let's watch a movie."

She put away the cleaning materials and surprised him by coming into the living room instead of scuttling off to hide in her bedroom. Perhaps he could thank the picnic for this new acceptance of him. Though she'd fallen into some kind of mood at one point, they'd had a great time.

He still couldn't imagine that a woman her age had never experienced a picnic. Must have come from a weird family. He pointed the remote and clicked. Who was he kidding? His hippie mother had been super-weird. They'd gone on lots of picnics, though hers had usually been Woodstock-style outings that had lasted days during which he and Dominic had wandered around on their own.

He flipped through the channels, stopping at a comedy program.

"How's this?"

"Anything's okay with me. A brainless way to relax."

"You actually do that on occasion?" he asked.

She made a face at him. The curled nose and squinted eyes looked cute. The long legs curled under her looked pretty interesting too. Who knew naked toes could stir a man's libido?

Better concentrate on the comedy instead. He did, but his attention kept straying back to his companion each time she laughed.

Eventually, the program finished and the barrage of advertisements began. When he was about to give up and go back to his desk, a news brief flashed across the screen. A beautiful little girl, no more than six, smiled from a photo while the reporter intoned a gruesome story of neglect and abuse and violent death.

Stephanie slapped both hands against her ears and squeezed her eyes closed. Daniel was tempted to do likewise.

"Horrid, isn't it?" he asked, stomach roiling.

"Dreadful." She pushed off the couch and turned away from the television, her complexion gone pale, tears glistening in her eyes. "That poor little angel."

He knew she had a heart for troubled kids and sometimes taught an art class for some kind of scheme. Naturally, she'd be disturbed. Who wouldn't be?

"Yeah." He scrubbed a hand over his face, repulsed at the inhumanity of some people. If a hard-heart like him was troubled, tender-hearted Stephanie would make herself sick if she dwelled on the story.

He switched the telly off. The room went dark except for the dim hall light. Quiet, broken only by the traffic on the road below, enveloped them.

"Would you like some tea?" he asked, feeling the inexplicable need to comfort her.

She shook her head. "I need to run downstairs."

Her comment felt odd somehow. He squinted at her, tall and slim and composed, and wondered if he'd missed something. "At this hour?"

"One of the dishwashers was acting up earlier, had a small leak. I want to check it."

Daniel frowned at her. Why hadn't she mentioned this earlier?

"I could have a look. I'm handy with water pipes and such."

"No need. Really. I'll handle it."

In other words, she didn't want his company, a truth that caused an unwanted curl of disappointment.

"All right, then. Ring me if there's a problem."

Without answering, she headed out the door.

Daniel jumped into the shower for a quick scrub and had just stepped out when the telephone rang. He grabbed for the receiver.

Stephanie's breathy voice said, "Daniel, come quick. I need you badly."

He didn't hold back the chuckle. "Well, that's more like it."

"I'm serious. Please, if you think you can help, come down here."

A surge of renewed energy zipped through him. "The dishwasher?"

"Leaking everywhere. I'm slopping up water now."

"Will you feed me cheesecake afterwards?" referring to the time he'd asked her to take him down for a midnight snack and she'd frozen him with silence.

"What?"

"Never mind. Be right down."

Stephanie squeezed out yet another mop full of water and watched in dismay as more seeped from beneath the industrial-sized dishwasher. She'd called the plumber again about this a week ago and still he had yet to show up. Ordinarily, she'd have followed up and called someone else, but she'd had too many other problems on her mind. One, the money missing from the accounts.

Two, Daniel Stephens. Since the moment he'd arrived, the man had occupied her thoughts in the most uncomfortable way. Then he'd taken her on that picnic and she'd realized why. She liked him. His passion for Africa stirred her. His relentless pursuit of an incredibly lofty goal stirred her. Looking at him stirred her.

A voice that also stirred her broke through the sound of sloshing water. "Ahoy, mate. Permission to come aboard."

Stephanie looked up. All she could think was, *Ohmygosh. Ohmygosh.*

She'd known he was coming. She'd been expecting him. But she hadn't been expecting this.

Barefoot and shirtless, Daniel waded toward her in a pair of low-slung jeans, a tool belt slung even lower on his trim hips.

Close your mouth, Stephanie. Mop, don't stare.

But she stared anyway.

Daniel Stephens, dark as sin, chest and shoulder muscles rippling, black hair still wet and carelessly slicked back from a pirate's forehead, was almost enough to make her forget the reasons why she could not be interested in him. Almost.

Slim hips rolling, he sloshed through the quarter inch of water to the dishwasher. Dark hairs sprinkled his bare toes.

The sight made her shiver. When had she ever paid any attention to a man's toes?

"You forgot your shirt," she blurted, repeating the slogan seen everywhere in American restaurants. "No shirt, no shoes, no service."

He grinned at her, unrepentant. "You said you needed me. *Badly.* How could I not respond immediately to that kind of plea from a beautiful woman?"

He thought she was beautiful? The idea stunned her. Beautiful? Something inside her shriveled. How little he knew about the real her.

He, on the other hand, was hot. And he knew it.

"Are you going to fix that thing or annoy me?"

One corner of his mouth twitched. "Both, I imagine."

He hunkered down in front of the washer, tool belt dragging the waist of his jeans lower. Stephanie tried not to look.

"Do you think it's bad?"

"Probably have to shut down the restaurant for a week."

Stephanie dropped the mop. It clattered to the floor. "You've got to be kidding!"

He twisted around on those sexy bare toes and said, "I am. It's probably a leaky hose."

"Can you fix it?"

He smirked. "Of course."

"Then I really am going to fire that plumber."

"Go ahead and sack the useless lout. Tell him you have an engineer around to do your midnight bidding."

Now, *that* was an intriguing thought.

She retrieved the mop. "Which is more expensive? A plumber or an engineer?"

White teeth flashed. "Depends on what you use for payment."

Time to shut up, Stephanie, before you get in too deep. Do not respond to that tempting innuendo.

Metal scraped against tile as he easily manhandled the large machine, walking it away from the cabinet to look inside and behind. Stephanie went back to swabbing the decks. Watching Daniel, all muscled and half naked, was too dangerous. Thinking about that cryptic payment remark was even more so.

"Could you lend a hand over here?" he asked.

Oh, dear.

The floor, dangerously slick but no longer at flood stage, proved to be an adventure. But she slip-slid her way across to where Daniel bent over, peering into the back of the machine.

"What can I do?"

"See this space?"

Seeing required Stephanie to move so close to Daniel that his warm, soap-scented and very nude skin brushed against her. Thankful for long sleeves, she swallowed hard and tried to focus on the space in question.

"Down there where that black thing is?" she asked.

"Your hands are small enough, I think, to loosen that screw. Do you see it?"

"I think so." She leaned farther into the machine, almost lying across the top. Daniel's warm purr directed her, too close to her ear, but necessary to get the job done.

"That's it. Good girl."

His praise pleased her, silly as that seemed.

He pressed in closer, trying to reach the now-unfastened hose. His breath puffed deliciously against the side of her neck. Stephanie shivered and gave up trying to ignore the sensation.

Their fingers touched, deep inside the machine. Both of them stilled.

Her pulse escalating to staccato, Stephanie's blood hummed. As if someone else controlled her actions, she turned her head and came face-to-face with searing blue eyes that surely saw to her deepest secrets.

She needed to move, to get out of this situation and put space between them. But she was trapped between the machine, the hose, and Daniel's inviting, compelling body.

"I think I have it," she said, uselessly. Foolishly.

Daniel's nostrils flared. "Yes. You certainly do."

His lips spoke so close to hers that she almost felt kissed.

Daniel held her gaze for another long, pulsing moment in which Stephanie began to yearn for the touch of his lips against hers. How would they feel?

All right, she told herself. That's enough. Stop right now before you venture too close to the fire and get burned.

With the inner strength that had kept her going when

life had been unspeakable, she withdrew her hand and stepped away.

As though the air between them hadn't throbbed like jungle drums, Daniel didn't bother to look up. He finished repairing the hose while Stephanie completed the mopping-up and tried to analyze the situation. Daniel was interested in her. Big deal. In her business, she got hit on all the time.

But it wasn't Daniel's interest that bothered her so much. It was her own. Something in Daniel drew her, called to her like a Siren's song. One moment he was cynical and tough. The next he was giving and gentle. There was a strength in him, too, that said he could—and would—move a mountain if one was in his way. He was different from anyone she'd ever met.

Metal squealed against tile again as Daniel shoved the washer back into place.

"All done." He gathered tools, dropping them into the proper slots in his belt. "You'll need to order in a new hose right away, but that should hold for now."

"Thank you. I really appreciate this."

He came toward her, all cat-like muscle and unquestionable male. "How much?"

"What do you mean, how much?" She took a step back.

He took one forward. "Remember your promise?"

Mind racing, she held the mop out like a skinny shield. What had she promised?

He stopped. "Cheesecake?"

"That's it? Cheesecake?"

"Why, Stephanie, whatever were you thinking?"

She laughed and playfully shoved the mop at him. He ducked, one hand out to ward off the pretend blow.

And then the slick floor took control. Daniel's bare feet slipped. Tools rattled and swayed, throwing him more off balance. He reeled backwards, caught the counter with one hand but not before his head slammed against the jutting corner.

Stephanie dropped the mop and rushed to his side. "Daniel. Oh, my goodness! Are you hurt?"

He righted himself, rubbing at the back of his head. He felt ridiculous. One minute, he was about to kiss a beautiful woman. The next he was thrashing around like a landed salmon.

"Only my pride," he admitted.

But when he brought his hand forward from the aching lump on the back of his head, blood covered his fingers. "Uh-oh."

"Let me see." Stephanie tugged at his shoulders. "Bend down here, you big lug."

With a half-grin, half-grimace, he lowered his head. A minute ago she'd been backing away as if afraid he'd touch her. And now her hands were all over him in gentle concern. Puzzling, infuriating woman.

"A scratch, I think. It's nothing." But her cool fingers felt good against his skin.

"Let me decide that." All business, she guided him to a chair. "Sit. We keep a first-aid kit beside the stove."

"I'm all right. It's only throbbing a bit."

But he sat anyway while Stephanie got the kit and went to work cleaning up the wound.

As soon as her fingers touched his hair, he forgot all about the throbbing pain. When had a woman last touched him with such gentleness?

The throb in his head moved to his heart.

"How bad is it, Doc?" he managed, though her touch was causing more reaction inside his head than outside.

"Irreparable brain damage. I fear there's no hope."

He hid a smile. If this was what it took to get her to touch him and joke with him, he'd bash his head every day of the week.

"Can't you kiss it and make it all better?" A man could always hope.

Her fingers stilled, only a fractional second, but enough for Daniel to know the question got to her. Good. She was thinking about it, too. He'd thought of little else tonight. Well, other than cheesecake. He still had hope in that department.

"Kissing spreads germs," she said lightly. "Can't chance infection."

"I'm already hopelessly damaged. A few extra germs won't hurt." He twisted around. "What if I said please?"

Their eyes met and, for once, held. Yes, she was thinking about it every bit as much as he was. What he couldn't work out was why he didn't just go ahead and kiss her. He wasn't shy with women. He didn't feel shy with Stephanie. But she kept a barrier up at all times, a wall that held him back, that scared him a little, as if kissing her would open a Pandora's box he was unprepared to handle.

Stephanie broke the stand-off by bopping him playfully on the shoulder. "Behave yourself or I'll use this alcohol cleanser."

"Evil woman." But he leaned his head forward so she could examine the cut.

Her stomach brushed against his bare back as she gently

separated layers of hair to dab away blood. Her scent, as clean and elegant as the woman herself, wrapped around him. Her fingers, light, deft, flitted over his scalp with exquisite care, as if she feared hurting him.

Daniel closed his eyes, soaking in the sensation. His own mother had never touched him with such infinite tenderness, and the truth of it brought a lump to his throat. A yearning, far greater and more complicated than desire, expanded his ribcage with a hot ache.

He wanted her never to stop, and that worried him. He, who'd made a point never to need anyone ever again, needed something from Stephanie.

He slept in the same house with her, breathed in her perfume, wondered what she wore to bed. But while he knew her on the surface, he sensed a secret heartache hidden behind the serene face. He needed to know what had hurt her. And that worried him even more.

"This would be easier if you had less hair."

Instantly, Daniel roused out of the pleasant lethargy that enshrouded him.

"Are you saying I need a haircut?"

He hadn't expected her to be like his sister-in-law, so concerned about appearances. But then, of course she was. Didn't her magazine-perfect flat prove as much?

"Maybe a trim."

She was probably right. He rubbed at the whiskers around his mouth. Lately, they'd taken the shape of a Fu Manchu. "What about this?"

"Your stubble? I like it."

Once again, he twisted around, this time surprised and far too pleased. "You do?"

"Sit still." She pressed gauze against the back of his head and held tight. "Yes, I like it. Very much. It's…" Her voice trailed off as if she had already said too much.

"Sexy?"

"Roguish." She gave his shoulder a soft pat. "There. All done."

Daniel caught her wrist. "Roguish?" Slowly, he pulled her around the chair to stand in front of him.

"Daniel—" She lifted a finger in warning.

He was tempted to bite it. "I only want to say thank you."

"Workman's compensation," she teased. "You were wounded on the job."

She started to pull away but he held fast. Her playfulness became a flicker of worry. Puzzled, he released her. He didn't want her to be anxious. He wanted her to be… What *did* he want?

She didn't move, and he was even more puzzled.

He studied her, trying to gauge what was going on inside her head, wondering why she fascinated him so much.

He wanted to reach out and bring her closer, but, more than that, he wanted her to come to him. He wasn't even sure where this was going, but, for purely selfish reasons, he longed for her to make the first move.

Something was churning behind that pretty face and he was willing to wait her out.

In that split second when he thought she might relent and move closer, a commotion erupted outside the restaurant.

CHAPTER FIVE

STEPHANIE jerked as if she'd been shot.

"What on earth—?"

Daniel leaped to his feet, grabbed a pipe wrench from the counter, and stormed through the swinging doors toward the back of the restaurant.

"Be careful, Daniel." Seeing no other weapon, Stephanie yanked a copper pot from the overhead rack and followed closely behind, too jittery to remain in the kitchen without him. After all, the hour was late, they were alone, and someone *had* been stealing money from the restaurants.

"Stay back," Daniel cautioned, putting one hand behind him in the dark hall to stop her.

"No," she whispered fiercely, bumping up against those wide, strong fingers.

Her own hands trembled on the pot handle, though she wasn't certain if they trembled from fear of the noise or from the unsettling episode with Daniel. She couldn't stop thinking of the feel of his hair, the soapy scent of his skin, or his bereft expression when she'd started to pull away.

Yes, something in him called to her, a loneliness she understood and wanted to erase.

"Stay behind me, then," he murmured. And the command made her feel protected in a way she'd seldom experienced. No one ever protected her except herself. And many times she'd done a sorry job of it.

At the back exit, they paused to listen. The racket had subsided. Slowly, Daniel eased the door open. In one swift motion he flipped on the light and leaped outside, wrench at the ready.

Then he laughed.

"Daniel?" Stephanie lowered the pot.

"Come out here."

She did. Two garbage cans lay on their sides, spilling trash on the concrete. A tiny kitten tore at a discarded meat wrapper.

Stephanie gazed at the pot in her hand and the wrench in Daniel's. "Look at us. Aren't we brave?"

"Positively formidable."

"Two giants bearing weapons against this terrifying intruder."

They both looked at the little kitten and burst into laughter.

In the crisp autumn darkness, with a soft breeze carrying scents of exhaust and the promise of winter hovering above, Stephanie and Daniel stood in the alleyway and laughed like lunatics left too long beneath the moon.

The kitten took note of their presence and, with a plaintive cry that resembled recognition, abandoned the trash heap to weave zigzags through Daniel's legs.

"Daniel," Stephanie said, pretending scandal. "Have you been feeding this cat?"

"Apparently not enough." And they laughed some more,

letting the tensions and questions brewing between them be washed away in the ridiculous.

"Come on," she said when she could once more breathe. "Let's feed your protégé."

"What about me? I'm still craving that payment you offered. Engineers don't work for free, you know."

Stephanie figured the moon had stolen her sanity. "Cheesecake?"

"Unless you have something else in mind." He grinned wickedly. "Terms are negotiable."

Her stomach fluttered. She really should send him upstairs for a shirt, but, at this point, what did it matter?

They scavenged the kitchen, found some smoked salmon for the kitten and two large pieces of cheesecake and a jar of chocolate sauce for themselves.

Rather than turn on the lights of the dining room and alarm security patrol, Stephanie lit a candle. Encased in a ruby globe, the candle glowed red and fragrant on the small table next to the kitchen door.

"Good cheesecake." Daniel laid down his fork. "But I need more chocolate."

She handed him the jar. "Karl is an excellent chef, especially with the desserts. They tell me your cousin Emma is every bit as good. Too bad Bella Lucia has lost her."

"She's the one that married the king, right?"

"Yes. In Meridia. Wherever that is."

Daniel poured the sauce on his plate, watching the chocolate drip with a mesmerized expression. "If I were the King of Meridia, there's no way my new wife would be commuting to a job in England. She'd definitely stay at home."

"Hey, don't hog all that." She playfully grabbed the jar

from him. "So you're going to make someone a very bossy husband?"

"I'll never know the answer to that." He caught a final drip of gooey sauce on his finger and licked it. "Daniel's rule number two. Never waste good chocolate."

She added another dollop to her plate. "What's rule number one?" she asked, expecting him to elaborate on his marriage comment.

"Empty your boots before putting them on." When she laughed, he said, "I learned that one the hard way. Scorpions." He gave a fake shiver.

"Africa must be an astounding place."

"You'd love it, Stephanie. The different countries, all the colors and sounds and smells. And the people I met. Amazing. Especially in the small villages. They may only have a small bowl of food for the entire family, but they'll insist on sharing with a stranger."

Everything about him changed when he spoke of Africa. The cynicism slipped away. His face lit up with an energy that came from loving what he did.

"How did you end up working so far from home?"

"Adventure. A chance to get away from a troubled upbringing." He hitched a bare shoulder, an action that flexed the muscles of his chest. "All the usual reasons of reckless youth."

"Interesting that your twin didn't join you."

"Dom and I have always been different." He licked the back of his fork and then studied it. "He's even more different these days, though. More intense, stressed."

She could hear the concern in his voice and admired him for that. Never having had a sibling, she couldn't imagine the bond twins might have. "I assumed that was his personality, him being an accountant and all."

"Didn't used to be. Oh, he's always been a stickler, always following the rules."

"Unlike you?" Stephanie teased.

"Exactly. That's why he's a great accountant and I'm not." Daniel's mischievous eyes twinkled. "But in the past, he was looser, more relaxed, a real joker at times." He shook his head and made another stab at his cheesecake. "He has a lot on his mind, I guess. A baby on the way, teenagers."

"That's trouble enough right there. But the restaurant has also added to his workload. That could be part of the problem. John has him auditing all the accounts in search of the money that's gone missing." She leaned her elbows on the table and admitted, "Did you know I thought you were a spy?"

His fork clattered to the table. He touched his chest, an eyebrow arched in question. "A spy? Like 007?"

Stephanie laughed. "Not quite, but I wondered if John thought I had something to do with the missing money."

"You do have access."

His words stunned her. Did he think she was responsible? "I don't need money, Daniel. And I love my job. I would never do anything to jeopardize these restaurants."

He held up a hand to stop her defense. "I know that now, Stephanie. I didn't when I first came here."

"So you *were* a spy? John set this little arrangement up as a means to keep an eye on me?" The notion mortified her.

"Not even close. In fact, it's a silly idea. John and I aren't on what you would call intimate terms."

"Am I a suspect?" Her stomach hurt just thinking such a thing.

"The subject came up, but Dominic doesn't believe you're involved, and he says John feels the same."

Some of her tension ebbed away in the gentle reassurance. She respected her boss. To think he might suspect her hurt. But she appreciated Daniel's honesty in telling her. "You had me scared for a minute. I thought the Valentine clan had turned on me."

"I don't consider myself a Valentine, Stephanie. John hasn't discussed any of this with me at all. I'm not part of the inner circle."

She could see that bothered him. "You really should try to get to know them. Especially your father and your sister."

A shadow, caused by more than the candle, fell across his handsome face.

"Adopted sister," he said firmly.

"And pretty upset to learn that, from what I hear. She's always been the darling in that family, Daniel. The sweet, good child doted on by all. To suddenly discover she's adopted must have totally rattled her foundation, her sense of self."

"I can relate to that," Daniel said. "But I can't understand why John and Ivy kept the adoption secret in the first place. Now they have to deal with the unpleasant consequences."

Glad to leave the unsettling subject of the missing funds, she said, "You mean the trip to Australia to find her biological sister?"

He nodded. "That's great from my viewpoint, but John's ranting that he doesn't want her poking into the past. Thinks she should be content with the life he gave her. Rather selfish of him, don't you think?"

Stephanie shook her head. "I think he's afraid she'll get hurt. That these biological relatives won't be what she expects or that they'll somehow take advantage of her."

His mouth curled cynically. "He's more likely worried about how this will affect him and his business. He doesn't need Louise creating more difficulties for him."

"So bitter, Daniel. John's made mistakes. Who hasn't? But he cares for Louise. You and Dominic, too, if you'll give him a chance."

Daniel twirled circles in the chocolate sauce on his plate. "Why bother? He seems to make a habit of hurting his children. Louise had a right to know she was adopted, just as Dominic and I had a right to know who our father was."

"Agreed. But that's the past. There is nothing you can do about it now." She was a fine one to be talking. "But you *can* affect the future."

"My future is set." But his tone was defensive, uncertain.

"Is it? Don't you want family, Daniel? Don't you need people around you? People who care for you and will be there for you when life sends a crushing blow?"

He grew quiet, thoughtful, and she knew, for all his arguments to the contrary, Daniel needed to connect with his family. Like her, he was held back by the fear of getting hurt. Strange how knowing that made her feel closer to him.

Who was she kidding? She felt closer to Daniel than she'd felt to anyone in a long time. They were kindred spirits, both having childhood hurts that still hampered them as adults. A bond like that was a powerful thing.

"Change of subject, okay?" he said gently, tapping her

fingernail with one tine of his fork. "My strange life doesn't concern you."

Oh, but it did. More and more every day.

The dark restaurant, the ruby candle glow, created an ambience of intimacy and, inevitably, personal conversation began to flow, moving away from the hazard of discussing his estranged family. He told her more about his gypsy lifestyle growing up. Stephanie sensed the hurt and loneliness interspersed with the funny stories.

In turn, she told him bits and pieces of her life in Colorado, her work in Aspen before coming here. But some things didn't warrant discussion, even with Daniel.

Long after the cheesecake was gone and the saucers pushed aside, they talked on. Stephanie knew the hour must be terribly late, but she didn't want to move, didn't want to leave this cocoon that had spun around them in the darkened restaurant.

Daniel leaned corded forearms on the table, his folded hands inches from hers.

"Tell me about the art classes."

"They're great. The kids—" She shrugged. "I like to think I'm helping, but I don't know." Some of them had been through far more than she had. "I want so badly to make a difference. Sometimes I dream about them, about their situations, about the things that have happened to them."

"You're doing a good thing, Stephanie. A good thing." He touched the back of her hand. "How did you get involved in that to begin with?"

"I've always had a heart for people who were down and out. I guess it stems from—"

She'd gone too far this time, letting the intimate setting and fatigue affect her usual reserve.

"Stems from what?"

Playing the pretense game didn't work too well with a bright man like Daniel. And in truth, she wanted to tell him. She was just too afraid, so she took the easiest way out.

"There was a child once, a little girl. A victim of abuse." The inner trembling started up, but Stephanie didn't let the nerves stop her. She could tell Daniel this much. And maybe by doing so, some of the lingering shadows would be driven back. "I should have told someone. But I didn't."

His voice deepened, incredibly gentle. "Why not?"

She lifted a shoulder. "She was afraid telling would make the problem worse. I didn't know what to do." And she still didn't.

Sometimes that was the worst shame. Knowing she might have stopped it, but she'd been too young to understand that.

As if he read her thoughts, Daniel asked softly, "How old were you?"

"Nine." She shook her head, recognizing the denial in his eyes. "But I should have told someone."

"You were a child. You can't feel responsible."

"I know. But it bothers me." Ate at her, if she told the truth. Had turned her into a woman who couldn't let anyone close enough to see the real person inside. "Children are powerless, Daniel."

He reached out, covered her hand with his. She soaked in the comfort of his spontaneous gesture.

"You were a child, too, sweetheart, as powerless as that little girl."

"I know. That's why I want to make a difference now. To help these kids, to show them a better way, a way out. I can't change the past, but I can help now."

The warmth of his skin against hers, his quiet under-standing seeped into her battered heart like fresh rain into the cracked, parched earth. And like that dry ground, Steph-anie felt renewed, refreshed, almost whole again.

For a split second, a blink in time, Stephanie considered telling him the rest, but as courage formed the words Daniel spoke again. "Life's injustices drive me crazy."

"Me, too. Obviously."

"Why is it, do you suppose, that some people have ev-erything going for them and others have nothing?"

With relief, Stephanie recognized that she'd raised no suspicions. Daniel saw the conversation on the surface, as two adults discussing a troubled world.

"You're doing all you can to make a difference, Daniel, just like I am. In fact, more than I am. You've spent your whole life trying to help. That has to mean something."

"But the need is so vast, sometimes I feel like I'm trying to empty the ocean with a spoon."

Tenderness gripped her. "You have such a good heart."

"Stephanie, my love, let me tell you a fact about your flatmate. He doesn't have a heart." He said the words lightly, easily as though teasing, but she knew he was serious. "I'm a civil engineer. Developing water projects is what I do."

Stephanie didn't accept his reasoning. Pure self-inter-est would have lined his pockets long ago.

"What about feeding that kitten? Or coming down here in the middle of the night to fix my dishwasher? Is that for selfish reasons, too?"

"No. That's cheesecake."

The silly answer made them both chuckle.

"You ate that entire jar of chocolate," she said, smoothly, glad to move away from topics that could only lead to trouble.

Daniel took the empty container and scraped the inside with a spoon. "Wasn't I worth it?"

"Absolutely." She stole the jar from him and ran her finger around the edge.

Daniel grabbed her finger and licked it. The energy from the touch of his tongue against her skin raced through her body faster than a breath. For a guy without a heart, he had a habit of doing strange things to hers.

She pulled her hand into her lap, but the feel of that warm, moist tongue wouldn't go away.

"Don't try to steal my chocolate, buster."

Was her voice really that breathless?

"All's fair in love and chocolate."

"Now there's a subject we haven't discussed." She blamed the dark, intimate atmosphere for her bravado. But why not talk about love? They'd discussed everything else.

"Love?" Daniel shook his head. His hair, now dry and in need of a comb, flopped forward. "I'd rather have chocolate, thank you."

Her heart began to beat a little faster. "Haven't you ever been in love?"

"Thought I was once, but it didn't work out. Since then. Well, a man realizes his shortcomings. What about you? Any boyfriends wanting to bounce my head against the concrete?"

His airy tone gave her the courage to answer honestly. "I suppose I've realized my shortcomings as well."

"I beg to differ. No shortcomings from my perspective."

Though his observation did wonders for her self-esteem, it showed once again how little he knew of the real Stephanie.

"I was in love once, but…" Her voice trailed off. Why had she admitted that?

"And he hurt you."

The sentence was a statement, not a question, and Stephanie accepted that he understood what she'd left unsaid.

"Yes. In the worst possible way." Brett had rejected the real Stephanie, unable to see beyond the scars.

Compassion flared in Daniel's flame-blue eyes. She thought he might touch her. And she realized just how much she yearned for that. He, like no one else, found a way past her guard and into her heart.

"What did he do? Cheat on you?"

"No. Not that." Stephanie wished she hadn't brought up the subject, but didn't know how to stop now without drawing suspicion. They were tiptoeing far too near her secret shame.

Daniel's fingers flexed against the tabletop, his expression fierce and dangerous. "Don't tell me he hit you."

Stephanie tried not to react too strongly. She should have known he'd follow that line of thought. He was too smart not to make the leap of logic from cheating to abuse. She had to end it now.

"Let's don't go there, okay? This is not something I like to talk about."

He studied her in the dim candlelight for several heartbeats while her pulse thumped in warning. Finally, his rich voice quiet, he said, "All right. I'll let it go for now. But a woman like you shouldn't give up on love just because some fool didn't have sense enough to recognize a treasure."

"I thought you didn't believe in love."

"For myself, Stephanie. Only for myself."

Was he warning her off? Telling her not to feel anything for him? Not to fall for the gentle and kind man beneath the pirate's tough exterior?

If he was, she had a very bad feeling that his warning came too late.

From somewhere on the dark streets of London a clock chimed the hour. "Oh, for goodness' sake, Daniel. It's two o'clock."

She hopped up and began clearing away their dishes.

Daniel followed her into the kitchen where he stretched like a waking lion. "Doesn't feel a moment after one to me."

"We'll both be terrors tomorrow on so little sleep." She dumped the dishes in the sink and turned toward him. "Let's go. These will wait."

Daniel pretended shock and disbelief. "You're leaving the dishes undone?"

Stephanie raised a defiant chin. "Yes, I am."

"Will wonders never cease?" he said mildly. A smile quivered at the corners of his mouth.

As they left the kitchen, heading to the elevator, Daniel reached out, palm upward in invitation.

The night had been revealing and wonderful. And she'd begun to feel things she didn't want to feel again. Things that could get her hurt. Only she worried that this time, with this man, the hurt would be too much to bear.

She slipped her hand into his, accepting the fact that, regardless of what the future held, Daniel Stephens might be worth the risk.

CHAPTER SIX

"SCISSORS. Scissors. My kingdom for a scissors."

Daniel rummaged through the kitchen drawers, came up empty and decided to breach the inner sanctum of Stephanie's bathroom. Surely the woman owned a pair of scissors.

Without a second thought, he charged into her bedroom and came to a sudden halt. Though he had passed by and glimpsed the sleek blue and gray interior, he'd never come inside this room. The essence of Stephanie filled the space.

The bed was fluffy, white, and feminine. A dressing table against a wide window that looked out over the city contained the usual pots and jars that he couldn't comprehend. The curtains were open; light flooded the room.

He drew in a lungful of Stephanie-scented air. That gentle, expensive scent had driven him quite mad last night in the restaurant. He could stand here all day breathing it in.

Above a white painted chest of drawers, a single painting compelled him to a closer look. In startling contrast with the elegant, oriental-influenced artwork in the rest of the flat, slashing colors tore at the canvas in a violent assault. Perfectly centered within the storm of blues and violet was a shattered heart. On each broken piece was a tiny tormented face, dripping blood and tears.

Puzzled over why Stephanie would choose such a disturbing print for her bedroom, he squinted at the name scrawled in one corner.

His mouth fell open in surprise. "S. Ellison."

He'd known she painted, but this turbulent look inside the artist was startling to say the least. As if beneath the aloof exterior lay an unreachable depth of emotion screaming to be released.

Intuitively, he knew she would not be pleased by his observation. Backing away, he went into the bathroom, once more to be assaulted by her scent. Perfume. Shampoo. Soap.

"Scissors, Daniel. Scissors." Annoyed, maybe even unnerved that Stephanie occupied so much of his thinking, he found the scissors and got out of her private space. The hall bathroom was safer.

"Where to start…" he murmured, peering intently into the mirror. He lifted one long section of hair and snipped. Not so good. But it was too late to turn back now.

A few chops and curses later, he heard the front door open and close.

"Daniel."

He poked his head around the doorway. "In the hall bathroom."

Stephanie's heels tapped against the tile.

"I just wanted to tell you—" She paused in the open doorway. "Oh, dear."

Their eyes met in the mirror. "That bad, is it?"

Her mouth twitched. He gave her his fiercest glare,

which only made things worse. The twitch became a full-blown smile.

She took the scissors from his hand, an action that ensured he looked every bit as bad as he feared.

"Come in the kitchen and sit down."

"Why?"

She laughed. The woman actually had the audacity to laugh. "I'm going to save you."

"Can you?" he asked hopefully, feeling like an utter idiot, but relieved to know she could, and would, help out.

"I think so." She pulled a chair out. "Sit."

"Didn't we do this last night?" He squinted one eye up at her while she wrapped a towel around his neck and secured it.

"You seem to be having problems lately with your head."

"Tell me about it." She had no idea just how bad the problems *inside* his head were becoming. He looked doubtfully at the towel. "Does this have to be pink?"

"I will never tell a soul that the great Daniel Stephens, conqueror of Africa, marauding kittens and leaky dishwashers, wore a pink towel." She slid a comb through his hair, taking extra care over the cut from last night. "May I ask what brought this on?"

Hadn't she said he needed a trim? Not that he'd ever cared about appearances, but some people did. "Need to spruce up for that lunch meeting with my father."

She dipped around him, pleased. "You've decided to go?"

Thanks to her influence, but he didn't mention that. "Good business sense, don't you think? Those men own companies that could easily fund a water system for an entire village."

"Good sense, indeed." She combed his hair toward his face. It fell over his eyes. "How much of this do you want off?"

"My fate is in your hands."

She giggled. "Oh, Daniel. Pink towel and all, you do live dangerously."

Curiously happy, Daniel settled back into the chair and closed his eyes. Having Stephanie's hands on him, however he could get them there, was worth the humiliation of a botched haircut.

He let that thought linger for a while, studied on it. She was good for him as well as good to him. Being with her settled some of the restlessness. Maybe even some of the anger.

Last night had been a turning point of sorts when she'd let him come close, and he'd exulted in the knowledge that she'd trusted him, at least a little.

Though she'd stopped short of telling him all he wanted to know about her former lover, Daniel wasn't obtuse. The man had hurt her badly, maybe even physically abused her, though he hoped he'd misinterpreted that part. The idea of a man hitting her sickened him, but it explained why she'd been jumpy and wary in the beginning. Trust wouldn't come easy after that.

Stupid as it was, he'd been glad for that leaky dishwasher. Was even tempted to tear up some of the other pipes so he could fix them for her and watch her face light up with gratitude and admiration. Sharing secrets and cheesecake with Stephanie was worth the lump on his head.

"You have wonderful hair." Her voice had grown quiet.

He tried to think of a witty comeback but failed. How could he when her slim, sweet-scented body kept inadvertently bumping his as she moved around the chair, snipping and combing?

He'd had plenty of haircuts in his life, but none like this. None with a woman who interested him so much, whose touch warmed a cold place inside him. He tried to shake off the feeling. He didn't do emotional commitments and, from what Stephanie had told him last night, he sensed her reluctance in that area as well.

He couldn't understand why the idea of commitment even occurred to him. He enjoyed women. Always had. So what was the big deal with this particular one?

A lock of hair tumbled down, tickling. Stephanie brushed it away, then unfastened the towel and whipped it off.

He opened his eyes.

The tingling in his scalp moved lower.

She was bent at the waist sweeping a mountain of black hair into a dustpan. He silently cursed the calf-length dresses she always wore.

"There you go. All presentable…" Her voice trailed off. Must be the dopey expression on his face. She slowly put the dustpan aside.

At the moment, Daniel didn't care if he had hair or not. He did care that Stephanie was standing in front of him looking incredibly kissable.

He wrapped his fingers around her wrist. The bone felt fragile, delicate within his work-strengthened grip.

"We started something last night that we never finished," he said. "I'm a man who leaves nothing undone."

"Daniel," she warned without much conviction.

Stormy green eyes held his and he saw a yearning there as strong as the one in his own heart. He waited until she made the decision to come to him and then guided her onto his lap.

He wanted this moment to last. Wanted to watch her face and eyes. Wanted to see the desire flame up in her. He'd seen the painting. He knew she was a woman who hid deep passion behind this perfect, cool demeanor.

She touched his cheek. Fingers of silk stroked from cheekbone to the corner of his mouth and rested there. And then she smiled. Tremulous. Uncertain.

Uncertainty?

An ache of exquisite tenderness squeezed the breath from him. No, it couldn't be tenderness. He didn't *do* tenderness. Must be desire.

And to prove as much, he kissed her.

She was more than he bargained for.

Her mouth was far sweeter, far hotter, and far more willing than he'd imagined. She kissed him back with so much passion, his head reeled. His pulse thundered like rampaging elephants, and a swirl of some frightfully unfamiliar emotion pushed inside his chest. *Sweet, sweet, sweet* was all he could think.

And then as quickly as the kiss had begun, it ended. Stephanie yanked back from him, her mouth rosy and moist and horrified. Her eyes, wide and stormy as the Indian Ocean, darted frantically around the kitchen as if she had no idea where she was. She was shaking, though he didn't think from passion.

She leaped from his lap and rushed out of the room. Her bedroom door clicked shut with a little too much force.

He blinked at the empty kitchen. "What was that all about?"

With a vengeance, he kicked aside the chair and followed.

"Stephanie." He rattled the doorknob. Locked. "Let me in."

"Give me a minute." Her voice was shaky, strangled.

Oh, boy.

"Look. I'm sorry." Only that he'd upset her, not that they'd finally kissed. He shoved a hand over the top of his head, startled to have considerably less hair. "Will you tell me why you're upset?"

"I'm not upset."

An obvious lie. He blew out a breath.

"If you're worried about what people will think if we get, um, involved. I mean, because we're sharing a flat…"

"I'm not worried."

He gripped the back of his now hairless neck. "Okay, then. Good. I'm not, either."

When she didn't answer, he pecked at the door. "Steph. Listen. Remember what you told me last night, about the idiot that broke your heart?"

"Yes." Was that a smile in her voice? Maybe he was getting somewhere.

"No need to worry. The last thing I would ever want is to get involved. Emotionally, I mean. We both know up front that we aren't interested in that sort of thing. So we're safe. Right?"

With an abruptness that had him backing up to the far wall, the door opened and Stephanie came breezing out, every hair in place, lipstick refreshed, and no hint that anything had occurred. A warm, impassioned woman had gone into that room. The elegantly untouchable restaurant manager came out.

"Everything's fine, Daniel. Sorry for the overreaction to a little meaningless kiss." Tiptoeing, she kissed him on the cheek and then tip-tapped down the hall. "Gotta run."

A little meaningless kiss? Meaningless?

Daniel blinked at the slender backside disappearing around the corner.

He had never been so confused in his entire life.

Stephanie still shook as she entered the empty elevator. She hoped she looked more composed than she was feeling at the moment. Daniel had rocked her world. Completely. One kiss and she was lost for ever. Dear heaven above. She'd wanted the kiss to go on for ever, to always have Daniel's strong arms hold her as if he could shield her from the whole world. She'd felt so secure, so protected.

"I'm falling in love with him." Her throat tightened around the muttered words.

She'd suspected as much last night when they'd teased and talked in the restaurant. When the real man behind the pirate's face had revealed his true colors. Oh, she'd suspected her feelings for a while, but today had clinched it.

That was why she'd been so anxious not to let him ever touch her, kiss her. Deep down she'd known he had the ability to break down all her barriers and make her vulnerable again. Vulnerable, the one thing on earth she could never afford to be.

Daniel didn't want any part of love. Had even told her as much. She should be glad of that, considering her past. He probably wanted an affair. She didn't. Not that she didn't want him. But an affair meant revelation, and she couldn't allow him to discover the real Stephanie and be repulsed, as Brett had been. Besides, in the light of her deepening emotions, an affair that led to nowhere would never be enough.

What was she going to do now? He was her roommate, for crying out loud. She would see him every day without fail and fall more and more in love with him.

With a groan, she banged her head against the elevator doors. As if awaiting that cue, the lift stopped and rattled open. No one was in the hallway, thank goodness.

More out of habit than need, she straightened the neckline of her dress and started toward her office.

Her heels tapping along the tile corridor, her mind raced with indecision. What should she do? Tell Daniel the truth and risk rejection? Lie and say she wasn't interested so would he please not kiss her anymore? Admit her feelings? Find another flat?

One by one she examined each idea and tossed it aside. There was no answer to her dilemma.

For years, she'd kept an arm's length from every man. Now, in the space of a short few weeks, Daniel had crowded past her guard and seeped into her heart. She couldn't escape that fact any more than she could escape him. She wanted to be with him. She wanted to be kissed and held and loved again.

Okay. There was her answer. Not a perfect solution, but one she could live with. She could enjoy his company, accept his kisses, but make her intentions clear—she would never agree to an affair. That was the only way she could keep her sanity and also keep her secret. When he tired of her and moved on, she would survive. She always had.

As she passed the accounting office raised voices caught her attention. She slowed to a stop, listening, relieved to focus on something besides her tumultuous emotional state.

"Don't worry about it," Dominic was saying, his tone strained. "I can take care of the problem by Friday."

A voice she didn't recognize muttered something in reply. She couldn't make out the words, but the tone was tense. Curiosity lifted the hairs on the back of her neck.

What was going on in there?

She moved closer but noise from the kitchen blotted out the conversation. She caught bits and pieces, a word here and there, and, after a few minutes of unsuccessful eavesdropping, began to feel silly. If she wanted to know what was going on, she could ask, not stand in the hall lurking like a criminal. Ever since John had questioned her about a vendor transaction she'd made from her flat, she'd been suspicious of everyone and everything. Add Daniel's confirmation that her name had come up as one having access and she was jumping at shadows.

She went into her office and waited until she heard the door of the accounting office open. Then she stepped back into the hallway.

Dominic stood in the entry of his office watching the pair depart. He ran a finger beneath his shirt collar and took a deep breath.

"Dominic."

He whirled around, noticing her for the first time. "Stephanie, hullo. You startled me."

"I thought I heard angry voices. Who were those men?"

His eyes, so like Daniel's and yet so different, shifted toward the back door. "Those men? Mr Sandusky and Mr Richardson?"

He seemed reluctant to tell her more, but she remained silent, waiting. Finally, Dominic gave a short laugh and rubbed a hand over his head. Daniel had that same habit, but the effect was quite different on a balding pate. "That wasn't arguing. That was debate over a very important topic. My brother."

Now she was taken by surprise. "Daniel?" What did he have to do with this?

"Sandusky and Richardson are investors. I'm trying to convince them that Dan's water ventures could eventually be nice moneymakers for their group."

And here she'd been thinking bad thoughts. "What a wonderful thing to do, Dominic. Daniel will be touched."

A modest blush stained his cheeks. "He's my twin. I want the best for him. And if sweetening up some business investors will help, I'll do it."

"You really should tell him. He has videos, photos, statistics, all kinds of information that could seal the deal."

"No. No. Not yet." He stood up straighter, fidgeted with his tie. "I'd rather wait until they've committed. I don't want Daniel disappointed if they don't come on board."

"Oh, I see." And she did. She also felt terrible for the ugly doubts that had popped into her head. "Well, let me know if I can be of any help. Daniel will be thrilled by this."

Then she went inside her office and shut the door.

Poor, sweet Dominic.

All day she'd been worrying about the tampered

accounts and trying to pinpoint suspects. In hopes of affirming her own innocence, she'd begun to wonder about Dominic.

The problem had begun shortly after Dominic came to work for the restaurants. But that was all the so-called evidence she had. Well, except for the two times she'd walked into his office unannounced and seen him scramble to log off the computer.

She chided her runaway imagination. The guy was probably looking at sexy pictures and was embarrassed at being caught. She had no business thinking the worst of Daniel's brother.

Thank goodness, she hadn't said anything. An unfounded accusation could alienate both John and Daniel. Worse yet, it could hurt them. And the last thing she ever wanted to do was hurt her boss or the man she was falling in love with.

But someone was responsible. If she wasn't guilty, and Dominic wasn't guilty, it could very well be, as John feared, someone else in the family. But who?

CHAPTER SEVEN

LIFE was starting to go his way.

Daniel softly punched a fist into his palm, excited about the new agreement with AquaSphere Associates. Even the cloudy day couldn't dampen his enthusiasm.

He stopped in the restaurant's back doorway to scratch the kitten under the chin.

Stephanie had been right. Meeting with his father's business contacts had resulted in the first of what should be many more contracts for his fledgling company.

For all his reluctance to attend the lunch meeting, Daniel had to admit his father seemed genuinely committed to helping him. The issue still made him uneasy. A lifetime of neglect couldn't be made up in weeks, and money wouldn't fix the hurt of having no boyhood father. He wasn't sure what to feel for John. One thing for certain, trust had to be earned. And the jury was still out on that one.

The kitten arched her back and rubbed against his calf as he walked away, leaving stray hairs on his dark trousers. It had been a long time since he'd dressed in a suit and tie. He didn't much care for the discomfort, but the new haircut seemed to demand more conservative attire.

His thoughts drifted pleasantly from the meeting to the afternoon Stephanie had trimmed his hair. He ran a hand over his head, grinning at the memory. Not surprisingly, she'd done a good job of taming his unruly locks, at least to some degree. A perfectionist like her wouldn't have offered if she wasn't sure of the outcome.

It was the minutes after the haircut that stayed with him, though. That first kiss was imprinted on his mind as permanently as a tattoo. At the time, he'd thought it was the only kiss he'd ever get, but she'd surprised him the next day by kissing him. Not on the cheek as she'd done before, but on the lips, proving that she'd forgiven whatever wrong he'd done.

He didn't know why that pleased him so much, all things considered.

Now that she didn't jump every time he came near, Stephanie was great company. She was intellectually stimulating, witty, and generous to a fault. He knew she befriended her staff almost to excess, loaning money, listening to sob stories, filling in when someone needed time off. But she was also generous to him in ways that boggled his already confused thought processes. Without his knowledge, she'd spent hours developing a PowerPoint presentation from his slides. The exceptional work had most certainly made the difference in today's meeting.

If that wasn't enough to get any man thinking about her, she was also the most coolly gorgeous thing he'd ever seen. He could deal with that. But living under the same roof with a woman who stopped at kisses was driving him quite mad. And she would never agree to the only kind of relationship he could give, a physical one. He wished he had more to offer, but he didn't.

Ah, well, kisses were better than nothing.

Maybe he'd ask her to celebrate today's success with him. Perhaps take her to a football match, or they could head to the West End for dinner and a play. Stephanie would like that, he was sure, and he did own a decent suit now.

Happy and full of excess energy, he decided to take the stairway up to the flat. Pounding the steps two at a time, he reached the top without breaking a sweat.

Stereo music blasted through the glass balcony doors. Classic hard rock. Daniel laughed as he stepped inside the living room. The insistent, driving sound was so unlike the smooth jazz Stephanie preferred in the restaurant.

Only slightly winded, he drew in a deep breath. Stephanie's perfume swamped him.

Yes, it was a good day. A good, good day.

"Stephanie," he called, but wasn't surprised when she didn't answer. Superman couldn't hear over that music.

He followed the sound down the hall, thinking to knock on her bedroom door until she heard him.

When he saw that her door was already open, he slowed.

And then he froze.

Back to him, she stood at the closet, rifling through a rack of clothes encased in clear plastic cleaner bags. Her long wavy hair was piled on top of her head with the usual stray curls tumbling down. Tall, slim, and lithe, the beautiful redhead was nude.

But it wasn't the nakedness that had his heart slamming against his ribcage with the force of a freight train.

It was the scars.

From shoulder blades to mid-thigh, long, white scars marred the perfection of an otherwise beautiful body.

Daniel rocked back. What on earth—?

He stood in the dim hallway for several more stunned moments before realizing he had to get away. He couldn't let her catch him here, not like this, not when his face must register the storm raging inside.

Wheeling on the heels of his shiny new shoes, Daniel raced out of the flat and thundered down the stairs. Right now, he couldn't face anyone. He needed time alone to assess what he'd just witnessed.

The alleyway was thankfully empty except for rubbish bins, the kitten, and an illegally parked car. Weak in the knees and breathless, he leaned against the brick wall at the back of the restaurant and closed his eyes. The image of Stephanie's battered skin arose like a bad dream.

What had happened? Fire? A car crash?

He saw the scars again, the long, slashing stripes that lay like ritualistic lashes across her entire backside.

Ritualistic lashes.

As if he'd been slammed in the gut with a sledgehammer, all the air whooshed out of him.

Oh, my God.

A trembling started down his soul. He fought the tide of emotion, scared of what it meant. Pity. This must be pity. And rage. He had never been so angry. Not at his mother. Not at John. Not even at the inhuman conditions he had witnessed in the course of his work.

Some vile, evil maniac had intentionally beaten Stephanie until she was terribly, irreconcilably scarred. Not once, not even twice, but many times in a ritual of abuse.

Their conversation in the restaurant came back to him, sharp and in focus, making sense now. When she'd said her boyfriend had hurt her badly, he'd suspected violence, but this was unfathomable. Only a monster could have done this.

Why had she stayed with him? Why had she let this happen, not once but many times? Had she been controlled by him in some way? Threatened and afraid? Was this why she'd come to England? To escape a maniac?

His temples throbbed with a dozen questions he couldn't ask. Stephanie didn't want him to know. She'd be destroyed if she thought he had discovered her secret.

The scars explained so much. The reasons she had avoided physical contact with him, the fear in her eyes until he'd finally proven himself trustworthy. Even the elegant dresses that showed so little skin now made sense.

Stephanie's wariness wasn't from a cold heart. It was self-preservation.

He squeezed his eyes shut against the onslaught of emotion rising up inside him, swallowed the vile sickness in his throat. His poor, beautiful, broken Stephanie.

The devil who had committed this heinous crime deserved to die. And Daniel would have gladly done the deed without a blink of remorse.

Daniel walked the streets of Kensington for more than two hours before returning to the restaurant. Long shadows of evening fell across the alley. The kitten greeted him as usual. This time he picked her up and rubbed his face against her fur, soaking in the purring comfort before opening the back door.

His shirt was rumpled and untucked. His shoes were

now scuffed and dirty. He'd long since shoved the silk tie into a pocket and loosened the top shirt button.

The smells emanating from inside the Bella Lucia made his stomach growl. To a man who hadn't eaten since lunch, the scent of Italian food was pure heaven—ironic considering how sick he'd felt earlier.

The need to talk drove him to stop at Dominic's office, but his brother had already gone home to Alice and the kids. The knowledge that his twin had someone to go home to struck Daniel with a loneliness he seldom experienced. He'd never know that pleasure of family, never have someone to share his life and troubles.

The moment he walked into the dining room, he spotted Stephanie. His gut clenched.

Cool and smooth as the terracotta tile beneath her feet, Stephanie moved from table to table, dropping a warm greeting, a welcoming smile, a complimentary bottle of wine. The restaurant pulsed around her with the beat of unobtrusive jazz, trendy, chic, a respite from the busy streets outside.

No one would ever guess the pain and betrayal she'd lived through.

His admiration edged upward. She'd suffered far more than he ever had and yet she'd chosen not to wither, but to bloom.

Out of sight of customers, Daniel leaned in the doorway, watching her, the perfect manager, perfectly groomed, perfectly poised, perfect in every way except for the terrible sorrow she hid from the world.

Tenderness threatened to choke him.

Regardless of what had happened to her, Stephanie had

made a success of her life. She went right on caring about the people around her, nurturing those in need, giving, loving.

And unless he'd missed something, she had no one in her life to reciprocate. Who tended her when she was sick? Held her when she cried?

With a sigh, Daniel wondered if life would have been different if he'd ever learned to love someone other than himself. But no matter. He hadn't. His heart was as empty as the devil's soul, whether he liked it or not. He wasn't the kind of man Stephanie needed. He wasn't the kind of man any woman needed for more than a night or two, an admission that left him emptier than ever.

Stephanie disappeared into the cloakroom. Unfamiliar tenderness crowding his better judgment, Daniel pushed away from the wall and followed.

He eased up behind her and placed a kiss on the back of her neck.

"All work and no play—"

Stephanie spun around. Her skin tingled from the feath-erlike touch of Daniel's lips, from his warm breath on her skin. Since the first time they'd kissed and she'd realized she loved him, something had broken loose inside her. Though she would eventually pay with a broken heart, she hungered for the touch of another human being. But not just anyone. Daniel.

"I wondered where you were. How did things go today?"

"Great." He told her about the contract, but his mind seemed somewhere else. "I need someone to celebrate with me. How about you?"

A celebration with Daniel sounded lovely. "I'm working."

He took her hands and pulled her toward him. The

usual mischief danced in his eyes, but tonight she saw something else in those blue depths that she couldn't quite define.

"So," he said as he nuzzled her temple. "These excellent employees of yours can't finish the evening without you?"

Stephanie resisted the longing to lean closer and soak him up like the dry sponge of need she was. "Of course they can."

"Good." He stepped back, still holding her hands in his warm, calloused grip. "Grab your coat and let's go. I'll take you anywhere you choose. Say the word and I'll even put the cursed tie back on."

She laughed. "This is your celebration."

"Right. So indulge me. You choose."

He stroked a finger along her cheek, smiling at her in the strangest way. There it was again, that subtle difference, as though he really cared about what she wanted.

"You're in an unusual mood."

"Nothing unusual about taking my favorite lady out for a good time."

His favorite lady? Where had that come from?

He ushered her from the cloakroom, skirting around the diners to slip out the front door.

"I need to let Sheila know I'm leaving," Stephanie protested.

"Call her from the flat." Without warning, he backed her against the wall. On the streets, traffic pulsed and somewhere a car honked, but the air around the two of them grew silent. That gentle, questioning expression appeared on Daniel's face again. Then his lips covered hers with such exquisite tenderness Stephanie almost felt loved.

What in the world was going on with him tonight?

* * *

Whatever was going on didn't relent in the days to come.

On a blustery afternoon when November had shortened the days and the sky threatened a cold rain, Stephanie donned slacks and sweater for yet another outing with the indefatigable Daniel. The man had more energy than an electric company. He could spend the morning schmoozing clients, visiting job sites, and frequently working himself into a dirty, sweaty mess, then come breezing in to whisk her away from the restaurant for a few hours of adventure. Invariably, she protested out of duty to her job, but her protests grew weaker with every soft kiss and tender caress. She was helpless to turn down these special moments with the new, solicitous Daniel.

Coat and gloves in hand, she met him in the living room. All cleaned up in blue jeans and a turquoise sweater that turned his eyes to jewels, he helped her into her long leather coat. When he began to button it up with his large, competent fingers, a swell of pure pleasure filled Stephanie to the point of no return.

Head bent, a wayward lock of his dark hair fell forward. Stephanie pushed it away, then let her fingers drift down to the warm, whisker-rough curve of his cheek.

Lord, she loved this man.

"All done." But he didn't step back. Instead, he took her scarf, draped it around her neck and used the soft flannel to bring her face in line with his. The whisper of his breath, minty and fresh, kissed her lips. "Ready, then?"

"Ready." She was as breathless as if she'd run six flights of stairs.

Hand holding hers, he led the way to the elevator.

"Where are you kidnapping me to?" she asked when they were inside the lift.

He pressed the floor indicator and, with a wicked grin that set her heart thudding, said, "Secret."

He'd told her only that they wouldn't be back until late and she should dress casually. A twinge of guilt said she shouldn't be gone during the dinner rush, but John had told her more than once lately that she worked too much and should take more time off. She wondered if Daniel had anything to do with that.

"Let me check in with Sheila and make sure everything is running smoothly before we go."

Still grinning in that wicked, wicked manner, he backed her against the metal wall. "No."

She pushed at his chest. "I can't enjoy myself unless I'm sure everything is covered."

Sighing an overly dramatic martyr's sigh, Daniel slumped. "Woman, have you never in your life done anything irresponsible?"

On tiptoe, she kissed him. "Humor me. I might be worth it."

"Kiss me again and I'll believe you."

She obliged, and Daniel, the naughty man, deepened the kiss, holding it while the elevator pinged open and then closed again.

"Daniel!" Stephanie cried when he finally let her come up for air. Something had definitely come over him tonight.

"What?" His handsome face was a study in innocence.

She whacked him playfully on the arm. "Are we going to spend the entire evening in this elevator?"

He cocked his head as if giving the idea serious thought. "Can't beat the privacy. Let's do it."

Doing it would be wonderful, but Stephanie couldn't ever go there again. Not even with Daniel. She leaned around him and pushed the down button.

"Spoilsport." But he draped an arm around her waist and snuggled her close, nuzzling her neck in the seconds from her flat to the restaurant.

"You're making this very difficult."

"That's the plan."

When they finally exited the elevator, laughing like two sneaking teenagers, Stephanie felt lighter and happier than she had since the day she'd left Denver.

With Daniel's hand at her back in the most protective way, they went into the restaurant, spoke briefly to the competent Sheila, and then retraced their steps to the back door.

"We could use the front entrance, you know," Stephanie said.

"What about the motorcycle I have waiting?"

"You do not," she said, but, knowing Daniel as she did, he probably did.

His eyes gleamed with mischief. "Try me."

A thrill of excitement raced along Stephanie's spine. She couldn't think of anything more wonderful than riding behind Daniel, her arms around his waist as the cold wind whipped her hair and stung her cheeks.

He paused outside Dominic's office and reached inside his coat pocket to extract a small box. "Let me drop this off first. Dominic's eldest is having a birthday."

Before Stephanie could comment on his thoughtfulness, Daniel pushed the door open. Two men whirled around. Anger sizzled from them as palpable and menacing as a nest of vipers.

Stephanie's breath froze in her throat. The investors were back and none too happy. Dominic sat behind the desk perspiring profusely.

She didn't know what was going on, but something was badly wrong. The tension in the room was thick enough to choke an elephant.

Daniel's hands fisted at his side. He looked from his brother to the two men. "Is there a problem?"

His tone was tough and protective, leaving no doubt about whose side he was on.

A pair of the hardest, coldest eyes she'd ever seen glared back. "No problem at all." The reptilian glance shifted to Dominic. "Isn't that right, Dom?"

Dominic pushed up from the squeaky chair. Stephanie couldn't help noticing a tremble in his hands. "Everything is fine. Just a bit of unfinished business." He hustled around the desk to usher the two men to the door. "I'll call you tomorrow about that project. You have my word."

Daniel looked at Stephanie and murmured, "What's going on?"

She lifted her shoulders, afraid he wouldn't appreciate her thoughts.

The rumble of voices in the hall told her that Dominic's unfinished business was quite a serious topic.

When Dominic returned to the office visibly shaken, Daniel asked, "What was that all about? Who were those guys?"

"Old friends." His face was pale. "No one you know."

Now Stephanie knew he was lying. The ugly suspicion

rose again, this time with enough strength to give the doubts validity. Dominic wasn't soliciting investors for his brother's business. He was up to no good. He had to be. Otherwise, why behave so strangely and lie so blatantly?

This time, Stephanie had no choice. She had to inform John that something was not right with the accountant. Maybe he wasn't embezzling funds, but something was definitely amiss.

Stephanie glanced at Daniel, her heart sinking lower than the Alaskan sun. She was about to accuse his brother of a crime.

He was going to hate her for this.

CHAPTER EIGHT

"LIKE it?" Daniel shouted over one shoulder, his voice yanked away by the force of wind and speed.

Stephanie leaned forward, mouth all but touching Daniel's ear. "It's wonderful."

The motorcycle sped through the streets and alleys of London, dodging in and out of places they probably shouldn't have ridden. But Daniel, confident and competent, had no fear. With him in control Stephanie didn't either. Hands locked over the smooth, supple leather of his jacket, she reveled in the energy racing through her bloodstream. For the first time in a long time, she felt carefree and alive.

She could have ridden for ever and been happy, but Daniel slowed and pulled into a parking bay.

"We're going to be tourists tonight," he said, helping her off the bike.

"Like this?" She shook her hair out, knowing she looked wild and wind-kissed.

"You're beautiful." Daniel bent to kiss her nose. "But your nose is cold."

She tiptoed up and returned the kiss. "So is yours."

He growled deep in his throat and made a teasing grab

for her. With a squeal, she jumped back, stumbled and was quickly righted by his strong hands.

"Careful there. We have lots of walking to do."

Pulse tripping, more from Daniel's touch than the near fall, Stephanie slipped her hand into his. "Where are we headed?"

"There." He pointed upward at the huge, rotating London Eye. "And then other places."

Even this late in the fall, the area along the South Bank of the Thames was alive with visitors, the smells and sounds almost carnival-like. They bought tickets, joined the growing line, and boarded an enclosed glass pod of the giant observation wheel. Buildings and people grew tiny as the Eye slowly ascended.

"I feel like I'm inside a bubble," she said.

Daniel smiled his reply and moved them closer to the window. Other visitors sharing the pod oohed and ahhed, pointing out landmarks as the wheel continued its climb.

A little boy with a posh accent carried on a running commentary to his parents as various sites came into view. Daniel shrugged and stuffed his guidebook into a pocket.

"Nothing like a personal tour," he muttered against her temple.

For Stephanie, the landmarks weren't the important part of the ride. Being with Daniel was. Yet, the panorama was breathtaking.

Through a moisture-smeared veil, she glimpsed London spread in every direction around the mighty river. In the west, the sun was setting. Though the fog and haze obscured the sunset, rays of diffused light penetrated just enough to cast a glorious glow over the city.

The South Bank, a cultural Mecca for art, music and

theatre, was a place she'd been wanting to visit since coming to London, but had never had the time. She was glad. Seeing the area with Daniel made it even more special.

Positioned behind her, her favorite barbarian rested his chin atop her head and pulled her back against him. Through her coat she felt the press of his jacket zipper, the mold of his muscled chest and belly, and the strength of his arms lightly bracketing her waist, and marveled at how safe she felt. She, who never felt safe in a man's arms, wanted to stay here for ever, loving him always as she did this moment.

She closed her eyes, the panorama briefly forgotten, and focused on the essence of Daniel. He smelled of leather and fresh air and that manly scent that was uniquely his. Though a dozen or so other people occupied the pod, Stephanie felt as if they were the only two people around. Something magical had happened when he'd come into her life, as if the thick miasma of fear and distrust had blown away in the fresh breeze of a man without false motives.

She knew where she stood with him. He'd made no secret that they could never be more than they were now, a fact that both comforted and seared. Comforted because he would never see the scars and be repelled. Seared because she loved him and knew these moments with him could not last.

The quiet burr of his voice forced her eyes open.

"According to our worthy guide," he said wryly, "we can spy Buckingham Palace right over there." He dipped closer, his cheek to hers, and pointed in the general direction.

The touch of his skin against hers was electric. She

turned to face him, resisted the urge to kiss the corner of that sexy mouth. "I think we could see the entire city if the weather was clear."

"The view from right here is even lovelier." As if he wanted to memorize every feature, Daniel scanned her face.

"Why, Mr Stephens, are you trying to flatter me into another late-night trip for cheesecake and chocolate sauce?"

"Is it working?"

"Could be," she answered and was rewarded with a quick flash of white teeth against his dark skin.

And then the rest of the trip around the wheel was lost as they focused on each other instead of the London skyline. For Stephanie those moments staring into Daniel's handsome face defined the evening. Inside their own glass bubble, a real romance with the man she had fallen in love with actually seemed possible.

When the ride ended, they strolled the promenade along the waterfront, stopping to watch the cruise ships pass. Darkness had come and streetlamps illuminated the tree-lined path and reflected off the river's edge in a dance of shadows and light.

"It's a long walk around," Daniel said when she opted to walk to the Millennium Bridge.

"I don't mind." The longer they walked, the longer she would be with him, alone and having fun. And the longer she could pretend they had something special together.

"We can hire a cab back to the bike."

"Or walk." Like a happy child, she wrapped her arms around herself and spun around in a circle. "This is so awe-some."

Daniel caught up to her, grabbed her hands and whirled

her again. "I thought you would fret over the restaurant all night."

"Shh. Don't tell a soul. I'm relieved to be away for a while." The Bella Lucia didn't worry her, but she couldn't get Dominic, and the coming conversation with John, off her mind. Daniel hadn't said a word more about the incident in the office, but he had to be concerned as well. Even if Dominic hadn't taken the money, something was not quite right with Daniel's twin.

She stopped spinning and the open lapels of her long coat swished against her boot tops. "What do you think is going on with Dominic?"

Daniel grew serious. "I think he may be in trouble, though he doesn't confide in me the way he once did."

"No guesses? No twin's intuition?"

He frowned, deep furrows in his sun-bronzed brow. "None."

She wanted to ask if he thought his brother would embezzle money, but feared Daniel would take offense. And the last thing she wanted tonight was to spoil the magical evening.

"It worries you. I shouldn't have brought it up." They started walking again. "Change of subject. Tell me about your work today. About the projects. What's happening?"

"One of the reasons for my good mood." He seemed relieved to sidestep the topic of his brother. "Today I hired two water technicians and another engineer to help carry the load on all the waste-water management projects I've taken on. Plus, I have a meeting set up next week with Lord Rathington."

She blinked up at him. "Should I be impressed?"

"Very." Daniel's proud smile pushed the Dominic dilemma to the back of her mind. "The man owns half of Britain, including WS Associates, the consulting firm that can make or break an upstart company like mine. And, rumor has it, he's made a few safaris to Africa."

"Ah."

"Exactly. He seldom meets personally with anyone, but he's agreed to see me."

Stephanie smiled. "You are the most amazing man to have achieved all this since coming to London."

He laughed. "You give me too much credit. I'm sure my father had something to do with it."

"Be that as it may, I think you're amazing, and I'm proud of you."

"Keep talking. You're good for my ego."

She was in the process of forming a snappy comeback when they rounded a curve in the river and a glorious display of lights blazed in the darkness.

"Is that St Paul's?" Stephanie stared in wonder at the elegant old cathedral.

"Glorious, isn't it?"

"I had no idea it was this impressive. I suppose it's closed at this time of night?" she asked, hoping.

"I'm afraid so. But there *is* something here in the neighborhood I want to show you."

Her disappointment at not seeing the interior of St Paul's turned to curiosity. There were so many landmarks in this section of London, she wondered what he could have in mind. Perhaps the Globe? Or the Tate Modern? He knew she loved contemporary art. He'd even teased her about it when she'd said she hated the masters but loved the abstract and avant-garde. Of course, she hadn't told him why she despised those classic paintings. Another secret better kept.

Instead of the Tate, however, he turned down a side street toward a closed and darkened business section.

"Where are we going?"

"You'll see," he said mysteriously, suppressed excitement in every word.

"Now I really am curious."

Boots echoing along the quiet street, Daniel stopped in front of a lovely older brick office building.

"Here we are. She has character, don't you think?"

"Yes. But exactly who is she?"

"*She* is the office space I leased today for Stephens International Water Design."

"Daniel! Oh, my goodness." She didn't know whether to laugh or cry. He looked so proud and so much like a small boy wanting approval.

She threw her arms around him in an enthusiastic embrace. "This is marvelous. A real office. Can we go in? Please."

Her reaction clearly thrilled him. He threw his head back and laughed. "Whatever the lady desires."

She desired, all right, something far more precious than a tour of an office building. But seeing Daniel happy was enough for now.

Inside the small but pleasant office space, Daniel stood with hands on hips waiting for her to comment.

"I can see a pair of plush chairs here along this wall, blue, I think," she said, moving around the room as decorating images flashed in her head. "And a nice wall grouping above them. Perhaps a black and white photo display of some of your projects. And the desk will go here. A very modern computer desk and—"

Daniel caught her in mid-sentence and spun her around. "You're a special woman, Stephanie."

Her heart caught in her throat. "Because I like to decorate?"

His chuckle raised warm goose bumps on her arms. "Because I needed you to approve."

Was that uncertainty? In a man as confident and strong as Daniel?

"This office is perfect. And what better place for a water-project engineer than along the shores of the Thames?"

"I knew you'd appreciate the symbolism."

Hand in hand, they took a brief tour of the office, then made their way back out on the street. All the way to the Millennium Bridge, Daniel talked nonstop about his plans and ideas for the fledgling business.

"You will succeed beyond your wildest dreams, Daniel," she said when he expressed a concern to the contrary. "I believe that with all my heart."

The long, water-washed pedestrian bridge stretched across the river and welcomed strolling couples. Stephanie and Daniel walked to the center and stopped to look down at the river below.

Lights from the shore gleamed on the water, and fog twisted and smeared the panorama into an impressionistic painting. Gentle music from a passing cruise ship wafted up to them. With a half-smile that made her pulse race, Daniel inclined his head.

"Dance?"

A few other strollers passed by, but Stephanie paid them no mind. She lifted the edge of her long coat and dipped a curtsey, then stepped into Daniel's beloved arms. For a few glorious minutes while the boat hovered nearby, they swayed and swirled on the pedestrian bridge. Resting her cheek in the crook of his neck, she reveled in the scent of his skin and delighted in the beat of his heart echoing hers.

Could he be feeling the same thing she was? This incredible surge of joy, this new willingness to be vulnerable to another person regardless of the past? Her heart swelled with the hope that both of them could lay aside their hurts and move forward together. She loved him. Dared she admit her feelings?

Everything he did tonight spoke of caring, but he claimed to have no love to give. With each passing moment in his company, Stephanie found that harder and harder to believe. If this continued, she would have to tell him.

But not tonight. She couldn't chance shattering the lovely fantasy of tonight. Here in Daniel's arms along the bank of the Thames, she could pretend that he loved her, too.

"Telephone call, Stephanie. The man says it's very important."

The evening rush was on and the restaurant was alive with trendy Londoners. Stephanie didn't mind. She was still walking on air from the incredible date with Daniel the evening before.

"Okay, thanks, Sheila."

She scribbled "zucchini" on a notepad beside the kitchen door, then caught herself and wrote "courgette" instead. The dish had come back to the kitchen uneaten on several plates. And whether she called the vegetable courgette or zucchini, less than marvelous food was not acceptable in her restaurant.

"He's calling long distance. From Colorado."

Her pen clattered to the tile.

"Colorado?" Was that squeaky sound coming from her? "Tell the waiting staff to downplay the courgette and recommend the potato-aubergine tart as an alternative. I'll be right back."

With a heavy dread, Stephanie went into her office, closing the door behind her. She took several long, steadying breaths, then punched the hold button.

"Stephanie Ellison speaking."

She braced herself for the horrid voice.

"Miss Ellison?" Relief shimmied through her. It wasn't him. "George Howard Whittier here. I hope I haven't caught you at a bad time."

Her stepfather's law partner. She glanced up at the clock, calculating the time in Colorado. Afternoon, if she figured correctly, though the sun had set in London. "Is something wrong?"

"I'm sorry to break the news so abruptly, but I've had difficulty tracking your whereabouts. I do hope you're not alone." Gentlemanly hesitation hummed across the ocean.

"What is it, Mr Whittier?"

"My dear, your father passed away two weeks ago."

Stephanie dropped the telephone and slithered to the floor.

Daniel tossed restlessly in his bed. He'd had a bad feeling all day, a kind of premonition that something was amiss.

In the sometimes dangerous situations he had been in while working abroad, he'd learned to trust his gut instincts. The simplest clue, such as a sudden hush of animal sounds in the darkness, often meant trouble ahead.

Tonight he felt that same hush brooding over the flat. Stephanie had come in an hour ago, claiming exhaustion, and had gone straight to bed. He knew the restaurant had been hopping tonight, but he was disappointed. He looked forward to the evenings when they had time to talk.

All day, she'd been on his mind. Her sweetness, her scent, the taste of her skin. When he'd shown her his future office space, she'd reacted just as he'd hoped, with the same excitement he'd experienced when he'd signed the lease.

He flopped over on the firm mattress and punched his pillow into a fluffier lump. If the noise wouldn't bother Stephanie he'd get up and work on the new monitoring design for flood control in North Yorkshire.

If she weren't so tired, he'd wake her and they'd sneak down to the kitchen for a midnight snack.

He slammed the pillow again. Might as well admit, Stephens, you're miffed. After last night when they'd had such a great time, he had expected a repeat performance or, at least, a recap. There had been that moment on the bridge when they'd danced and the world had seemed to fade away, leaving only the two of them. He relished the idea of being alone with her, frequently and for long periods.

He sat up, feet over the side of the bed, and shoved five fingers through the top of his hair. What was happening to him? His mind should be on work and water and fund-raising. Those things were his life. A woman was only a passing fancy, but Stephanie no longer fit his carefully structured view of women.

Frustrated, he flopped backwards on the bed and lay staring at the shadows dancing on the ceiling.

A sharp cry yanked him up again.

"Stephanie?" he called, knowing she couldn't hear from this far away. He got up and opened his bedroom door. A scream pierced the night. Whimpering sobs began. And then a terrible pleading.

"No. Please. No."

Hair rose on his arms.

He'd heard her nightmares when he'd first arrived and had done nothing. In time, the bad dreams had subsided. But now he couldn't stay away. Not after he'd seen the scars.

Heart thundering, he rushed into her bedroom.

"Stephanie. Love. Wake up."

Eyes accustomed to the darkness, he could see her, feel her thrashing in agony. Without a second thought, Daniel climbed onto the bed and pulled her into his arms.

"No. Please." She fought him like a wild thing, but his strength was far greater—just as someone else's had been. An awful sick lump formed in his throat.

"Stephanie. Love. It's Daniel. Wake up. You're safe. You're safe." He held fast, pressing her face into his naked shoulder until she went limp against him, and he knew she had awakened.

Her body trembled while Daniel crooned meaningless words of comfort against her hair. Even sweat-soaked, she smelled of exotic flowers.

When at last she quieted, he stroked the damp hair from her face and kissed her forehead. "Tell me."

She shook her head and shrank back as if only now aware that they were in a bed together. "A nightmare."

That was obvious. "About?" he urged as gently as he knew how.

Using the sheet for a tissue, she dabbed her damp eyes, then drew in a long, shuddering breath. "Something happened tonight. A phone call from my family's attorney."

Daniel waited, saying nothing, but trying to put the two events together.

"My father died two weeks ago." The words came out flat and wooden. "And I didn't even know."

For Daniel, missing his father's funeral wouldn't have mattered even a month ago, but now that family had intruded into his life he knew he would care if something happened to John. He didn't want to care and wasn't about to let John know as much, but he would. Stephanie hadn't been home for her own father's funeral. Understandable that news of his death would set off a bad dream.

"I'm sorry, love. Truly." He wanted to hold her, but she seemed not to want that, so he settled for touching the back of her cheek with his knuckles.

"I have to go to Colorado," she whispered, "and settle the estate."

"So soon?" Daniel flipped on the bedside lamp.

Stephanie's eyes were red and wild as she blinked against the sudden flood of light.

"Yes. Now. Tomorrow." Her hands began to pick and twist at the sheet in a way that Daniel recognized as deep anxiety.

"Is it that urgent?"

"I don't want to go back, but I have to."

A quiver of worry intruded. "Is he still there? Your ex?"

"Brett?" She looked bewildered. "No. No. Not any-more."

He felt a measure of relief. If the monster who'd abused her wasn't there, she'd be safe.

She shoved off the bed. Silk pajamas whispered against her skin. She paced to the window and back. The trembling started again and Daniel wasn't sure what she needed.

He offered all he could. "You've had terrible news. You're distraught. Come here. Let me hold you."

As if he were the lifeboat in a stormy ocean, she fell upon him, knocking him onto his back. He took her with him.

Her wild tangle of curls fell across his face. He pushed them aside, trying to read her expression, to understand what she was feeling.

"Come with me, Daniel," she murmured, the request urgent, almost frantic. "I can't do this alone."

"Love." Beyond that, he was at a loss. The old fear rose up. What was she asking?

"Please, Daniel. I need you beside me. I need your strength. I love you. You have to know that by now. And I need you with me. I can't get through this alone."

Daniel stiffened. She loved him?

Oh, no.

Stephanie's warm, slender body lay atop his and yet he had no sexual urgings, just the terrible need to run. He was a coward of the worst kind, but the word love scared him out of his mind.

"Stephanie, sweetheart. Listen to me." He rolled them to the side so they lay face-to-face. Her stormy sea eyes were wild and distraught. "You don't love me. You can't."

He wasn't lovable. And he had no love in him. Hadn't he told her as much?

"But I do," she whispered. "I didn't mean to. I didn't want to. But I love you."

Daniel released a groan of dismay. What had he done? Stephanie needed far more than he had to give. She deserved far more than a man with no heart, no soul.

He squeezed his eyes closed against the onslaught of despair. No matter what he did now, she would be hurt even more than she already was.

The best thing he could do for both of them was get away. He sat up, putting distance between them. If he touched her much longer, he'd do something stupid. She didn't deserve the kind of misery a life with him would bring. He was too empty. He had nothing to give her. Nothing.

"We agreed early on that neither of us wanted emotional commitment." He couldn't look at her. "You can't love me, Stephanie." His own mother hadn't. How could she? "I can't love you. I don't know how. I don't have it in me."

She touched his bare arm. "You're wrong. You have so much love, it scares you."

He shook his head. She didn't understand. He didn't expect her to.

"Don't you see, Daniel? A man who gives his entire life to improve life for others has plenty of love. You're afraid. That's all. So was I, but you're not like him."

She was afraid of loving, too, and now he'd ruined her for good. She would never chance letting another through her force field of protection.

"I'm sorry, Stephanie. Truly." She'd never know how sorry.

"Go with me, Daniel. No strings. I can't do this alone."

But she loved him and love always expected something in return.

"The meeting with Lord Rathington," he said feebly.

Drawing the sheet up like a coat of armor, she sat up straighter in the center of the bed. Her expression went cool, her body still as stone. "Of course. How thoughtless of me. You can't miss that."

He stood like the stunned fool he was, wishing he had something more to give her. Something that mattered. In the end, he said the only thing he could. "I'll move my things into the new office while you're gone."

Red-eyed and flushed, she nodded with the regal grace of a queen. "I think that's best."

She was right. It was for the best. He had nothing to offer her, and prolonging the relationship would serve no good purpose.

Then why did he have the strongest need to crawl back onto that bed and beg her forgiveness?

CHAPTER NINE

COLORADO was as beautiful as ever. But even the majesty of the snow-covered Rockies couldn't lift the dark mood hanging over Stephanie like a London fog as she maneuvered her rental car through the streets and inclines of downtown Denver.

As much as she dreaded the days ahead of settling the family estate, the heartache of that last fight with Daniel tormented her most.

Why had she said those foolish words? Why had she tossed her heart out on that bed for him to reject? What was it about her personality that navigated toward men destined to hurt her?

And yet, Daniel was nothing like Brett or Randolph. For all his denials and sharp cynicism, Daniel cared deeply about people. And after that wonderful, magical night along the Thames, she'd even believed he cared about her.

Over and over, for the entire international flight, she'd puzzled over Daniel's behavior and called herself ten kinds of fool. She'd walked right into that opportunity for Daniel to break her heart.

But Daniel had suffered hurt, too. Somehow, from his

mother's and father's mistakes, he'd come to think of himself as unlovable and unloving. He was wrong. But Stephanie was too tired and weak to fight anymore. She wasn't even sure she had the emotional strength to face the meeting with the Ellison family lawyer.

Her grip on the steering wheel tightened as the tall glass and steel building came in sight.

Might as well admit the truth. She was scared out of her mind.

She pulled the rental car into a parking garage filled with cold air and exhaust fumes, then rode the elevator up to the eighteenth floor to the law offices of Whittier, Ellison, and Carter. The suites, ultra-conservative, just like her stepfather, occupied one end of the floor.

An immaculately groomed brunette receptionist and a security guard manned the entrance. Randolph had always been paranoid about security. To Stephanie's way of thinking, his own conscience had known he deserved to be shot.

"Stephanie Ellison to see Mr Whittier," she told the receptionist.

The action was nothing new. Even as a child, she and her mother had been expected to check in at the desk and wait their turn as if they were nothing but business appointments instead of family. Randolph Ellison had never cut her a bit of slack. Not in any way. She wasn't expecting today to be any different.

"Miss Ellison?" The brunette assessed her with an open curiosity that would have displeased her now-dead employer. Underlings were to maintain professional decorum at all times. "Mr Whittier is expecting you. I'll buzz him and you can go right in."

"I know the way, thank you." Without waiting, Stephanie pushed through the heavy double doors and knocked at the inner office marked "George H. Whittier, Attorney at Law."

"Stephanie, my dear child, come in. Come in." Mr Whittier, tall and angular in his gray business suit, came around an enormous oak-and-glass desk to greet her. As bony as he was, she expected him to rattle.

He seated them both. "You look wonderful, positively luminous. London must agree with you."

"Thank you. I'm happy there." Or she had been until she had allowed Daniel to break her heart. She ran damp palms over her royal-blue designer suit, chosen specifically to provide the confidence needed to get through this meeting. "If you don't mind, Mr Whittier, could we get down to business? I'd like to get back to England as soon as possible."

The jovial expression turned somber. "You do realize that there is a great deal to be done before the estate can be settled. I'm afraid this may take some time."

She gripped the tiny designer purse in her lap. "How long?"

"Several weeks at least. Maybe longer with the holidays coming on. Business moves much slower at this time of year."

The holidays. She'd hardly given them a thought with all that was happening in London. But here in America, business came to a near standstill from late November through the New Year.

Her stomach began to churn. How could she face dealing with Randolph's estate for more than a day or two? The nightmares had come nonstop since she'd first gotten word of his death. It was as if he had the power to reach from the grave to torment her.

"I don't want any of it, Mr Whittier. Give everything to charity."

"That's not possible, my dear. Your father made certain you couldn't do that. You see, he was very concerned about your state of mind after you went away to college."

Concerned? Yeah, right. He was concerned that she'd tell someone the truth about the powerful, respected attorney turned local politician. But she never had. She'd been too ashamed then and she was too ashamed now.

Face carefully composed, she asked, "What do I have to do?"

"Randolph set the trust up very carefully. There are stipulations regarding distribution of certain properties."

A chill circled her heart like cold fingers. "He couldn't touch the trust my mother left me, could he?" Knowing Randolph as she did, he had tried.

"No, of course not. But the bulk of the estate is in a trust of Randolph's creation. You have control, of course, but some of the holdings come with stipulations." He picked up a sheaf of papers and cleared his throat. "Your father left a letter addressed to you."

Stephanie wanted to ask him to stop calling Randolph Ellison her father. But there was another carefully pre-served lie that she wasn't ready to admit to the world.

She reached for the letter and was surprised when the attorney did not hand it over. "I'm sorry." She dropped her hand. "I thought you said it was addressed to me."

"It is. But your father instructed that I read it aloud in your presence." He shifted, clearly uncomfortable. "I know the contents, Stephanie, and I want to apologize in advance. I tried to convince Randolph not to include this, but he insisted. Just as he insisted that it be read aloud."

One last opportunity to humiliate her, no doubt.

"You have to understand," Whittier went on. "After you left, Randolph became quite bitter. I'm afraid he never got over your abandoning him after your mother's death."

Stephanie held back an angry retort. She hadn't abandoned him. No longer afraid for her mother, she'd escaped from hell. But knowing Randolph as she did, she wasn't surprised that he had become the injured party, playing her as the ungrateful, heartless daughter.

Her head began to pound, but she kept her expression empty and her voice cool and calm. "Read the letter, please."

"Very well." Whittier gave her another long look before bowing his head to the missive and beginning to read.

My dear Stephanie, he read.

Your best interest and that of your beloved mother has always been the focus of all I do. You know this is true. I never wanted anything but the best for you.

The old hypocrite. If he'd wanted her to react to that outright lie, he would be disappointed. She sat still and straight. Randolph, good lawyer that he had been, had begun his attacks gently, saving the zinger for last. She had to be ready for anything.

Your mother and I gave you the best life possible. We raised you in the best society, with the finest education and all the material things money could buy.

Yet, you never appreciated any of it. You are an ungrateful, disobedient young woman who does not deserve my generosity.

Thank you, Daddy Dearest. You always were so very, very generous with money as long as the other price was paid.

The lawyer's gray gaze flickered up to hers, a warning that the worst was yet to come. Stephanie braced herself. The cold trembling started deep in her stomach.

The letter went on for several pages of hideous vitriol until Stephanie wanted to bolt from the room and never return. But, after all she had suffered at Randolph's hands, she was not about to give him that satisfaction.

The trembling spread to her knees. Though her face blazed with humiliation, she sat straight and stiff in the armchair and waited until the diatribe ended.

Mr Whittier lay the paper aside and looked up. "Again, my apologies, Stephanie, for the remainder of this document. Would you like some refreshment, tea perhaps, before we continue?"

"No, thank you. Just get it over with. After the last few pages, I can handle anything."

She wasn't sure if that was exactly true, but she had no choice. On the outside she remained poised. The inside raged with anger and hurt and a sick dread.

After another moment of hesitation, Whittier pushed his glasses on and finished.

Under the circumstances, I should turn you out in the street penniless. But I am a generous man whose charity extends beyond the grave. Considering that your real father was nothing but trash who seduced your mother and left me with his bad seed, I am not surprised by your disgraceful behavior. I'm only thankful that my blood does not flow in your veins. Nevertheless, I tried to keep you from following your mother's same wanton path. But just as I forgave her, I am forgiving you.

Whittier glanced over his bifocals. "You can rest assured, my dear, that this meeting is entirely confidential. Nothing in this letter will ever leave this room."

The heat of embarrassment deepened. She swallowed past the cotton in her throat. No one outside of her mother, herself and Randolph had ever known the truth about her parentage—until now. "Thank you."

The quiver in her voice angered her. She would not let Randolph get to her, not now.

Whittier carefully folded the letter in thirds and replaced it in the vellum envelope. "I need your signature to indicate the letter was read to you. Then I must sign before a notary as proof that I followed Randolph's instructions to the letter."

"He was always thorough." Hands trembling, she dashed her signature across the indicated line. "Is this all?"

The sooner she had this settled, the sooner she could sell that house of horrors and go home to England.

"The will itself is quite straightforward. We've only to clear the house, decide on what you want done with other properties, and wait for probate. All the properties, bank accounts, and holdings are already in your name."

She stared at him, stunned. "You're kidding. After that horrible letter, he left me everything? No strings attached?"

His expression was sympathetic. "He left you everything, but Randolph always attached strings."

Of course. The loud banging inside her head intensified. "And that would be…?"

"You are to personally clean out the family home, and neither it nor the acreage around it can ever be sold as long as you live. Randolph said you would understand his reasons."

Black spots danced in front of her eyes. The devil. Oh, yes, she understood why he had done this. He knew how much she hated that house. That she never wanted to cross that threshold again. So he connived to punish her one final, lifelong time.

Daniel slapped the lift button and waited impatiently for the door to ping open.

He didn't think his week could get any worse. After supervising a job site east of the city, he'd come back to find problems with another project. Then word came that his furniture couldn't be delivered for at least a week, and now this urgent call from his brother.

His black mood deepened. Annoyed with waiting, he abandoned the lift and pounded down the stairs.

Stephanie had been gone a few days and since she'd left, his mood had been black as midnight. Nothing was going right, and he was going crazy living in that flat. If he had to sleep on his bare office floor, he was moving out.

The flat screamed Stephanie's name, her scent, her belongings. Even her art and the fastidious organization of her kitchen cabinets reminded him of her.

He couldn't sleep either, something he'd always been

able to do, even under the most adverse environmental conditions. Then last night, he'd completely lost it. He'd suffered the stupid urge to crawl into Stephanie's empty bed. At the last minute, he'd camped on the floor of the living room, her pillow cradled in his arms for the entire sleepless night.

Yup. He was losing his mind.

And to top it all off, something serious was happening with his brother. In the urgent phone call just now, he'd heard fear and desperation. All Dominic would say was, "I'm in trouble, Dan. Get down here fast."

So here he was, out of breath, cranky, and worried as he entered the small accounting office.

Dominic sat at his desk, complexion gray as ashes. Their father, John, sat across from him. Daniel glanced from one to the other and back again. They were both as grim as a double murder.

He felt a protective need to stand between the two.

"What's going on?" he asked.

The question was meant for Dominic, but John replied.

"For the past few weeks money has slowly disappeared from the Bella Lucia accounts."

"Yeah?" He knew that. Stephanie worried about the issue all the time. He also suspected what was coming, and the idea that his own father would accuse Dominic of stealing got his hackles up.

"Stephanie came to me with her suspicions," John said quietly.

Daniel felt as if he'd been struck by lightning. "Stephanie?"

How could she do that? Why hadn't she at least warned him?

John waved off his protestation. "Don't blame her. She didn't want to say anything, but she had to. It took a bit of work, but we finally figured out how the money was being diverted."

John's sad gaze settled on Dominic. With a start, Daniel saw the physical similarities between his fraternal twin and their father. "Your idea was both simple and brilliantly clever. Set up false service accounts into which the money, in the guise of payments, was electronically diverted from a remote location, so that any of the other people with access could be blamed. Why, son? Why would you do this?"

Eyes downcast, Dominic rested his forehead on the heel of his hand, his voice desperate. "I only meant to borrow the money. I was going to put it back, I swear." He lifted his head and looked at Daniel. "You have to believe me, Dan. I was in a pinch for cash and borrowed heavily from some individual investors. After that, things got out of hand."

"Loan sharks," John said flatly. "They always find a way of making you pay and pay."

And suddenly Daniel recalled the two men he and Stephanie had encountered in Dominic's office.

"I didn't know they were shady. And even if I had, I was so desperate for the cash, I would have agreed to any amount of interest. The problem came when I couldn't repay them fast enough and they began pressuring me, threatening to hurt Alice and the children."

Daniel slid down into a chair. Hell. His brother was in deep trouble. If he hadn't been so focused on his new business and in pursuing Stephanie, maybe he would have noticed in time to help. "Why? You're well-heeled. Why would you be in a pinch?"

"You don't understand," Dominic said miserably. "When the economy began to flounder my company cut back. I was one of the higher salaries, so I was expendable. And with the new baby coming and Jeffrey entering university, Alice spent more and more. I couldn't bring myself to tell her that I'd been sacked. She's always expected the best. She wouldn't understand."

Yes, Dominic's wife was quite a spender and, though Daniel hated to think it, she was a self-centered social climber who might not stand by her man in a financial crisis. Not like Stephanie, who didn't care how much money Daniel invested or how much he gave away. She'd liked him—correction: loved him—for who he was.

A sharp pain stabbed through his heart, cutting off his air. He couldn't think about Stephanie. He was here to help his brother. With concerted effort, he focused in on the terse conversation between John and Dominic.

"So working here wasn't a means of getting acquainted with the family?"

"I'm sorry, John. It wasn't. This job was all I had."

John leaned forward in the chair, elbows on knees, fingers steepled out in front of him. Intense emotion, whether anger or disappointment Daniel couldn't say, radiated off him. "So you set up false service accounts and embezzled money from your own family?"

Daniel tried to read John's face. What was going on behind their father's tired eyes? What would he do with this information? Was he the kind of man who could send his own son to prison?

Daniel clenched his fists. Probably. But he'd have to do it over Daniel's dead body.

"I'll pay the money back. I swear." Dominic's voice was hoarse with desperation.

"This is a huge sum, Dominic. The restaurant is in serious jeopardy because of the losses. We have little choice. We must take action and we must do it now."

Daniel leaped from his chair, jaw tight, blood rushing to his head. "I'll repay the money myself, but I won't see my brother in prison."

He could cancel the furniture. As much as asking for favors would grind against him, he would even cancel the office lease and ask John for a small office space in one of the restaurants.

Energized by the hope that he could help, he spun toward Dominic. "I have a little savings put back and my company is under way. I can borrow against it."

"Absolutely not!" John's reaction thundered through the room. He rose and moved to stand next to Dominic, clasping a hand upon his son's shoulder. "I'm your father. Helping you is my place, not your brother's."

Dominic's mouth fell open. "Sir? Are you serious?"

Daniel had the same reaction, staring in speechless bewilderment. Was the man serious?

Jaw set in determination, John nodded. "When you were small lads, I wasn't there. And I regret every day and every year that I missed. I never had a chance to buy you a bicycle or your first car. I never bought your school uniforms or paid for your food or took you to a football match." His voice dropped as he studied Dominic's face. "Don't you understand, son? I need to be the one to see you through this difficulty. No matter how great the expense, I will find a way to cover the loss."

All the air went out of Daniel. Deep inside, in that place that had been frozen for so long, a layer of hurt and anger melted away. Was this what family was supposed to be? Was this what he'd shut out of his life for so long?

John had every right to be furious and to call the police. But instead, he behaved as if—as if—he cared. He behaved like a loving father.

Dominic, as stunned as Daniel, slowly rose from his desk chair. "Sir. I don't know what to say. I'm grateful beyond words."

Moisture glinted in John's eyes. "I don't want gratitude. I want my sons."

In that instance, Daniel watched a weight of worry lift from his brother as he experienced for the first time the healing power of a father's love.

His own chest expanded to the point of bursting. He, who hadn't cried since grammar school, blinked back tears.

Maybe family was a good thing after all.

Forty-five minutes later, still reeling from the scene in Dominic's office, Daniel finished packing his business materials in preparation for the move. He'd promised to have dinner with the family at John's house later tonight. The idea that he looked forward to an evening with his father no longer surprised him. Stephanie was right. John was a good man. Daniel felt privileged to have that good man's blood running through his veins.

Regret pulled at him. He'd realized something else, too.

He wasn't half the man his father was. Unlike John, he'd let someone down in her hour of need. When Stephanie had needed him most to help her through the loss of her only parent, he'd walked away.

"Nice guy, Stephens," he muttered.

Maybe he should call her, apologize. See if she was all right. Make sure her ex hadn't discovered her return to Colorado.

He gnawed on the idea, all the while jamming items in boxes. Somewhere in this mess of papers was a number she'd left in case the restaurant needed her. A tiny smile tugged the corner of his mouth. Stephanie would have a fit if she could see the mess he'd made of her flat.

The telephone jangled. He dropped a handful of files into a box before answering.

"Stephens International Water Design."

After a momentary pause such as is common to over-seas transmission, a very feminine American voice spoke. "Oh, hello. Is that you, Daniel?"

"It is. Who's this?" He balanced the receiver between chin and shoulder and went on packing.

"Rebecca Valentine. Well, Rebecca Tucker now. Your first cousin, I believe?"

Rebecca. Another relative that he had never met. But Stephanie spoke fondly of his uncle Robert's oldest daughter, and they chatted regularly by telephone.

"Rebecca. Hello, then. How's married life?" Stephanie had talked with excitement about her friend's unexpected romance with a Wyoming rancher. He'd even seen some wedding photos.

A soft laugh danced over the long-distance wires. "Wonderful. There's nothing like love to slap you upside the head and make you look at life in a whole new way."

Talk of love made him uncomfortable, especially considering the crazy thoughts he was having lately.

"If you're calling for Stephanie, I'm afraid you've missed her. She's in Colorado."

This time the pause was pregnant. "You're kidding."

He wished. "She left a few days ago. Her father passed on, and she had to go back to settle the estate."

"Not alone. Promise me she didn't go alone."

The stab of guilt was all too real. "She did."

"Oh, but that's horrible, Daniel. Someone should be with her. She shouldn't have to face that house alone."

Cold fingers of dread crawled up his spine. "That house? What do you mean?"

"Something terrible happened to Stephanie in that house. I just know it. She never talked about it. You know how she is. Very private, almost secretive about her past. But she said enough for me to guess that her father may have abused her. She despised him and she despised that house."

"But I thought…" His stomach rolled in revulsion as the truth hit him. He'd blamed the ex-boyfriend when all along the scars, her fears, her nightmares, all stemmed from whatever had happened to her in the family home in Colorado. She was that little girl, the victim of abuse. "Oh, no."

She hadn't begged him to go with her out of grief for the loss of her father. She'd been afraid to face the past alone.

"I am a fool," he breathed. "I should have gone with her."

"Go now, Daniel." Rebecca's voice deepened with

emotion. "If you care about her, please go. She needs you. Go."

She needed him, in much the way Dominic had needed John. And, heaven help him, he needed her, too. His very bones cried out for her and he'd been too blindly wrapped in self-preservation and selfishness to realize the truth.

If he cared, Rebecca had said. Oh, he cared all right. He loved her. Daniel Stephens, man without a heart, loved the strongest, most amazing woman on earth.

He sank to his knees amidst the mess of papers on the living-room floor. As soon as he could breathe again, he was going to America.

CHAPTER TEN

SHE couldn't do it.

Stephanie lay on the bed in her room at the Adam's Mark Hotel. The room had grown too cool, but she hadn't the energy to get up and adjust the heat. Outside the window a soft snow fell, pure and white and silent.

Fully dressed in a turquoise and black ski sweater, black pants and boots, she had readied everything needed to make the trip out to the suburbs. The portfolio of legal papers. Telephone numbers to call. She'd even contacted the auction house to sell off Randolph's extensive art collection and her mother's collection of antiques. They were prepared to begin cataloging as soon she could let them into the house.

Until the house was cleared of all furnishings and personal belongings, she couldn't leave Colorado. But after a few days of watching the Weather Channel she still hadn't mustered the courage to drive out to Littleton.

Randolph's final, hideous attack on her emotions had taken a toll. Immersed in a depression unlike anything she'd ever experienced, she wondered if her mother's mental fragility was a part of her internal makeup, too.

She squeezed her eyes tightly shut, only to find her mother's haunted eyes and Randolph's mocking smile behind her eyelids.

"You killed my mother," she whispered. "I won't let you kill me, too."

With every bit of effort she had, Stephanie tried to rise from the bed.

Halfway up, she dropped back with a sigh. Maybe tomorrow would be better.

Turning on her side, she stared out the window at the drifting snowflakes.

When her room phone rang, she jumped. For a nano-second, her foolish heart hoped the caller might be Daniel. But she knew better. Daniel was gone from the Bella Lucia flat by now, and that was for the best. He would have turned away from her eventually anyway. Better now than later.

More likely the call was her attorney, urging her to get on with it. She let it ring into silence.

Five minutes later, someone tapped at her door.

"Who is it?" She wasn't in the mood for housekeeping.

"Open the door and see for yourself."

Her heart slammed against her ribcage. Only one man possessed that purring burr in the back of his throat. "Daniel?"

Here? In Colorado?

What could he want? Had something happened in London?

Her stomach twisted into a knot. No matter what his reasons for coming, seeing him was going to hurt. And she just couldn't take any more of that today.

Trepidatiously, she opened the door.

At the sight of him, big and dark and all man, she felt her knees wobble and the ache of love she wanted to escape rose up like a tidal wave.

"Why are you here?" Darn her voice for quivering. She blocked his entrance. No way was he coming into this room.

Daniel had different ideas. Gently, he pushed inside and closed the door behind him. "I made a terrible mistake and I want you to forgive me."

Stephanie crossed her arms protectively and turned away, going to the window. She felt him, all six feet four and muscles, move pantherlike up behind her.

Eyes squeezed tight, she prayed he wouldn't touch her. She'd crumble like a dry cracker if he did.

He didn't. And she was both relieved and disappointed.

"Stephanie. I've come across the ocean to find you. Hear me out."

A snowflake the size of a silver dollar swirled like an autumn leaf in front of the window. She focused on it. Cold, fragile, dying.

"You were right all along. I do have the ability to love. You taught me that. Maybe I'm not all that lovable, but I believe you love me. I've just endured four plane changes and six thousand kilometers without sleep to tell you that—" he paused and the air pulsed between them "—I love you."

Not now. Please not now. She'd spent almost a week coming to grips with the fact that the breakup was inevitable and for the best.

Feeling colder than death, Stephanie rubbed her hands up and down the soft mohair sleeves. Her father's voice yelled inside her head. "Worthless. Bad seed. If he knew the real you, if he saw the scars, he wouldn't be here."

Better to leave the break in place and move on than to chance rejection again when he discovered her ugliness.

"No, Daniel. You were right. It's over between us."

"Don't do this, Stephanie." He sounded as ragged as she felt and so desperate, she hurt for him. "I beg you. I know I made a mistake. I know I hurt you. But please don't give up on something as good as what we have."

"You can't love me, Daniel. It won't ever work."

"Why?" he whispered and moved closer.

"Because you don't really know me. The real me. If you did, you'd run back to London."

He touched her shoulder, tugged gently at the loose, stretchy neck of her sweater.

Horror tore like a whip down her back. She dipped away, pushing at his hand. "Don't."

But Daniel proved relentless.

With a tenderness that melted her resistance, he pulled the neck of her sweater down just enough to reveal the crisscross of flayed, damaged shoulder.

Afraid of the revulsion she would see, Stephanie couldn't look at him. Blood rushed to her head, pounding, swishing, pressing until she thought she would faint. Shame filled her.

"Look at me," his beloved voice demanded. "I love you, Stephanie. I love you. All of you."

"I'm so ashamed," she whispered, her voice raw and thick with the need to cry.

When she didn't look up, Daniel forced her chin up with his opposite hand. She felt humiliated, shamed, and afraid; tears filled her eyes. She shook her head and tried to pull away.

"Don't hide from me, love. I know. I saw." Head bent so the dark, unruly locks of hair tickled the side of her neck, Daniel kissed her shoulder.

"And you can still say you love me?"

"I love you even more. Your strength. Your courage. A man who didn't appreciate you would be a fool. I've been a fool."

A dam burst inside her then. With a sob, she fell against him. His two powerful arms caught her up, kissing her face, her tears, her hair; murmuring all the words she'd longed to hear.

After the first fierce storm had passed, Stephanie pulled away. Drawing in a shuddering breath, she asked, "Do you want to know?"

Daniel took the question as a test. She had to know if he would balk now, when the worst was yet to come.

Determined not to blow this chance to prove his love, he kept his gaze steady and sure, his eyes not leaving hers as he led her to the bed.

He was scared out of his wits to know the horror she'd been through. But he loved her. And he wanted to be strong enough to carry her pain so she could let it go.

He lay down, then pulled her down beside him. She stretched out, full-length, staring up at the ceiling.

Daniel leaned up on an elbow to look down into her aqua eyes and told her about the day he'd come into the flat and seen the scars. Then, he said, "Tell me what happened."

She studied his face for the longest time. He could read all the fears, the worries, the doubts that telling the story held for her. But gradually the wall of wariness slipped away and was replaced by trust. She trusted him. At last. And in the power of that realization, his love grew tenfold.

"I loved my mother," she said simply. "She was kind and sweet, but emotionally fragile. I blame Randolph for that."

"Your father?"

She shook her head and red hair fanned out over the white pillow. "No. Thank goodness. He was my stepfather, though I didn't know until I was nine years old. That day I came home from school and heard them arguing. My father was browbeating Mother as he always did in his snide, cruel, controlling way. He called her a whore. I'll never forget how awful the word sounded, though I barely understood its meaning."

"What were they arguing about?"

"Me, it turns out. Mother thought he was too strict, too harsh. And he was. He would punish me for the least thing. A book left lying on the table. A spot of dirt on my dress." Her gaze glued to the ceiling as if she watched a movie overhead. "The night before he'd whipped me with his belt because I couldn't remember the title of a painting."

"All this time I thought your ex—" He slid down to lie beside her, hiding the horror he felt.

She shook her head. "No. Brett did hurt me, but not that way. He couldn't handle my past. And I was afraid you'd be the same."

"Oh, my sweet." With an arm around her back, he rolled her towards him. Tremors rippled through her, tearing at Daniel's self-control. "You've carried this burden alone for too long. The man must have been a maniac."

"Yes, he was. But only Mother and I knew. He was so

smooth, a politician, a social success. He took pride in parading his possessions, especially his collection of the great masters, before company. My job was to recite the names and artists in his vast repertoire. Heaven help me if I forgot one."

Daniel fought to stay silent though he wanted to rage at the evil man who'd hurt her so. Randolph Ellison had scarred more than her body. He'd scarred her soul.

"He'd always told me I was bad and worthless. That was why he punished me so much. I could never understand why he didn't love his own daughter. That day, he brought all my mother's sins out to throw them in her face. She'd had an affair, got pregnant with me, and Randolph used that indiscretion to control her—and me—for the rest of her life."

Now Daniel understood her obsessive tidiness. Keeping things in order gave her a sense of control. The more anxious she became, the more she needed the environment around her under control.

"How did he know you weren't his child?"

She gave a small, sad laugh that was no laugh at all. The warmth of her breath soughed against the skin on his neck.

"The great and mighty Randolph Ellison was sterile. An accident of some kind when he was a boy. He and Mother had never planned to have children."

"Surprise, surprise," he said softly.

"From what little she told me, he didn't seem angry at first. He'd told her they would pretend the child was his and no one would ever know. That was the way Randolph worked. His revenge knew no bounds, but he wanted to punish her slowly and completely. And that's what he did. Over the years, he picked away at her self-esteem, convincing her that she couldn't survive without him. He controlled her every movement, her social life, everything. She grew depressed and nervous, an emotional wreck until she had a breakdown. After that, I had to protect her, too. She was so fragile."

"Couldn't she have gone to your real father for help?"

She pressed one hand against his chest as if he was her lifeline. The urge to protect her hit him like a freight train.

"He was married, too."

"What a nightmare." He twined one of her curls around the end of his finger, calming the storm inside with the repetitive action. He'd be no good to Stephanie at all if he let go of the building rage.

"My finding out the truth infuriated Randolph. He didn't have to hold back his hatred anymore. That's when the real beatings began."

Daniel had seen the ritualistic scars. She didn't need to describe the torture for him to know what had happened.

"What about your mother?"

Stephanie swallowed hard. Her voice fell to a sad whisper. "She overdosed on antidepressants when I was seventeen. I still feel so guilty about that."

"You? Why? Your stepfather was the one who drove her to it."

"She was upset because of me. She'd tried to interfere during one of his…" Stephanie's voice trailed off. She stared out the window, unable to go on. Daniel wasn't sure he could bear to hear anymore.

"I understand, love. No need to elaborate." He stroked her hair over and over, offering the only comfort he could. "Why didn't you tell someone? Why didn't anyone stop him?"

"I tried to tell once. But Randolph was a very smart, very powerful man. He knew how to work the system to his benefit. No one believed the fabulous, charismatic attorney would ever do such a thing. I was branded a spoiled, lying child. And after he finished with me that time, I was afraid to ever tell again."

"So you kept the abuse inside all these years."

"Except for Brett. And that was a disaster. He was horrified, revolted by the scars and abuse. I felt ugly, untouchable." Her voice dropped. "Unlovable."

"He was an idiot. You are the most beautiful, incredibly lovable woman in the world."

She smiled, a tremulous, teary smile that broke his heart. And he felt such joy to know he could love someone this way.

"After Brett, I gave up on love for good."

"Not for good. I'm here now. And you will not give up on me. I won't allow it."

"What changed your mind?" she asked, stroking a hand over his bewhiskered face. He'd had the devil of a time getting here and no time to shave.

"You."

She raised an eyebrow.

"You haunted me. I couldn't sleep. And then something happened that woke me up to the power of loving someone." He told her about John's reaction to Dominic's embezzlement.

"So it *was* Dom. Oh, Daniel, I'm so sorry."

He was sorry ,too, but didn't want Stephanie to see how worried he was. "John seems set on seeing him through this."

"He will. Your father is both powerful and decent, a rare combination."

"Yes, I'm sorry for all the times I resisted getting to know him. My mum had poisoned our minds about him." But Stephanie already knew about his troubled relationship with his mother. No need to go through that again.

Tugging on a lock of her hair, he aligned her body with his. "Enough about them," he whispered against her soft, lush lips. "Let's talk about us."

"Is there an us?"

"Absolutely."

With a happy sigh of surrender, he lost himself in the pleasures of her sweet mouth. She responded so sweetly, so passionately that he was hard-pressed to break away.

"I have to ask you something."

"Mmm," she murmured dreamily, tracing his lower lip with one finger.

"You're distracting me, woman."

"My intention."

He grabbed her finger and kissed it, then held her hand prisoner against his chest. "Will you marry me? Will you put up with this moody Englishman who has nothing to offer except the promise that I'll spend the rest of my life giving you all that I am and all that I have?"

He loved the way her eyes, so sad moments before, sparkled now. He loved the way her face softened with happiness. He loved everything about his Stephanie.

"Well?" he persisted.

"When?"

"What do you mean, when?"

"When do you want to get married?"

"This afternoon."

She laughed. "This afternoon? Daniel! A girl has to plan."

He heaved a beleaguered sigh. "Okay. I'll give you a week."

"After the estate is settled. I don't want that or anything else to spoil our wedding day."

Yes, getting that painful experience behind her was necessary to her peace of mind as well as his.

"Deal. I'll help you get things settled. Meanwhile make your plans, because you are going to be my bride as soon as possible." He rolled to a sitting position and reached for the phone. "Let's call London. After the week he's had, I think my father could use a little good news, don't you?"

Smiling her answer, his beautiful bride-to-be sat up, too, wrapped her arms around his waist and gazed up at him with an expression that made him believe he could conquer the world.

Drawing her against his side where he always wanted her to be, he connected with the overseas operator and waited until he heard his father's voice.

"Hullo?" he said.

"Daniel? Son? Is that you?"

"Yes, Dad. It's me." And the joy that burst in his chest at finally saying that simple word erased the years he'd been a fatherless son.

CHAPTER ELEVEN

HE WAS whistling in the shower.

Stephanie pinched her arm to be sure she wasn't dreaming. Daniel, her love, her heart, had come all the way from England to propose. Imagine that! All the way across the Atlantic to tell her of his love.

Dressed in her usual long flannel pajamas, she stood at the hotel window, watching the snow dance around the streetlights and cast a white glow in the darkness. In a matter of a few hours, she'd gone from depressed to joyous, all because of Daniel. With him at her side, she could face anything, even the task of cataloging and dispensing the contents of her childhood prison.

A deep, rumbling baritone replaced the cheery whistle.

Stephanie smiled.

He had to be exhausted, suffering from jet lag, but he'd taken her to an elegant, wonderful tea at the gracious old Brown Hotel. Over tiny finger sandwiches and Earl Grey tea, he'd told her over and over again that he loved her. They'd talked and talked until their hearts were full and their jaws aching. The burden of her disturbing responsibilities had lifted just by sharing them with him.

Afterwards, they'd walked the snowy streets of Denver to the Molly Brown House and made the trek upstairs, amused at how such a tiny nineteenth century place could have once been considered the grand house of Colorado's wealthiest citizen.

Just then, Daniel came out of the bathroom, rubbing his face with a towel.

"How's this?" he asked, rubbing her cheek with his.

"Smooth." She sniffed. "You smell good, too."

He flipped the towel over one bare shoulder. "I suppose I should have done this before going to tea."

"We would have missed it if we'd waited any longer."

"The phone call to London took more time than I expected."

Stephanie smiled. "Good news takes time to share. Speaking of London, now that Louise is back, do you think she'll invite her new family to the Christmas party to meet the Valentines?"

"Can't say. I fear I don't know Louise that well. At least, not yet."

All either of them really knew about Louise was her reputation as the kind-hearted, conservative, good daughter of John and Ivy Valentine. She'd been traveling so much lately, having only returned to England the day before Daniel had left for America, that Daniel had had no time at all to become acquainted.

Whatever Daniel was about to say next was smothered by a huge yawn, and Stephanie laughed. "I think your body must be losing its battle with jet lag."

"Are you complaining about my body?" He flexed a muscled arm.

Playfully, she squeezed his biceps and gave an exagger-ated shiver of admiration. "Your physique is magnificent, as you well know, Mr Conceit. But you *are* tired."

"Yes, I am. Exceedingly." Naked chest and all, he pulled her to him for a kiss. His skin was cool and damp and fragrant with soap. "My internal clock doesn't know where I am or what time it is."

He flopped onto the bed and tugged her down. "Come here."

Her pulse stuttered. She knew he expected to spend the night, and that was fine with her. Having him here was all she really wanted. But she hadn't spent the night in the same bed with a man in a very long time.

All her old fears and anxieties flooded in. What if he changed his mind? What if he only imagined he could handle the way her body looked?

As if he understood, Daniel clicked off the lamp, leaving only the dim lights from the streets. "Just lay beside me, love. Let me hold you."

The tension in her shoulders eased. Being held by Daniel was exactly what she wanted. And she knew he loved her. He wouldn't force anything she wasn't ready for.

Glad to be covered from neck to ankle, Stephanie slid beneath the sheet and nestled against Daniel's broad chest. It felt so good to be wrapped in his embrace, protected by his strength.

His calloused hand rubbed up and over her hair, her neck, her shoulder, then drifted down to massage her back. "Did I tell you lately that I am totally, madly in love with you?"

"Not in the last two minutes."

He shifted to his side and bracketed her face with his fingertips. "I love you. You can't imagine how good it feels to be able, finally, to say that. To feel that."

"I know."

"Are you worried about tomorrow?" he asked, eyes searching hers in the semi-darkness.

She swallowed a lump of tenderness. He was so wonderfully thoughtful.

"A little." A lot. Tomorrow she had to face the house. And she was scared. "But I don't want to talk about that. Not tonight."

Today had been too special to mar with tomorrow's worries.

"Enough talk then," he murmured, and his mouth found hers.

The kiss was sweet and hot and hungry. His intention was clear. He loved her; he wanted her.

And she wanted him. The rest should come naturally. For a normal person it would. But not for her.

"Daniel," she said, plucking nervously at the collar of her pajamas. "Please don't be angry, but I'd rather wait until our wedding night."

He looked pathetically disappointed. If she hadn't been so worried, she would have laughed.

"It's just—" She hesitated, afraid to say what was on her mind. Regardless of Daniel's claim to the contrary, Stephanie had a horrible fear that, somehow, the ugliness could still drive him away.

Daniel stopped her fidgeting hands with his.

"The scars?" he asked.

She nodded.

"I've seen them, remember? And you're still beautiful to me."

The awful truth rose in her throat like a sickness. She wanted to tell him. He deserved to know.

While she hesitated, he said, "My love, if you were scarred from head to toe, I would still love you. And because I love you so much, I'll try to be patient. I'll even take another room after tonight. Just remember, though, on our wedding night—" he tugged gently at her pajama top "—this will go. All of it will go. And I will see and love all of you. There will be no more secrets between us."

Long after Daniel's magnificent chest rose and fell in exhausted slumber, Stephanie lay staring at the ceiling.

He was so sweet, so understanding. And he'd asked so little of her. She only hoped that when the time came, she would have the courage to give him what he asked.

Daniel awakened disoriented. A sliver of glare had snaked between a pair of green drapes to laser him right in the eyes.

As he rolled over memory flooded in stronger than the glare. He was in America. With Stephanie.

Contentment expanded his chest. If he didn't have such a jet-lag hangover, he might shout with happiness.

Thrusting out one hand, he searched the sheets for his lady.

"Stephanie?" His voice was a morning frog.

No answer.

He pried open one eye, saw nothing, and opened the other.

"Stephanie?" He sat up, looking, listening.

With a frown, he shoved the covers away and padded through the room. "Where are you?"

The bathroom door stood open. No Stephanie, but a yellow note was stuck to the mirror. He yanked the paper down.

Just as he'd suspected. She'd gone to the property to begin sorting through her nightmare.

"Stubborn, independent female," he muttered, then stomped around the room, grabbing clothes and shoes in a fit of temper. "No business going out there alone."

In record time he dressed, found the address, and called a taxi. Stephanie shouldn't face that house alone.

The ride to the suburbs was beautiful and the snowy scenery cooled his hot temper. The snow had stopped and sun glistened off the fields of white. Kids had ventured out to roll huge balls into snowmen. City workers in oversized machinery pushed piles of the fluffy stuff to the sides of the road.

But while his eyes admired the Mile High city, his mind recalled last night.

He'd been disappointed. What man wouldn't be? The woman he loved had been in the bed beside him all night and he hadn't been able to do more than kiss and hold her. If his body hadn't been so tired, he'd have spent the night in a cold shower.

He hated what had happened to her. And he was going to prove his love by waiting until she was ready to trust him. The scars were horrid, not because of how they looked but because of how she'd come to have them. But they truly didn't matter to him.

The taxi slid to a halt outside a gated residence. "This is it."

Daniel paid the driver and got out. He stood at the opened gate, staring down a long, curving, snowy driveway toward a mansion set upon a knoll.

What a place!

An enormous house, built of some sort of golden-red wood, cedar perhaps, rose three stories high against a backdrop of the Rocky Mountains. The fresh snow decorated the roof and shrubbery, giving the place a fairy-tale appearance. Who would believe such a stunning home could hold such an ugly secret?

He spotted her then, standing beside her silver rental car. The driver's door was open as if she'd just stepped out. One hand shading her eyes, she stared up at the house.

Daniel broke into a trot and his boots crunched at the dry snow. Before he reached her, she whipped around.

Dressed in the long black leather coat, red hair spilling around her shoulders, cheeks kissed pink by the cold, she took his breath away.

"Daniel," she said simply.

"Why didn't you wake me?" he panted, out of air from the run and the unaccustomed altitude. "I didn't want you coming here alone."

She smiled. "This morning, for the first time, I finally believed that Randolph Ellison can no longer hurt me." A peace she'd never had before emanated from her. "You did that for me, Daniel. You made me strong enough to face anything." She reached out a hand gloved in black leather, and touched his cheek. "This house is my burden to bear, not yours."

He squelched another burst of temper. If she thought for one minute he would walk away and leave her to face this house alone, she was sadly mistaken. "Call me chauvinistic, but when you agreed to marry me, your problems became mine. I'm here. And I'm staying. Get used to it."

Her smile grew brighter than the glaring snow. She threw her arms around his neck. "You look positively fierce. And you've just reminded me of why I love you so much."

She kissed him, a full, smacking kiss that made him laugh.

"Come on, then. Let's get this job done."

She turned to face the house again and Daniel saw her hesitate as some of her bravado slipped away. She really was terrified of this building.

He took her gloved hand in his. "Together, my love."

With her cheeks a little rosier than usual, her eyes a little brighter, and her face set like stone, she led him up on the porch and inside the house.

The immaculate, enormous vaulted great room looked as if the owner were only away for the day. As neat and tidy as Stephanie's flat, the furniture was uncovered, the huge stone fireplace laid with logs, and the wood floors polished to a sheen. Even the potted plants lining the foyer looked green and healthy.

"Someone has been caring for the house?" he asked.

"I discontinued the service yesterday."

"So, what's the plan today?"

"Inventory. I brought a laptop." Her voice was quieter than usual. Her eyes moved from side to side as if watching, waiting for the bogeyman to appear.

Daniel ached for her, but he didn't comment. She had to confront this symbol of her past on her own terms before she could put it behind her for good.

As they moved through the rooms he noticed the magnificent collection of paintings and sculptures decorating the lavish interior. Unlike Stephanie's thoroughly modern works, these pieces were classics, several that he was surprised to see outside of museums. Stephanie saw them, too, and her hands twisted restlessly against the slick leather of her coat. This artwork, some pieces near priceless, had cost her far more than it would ever be worth.

When they passed in front of the massive stone fireplace, Stephanie took down a photograph of a beautiful red-haired woman.

"My mother," she said simply.

He stepped up close and looked over her shoulder.

"You look like her." Right down to the haunted eyes.

"A little maybe. Randolph said I resembled my worthless father."

"Randolph, as we well know, was an unmitigated fool." Anger hovered around the edge of his words. He wished Randolph Ellison were still alive because he personally wanted to make him pay for all the harm he'd done.

Picture held tightly against her chest, Stephanie continued to roam the house, saying little, doing nothing as far as inventory. Daniel held her hand and tagged along, letting her take the lead. This was her show. He wanted to do it her way. And he'd be here for whatever she needed.

Through two dining rooms, an enormous kitchen, a sun room, a hot-tub room complete with skylight, and a massive games room, Stephanie seemed to hold up well, though she was far quieter than usual. The old familiar way she had of distancing herself from other people returned, and it was as if she knew he was there, but he wasn't.

They started up the wide spiral staircase.

"Five bedrooms up here," she said woodenly. "All with private baths. Wasn't that wasteful in a family of three?"

They looked inside each one and Daniel noticed that each had its own balcony with exterior stairs leading down to a small garden. Beyond that, a wooded acreage led into the mountains.

"What about the third floor?" he asked.

She hesitated. A pinch of white appeared around her lips. "One dormer room. Mine."

"You were up there alone?"

"Yes. With no way down but these stairs that led right past the master bedroom. He made sure I couldn't run away."

Daniel bit back an angry curse. His poor, precious little rich girl. Alone in her ivory tower prison, except for the madman downstairs.

She hesitated another second longer, contemplating the dark landing above. Then she dropped his hand, put her mother's photo on the bottom step, and started up. She looked for all the world like a condemned queen on her way to execution.

A terrible foreboding started Daniel's blood racing. Suddenly, he didn't want her up there. He could inventory and empty this part of the house.

"Stephanie?" he said, just as she pushed open a cherry-wood door and stepped inside, out of his field of vision.

In the two strides he took to be inside the room, she had

started to come undone. She shook violently. Her chest rose and fell in agitation.

And then Daniel understood. This had been the room of her torture, of her beatings, and God only knew what else. He had to get her out of here.

He reached for her elbow. "Sweetheart—" he started.

She jerked away.

"Why?" she asked in a voice so anguished that Daniel's knees began to shake.

"Why did you hurt me? I was just a little girl."

As if in a daze, she moved forward, trembling, whimpering. When she reached the fairy-princess bed, she fell to her knees, arms thrust forward across the white bedspread in a posture of submission.

And then she raised her head and screamed.

"I hate you. I hate you! Do you hear me, you evil monster? I hate you! I'm glad you're dead. I'm glad you're dead. You had no right to hurt me."

Daniel slid to the floor beside her but she didn't seem to know he was there. His heart said to stop her, but his gut said she needed this. Throat aching, he bit down on his fist and kept quiet.

Stephanie shook so hard the bed quaked, but still she railed on against the criminal who'd made her childhood a living hell. Sweat broke out on her face. Her eyes streamed tears. Her voice grew raw and raspy, and yet she raged.

Her total brokenness terrified him. He'd never felt so helpless.

When at last the torrent ceased, Stephanie's exhausted body went limp. Daniel gathered her to him, heart shattered in a thousand pieces with the tender concern he felt for his woman.

"Shh," he crooned. "Shh. He can't hurt you ever again. Not ever."

"Daniel?" she said, still quivering.

"I'm here, love. Everything is okay, now."

"He's dead, isn't he? He's really dead?"

"Yes, love. Yes."

"I'm glad." She looked up at him, aqua eyes red-rimmed and teary. "Oh, Daniel, am I a bad person because I'm happy that someone is dead?"

The pressure inside Daniel's chest reached breaking point. "If you're bad," he ground out, "I'm worse. I wanted him to be alive so I could have the pleasure of killing him myself."

"Daniel," she whispered, her fingers touching his cheek. "You're crying."

Crying? Him? The tidal wave of emotions, love, anger, sorrow, overwhelmed him then. Now he knew he had a heart because it was broken. For her.

He crushed her to him, rocking her back and forth. He kissed her hair, her swollen eyes, her wet cheeks, and after a while he simply held her.

He wasn't sure how long they sat there on the floor, but eventually, Stephanie stopped trembling and sat back.

"Better?" he asked.

She nodded. "Much."

And then his brave, strong woman dried his tears and hers, and smiled. A wet, wobbly, sad effort, but still a smile.

"Let's go back to the hotel, Daniel. The nightmare is over. And I'm so very, very tired."

* * *

Three weeks and an enormous amount of work later, the last of the valuables from the mansion had been inventoried and readied for auction. Some days, after they'd done all they could with the property, Stephanie relaxed by shopping or jogging while Daniel spent hours by phone and computer doing business back in London.

The days passed, and as the remnants of her early life were catalogued and set aside Stephanie was amazed at how her inner spirit slowly healed. Confronting the memories locked in that house had freed her.

Even Thanksgiving, a holiday that normally held little meaning for her, had taken on a special significance. She'd told Daniel over a quiet dinner in the hotel, "I have you this year. For that, I will ever be thankful."

Now, as she sat on the hotel bed, up from a power nap, Stephanie sorted through the final pile of legal papers.

"I'm still not sure what to do with the house," she admitted, gnawing the end of a pencil. "I had originally planned to set it on fire and watch it burn."

Daniel, who sat at the small round hotel table perusing the newspaper, didn't seem the least troubled by that revelation.

The newspaper rustled as he lay it down. "A waste of perfectly good lumber."

"And some very costly furnishings." She pushed the papers aside and padded to the exterior vanity. "Ugh. Bed head."

"A charming sight, I assure you." Daniel grinned, causing her heart to flip-flop. "Let me."

He took the brush and gently began the job of untangling the mass of curls. "I have a thought about the house. Are you open to suggestions?"

"From you?" She gazed up at him in the mirror. His eyes were serious. "Of course."

"The estate has a legacy of hurt. Change that. Make it a place of helping."

And as suddenly as that, an idea popped into her head.

"Daniel, that's brilliant. I know exactly what I want to do." Excitement zipped through her blood stream. "I'll call my attorney and have him investigate our options."

"For what? Tell me."

"A safe house for abused women and children. A place for them to come without fear, to heal and get on their feet. There's enough money with the estate to keep it in perpetuity."

"What a terrific idea."

"I would never have thought of it without you." She whirled around and took the brush from his hands. On tiptoe, she kissed him. "I love you. You are so smart."

"Keep talking." He walked her backward toward the bed. "On second thought, don't talk. Kiss."

With a laugh of happiness, she did exactly that as Daniel tumbled them down.

After far too much kissing that left them both frustrated, Daniel groaned, "If you want to wait until our wedding night, we'd better get married today."

"Think you can wait until Monday?"

"This coming Monday?"

He looked so wonderfully hopeful that Stephanie laughed. "Yes. Most everything I have to do is taken care of now. My mind is clear of all those stressors. And I don't want to wait any longer to be your wife."

The corners of his eyes crinkled. "I hear Aspen is beautiful this time of year."

"Aspen?" A bubble of happiness rose in her chest. "I still have friends in Aspen." But Daniel knew that already, a reminder of how thoughtful and considerate her husband would be. "It's the perfect romantic spot for a wedding, however impromptu."

He pumped his eyebrows. "And a honeymoon?"

"Yes." She jumped up, pulled him up with her, and danced them around the hotel room. "A Christmas wedding in Aspen."

Unlike Denver, Aspen held good memories and a few friends she'd kept in touch with. A phone call or two to the Snowbound Lodge could set things in motion.

And if she had any worries about the wedding night, Stephanie was too happy at the moment to think about them now.

CHAPTER TWELVE

THE bride wore Christmas green.

Daniel's stomach dipped the moment Stephanie stepped out of the chapel's tiny dressing room to join him in the short walk down the aisle. She'd warned him that her dress was not traditional, claiming she looked terrible in white. Modest cut, chic and elegant, the long emerald velvet was the perfect complement to her flowing red hair. Her mother's diamond choker and matching earrings sparkled like Christmas lights against her peach skin.

He cleared his throat, found it uncommonly dry, but managed to say, "You are beyond gorgeous."

She smiled up at him, her aqua eyes gone as green as her dress. "Wanna marry me?"

Fighting the need to crush her to him and carry her off like some barbarian, he breathed, "Oh, yeah."

He was either going to marry her or kidnap her. One way or the other, she was going to be his today. He'd waited as long as he could stand it, a notion that still astounded him. He had never expected to marry, let alone love a woman the way he loved Stephanie.

"Then lead the way, handsome man. I wanna marry you, too."

He folded her hand, soft and smooth as the velvet fabric, over his elbow and led her toward the minister waiting at the front of the chapel. Behind the clergyman, floor-to-ceiling windows offered a spectacular view of the forest, and beyond that, the snow-covered Rockies. Stephanie had chosen this quaint little chapel, nestled in the trees near Aspen, for this view. But Daniel found the vision beside him far more breathtaking.

From somewhere came the sound of a harp playing "Ave Maria", so gentle and heavenly that he felt transported by the sheer beauty of the place, the melody, the moment. One glance at Stephanie's enraptured face told him she felt the same.

When they reached the minister, a graying, middle-aged man with smile lines, the music ceased and the ceremony began. The minister read from the Bible and spoke lovely words that roared in Daniel's head like the sound of the sea rushing in. He didn't care what was said as long as the end result was the same. But Stephanie deserved a special memory and he intended for her to have it.

The ceremony seemed to go on for ever and yet be over in a moment. During the exchange of rings, Daniel's hands trembled, not with anxiety or fear, but with an emotion so powerful he thought he might go to his knees. He, a man who had braved floods and droughts and so much more was reduced to tremors by the sound of Stephanie whispering her eternal promise of love.

At last, the moment came when she was his for evermore, and, with his heart near to bursting, Daniel kissed his bride. Not once, but over and over again until all of them, minister, witnesses, and the newlyweds, were laughing.

The harp music began again and to the accompaniment of "Ode to Joy", a fitting piece if ever he heard one, Daniel and his bride completed the formalities and prepared to leave.

"I have a surprise, Mrs Stephens." Daniel draped a long fur cape over her shoulders and opened the door.

A pair of large, hairy-footed golden horses waited docilely in front of a curved white sleigh.

Stephanie gasped and looked up, expression so full of love and excitement he knew he'd made the right choice. "Daniel, I love it. I love you."

She kissed him.

"Just the reaction I was hoping for."

A sleigh ride might be clichéd, but it was exactly the kind of romantic gesture he wanted to do for her. The sleigh was only the first of several surprises he had planned for this special night…and for his special bride.

Snow kissed their faces as the driver "tsked" the horses into motion. Snuggled beneath a heavy fur lap robe, Daniel held his lady-love close. All the while, his heart was singing.

Horse hoofs thudded softly against the packed snow; harness a-jingle, they journeyed out of the pines and into town.

"Aspen is a fairy tale at Christmas," Stephanie said as the sleigh glided down Main Street.

Every building in the quaint resort of the rich and famous was bathed in lights so that the town glowed with warmth and holiday cheer. Festive green and red decorated the storefronts, the streetlamps, the windows, the doors, and, as if the human effort weren't enough, nature supplied the constant cover of snow and the backdrop of majestic mountain peaks and stunning star-sprinkled sky.

Cheek against hers, he pointed upward. "Did you see that?"

"A shooting star," she said and he could feel her smile curve upward. "We have to make a wish."

But Daniel's wishes, even the ones he hadn't known he wanted, had all come true. A father. A family. And now a wife. He gazed down at her. Her eyes were squeezed tight in the pale moonlight. "What did you wish for?"

"You already know," she murmured, opening her eyes. "I wish for us to always be as happy and in love as we are tonight."

"Your wish is hereby granted." He sealed his promise with a kiss.

They rode along in silence for a while, snuggled close sharing warmth and smiles. The scent of wood smoke from nearby homes teased the air, and an occasional car motored past. Once, they heard snatches of Christmas carols coming from a brightly lit building—a country club party, he surmised.

The cold of Colorado made Daniel's skin tingle. He used the chill as an opportunity to hold his wife a little closer.

When at long last she shivered, he said, "You're getting chilled. Maybe we should go to the cabin now."

"This is so wonderful. I hate for the night to end."

"We'll ride as long as you choose, but remember, love…" he rubbed her nose with his "…the night has only just begun."

Stephanie's skin tingled, too, though not from cold. She loved the invigorating smell and feel of cold mountain air.

She tingled from the delicious suggestion in Daniel's voice, and the notion thrilled her. Even though the nagging worry about tonight didn't leave, with all her heart she wanted to be Daniel's wife in every way.

"I'm ready to go to the lodge when you are," she said and was rewarded with a heart-stopping kiss.

Daniel spoke to the sleigh driver and they began the trip away from the city proper.

When the sleigh turned north, Stephanie sat up to look around. "This isn't the way back to the lodge, is it?"

"We're not going to the lodge." Daniel's expression was smug and secretive.

"But our things are there."

"Not anymore."

A zing of excitement heated her blood. Daniel, her husband, her love, was making tonight a beautiful adventure.

The sleigh turned down a narrow, tree-lined lane and headed deeper into the woods. The horses slowed to a gentle stop in front of a small cabin, illuminated from without and within.

"Your honeymoon cottage, my love." Daniel hopped down and playfully bowed toward the small cabin nestled in the snow-laden pines.

"It's perfect."

And it was. From the wreath on the door to the romantic interior where a small fireplace already crackled.

Inside, Daniel slid the fur cape from her shoulders and dropped it onto a stuffed chair. "This is our little hideaway for the next week."

"How did you do this? Everything was booked when I called."

"That's because I called first."

"Sneaky." She trailed her fingers over a small wooden bar where a large basket of Christmas cookies, gingerbread men and foil-wrapped chocolates awaited them. "But very wonderful. I think I might fall madly in love with you if you keep this up."

"Admit the truth. You fell for me the minute I invaded your flat."

She smiled. "Maybe I did. But you also scared me to death. Such a barbarian, all dark and wild with those big muscles."

He stalked toward her. "Are you scared now?"

"Terrified." With a squeal, she danced away from his outstretched hands, laughing. Her heart raced a little faster.

She grabbed for the cookie basket. "Want a cookie?"

His grin was absolutely feral. "Nope. I want you."

He caught the sleeve of her dress and tugged. She catapulted into his arms, stomach fluttering with excitement.

"There's hot mulled cider," she teased, knowing that neither of them was at all interested in food. At least not right now.

His eyelids drooped to a sexy stare. "I'd rather have hot married you."

Stephanie felt the heat of a blush but loved knowing that her new husband wanted her so badly.

"So impatient," she said, a complete untruth. He'd been a paragon of patience since their engagement, giving her all the time and space she needed.

"Love the way you look in this dress." He ran a finger beneath the sweetheart neckline. She shivered with the thought that soon he would see her, touch her, everywhere. "I'd love it even more if you'd take it off."

Stephanie laughed, a husky sound that surprised even her. She tugged at his tie, enjoying the mating ritual.

"And you look so handsome and sophisticated in this suit."

"Handsome? Sophisticated?" He gave her a mock frown. "What about virile? Tough? Strong?"

She struck a pose, vamping for him, her voice intentionally seductive. "Manly, rugged, and, oh, so sexy."

"Want to find out how sexy I can be?"

"Maybe." She touched the diamond choker at her throat. "Would you help me with this?"

"We have to start somewhere," he murmured wryly. Then he unclasped the necklace, whisked it from her, and replaced it with his lips. His soft whiskers tickled deliciously. Stephanie let her head fall back. A low hum vibrated from her throat to his mouth.

"Are you trying to seduce me?" she asked when she could finally speak.

"How am I doing?" he murmured against the pulse dancing wildly beneath her collarbone.

Stephanie couldn't answer. She was too busy angling her neck this way and that to capture the luscious feel of his hot mouth and tongue on every inch of her skin.

"I have earrings too," she finally managed to say, though the words were breathy.

He chuckled. "Yum."

In turn, he removed each one and suckled her earlobes, nuzzled the sensitive skin beneath her ear, kissing her until they were both breathless.

"Anything else you want removed?" he whispered, his voice a throaty purr.

She loosened his tie and in a slow, sexy dance slid it from his neck. She trailed the narrow band of silk across his face. He caught the end with his teeth in a sensuous tug-of-war.

"Maybe I should slip into something more comfortable," she said.

Eyes widening, he dropped the tie like a hot potato.

"Meet you in the bedroom in five minutes?" he asked hopefully.

A tiny knot of anxiety formed in her stomach. Even though they'd been working toward this moment for weeks, some of her playful eagerness drained away. As much as she loved this man, she dreaded the moment he would see her.

"I'm a little nervous," she admitted. Actually she was a lot nervous, but telling Daniel the truth helped. He knew and he understood that her reasons were not about him, but about herself.

"Don't be, love. Don't be." He took the tie and looped it around her neck, using the strip of cloth to pull her close, swaying them from side to side. "I love you more than I can say. And want you just as much. Nothing is going to change that."

She hoped he was right.

"I want you, too. So, so much." Gathering her courage, she kissed his jaw. "Five minutes."

When she came out of the bathroom in a robe she'd bought especially for tonight, Daniel already waited in the bed, his broad chest nude and golden in the glow of the fireplace. The overhead lights were out and only a small lamp lit the room. She silently blessed his thoughtful concession to her modesty and fear.

"We can turn out all the lights if you'd rather," he said.

"What do you want?"

"Whatever you do."

Though she knew his preference, she loved him for giving her the choice. "Leave them on."

He reached for her, but she backed away, standing in the full light from the fire. If she was going to do this with lights on, she would do it all.

Gaze locked on Daniel's face, she untied the belt of her robe and let it drop. She had to watch his reaction.

"I haven't told you everything, Daniel."

"You don't have to."

"Okay, then. I'll show you. No secrets, remember?" She let the shoulders of the satin robe slither halfway down to her elbows.

Daniel levered up to watch, his pupils large and dark in the fire-glow, the sheet falling to his trim, rippled belly.

"More than my back is scarred," she whispered.

"Let me see." His voice was soft, compassionate, loving. She could do this. For him. For herself.

She let the robe slide ever so slowly past her arms, over her hips to puddle at her feet.

She stood, naked and vulnerable, heart pounding wildly as she watched his reaction. The revulsion she expected never came.

"You…are…so…beautiful," he ground out between jaws clenched with desire.

In that moment, Stephanie knew she had found the impossible. A man who looked past the horrible scars of her childhood to the woman inside.

All her doubts and fears fell away to join the robe at her feet when Daniel's nostrils flared and his eyes darkened in passion.

"Come here, woman," he growled.

Slowly, proudly, she moved toward him, reveling in the mounting passion she evoked in her new husband. Not pity. Not revulsion or sympathy or even anger. But love and passion.

"I love you," she said as he pulled her onto the bed with him.

His body trembled against hers, and she loved him even more.

And then with an exquisite tenderness that brought tears to her eyes, Daniel laid her back against the downy pillows and gently kissed every scar on her body until she no longer thought of anything except becoming one with her forever soulmate.

Daniel awoke to the warm, delightful smell of fresh coffee. For three glorious days now, his beautiful bride had managed to awaken before him and fill the cabin with delicious smells. Tomorrow he simply had to wake up first and make her breakfast in bed.

"Morning, my love." She swept into the bedroom, carrying two steaming cups. Her face scrubbed clean and pink, her hair tied back at the neck, she looked fresh as the mountain air.

He took the mug, sipped at the warm brew, and then said, "You're interfering with my plans."

She perched on the edge of the mattress. "How so?"

"I want to do the spoiling, but you don't give me a chance."

She pushed the hair back from his forehead with one cool, soft hand and kissed him. He loved it when she did that. "Daniel, you made our wedding day—" she paused to smile "—and night perfect. You've made every day since perfect. Fixing breakfast makes me feel like a real wife. I love it."

"Do you love me, too?" He could never get enough of hearing her say it.

"Oh, a little, I suppose." She grinned, and seeing her relaxed and carefree enough to tease filled him with enormous joy.

He was still on an emotional high from their wedding night. As hard as it must have been for her, Stephanie had undressed for him—had wanted to. And by that action, his beautiful, brave wife had given him the finest wedding gift of all—her trust. No one had ever sacrificed anything for him that he remembered. But she had.

After the initial shock of seeing what her stepfather had done to her body, he'd seen only the woman he loved more than life. With his heart bursting, he'd vowed at that moment that no one would ever hurt her again, beginning with him.

"What do you want to do today?" he asked, setting his cup on the bedside table. "The world is yours. I'll even get the universe if you want it."

"I'm sorry to bring this up, but—" she ran a fingertip around the rim of her cup "—we're going to have to think about going back to London soon."

"No-o-o." He flopped backwards on the bed in protest. But he knew she was right. They both had work to do that couldn't be done long distance, but being here with Stephanie was magical. He'd never been so fulfilled.

"Louise phoned earlier."

"My sister?"

She smiled, and Daniel lifted one shoulder in response. Referring to Louise as his sister was starting to feel okay.

"Things are chaotic. Your father and Robert are arguing constantly because Robert thinks Dominic belongs in jail. John won't hear of it, of course. Money is very, very tight and there is talk of closing one or more of the restaurants. She thought we should know."

The problem, thanks to his brother, was approaching crisis state.

"I talked to Dominic yesterday. He's worried, too. As he should be, but still…" He let the rest ride. Dominic was his twin. Regardless of the mistake he'd made, Daniel would stand by him just as John was doing. In the face of such desperate odds, Daniel was amazed at their father's steadfast loyalty.

"So what do you think we should do?"

He sighed. "Book our flights."

"Agreed." She rose from the bed and set her coffee cup beside his. "But first, I have a present for you."

He pumped his eyebrows. "You're coming back to bed?"

She laughed. "Maybe. But something important came by messenger a few minutes ago, and I can't wait to share the news with you." She left the room, only to return a moment later carrying a brown envelope.

"Remember all that fabulous art my stepfather collected?"

Yes, he remembered. And he also recalled the abuse she'd suffered when she hadn't been able to remember the titles and artists. He'd wanted to tear the paintings from the wall and rip them apart with his bare hands.

She handed him a legal-looking document. "That collection auctioned for an enormous sum of money."

"Good. Are you planning to add that to your Hope House?"

She shook her head. "This document creates a trust to help fund Daniel Stephens' water projects in Africa."

Incredulous, he stared from her to the document. "You're serious. That's really what this is."

"Yes. If I'd known a crisis would arise in the family, I would have saved some out for that. But I didn't. And this is already in motion. A trust of this kind can do an enormous amount of good."

"You put your inheritance into this? For me?"

"My wedding gift to you. I know how important those projects are to you. Now they're important to me." She climbed on the bed beside him, touched his cheek with her fingertips. "You changed my life, Daniel. You made me feel beautiful and desirable and worthy. You took away my shame. Nothing I give you will ever be enough."

Love, almost more than he could contain, exploded inside him. This woman, this incredible, generous, valiant woman had taken the ugliness of her childhood and created something beautiful. And in the process, she'd changed him, an empty, heartless shell of a man.

And as he contemplated the priceless gifts Stephanie had given him—her love, her fears, and now her inheritance—Daniel let go of the bitterness he'd carried so long.

CHAPTER THIRTEEN

"IT'S a Christmas party." Over the softly crooning music of "White Christmas," Daniel spoke close to Stephanie's ear. She was understandably nervous about tonight. "What bad thing could possibly happen?"

Daniel gazed around at the gathered assembly. Seated with them at the corner table were Daniel's cousins, Rebecca and Rachel, both pregnant and with their new husbands by their sides. Across the room, Rebecca's stepchildren played wide-eyed under the Christmas tree. A host of Valentines, of whom Daniel and his bride were both now a part, swarmed the gaily decorated interior of the Bella Lucia Mayfair. Beneath the outward gaiety, the strain was almost palpable.

"A Christmas party that is also an emergency family meeting. Things could get sticky before the evening is over."

She nodded toward Robert and his wife, ensconced at one end of the room, and then toward John, who'd taken a table at the other end. The two brothers, who'd never gotten along, were really at odds now.

"This is my first ever family Christmas," Daniel said. "I think I'll enjoy myself and forget the rest." He dropped a kiss on her hair, and filled his lungs with her fresh designer fragrance. He was only telling half the truth. He was worried, too. As hard as he'd tried to remain detached from his blood relatives, they had a way of sucking him in. And now they were in trouble.

Regardless of some happy news, including Daniel and Stephanie's elopement, bad news seemed to be the order of the day. Dominic's embezzlement had caused much greater damage than John had anticipated.

Without a huge infusion of money from Lord-knew-where, the Bella Lucia chain would be bankrupt. John was striving valiantly to protect Dominic and had drained his personal accounts in the effort. Robert was furious with them both and threatening everything from lawsuit to strangulation. All involved, including Stephanie, were concerned about their livelihoods. Daniel felt guilty to see his own dreams coming true when others were losing theirs.

"You two look cozy," Rebecca said, smiling toward Daniel and Stephanie. "How was the honeymoon?"

"Perfect," they answered in unison and then burst out laughing. No one would ever know how perfect. They'd skied, hiked, and gone sledding. They'd dined out and in. They'd strolled the woods and the streets of Aspen. But mostly they'd stayed in the secluded cabin and reveled in the joy of their love.

"Did I ever thank you for sending me to America?" Daniel asked.

Rebecca reached across the table to squeeze Stephanie's arm. "Seeing my friend happy is thanks enough."

"You look pretty happy yourself," Stephanie said, returning the squeeze.

"Delirious." Suddenly, Rebecca's eyes widened. "Daniel," she said in amazement, "is that your sister?"

They all looked in the direction of Rebecca's gaze. A tall blonde in a white angora crop top and red micro mini had entered the dining room. Mistletoe jewelry flashed from her belly button. At her side was a tall, tanned fellow who probably had every woman in the place staring at him.

Daniel choked on his drink. "That's not the Louise I remember."

Gone were the classic designer suits, subtle makeup and hairstyle. Miss Goody-Two-Shoes looked red-hot.

"We're not the only ones noticing her new look." Stephanie hitched her chin toward Max. Daniel's cousin, who helped Robert run the Bella Lucia Chelsea, glowered at the outrageously clad Louise and her escort.

"Don't mind Max," Rachel said. "The two of them have never gotten along."

"Hmm. I wonder." Rebecca's eyes sparkled beneath the white blinking Christmas lights. "Sometimes all that fighting is a mating dance."

Mitchell, Rebecca's husband, chuckled indulgently. "I'm afraid you'll have to overlook my wife. She sees romance everywhere these days."

Rebecca grinned up at him. "You complaining?"

He hooked an elbow around her neck and pulled, his besotted expression clear to all. "Nope."

"Romance or not, Louise is here for the same reason we are. Because this family has big problems." Rachel seemed set on fretting. And rightly so. She'd been a favorite of Grandfather William's and had invested her adult life in these restaurants. "I, for one, don't know what we're going to do."

"I've offered to take a cut in salary," Stephanie said. "Others have done the same."

"The business needs a lot more money than salary cuts can generate. Unless Uncle John and Dad come up with a plan soon, the entire chain will have to close. But the way those two quarrel, I can't see that happening."

"Surely, they can find an investor, Rachel. Doesn't anyone in this huge family have that kind of money?"

"There is one. But he won't help."

"Who's that?"

"Jack. Dad's other son, my other half brother, the estranged one. But he washed his hands of this place and all the Valentines a long time ago."

Odd. Daniel had never heard of this cousin. "Will he be here tonight?"

"Are you kidding?" Rachel shook her head. "Jack hasn't been to a family gathering in years. He hates this place. All the others may put aside their differences at Christmas, but not Jack. If this place sinks, he'd be the last person on earth to throw out a life-preserver."

Above the lilt of "Have Yourself a Merry Little Christmas" came the tinkle of metal against glass. Soon the room took up the chorus of tapping and conversation hushed.

John rose. His face was drawn and weary, his usual ruddy vigor gone, and Daniel thought with a start that his father looked old. He'd had a mild heart attack a few months back and now the strain of Dominic's misdeed was taking a heavy toll.

Still, he carried himself erect, and, with a determined set to his chin, he started across the room toward Robert.

"I would like to propose a toast," he said. The sound carried among the assembly now gone quiet except for the soft Christmas carols playing through the sound system. All eyes watched as John approached his brother's table.

Robert looked startled; an inward struggle played across his features. Finally, as if he had no choice, he rose, wineglass in hand. The rest of the crowd rose as well.

"Tonight," John said, his gaze intent on the other man's face, "is Christmas. All of us are here because we're family. If only for this one night, let's forget our problems, and celebrate all the good things that have happened to us this year." When Robert didn't protest, he went on, gathering momentum. "Here is a toast to all of us. Young and old. Old and new. We face some challenges, but the indomitable spirit of the Valentine family will prevail. Somehow, some way, we will prevail. May the coming year bring happiness, peace, and prosperity to us all."

"Hear, hear," someone in the crowd called. And a chorus of the toasts rose and fell. Glasses clinked.

Daniel used that diversion as an excuse to maneuver his bride beneath a sprig of mistletoe. "Merry Christmas, wife."

"Merry Christmas, husband," she said as his smiling lips melded with hers.

When the kiss ended and the clinks and good wishes faded away, the front door of the restaurant, closed to all but family, whooshed open. Cold December air flooded in.

The party, wineglasses held high, turned as one to see who the latecomers were.

A collective gasp emptied the room of oxygen.

For there in the doorway stood Madison Ford, Jack Valentine's assistant. And next to her, a cynical half-smile on his face, was none other than the prodigal son himself, Jack Valentine.

* * * * *

CRAZY ABOUT
THE BOSS

TERESA SOUTHWICK

Teresa Southwick has written over twenty-five books and calls it the best job in the world. She lives in Las Vegas, where she's hard at work on her next romance novel.

For the Romance readers – without you there would be no happy endings!

PROLOGUE

New York—December 23

HEARING his sister's voice always made Jack feel like that eighteen-year-old who'd left home in disgrace.

How bloody stupid was that? He was Jack Valentine of Valentine Ventures, the reckless genius who had challenged conventional wisdom and made a fortune. And she was asking him to come home again.

Jack squeezed the phone until his fingers ached. "It's been twelve years, Emma. That's a lot of Christmases. Why should I come home for this one?"

"Do you have something better to do?" she said, her soft, cultured voice dripping with irritation.

A muscle jumped in his jaw. It was almost as if she knew he had no plans at all. "Anything's better than that."

"It's time, Jack."

He heard London in her voice. Americans loved the accent. But he heard silk and steel in the soft, firm tone that tapped into an accumulation of loneliness he hadn't realized was there.

Swiveling his chair around, he stared out his office window and concentrated on the New York skyline instead. It was dark, but across the city lights dotted the windows in the tall buildings. Out there someone was staring at *his* window and coveting this office with its expensive art, plush carpet, fine furniture and the latest electronics. Standing on the street they were cold and scared and staring, wondering what it felt like to have everything you ever wanted.

He knew because twelve years ago this city was where he'd run and he'd once been down there with nothing. He'd looked up and vowed that one day he'd own the whole damn building. Screw-ups didn't grow up to be millionaires, but he had.

"It *has* been twelve years, after all. Are you listening, Jack?"

"Yes. And what I hear is that something's wrong. What is it, Em?"

There was a big sigh from the other end of the line. "All right. There is a problem here. The business is in trouble. We need your help."

The precious business Robert Valentine prized above everything? Good. It was about time the womanizing bastard paid for his sins where it hurt him most. "I'm not sure why I should care."

"Because no matter how stubborn you insist on

being, you're still part of this family." This time censure mixed with the steel in her voice.

"Did he put you up to this?"

"No." Another big sigh. "Jack, what happened between the two of you?"

Jack had protected his mother. And it had cost him.

"It doesn't matter any more, Em."

The unladylike snort on the other end of the line told him his sister was probably rolling her pale blue eyes in disgust as she fiddled with a strand of curly light brown hair. The vivid image made him miss her.

"I hear in your voice that it still *does* matter," she said quietly.

"You're wrong. Now, if that's all—" He turned away from the window and leaned back in his chair.

"It's not," she snapped. "We need you, Jack. Your job is investing in companies. The family business needs money and quite literally you're our only hope to keep it going."

"Lots of investors would love to get their hands on a piece of the action."

"But they wouldn't be family. And none of us want to give a non-Valentine a piece of the action because you don't turn your back on family. It simply isn't right."

Even if family turned their backs on him? he wondered. "They'll survive, Em."

"I wish I could be as sure." Sadness shaded her voice. "As you said—it's been a dozen years. Twelve seems like a good round number to make peace. Tis the season. Peace on earth. Charity begins at home and all that."

"I'm not feeling charitable." Jack rested his elbows on his cluttered desk.

"Neither am I." Frustration laced with anger making her tone more clipped. "You disappeared," she blurted out. "Dad wouldn't discuss it and Mum was fragile. I was sixteen when you left me with the whole mess. Big brothers are supposed to take care of their little sisters."

Little sister knew how to stick the knife in and twist. He'd loved her. Hell, he still loved her.

"I had no choice, Em. I had to leave."

"That doesn't change the fact that you abandoned me, but you did what you needed to, I guess. Now I need something from you." She hesitated a moment, then said, "I got married, Jack."

It took him two beats to pull himself out of the past. His little sister was a married woman? He hadn't heard. "Congratulations. Who's the lucky man?"

"He was a prince—"

"Of course he'd be a prince of a guy," he teased.

She laughed, a happy sound, so different from a few moments ago. "No, Sebastian was actually crowned King of Meridia."

Meridia. Jack knew it was a small European country and recalled something in the news recently about a scandal in the line of succession. "I've heard of it."

"It's very important to me that you meet him."

"Look, Emma—"

"I've never asked you for anything," she interrupted, her voice firm. "But I want this and, quite frankly, I think you owe me, Jack. Come for Christmas. The usual place for the family toast. I'll be expecting you."

Before he could decline again, the line went dead. Jack let out a long breath as he replaced the phone. His little sister married a king?

And he'd missed it.

That made him wonder what else he'd missed. But Emma had never told him that she'd felt abandoned. And she *hadn't* ever asked him for anything. Until now.

"Jack, you're out of your mind." His associate, Maddie Ford, walked into his office without looking up from the proposal he'd given her earlier. "You can't seriously want to put money into this. It's crazy. It's risky. And so like you it makes me want to shake you until your teeth rattle."

She kept talking, but he was only half listening to blonde, blue-eyed, brainy Maddie. His sensible and down-to-earth, tell-it-like-it-is Maddie. In the two years since he'd brought her into his company, she'd become more his partner than his assistant. He'd come to rely on her sound judgment. For better or worse she'd become the voice in his head.

She was also the only stunningly beautiful woman he'd never hit on. And he planned to keep it that way because the women who gave in to him were here today and gone tomorrow. Sometimes they were gone in the same day. He wouldn't do anything to lose Maddie because he needed her around, although what he had in mind wasn't business related. The thing was, he hadn't made a fortune by *not* listening to his gut and it was telling him now to take her with him to meet Emma's husband.

When she stopped talking to catch a breath he said, "How do you feel about Christmas in London?"

CHAPTER ONE

London—Christmas Day

"I suppose millionaires have problems, too."

Maddie Ford waited for a reaction from the bachelor millionaire in the town car beside her and Jack Valentine didn't disappoint.

He glared at her. "What's that supposed to mean?"

"I'm sorry. Did I say that out loud?" she asked, making her eyes as wide and innocent as she could manage.

"You know good and well you did. Was that a blonde moment? Don't go blonde on me now, Maddie," he said, irritation in his voice. Or was it tension?

Definitely tension and that wasn't like Jack. Whatever business had made him insist she come along on this trip must be really important because the strain was showing.

And that was starting to concern her. Jack Valentine was rich, handsome, charismatic and often touted as New York's most eligible bachelor. He did the charming

British thing with overtones of brash American and it worked way too well. From his short, black, carefully mussed hair to his dark blue eyes with the bad-boy gleam that promised trouble in a most appealing way, he exuded the same exciting vibes that had brought down her heart not once, but twice.

In the beginning, she'd had a crush on him but quickly learned he wasn't a one-woman man. So the fact that he'd never tried anything had convinced her she wasn't his type. He wasn't likely to turn his charm in her direction, which was just fine with her. She liked her job.

For the last two plus years she and Jack had worked well together. Her sensible side balanced Jack's tendency toward rashness. They had been a team. Until he'd messed with her Christmas plans. Although he hadn't smiled or teased her since leaving New York. The way he was acting made her feel guilty for giving him a hard time. Maybe a little teasing of her own could lighten him up because he normally didn't do tension.

"If by 'going blonde' you're referring to my current state of irritation, let me assure you I have a very good reason. It's Christmas. And I'm on the wrong continent. Is there a reason this trip couldn't have waited?"

"It's one day and I did promise to make it up to you."

That was a non-answer. "How do you make up for missing Christmas? I had plans."

"I know. You've made that quite clear."

He didn't need to know that her plans hadn't been with family. Her married siblings alternated holidays with their spouses' families and this year her parents had taken a cruise. They'd invited her because they felt sorry for their twenty-eight-year-old unmarried-and-not-dating daughter. She'd declined because it seemed too pathetic for words, but she hadn't shared any of that with Jack. He'd have teased her unmercifully and teasing from Mr Bachelor-about-town regarding her non-existent love life would be too humiliating.

"It's good of you—"

"No, it's not. I'm not good."

"Okay. You're bad. I can live with that." For a split second, he flashed his carefree, charming Jack Valentine grin.

Was his grin always that potent? Or did his uncharacteristic tension just make it seem more thrilling than usual? Not going there, she thought. "I can't believe you played the because-you're-the-boss card to get me here."

"Our difference of opinion showed no signs of letting up. In the interest of time, it seemed the expedient thing to do."

She'd disagreed because she hadn't liked his attitude and now it was time for his reminder that he couldn't walk all over her. "My being here makes no more sense now than it did before. Since when do you want me to come along? And what business couldn't wait a day? More important, who does business on Christmas? It's un-American."

"Then it's a good thing we're in Britain."

Did he just snap at her? That was out of character, too. But before she could demand to know what was going on with him, the car smoothly pulled to the curb in front of a restaurant. It was then she realized that by continuing their disagreement on a different continent, she'd missed seeing anything of London. It didn't matter that it was too dark to see all that much, she really wanted to see London. At least he'd promised her a couple days there. That had finally broken down her resistance.

"Why are we stopping here?" she asked.

"It's something I have to do." There was an edge to his voice that said whatever he had to do was tantamount to a firing squad at dawn.

There was an angry, dark look on his face that frightened her, mostly because she'd never seen it before. "What's going on, Jack?"

"I have to see my sister."

"Your sister?" If Maddie hadn't been so shocked, she'd have come back with a brilliantly clever retort. But she *was* shocked and said exactly what she was thinking. "I didn't know you had a sister."

"Well, now you do."

"What else don't I know?" she asked as the driver opened the door for them to get out.

A lot, Jack thought, and he ignored the question, as he didn't plan to enlighten her. He would see Emma and meet her husband. Duty fulfilled and he'd leave.

Cold London air filled his lungs as he slid out of the car before her. He walked slowly toward the Bella Lucia restaurant he hadn't been able to get out of fast enough twelve years ago. The gate he pushed open was familiar, as was the courtyard in front of the building. Small white lights twinkled in the shrubs and a subdued glow coming through the frosted windows pooled gold at his feet. There were people inside.

His family. And he was on the outside looking in, a thought that opened up an empty feeling deep inside him.

"Jack?"

He looked at Maddie, grateful for her presence and determined not to let her know. It was just this once, because he wouldn't let himself need anyone.

"Let's get this over with," he said.

"Way to make me even more joyful about missing out on the biggest holiday of the year."

Her sarcasm made him smile. Brutal honesty was what he counted on from Maddie. She'd never been more indispensable to him than she was at this moment.

He pushed open the door, walked inside the restaurant and looked around. It was all different. Gone was the original Italian style and in its place was a trendy, smart, fashionable restaurant. A restaurant that went dead quiet as everyone turned and silently stared at him.

He recognized his uncle John, in the center of the room with glass in hand for the traditional holiday toast. Robert Valentine stood beside him and Jack met his father's gaze across the room. The rest of the family clustered on either side of the two men and looked from him to Robert. Jack would swear every last one of them were holding their breath. He could almost reach out and grab the friction out of the air.

Maddie leaned over. "They're all staring at us, Jack."

"I know."

"Do you realize everyone is looking at us as if I'm Scrooge and you're the Ghost of Christmas Past? Are we crashing a private party?"

"We are, yes."

Jack didn't take his eyes off his father. Every muscle in his body tensed as he waited for the man who'd sent him packing to make the first move. The young woman beside Robert looked anxiously between them and the seconds ticked off like the timer on an explosive device.

Finally she rushed over to him. "Jack, you came. I didn't think you would."

"Emma?" He recognized the voice, but the petite, curvy young woman in front of him had been a gawky sixteen-year-old when he'd left. Now she was glamorous and sophisticated, her hair no longer light brown, but blonde shot with honey-colored highlights. "You're all grown up."

"As are you. You're just in time for the family toast." She handed first him then Maddie a flute of champagne.

"Merry Christmas, everyone." His uncle John continued as if nothing out of the ordinary had happened. "Here's to a holiday season filled with health, happiness and success." He held up his glass. "To family."

Murmurs of agreement filled the room as everyone

sipped from their crystal flutes. Without drinking, Jack set his glass on the white linen cloth covering the table beside him.

"Welcome home, Jack," Emma said, even as she frowned at the champagne he'd abandoned.

"This isn't my home."

And as soon as he met his sister's new husband, he and Maddie could get the hell out of here. He looked at her bright blonde hair and big blue eyes, letting himself feel the familiar tug for a beautiful woman. In her case he'd never given in to it because he respected her too much. She was different from the women he dated and his relationship with her was as sacred as the separation between church and state.

Emma ignored his sharp words as she looked at Maddie. "Who's this, then?"

"Madison Ford. I'm Jack's assistant." Maddie held out her hand. "Call me Maddie. Or better yet, Scrooge," she finished.

"No Christmas spirit?" Emma asked.

"I left it back in New York. I had plans."

"After you called," Jack said to his sister, "I decided to move up a scheduled business trip and convinced Maddie to come along. Where's your husband?"

Emma turned to look, then smiled at the man just joining them. He stood military straight, even as he slid his arm around her waist. Not quite as tall as Jack, he had wavy dark hair and brown eyes.

Adoration shone on Emma's face as she leaned into

the man. "His Highness Sebastian Marchand-Dumon-
tier of Meridia meet Jack Valentine, my brother."

They shook hands and Jack noted the prince's firm
grip. *Always squeeze a man's hand as if you mean it. No
one respects you if your hand feels like a limp codfish.*

When his father's words flashed through his mind,
Jack knew it had been a mistake to come. Then he
looked at Maddie as the prince kissed her hand.

"It's a pleasure to meet you, Your Highness,"
Maddie said.

"Please, Sebastian is fine," he said graciously.

Maddie looked at Emma. "That would make you what?
Queen? Princess Consort? I can never keep that straight."

"Emma will do," she said with a twinkle.

"Quite nicely," her husband added, smiling down at her.

Maddie was studying his sister. "I think there must
be something in the royal rulebook about fabulous
jewels. If you show me your tiara, it might almost make
up for the fact that I'm missing Christmas in the States."

Laughing, Emma leaned into her chuckling prince.
"I'm afraid the tiara's at home in Meridia's royal vault.
But do come for a visit, Maddie. I've a feeling you and
I would get on very well together."

"I'm not sure I could spare her," Jack cut in.

"I'd love to visit Meridia," Maddie countered,
shooting him a look. "His Lordship will just have to get
along without me."

"Jack."

He turned and recognized his older brother, Max,

and pleasure shot through him. He put out his hand and Max took it, then the two of them grinned at each other.

Emma cleared her throat. "I'll let you and Max catch up, Jack."

"How long will you be in London?" Maddie asked her.

"We're on holiday for several weeks." She looked at Jack. "And you? How long will you be here? Are you planning to see Mum?"

"I hadn't thought about it," he said.

"You should." Emma stood on tiptoe and hesitated a moment before kissing his cheek. "You look well but not happy, Jack."

The casual comment brought the same rush of emptiness that had washed over him when he'd looked through the window. Why now? He'd managed fine without them all these years, proving he didn't need them or anyone else.

"Not happy? And you can tell that in five minutes?"

"Less." She slid her hand into her husband's and their fingers intertwined. "Now that I know what happiness looks like, it's easy to see when it's not there. We'll talk later."

She and her husband walked away and mingled with the rest of the family. Then he looked at Max and felt again that soul-deep, overwhelming loneliness. They were half-brothers and had been best friends. Max had been the one to introduce him to parties, girls and fast cars.

Jack realized how much he'd missed him. "It's good to see you, Max."

"You, too." Max looked at Maddie. "Aren't you going to introduce me to your significant other?"

"I'm significant and Jack has many 'others', but I'm not one of them," Maddie retorted.

"Excellent news. I'm Max Valentine."

"Jack's brother?" she guessed.

"Indeed."

"Maddie Ford," she said. "Jack's assistant as opposed to his significant other. Upon occasion, to my dismay, I've dutifully smoothed the ruffled feathers of his significant others. Which I guess would then make them insignificant."

Max grinned. "You're a feisty one."

Jack was taken by surprise when an unreasonable flash of resentment ripped through him. "You're not her type, Max."

"How do you know?" she asked.

"Max actually has a personality."

Maddie finished off the champagne in her glass. "Then maybe I should get to know him and his personality better," she shot back.

Before Jack could figure out how he could be so pleased to see his brother at the same time he wanted to wring his neck for flirting with Maddie, his father joined them.

The older man rested his hand on his Max's shoulder. "And so," Robert Valentine said, "the prodigal son returns."

CHAPTER TWO

THE last time Jack had been face to face with his father, Robert Valentine had been enraged. Now he showed no emotion, not even surprise. He was still handsome, the silver flecks in his black hair giving him a distinguished look. His black eyes revealed nothing about his feelings for the son who had spent eighteen years trying to get his notice. The son who had struggled to control his natural enthusiasm. The son who now controlled the fate of this restaurant.

The irony of that almost made him smile.

Jack had literally looked up to his father twelve years ago, but now he looked him straight in the eye. He'd made himself a powerful man and was no longer that unsure boy who craved his father's good opinion.

"Hello, Dad."

"Jack." Robert smiled his practiced smile. "It's been a long time. To what do we owe this unexpected surprise?"

"Emma called."

Something flickered in Robert's eyes. "Did she now?"

"Yes. To tell me she got married."

"Did she say anything else?" A muscle jumped in his father's jaw.

In anyone else that tightening of the mouth would be nothing. For his stiff-upper-lipped father it signaled nervousness in the man Jack had once thought invincible. Satisfaction surged through Jack. If it made him a bastard that he took pleasure in the old man's problems, so be it.

"She said she wanted me to meet her husband," Jack answered.

"Sebastian. Nice chap."

Jack shrugged. "Hard to tell in a few minutes, but my sister seems happy."

"She's blossomed, our Emma has, into a beautiful, self-confident young woman."

"She has, yes."

Funny how leaving Robert Valentine's shadow had that effect.

"I hear you've done well for yourself, Jack," Robert said.

"Does that surprise you?"

Instead of answering, Robert turned his gaze to Maddie. "And who's this, then?"

She held out her hand. "Maddie Ford. Jack's assistant," she added before his father made the "significant other" assumption.

"Robert Valentine," he said, shaking her hand. "It's a pleasure to meet you. Welcome to Bella Lucia."

"Thank you."

"Have you been to England before?"

She shook her head. "This is my first visit."

"And Christmastime in London is a fine introduction." Robert smiled at her.

"I have business," Jack said.

"I do hope work won't keep you from seeing some of London." His father's voice oozed charm.

"It won't. Jack promised." Maddie smiled brightly, a clear indication that the Valentine charm was working on her. "It would be a shame to come all this way and not take in the sights. Traveling has always been on my list of things to do."

"Don't put things off, Maddie," Robert warned, "All work and no play…"

Hypocritical bastard! Vibrating with anger, Jack took a step forward and stopped inches from his father. "And how would you know about balancing work and play? For all the time you gave your family, we might have been pet frogs. When you weren't buried in work, you played with women who were not your wife."

Maddie put a hand on his arm. "Jack—"

He barely felt the touch, but her tone got his attention. The shocked expression on her face cleared the red haze of rage from his head. He blew out a long breath. "We're leaving, Maddie."

Shock turned to surprise and there were questions in her eyes. "But it's just been—"

"We can't stay," Jack interrupted.

Robert frowned. "You've come a long way. Surely you can have dinner—"

"We have other plans," he snapped.

Jack had come because of Emma, but he didn't owe this man a thing and this place held no good memories for him. Right here the world as he'd known it had come apart. He'd rebuilt his life, but no one would be that important to him again.

As Jack hustled Maddie back out into the cold he acknowledged irony for the second time and didn't appreciate it. Just like that night a dozen years ago, he couldn't get out of Bella Lucia fast enough.

The difference was that this time he was leaving with Maddie, the only woman he trusted.

After checking into a suite at Durley House, Maddie couldn't wait to get out of her travel clothes and into something more comfortable. If only she could get out of her thoughts as easily. The scene at Bella Lucia had really shaken her.

She'd never seen Jack like that. The repressed violence she'd felt in him had shocked her because she was accustomed to his easygoing charm, a trait she suspected he'd inherited from his father after meeting the man. This darker Jack with an aura of danger hanging over him was someone she didn't know at all. And she couldn't stop thinking about him.

She didn't like thinking about Jack outside of business because, by definition, outside of business meant personal. On a personal level, men like Jack were toxic to her. After getting to know him, she'd filed him in the well-to-do womanizing wastrel category. But after seeing his volatile reaction to his father, it was harder to keep him there. The little he'd said revealed that Jack had probably inherited his father's fondness for women as well as the charm to reel them in.

And here she was sharing a suite with the man. He had the master bedroom with a living room in between, but suddenly it was too close.

Damn it. She should have told him what he could do with his Christmas in London.

An unexpected knock on her door made her jump. She walked over and opened it. "What?"

"I've taken the liberty of ordering dinner." He indicated the dining table behind him set with linen, china, candles, flowers and two plates.

That was all very lovely, as was Jack. He'd slipped into something more comfortable, too—jeans that fit his toned body as if they'd been made for him. As they probably had. The navy pullover sweater made his eyes look very blue especially with traces of his earlier hostility still darkening them. And it hit her like a bolt of lightning from a clear blue sky that her crush could be resurrected without him lifting a finger.

His brother had called her feisty, but she didn't feel that way at the moment. She could meet men in business and go toe to toe. She could talk capital and investments with Jack and give as good as she got. But something had shifted for her tonight and she wasn't entirely sure what it was or how it happened. She just knew the sight of him produced a tickle low in her belly and she was aware of him in a way that she shouldn't be.

"I'm not very hungry. It's getting late. I'll just—"

"We're still on New York time. And after leaving the restaurant you clearly expressed your displeasure about not staying because the unbelievably scrumptious smells made your mouth water."

Not as much as now, she thought, forcing her gaze from the width of his chest. She'd seen him in sweaters before. She'd seen him in jeans. But she'd never seen him angry enough to do battle. And after battle warriors had an overabundance of adrenaline to channel into other activities. Physical, intimate activities. How inconvenient for her that she was handy, yet exciting for her at the same time, which just meant that she needed serious therapy.

"The scrumptious smells are gone. And since when do you pay attention to my whining?"

"Did I say whining?"

"No, but that's what you meant. It's a flaw. I'm working on it," she informed him.

"Speaking of work, I'm the boss. And you need to eat. I'm not a heartless slave-driver."

"And you're attempting to prove that by making sure your indentured subordinate is well nourished and has the strength to give you the last ounce of blood?" she asked, indicating the food on the table.

One of his dark eyebrows lifted. "When did you develop a flair for the dramatic?"

"I've always had it."

But seeing a different side of Jack had unleashed it. She knew his business background and venture-capitalist-on-the-rise story, but until today she hadn't realized how little she knew about him personally. She'd shared details of her life but he never had, unless it had been about the female of the month. The arm candy never lasted much longer than that before he ended things and it didn't affect her. Except for the occasional overly emotional cast-off who had trouble dealing with Jack's rejection and came to Maddie for consolation, in the form of an old-fashioned session of male-bashing.

But this male didn't look as if *he'd* take no for an answer. If he ever made up his mind that he wanted more from her than simply sharing a meal, she'd be in a lot of trouble. She'd never been more grateful that she wasn't his type.

"Okay, Jack. Let's eat." She picked a chair, then sat and lifted the metal covering over the plate. "Christmas dinner," she said, surveying turkey with all the trimmings.

When she started eating, Maddie found she was hungry and the food was delicious. "Who'd have guessed hotel room service on a holiday could be so yummy?"

"In a five-star hotel one doesn't have to guess. One counts on it, which is why one stays there."

"If one can afford it." She knew Jack could afford it. They ate in silence for a few moments, then Maddie made the mistake of looking at him. The brooding expression on his face tugged at her, because Jack didn't brood, and again she was amazed by how little she knew him. On the one hand she was safer not learning anything new. On the other, that damn dark expression on his face made her want to do something to make it go away.

"So can we talk about your family?" she asked.

"No."

She dragged her fork through the mashed potatoes so the dammed up gravy could escape. Glancing at Jack, she realized he looked like a man with dammed-up feelings in need of release. And that was why *she* couldn't take no for an answer. "I thought you were going to deck your dad."

His gaze narrowed on her. "Did you now?"

She noted that he'd elevated the non-answer to an art form. "You never told me you had parents."

"Everyone does. It seemed that confirming the obvious was an insult to your intelligence."

His smile held no humor and made her shiver. But that didn't stop her. "I guess your parents are divorced? So where's your mother?"

"Dublin." He cut a piece of turkey and forked it into his mouth, his gaze not leaving hers as he chewed.

"Are you going to see her?"

"I suspect I'll have occasion to visit."

She took a hearty drink of the wine he'd poured. "I meant while we're here."

"Technically this isn't Ireland. London is in England."

"Thanks for the geography lesson." She knew he was deliberately trying to sidetrack her. She knew he could chew her up and spit her out if the focus he turned on her got personal. But she'd developed a tough façade so that he didn't walk all over her and was never more grateful than right now. "Just so you know, the British accents were a big clue for me. To put a finer point on it, I meant since we're so close, are you going to visit?"

"There's a time issue. I'm not sure—"

"For God's sake, Jack, we came all this way. To pop over to Ireland is like going from New York to New Jersey."

"I'll think about it."

Maddie studied the dark look. Jack acted on instinct, gut feeling, deciding yes or no in a split second. He didn't think about it. That was her job. She knew he'd already made up his mind and decided to change the subject. For now.

"I liked Emma." She finished the wine in her glass and he refilled it. "She seems nice."

"I don't want to talk about my family."

As if she needed it, there was another red flag that something wasn't right with him. He was normally open and honest, too honest. On a regular basis he told her more than she wanted to know about his current woman. But now he was closed off and detached. What was up with that?

And the way he was looking at her... Maddie had shared dinner with him before, but not like this. They'd ordered in at work, and on the intimate scale it had never even registered. But this was *intimate*. God knew she wasn't experienced, but she'd have to be a moron not to feel the pent up sexual energy in him. And all that energy directed at her seemed to be affecting her brain function, which no man had managed to do since college. She had to deflect it somehow.

"Tell me about Max?"

Something flared hot in his eyes, burning through the shadows. "What about him?"

"Well, for one thing, he's very cute."

"Looks can be deceiving."

"Speaking of looks," she said, "there's a family resemblance. Does he treat women like tissues, too?"

"Tissues?"

"Disposable—like tissues."

"Max isn't your type," he said again.

"How do you know what my type is?"

"I've met one or two. The accountant." He sipped his wine as he thought for a moment. "The computer geek. The chemistry professor. There was no chemistry. With any of them."

"Like they're going to show chemistry in front of my boss."

"If the spark is there, one can't hide it."

"A lot you know." She was hiding her feelings from Jack right now she thought, as he focused those amazing eyes on her. Her pulse stuttered and she took a deep breath. "Going from one woman to the next doesn't exactly satisfy the prerequisites for advanced chemistry."

He leaned back in the chair and twirled his wineglass. "Just think of me as a scientist—experimenting until I get it right."

"Don't even go there with me. You wouldn't know chemistry if a science experiment blew up in your face. And it does on an annoyingly regular basis."

"And you know this how?"

"Two words. Angelica Tedesco."

"Ah. A lovely girl." He rested his elbows on the table and smiled his big-bad-wolf smile.

"Girl being the operative word." She shook her head. "I had to pick up the pieces when she came to the office in tears."

"While it lasted, the relationship was mutually satisfying."

"It never lasts, Jack. Why is that?" She folded her arms on the table.

He lifted one broad shoulder dismissively. "I'm not looking for anything permanent. Don't I get points for sending roses and breaking it off before someone gets hurt?"

"You're a hit-and-run player. How do you know there's no such thing as love at first sight?"

A dark eyebrow arched. "Maddie, I had no idea you were such a romantic."

She ignored the way his words pricked her. "You may not get hurt, but how do you know others don't?"

Maddie hurt for all the Angelica Tedescos in his life. And roses wouldn't mend a broken heart. She knew for a fact only time would do that. Time and a promise not to make the same mistake. Jack had mistake written all over him.

She met his gaze. "It occurs to me that you're a lot like your father."

"You're wrong." His voice was sharp enough to cut glass.

"Am I? What was it you said to him tonight? Buried in work and playing with women? You described yourself, Jack."

His gaze jumped to hers as the muscle in his jaw flexed. "Aren't you just full of questions and observations."

"It's part of my job and what you expect from me," she shot back. "And here's an observation for you. In spite of that, he seems like a charming man."

He scowled. "Believe me, he's not the nice man you think, Maddie."

She waited and hoped he'd say more, but he'd shut down tighter than an airport in a blizzard. If he expected them not to talk about what happened tonight, he'd brought the wrong woman to London.

"Jack, we all have flaws. Yours is a reckless streak that makes you very good at what you do."

"Your point?"

She stopped and waited until he looked at her. "Your father is no doubt imperfect, but he loves you."

The dark look got darker still and his blue eyes glittered with something dangerous. "And you got that from an observation?"

"No. I got it when he told you it's been a long time."

"I'm not following," he said, shaking his head.

"That meant he's missed you."

"Oh, really?" He leaned forward.

"Yes, really. And when he said you've done well, that meant he's proud of you."

"I had no idea you were gifted in reading between the lines."

"It's easy to read between the lines when one isn't emotionally involved," she told him. She set her fork down on her empty plate.

"And you think I am?"

"Oh, please." She rolled her eyes. "He's your father. You love him and he loves you."

"And you know this—how?"

"When you abruptly announced it was time to go, he tried to get you to change your mind."

"Translation?"

"I love you. I've missed you. I'm not ready for you to leave so soon."

He laughed, but the sound was bitter and harsh and completely humorless. "Not that I buy into such a lunatic theory," he said, "but how do you know this?"

"My father." She pushed her plate aside. "He used to tell me I looked like a college football quarterback and I found that fairly offensive as I prided myself on being feminine."

"And doing a fine job."

There was that gleam in his eyes again as he let his

gaze boldly roam over her. Along with the compliment, it produced a warm glow in the wasteland of her heart. She wished she could blame the feeling on the wine, but that simply explained the buzz. This sensation was so much more. It was all that attention zeroed in on her. It was exciting. It was scary. It was a stepping-stone to heartbreak.

"I complained to my mother and she explained it was approval. That he was actually saying that I'm trim and fit."

"I couldn't agree more." Jack's gaze lowered for a fraction of a second.

His attention was more than scary. It made her want to run but she wouldn't because she'd be humiliated and Jack would win. She forced herself not to look away. "That's when I started translating male speak," she explained.

"Fascinating."

"I'm convinced your father was trying to reach out—"

"I don't want to talk about it." He stood abruptly. "Did you leave room for pie? I had it made specially. Let's have it in the sitting area." He took one of the pieces on a dessert plate and walked over to the sofa.

And just like that the conversation was over. "All right."

She took the other piece of pie and followed him. The suite, ironically enough, was decorated in the color of money. Thick jade carpet cushioned her bare feet and furniture covered in varying shades of green was arranged in a conversation area on one wall. Maddie sat on the sofa at a right angle to him and concentrated on eating her dessert.

"This is really delicious. Almost as good as my sister Susie's. The whipped cream is to die for," she said, closing her eyes. Memories of a past holiday flitted through her mind and she started to laugh.

"What?" Jack set his untouched pie on the table, then rested his arm on the end of the sofa.

"I was just remembering the time my mother caught us squirting the whipped cream straight from the can into our mouths."

"A hanging offense if I ever heard one." This teasing man was more like the New York Jack.

Relaxing, she set her plate with half the pie uneaten beside his, then curled up on the love seat. "It's funny now, but my mother was not amused." She rested her chin in her palm as she looked at him. "Do you remember what your favorite Christmas present was?"

He grinned. "A bike. Top of the line. I'd been lusting after it for months. Cut a picture out of a catalogue and hung it in my room. What about you?"

"A doll house. With furniture." She sighed. "It was—"

"What?"

"You'll think it's silly."

"No, I won't," he vowed. "Give me a chance to screw up before you make me guilty."

"You've got a point," she agreed. "Okay. It was that tweener time—"

"Excuse me?"

"That time between when you believe in Santa Claus

and when you suspect the truth. I wanted to believe, but I'd heard the ugly rumors."

"Gossip does spread."

"I was like you and the bike, wanting that doll house so badly it was all I could think about. But I knew my parents couldn't afford much that year. My sister got braces. We needed a new car. Money was tight." And why was she spilling her guts? It wasn't what she and Jack did. But she'd started this. "Anyway, I decided to go see Santa with my younger brother, Dan."

"Dan was a believer?"

"Yeah. But he was intimidated by the beard and suit. I sat on Santa's lap to coax him into it. Mom wanted a picture."

"And you told Santa what you wanted?" he guessed.

"On the off chance that he was magic, I sort of whispered it in his ear." She shrugged and self-consciously toyed with a strand of hair. "Pretty silly, huh?"

"On the contrary—" He reached over and put his hand on hers.

The touch was warm, strong, sweet, and stopped her heart. It could have been the wine, the buzz, or sharing a suite with Jack, but the feel of his hand on hers was like a punch to the gut and it took two deep breaths to get everything moving again.

That had never happened before.

"Did you get it?"

"What?" she asked.

"The doll house?"

"Oh. No. Anyway—" she eased her hand from beneath his "—tell me about your bike."

"It was blue. And it didn't come from Santa," he teased.

"I knew you thought I was being silly. It's very sad when you have to grow up."

"It is, yes." He looked at her, an odd expression on his face. "If you still believed, what would you ask Santa for this year?"

"Florence," she said.

"Who?"

"Not who," she said, laughing. "Italy. I've always wanted to go there." She shrugged. "I'm not sure why. I've seen pictures, but I just have a feeling it's one of those places you have to see with your own eyes."

"Who knows? Maybe Santa will make it happen."

"Maybe."

When he smiled, the scary exciting feeling came back with a one/two punch. It was time to call it a night before she said something else she'd regret.

"I'm exhausted. Funny how sitting for hours on a plane can do that. I think the traveling has caught up with me."

Amusement disappeared from his eyes, replaced by what looked like regret. "I'm sorry, Maddie. I shouldn't have made you travel on Christmas. You had plans. With someone special?"

"Yes." Not quite a lie; her friends were special. "But it's okay. Actually, this turned out to be a nice holiday after all."

The brooding look was back, as if he were remembering the ghosts of Christmas past. Quite frankly she'd never seen a man more in need of a hug.

He stood and held out his hand. When she took it, he tugged her to her feet and into his arms. They were pressed together from chest to knee and it felt really good. If he hadn't looked so lonely, she might have been able to resist but she couldn't help herself. She put her arms around his neck and held him close.

"No matter what you think," she said, "your family was happy to see you."

"I'll take your word for that."

She looked up and his eyes flared with something hot as his gaze settled on her mouth. Was he going to kiss her?

She held her breath, suddenly wanting to feel his lips on hers more than she'd ever wanted anything—including that doll house. But she didn't dare toy with Jack.

He looked at her for a long moment, before lowering his head to settle his mouth on hers. One soft touch and her breathing went from zero to ragged in a heartbeat. He tightened his arms around her, fitting her body more closely to his, setting off sparks inside her. The needy moan trapped in her throat threatened to make her go up in flames. This was a place she'd never been before and didn't want to ever leave.

But this was Jack. Her boss.

She would never know how she managed to find the willpower and presence of mind to pull her mouth from his and disentangle herself from his arms. "It's time to turn in."

That breathless, needy voice couldn't really be hers, could it?

He ran his fingers through his hair. "Merry Christmas, Maddie."

"Same to you, Jack."

She hurried into her room and shut the door, heart pounding as if the devil were after her. The devil in the form of Jack Valentine? She'd certainly seen his dark side, a side she hadn't known he had. A side she'd have been better off never finding out he had because she was drawn to it. The dark side was what made her hug him. And that led to…

She leaned against the door and pressed her fingers to her still-tingling lips. If only it hadn't been a good kiss. But it was without a doubt the best kiss she'd ever had.

Now she hoped there wouldn't be the devil to pay.

CHAPTER THREE

ALL Maddie had wanted was a dreamless sleep and to wake up and have the old Jack back. She hadn't seen him yet, and she could say the same thing for sleep thanks to that kiss. After two years, why now? And what did it mean? Probably nothing. By sheer numbers, the women in his life proved that. Maddie wanted more. Jack teased her about the men she dated, but she'd never hear the end of it if he found out she was a virgin.

Her current state of purity had everything to do with crappy judgment in men. She'd fallen head over heels once, with a bad boy of course. She'd almost given him what she'd been saving for marriage but had found out just in time that he'd bet his buddies he could get her into bed. He'd lost the bet.

So now her taste in men leaned toward the ones who showed no obvious signs of bad boy-itis—no earrings, tattoos or long hair. The problem was she didn't want to sleep with any of them either. Up until last night, Jack hadn't tempted her but she couldn't let a nothing kiss change anything because he didn't want a permanent relationship.

She looked in the full-length mirror on the closet door to check her appearance, then gathered up her notes on the dresser beside Jack's gift. She'd forgotten to give it to him yesterday so she grabbed it, too. The door separating her room from the shared living space was in front of her and she tried to tell herself that this was no different from going to the office in Manhattan every day.

But herself didn't buy the lie because she knocked once. She never knocked when she entered her office. "Ready or not, here I come."

"I'm ready." Jack was sitting on the sofa where he'd been last night. His laptop was on the coffee table and in the dining room there was an array of food ranging from scrambled eggs and bacon to pastries, croissants and fruit.

"This is very nice of you, Jack," she said, looking at the spread.

"I'm a nice man."

Like his father. But he wouldn't want to hear that and he was looking like the old Jack. No need to bring out the dangerous side of him that thrilled the part of her susceptible to his type.

She set her notes and his gift down on the coffee table and helped herself to eggs, a croissant and fruit, as well as a cup of coffee. Moving back to the sitting area, she took the same space she'd occupied the night before and settled the plate in her lap and the coffee on the table.

She picked up the gift and held it out. "Here. This was in my suitcase. I didn't get a chance to give it to you last night."

He hesitated to take it. "Maddie, I— You shouldn't have."

"Why? We exchange gifts." She took a bite of croissant, then a forkful of eggs.

"That's just it. I—"

"You left my visa gift card in New York?"

"Well, yes," he admitted. "I don't have anything for you to open."

"It's all right. You brought me to London."

"Under protest."

"About that," she said.

"What?" His gaze narrowed suspiciously.

"I may have slightly exaggerated my plans with that someone special."

One dark eyebrow lifted questioningly. "And yet you were still annoyed."

"Besides the whining, how do you figure?"

He held up the plain-wrapped package. "No dangling candy canes. Or snowmen. No cute little santas or reindeer." He shook it gently as he studied the wrapping. "And the paper isn't shiny."

Yet another Jack Valentine revealed. He noticed and remembered how she wrapped Christmas packages. That was endearing and she'd never figured him for the endearing type. It was information that wouldn't help to snuff out her emerging and disturbing feelings. But he *had* apologized for spoiling her plans so the least she could do was be gracious.

"I was annoyed at your timing, Jack. And the fact that you think you can say jump and I'll ask how high. But I'm over it now. I sincerely mean that. Now open your present."

He ripped off the paper and nudged up the lid on the box, then lifted out the eight and a half by eleven butter-soft leather portfolio with his initials embossed in the bottom right corner. His gaze jumped to hers. "This is beautiful, Maddie."

"And it's personalized so you can't take it back," she pointed out. She finished her fruit.

"I wouldn't dream of it." He looked sheepish and darned if it wasn't charming. "This makes me feel even worse about not giving you a gift. I'll make it up to you."

"Not necessary. You promised me London."

"Thank you for this," he said, then set it on the table beside the laptop. "So, let's get to work. Old business first."

"Okay." She set her empty plate aside, then took a sip of lukewarm coffee before handing him the file on a software company they'd been nurturing. "They just signed a deal for shelf space in one of the country's largest office supply stores."

He scanned the notes, then looked through the spreadsheet. "Excellent. The internet sales are good, too."

"Yes. The company is performing better than we expected."

"I see that." He looked through every file. The results were all positive.

"Good work, Maddie." He put the folders on the table. "What else have you got?"

"We had twenty proposals submitted and I whittled them down to five for market evaluation. I have the top three for you to look at."

He took the first file she handed him and read carefully. "Mothers of Invention."

"I'd like to start a company to market the creations of problem-solving mothers."

His gaze captured her own but she couldn't read the expression in his eyes. "Mothers who *solve* problems?"

"You sound surprised by the concept."

He just shrugged in reply. The brooding look was now back and Maddie decided not to ask any further questions. If anything, it was silly to be disappointed that he didn't elaborate. Knowing more had made her hug him. And he'd kissed her. It would be better not to know more. She needed to concentrate on business and forget the dangerous man she'd glimpsed last night.

She cleared her throat. "As you'll see in my notes, the items range from videos that entertain toddlers, a gizmo that prevents said unentertained toddlers from unrolling a toilet-paper roll, to the obsessive compulsive mother who created a washable fabric cover for a grocery cart."

"These are problems?"

"For the average mom," she clarified.

"What about the ones who aren't average?" he said, still inspecting her report. But the muscle in his jaw contracted.

Did he mean above or below average? His frown made her wonder again what he was thinking. Something about his own mother? And again she reminded herself this was business, not personal. Up till now they'd concentrated heavily in the technological market and this was an area they hadn't tapped into yet. Diversification was good—in business. There was a lot of wisdom in not putting all your eggs into one basket. In love? She didn't want diversification and Jack was a master on the subject.

"Rather than investing in a single item," she said, "it occurred to me that one company with a line of unusual items to address the nagging chores and concerns of motherhood would be fresh and original."

"I agree," he said. "Pull it all together."

"Okay." She made notes to herself before handing over another file. "Here's one I thought would appeal to your inner technological geek."

"Cell phone central," he said, nodding as he looked it over.

"It adds even more functions to a device most people are already carrying. I've had it analyzed by our expert gadget guy and he says it looks promising."

Jack nodded and made notes in the new portfolio she'd given him for Christmas. "Whatever you think."

That was what she'd figured he'd say. Nine times out

of ten he approved her ideas, and it pleased her. She
handed over a file with the last of her recommendations.
This was another area where Valentine Ventures had yet
to venture. She'd met with the young entrepreneur and
his enthusiasm was contagious. She'd assured him that
Jack's go-ahead was in the bag.

"This is a restaurant proposal—"

"No." He frowned again.

Jack Valentine wasn't a serial frowner. Twice in one
meeting never happened. How could she not want to
know more if he kept doing that? First mothers, now restaurants had touched a nerve with him. Although she
couldn't see the connection, and it made her want to
know more.

"I'm aware that restaurants are uncertain, but look at
the location. It's midtown New York, yet the rent is
really reasonable and the concept young and fresh. With
backing it could be the next hot spot for Manhattan
singles looking to hook up."

He shook his head. "I don't want anything to do with
a restaurant."

"Why?"

That muscle in his jaw jerked again. "I don't know
anything about it."

His tone caught her attention. She'd only heard that
particular edge to his voice one other time—yesterday
when he'd confronted his father. "You don't know
anything about guards for the toilet-paper roll either.
That's my job. I believe in this one, Jack. Very strongly."

She sat up straighter. "And I'll go to the mat on it. I all but promised this guy."

"That's not like you." He took her measure for a long moment. "I guess you'll have to find a way to un-promise."

They'd worked together for two years. It was fun and she liked helping him decide what to spend his millions on. She'd gotten used to Jack taking her advice and she was surprised bordering on offended that he'd arbitrarily said no. But this was more than ego. Her gut was telling her his negative on this particular proposal was deeply personal.

"It's not like you to turn me down without a good reason. Care to enlighten me?"

"Not really. No."

"Then I don't understand," she said, unwilling to take his no without a challenge. "This project has the potential to be big, to franchise in Chicago and Los Angeles. It could catch on with serial daters not unlike yourself—"

That was uncalled for; she had no right to judge. Except she'd never seen him as he'd been at the restaurant last night and she couldn't help wondering if he had his reasons. But finding out Jack wasn't as shallow as she gave him credit for had its own risks.

"I'm sorry, Jack."

"Forget it. What we have here is a stalemate." One corner of his mouth curved up. "It's my experience that the best way to handle an impasse is with delicate diplomacy."

"Define delicate," she said.

"Let's table this proposal until we get back to New York."

"Okay. Fair enough."

"We're leaving this evening."

Her gaze snapped to his. "What about the business you had here in London?"

"We have a meeting later today," he said vaguely. "Then we're going home.

"You promised me a couple days here."

"I'm sorry. I have to get back."

"So apparently I should take lessons from you about un-promising."

"I have business waiting."

"Fine. I understand."

Who was she kidding? She didn't understand any-thing. This wasn't like the fearless, reckless Jack she knew. This wasn't the confident bad boy who oozed charm. This same man she'd relegated to the bad-boy section had come to London to meet his sister's new husband and now was just as anxious to leave. What was he running from?

He lifted his gaze to hers and there was confusion with a generous dose of wariness in his eyes. "As easy as that?"

"You're the boss." She gathered up her notes and started out of the room. "I'll be back in time for the meeting."

"Where are you going?"

She glanced over her shoulder because she didn't want to miss his reaction. "To lunch at Bella Lucia."

* * *

Jack sat in the town car with Maddie beside him. He'd much rather have lunched with her at the hotel. Last night's intimate meal had been something of a surprise. He always enjoyed bantering with her, but there'd been something different—intimate—something about sharing memories had pulled them closer. She'd hugged him, for God's sake, then he'd kissed her. In that moment he'd *wanted* her. But it was *Maddie*.

They were the same two people. They'd worked together over two years. In all that time, he could have put the moves on her, but he'd been careful not to cross that line and change the good working relationship they had. Five minutes with his father had brought out something in him that had moved her to hug him. He didn't want to risk a repeat of that kiss which was why he'd rather lunch with her anywhere but Bella Lucia.

"It probably isn't open today," he said.

"Why wouldn't it be?"

"Government buildings and small businesses are closed." At least one could hope. After being in New York all this time, he hadn't thought about the holiday. "It's Boxing Day."

Maddie stopped staring out the car window and looked over her shoulder at him. "As in fisticuffs? As in no hitting below the belt and go to your corner Boxing Day?"

"No. As in boxes of food, clothing and gifts that are distributed to the less fortunate."

"I thought that was done at Christmas," she said.

"It is. This is an extension of the holiday and keeps

the spirit of giving alive one more day. So, there's a good possibility the restaurant may not be open."

The car pulled up to the curb in front of Bella Lucia just as four people were walking out the door with leftover containers in their hands.

Maddie looked at him. "Either it's not closed. Or those people are some of the less fortunate who just got lucky."

Jack refused to comment as he escorted her inside the restaurant where they were seated at a cozy table for two.

He didn't want to be here, but he didn't want Maddie here by herself.

"This is nice." Maddie's voice interrupted the bad memories that were threatening and he looked up from the menu he'd been pretending to peruse.

"It's all right."

So far today he hadn't seen a single member of the family, which suited him just fine. There was always the chance of a Valentine sighting, but he hoped to avoid it.

The restaurant was busy, crowded. And he and Maddie were tucked away in a quiet corner. The white table linens were perfect, as were the flowers and red tapers in crystal holders. It had five-star ambience, although he hadn't tasted the food yet. If it passed muster, he'd be damn curious to know why the business was in financial trouble. Impatient, he tapped his fingers on the pristine tablecloth, then looked at his watch.

Just then a waiter appeared with a basket of linen-wrapped bread that he set down on the table. "Good afternoon, sir, madam. Are you ready to order?"

After the waiter had taken their orders and left, Maddie broke off a piece of Italian bread and steam escaped as she dropped it on her plate. "Something bothering you, Jack?"

"Of course not."

He didn't miss the expression on her face that said she was waiting for him to explain what had happened last night. He knew she was curious; he knew all of her expressions. Including the new one that had told him she'd wanted him to kiss her last night. That's why he was cutting short the trip. He'd paid his debt to his sister and soon he and Maddie would be on their way back to New York.

"Mmm," Maddie said, taking a bite of the bread. She closed her eyes and her curious expression changed to one of sheer pleasure.

The look was positively erotic and heat shot straight through him. An image flashed through his mind of him, Maddie, tangled legs and twisted sheets and he couldn't begin to explain why now. Why the scent of her was suddenly so…vivid. Sexy. That was just one more reason why he was impatient to get the hell out of here. What was supposed to be a quick trip to clear his conscience had turned complicated. Seeing Emma and Max had generated feelings that were complicated. Now feelings for Maddie had turned complicated.

Jack hated complicated.

And that didn't sweeten his temper. "Actually, there is something bothering me."

"Oh? Fire away." She wiped crumbs from her full lips with the linen napkin and waited expectantly.

"I take exception to the serial-dater crack," he said, trying to take his gaze from her mouth.

"Okay," she said slowly, her tone implying she was humoring him. "I believe we talked about this. Sometimes the filter between my brain and my mouth isn't as efficient as it should be. Another flaw I'm working on. It won't happen again."

"Yes, it will. Because you can't help yourself."

"I promise to try."

"If you say so."

He didn't really want her to hold back, but it was a mixed blessing. Mixed because she'd voiced her observations, but she didn't know his father as he did. Mixed because he'd seen the disappointment in her eyes when she'd asked why he treated women the way he did. For reasons he couldn't explain, he didn't like that Maddie was disappointed in him.

Her gaze moved away from his and followed a slim figure moving toward the exit. "Isn't that your sister?" Before he could respond, she called out, "Emma?"

Where was that filter when he really needed it? Jack thought as his sister turned, looked, then came toward them.

"Hello, you two." Emma smiled at Maddie, but the look she gave him was guarded.

"What are you doing here?" Maddie asked.

"I just came in to see some old friends. They wanted

to hear all about how the Meridian monarchy commissioned my services for Sebastian's coronation, which is how we met."

"Very romantic," Maddie said.

"Very," Jack echoed, wryly. These two had bonded over tiaras and he could only wonder what might be next. But his sister must be very good at what she did to have snagged such a high-profile assignment. Nagging guilt twisted. He was a powerful man who could make or break a career, yet he didn't know as much as a brother should about his own sister's career. The thought tweaked his temper.

"So where is the king?" he asked.

"He's waiting for me at our hotel."

"Don't let us keep you," he said.

"Jack." Maddie looked surprised before glaring at him. "Have a seat, Emma," she invited, indicating the chair to her left.

Emma sat. "I'm going to miss working with Max." She sighed.

Maddie looked puzzled. "Is Max a chef too?"

"He's manager at Bella Lucia Chelsea, along with my father. He—Max, that is—advised me to live my own life and not worry about things here, but I feel badly adding another headache for him to deal with, he's such a workaholic as it is."

Jack knew she was simply sharing information with Maddie the way women did. Like tiaras. But he felt the words scratch at something buried deep inside and he didn't want to go there. "His work ethic must please your father."

"He's your father, too," Emma shot back. "And Max takes the business very seriously."

"So the family owns this restaurant?" Maddie asked.

"Jack didn't tell you?" Emma glanced at him. "There's three in all, Bella Lucia Chelsea is the flagship property."

"I see." When she looked at him, Maddie's gaze held censure mixed with a dose of hurt. As if he'd kicked a kitten. He disliked the look.

"What's this about a time of need?" she asked.

Hesitating, Emma looked at Maddie, then him. Jack knew his sister was being discreet in front of non-family, but there was no one more trustworthy than Maddie. He could have blown it off, but he wanted to know what had caused the flourishing business he remembered to flounder.

"What's wrong, Emma?"

She nodded, recognizing he was giving her the okay to discuss it. "There's a serious cash-flow problem. To make a long story short, money was embezzled and the business is nearly bankrupt. Without an infusion of capital it won't survive."

"That definitely qualifies as a time of need," Maddie said. "What are you going to do?"

"The question is what Jack's going to do," Emma countered. "I didn't want to bring up anything unpleasant last night, but we have to talk about it."

"I'm going back to New York tonight," he said.

Emma's mouth pulled tight. "So you don't care that a business begun from our grandfather's love for his bride, and nurtured with the blood, sweat and tears of two more generations of Valentines, will cease to exist?"

"In a word? No."

Emma shook her head. "The Jack I remember wasn't so unfeeling and he was deeply committed to proving he had a future in this business."

"You could have said all this on the phone, Emma."

"I could, yes. But I wanted you to have to look me in the eye."

Anger churned through him. "So that crap about wanting me to meet your new husband was nothing more than manipulation?"

"Call it what you want."

"That's what it is. This family doesn't need me to bail them out. They've got the Queen of Meridia."

Emma's gaze turned steely. "There are so many things wrong with that statement, I don't even know where to begin. Suffice it to say that Sebastian is family by marriage, but you're family by blood. Who has more responsibility?"

"Are we talking about the same family that turned its back on me twelve years ago?"

"You left. I think there's some gray area in terms of who turned away from whom," she said tightly.

"It's black and white for me. I'm just supposed to forget about the past and hand over money."

"Not forget," Emma said softly. "Learn from it, then take the high ground. There's more at stake than money, Jack. It's about mending fences with family."

Jack had never thought of himself as vindictive, but it was a heady feeling to know that he held his father's fate in his hands. He could almost taste revenge and wondered how sweet it would be. The thing was, all he had to do was nothing.

Emma's glare intensified as the silence dragged on. "You're impossible, Jack, so much like Dad it's really quite amazing."

"And you're still trying to please him," he ground out, deliberately not looking at Maddie.

"For goodness' sake, Jack, don't be such an idiot."

The friction between him and his sister was almost a tangible thing and Jack had nearly forgotten Maddie was there until she applauded. They both stared at her.

"Do you know how many times I've wanted to say that to him?" Maddie wasn't the least bit intimidated by his glare.

Emma smiled but there was a stubborn glint in her eyes. "Have at him, Maddie, with my compliments."

Maddie met his gaze across the elegant table. "Your lordship, you're being a complete idiot."

"That said—" Emma stood "—I have to run. Sebastian and I will be here a while longer if you change your mind and want to talk." She looked at Maddie. "It's been a real pleasure meeting you. I hope I'll see you again soon."

"Count on it."

"Excellent."

Emma turned away, but Jack was staring at Maddie, wondering about her comment.

"I've never known you to say something you don't mean," he said.

"I don't."

"Well, how can you see my sister soon if we're leaving?"

"It's quite simple, Jack."

The stubborn expression on her face gave him a bad feeling there was going to be a problem and he'd been told that millionaires had them.

Maddie met his gaze. "You promised me time in London and I intend to have it. I'm not leaving."

CHAPTER FOUR

JACK hadn't said much after she'd made her announcement, but Maddie knew he'd been thinking about it. All through their afternoon meeting he'd been giving off tension like radiation from a leaky nuclear reactor. On the way back to the hotel, he kept glancing at her and frowning. They'd just returned to the suite and Maddie slipped out of her cashmere coat. After setting it on the back of the love seat, she faced Jack, who was studying her intently. The look was dark, dangerous and her heart responded with a quick, automatic stutter before settling into normal rhythm again.

"So, the meeting went well, don't you think? A technology company is right up your alley, but tech toys for kids is a new area for you. I bet you liked that new shift tricycle design."

"Back wheels that move closer together as it picks up speed is a pretty innovative way of incorporating training wheels." He folded his arms over his chest and leaned a hip against the arm of the love seat.

The gaze he settled on her sizzled with something unsafe and she couldn't help thinking about that kiss. The memory of all that heat warmed her deep inside, a frozen place she'd abandoned.

She moved around him and sat on the love seat. "I was amazed at the advancement of doll-house technology. And what I thought was an especially brilliant touch was hooking two houses together and one teenage girl calls the other."

"Things do happen when women talk."

Maddie had no doubt that was a not-so-subtle reference to her and his sister. And probably her own announcement that she was staying. Waiting for him to say what he thought about it was driving her crazy. "I was thinking that this technology company might integrate well with Mothers of Invention," she said.

"It seems like a good risk."

She met his gaze. "As opposed to a restaurant venture?"

His mouth pulled tight before he said, "Just tell me what's on your mind, Maddie."

The more important question was what was on his. "I'd like to talk about your family being in restaurants and how that relates to the fact that you refused to put capital into a promising restaurant venture because you don't know anything about the business."

"I don't. Not any more."

"Not since your family turned its back on you twelve years ago?" she asked.

He straightened away from the sofa and started pacing. "Do you remember everything I say?"

"Yes." For over two years she'd learned nothing about him and now seemed to soak up every tidbit of information like a super-absorbent paper towel. "So you were, what—" she did the quick math calculations "—eighteen when you got out of the restaurant business?"

He stopped in front of her and looked down. "I left home and went to New York."

"That's some teenage rebellion."

"My father and I don't get along."

"I noticed. But it must have been a heck of a fight to make you leave home." She watched him carefully, trying to read into his tight expression. "What happened?"

"It was so long ago I don't even remember."

The flash of anger in his eyes told her he was lying. But she decided not to push. She might not know facts and details about Jack's past, but it didn't take psychic ability to realize his past and family tensions were responsible for bringing out the dark side of him. But easygoing or enigmatic, she didn't think his stubborn streak would change. When he made up his mind about something she'd learned it was pointless to scale his position head-on. She'd find a roundabout way to get in.

"Okay." She nodded. "If you don't want to talk about that, can you at least tell me about your grandfather and the love story that started the family business?"

He shrugged. "William Valentine was sent to Naples

as part of a British campaign in World War II. He met Lucia Fornari and married her in nineteen forty-three."

When he stopped, she wanted to shake him. How like a man to leave out details. "And?"

"When they returned to Britain, he opened a restaurant in Chelsea in honor of his new wife and called it Bella Lucia."

"Beautiful Lucy," Maddie whispered. She met his gaze and waited expectantly. "And?"

"Eventually he opened two more locations. One in Knightsbridge, the other in Mayfair." At her exasperated look he added, "Apparently William managed the business until he died in June."

Maddie processed the information and was taken aback. "So you haven't seen your family in all this time?"

He shifted uncomfortably and rested his hands on his hips. "Before you start, keep in mind that I was busy surviving. Not having a dime to your name makes it tough to keep in touch."

He'd had nothing, had been only eighteen and in New York on his own. Oh, Jack, she thought. Why did you put yourself through that when you had a family who loves you? But all she said was, "What happened?"

"I survived." He shrugged. "Eventually I received a small inheritance from an uncle on my mother's side and I turned that into Valentine Ventures."

"Okay." Maddie could understand being busy. "But after your business was successful what excuse did you give yourself for not seeing Emma?"

"She was working on her own career as a chef for Bella Lucia."

"So what made you come back now?"

"Do I need a reason?"

"After twelve years? I think so," she said. "I can see it on your face. Looks a lot like guilt."

Jack shifted and in anyone else it would be called squirming. But the mighty Jack Valentine didn't squirm. "Okay. Our parents split up and I took off. Emma was left to deal with the whole mess. She asked and I owed her." He shrugged as if that explained everything. When she simply stared at him he frowned. "What?"

Maddie folded her arms over her chest. "So you don't get along with your father."

Jack looked at her as if she had two heads. "You heard what I said. He neglected his family and was unfaithful to my mother with his many women."

"Many women? And yet you think you're nothing like him." The thought of Jack's women touched a nerve in that frozen place inside her. She wanted to keep herself numb and feel nothing, because the way she'd responded to his kiss told her the potential for pain was there in a big way. "The only difference is that you never married one of *your* many women. Why is that?"

His gaze narrowed on her. "Because I like women."

"That's not an answer."

"Let's just say I have more to offer as a friend and lover than a husband." When she opened her mouth to ask more, he held up a hand. "Enough said."

Common sense and self-preservation were sending the same message. She couldn't afford to let the attraction he'd stirred up boil over. That would be bad because he was industriously avoiding marriage and she wouldn't settle for less. In college she'd been used as a bet. She'd tried again and learned the guy was using her to get to Jack for project capital. She wanted a man to love her and commit to her. She hadn't yet given herself to a man because she wanted it to really *mean* something.

She nodded. "Okay. But probably you should be heading to Heathrow."

"Because?"

"You're going back to New York today."

He looked down at her. "You're determined to stay?"

"Yes. I have vacation time coming and I'd like to see some of London."

"By yourself?"

"Yes." And she simply couldn't resist tweaking him. "Or maybe Max would consider showing me around."

"Any tour my older brother would give, you wouldn't want to take." His voice was nearly a growl as he bit out the words.

"You haven't seen him in a dozen years, Jack. How would you know this?"

"Because when I was here, Max was the older brother every guy wanted. He knew how to party and took me to the best of them. He introduced me to fast women and faster cars."

His reaction didn't disappoint her, but it did make her

curious. He'd never shown the slightest bit of emotion before when discussing her dates. What was different? Was it London? Or was it family tensions that brought out this side of Jack? This side was one she liked too much.

"It sounds like Max would know where to take me. Don't you worry. I'll be fine. You have a good flight back." She stood and started to go back to her room. "I'll check out of the hotel after I find a place to stay."

He stopped her with a hand on her arm. "Don't bother."

"No bother. I'm sure I can get a room—"

"I'll stay."

"Are you sure? Business is waiting."

"We'll work here."

"Good." She smiled sweetly. There was just one more shove she wanted to give him. "Then you'll have plenty of time to call your ultra cool older brother and he can get you up to speed on all the latest techniques with fast women."

"We caught up last night."

"Oh, please. I can't believe you wouldn't want to see him and reminisce about those women." She lifted an eyebrow.

"Not really."

"Here's the thing, Jack. Either you get in touch with Max. Or I will."

"Why are you being so stubborn about this?"

"Just because." Because she felt the conflict in him and sensed he didn't know what to do about it. "And I'm serious."

He stared at her for several moments, taking her measure. Then he nodded grimly. "All right. I'll call Max."

Jack was glad his brother had suggested they meet at a non-Valentine restaurant. Definitely neutral territory. Near Grosvenor Square, the restaurant Max had suggested was an elegant location oozing art-deco ambience—from its three-tiered light shades to the delicately etched glass panels in the windows.

With Maddie between them, he and Max were seated in a quiet corner. As he studied his brother across the table that damn empty feeling twisted inside him again when he wondered where all the years had gone and what he'd missed.

Max had ordered and approved a bottle of Alsace Pinot Blanc. He lifted his half-full wineglass. "To reunions."

"Reunions. Preferably not high school." A musical tinkle sounded when Maddie touched glasses with each of them. "So, Max, unless I miss my guess you were flirting with me the other night. And I have to ask—is there a Mrs Max?"

"No."

Jack wished there were, especially when he noticed his brother's gaze lower to the neckline of Maddie's black chiffon dress. If only it were up to her neck instead of low enough to reveal a tempting hint of cleavage. This was not a good place—torn between pleasure at seeing his brother again and a tightening knot in his gut that could be jealousy.

He wasn't sure why he felt the need to keep her away from Max, but thought it might have something to do with seeing a glimpse of that little girl who loved doll houses and believed in Santa. But he was well aware that Maddie was all grown up now. He'd given in to temptation and kissed her, a kiss that never should have happened.

Maddie had accused him of being like his father, and she hadn't meant it in a good way. The truth was, Robert Valentine had sired Max, too, and Jack didn't know his brother any more. He had no idea if his brother was a womanizer like their father. But he wouldn't let Maddie be hurt—not by Max or himself.

"I can't believe there's not a special woman in your life, Max." Jack wondered at his brother's frown.

"Believe it."

Maddie sipped her wine, then said, "Jack told me you taught him everything he knows about women."

"Did he now?" A gleam stole into Max's eyes. "Did he happen to mention the line he used to meet women?"

"No." Maddie's blue eyes were bright with curiosity. "What was it?"

Jack groaned. "We don't really need to talk about that."

"If I remember correctly," Max said, ignoring him, "it was, 'Haven't I seen you somewhere?' Followed two beats later by 'Oh, yes. You were in my dreams.'"

"No!" The look she settled on him was both appalled and amused. "Tell me he's making that up."

"I wish I could," Jack said ruefully, but the memory made him laugh. The times with his brother stood out bright and happy in a past that was littered with darkness and pain.

"Did it work?" she asked.

"Brilliantly," Max answered. "He made me so proud."

Maddie shook her head. "I'm deeply ashamed of my gender, to fall for a line like that."

"The line had nothing to do with it," Max said. "It was the legendary Valentine charisma."

"Oh, please," she protested. "Jack was eighteen. And teenage girls are notoriously vulnerable."

Jack didn't like to think about a vulnerable Maddie fending off men. No one knew better than he how single-minded a man could be when he wanted a woman. "Is that experience talking?" he asked her.

"I like to think I was smarter than the average teenage girl." Maddie smiled, but it didn't reach her eyes.

Jack leaned back and rested his arm along the top of the leather booth, very near her smooth-as-silk shoulder. He struggled to keep his mind on the conversation and off imagining what the bare flesh under her black chiffon was like. "Max tutored me, but there was some skill involved. I had to pull out all the stops to compete with him."

"I'm seven years older," Max scoffed. "It was no contest."

"For you." The words were out before Jack thought and he hoped no one picked up on it.

Maddie took her linen napkin and settled it in her lap. "So you felt competition?"

He should have known she'd zero in on the slip since

not much got by her. Still, it had been a long time ago. He had nothing to lose by admitting the truth. "Yes, I felt it."

Max frowned. "I wish I'd known. The truth is that the age difference made it an uneven playing field." He turned a grin on Maddie. "And that wasn't his only disadvantage. I got all the Valentine charm and I'd be delighted to give you an opportunity to judge that for yourself."

"Back off, Max." Jack was consumed by another unreasonable flash of jealousy mixed with a healthy portion of protectiveness. "Maddie's working. She doesn't have time for—"

"A personal life?" she interrupted. "Maybe it's time I made an exception."

"Not with Max," he snapped.

"Apparently you haven't outgrown your competitive streak." Max lifted one dark eyebrow. "Just so the rules of engagement are clear, are we rivals over women in general? Your assistant in particular? Or does the competition include anything else?"

"Not any more," Jack snapped, refusing to discuss Maddie.

"Meaning?" Max asked.

"Nothing. It's not important."

Maddie stared at him. "If it's not important, what's the harm in telling him?"

Jack knew the issue would have more importance than it deserved if he didn't answer. He met Max's gaze. "I always felt as if I was competing with you for Dad's attention and respect."

"If that's the case," Max said evenly, "fate has given you the perfect opportunity to get the upper hand."

Jack glared at his brother. "Here comes the pitch for money."

"Emma told you about the financial problems we're having," Max guessed.

"She did." Jack noted the steely look in his brother's eyes. "If I got involved, I'd expect controlling interest. Taking the business apart and selling it in pieces holds some appeal."

"How can you even consider that? You're a Valentine," Max snapped.

"By birth, yes." Jack tensed. "But in practice I haven't been one for a long time."

Max scowled. "It's more than business. It's a heritage."

"Not from my perspective."

"So you're turning your back." Max's mouth pulled tight. "I should have expected that."

"Meaning what?" Jack demanded.

"It's what you do best. You wanted Dad's respect but all you managed to get was his attention—and not in a good way. Screwing up a big event at the restaurant, then taking off to parts unknown, is irresponsible. Me, Emma, the rest of the family—" Max shook his head. "We didn't know for a long time if you were dead or alive. You wanted respect? Selfish, self-centered behavior isn't the way to get it."

Jack curled his hands into fists. "You have no idea what happened."

"Enlighten me."

For a moment, Jack recalled what his mother had done, what he himself had done to keep the truth from his father. He could still see the furious contempt on Robert Valentine's face when he'd said Jack wouldn't amount to anything. That he couldn't stand the sight of him. That he was his mother's son because no son of his could be so incompetent.

"Forget it." Jack felt the rage surge through him—red and righteous and consuming. He started to rise, then felt Maddie's hand on his.

"Jack, put yourself in your brother's place. How would you have felt if Emma had disappeared without a word? Or Max? Or someone else you cared about?"

He looked into her blue eyes, filled with concern and compassion. The softness and warmth of her fingers seared through him and touched that cold, empty place that never seemed to fill up. Her words, her cool logic slowly penetrated and cooled his anger.

Something unfamiliar pulled tight in his chest as he thought about her disappearing from his life. He relied on her in business. He respected and admired her. On top of that she was a beautiful woman. But this...attraction...wasn't about business. And if it wasn't about business, he wouldn't let it be anything. He was a risk-taker, but he wouldn't risk losing her.

Jack flexed his fingers, forcing himself to relax. "Okay, Max. You have a point. I left without a word."

"Did you just admit you were wrong?" she asked, one slender eyebrow lifting.

He met her gaze and grinned. "No."

Max laughed, lightening the mood. "Another Valentine characteristic, I'm afraid."

"A blessing and a curse," Maddie commented.

Max smiled at her, then met his gaze. "Seriously, Jack. The business was profitable once. The cash flow problem is simply the result of money being misappropriated. Dad is a brilliant businessman."

"I never said he wasn't."

"They say you're a lot like him."

"I've heard that, too." And he was sick and tired of hearing it.

"You need to go see him," Max continued. "Obviously you didn't get where you are by being stupid and it would be stupid to let emotion influence your good judgment. Bella Lucia is a good investment. Trust me."

Jack nodded. "I'll give it some thought."

He saw the look in Maddie's eyes and knew "it" was going to get more than thought.

CHAPTER FIVE

BACK in the suite and comfortable in velour pants and matching cardigan jacket, Maddie cradled a snifter of brandy in her hands. It was cold outside and she was grateful for the liquid fire that warmed her clear down inside. She'd been warmed in a different way when Jack had instructed the driver to take them on a tour of London at night, which was probably the best time to see any city. Darkness and strategically placed lights hid flaws and highlighted perfection. Kind of like Jack. He was the kind of man whose perfect looks turned heads, but she was finding out his life was anything but perfect.

She was sitting on the sofa with her feet tucked beneath her watching him pace back and forth in front of the windows. "So you'll think about seeing your father?"

"I said I would."

"Have you made up your mind already, or is there really something to think about?" she persisted.

"Always."

"Is that why you're pacing like a man in charge of quality control in carpet durability?"

He stopped mid-pace, then walked over and sat beside her. The sofa cushion dipped from his weight and his nearness seemed to suck all the oxygen out of the air. She wondered why she'd never noticed that at the office in New York, or if oxygen deprivation was a fact of life after kissing Jack. If so, that would make it difficult to continue doing the job she loved.

"Pacing helps me get rid of excess energy," he said.

She tapped her fingernail against the side of her glass and a crystal tinkling sounded. "Hmm."

"What does that mean?" he asked sharply.

She shrugged. "Just a noncommittal response to let you know I'm listening. It's supposed to encourage you to continue talking."

"I don't want to talk."

"How do you feel about listening, then?"

"Depends on what you have to say."

"For starters, that pickup line from Jack Valentine the early years really stinks."

The grin he flashed warmed her faster than the brandy. It was the same grin from the same man she'd known for over two years but, like oxygen deprivation, after kissing him the potency factor had increased exponentially.

He rubbed his eyebrow. "Do you want to talk about being a vulnerable teenage girl?"

"Not even for money."

"Okay, then, let's agree to put the past to rest."

"Not so fast. I do want to talk about Max's sugges-tion that you see your father."

"I had a hunch you would." Jack leaned back and settled his arm across the back of the sofa. The casual pose was at odds with the dark, restless, reckless look in his eyes.

"The thing is, Jack, you have to go."

"Actually, I don't."

Maddie figured this wasn't much different from taking sides when they had a difference of opinion about business. She decided to approach it the same way.

"Then tell me why you're so opposed to seeing your father after coming all this way."

"Besides the fact that we had a falling-out?"

"That was twelve years ago. Don't you think it's time to get past it?"

"What if I don't want to?"

"Why wouldn't you?" she asked.

"I already told you."

She tapped her lip. "You said he was unfaithful to your mother with many women and a workaholic who ignored his family," she said. "That's in addition to the falling-out for which I have no specific details." She sipped from her glass and felt the burn in her throat. "Care to tell me what happened?"

Jack abandoned the casual pose and stood. "Just drop it, Maddie."

"No." She swallowed the last of her brandy, then set the snifter on the coffee-table.

"I'm ordering you to lay off the subject of me and my father."

She stood and crossed her arms over her chest as their gazes locked. "No."

His mouth pulled tight as something flared in his eyes. "Disobeying a direct order is insubordination."

"If this was about work, I'd agree. But it's not."

"Exactly. It's not business. So why are you getting involved?" The edge in his voice was sharp enough to cut glass.

"You involved me when you insisted I come along on this trip."

And Maddie wished she'd been smart enough to say no then. Everything she'd thought she knew about Jack was changing. He was far more complicated than she'd given him credit for and that was frustrating and fascinating in equal parts. Frustration with Jack wasn't new, but she didn't want to be fascinated by him. He was too much like the guy who'd hurt and humiliated her.

She could overlook her attraction to Jack when she painted him with the same brush as the jerk who'd pretended to care for her. But because she'd come along on this trip, she was learning things about Jack. He had a past filled with secrets. He was pushing away the family reaching out to him. The more she learned, the more determined she was to help him reach back.

Jack stared at her. "I wanted you here because I had business and I rely on your advice."

She chose to ignore the "business" qualifier. Whether

he wanted to or not, he was going to listen to what she thought he should do with his family.

"Here's my advice," she said. "Invest in Bella Lucia. You'll get more than money in return."

"I don't want more than that."

"Money doesn't keep you warm at night," she blurted out, regretting her phrasing almost instantly. Jack was never at a loss for a woman to warm his bed, and that bothered her.

"That's true, but it buys lots of blankets."

"It's family," she protested. She thought about what he'd said to Max, but Jack had always been about building a business, not tearing it apart. "How can you even think about breaking up the restaurants and selling them off in pieces?"

"Because in this case the pieces are worth more than the whole."

"You can't look at this from a professional level. It's obviously personal. You might make more money, but it could cost your soul."

"My father cut out my soul twelve years ago. If I buy it back, it will be on my terms."

Jack's eyes glittered dangerously and Maddie shivered. "You need to talk to your father."

Two people alone in a room were like a blank computer screen. If you sat in front of it long enough, there was a good chance you'd put something on it. If Jack and his father were forced to face each other, they would talk about the past and iron out their differences.

"What if I don't want to?" Jack asked.

For just an instant she got a flash of the stubborn little boy he must have been. Charming and strong-willed, he had probably given his parents fits. He was still charming and strong-willed and giving her fits. One had to be strong to handle him. If one wanted to handle him, which Maddie most definitely did not.

"If you refuse to listen to my advice, I plan to involve myself incessantly until you do talk to him," she warned.

He shot her an obstinate glare, took her measure and apparently decided she wasn't bluffing because finally he nodded. "Have I ever told you how annoying I find you?"

"The feeling is mutual."

Maddie hoped a meeting would put things right because she found herself between a rock and a hard place. She didn't like loose ends and couldn't go until Jack made some attempt at peace with his family. But if she didn't return to New York soon, finding him annoying would be the least of her problems.

That kiss could become a big problem if they were here too much longer. She wasn't sure she could resist if he turned into a stubborn man who wanted her.

Jack looked at his father's large white stucco town house in South Kensington. Leaving the bad memories behind hadn't been easy and he wasn't looking forward to the reminders he knew were inside. But he'd seen Emma, Max and shown Maddie some of London. He'd get this face-to-face over with then take his stubborn assistant back to New York so they could both be home for New Year's Eve.

Maddie pressed the bell, then glanced at him. "This might be easier if you didn't look as if you're going to your own execution by firing squad."

Her wry expression and trademark tartness almost made Jack smile. He trusted her, in spite of the fact that she was the one who'd insisted he call his father.

The door opened and a slim, petite brunette stood there. Her green eyes assessed them seconds before a friendly smile brightened her face. "You're early. If you're Jack."

"I am, yes. And you are?"

"Melissa Fox. I guess we're sort of related since my mother married your father."

Maddie quickly stuck out her hand. "Maddie Ford. Jack and I work together."

"A pleasure." Melissa shook her hand. "Mum and Robert are expecting you. Please come in."

She stood back and they entered a wide foyer just off the living room. At that moment a buxom blonde in an emerald-green lounging outfit descended the stairs with a small white dog in her arms. The woman's hair fell just past her shoulders and was stick-straight.

She crossed the foyer and held out her hand. "I'm Beverley. And you must be Jack. You look a lot like your father."

No need to ask if that was good or bad. He already knew the answer. "Hello."

"Mother, this is Maddie," Melissa said.

"It's nice to meet you both." She held up the dog. "And this is Saffy."

Jack refused to shake the dog's paw. He had limits, ones even Maddie couldn't prevail over.

Melissa grabbed the coat slung over the banister. "I'm glad you're early so I had a chance to meet you."

"You won't be joining us for dinner, Melissa?" her mother asked, stroking the dog.

"Sorry. I've got plans." She shrugged. "I hope we'll see more of you, Jack," she said, opening the front door.

Not if he could help it.

Beverley frowned at the door her daughter had just closed, then turned a smile on them. "Why don't we have drinks in the living room?"

"I just want a few minutes with my father."

Her smile faltered but she recovered quickly. "Robert is probably in his game room."

Jack remembered it. "I know the way."

"We'll join you," Beverley said.

"Why don't we let the men talk?" Maddie brushed a hand over the dog's head. "I'd love for you to show me around, Beverley."

The other woman looked doubtful. "Are you sure?"

"Absolutely," Maddie confirmed.

Jack agreed because he didn't want Maddie to witness another unpleasant scene and didn't doubt that was what would happen. It was his father after all.

Jack stepped into the living room and it was like a walk down memory lane. The Bohemian rugs scattered

over the carpet had belonged to wife number one—
Georgina. Diana—wife number two—had been into
American kitchens. The O'Briens' Irish coat of arms
hung on the wall—a memento of wife number three:
Cathy. His mother.

Before the grinding resentment took hold, he noticed
the life-sized ceramic tiger, panther and giraffe. Since
he didn't remember them, they must reflect the ques-
tionable taste of wife number four. Dominating the
room was a glass coffee-table resting on four gold elephants and he couldn't quite suppress a shiver as he
moved through the room. No wonder his father was
happiest in the game room.

And no wonder Jack was alone. He'd grown up in a
house that was like a museum to bad relationships. It
didn't take a PhD in psychology to understand that he
always broke things off with a woman before anyone's
heart was seriously damaged. With Jack it was all about
wining and dining and fun. Then he was gone before he
could destroy a woman the way his father had his
mother. He wouldn't put a woman through that.

Winding his way through the house, Jack followed the
faint smell of chlorine to the indoor pool. The air was
humid and the windows fogged with moisture where they
met the cold outside. Robert was sitting in a lounge chair
by the pool—with a glass of whiskey beside him and a
cigar in his fingers. He was dressed in slacks and a pullover
sweater with the white collar of his dress shirt sticking up
at the neckline. When the older man saw him, he smiled.

"Hello, son." He stood. "You're early. Why don't we go into the living room and have drinks before dinner—?"

"No." Jack ignored his father's outstretched hand.

Robert looked momentarily surprised, but nodded. "All right. I can get you something from the bar." He indicated the game room, separated from the pool by French doors.

"Don't make this into a social occasion."

His father frowned. "What's more social than a son coming home?"

The anger knotting inside him was familiar and welcome. "Since when am I your son? As I recall, you wanted nothing to do with me because no son of yours could be so incompetent."

"That was a long time ago."

"I screwed up," Jack said bluntly. He was itching for a fight. He could feel it clawing through him.

"You were young. I said some harsh things. You said some harsh things." He shrugged.

"Yeah." Jack still remembered calling his father a son of a bitch and it hadn't made him feel any better.

"That wasn't the first time we had words. But there was something different that night. What was it, Jack?"

He'd covered for his mother because there had been no one else to protect her, but he was surprised his self-absorbed father had noticed anything out of the ordinary.

"The difference was that I realized nothing between us would ever change."

"Why did you disappear, Jack?"

"Why didn't anyone look for me?" he countered.

"I hired a private detective," Robert said.

That stunned him, but he hid the reaction. "Oh?"

"He located you and confirmed that you were in good health."

Jack found that hard to believe. "Right."

"The man reported back to me that he'd tracked you down where you were living in a despicable little room in New York. You were working as a busboy in a restaurant that I can't remember the name of. Quite a comedown, my boy."

Jack remembered the room—rats and bugs and yellowed walls. He'd cooked on a hot plate or survived on peanut-butter sandwiches. Or brought food from Gimme Sum—the Chinese restaurant where he'd worked. When he'd had no money, he'd learned where meals were served at a rescue mission. And every moment had been consumed with proving his father wrong, proving that he would be a success.

"I'm not your boy. And I was never contacted by a detective."

Robert tamped out his cigar in the ashtray on the wicker table beside his lounge chair. "His orders were simply to find out where you were. Clearly you wanted your space. You knew where the family was. If you needed help, you only had to ask."

Jack curled his hands into fists as anger swelled. Come crawling back? No way. "Is that your segue into asking for money to bail out your failing business?"

Something flashed in Robert's eyes. "If it were *mine*

it wouldn't be failing. My brother got us into this fix. John covered for his son the embezzler."

That confirmed what Max had said. "So it's all Uncle John's fault for helping his son?"

Robert's mouth pulled tight. "If your uncle had the same connection and commitment to the business that I do, he'd have found another way. My father started that restaurant for *my* mother, not his. John always resented that."

Ironic, Jack realized, that he and Max had different mothers yet had maintained a warm relationship in spite of their competition and desire to please their father.

Robert set his whiskey on the glass-topped table beside the ashtray. Cigar smoke still hovered over it. "Just think, Jack. If you invest the needed capital it will give us an edge. We can run the company. Father and son."

"Ease Uncle John out?" Jack asked, struggling to keep his voice bland. "What about Max? And Emma?"

"She's the Queen of Meridia now. I think her days as a chef are behind her. And Max wants what's best for the business."

That was probably true about Emma. But the Max Jack remembered wouldn't like the idea of squeezing out a family member who'd worked his whole life in the business.

"What do you say, Jack?"

"Would you really trust me with controlling interest?"

Robert's gaze narrowed. "Why shouldn't I?"

"Because I could take it apart and destroy you."

"Is that what you're planning?"

"What would you do in my place?" Jack demanded.

His father had the reputation of being a brilliant businessman and Jack had been told he was like him. His father was a cold-hearted bastard who would screw anyone—even family—for the sake of the business. Was Jack like that, too?

"Never mind. I don't want to know." Jack saw the surprise that flashed in his father's eyes, then turned away and left the room. He found Maddie where he'd left her in the foyer with Beverley.

"Jack?" Maddie's blue eyes filled with concern when she looked at his face.

"We're leaving," he said curtly.

"But—"

"Now." He was in no mood for more of her advice. Taking her arm, he led her to the door.

"Nice to meet you, Beverley," she said over her shoulder as he hustled her outside. "Give Robert my regards."

When they were back inside the town car, she turned on him. "That was rude."

"Quite."

"What happened with your father?"

"He said with my money and his brains we could rule the world as father and son."

"Don't be sarcastic," she said. "Tell me what really happened."

"I told him what I would do with controlling interest in the business."

"But, Jack, you don't mean—"

He held up a hand to stop her. "I'm not in the mood for you to defend him. Have I ever told you how obnoxious I find this glass-is-half-full attitude of yours? Why can't you just hate him like I do? Just on general principle?"

"That's just silly." She shook her head. "I don't even know him. And neither do you. Not any more."

She was right about that, Jack thought. And he didn't want to get to know Robert Valentine. He was afraid he'd find out more to hate about himself.

In spite of what he'd said, most of the time he liked Maddie's attitude. It balanced him. Balanced him right into this disastrous meeting with his father. He couldn't think of anyone besides Maddie who could have talked him into coming here. At least it had taken his mind off kissing her. Ever since that kiss, he'd felt his attraction growing stronger.

It was time to get back on familiar ground. Now that he'd seen his father, they could go home. They could resume their comfortable working relationship and life would be good again.

After instructing the driver to take them back to Durley House, Jack looked at Maddie. "I'm going to have the company plane ready in the morning to take us back to New York."

"But—"

He held up his hand. "I'm ready to go."

"Not so fast, your lordship. There's something I forgot to tell you."

He had a bad feeling he wasn't going to like it. "What?"

"Emma called earlier. She invited us to a New Year's Eve party at the Meridian Embassy in London. I accepted on your behalf."

"You'll just have to un-accept."

"But I really want to go. I've never been to an embassy, let alone a party there. You should know that I'm prepared to go by myself, even if it looks weird to not have a date. Before you answer, give it some thought."

He hated that he couldn't flat out say no because he recognized in her the essence of the little girl who'd once believed in magic. "All right. I'll think about it."

CHAPTER SIX

"Jack, this has been the best day." Maddie sighed and leaned back against the cushy leather of the town-car seat.

"So you're not sorry we played hooky from work and went sightseeing?"

Not sorry. Surprised. Apparently he'd gotten over being angry at her for talking him into seeing his father.

"Sorry? Oh, please. This is me."

"I know," he said, a *faux* serious expression on his face. "I was afraid you'd implode when I suggested breaking the rules and taking a day off."

"I'm organized, not inflexible."

Her heart stuttered and skipped when she glanced sideways at him. He looked so good. That dark hair, mussed as if he'd carelessly run his fingers through it, yet so perfect for him. Blue eyes that danced when he laughed, brooded when he didn't. In jeans and navy sweater, he looked every inch the wealthy bad boy. Staying in London had put them in contact 24/7 which was probably why she was beginning to overdose on his appeal. She'd enthusiastically embraced the opportunity to leave the seductive confines of their suite.

"Let's just say I appreciate your dedication," he said. "And I think it should be rewarded."

"Well, there's nothing like a trip to Buckingham Palace to let a girl know she's appreciated."

He rested one arm along the back of the leather seat. "You do realize you're not the first person to try and get a rise out of the guards?"

"You mean the guys in the funny hats and bright red jackets?"

"They're very well trained."

"They'd have to be," she scoffed. "In the states, any guy who went out in public dressed like that had better be able to defend himself. Or run like the wind."

Jack laughed. "Actually I meant they're trained not to show emotion, or give any indication what they're thinking."

Just like you, she thought. Maybe he had been a palace guard in a past life, because she rarely knew what he was thinking. He'd put her off about the embassy party and she wondered if this whirlwind day was her consolation prize because going solo to the ball would make her look like a loser.

"Well, it was a lot of fun, Jack. Thanks for taking me."

"You're welcome."

The car slowed and pulled smoothly to the curb. Maddie looked outside at the fashionable row of shops. "Why are we stopping here?"

"An errand."

The driver opened the door and the cold air made her shiver as Jack got out. He reached a hand back to her, then wrapped his fingers around hers and tugged her into Stella's, an upscale dress shop. The inside was brightly lit by crystal chandeliers. In the center of the room was a carpeted dais surrounded on three sides by paneled mirrors. Around the perimeter, fancy dresses in vibrant colors and different materials hung on racks.

A twenty-something brunette in a sweater and skirt with a flirty, flared hem smiled. "Mr Valentine?"

"Yes. And this is Maddie."

Maddie gave him a wry look even as a twinge of annoyance tightened inside her. Until now it had been such a perfect day.

"I'm Rhona. We spoke on the phone and I've picked out some lovely dresses for you to choose from. Size four, I believe you said?"

Dresses? Choose? Maddie pulled her hand from his. "You don't need me for this."

"Actually, I do," he said. "As you'll be the one wearing the dress to the party tomorrow night, the fit could be important. And since I'll be your escort, the public at large will have to look elsewhere for proof of your weirdness."

Her eyes widened as his words sank in. "You're going to the party?"

"With you. Yes."

Inside her, happiness swelled and spilled over.

Maddie threw herself into his arms and hugged him. "Thank you, Jack."

He pulled her tight and she thought she heard a soft sigh before he let her go and smiled down. "Now then, you need to try on dresses. This place comes highly recommended."

"Says who?"

"Says my sister Emma who confirmed it with my cousin Louise. So, off you go with Rhona."

Maddie followed the saleswoman down a corridor to a large mirrored dressing room containing several racks of dresses and two overstuffed chairs with a table in between.

Rhona sighed. "I must apologize in advance, Maddie. We normally schedule fittings in order to give clients our undivided attention. But Mr Valentine was quite insistent that you need something for tomorrow night and apparently so does half of London. It is New Year's Eve. We're a bit short-staffed today, but I'll—"

Maddie held up her hand. "Don't worry about it. I'll be fine."

"Then have fun," Rhona said, indicating the dresses. "I'll be back as quickly as I can."

When she closed the door, Maddie went through all the racks and organized the dresses into priorities: the ones she loved, the ones that might be flattering, possibilities, and not in this lifetime. There was no way to eliminate by price because none of the creations had tags and were probably all outrageously expensive. She would just have to cross that bridge when she fell in love with something.

After slipping out of her jeans and sweater, she welcomed the challenge and quickly eliminated dresses that were unflattering or the color was wrong for her hair and skin. She'd just pulled on a strapless black chiffon and practically twisted herself into a pretzel trying to zip it without success. Maybe she could track Rhona down. Barefoot and holding the bodice of the dress up, Maddie opened the door and scanned the corridor. She followed it the way she'd come, hoping to find the saleswoman in the main area of the shop.

Rhona was nowhere to be seen, but Jack was there and spotted her before she could dart back. "Hi," she said, feeling self-conscious. "I—I was just looking for Rhona to—"

"Need some help?"

"No—it's just a zipper. I think it's stuck."

"I think I can handle that."

She'd just bet he'd done up a girl's zipper a time or two. This would never have happened if she'd stayed in New York, but Maddie didn't think she had a choice. There was no delicate way to tell him he made her nervous in the way of a woman who was too attracted to a man who didn't think about her that way. That kiss on Christmas was simply that—a holiday sweet nothing.

"All right, Jack."

She came out into the room and turned her back to him. It seemed there were mirrors everywhere and she was mesmerized by the sight of his tanned hands dealing with the delicate back of her dress. His fingers skimmed the bare flesh of her lower back and raised tingles of awareness. It felt as if he were touching her everywhere. His gaze met hers in the mirror and it was intense, stunningly intense, and all the more exciting because of that. Her breath caught, then speeded up as she struggled to conceal it. Not easy when the bodice of the dress was cut daringly low and the swell of her breasts clearly visible.

She tried to think of something to break the tension, but couldn't since her brain had also taken the day off. Fortunately Rhona came bustling into the room.

"Maddie, there you are." She looked harried and blew out a breath as she critically studied the black dress. "I don't know about that one."

"I know," Jack said. His voice was deeper than usual and there was a raspy sort of quality to it.

"I agree, it certainly looks lovely on her," Rhona said, gazing at Maddie thoughtfully, "but I've got something in white that I think would suit better."

Jack's eyes grew dark and hot and sent desire dancing up and down Maddie's spine. "I don't know if my heart can handle better," he said hoarsely.

Rhona laughed. "Come with me, Maddie."

A short while later, Maddie was dressed and standing beside Jack as Rhona set the hanger of the dress on a hook. The dress, a strapless white silk creation, had fit perfectly. Now that she thought about it, how did Jack know her size? Because he'd had women in all shapes and sizes, of course. She refused to acknowledge the twinge. This was a lovely gesture. One she'd keep in perspective, though it threatened to expand. But this was Jack, after all.

Maddie took a deep breath, preparing herself for the exorbitant price of the dress she'd fallen in love with. "What's the damage, Rhona?"

"I'm taking care of it," Jack said.

The saleswoman smiled at him. "I assumed you would."

"No," Maddie said. "We're not— I mean I'm not his—" Wasn't this awkward? "I work for him."

That hadn't come out right. When heat crawled up her neck and flushed her cheeks, she didn't miss Jack's grin.

"I can't let you pay for this," Maddie protested.

Jack assumed battle stance as he folded his arms over his chest and stared her down. "Okay, we can do this the easy way or the hard way."

"What's the hard way?"

"That's where we argue for ten minutes and I pull rank and do whatever the hell I want."

"What's the easy way?" she asked.

"You graciously give in and let me buy this for you as a belated Christmas gift." One corner of his mouth curved up. "I prefer the easy way. I ruined your holiday and dragged you into all this stuff with my family. I've been an insensitive jerk. Let me make it up to you."

When Maddie glanced at Rhona, she knew the woman was half in love. Join the club, she thought. Who wouldn't fall for a man being so charmingly sweet, even after Maddie had assumed he'd stopped here to get something for one of his women. If she let him buy, did that make her one of his women? Not in this lifetime.

"All right, Jack. You win." She smiled. "And thank you."

December 31—Meridian Embassy

With her hand tucked into the bend of Jack's elbow, Maddie walked into the ballroom. The white silk she'd fallen for at first sight made her feel beautiful and she had to admit Rhona had been right about it. Jack had been rendered speechless the moment he'd seen her in it and she wasn't sure why that mattered so very much.

"I feel like Cinderella at the ball." Maddie looked up. "Pinch me, Jack, so I know I'm not dreaming."

He covered her cold hand with his own warm one. "You're not, Princess."

That was the closest Jack had ever come to an endearment and it meant a lot, especially when she knew he wasn't delirious with joy about being here. It wouldn't be wise to read too much into this, but he *had* come because she wanted to. And he'd surprised her with this dress. The thought produced a glow inside her.

"So, if I'm Cinderella, that would make you what? Prince Charming?"

"If the crown fits—"

His grin, sudden and spectacular, went straight to her head as surely as alcohol on an empty stomach. The tuxedo and the fact that he looked amazing in it certainly multiplied the intoxication factor.

"Thank you for bringing me tonight," she said.

"You're welcome."

She'd expected a teasing comeback and was both pleased and surprised when it didn't come, indicating he was on his best behavior. This was new.

"So," she said, "should we get in the receiving line?"

He didn't look happy. "Do we have to?"

"She's a queen now. I'm sure there are rules. Something you're not very good at."

And she must have a screw loose because the man who thumbed his nose at rules appealed to her in or out of a tuxedo. Jack was no prince, but she'd seen his charming and successfully resisted. It was the man he'd become in London who could really hurt her. But what was the harm in relaxing her guard just for one night? They were in public. What could happen?

"I'd like to say hello."

"The way you look tonight…" Blatant male approval was in his eyes as his gaze lowered, settling on a place in the vicinity of her cleavage "…how can I deny you anything?"

Maddie felt as if she were floating on air as he escorted her across the room and they took their places in the receiving line. Tables with candles, flowers and white linen cloths graced the perimeter of the room. Overhead chandeliers dripped golden light on a wood floor already polished to a high gleam and poinsettias adorned tables standing in front of walls painted pale blue and decorated with window-frame molding. A Christmas tree with splashes of red, golden bows and white lights dominated one corner of the reception area.

Their arms brushed as they continued to move forward and Maddie could almost see the sparks. She definitely felt the heat as Jack focused his attention on her and she wanted to be in line with him forever. But eventually they reached Emma and Sebastian, who both smiled with genuine pleasure.

"Maddie. Jack. I'm so glad you came," Emma said. She looked like a queen in a one-shoulder, full-skirted black chiffon gown.

"Nice of you to invite the peasants," Jack teased.

"Nice of the peasants to come," Sebastian said, but his eyes were warm with humor.

Emma looked at him. "Max tells me you agreed to look at his business plan for the restaurants."

"I did, yes. I'd discuss it with you, but, frankly, I'd rather get Maddie into a dark corner."

"Don't you just love his sense of humor?" Maddie said. But the idea of Jack and a dark corner held too much appeal.

"Who's joking?" He nodded at the other couple. "See you later."

He moved her off and slid his arm around her waist, drawing her closer against his side. A possessive gesture, she thought. With overtones of protectiveness. Jack didn't do protective. He also didn't do dark corners.

Not with her, but she thought she'd like it. A lot. His best behavior could deal a major blow to her willpower. While Maddie and Jack stood on the sidelines, musicians took their places in a corner of the room opposite the Christmas tree and began to play a waltz.

He bowed slightly. "May I have this dance, Princess?"

"You may, your Lordship."

On the outside, Maddie pulled off cool, calm and collected, which was a miracle because her heart was going a hundred miles an hour. Somehow she managed to move gracefully into his arms even as tingles skipped over her skin. But she thought her knees would give out when he settled her snugly against him.

With her fingers on his broad shoulder and the other hand swallowed in his, Maddie tried to relax and follow his lead. This was another first—she'd never danced with Jack. Was *that* a good way to start out the new year? Not if she wanted to keep from getting hurt.

She forced herself to meet his gaze and tried to think of something innocent to say. "So, have you made a new year's resolution?"

"I honestly haven't given it much thought." One corner of his mouth curved up. "Is there one you think I should make?"

She remembered what his sister had said on Christmas. "I just want you to be happy, Jack."

Surprise flickered in his eyes. "I expected something about not being a scoundrel."

"Your words, not mine." She liked the scoundrel

because that made him resistible. She didn't want to know he could be more than that.

He touched a finger to her chin and nudged it up. "What about you? Any resolutions?"

Other than to keep her heart in one piece? "Continued success," she said.

A waiter was just passing with a tray of champagne and Jack let her go in order to grab two. He handed her a crystal flute. "Here's to many years of success working together."

"I'll drink to that," she said, touching her glass to his.

Food was served buffet fashion from silver chafing dishes and platters. The music was alternately lively and lovely. Jack was solicitous and suave as he stayed by her side and pretended he didn't notice any of the beautiful women in the room. Although they both smiled at Louise who was busy networking with the prestigious guests. Maddie had been to some of the most exciting parties in New York, but couldn't remember having a more elegant, enjoyable evening. She had a bad feeling it had nothing to do with the environment and everything to do with her escort.

Not unlike Cinderella, before she knew it midnight approached. The wait staff circulated with trays of champagne until each person had a glass for the toast. When the time came, everyone in the room counted down to midnight.

"Five, four, three, two. One," Jack said. He looked down at her. "Happy New Year, Princess."

"Same to you, Jack."

They sipped from their glasses just before he lowered his mouth to hers. It should have been a quick, chaste, traditional kiss, but the moment their lips touched something sizzled between them that had nothing to do with static electricity and everything to do with a sensual connection. He met her gaze and his own was filled with dark intensity as he cupped her cheek in his palm and kissed her again.

Maddie rested her free hand on his chest and curled her fingers into his satin lapel. The softness of his lips was exquisite and her heart pounded as excitement poured through her. When he traced her lips with his tongue, she instinctively opened to him, then heard his quick intake of breath. He took what she offered and plundered her mouth thoroughly, leaving her breathless and clinging to him, wanting more yet unsure what more there was.

Her chest rose and fell rapidly though she couldn't seem to get enough air into her lungs. When he dragged his mouth from hers and stared down, he was breathing hard. Maddie swore she saw yearning mixed with the tension in his eyes. He downed the rest of the liquid in his glass in one gulp.

"We've done our duty," he whispered, not taking his eyes from hers. "Let's get out of here."

In the car, on the way back to the hotel, Jack savored the anticipation flowing through him like wine. Maddie

Ford turned him on and the realization blew him away. Her beauty was a given, but at work she'd always pulled primness around her like a force field.

But tonight... In the strapless dress that hugged her curves like a second skin, there'd been nothing prim about her. He was filled with the sight, sound and scent of her. If those were the only senses she'd engaged, he might have been able to hear his sensible side trying to warn him about rocking this particular boat. But the taste of her was still on his lips and that was his undoing.

When the door to their suite was closed and locked, Jack turned. "So, where were we?" he murmured. He reached out, and pulled her into his arms, then felt her tremble and heard a throaty little moan that turned the blood in his veins to fire. He knew women as well as he knew money and Maddie wanted him as much as he wanted her. "Now I remember," he said, just before settling his mouth on hers.

Another tremor of desire rippled through her and he felt wonder and a deep satisfaction at tapping into the unsuspected depths of her passion. Their bodies were molded together and her breasts pressed into his chest. Her hips tilted up against him in an almost instinctive movement that signaled her melting into him, a sure indication that he could make her his.

Jack continued to kiss her as he toyed with the little tab that would lower the zipper and part the back of her dress.

"Jack?"

He trailed kisses over her cheek as he slowly slid the closure down. "I like this much better than zipping it up."

"We better stop." Her voice was breathless.

He touched his tongue to a spot just beneath her ear and felt her tremble. Her body said everything he wanted to hear.

"That's enough, Jack."

It was the way she tensed, not the words, that finally penetrated his sensual haze. He straightened and met her gaze. "What?"

"We can't do this." With her palms on his chest, she exerted gentle pressure to push him away.

"Yes, we can."

"I'd be lying if I said I wasn't attracted to you." She swallowed.

"But?" He didn't like the sound of this.

"It can't happen."

"Why? We're consenting adults. I want you. You want me." With his hands at her waist, he brushed his thumbs up and down, just beneath her breasts.

"You want another conquest." The words were soft and laced with that damn primness.

"That's not fair, Maddie. Tell me I'm wrong. Tell me you didn't kiss me back."

Something shattered in her crystal-clear blue eyes and she looked ready to run. Then she said in a brittle voice, "I can't. And I'm sorry, but it was a mistake."

Jack shook his head to clear the rushing sound in his

ears. "It didn't feel like a mistake. It felt honest, and pretty damn good."

"I agree. But we have a special relationship and this would spoil it."

"How?"

"I can't believe I have to explain this to you."

"Believe it," he all but growled.

She sighed. "Women are wired differently. Unlike men, we don't treat sex like a competitive sport. We don't jump in and out of bed without our feelings being engaged."

"So you don't like me?" Good God, now he sounded as if he were in high school. This wasn't at all what he'd envisioned.

"Liking you isn't the issue. I'm saying that when you move on to the next woman, and everyone in this room knows you will—"

"How do we know?"

"It's what you do, Jack. As soon as a woman gets the least bit serious and wants more from you, you are so out of there."

As usual, she was right. But that didn't sweeten his temper or take away the ache of wanting her. "But this could be fun while it lasts."

Maddie's hands were shaking as she crossed her arms over her breasts, holding the front of her dress up. "And what happens when it's over? Think about it. There could be hurt feelings. That could lead to tension in the workplace. I like my job, Jack. And I know how it feels to be disposable. I don't need another lesson from you. Tonight's been fun. Let's just leave it at that."

Jack felt a lot of things, but fun wasn't one of them. However, the need to put his fist through a wall was on the top of his list.

"What makes you think men view sex as a competition? Who made you feel disposable?" It was a shot in the dark, but there was a bruised look in her eyes and he didn't like it.

"College." She looked down for a moment. "I was away from home for the first time and fell in love. I thought he loved me, too, and felt it was time to show him how much I cared for him. I'd made up my mind to take *the* step."

"What stopped you?"

"One of his fraternity buddies slipped up and I found out he'd made a bet that he could get me into bed. All I was to him was a wager. And the whole time we were together he was dating someone else so he was two-timing me on top of everything else." She held up her hand to stop him when he opened his mouth. "Before you say it, I did try again. A brief fling with another fidelity-challenged man. That's when I realized the type of man I'm attracted to is bad for me. He didn't just break my heart. He broke my trust."

Her mouth trembled and for just a moment she caught the corner of her bottom lip between her teeth. Emotions kaleidoscoped across her expressive face. Betrayal. Bewilderment. Disillusionment. But, most of all, a hurt that went soul deep. The primitive need for retribution slammed through Jack. He wanted to hurt the bastard who'd put that look in her eyes.

"The thing is, Jack, your track record with women proves that your relationships are all about quantity instead of quality. You send roses and think that makes it okay. But it's not okay for me."

She thought he was just like the bastard who'd put that look in her eyes? Good God. She thought so little of him? "Maddie, I—"

"What else is there to say? You made it clear that you don't want anything permanent. And I won't settle for anything less."

"You mean marriage?"

"It's not a dirty word."

"It's not a guarantee," he ground out.

"Maybe not. But I guarantee you're a bad risk. You'll never settle down with a woman you love, because you'll never love any woman. As they say, the fruit doesn't fall far from the tree."

"Meaning?"

"You're just like your father."

He'd lived his life trying to be different, struggling to overcome Robert Valentine's DNA. It seemed everyone made a point of telling him that he'd failed. He was sick and tired of hearing it, but most especially hearing it from her.

"Don't *ever* say that to me again, Maddie."

"I thought you always counted on me to tell you the truth."

"I count on you in business."

"Then we agree." Her mouth pulled tight. "Our relationship needs to stay strictly professional. That's settled, then. I'm tired, Jack. I'm going to bed."

When she turned and left the room, Jack saw her smooth, satin skin in the vee of her half-open dress. His hand ached to touch her, the rest of him ached to take her. All of the above proved he was a scoundrel.

He was no good for her; he'd only make her unhappy. As his father had done his mother. She was right to walk away from him.

But something told him he would regret letting her go for as long as he lived.

CHAPTER SEVEN

MADDIE knew Jack must never find out she'd exhausted her willpower in resisting him. They were a week into the new year, but she couldn't forget the way his kisses had made her hot all over. She'd never wanted the way Jack had made her want and the strain of not letting him know was taking a toll.

Jack had put on his charming face and never said a word about what had happened, but she could feel an invisible wall between them. Sometimes, when he didn't know she was watching, his eyes would grow dark and questioning, tortured, and she wondered what he was thinking.

He'd told her they would work in London until Max delivered his business plan. And every afternoon, Jack took her to see whatever touristy thing she wanted.

What she wanted was to get back the easy, working relationship she and Jack had once shared. What she wanted was to rewind to the moment when Jack had asked her to come with him on this trip. This time she would say no. Because he was different here.

And she was different, too. She'd kissed him back and wanted more.

Since that night she'd given it a lot of thought and realized he hadn't taken her to the embassy party to be nice. Although, buying her that gorgeous dress was definitely nice, but beside the point. The party was about reaching out to his sister—to family—and he probably didn't even realize. The differences in him had to be about his past, the part of his life he'd never discussed. Maybe if—

When the phone rang, Maddie set the untouched file she'd intended to review on the coffee-table and rose to answer it. "Hello?"

"Maddie, it's Emma."

She looked at the closed door to Jack's room. "Emma, I'll get Jack for you. He's on a conference call, but he'll—"

"Don't bother him. Since I've got you," Emma continued, "I just wanted to say that I hope you enjoyed your visit to the embassy and had a good time at the party. You and Jack disappeared so suddenly we never had a chance to say goodbye."

A flush crept into Maddie's cheeks. Etiquette had been the last thing on her mind after Jack's kiss. "It was— I've never had such a— I'll never forget it," she finally managed to say.

It was the truth. She wouldn't ever forget the breathtaking kiss. Talk about chemistry! Unfortunately it had changed everything with Jack, making

it an uphill battle to salvage their former working relationship.

"Is everything all right, Maddie? Did something
happen?" There was concern in Emma's voice.

Oh, yeah, she wanted to say. But then she'd have to
provide details. "Not really," she lied.

"It's about Jack, isn't it?" There was a slight pause
on the other end of the line before she said, "Let me
put a finer point on the question. Are you in love with
my brother?"

"Good heavens, no." Maddie sincerely hoped that
was the truth. "Emma, I know you're trying to be nice,
but Jack doesn't do commitment and that's what I want."

"Sorry. I'm prying. But," Emma added, "you should
know that our—Jack's and mine—formative years were
difficult. Be patient with him, Maddie. He could very
possibly be worth the effort."

"He's not going to change."

"I'm sorry you feel that way." There was a pause,
before Emma said, "Do me a favor, will you? Tell Jack
I talked to Mum. It took me a while, but she told me
what he did for her twelve years ago."

"And?"

"You'll know what to do. Goodbye, Maddie. It was
a pleasure meeting you."

Before Maddie could say anything, there was a click
on the other end of the line. Just then the bedroom door
opened and Jack was there. His hair was mussed, as if
he'd dragged his fingers through it. His sweater and

jeans were charmingly casual. And her heart stuttered and bumped at the sight of him.

"Who was on the phone?" he asked.

"Your sister. She didn't want me to disturb you. She and Sebastian are going home and called to say goodbye."

"I see." He frowned. "That sounds pretty innocuous. Why do you look like the stock market just crashed?"

Maddie repeated what his sister had said and had a clear view of Jack's face. The intense expression put every nerve in her body on alert. What made *him* look as if he'd lost everything, as if he had no one? As if he were empty? Her heart squeezed painfully tight and made her want to put right whatever it was. Damn. She wanted to hug him again.

Hugging would lead her into temptation, a place she couldn't afford to go. But she had an alternative destination in mind. Emma was right. She did know what to do.

"So, is it cold in Dublin this time of year?" Maddie asked.

"Why?"

Maddie stared at his stubborn expression for several moments. His past was catching up with him. His grievances with his family were surfacing and she couldn't shake the feeling that it was at the heart of his restlessness. Maybe if he resolved his conflict—whatever it was—the two of them could go back to the perfect boss/assistant relationship they'd enjoyed. The relationship where she kept him in line and he didn't cross it and kiss her. The one where she didn't wonder if she was falling for him.

"The weather in Dublin matters very much because I need to know how to dress when we're visiting your mother, Jack."

Jack wasn't sure how Maddie managed to have her way with him, but she damn sure didn't use sex. Yet here he was in Ireland. He'd called his mother and she was expecting them.

After flying to Dublin, he'd hired a car and driver and they were heading up the long road to Cathy's place, about fifteen minutes from the city. The house was just coming into view. A patchwork of white-fenced corrals fanned out behind the barn. On the gently rolling green hills, scattered horses lazily nibbled grass. The setting was bucolic and made him uneasy.

Cathy O'Brien Valentine's family home was a modest, two-story structure nestled in the center of a shallow valley. It was a tranquil and serene setting, not at all the way Jack remembered his mother. High-strung, unstable—emotionally needy would describe her best. If, as his father had said, he was his mother's son, what did that make him?

In his earliest recollections, he could recall her making it clear she needed him—to behave. Be quiet. Listen to her or his father would make him listen. And he had behaved, and worked harder than ever before, after listening to his father tell him hell would freeze over before he would get another chance to screw up Bella Lucia. Max was right. Fate had given him the ultimate means of revenge.

Maddie sat silently beside him in the car. He glanced at her and saw the rigid set of her shoulders, the tension in the delicate line of her jaw.

"You're not nervous about this meeting? Are you?" he asked.

"No." She waved her hand dismissively, then clasped her fingers in her lap. Tightly. "Are you nervous?"

"Of course not." But he wanted it over.

After the driver stopped in front of the house Jack got out of the car and held the door for Maddie. As he waited he heard voices and laughter. A couple, side by side with their arms around each other's waists, came around the house.

His mother's blonde hair was much as he remembered—long and wavy. She was still plump in her jeans and thick, baggy olive-green sweater. But her smile made her seem younger somehow as she looked up at the tall, black-haired, blue-eyed man who grinned down at her. What love looked like...

Jack's guard went up instantly.

Cathy saw him then and glanced up at her companion who gave her what looked like an encouraging nod, followed by a supportive squeeze. The two of them stopped on the cobblestone walkway in front of Jack.

Cathy studied his face. "The last time I saw you, you were a mere boy. You're all grown up, Jack."

"Hello, Mum."

"It's wonderful to see you. You look really good. So handsome." The Irish accent was thicker in her voice.

She lifted her hand, as if to reach out, then dropped it. When she looked at Maddie, a speculative gleam slipped into her light blue eyes. "Who's this, then? Your wife?"

Maddie's mouth thinned for a moment as she held out her hand. "Madison Ford. Maddie. I'm Jack's assistant."

Jack eyed the tall stranger. "Your turn."

"Aidan Foley." The deep tone was thickly accented and couldn't hide that he was Irish through and through. "Your mother and I are—"

"Good friends," she interrupted, putting her hand on his arm. "Please come in, Jack. Maddie. I'll make a pot of tea. We can catch up."

"We'd like that," Maddie said. "Right, Jack?" She nudged him in the ribs with her elbow.

"Yes. We'd like to know what you've been up to." His gaze narrowed on the other man.

They went in the house and Jack saw that it was comfortable and cozy, not flashy, not the way it had been when she'd been with his father. Photographs of him and Emma were scattered on the end tables and hung on the walls. A brightly colored afghan was slung over the back of the floral-covered sofa and reading glasses were carelessly resting over a facedown book on the coffee table.

In the kitchen, Aidan poked at the banked embers in the fireplace and coaxed it into a small blaze before adding several logs. Cathy invited them to sit at the pine table, then set about putting tea together. Her *good* friend helped in what clearly was an intimately familiar choreography, movements that showed they made tea together often.

They smiled at each other and their hands touched, bodies brushed. This was a long-term connection and the realization had unreasonable anger coursing through Jack.

The man in question watched carefully even as he stood back, folded his arms over his chest, and leaned against the counter. Cathy poured from the teapot, then set steaming mugs in front of him and Maddie.

"That'll chase away the chill," she said, smiling brightly, as if determined to ignore the awkwardness.

"Thank you." Maddie wrapped her hands around the cup.

"What's it been? Twelve years?" Jack rested his arms on the table and glanced at his mother's lover. Tension crackled in the air and Jack didn't give a damn. "So, how've you been, Mum?"

Aidan's deceptively casual manner disappeared when he moved and stood by Cathy, pulling her against him. "You're a guest, Jack. And Cathy's son. But when you speak to your mother you'll be puttin' some respect in your tone or I'll ask you to leave our home."

Jack stood and faced them both. "And I'd like to know who you are to my mother."

Aidan met his gaze without flinching. "I'm the man who loves her."

"So do I." Jack took a step forward.

Cathy put herself between them. "Aidan, why don't you take Maddie down to the stables and show her our horses while Jack and I talk?"

"I'm not leaving you with him in a mood—"

"It's all right." Cathy smiled. "This conversation is long overdue."

Aidan hesitated, then forced a smile for her. "If that's what you want, love."

Maddie stood and put a hand on his arm as she met his mother's gaze. "I think I'll stay with Jack."

Cathy took her measure, then finally nodded. "That's fine, then."

When his mother's lover was gone, Jack said, "Is he good to you?"

"Aidan?" Her smile was soft. "Very."

"Are you married?"

"He's proposed many times and I've turned down every one."

"Why?" Maddie asked softly.

Cathy gripped the top of the ladder-back chair. "The truth? I married your father because I was pregnant with you, Jack, and had to. I'm with Aidan because I love him and for no other reason."

"Maddie says marriage is a measure of commitment."

"I said," Maddie interjected, "that it's the right thing for me. I don't judge anyone else."

Cathy smiled. "She's a wise one. Aidan tells me he loves me and shows me as much in everything he does. It's all the commitment I need."

"He's younger," Jack pointed out, not sure why that was important.

"He is, yes. And he keeps me young. He respects me

and my opinions. He has expectations of me that I find myself wanting to meet."

The words touched a nerve and Jack wasn't sure why. "What about your drinking?"

"Jack—"

Maddie put her hand on his arm again and the touch steadied him. But the words were already out there. He refused to feel like a bastard even though the blunt question bleached the pretty pink from Cathy's cheeks.

Her chin lifted and she met his gaze squarely. "You're confident and self-assured, Jack. You always have been. Though you can't understand, I'll tell you because you asked. I did drink too much in those days—to help me cope. I was barely twenty-one and overwhelmed by the demands of being a mother. Living in the shadow of my husband's love for another woman."

"More than one," Jack murmured.

"Yes." Her mouth compressed slightly. "But there was only one he loved. Diana."

Jack knew about her, his father's second wife. He had half-sisters, Rachel and Rebecca, who'd been raised by their mother in the States.

"When she passed away," Cathy continued, "Robert told me that he would never love another woman the way he loved her. The day I drank too much and…did what I did…at Bella Lucia was the day I received the divorce papers. I was losing my husband and there was nothing I could do."

This wasn't the same defenseless woman who'd

begged him not to let Robert know what she'd done. This woman didn't need him to protect her. She had Aidan, although Jack suspected she didn't need him either.

"You've changed." Resentment tinged his tone.

"I have, yes, hopefully for the better." Her smile was sad and apologetic.

"You told Emma what happened," Maddie said gently.

"That Jack protected me?" Cathy nodded as she met his gaze, her own troubled. "I know you promised to keep my secret but I'll always hate myself for asking it of you. I'm your mother. I should have protected you."

"Yes."

"Jack, I don't know what happened," Maddie said, gentle censure in her voice. "And I don't need details. But your mother is trying to apologize."

"It's all right, Maddie." Cathy sighed. "He has every right to be angry. Jack paid too high a price."

Damn right, he thought. She'd lost a husband that night, but he'd lost his family. He'd lost everything.

The look in his mother's eyes pleaded for his understanding. "Your father's not a bad man, just flawed. He couldn't love me, and I don't think I was in love with him either. He didn't make me happy, anyway."

Now that she knows what happiness looks like, he thought, remembering Emma's words.

"What happened with your father and me had nothing to do with how he felt about you and Emma. He always adored his children. He especially thought the sun rose and set on you, Jack."

"He had a funny way of showing it," Jack bit out.

"I've forgiven him, son. It's time you did, too."

Maddie took his hand in both of hers and forced him to look at her. "Your mother is right, Jack. The past is eating away at your present and robbing you of a future. You need to let it go so you can move on. For your own sake."

Move on? Jack felt as if he'd been stranded on a desert island for the last twelve years and was just rescued, only to find out everyone he cared about had moved on without him. His mother was happy and at peace, yet he was angry and resentful. What kind of a son was he? What kind of man?

He looked into Maddie's trusting eyes. Beautiful Maddie. His sensible, stubborn Maddie. He was a selfish bastard for dragging her into this mess. The very least he could do was protect her from himself.

CHAPTER EIGHT

JACK had left her stranded!

Not stranded, exactly, Maddie admitted. Aidan had dropped her off at the hotel. But what was up with Jack? He had his faults, a great many, but leaving her without a word of explanation was not at all like him. And she was really uneasy.

She hurried inside and punched the up button to summon the elevator. When the doors didn't open instantly, she jabbed several more times. "Stupid lift," she muttered.

His mother had been upset and said he had every right to be angry and it was completely her fault. But when Maddie had pressed for details, Cathy had firmly told her she'd have to ask Jack.

"Darn right I'm going to ask him." She jabbed the call button again for the elevator that would take her to the suite. Assuming he hadn't left her stranded in Ireland as well as the outskirts of Dublin.

Fear knotted inside her. This wasn't just out of character for Jack, it was scary out of character. She'd seen the disapproval rippling through him for Aidan, but didn't understand what fueled it. His parents were divorced and had been for many years, which explained a lot about why Jack didn't do commitment. But anyone could see that Cathy looked happy and a ring on her finger wouldn't make a difference. So what was Jack's problem?

The elevator doors finally opened. "Thank God."

When it arrived on the top floor, Maddie hurried down the hall to the suite. She unlocked the door, then walked inside, flipping on the light. She stopped suddenly when the shadows disappeared and she saw Jack sitting on the love seat. Had he been alone in the dark all this time?

"That was low, Jack." She dropped her coat and purse on a chair. "Why did you take off like that?"

The layout was not unlike their suite in London, with the exception of a corner fireplace. Flames crackled there now. But Jack still hadn't acknowledged her.

"Jack?" Hands on hips, she stared at him.

In front of him on the coffee table was a bottle of Irish whiskey and a tumbler half full of the stuff. It looked untouched.

"You left me, Jack."

"I had to get out of there."

"No kidding. Why?"

He picked up the whiskey glass and turned it, studying the amber liquid as if it were the cure for a dreaded disease.

What had been unease blossomed into full-blown worry. "Jack, are you all right?"

"I don't think so."

The Jack she knew would never admit that. This more introspective man reached in and grabbed her by the heart. In seconds she was sitting beside him. She touched his forehead, testing for fever. Then she looked in his eyes and saw his wounded soul.

"What's wrong?"

"You were right about me, Maddie. I'm a despicable person."

"I never said that," she protested.

He turned his head and his gaze locked on hers with mesmerizing intensity. "You said I was like my father. It's the same thing."

She'd said that in a moment of anger, embarrassment, and self-preservation. She'd needed to push him away. This wasn't the time to point out that most likely his father had many positive qualities. "You're a good man."

"See, that's where you're wrong. My mother is happy and it ticked me off. If that isn't despicable, I need to look up the meaning of the word."

"What drove you away twelve years ago, Jack?"

He said nothing, although the look he turned on her was dark, desperate and dangerous, but she was determined.

She rested her hands in her lap. "Since we arrived on Christmas everyone has been dancing around it. Whatever 'it' is. You might as well tell me because I won't let up until you do."

He stared at her wordlessly, so long she was sure he would call her bluff. Then he set the glass of whiskey on the table without drinking.

"I badgered my father to give me some responsibility at Bella Lucia. There was a big event, very high profile. A wedding, some politician's daughter." He stared straight ahead and his voice was monotone, hinting that he was barely keeping his emotions in check. "The flu was going around and restaurant staff was getting sick. Dad was desperate, but he gave me a chance to prove myself."

He stopped and she could almost see the memories playing through his mind. His mouth pulled tight and Maddie wanted to say something, encourage, but she was afraid to interrupt and break the spell.

"I was focused and in control," he continued. "The food was prepared, liquor on hand, wedding cake waiting—"

She put her hand on his arm, encouragement and support. But she didn't say anything.

"The day of the event I got to the restaurant early in the morning. To go through my game plan, make sure things were absolutely ready. Leave nothing to chance. But chance has a way of biting you in the ass."

"What?" she asked softly.

"My mother was there. Passed out drunk. She'd lashed out at my father because of the divorce. It looked like the kitchen threw up. Food was destroyed. The cake—"

"Oh, Jack." She shook her head, pity for that eager,

ambitious young man coursing through her. "But I don't understand. Why was your father angry with you? When he saw your mother and the mess—"

"He never did. I managed to get her out and clean the place up. It looked like nothing happened. And I mean nothing."

Maddie thought about it and connected the dots. "He thought the food had never been prepared in the first place."

"It was pathetically easy for him to believe the worst," Jack confirmed bitterly.

"Why didn't you tell him the truth?"

"She was so fragile. The divorce was a fresh wound." His voice was distant, as if he could still see Cathy that night. "He'd have completely destroyed her if he'd found out. I couldn't let that happen."

"What did he say?" Maddie was afraid to hear his answer, but knew he had to tell it.

"That I was incompetent. A screw-up. No good to anyone. And I'd never amount to anything."

And ever since, he'd paid with his heart and soul trying to prove the man wrong. "Oh, Jack—"

"He told me to get out and I obliged."

And he'd never been back after lying to his father with the noblest of intentions. Her heart ached for Jack, for the years of loneliness and pain he'd suffered.

"How does protecting your mother make you despicable?" she asked softly, hoping he would see in himself what she did.

His gaze was overflowing with wry self-incrimina-tion. "She moved on. She's forgiven my father. She's content with her significant other. Don't get me wrong." He surged to his feet and moved to the window, staring out while the muscle in his cheek flexed. "No one knows or understands the toll that living with my father took on her better than I do. But I resent her happiness."

His mother had found love and companionship while the son who'd shielded her had gone on alone. Contrary to his father's prediction, he was incredibly successful. Admiration and something far deeper grew inside her. But she couldn't deal with that right now. This was about Jack and he needed her.

Maddie rose and walked over to him. "That only makes you human, Jack."

He didn't look at her. "The irony is that I was only trying to prove to my father that I was worth some-thing. And I failed."

"You're wrong, Jack. You protected your mother. You proved you're worth more than all of them put together."

He didn't acknowledge the comforting words. "So that's it. The whole ugly story. Aren't you sorry you asked?"

"No. Your mother should never have asked you to do what you did. But I'll say this again because it's very im-portant. You need to forgive your father. If you don't, the ugly past will continue to have the power to hurt you."

"I don't think I can do that."

She put her hand on his arm, needing to touch him,

hoping it would make him hear her—believe her. "You built a multimillion-dollar company with practically nothing. In my opinion you've amounted to something—and more. It's time you stopped working to prove your worth and work on allowing yourself to be happy."

He shrugged off her hand. "I'm tired of this." He sighed. "I'm tired, period. Goodnight, Maddie."

She stared at his broad back as he abruptly walked into the master bedroom. It was said that a woman could judge the character of a man by the way he treated his mother. She was stunned by the fact that Jack Valentine, the man she'd assumed was shallow as a cookie sheet, had depths and dimensions and more character than she'd ever suspected. He'd *protected* his mother, taken the blame for her angry, vindictive actions, and his reward was exile.

He wasn't simply a good-looking man she was attracted to. He was the man she was falling in love with. And he'd been left alone too much. She wouldn't do it to him, too.

Before Maddie could think it to death and talk herself out of it, she followed him. She crawled up on the bed to kneel beside him, then put her arms around him.

They sat like that for a long time before he reached up and pulled her into his lap and held her close. "I've never told anyone about that night, Maddie."

"I'm glad you told me." She rested her cheek on his shoulder.

Jack clawed his way out of sleep with the feeling that everything was wrong, starting with the fact that he wasn't alone in bed. A woman was lying half on top of him, her gently rounded breasts nuzzling his chest. He opened his eyes. A sliver of light from the living room caressed Maddie's tousled blonde hair and created a nimbus. One of her shapely jean-covered legs was carelessly thrown over his and her small hand rested on his chest. He let out a long breath, one part tension, three parts relief.

Maddie hadn't left him.

She felt sweet and so right just where she was. He tightened his arms around her and there was another breathy sigh of contentment, as if she connected with him on some elemental level and was at peace here with him.

Him. Jack Valentine, bachelor bastard.

They must have fallen asleep. He'd told her his secret, shared his dark resentment and it had been draining. God knew he'd felt as if someone had pulled the plug on his emotional power source. Yet, she hadn't turned away. In fact, she'd defended him and his actions. Maddie didn't hesitate to call him on the bad stuff he did, and there were times it annoyed the hell out of him. So annoying, in fact, that he'd wondered more than once why he'd brought her with him to London.

But her honesty made this moment all the sweeter because it made the good stuff she said about him almost believable. And he'd needed her, needed someone to talk to after seeing his mother.

He gently pressed his lips to the top of Maddie's

head and breathed in the intoxicating scent that was perfume and sensuous, seductive woman.

She stirred against him, pressing her body to his, mumbling as if trying to get closer. He could almost feel the heat of her feminine center caressing him. All the blood drained from his head and pooled south of his belt. He was hard. He was ready.

He wanted her.

Her fingers flexed on his chest and she started to pull away until he covered her hand with his own to hold it in place. His heart was beating, pounding, a roaring sound in his ears.

Maddie stretched again and he could feel her go from complete relaxation to groggy awareness. "Jack?"

"I'm here, Maddie."

She was silent for several moments, thinking. Figuring out where she was. Remembering what he'd told her. She nestled her cheek on his chest. "Are you all right?"

Since he'd expected her to pull away as soon as it sank in where she was, the question regarding his state of mind took him by surprise.

"I'm fine." Better than fine. Not alone.

He was New York's most eligible bachelor. A ladies' man who'd had a great many women and awakened with most of them, yet still felt isolated. It disturbed him that he didn't feel that way now.

"Thanks for—"

She touched a finger to his mouth, silencing him. "Don't say it. I'm glad I was here. I hope it helped."

In answer, he took her wrist in his hand and pressed her palm to his mouth. Her body went still, frozen in anticipation. One by one, he took her fingers into his mouth and sucked gently. When he touched the tip of his tongue to the tender, sensitive skin between her index and middle fingers, he heard her sharp intake of breath. Her chest rose and fell rapidly, a rhythm she'd probably picked up from him.

"Jack—" Her voice was a breathy whisper full of need and hunger. "Jack, please kiss me. I liked it so much when you did."

"But, I didn't think you—"

"I couldn't let on. Because— Well, it's not important now. Things are different. After—" She cupped his cheek in her hand. "Never mind. It doesn't matter. Just kiss me."

"Are you sure?" he asked, but his lips were already taking hers. He wasn't sure of anything except he couldn't seem to stop himself.

The touch was spontaneous combustion as she surged against him, sliding her fingers into his hair. It was like holding fire in his arms. The small sounds of pleasure she was making heated his blood. Desire exploded through him as he pressed her into the mattress, his body half covering hers.

When he traced her mouth with his tongue, she opened to him and he could no more stop himself from taking what she offered than he could hold back the sunrise. He plunged inside, stroking and staking his claim, invading her, imitating the act of making love. He teased the roof of her mouth and felt her squirm, rubbing her bare foot along his thigh.

As naturally as breathing, he moved his hand from her waist, up under her sweater, to settle on her abdomen.

"Oh, Jack," she said, her voice husky with passion.

"You feel good, Maddie."

The words were pathetically inadequate to describe the silky softness of her skin, the exquisite sensation of her bare flesh. He rubbed his thumb back and forth, just underneath her breast, just grazing the underside. Her pleasured whimper fueled his own excitement, feeding his need to feel her naked body against his own.

He slid his hand higher, resting his palm on her breast. Through the wisp of lace that was her bra, he felt her tighten at his touch and savored the wonder of her response to him. In the dim light, he could see her head thrown back in abandon, the slim column of her neck exposed, there for the taking.

A small smile played on her lips as she squirmed in his arms. "Oh, Jack. That feels so— Good."

"I love touching you."

Acting on pure instinct, he pulled far enough away to grasp the bottom of her sweater, then drag it up and off. She sat up, and with a smoky glance over her shoulder let him know to unhook her bra, which he could now see was black and sexy. His hands shook slightly as he released the fasteners and the sides parted, revealing her slender back.

"Love *me*, Jack."

"No need to rush." Except he'd never heard quite that level of need in his own voice before.

Dropping his head, he kissed her neck and relished the shiver that shook her. He touched his lips to her shoulder as he reached around and took her bare breasts in the palms of his hands. The fit was perfect, the feel delicate, lovely, intense. He rubbed his thumbs over her nipples and felt them pebble at his touch. She was amazingly receptive and so immediately quick to respond.

Her responsiveness drove him crazy. But she'd stopped him before, insisting that making love would destroy the good thing they had.

"Maddie?" He kissed her neck and smiled when she shivered. "I have to ask. Are you sure about this?"

"Very sure." Her voice was laced with desire. "It never felt right before. Doubts crept in. And I just couldn't do it."

"So there's not a doubt in your mind?" he persisted.

In answer, she tilted her head to the side, giving him the freedom to roam her neck at will. "None. I've waited for the right man and never thought you'd be the one. But this feels right. It feels perfect."

Waited? Right man? The one? His head pounded along with other body parts that urged him to ignore the words. But he couldn't. Doubts crept in, but surely he was wrong. "Have you ever done this before?"

She twisted her fingers together and hesitated a moment before answering. "No."

"You're a virgin?"

"That would be the correct term for someone who's never had sex." Her tone was sassy, but the underlying vulnerability leaked through.

She'd never been with a man.

Good God. What the hell was he doing?

Maddie was an innocent. He cared about her. God, he *was* despicable. He couldn't treat her the way he treated other women, experienced women looking for a one-night stand.

He dropped his hands as if he'd been burned and backed away. Sitting on the mattress, he rubbed both hands over his face as need and frustration warred inside him.

"Jack?" Maddie glanced over her shoulder. Her gaze was hidden in shadow but there was a tremor in her voice.

"You were right, Maddie. On New Year's Eve when you said this would spoil us."

"I was wrong. I want this. I want you." She turned to face him.

He looked at her, so proud, so beautiful, and didn't think he could stand much more. Maddie wanted love and marriage. She wanted someone who could make her happy. This was her gift to that man. It was special. *She* was special. If he took it from her, she'd hate him. And he didn't think he could stand it if Maddie hated him. If she didn't leave, he didn't think he could stop himself.

"It's been great, Maddie. Seeing London with you. The laughs. Spending money on you."

"But— The things you said— About kissing me."

"I meant everything." And more, he wanted to say.

"It's been fun. You're terrific. And I don't want you to misunderstand because sex complicates everything."

The bruised look was back in her eyes. "I don't understand. Is it because I've never done this before?"

"It's because there's nothing between us, Maddie." He rolled off the bed, as far from her as he could get. He didn't trust himself near enough to touch her.

She crossed her arms over her breasts, embarrassment chasing away her passion and pleasure. He hated himself for making her look like that, for making her ashamed. But he couldn't do this. Not to Maddie.

"You need to go," he ground out. He needed her to leave before he couldn't let her go at all.

She gasped, a small cry, then scrambled off the bed and gathered up her sweater, covering herself as she rushed from the room. Destroyed.

Way to go, ace, he thought. DNA had reared its ugly head, proving he was like his father after all.

Jack ran his fingers through his hair, then pressed his fists to his eyes, trying to block out everything, without success. He would never be able to block out the shock, surprise, and hurt he'd put on Maddie's face. But sending her away had been the right thing. And not just for her. He'd needed her today, and not in the physical sense.

Well, that was a lie, he thought. He'd needed her that way, too. Apparently he needed her in every way it was possible to need a woman. And he couldn't stand that he did. He didn't want to need anyone ever again. If there was any positive in dredging up the past, it was the reminder that he could only count on himself.

He'd sent Maddie away for her own good. She would thank him in the morning. And they could forget all about this.

CHAPTER NINE

MADDIE was numb when she closed her door and locked
it. As if she needed a lock to keep Jack out. She could
leave the door wide open, dance around naked and still
be safe from him. How ironic was this? she thought
bitterly. She'd waited to give herself to a man, and
finally decided to go for it. She'd wanted Jack to be the
one, and she hadn't given any thought to having a ring
on her finger first. She wanted him simply because she
loved him. And he'd turned her away.

Anger sneaked past the numbness and she stoked it to
hold back the pain she knew was coming. She threw her
black bra across the room, then yanked her sweater over
her head. Putting it back on in front of him would have
been too... Too humiliating. All she'd wanted was escape.

Maddie wished the earth would open and swallow
her. She'd been humiliated when the man she'd loved
had bet he could get her into bed. She'd been mortified
when the story had spread all over her college campus.
But that was nothing compared to this.

She was in love with a man who didn't want her. New York was teeming with models and actresses—some of the world's most beautiful women. They were the core of his dating pool.

"Dating my foot," she muttered. "A euphemism for sleeping with them." Her eyes burned, then filled with tears. "But he wouldn't sleep with me. Not even for money. He doesn't need it."

She didn't know from personal experience, but it was generally understood that men wanted sex pretty much all the time. And it was also a generally accepted fact that they took it wherever they could find it. Which made his rejection all the more pathetic. Jack didn't even have to look for sex. She'd been right there, in his arms, in his bed. Willing and ready. Boy, had she been ready. And he'd still turned her away.

Was she not thin enough? Not pretty enough? Too blonde? Not blonde enough? What was wrong with her? He'd kissed her and it had been good. Better than good.

She'd never been swept away, not even in college. Her choice to sleep with the jerk had been logical—a conscious decision to go to the next level. But when it had been over with him, she'd never felt this physical ache. And somehow she knew it was more than sex. It was the need to make love, to give herself only to Jack.

Unfortunately the thoughts pouring through her melted the numbness and she began to feel. The pain knotted in her stomach and spread everywhere, until finally lodging like a rock in her chest. It pressed against her heart.

His rejection had nothing to do with her looks. It was chemistry. She felt it; he didn't. She'd probably been nothing more than a diversion. At least he'd had the decency to push her away before she'd made an even bigger fool of herself. Maddie breathed deeply, dragging air into her lungs along with the scent of Jack still clinging to her sweater.

"He can't love me. He can't love anyone—" Her voice cracked.

That was when her heart shattered and she knew the shards would prick her forever.

The next morning Maddie still wanted to fall through a hole in the earth. Probably not the best thing to think before getting on a plane. But she couldn't help it. After a night spent crying into her pillow to muffle the sobs, her eyes were tired and puffy. She no doubt looked hideous. If he rejected her now it would be understandable. But they'd ridden to the airport in stony silence and that showed no signs of changing.

It was no consolation whatsoever to realize she'd been right. He was toxic for her. If he'd turned on the charm like any self-respecting bad boy she'd have seen the dismissal coming and shut him down before he could draw first blood. But he'd done something worse than be straightforward. He'd opened up to her emotionally and that had been her undoing.

So here they were. Maddie, queen of till-death-do-us-part, was in love with Jack, king of one-night stands, in the airport waiting area. He sat in a row of chairs across from her, working on his laptop as if the information would bring about world peace or a cure for cancer.

She stole looks at him, even though each and every glance produced a pain that went soul-deep. If only he looked tired and puffy, too. Or tortured. That would be good. But he just looked like… Like Jack. Handsome, intense, dark, hunky Jack. She wished…

Her cell phone rang and she saw him glance over. When their gazes met, his own was hooded before he looked down at his computer again.

Maddie flipped open the phone. "Hello."

"Hi, honey. It's Mom."

"Mom—" Maddie's throat closed as the familiar warmth seemed to reach out and wrap around her, chasing away the cold. How stupid would it be to lose control now, when she'd managed to hold it together from the hotel to the airport?

"Maddie? Are you there?" A worried note crept into Karen Ford's voice. "Is everything okay?"

Maddie got up and walked over to the window looking out at the jet and the maintenance crew in overalls checking it over.

"I'm fine, Mom." But her throat closed again.

It felt like that time she was ten or eleven and had somehow gotten separated from the rest of her family at a big amusement park. For a long time, she'd wandered around alone and scared, looking for them. But she'd held it together until she'd finally spotted her mother and burst into tears. As a grown woman she realized she'd let go because it had been safe. With Jack so close, nowhere felt safe.

"What's going on?" Karen asked.

"I'm at the airport. In Dublin," she added. "We're on our way back to London."

"What are you doing in Ireland?"

"Jack came to see his mother. It's close to London."

"I'm aware," her mother said wryly. "You never said anything about his family."

"Because I didn't know anything."

She wished she didn't now. Seeing them again had changed Jack. The past had unleashed the darker man, intensifying the reckless streak that had made him successful. She'd also seen the thoughtful, protective side. Now she felt she knew the whole person, the three-dimensional man with flaws and frailties, strength and a depth of nobility she'd never suspected.

He was the man she'd been waiting for all her life and could never have.

"Maddie?"

"Sorry, Mom. Why did you call? Is everything okay there? Dad?"

"Everyone's fine. I just hadn't heard from you."

That was when Maddie realized she'd never appreciated her parents and family enough. She'd always taken their love for granted. A few weeks without talking and the woman was on the phone. Jack had left home at eighteen because his mother had been a basket case and his father a bastard and no one had bothered to go after him.

"I've been kind of busy, Mom. How was the cruise?"

"Amazing. You should have come with us."

Maddie couldn't agree more. "I'm glad you had a good time. Can't wait to see the pictures."

"When are you coming home?"

She wished she'd never left; she wished she were there now. The tears were threatening again. She heard a cell ring behind her and glanced over her shoulder to see Jack take a call, then signal that it was time to board. "I'll be home soon. I've got to go, Mom. It's really good to hear your voice."

"Same here. Can't wait to hear all about your trip and how things are with you."

No more than Maddie could wait to unburden her heart. "I miss you so much. Bye, Mom. Love you."

"Love you, too, sweetie."

She followed Jack onto the plane then and took her seat. After landing in London, she unbuckled her seat belt and stood. Jack was retrieving a bag from the overhead bin and the sight of his broad back and flexing muscles brought a sharp, fresh wave of pain. She missed home; she missed her family. And she made up her mind about something else.

"Jack, I'm not going back to the hotel with you."

"Why not?" he asked, one eyebrow lifting.

"There's something I have to take care of."

He frowned. "Everything all right?"

No, she wanted to say. He'd completely mortified her. On top of that he'd hurt her terribly and she couldn't be around him.

"Everything's fine," she lied.

He stared at her for several moments, but his expression was unreadable. "All right. I'll see you later."

He acted as if nothing had changed between them and nothing could be further from the truth. For her everything was different.

Maddie took a deep breath, bracing herself to face Robert Valentine. Her first thought had been to stop by the house, then she'd realized Bella Lucia was probably where she'd be more likely to find the workaholic. She knocked once on the office door, and after hearing a muffled "Come in," she entered the room. Jack's father sat at his desk, staring at the computer monitor.

"Hello, Mr Valentine."

Surprise flashed across his handsome face. "Maddie. How nice to see you."

She cocked a thumb over her shoulder. "Max was downstairs and sent me up. Am I interrupting?" If she was, she really didn't care.

"Not at all, my dear. Do sit down." He swiveled his chair to face her and held out a hand, indicating the chair in front of the desk.

She settled her jacket and purse on the other chair, then sat and crossed one jean-clad leg over the other. "Thank you."

"I assume Jack is downstairs?" If he was worried about Jack's intentions, it didn't show.

"No." She shook her head. "I came here alone."

"What a nice surprise." He linked his fingers and rested his hands on his desk. "You're looking lovely as ever. London agrees with you, I think."

That was baloney. She was aware that she looked as if she'd been run over by a truck. Effortless charm. Like father, like son. Maybe like the son, there was more depth in the father than anyone knew, and she was about to find out. Although the part of her that was hurting just wanted to walk away. That part wanted to be bitter and angry.

But she couldn't forget that Jack had wanted her here with him when he faced his family. Since the night they'd arrived in this restaurant, she'd been a bridge between him and them. She'd cross it one more time because she loved Jack. When you loved someone, you wanted them to find happiness. He couldn't do that until he resolved his past. She'd do this one last thing for him.

"I think London is a lovely city, but I wouldn't say it agrees with me. Or Dublin, either." Especially not Dublin. She drew in a deep breath.

"What about Dublin?" Robert asked sharply.

"This isn't actually a social call."

His dark eyebrows drew together. "No?"

"Jack and I returned from Ireland just this morning. We saw his mother." She pressed her lips tightly together, then decided to just say it. "I came here, Mr

Valentine, because I just learned the truth of what happened twelve years ago. It's time you knew, too."

"What are you talking about?"

When Maddie finished the sorry tale, the older man looked taken aback. "You're saying that Jack deliberately let me think he was an irresponsible slacker?"

"Jack said it was quite easy for you to think the worst of him."

"I see." Robert leaned back in his chair. He stared at the papers on his desk, but couldn't hide the shock and surprise of this revelation. As he processed the information and the ramifications the frown on his face deepened. Then the intense expression took on traces of shrewdness. "Why do you care, Maddie?"

She shouldn't, but she couldn't help it. "Who said I care?"

"I was just asking why you're involving yourself in Jack's past."

Jack had asked her that once and she'd told him it was his fault for insisting she come with him for Christmas. Now she knew it was deeper than that, but she wasn't going there with his father.

"Jack is my boss."

"Forgive me, but this seems above and beyond an assistant's duties."

She wasn't going to let him make this about her. This was about Jack and his family. She'd seen for herself that Max cared about him. Emma did, too. Talking to her mother had reminded Maddie how lucky she was to have a loving family. Jack had one and he was throwing it away. Not if she could help it.

"Mr Valentine, you have no idea what my duties entail and I'm not about to discuss it with you. Unlike Jack, I don't really care what you think of me. I'm not after your respect."

"That's quite clear." His tone was clipped.

"I simply felt that it was past time you knew the truth." She stood and gathered up her things.

"No offense, my dear, but I barely know you. Why in the world should I believe this preposterous story?"

She shrugged. "No reason except that it's the truth. The problem is that if you do believe, you'd have to admit you were wrong. And it cost you a lot of years with Jack. It's past time for you to stop being an idiot and be a father to your son."

Maddie walked out of the office in a haze and that didn't clear until she passed the table where she and Jack had had lunch on Boxing Day. The spot where she'd called him an idiot, too.

The very place she'd begun to fall in love.

Another couple sat there now and smiled into each other's eyes. They didn't notice anything around them, not even her standing and staring.

Or the tears trickling down her cheeks.

Maddie pushed the button for the elevator to take her up to the Durley House suite. She'd just called Jack's father an idiot and she wasn't sorry. Although she didn't think that mattered one way or the other since the man had shown very little emotion to her tirade on Jack's behalf.

She'd thought she would feel some sense of relief, but she simply felt drained. On top of that, she dreaded facing Jack after throwing herself at him the night before. He'd saved her the humiliation of "going all the way" but that was little comfort. In her frame of reference, humiliation was a campus full of college guys pointing and laughing because your virginity was the stakes in a fraternity bet. What she felt now was so much deeper. It was as if all the light in her world had just gone dark. It was as if the carrot of happiness always dangling just out of reach had suddenly disappeared forever.

She'd offered herself to Jack without considering marriage or long term. It was a principle she'd held dear, then compromised without a second thought because it was the simple, logical next step when one was hopelessly in love. In a weird way, she would almost feel better if she'd slept with Jack before he'd told her there couldn't be anything between them. Then she could hate him with all the force of this awful pain. But he'd stolen that from her too.

What a lousy time he'd picked to be noble.

The elevator doors whispered open and she stepped inside. For the first time ever, she wished it would get stuck. Put off the inevitable.

But it smoothly and efficiently carried her to the correct floor as expected of an elevator in a five-star hotel. She walked to the suite and opened the door. Jack was sitting at the coffee table with his open laptop in front of him.

He looked up. "I'm glad you're back."

Had he missed her? Hope sprang eternal... "Oh?" she asked as casually as possible.

"I've got a proposal that I'd like you to take a look at." He glanced down at the screen. "I know you've made up your mind, but this is a new and promising laser communications technology. The guy's been working on it a number of years but can't make significant progress without financial backing. I'll print out—"

"Don't bother."

Without taking off her coat, she walked into her bedroom and pulled her suitcase from the closet and started packing.

"What are you doing, Maddie?" Jack stood in the doorway.

She only sensed it, because she couldn't look at him. She'd cry and he wasn't worth it. How many hundreds of years would have to pass before that lie became the truth?

"Come on, Jack. You're brighter than the average bear. Surely you can see I'm packing."

"Why?"

"Because I'm going home." She threw several sweaters and a pair of jeans into the jumble of clothes.

"Why?"

Because she missed home. She missed her family. He was no longer the boss who teased and harmlessly flirted with her. That relationship was gone and she'd never get it back. Because he was the man she loved.

As soon as she'd walked in and looked at him the stab of pain had told her she couldn't go back to New York and pretend nothing had happened. She couldn't go into the office day after day and see him and know he would never return her feelings. The prospect of that was too grim to contemplate.

Now she did look at him. She pulled herself together and looked into his bad-boy blue eyes and said, "I can't work for you any more."

"I see." The tone was cool, but his gaze turned hot and angry. He was looking at her the way he'd looked at his mother when she'd admitted asking the unthinkable of him had been wrong. "I suppose there's nothing I can say to change your mind?"

Not unless he could say he loved her and mean it. "No. Nothing."

He nodded, then turned away without another word. The second he disappeared, Maddie knew with a terrible certainty that her heart would never be whole again.

CHAPTER TEN

JACK prowled the suite at Durley House and brooded over the fact that not only *hadn't* Maddie thanked him in the morning, she'd quit.

Frustration twisted inside him, and not for the first time. A vision of the few moments she'd been in his bed slammed through him. She was so lovely in every way, inside and out. He'd wanted her then. The wanting was worse now, but nothing changed the fact that he didn't deserve her. Closing his eyes, he tried to shut out the hurt and humiliation on her face when she'd run from him. Yet he'd been stupid enough to believe she would thank him in the morning.

But she'd left.

Good riddance, he thought, deliberately fueling his anger. It was all he had.

There was a knock on the door and he was grateful for the welcome distraction, until he opened up and saw who it was.

"Dad."

"Jack." The old man smiled. "May I come in?"

"I don't think we have anything left to say." Jack really didn't need this. The way he'd treated Maddie, he'd lived up to his father's low expectations. Another round with the man who believed he could do nothing right wasn't high on his list.

But he heard Maddie's voice in his head saying his father loved him, preaching forgiveness. "Come in."

Robert walked past him and looked around the suite, nodding with satisfaction. "This is nice, Jack."

"I've been comfortable here." Maddie had liked it, he remembered. All their comforts had been taken care of with competent efficiency. The room service options—quiet delivery by private lift, or the personal touch of a proper, polite butler. He remembered her pleasure during Christmas dinner.

Speaking of polite, he should invite his father to sit, but he couldn't get the words out. "What do you want, Dad?"

Robert turned and met his gaze. "Maddie came to see me yesterday."

That stunned him, but it also explained where she'd been before coming back to give her notice. When he finally responded, all he could say was, "I can't imagine what she would have to say to you."

"Maddie decided it was time for me to know that I held you accountable for something you didn't do."

Jack had never told another soul. Not ever. He'd trusted Maddie as he'd never trusted another woman and shared his most personal emotions. And she took the information straight to the one man on earth who wasn't to know.

"Maddie had no right to tell you that," he ground out.

Robert slid his hands into the pockets of his slacks, lifting the bottom of the matching jacket. "Ease off, Jack. She was trying to help."

Help? Or punish him? "That was my mother's secret. She begged me to keep it from you."

His father looked thoughtful. "How is your mother?"

The question came from out of the blue and surprised Jack. "Not that you'd care, but she's fine. She and Aidan."

"Aidan? So she's not alone." Robert nodded thoughtfully. "I'm glad. Despite what you think, I do care. I was no good for her. Never made her happy."

In a vulnerable moment, Jack had told Maddie something private, something no one else knew. "Maddie's never betrayed me before."

"She didn't now, son. She's right. It's time I knew. Time to put it in the past where it belongs and forget."

Twelve years of being alone, cut off from the people he loved. Jack shook his head. "That's not possible."

"I probably deserve that."

"You were destroying my mother," Jack shot back.

Robert sighed. "I'd like to say you're wrong about that, but I can't. I was selfish. I hurt your mother."

"And I am my mother's son," he said bitterly.

"You're a good son, certainly not because of me. Obviously your mother is responsible for the man you turned out to be. But you're a grown man now, a gifted businessman in your own right. What would you do if an employee shirked an important responsibility and all the evidence you had said they didn't lift a finger to do the job?"

The dark memory of being caught between his parents twisted inside Jack. Having to choose his mother but desperately hoping his father would somehow know he'd tried his best. "It was as if you expected me to screw up."

"You gave me no facts to the contrary, never offered a word of explanation. What else was I to think?"

His father had a point, although under the same circumstances Jack knew he would make the same choice. "I had to protect her from you. And *that's* your fault."

"I wish I could say you're wrong." Robert nodded grimly. "Your mother did get her revenge. The failure was very public and cost the business a great deal of money. It was a long time before we regained the reputation that was lost." He met Jack's gaze. "But the worst was that it cost me you."

Jack struggled through years of bitterness and blame as he thought. "I did what I had to do."

Robert's smile was sad. "I would give anything to undo what happened and take back the things I said to you that night. If I'd been a better parent, if we'd been able to talk, you might have trusted me with the truth. I'd like the opportunity to try again, Jack. It's time I stopped acting like an idiot and started being a father."

Jack stared. "I've never heard you talk like that before."

"Your assistant is quite straightforward, isn't she?"

Maddie had said that to him? Good for her. "She says what's on her mind, yes."

"We could both take a lesson from her. And I hope it's not too late for us to work on our communication." Robert's gaze was direct and unwavering. "It's time I told you how proud I am of you, son."

Again Jack was stunned. The words tapped into a place that was dark and empty. Sarcasm, the verbal weapon he'd learned from Maddie, made him want to say, Who are you and what have you done with Robert Valentine? But all he managed was, "Oh?"

Robert nodded. "In my world, business came before family. I suppose because it came easily to me. But I'm a failure as a father. And relationships with women?" Robert shrugged. "I'm not good at those either."

"What tipped you off? Four marriages?" Jack said.

Robert's mouth twisted in a smile. Then he was serious. "It's cost me more than you'll ever know. Business is important. But love should come first."

"That's rich coming from you."

"Isn't it, though?" The man seemed unperturbed by the criticism. "If I'd put love first, I wouldn't have made so many mistakes. With Max. Emma." He met Jack's gaze directly. "With you especially."

Jack didn't know what to say. He'd held his anger and bitterness up as a shield for so long, he felt as if he had nowhere to hide. And Maddie was responsible for this mess.

"While this is all very interesting, Dad, none of it

excuses the fact that Maddie went to you with information that wasn't hers to share."

"Don't be angry with her, Jack." Something in his father's eyes pleaded for understanding. "She did what she thought was for your own good, my boy. You know she's in love with you."

"You wouldn't know love if it came up and shook your hand."

"She defended you like a mother cat protecting her young."

"She did?"

"Quite. I have a feeling you love her, too." His look was thoughtful, as if he was remembering. "I loved a woman once, and only when she died did I realize how much I'd lost. Then it was too late. Don't make the same mistake, son. Tell Maddie how you feel before it's too late."

It's already too late, Jack thought. The fading glow of anger highlighted the awful truth. He'd ruined his chance with her.

Then he glanced at his father and the look on the man's face was something he'd never seen before. Pride. Love. Respect. Sadness. All the things Maddie had told him she'd seen in his father just from that short first meeting.

Jack had run from a lousy situation, but he would never know what might have happened if he'd stayed. The loneliness of twelve years lashed him and he admitted something he'd been trying to ignore. He'd missed his family—all of them, including his father. If he didn't make it up now, there might never be another opportunity and he couldn't live with that regret.

Maddie had brought this about. Maddie was the voice in his head. She told him what she thought whether he wanted to hear it or not. She did what she thought was right and let the chips fall where they might. He respected her. He admired her. He needed her. He…

Damn his father for being right. He *was* in love with her.

"All right, Dad. I won't be angry with Maddie."

Robert nodded. "Good. Now then. Can we discuss you staying in London?"

"I'm not here permanently."

"In spite of your threat to dismantle it, I was rather hoping you'd come back to stay and run the business."

Jack shook his head. "No. About the business… From what I've been able to gather, you and Uncle John are pulling it apart. Each trying to take control."

"I'm the logical choice. It's John's son who put us in this financial bind."

"Does it really matter now? The most important thing is to save Bella Lucia." Until this moment, Jack hadn't even realized he felt that way. Once the words were out, the feeling gained momentum. "The thing is, neither one of you is getting any younger. You need to think about retiring."

"If we do and you're not staying, who would run the restaurants?"

"Max is the logical choice. He's been there every step of the way. I'm waiting to see the business plan he's preparing for me." Jack didn't want to say anything yet, but with the capital he planned to invest the cash crisis wouldn't be an issue.

"You're sure you won't stay on?"

Jack shook his head. "My life isn't here any more, Dad."

The man actually looked disappointed and the fact that Jack could recognize the emotion was an amazing thing in itself. All thanks to Maddie.

"Of course." Robert's smile was sad. "But you can't blame a father for hoping."

The man was reaching out. Could he do any less than meet him halfway? Jack stuck out his hand. "I promise it won't be another twelve years. From now on I won't be a stranger here in London."

Robert took the hand, then pulled him close for a bear hug. It wasn't easy; it wasn't familiar. But the ice was broken.

Robert pulled back. "I'll look forward to seeing you again soon, then."

"Me, too." Jack smiled at his father, something he'd never believed he could do.

His mother had urged him to forgive, but Jack knew he wasn't quite there. Forgetting would be a disservice to both himself and his father and the progress they'd made today, but he was ready to leave the door open. He was ready to start the process of building a relationship with his dad.

The miracle of it could be laid directly at Maddie's feet.

* * *

Jack paced back and forth in the reception area at the solicitor's office. A lawyer's per-hour fee was stiff enough and he hoped there wouldn't be a charge for wearing out the thick green carpet. The walls were oak paneled and an information desk sat in the center of the large space. Glancing at his watch, for the umpteenth time, he hoped Max and Louise were on time. He'd ordered the plane to be ready for the flight back to New York. To Maddie. She wouldn't return his phone calls, so he would show up on her doorstep and camp there until he could make her listen.

The door opened and Louise Valentine walked in. A tall, athletic blonde with gray/blue eyes, she looked exceedingly professional in her power suit with the black skirt and red jacket. She glanced around and smiled when she saw him. "Hello, Jack."

"Lou. Thanks for coming."

She looked nervous. "What's going on?"

"I'll tell you when Max gets here."

"He's coming?" Her look said she'd rather be exposed to influenza.

"I called him and he agreed to be here."

Just then Max opened the door. He smiled at Jack, but when he saw Louise his expression became hooded. "Lou."

"Max," she said, coolly.

"Good. We're all here." Jack looked at his watch.

Max slid his hands into the pockets of his pin-striped slacks. "What are you up to, Jack? Why are we here?"

"I've decided to save the business, not take it apart,"

he explained, staring at Max. His brother nodded his understanding. "The solicitor is going to draw up the investment papers."

"Excellent news." Max grinned until his gaze landed on Louise. "But I don't understand why she's here."

"It's nice to see you, too," she said.

"That's why." Jack glanced between the two of them. "This family is tearing itself apart and I'm not going to let it happen. You're each here as a representative from the warring factions."

Louise settled the strap of her small black leather purse more securely on her shoulder. "What are you? The family fairy godmother?"

Jack grinned. "In a manner of speaking."

"When did this transformation come about?" Max demanded.

"I'm still a work in progress," Jack admitted. "I guess you could say Emma started it and Maddie nursed it along." He met his brother's gaze. "I saw Dad and we got things out in the open."

"I see." Max's tone said he didn't see at all.

"I've missed family. I didn't realize how much until coming back. You guys don't appreciate it because it's right here in front of you." Not unlike him and Maddie. He hadn't fully recognized the value of what he shared with her until she'd left. But he would fix that. First things first. "I'm going to bail out the restaurants, but both sides of the family have to work together to be successful." He looked at Max. "I think your first order of business should be to hire Louise."

His two companions exchanged a stunned look.

"Why?" Max asked.

Jack slid his hands into the pockets of his slacks. "She's a gifted PR and marketing consultant who can give you exactly the right kind of support. I saw her in action at Emma's embassy party and it seemed she wasn't intimidated by the rich, famous, powerful or royalty."

"But—"

"Really, Max." Louise glared at him. "Don't look so shocked. I'm not without skills."

"Let me remind you in case you've forgotten," Max said. "We tried working together. It was a disaster."

"He fired me," Louise explained to Jack.

"Ah." Jack studied the two of them and had the feeling that there was more to it. If he'd learned anything, it was that there were two sides to every story. They would have to work it out.

"Then you should rehire her," Jack persisted. "This family needs to learn to work together."

"What made you decide to put the money into Bella Lucia?" Louise asked.

Max slid her a look, then shook his head as if she were a bit slow. "It was because of Maddie."

"The woman who came to the Christmas party with you?" When Max snorted, Louise glared at Max. "Don't even go there again. I don't want to hear about my outfit."

"You mean the fuzzy white crop top, short red suede

skirt with boots? Oh, and the flashing mistletoe belly-button jewelry? It never crossed my mind," Max said.

"That was Christmas," Louise huffed. "You should be able to express yourself with your family."

"My point exactly," Jack said. He remembered his spur-of-the-moment decision to bring Maddie with him to London. Now he realized that he'd known she would be his bridge back to his family.

"Maddie had a lot to do with my decision," he admitted. "And you, Max. The business plan is brilliant—"

"Oh, please," Louise interrupted. "Don't feed his already inflated ego."

Jack studied his cousin Louise and couldn't help comparing her to Maddie although the two looked nothing alike. His cousin's air of confident business-woman and her sassy comebacks reminded him of Maddie. And when Max and Lou exchanged a look filled with sparks, Jack wondered about their relation-ship. He had a feeling it would be electric, not unlike his with Maddie. God, he missed her.

"Where is Maddie?" Max asked, as if he could read thoughts. "I expected to see her here."

"No." Jack felt her absence as if half of himself were missing. "She left for New York a couple days ago."

"Did you two have a problem?" Max asked, studying him closely.

"We had a—" His brother knew him too well. There was no point in glossing over the truth. "The problem is I was a jerk."

Sympathy brimmed in her eyes as Louise patted his arm. "Recognizing the problem is halfway to solving it, Jack. A bit of groveling wouldn't hurt either."

"A lot you know," Max scoffed.

"I know more than you think," she shot back, before meeting Jack's gaze again. "Is your business here in London finished, then?"

Jack nodded. "As soon as we see the solicitor, I'm heading back to New York."

"Give Maddie my regards," Max said.

"I'll do that." Jack was no longer jealous of his brother. Maddie had been waiting to give herself to the man she loved and wouldn't have come to Jack's bed unless she'd had deep feelings for him. Hopefully he hadn't crushed that out of her because he was counting on the fact that she still cared to win her back.

"Good luck," Max added.

Jack would need every bit of luck and all the charm he could muster. He had to believe it wasn't too late for him and Maddie. He'd faced the fact that he was his father's son, but that didn't mean he couldn't learn from his mistakes.

Jack had found the woman he wanted, the only woman in the world who could make him happy. And she'd been right under his nose all the time.

No matter how long it took, no matter what he had to do, he would convince Maddie that they should be together.

CHAPTER ELEVEN

A PLEASANT late-afternoon breeze drifted over Maddie as she sat on a lounge chair in the garden at the Hotel Villa Medici, sipping a full-bodied Cabernet. They said red wine was good for a person's heart and she was putting the theory to the test. Granted, she'd only taken a couple of sips, but she didn't feel better. She missed Jack and her heart ached with it.

That wasn't all. She missed her job at Valentine Ventures and hated that hindsight was twenty/twenty. She should never have gone to London. That trip, plus a jaunt to Ireland with some hot kisses in Jack's bed all added up to her worst nightmare. She'd had to quit the job she loved because she dreaded seeing the boss she loved.

On the upside, the generous salary from that job had allowed her to fulfill her dream of coming to Florence. It had been her mother's suggestion after Maddie had unburdened herself. She'd thought it a good idea and quickly made reservations. She'd just barely checked into her lovely room when she realized she could fly around the world, but she couldn't run away from her problems.

"Hello, Maddie."

At the deep, familiar voice, the hairs on the back of her neck prickled and every nerve ending in her body tingled with awareness. She looked up and put a hand up to shield her eyes from the glare of the setting sun. Speaking of problems... Jack stood in front of her and she wasn't completely certain he wasn't a figment of her imagination.

"Jack?"

"Maddie, I need to talk to you."

He'd followed her to Italy? "How did you know where to find me?"

"I talked to your mother when you didn't return my calls." He indicated the padded wrought-iron lounge beside her. "Do you mind if I sit down?"

"And if I do?" He'd followed her to Italy? She couldn't seem to get past that.

"It's important."

"I'm pretty busy," she said coolly, although her heart was skipping like a stone over water.

"I can see," he said wryly. "Please."

Had reckless Jack Valentine ever said please? She couldn't remember. More important, she couldn't turn him down. He'd come all the way to Italy. She took a deep, cleansing breath and braced herself to get this over with. She told herself it was like jumping into frigid water—the first sensation was bitter cold and shocking, then you got used to it. Then you could deal with it.

She couldn't backspace her life and delete her mistake, but she would do her darnedest to forget that anything personal had happened between them.

"Okay."

He sat on the lounge, but didn't stretch out. There wasn't a lot of space for his long legs between the chaises and his knees were only inches from her thigh. Was it her imagination, or could she actually feel the warmth of his body?

Was it true what they said about absence making the heart grow fonder? Because he looked better than any man had a right to look. His dark hair was artfully mussed and sexy as sin. His expensively worn jeans molded to muscular thighs and the long sleeves of his shirt were rolled up to just below his elbows. The light blue color brought out the scoundrel in his eyes.

It would be so much easier to resist him if he'd had the decency to wear a suit and tie, except that wasn't Jack. And this was Italy.

"What do you want, Jack?"

He reached out, as if to touch her, then rested his forearms on his thighs. "It's good to see you, Maddie."

"It's only been a week." It felt so much longer.

"Ten days," he corrected.

It felt like a lifetime. "Okay."

"I understand you visited my father."

Her gaze snapped to his. "How did you know?"

"He came to see me."

Something darkened in his eyes and she got a bad

feeling. Her decision to see Robert Valentine had been impulsive; she hadn't really thought about the ramifications. Someone had needed to mediate. She'd just gone with her gut; it was what Jack would have done. But what if she'd made things worse? And she couldn't tell whether or not Jack was angry. Not that it mattered. What was he going to do? Fire her? She didn't work for him any more.

"How did it go?" she asked, studying him, waiting for the intensity that mention of his father always generated.

He linked his fingers together. "It was…interesting."

That wasn't very helpful. She didn't want to be curious, but she couldn't seem to help it where Jack was concerned. "Would you care to elaborate?"

"He explained things from his perspective. I told him why I did what I did. He apologized and said it was time he stopped acting like an idiot and started being a father."

Maddie stared at him. "He said that?"

"He did." The corners of Jack's wonderful mouth turned up and she knew he knew she'd said it. "Dad and I are going to work on our communication."

"I'm glad, Jack. What about your mother?"

"I called to apologize for my abrupt exit. We talked and things there are on the mend, too."

Inside, Maddie was doing the dance of joy. It was good that he'd patched up things with his family. At least that part of the trip had been successful.

"That's good. What about Bella Lucia?" Beautiful Lucy, the business begun because of a man's love for a woman. The thought made her heart ache because it wasn't likely a man would ever love her that much. The only man she wanted was Jack and he'd made it clear how he felt.

"Before leaving London I made arrangements to infuse the restaurants with the capital necessary to keep them running and get the family business healthy again. Max is going to take over."

"I'm so glad, Jack."

He nodded. "I thought you'd approve."

"I do. You did a good thing. I'm sure your family is very grateful. They must be—" She forgot herself and leaned forward to touch him, then froze.

"What?"

"Nothing." She dropped her hand. This was why she'd quit. She couldn't keep her feelings from showing. "Why did you come all the way to Florence?"

"I want to talk about us."

Just like that his intensity was back. All that focus directed at her was unexpectedly sexy and stole the air from her lungs.

She sat up straighter. "There is no 'us'. I'm sorry you came all this way to talk about nothing."

"I have plenty to say."

"I can't imagine what."

"First, I want you to come back to work for me."

She swung her legs to the side and sat up straight, facing him. After setting her wine on the glass-topped table beside her, she said, "I told you why I can't do that."

"Because of what I said—that there can't be anything more than business between us."

How like Jack to surprise her. He was taking responsibility. "Give the man a gold star."

"I was wrong about that. I love you, Maddie."

"I don't believe you." She stood up and backed away.

"Don't look so shocked."

She didn't know how else to look. "You can't be serious."

"Dead serious," he answered.

"I guess on a professional, career level I should be flattered. Apparently you'll go to any lengths to keep me from quitting."

"I love you," he said, an edge to his voice.

"Oh, please. I bet you say that to all the girls to get what you want. The problem is that you've made it clear to me what you *don't* want—in a word, marriage and family."

"That's two words," he pointed out far too rationally.

"Whatever. It's a deal breaker for me." She'd had enough of him taunting her with the only words that could rip her heart out. Her eyes burned and it took every ounce of her control to keep back the tears. She stood. "You'll never change, Jack."

He loved her? What had made him say that? She'd told him once that she was waiting for love. Correction: someone to love her. He was using her words against her. Why?

"You're wrong, Maddie." Before she could walk away, he stood and took her arm.

He was far stronger than she and the grip was impossible to break without struggling, if then. "You hurt me, Jack. You threw my feelings back in my face and, unlike your other disposable women, I didn't even get flowers. Why in the world would I set myself up for that again? And why would you bother? The world is full of women who would be happy to play your game." She looked at his fingers on her arm, then glared.

Jack dropped his hand. "I'm not playing anything."

"Neither am I," she said and walked away.

His voice drifted to her. "We're not through, Maddie. I'll be back."

"To Bella Lucia," Jack said and touched his glass to Max's.

"Cheers." Max grinned, then sipped his wine. "It's just like old times. Except for the fact that you just saved the Valentine family's skin."

The two of them were sitting at a table in a pub around the corner from the solicitor's office where Jack had just signed the paperwork giving him a controlling interest in the family company. It was like old times and Jack experienced a contentment he hadn't known in a long while—if ever.

"How does it feel?" Max asked.

"Pretty damn good." And Maddie was responsible. She made him want to be a better man and part of that was doing the right thing by his family. The legal business with his family couldn't wait, which was why he'd taken this quick trip to London. That and Maddie needed some time to think about what he'd said. He was the doer and she was the thinker, which was why they were so good together.

Jack raised his glass again. "To the new head of the Bella Lucia restaurants."

"Who would that be?" Max asked.

Jack grinned. "You."

"Me?" His brother looked surprised. "You're sure about that?"

"I am, yes. Unless you think you can't handle it?" Jack teased.

"Try and stop me," Max scoffed. "My only reservations are Dad and Uncle John. Neither will gracefully take a back seat after wrestling so bitterly for control of the company."

"It's time the two of them retired," Jack said. "And they *will* retire. You'll be in charge. I promise."

"Excellent news." Max grinned. "I've been impatient to move the company into the twenty-first century for some time now."

"What do you have in mind?"

"Expansion," Max said. "I've been meeting quietly with a friend of mine from Eton—Sheikh Surim."

"How very James Bond of you."

"Yes, well. He has quite a lucrative tourist resort in the desert kingdom of Qu'Arim. And he's receptive to the idea of opening a branch of Bella Lucia there."

"I see."

Max leaned forward eagerly. "Jack, have you any idea how big this is?"

"How big?"

"It could be the first step in making the Bella Lucia empire global."

"That's big." Jack grinned.

Max looked annoyed. "Oh, buzz off."

"No, seriously."

"Seriously," his brother said. "You and I are in this together and it does feel good."

Jack could feel his brother's excitement and shared it—to a point. "I'm in this, Max, but not quite together. It's your baby now, not mine."

"What are you saying?"

That he wouldn't make his father's mistakes. "I don't want an active role. I intend to have a life."

Max studied him intently. "Would a certain beautiful blonde named Maddie have anything to do with that decision?"

"Am I that easy to read?"

"Yes."

Jack needed Maddie to believe he was telling the truth about loving her. He hadn't been this nervous since—well, never. Not even when he'd wagered everything he had into a computer software deal. He had more than money at stake now. "I've mended fences with family and I need to do the same with her. It won't be easy. I just left her in Florence and she was pretty adamant about not giving me a chance."

"Persistence, old chap. It works in business and romance."

"I hope you're right." She'd looked angry and hurt. That was a formidable combination even for persistence. Although Jack didn't have any plans to give up. Ever.

"Would I steer you wrong? Didn't I teach you everything you know about women?" Max grinned.

"That's what I'm afraid of." Jack teased, but he was raw with nerves. If Maddie wouldn't have him…

"Just tell her what's in your heart and it will be fine. I wish you all the luck," Max said. "And every happiness."

Jack knew he'd need every bit of luck he could get. Then he heard Maddie's voice in his head. He didn't have to work to prove himself; he had to work to be happy. And he'd work the rest of his life to make her happy, too.

CHAPTER TWELVE

FOR as long as she could remember, Maddie had dreamed of seeing Florence, but her dreams had never included seeing the beautiful city alone. And she hadn't realized that part until Jack had shown up.

Pain sliced through her and it was all his fault. He was irritating and sweet in equal parts. Tracking her down. Pleading his case. Then disappearing. Actually, she'd walked away, but he'd said he would see her again and he hadn't shown up all day. What was he playing at? And no matter what he said, she couldn't afford to believe this wasn't a game to him. But a part of her couldn't reconcile the fact that he'd come all the way to Florence to see her. It was nothing more than a man who wasn't used to taking no for an answer.

Now she was in the back of a car riding through the city thanks to the hotel's outstanding customer service. Just because her room-service breakfast had been late, they'd insisted on making it up to her with dinner at one of Florence's most highly recommended restaurants.

As they drove she looked at the buildings—historic churches and their ornate architecture, statues, *palazzos* and *piazzas*. All dressed up in bright lights.

It was everything she'd expected it would be and yet she'd never experienced quite this depth of loneliness. She didn't know where Jack was, but she carried him with her in her memories. Everywhere she looked there were reminders of him. The hotel suite—the last time she'd stayed in one, he'd been with her. Having a car and driver at her disposal was a Jack Valentine touch. Though she'd tried to protect herself from the type of men who were bad for her, she'd fallen for the rogue who'd been right in front of her.

"At least I'll always have Florence," she said softly as the car turned into a lot.

She looked at the white building with the red-tiled roof. In the distance was a panoramic view with the lights of Florence and the Arno valley that took her breath away. The sight distracted her for several moments and she didn't immediately realize that the parking lot was deserted.

Maddie sat forward and said to the driver, "Paolo, are you sure this is the right place?"

"*Sì*," he said in his heavy accent. He was a very handsome, thirtyish Italian with all the charm Italian men were reputed to have. "The hotel concierge personally gave me the address. This is Carpe Diem."

"Seize the day," she whispered. The name reminded her of Jack.

Paolo opened her door. "Shall I go in with you, miss?"

"I'll be fine." She slid out. "But it doesn't look like the place is open so I'd appreciate it if you wouldn't leave."

"Never," he vowed. When he grinned, his teeth were very white against his olive skin. "I am happy to drive such a beautiful lady."

He was charming; she was immune. And this was weird. It was time to find out what was going on. She expected to find the restaurant door locked, but when Paolo pulled it swung open easily.

Inside, the dark-haired, dark-eyed hostess in the chocolate-brown jersey dress smiled. "Miss Ford, I am Sophia."

"How did you know who I am?"

"The hotel told us to expect you."

It was dinner time at one of the city's top restaurants, yet the place seemed empty. "Where is everyone?"

Sophia's smile was friendly. "Follow me."

Maddie followed through the dimly lit corridor and several arched doorways. Somewhere there was a fountain and the trickling sounds drifted to her. The scent of flowers permeated everything and the sheer romantic ambience tugged at her.

The hostess stopped beside a table set only for two, covered with silverware, white linen, and a crystal vase containing a single red rose.

Maddie turned to Sophia. "I don't understand—"

"Hello, Maddie."

It was déjà vu. She whirled around—heart pounding. "Jack!"

He smiled at the young Italian woman. "Thank you, Sophia. I'll take it from here."

When they were alone, Maddie glared at him. "What's going on? You disappear without a word, then scare the wits out of me."

"I didn't mean to." He picked up the open bottle of wine on the table and poured some into the two glasses. "Let's drink to Florence—the city, not a person."

With the words came memories of Christmas in London and a whole lot of pain. "No."

He slid his hands into the pockets of his dark slacks. The cream-colored knit sweater highlighted the contours of his wide chest. "All right. Then, tell me what tourist attractions you've seen so far."

She was about to tell him what he could do with his tourist attractions, then thought better of it. If she knew anything about Jack, it was that he was stubborn. She would get this over with quicker if she went along with his program.

"I've seen the Piazzale Michelangelo with its reproductions of the Medici chapel statues from San Lorenzo and Michelangelo's David. I toured the Ponte Vecchio, which is a wonderful bridge that was the only one spared by the retreating Germans at the end of World War II. I saw Santa Maria del Fiore and the Duomo, which dominates the skyline of the city." She stopped to take a breath.

"So you've been busy in my absence," he commented. "Is the city everything you hoped it would be?"

No. And that was all his fault. He'd taken the joy out of her world and she didn't know how to get it back. "It's a beautiful city."

His eyes darkened. "Not as beautiful as you."

"Let's cut to the chase, Jack. Why is the restaurant empty?"

"I reserved it for our private use. And before you ask, I did conspire with the hotel concierge to get you here. I wanted to surprise you."

Maddie knew he wasn't mean-spirited and couldn't imagine what reason he could possibly have for tricking her. "Why go to so much trouble?"

"Because I have a lot riding on what happens." His eyes locked on hers until heat settled low in her belly.

"Such as?" Her voice was a raspy whisper that had nothing to do with the echo in the deserted restaurant.

"My life and happiness." He took her hands in his warm ones and glanced at the rosebud. "This time I don't want to end with flowers. I want to signify the beginning of our relationship. It's a single red rose, a single everlasting love. Despite what you believe, I've never said this to any other woman. I love you, Maddie. I want to marry you."

She didn't get it. He'd had his chance and sent her away.

"Just so we're clear, I fell into your bed once, but it won't happen again."

He dropped her hands. "That's not what this is about."

"No? What other reason could you have for showing up here and using the L-word? And the M-word?"

"I suppose I deserve that." His mouth thinned for a moment. "And, yes, I want you in my bed. I want you now as much as I wanted you when we were in Ireland. But it's more than sex, Maddie. I want you in my life. I want to have children with you. I want us to grow old together. I want to make you happy."

She couldn't take it all in and seized on the first thing he'd said. "You wanted me then?"

"Innocent, Maddie." His smile was fleeting as he tucked her hair behind her ear. "You have no idea how hard it was for me to let you go that night."

"Then why did you?"

"Because you shocked the hell out of me when you dropped the bombshell that it was your first time. Because you are an awesome responsibility and a profound gift. Because I'm not good enough for you."

For so long he'd wandered around alone and scared and trying to prove to his father that he wasn't a loser. It was time he started believing in himself. "I don't ever want to hear that again, Jack. You're a good and decent man."

"Not good enough for you." He let out a breath. "If I were, I'd walk away right now. But I can't do it, Maddie. I *need* you."

"You're not talking about business."

"That's the last thing I want to talk about," he said angrily. "This is very personal. I realized after you quit and left me in London that I've been in love with you for a very long time."

Maddie had seen the many faces of Jack Valentine—

from charming to tormented—but never this desperation. She could hardly believe—was afraid to believe—this wasn't a wonderful dream. "If this is a line—"

Anger flashed through his eyes again, turning them dark blue. "I'm not being smooth or charming. I don't have the reserves left to pull that off. Besides, it wouldn't work because you'd see right through me."

That was true. And this angry Jack convinced her more surely of his sincerity than charm or smoothness could have done.

Jack shoved his fingers through his hair. "I'm simply stating the honest truth of my feelings. I love you and I want to marry you. And I won't settle for less. No compromises."

"You really do understand me."

"No man could ever love you the way I love you. No man could possibly love you more than I do and will for as long as I live. You're perfect for me." He cupped her face in his palms and his gaze captured and held her own. "You have every right to torture me, but I know you love me."

"You do?"

Tension rolled from him in waves. "You were ready to give yourself to me. I've never respected a woman more than I do you. You have expectations that I find myself wanting to meet. If I hadn't been so stupid and clumsy… I'd give up everything I own to take back the hurt I caused you, Maddie. Give me a chance. Let me make it up to you."

She smiled at him as happiness surged through her. "You already have, Jack. And you're right. I'm in love with you. I love you with all my heart."

He closed his eyes for a moment, and when he opened them his gaze was clear and carefree and… happy. "This is the most important venture of my life and I want to do it right." He went down on one knee as he dug in his pocket and pulled out a ring with the biggest diamond she'd ever seen. "Madison Ford, will you marry me?"

"Yes."

"Will you marry me here? In Florence? And let me take you on a honeymoon in the city you always wanted to see?"

"Yes," she whispered.

Maddie had never really believed it possible that she could have everything she ever wanted and still stay true to herself. But when Jack stood and took her in his arms, then settled his lips on hers, she knew her bad-boy boss would make all her dreams come true.

* * * * *

THE NANNY AND THE SHEIKH

BARBARA MCMAHON

Barbara McMahon was born and raised in the south USA, but settled in California after spending a year flying around the world for an international airline. After settling down to raise a family and work for a computer firm, she began writing when her children started school. Now, feeling fortunate in being able to realise a long-held dream of quitting her 'day job' and writing full time, she and her husband have moved to the Sierra Nevada mountains of California, where she finds her desire to write is stronger than ever. With the beauty of the mountains visible from her windows and the pace of life slower than the hectic San Francisco Bay Area where they previously resided, she finds more time than ever to think up stories and characters and share them with others through writing. Barbara loves to hear from readers. You can reach her at PO Box 977, Pioneer, CA 95666-0977, USA. Readers can also contact Barbara at her website: www.barbaramcmahon. com

To Pat McLaughlin – a long-distance friend dear to my heart! Thank goodness for phones!

CHAPTER ONE

MELISSA FOX threw down her pencil and rubbed her eyes. Arching her back, she tried to relieve the tense muscles. Translating business documents wasn't the most stimulating activity. She shook her head and took a deep breath, glancing around the crowded office of Bella Lucia. The headquarters for the famous London restaurant group was a busy place. The accountants had their own row, quieter than where she was working. The general manager had a private office. She was seated in an extra desk near the receptionist who fielded a gazillion phone calls a day.

But she shouldn't complain. She was between jobs and thankful to have something to do. Her mother had obtained this assignment for her through her new husband. It was only temporary, until mid-February when she flew to the United States to take on a new family.

A professional nanny, Melissa had recently quit her job as childcare resident at a large international hotel in Lake Geneva. She'd been there for five years, and had loved every minute. Or, almost every moment. Until the debacle with Paul. Now she planned to move on to working as nanny to a single family. The McDonalds were expecting their third child in February. When they had met her last fall in Switzerland, they'd talked her into accepting an assignment with them when the new baby arrived.

After the end of her relationship with Paul, she was ready to change. Their current nanny was planning to marry in late January and the timing would be perfect.

Melissa looked back at the lengthy document. She was almost finished. She would complete the translation today before heading home. At loose ends since quitting her job just before the holidays, she was grateful for the chance to earn some money until she took up her new position. But she missed the children and the activities and her friends in Switzerland. Still, the chance to spend some time with her mother was great.

Staring at the page, she let her mind wander a bit. When her mother had prevailed upon her new husband, Robert Valentine, to offer Melissa a temporary job, Robert's oldest son, Max, had come up with a spot in the office for the exclusive Bella Lucia restaurant business. She'd started by filing, then answering the phones. Once Max had discovered she was fluent in French, he had immediately started her on translating a stack of documents he had received from Sheikh Surim Al-Thani who lived in Qu'Arim, an Arabic country on the Persian Gulf. Apparently the two men had been corresponding for some time about the feasibility of opening a Bella Lucia restaurant in Qu'Arim. Sheikh Surim Al-Thani and Max wrote their letters in English. It was the construction firm giving preliminary bids who used French.

Working with the translations, Melissa was learning a great deal about the restaurant business and how Max envisioned the operations to run. She cross-referenced the documents with the correspondence between Max and the sheikh. It was a new venture for the family-owned and -operated restaurants—expanding in a foreign market. She knew Max had mentioned opening a few more worldwide if this one proved successful. Maybe he'd open one in Boston one day—near enough that she could visit while she was employed by the McDonald family.

She picked up her pencil to begin again. Only a few more paragraphs.

The sheikh was building a luxury resort right on the Gulf. The restaurant would be the jewel in the crown of the new holiday destination, he'd said. He had plans to make the entire seaside complex the premier place to visit in that part of the world.

Melissa wished wistfully that she could visit herself. It was rainy and cold in London. Switzerland, where she'd lived the last few years, was buried in snow. How wonderful would it be to visit a tropical resort in January, laze around on the beach, visit souks and find exotic goods at rock-bottom prices?

The McDonald family lived in Massachusetts, which was also under snow. Apparently she was destined to live in cold climes.

Max came up to her desk.

"Got a moment?" he asked.

"Sure, what's up?" She still wasn't used to the fact that Max Valentine was her new stepbrother, but already liked him very much. He was tall, dark and handsome, and, though her own feelings toward him were purely platonic, she could see why Max had more than one woman in the office preening every time he walked through.

"Come back into my office if you would."

Melissa followed him into his office and sat on one of the visitor chairs.

He leaned back in his own chair studying her for a moment, a small smile playing around his mouth. "I have to fly to Qu'Arim on Sunday as I'm meeting Surim for a final session before we sign all the paperwork. They've already started building and I'd like to see the setup. It's thanks to the translations you've done that we've got a lot of the preliminary work behind us, so…" he paused "…how would you like to come with me?"

"To Qu'Arim? I'd love to!" Melissa felt a surge of excitement. Look out beaches, she was on her way! How terrific of Max to offer her the chance. It would be more like a vacation than work. And a fabulous opportunity to see more of the world.

"It will only be for a week and I expect to return home by

the following weekend. We'll stay with Surim.' Max smiled. "His home is large enough for a battalion."

"You've been there?"

"Several times. He stays with me when he's in London. He and I went to Eton together. Until our final year."

"What happened then?" Melissa asked, intrigued to learn she might get to meet a real-live sheikh and that he had actually gone to school in her country.

"His father died and he had to return home and assume the role of leader before we graduated."

"At sixteen or seventeen? How could anyone that young rule a country?"

"He was young, but had lots of advisors," said Max. "By diligently working with the various factions in his country over the years, he's been able to pull the country into a united front. Which probably saved its economy at the same time."

"Isn't Qu'Arim known for oil and pearls?" she asked. She'd read up on the country when she'd first begun the translations.

Max nodded. "And fishing. Their pearl industry used to contribute a bigger percentage to their wealth, but money from oil far outweighs it now. Consequently that industry gets bigger press. But high-quality pearls from Qu'Arim are well known and sought after by experts." He stood up, signaling the end of the conversation. "Anyway, plan on staying a week. And you'll need to bring something dressy—if I know Surim, we'll attend at least one reception. We'll leave early Sunday."

Melissa nodded and rose, almost dancing with delight. "I appreciate this, Max."

"You'll be helping me out. If that contractor has anything new to report, I'll need to have an instant translator. You're up to speed on where we stand, so you'll be more valuable than anyone new to the project who could translate," Max said, grinning at her obvious excitement.

Melissa smiled back and left, and as she tidied her desk her bright smile refused to fade. She was going to Qu'Arim! She loved to travel and see new sights. She'd visited much of Europe on holidays, but she'd never been to the Middle East with its exotic and mysterious settings. And what better time of year to escape the rain and cold of London?

It was dark by the time she left the building a short time later. She stared at the dreary January weather, wondering if she could catch a cab or was destined to take the underground and then walk the few blocks to the house. She had her umbrella, but the thought of splashing through cold puddles for several blocks held no appeal. Instead, she dwelt on the thought that in only a few days she'd be in sunshine and warmth.

When Melissa reached home, she was disappointed to find it empty. She was anxious to share her good news. Her mother and Robert had probably gone to an afternoon matinee or something. Robert and her mum were in the honeymoon stage, having been married less than a year. While she was glad for her mum—it had been far too long since her own father had died—nevertheless sometimes she felt left out.

Had things gone differently with Paul, Melissa might have been the one in the early stages of marital bliss. She'd been so wrong in her judgement. It made her wary now of trusting her instincts. She refused to think about the man any longer. He was in her past, and she was a wiser woman because of it.

Shaking off gloomy thoughts, she went upstairs to her room. She had time to shower and change before dinner. She wondered if she could find further information about Qu'Arim on the Internet. It was one thing to read casually about the country for work, something else to learn all she could before actually visiting the place.

Sunday morning, Max and Melissa caught an early flight to Rome where they changed for a plane to Qu'Arim. It was late afternoon when they landed. Immediately after exiting the plane, Melissa raised her face to the sun. Its warmth felt fabulous! The air was perfumed with the sweet scent of plumeria mixed with that of airplane fuel. The soft breeze that wafted across her skin felt as silky as down. Soon they'd be away from the airport and she could really enjoy scents that vied for identification.

"I already love it here," she said as they walked across the tarmac.

"Did you say something?" Max asked, a bit distracted. He was in full business mode, having worked on the plane and now carrying his briefcase almost as if it were a part of him. Melissa wasn't surprised. The man loved his work. He ate, slept and breathed it as far as she could tell. Though, he wasn't a hermit. He did his fair share of dating, according to her mother.

"It's nice here," she said, trying to match his businesslike attitude. Inside, however, she felt sheer excitement. She hoped she had some free time to explore while she was here. And maybe spend an afternoon at the beach. The Persian Gulf had been a heavenly blue when they had circled preparing to land.

They were met inside the terminal by a tall man with dark hair and almost black eyes. He smiled at Max when he spotted him and Melissa felt her heart skip a beat. She'd thought Max handsome, but this guy was something else! His charcoal-gray suit and red power tie were very western. She glanced around; most of the men wore suits, few wore the more traditional Arab robes.

In fact, she could have been in any airport in Europe. For a moment she was disappointed. She wanted to see more of the exotic aspects of this country, not find it was just like any other capital she'd seen.

Melissa spotted two men standing nearby, scanning the crowd. The local equivalent of guards, she guessed from the way they behaved.

Max turned and made the introductions. Sheikh Surim Al-Thani inclined his head slightly, reaching for Melissa's hand

and bringing it to his lips. The warmth of his lips startled her, but it was the compelling gaze in those dark eyes that mesmerized. She felt her heart race, heat flooded through her and she wondered if he came with a warning label—dangerous to a woman's equilibrium.

"Welcome to Qu'Arim," he said formally, his voice deep and smooth with the faintest hint of accent. "I hope your stay will be enjoyable. Please let me know if there is anything I can provide for you while you are here."

"Thank you," Melissa mumbled, feeling halfway infatuated by the sheer animal magnetism she sensed in the man. She could listen to him all day. His hand was warm and firm, almost seeming to caress before he released hers. She felt a fluttering of awareness at his intensity when he looked at her. Giving herself a mental shake, she tried to think of the mundane reason for her visit. She was definitely not here to get a crush on Max's friend.

She glanced back and forth between the two men as they spoke. Both carried an air of assurance and confidence that was as appealing as their looks. But it was Surim who captured her attention. Before she could think about it further, their host gestured toward the entrance.

Their small group began to move toward the front of the airport. She gladly let Max and Surim talk together while she looked eagerly around, taking in the crowds of travelers in the various dress. There was a mixture of languages, some she recognized as European. She wondered how hard it would be to learn some Arabic while she was here.

Melissa and Max were ushered into a luxurious stretch limousine while one of the men attending the sheikh went to fetch their luggage. Melissa settled back in her seat and gazed at the landscape, trying to ignore the growing sense of awareness she felt around the sheikh. He joined them after speaking to his men and Melissa was hard-pressed not to stare. Resolutely she gazed out the window.

Flowers and soaring palms lined the avenue, softening the austere lines of the airport terminal.

As the sheikh continued his discussion with Max as the limo pulled away from the airport she occasionally glanced in his direction, intrigued as never before. Surim Al-Thani was slightly shorter than Max, but at six feet still towered over her own five feet three inches. His dark hair gleamed. She wondered if it was as thick and silky as it looked.

When he met her gaze she felt flustered. She had been rude. Yet when his eyes caught hers for an instant she continued boldly staring—this time directly into his dark gaze. Growing uncomfortably warm, Melissa finally broke contact and again looked out the side window. Her heart skipped a beat, then pounded gently in her chest. Concentrate on the scenery, she told herself, meaning that outside view, not the handsome sheikh who sat opposite her.

She wished she'd questioned Max more about their host. While working with the children in the resort in Switzerland, she'd met all levels of society. This attraction wasn't due to his wealth, or even his power. He was simply one sexy man and Melissa wondered how much she'd get to see him during their visit. The less the better, she was starting to think.

The thoroughfares were wide and straight, with banks of flowers in the center islands. Because the limousine's windows were closed to contain the air-conditioning, she couldn't tell if the flowers she saw were the ones that smelled so fragrant at the airport. But their bright blossoms danced on the breeze.

She wasn't listening to the conversation, but became aware of when it stopped. Glancing away from the window, she saw both men looking at her.

"Did I miss something?" she asked.

"I was telling Surim that your fluency in French is why I brought you," Max said.

"It is the second language here in Qu'Arim, though English is gaining favor," Surim said in French.

She wondered if he was testing her. She replied in the same language, "It was the primary language where I worked before, so I have become quite proficient. I'm the one who translated the documents from the construction firm that you sent to Max recently."

He inclined his head in acknowledgment. Returning to English, he glanced at Max. "I hope you will be pleased with the site I've chosen for Bella Lucia. It is right on the water, with palm trees framing the view. We can drive by before heading home if you like."

Max quickly agreed.

Melissa felt she wouldn't mind seeing the site herself. Right on the water—it sounded fabulous.

And it was. The construction site was quiet. The framing of the main building had begun, concrete had been poured, pipes were sticking up in various locations. Max and Surim donned hard hats and headed for the far end of the building.

"You stay out of the construction site," Surim said to Melissa.

Another time she might have been annoyed at such a high-handed command, but she was too enchanted with the setting to care. She would much rather walk down to the water's edge than traipse through a construction zone any day.

The driver of the limo leaned against the hood and watched the men. The two men who had been with the sheikh at the airport had followed them in a separate vehicle. One remained with that car, the other hurried to catch up with Surim and Max. Apparently they took their security seriously, though there was not another soul in sight.

Melissa climbed out of the limo and headed for the water. Her shoes were not at all suitable for the sand, so she kicked them off. Her stockings would undoubtedly be sandy when she put the shoes back on, but she'd deal with that later.

The sugar-white sand was soft and warm. She found the going easier when she reached the damp hard-packed sand near the water's edge. The deep blue of the Persian Gulf stretched before her. She drank in the clean air, relishing the slight salty tang. Turning, she studied the outline of the resort. The main building would be three stories tall, with a high roof. She could see the men at the far end where the restaurant must be situated. Palm trees fluttered in the breeze. It was an ideal setting.

Looking left and right, she was amazed there weren't scores of families enjoying the beach. But as far as she could see in either direction, it was pristine and empty.

She'd love to go swimming, but that was totally out of the question. At least for today. Would she get time off while they were here? She needed to remember she'd come to work, not vacation. But the water was so tempting.

Glancing around, she saw Max and Surim heading for the car. Reluctantly, she returned as well, dusting off her feet as best she could before donning her shoes.

"Enjoying yourself?" Surim asked when they reached the limousine.

She met his glance as she slipped her feet into her shoes. Did she detect a hint of amusement? "It's fantastic. But I'm puzzled why the beach is so empty. I'd think hordes of people would enjoy a day here."

"That is my hope as well, once the resort is completed. In the meantime, construction holds certain danger, so I have closed the area for the duration of building," Surim said.

"I see." All that lovely empty beach. She sighed. There went her idea for swimming.

They resumed their places in the limo and in only a short time they turned into a long driveway flanked on either side by tall palms. Melissa looked with interest at Surim's estate. She had no idea of what kind of place a sheikh might own. Somehow she'd thought maybe a lavish tent like in *Arabian Nights*.

The edifice surprised her. Max hadn't been exaggerating when he'd said it was large enough for a battalion—it was huge. Whitewashed walls with terra-cotta trim reflected the bright sunshine. High arches of windows, outlined by ornate fretwork and mosaics inlaid in bright colours, provided symmetry on the front. A wide veranda seemed to encircle the entire three-story structure. Quite simply, it was stunning.

"It's beautiful," she said, now taking in the colorful flowers that grew in profusion right to the edge of the veranda. Gently waving palm trees encircled the house, while a lush lawn stretched out in all directions. Her gaze was drawn to an elegant fountain in the front, providing a focal point to the circular drive. The watery spray made dozens of sparkling rainbows. She sighed wistfully. What a magnificent place to live.

"Are you near the Gulf?" she asked, not seeing any signs of the sea, but still smelling that slightly salty tang in the air even in the car.

"There is a path from the back of the house that leads to a private beach. It is not far, only a short walk," Surim said. "Perhaps you'd care to go for a swim sometime during your visit."

She smiled at him. "Yes, I would. It's freezing in London right now." Would he join her if she went swimming? She looked away, afraid he'd see the hope in her eyes.

As she followed her host into the house a moment later, through large acacia wood double doors carved into intricate designs and polished to a gleaming shine, she wondered why Max had brought her since Surim spoke French fluently. To have an impartial person on his side? Not that she could imagine the sheikh being the slightest bit dishonorable. Of course he was probably too busy to translate mere construction documents.

Or, as her mother had suggested, maybe the trip was a treat for the work she had already done. It didn't matter; she was thrilled to be here.

The interior of the house was cool, though not apparently due to artificial means. Windows were wide open allowing a balmy breeze to flow through. The tall ceilings allowed the air to circulate freely.

Rich colorful furnishings filled the room to the left. She followed the men and stood in the doorway, her sandy stockings starting to annoy her. How soon could she escape to her room and change?

"You must be tired from the journey," Surim said. "I'll have my housekeeper show you to your room. Dinner will be at eight."

"Thank you," Melissa said, glancing at Max to make sure her departure would be all right with him. There wouldn't be any work today, would there? Surely if he and the sheikh were such old friends they had lots to catch up on.

"Good idea. That'll give you and me time to look over the plans. I've noted some changes I want in the kitchen area," Max said.

So much for catching up on their personal lives. Was work the only thing these men cared about?

Melissa pulled back the cool sheets from the high bed. It was after eleven and she was tired. Slipping beneath the light covers, she lay back on the mattress, her head still swimming from the conversation at dinner. It had only been the three of them in the ornate dining room that could have seated fifty-four easily. The primary topic of conversation had been the new restaurant and resort.

She would have preferred an alfresco meal on the veranda, with more talk about Qu'Arim to enable her to learn more about the country. Maybe with another guest or two to round out the numbers. It was apparent the sheikh liked things formal. It was a good thing she was only here a week; the protocol would drive her crazy.

After dinner, she'd excused herself to wander in the gardens. They'd been illuminated with subdued lighting. She'd walked down one path and then another, exploring little nooks and thoroughly enjoying herself. It was such a change from wintery London.

Melissa began settling on the pillow, her eyes closing as she reviewed what she needed to remember for the morning. They would eat at seven and head for Surim's offices where she and Max would meet with the contractor. Then they would—

A sudden shriek startled her. She sat up. What had that been?

Listening intently, she heard another shriek and then a child crying.

The sheikh wasn't married, at least not that she knew. But that was definitely a child. She got up and found her robe, pulling it on as she hurried to her door.

Opening it, she could clearly hear the wailing. It came from the third floor.

Her heart hurt to hear a child cry so wretchedly. She ran lightly down the hall to the stairs she had seen earlier and quickly gained the third floor. Rushing to an open doorway, the light spilling into the hall, Melissa halted at the scene before her.

Surim had shed his jacket and rolled up the sleeves of his dress shirt. His hands were on his hips and he glared at three young children huddled on a sofa. An older woman stood near a door on the opposite wall, wringing her hands. The oldest child looked to be seven or eight, a toddler leaned against her. It was the little boy, about four or five, who was crying so hard.

Without a thought, Melissa stormed into the room.

"What is going on?" she asked. Moving past Surim, she gathered the little boy in her arms, brushing back his hair and hugging him as she sat on the edge of the bed. "What's the matter, little man?" she asked in her most soothing tone.

The other two children looked at her with startled surprise, then glanced nervously at Surim.

Melissa turned, the little boy in her arms, and glared at the sheikh.

"These children should have been in bed long ago; it's after eleven," she said in her firmest nanny tone.

"That is what I have been telling them," Surim said, his own voice showing his frustration. "Their nurse has been unable to control them. When Hamid awoke with a nightmare, he woke the others. Now they won't return to bed. If they don't behave, I'll have to find new accommodations for them."

"That's the coldest thing I ever heard a father say!" she exclaimed.

"I'm not their father," he returned.

The little boy rested his head on Melissa's shoulder, quieting. She hugged him again and looked at the other two. They looked tired, scared and wary.

"Well, whose children are they and why were they left with you?" Melissa asked. The woman moaned slightly and lowered her gaze.

Surim lowered his hands and took a step closer, anger evident in his eyes.

"My household is not your concern. You are merely a guest. Here because Max requested it."

"Children are my concern, however, and if you can't take proper care of these children, I shall report you," she replied hotly. The foolishness of the comment struck her. Surim was the leader of the entire country. To whom would she report him?

Surim narrowed his eyes, anger threatening to choke him. Then the absurdity of what she'd just said penetrated. His anger immediately cooled. For a moment he thought he'd challenge her on that. He looked at Melissa, then at the children. They shrank away from him. He was not a monster. He would never strike a child. Yet they walked as if on eggshells around him.

No wonder—he had no clue how to care for children. He'd hired Annis to watch them. But they were proving too much for her. Not that he had any intention of sharing that information with his guest. Maybe boarding schools were the answer.

He looked back at Melissa. She might be petite, but she

looked as if she'd fight him to the death. And she didn't even know the children.

"These are my cousin's children. Nadia, Hamid, and Alaya. They have come to live with me recently and we haven't found our way yet. I would prefer you not report me." Surim let the humor of the situation defuse the tension. He had never heard anyone in Qu'Arim threaten to report him before. The novelty was priceless.

"Perhaps they should return home," Melissa said.

"Unfortunately, their parents were killed in a car crash and they have no home to return to. As their guardian, I now provide for them."

Surim watched as Melissa shifted Hamid in her arms. He had to be growing heavy. At least she had been able to stop his crying, for which Surim was grateful. The nightmares came regularly and Annis seemed incapable of doing anything to stop them. Not that he himself had been any help. Yet Max's little friend seemed to have the knack of quieting the child. He'd take any help he could get at this point.

He looked at her once more, surprised to see she was in a gown and robe. Her hair looked soft and touchable, her eyes sparkled with righteousness indignation. And the color that rose in her cheeks intrigued him.

Max had asked if his assistant could come, more for a holiday than for needed work. Was there something between the two of them? Surim had not seen anything. Which didn't mean she was totally unattached. Was there a man waiting for her in London?

"Perhaps you'd help get the children settled for the night," he said, dragging his speculation back to the matter at hand. With a glance at Annis, he shook his head. The nurse had proved most ineffective when dealing with these children. How hard could it be to put three children to bed at a reasonable time each night? Weren't nurses supposed to be able to deal with nightmares and other problems Hamid seemed to have?

"Perhaps I should." Melissa looked at the two girls. "Hi, I'm Melissa. Want to help me get Hamid to bed? Then I'll tuck you both in and read you all a story."

"Our room is across the hall," the older girl said. "Hamid couldn't hear the story from his room."

"Then tonight why don't we have all three of you sleep together, and then everyone can hear at once?"

"I wuv stories," the littlest one said.

"They speak English," Melissa said, looking at Surim.

"Their parents lived in England. They were all three born there," he replied.

"Ah, I'm from England, too," she told the children. "Let me tell you about the weather when I left, cold and rainy. They even thought there might be snow in the north before the end of the week. It's much nicer here."

Surim watched as the Englishwoman seemed to effortlessly gather the children to her and head them to the girls' room. In a moment all he heard was her soft murmur.

"I'm sorry they disturbed you, Your Excellency. The boy had a nightmare and the girls awoke to come to his aid," Annis said in Arabic.

Surim sighed. This was the fifth or sixth time since they'd arrived it had happened. When would it stop?

"It is to be expected, I suppose. We will discuss the situation in the morning," he said.

The older woman scurried away. Surim wished she'd shown a little of the backbone Melissa Fox had when she'd taken him to task. Annis had come highly recommended, but Surim didn't think much of her abilities with these children. Unlike Melissa Fox, who had miraculously charmed them all.

Himself included?

Report him, indeed.

He crossed the hall and paused near the opened door. The three children were snuggled together in the large bed. Melissa sat in a chair near the head, reading a story. Already little Nadia had her eyes closed. Hamid was fighting sleep.

Surim watched as Melissa seemed to calm them all, and bring much-needed rest.

He waited until she checked the children, gently closed the book, and turned off the light. She made it seem easy. Yet he had no idea of what to talk about to a child.

When she stepped into the hallway, she was surprised to see him.

"Thank you for getting them to sleep," he said formally. He was embarrassed a guest in his home had had to involve herself with his responsibilities. But the quiet was much appreciated. He hoped they slept through the night this time.

"I apologize for speaking to you as I did earlier. It was not my place," she said, equally formally, looking just beyond his left ear.

It was a perfect apology, but he didn't believe she really meant it. From the stiff way she held herself, he had an idea she'd like to tear into him and berate him for not being a better guardian for the children.

"I hope they will not interrupt your visit a second time," he said politely.

She flashed him an annoyed look and turned to walk down the hall. "Children don't annoy me."

Lucky her, that children didn't annoy her. Or baffle her as they did him. He expected them to do as they were told, but had found in the three weeks they'd been in his home that expectation was not met more times than it was.

He glanced into the darkened room once more, feeling a sharp pang at the thought of his cousin Mara's death. She and her husband had been too young. And he had never expected to be named guardian of three children under the age of nine. He knew nothing about children. He'd have his secretary begin researching boarding schools in the morning. There had to be some that would take children as young as two.

CHAPTER TWO

MELISSA dressed in a navy suit and sensible shoes the next morning. She and Max were meeting with the contractor at Surim's offices. Then they would all view the site again, with the foreman explaining each stage. She would begin to earn her salary today. That was if Surim would still let her work. Melissa sighed. She really shouldn't have threatened him last night. Would he mention the incident to Max? She needed to watch her tongue and not blurt out things before thinking.

Breakfast was served buffet-style in the dining room. Max was sitting in the spot he'd occupied last night when Melissa entered. After a quick glance around, she breathed a sigh of relief. Surim was not present.

"Good morning. I hope I'm not late," she said to Max.

"Not at all." He looked up from the English newspaper he was reading, hot tea steaming by his hand. "Surim left a while ago. He'll meet us when we get to the office. Help yourself to breakfast."

Melissa didn't know if Surim normally ate a hearty English breakfast or had had one set out for his guests, but she gladly dove in. The amount of food out on the sideboard for two people was staggering, yet she saw no sign of the children. She wondered if they'd slept through the night without further incident.

"What do you think of Qu'Arim so far?" Max asked when she sat opposite him. He folded his paper and laid it aside.

Melissa smiled. "About what I expected with a country that has such strong ties with Europe. The downtown buildings are taller than I expected and much more modern. Overall it looks very prosperous. And I especially love the flowers that grow in such profusion."

"Surim's done a terrific job. He was telling me about his plans for expanding their tourist market, which is the reason for the resort. He has an aggressive schedule devised to lure in European and American money. If anyone can pull it off, he can."

"That's why he wants Bella Lucia?"

"Of course. Anyone from the UK will recognize the name. As we stand for the highest quality it will be a strong draw he wants for the initial guests," Max said.

She nodded, glancing at the doorway as she strained to hear any sounds from the children. But the house remained silent. Were they still sleeping? She'd like to spend more time with them. She hadn't realized how much she'd miss children until she'd taken this extended break between her old job and her new. It was the longest she'd gone without interacting with small children since she'd finished her training.

"I'm ready when you are," Max said, folding his napkin.

Melissa took a final swallow of her coffee and stood. "Let's go."

They had the limo at their disposal and as they were driven through the city streets Melissa felt a hint of excitement at the thought of seeing Surim again. He hadn't paid her much attention yesterday, and she'd been rude last night. Still, there was a fascination that hadn't been quelled yet. She'd love to talk to him about his country, about how he felt taking the reins of leadership so young. What changes had he made? What were the plans for the future?

It wasn't his looks alone that fascinated her. He was a

challenge to talk to, seemed smarter than most men she had dated, and carried himself with confidence bordering on arrogance. Yet on him it sat well. She tried to pinpoint exactly why she felt drawn to the man. He definitely didn't have a way with children. But many men left most of the child-raising to the wife. He had lots more going for him than being father of the year.

"Max, did you know Surim has three children living with him?" she asked.

"Umm? Children? I don't think so; he's not married. Though I heard he's looking."

"Maybe because he has those three children," Melissa said. What did that mean, looking? Could she ask without giving the impression it was important?

"What children?" he said, looking at her.

"Their parents just died. They were raised in the UK and speak English as well as you or I do."

Max looked at her in puzzlement. "How do you know this?"

"Didn't you hear them last night? The little boy woke from a nightmare and was crying loud enough I heard him in my room."

"I didn't hear anything." He looked pensive. "I can't imagine Surim with children. Running a country, yes. Visiting Europe and squiring beautiful women around, yes. Kids, I don't think so."

"No surprise there. He didn't seem to have an ounce of sympathy for the little boy." She tried to maintain her indignation, but couldn't help thinking of Surim's side of things. If he wasn't used to being around children, becoming an instant guardian to three would be daunting.

The limo stopped in front of a large high-rise glass and steel skyscraper. Max led the way and Melissa hurried to keep up. Tall people never seemed to consider that those not blessed with extraordinary height would have trouble keeping pace.

Entering a mirrored elevator, they were soon whisked to the top floor. Stepping out onto a luxurious carpet, Melissa gazed around, noting the old paintings on the walls, the elegance of the furnishings and the quiet hum of business.

She and Max were ushered into a conference room. The outer wall was of glass, offering a spectacular view of the Gulf. Melissa wanted to stand there and drink in the sight, but Surim was already at the large table with three other men. Introductions were quickly made—the contractor and his assistant, and Surim's project manager. All the men from Qu'Arim spoke French, so they used that language, Melissa translating into English for Max.

When she wasn't speaking, she studied Surim. He had the capacity to totally focus on the situation at hand. Did he bring that focus to his new children?

Would he bring that focus to a woman? She could imagine being the center of his attention; his eyes would gaze into hers. His conversation would be on topics she liked. And the woman would feel like a queen. Not that she would ever know. Not that she wanted to even venture there. She'd been burned badly by Paul and had no intention of flirting with a friend of Max's. Max had trusted her enough to bring her as his assistant; she would do nothing to damage that relationship. How awkward it would be if Surim complained Melissa was flirting with him. She cringed at the thought.

But she couldn't help glancing his way again. And came up against his gaze focused on her. He didn't read minds, did he?

When it was time to go to the construction site, Melissa rode with Surim in his private car, which he drove. Max went with the others in the limo.

"I wished to speak to you privately," Surim said as they merged into traffic.

"About?" For a moment, despite her best efforts of keeping a businesslike demeanor, her imagination soared. Would he reach out and take her hand? Tell her he was delighted she'd joined Max and would she spend time with him alone before they returned to England? Maybe she'd like to see a quiet place only he knew?

"To thank you for calming young Hamid last night. He has been troubled by nightmares a great deal."

Her bubble popped.

"Not unexpected if he just lost his parents," she said, feeling foolish after all. Thankfully no one else knew of her dumb daydreams. She really had to get control of her emotions. Paul should have cured her once and for all of getting ideas about rich, powerful men and their interest in a nanny. Especially with the cultural differences added in.

Surim nodded, focused on driving.

"Perhaps. I hope they won't bother you tonight," he said.

"No bother. I'm sorry they are going through such a trying time. It was fortunate they have family to take them in."

"My cousin's mother, Tante Tazil, is not well. She is unable to care for them. But I don't believe they will remain with me for long. I have my secretary looking into boarding schools."

"What? They're too young to be sent away!" Good thing she didn't have any illusions about the man; this would have shattered any lingering ones. Who would think of sending babies to boarding school?

"I went to boarding school when I was nine, in England—which was a foreign country to me. We are looking at schools in England. That is their native country, even though their parents were from Qu'Arim. They have been raised there and I thought it would make them feel better to be back there."

"Nadia is still a baby, Hamid can't be five yet and Alaya is still too young to be sent away. Think, Surim, they are *children*. They have just suffered a horrific loss of both parents. Being here took them away from the only home they knew, and now you're proposing to shunt them off to some school—if you can even find one that will take them that young."

"I'm sure that will not be a problem."

The arrogant statement caused Melissa's blood to boil. Men who were obscenely rich thought money could buy everything. But not family ties, not love and loyalty, nor negation of his responsibility to his cousin's children.

"Maybe not to you, but think of them," she said. "It would be horrible."

"They are unhappy and disruptive. During the day they run wild around the house, yelling and breaking things. At night Hamid has nightmares and awakens the entire household. Their nurse cannot control them. I believe a more structured environment would be beneficial. It is not open for discussion; I was merely informing you of my plans."

They had reached the site of the hotel and he turned to park beside the row of cars and trucks near the building. The activity at the site was a stark contrast to yesterday. The lot was crowded with workers. Trucks of cement were dumping their loads. Men and machines worked as if choreographed, building a structure that would reflect the desires of their sheikh to expand tourism for his country.

Melissa ignored it all, however. She was so angry she could spit! How dared he mess those children around like that? They needed stability and love, guidance and assurance that they were part of a family—not to be sent away from the only relative who was apparently able to look after them.

She reached out and caught his arm, stopping him from exiting the car.

He looked at her with some surprise.

Amazed at her own audacity, she nonetheless held onto her courage. "There has to be other alternatives. Think, please. They're babies. They need comforting, love. You are their cousin, their guardian. Spend time with them or find other family members who can care for them. Don't send them to some institutional school so far away."

"I believe I know what is best for the children." He slipped his arm from beneath her hand and climbed out of the car.

"I don't think so," she muttered, opening her own door and getting out before he could come around to assist. Her opinion of the man dropped significantly! How could he do that to those precious children?

Max had said he was looking for a wife. Maybe his attitude was one of the reasons he wasn't already married.

Yet her heart ached for those sweet children. Maybe she'd find a way to make him change his mind.

Melissa was tired by the time she and Max returned to Surim's house in the late afternoon. Dinner would not be for a couple of hours. She quickly showered and put on some casual, light trousers. No one had said she couldn't visit the children, so she went up to the third floor.

They were sitting in front of a television, the program in Arabic. Why weren't they outside in the sunshine?

"Hi," she said, stepping inside the room.

All three kids scrambled to their feet and rushed to greet her.

"You came back," Alaya said in perfect English. "I didn't think we'd see you again. I'm sorry Hamid woke everyone up last night."

"I had a nightmare," the little boy said.

Nadia held up her arms and Melissa scooped her up, hugging her gently, then resting her on her hip.

"What are you doing inside on such a gorgeous day? I heard there's a path to the beach," Melissa said. She smiled at the older woman sitting with crochet work in hand.

"Do you mind if I take the children out for a walk?" she asked in French.

With the nurse's agreement, she told the children to get

ready. "We'll walk there and back. But only on the condition you are on your best behavior," she admonished, remembering what Surim had said about their running wild.

"We haven't been outside except to the gardens. Annis doesn't like to go far. She's old," Alaya ended in a whisper.

"Well, I'm not and I'm up for a walk to the beach. Sun cream first and then we'll leave," Melissa said. The nurse wasn't that old—she looked to be about fifty—but to a young girl she probably did seem elderly.

The outing proved to be full of fun. Melissa forgot about being tired and held Nadia's and Hamid's hands. Alaya walked on the other side of Nadia, chatting freely.

"We've been here a long time it seems and never seen the beach. Our parents died, you know. I really miss Mummy. Is the water cold?" Alaya asked.

"I think it's warm. We'll find out together." Melissa found the gate leading out of the garden and followed the neatly kept path. In only five minutes they reached a pristine stretch of beach totally empty in both directions. The children ran toward the water.

"Don't go in until I get there," Melissa called, running after them. It felt so good to be free of office clothes, to be running in the sunshine. The laughter of the children warmed her heart. She was glad she'd followed her instincts and sought them out.

The children kicked off their shoes and waded in the warm sea. Melissa quickly followed, getting the bottoms of her trouser legs wet, but she didn't care. She was happy to enjoy the excitement of the children.

"I want to go swimming," Hamid said, splashing his sisters.

"Whoa, not so much water. Another day we'll ask about swimming. How about we race along the water's edge? Who can run the fastest?" Melissa said, looking to channel some of their energy. They probably got into trouble in the house from sheer curiosity and exuberance. She'd make sure they got enough exercise to sleep soundly tonight.

"Me," little Nadia said.

"I can," Hamid said.

They were off, running at the edge of the water, splashing and laughing. Alaya took off after them, with Melissa following.

When they tired of that, Melissa suggested they build a sandcastle.

Alaya looked sad. "Mummy and Daddy built a fabulous one the last holiday we had. We went to Cornwall."

"I'm sure they'll be happy to see you are building a new sandcastle on this beach. It's a long way from Cornwall, but sand is sand. Won't you join us?" Melissa wasn't exactly sure what to say to grieving children, but she knew it was good for the children to talk about their parents.

"You can tell us how to make one like your mummy and daddy built. Did you help them?" she asked.

Alaya nodded. "I miss them." She started to cry. The other two ran to her, upset by their older sister's tears.

Melissa reached out to draw her into her arms, hugging her warmly. "I know you do. You will miss them all your life. My daddy died when I was five and I still miss him. But the aching, crushing hurt will diminish, I promise. One day you'll look back at all your memories so grateful to have them. They'll bring smiles to your face and a lift of love to your heart." Melissa wished she had more memories of her father. Alaya was older than she'd been. She would remember. But the others would not. It was so sad.

"I miss Mummy, too," Hamid said.

Melissa sat on the sand, pulling Alaya down with her, and keeping one arm around her shoulder. She patted her lap and Nadia climbed on, while Hamid crowded from the other side. She wished she could hold each one until the hurt eased.

"Of course you miss them. They were your parents and loved you very much. You know they didn't want to die."

"It was a truck, crashing into them," Alaya said. "The

brakes failed, that's what the policeman said. Why did it have to happen?"

"No one knows things like that, sweetheart," Melissa murmured. "But you will be cared for here."

"Nobody here knew our parents or talks about them. It's as if they were never alive," Alaya said.

"Your uncle knew your mother. Get him to talk about her and your father. I bet he has wonderful stories about when they were young," Melissa suggested.

"He's our cousin," Alaya said, bitterness tingeing her voice. "He doesn't want us. Mummy asked him long ago to be our guardian if something happened to them and he said yes. But he doesn't want us."

"He's your family," Melissa said, hoping it wasn't a total lie. "He's just not used to children. We need to find a way to have him feel more comfortable around you."

"He's getting married," Hamid said, looking up at her. "Will she be our new mummy?"

"No, we are not getting another mother," Alaya said firmly. Nadia slipped her thumb into her mouth, watching with large eyes.

"Because of the age difference, I'm sure the sheikh wouldn't mind if you called him Uncle Surim. His new wife will be your new aunt. Have you met her yet?"

"He's looking," Alaya said.

"Looking?"

"He needs to get married to have sons to carry on when he dies," Alaya said.

"But he's not going to die soon," Hamid said, looking at his sister. "Is he?"

"No, he has to get married first," Alaya said.

"How do you know this?" Melissa asked, curious.

Alaya and Hamid looked away.

"Sometimes we spy on him," she said in a low voice.

"We sneak down the stairs and listen at the door, then run like the wind when someone leaves the office room," Hamid said.

Melissa was torn between laughter at the picture, and telling them that spying wasn't really a good thing.

"So he wants babies. They'll be new cousins for you to play with," she said, wondering why he was planning to send these adorable children away if he wanted children of his own. She hoped he found his wife soon, and she'd insist on keeping the children.

Paul's scathing denouncement echoed in her mind. He hadn't wanted children at all. He considered her involvement with them immature and beneath a woman he'd want to marry. For a moment she was back in the small restaurant hearing his voice, feeling each word as a dart piercing her heart. She'd thought they had so much going for them, until she'd voiced that thought and been soundly corrected. How had she misjudged him so much?

Shaking off the melancholy, she smiled.

"Let's get going on those sandcastles. Dinner will be soon and we'll have to return to the house."

The children scrambled up and ran to the water's edge again. Soon they were all mounding wet sand, trying to sculpt it with fingers. Melissa made a mental note to see if there were sand toys in the children's nursery for future visits to the seashore.

Surim walked down the path to the beach alone. Annis had come to tell him the children had not returned in time for their supper. She was worried she'd done the wrong thing by allowing them to go off with his guest. Sometimes it was almost more than he could do to control his frustration. His aunt had insisted Annis be hired to watch her grandchildren. But however qualified Annis appeared on paper, her skill with the children lacked a great deal in his opinion.

As he approached the beach he heard laughter and happy chatter. Pausing by the last of the green grass, he observed four people caught up in building a sandcastle. Little Nadia for once didn't have her thumb in her mouth. Hamid was laughing so hard he fell over and rolled on the sand. Alaya stood, running to the water to scoop some in her hands and carry it, dripping all the way, back to the ditch they'd built around the castle.

But the person he had the most difficulty recognizing was Melissa Fox. She looked like one of the children. Gone was her suit and her business attitude. Her hair was flying in the breeze, and her trousers were damp and sandy. He could see the joy in her expression. He was struck by how beautiful she was. Suddenly he was gripped with an urge to see her dressed in a designer gown, with pearls from Qu'Arim at her throat.

Every one of them was having so much fun a pang of envy struck. Surim couldn't remember the last time he'd laughed like that. Or spent a carefree afternoon doing nothing more important than building a sandcastle.

Hamid rolled to his knees and caught sight of Surim. The merriment dropped instantly from his face. He said something and the others looked his way. Alaya stopped smiling and stepped closer to Melissa. Nadia popped her thumb back into her mouth and regarded him warily.

Was he frightening to these children? He remembered his cousin Mara fondly. They'd played together when he was younger—not any older than Hamid. He'd seen her often when home from school, before his father had died and his life had changed so drastically. He'd never expected her to die young, or for himself to wind up responsible for her children.

Melissa rose, dusting some of the sand from her clothes.

"Are we late?" she called. She spoke to the children and as one they turned to walk to the water and swish their hands clean. Picking up their shoes, they moved to stand just behind her. In a moment, the little line headed his way, almost like a mother duck with her ducklings following in a row.

Surim watched, fascinated at the change in his guest and the laughter he'd seen from the children. He had only seen them sad or scared or defiant. Melissa still looked carefree and happy, but the children had become solemn.

"Annis was worried when they didn't return for dinner," he said when Melissa drew close.

"Sorry about that. I forgot my watch. Guess my estimating the time from the sun isn't very accurate." She laughed. "But we were having such fun time seemed to fly."

He looked at the pile of sand, then at the children. "A very fine castle," he said awkwardly.

"I bet you and their mother made sandcastles when you were young," Melissa said.

He was startled. He hadn't said anything about Mara or her husband, fearing to upset the children.

"Did you?" Alaya asked hesitantly.

Surim regarded the little girl and nodded. "We did. And when we grew older, we had swimming races, and went water-skiing together. She and I were great friends during the summers when I was home," he said, remembering back before the world had changed and his childhood had ended abruptly.

"Where were you in not summer?" Hamid asked.

"I went to school in England. Where you used to live."

"I miss home," Hamid said forlornly.

"This will feel like home in no time," Melissa said bracingly. "Right?" She smiled brightly at Surim.

He raised an eyebrow at her comment.

She smelled like sunshine and salt air. He noticed the deep green of her eyes, the glossy shine to her hair. There was a faint hint of pink on her cheeks—from the sun? She was shorter than most of the woman he dated, and much too young. But for a moment awareness flared.

Intellect didn't rule the body all the time. He remembered how soft her skin had felt when he'd kissed her hand at the airport, a gesture foreign to him. Had he been making a show for Max's friend?

Instinctively it had seemed right.

The children marched quietly into the house, all evidence of the joy he'd seen subdued by his presence. Surim wished he could change that.

"I'll run up with the children and give Annis a hand getting them cleaned up," Melissa said when they reached the stairs.

"Our own dinner will be in thirty minutes."

"Then I'll have to hurry." She herded the children up the stairs without another glance in his direction.

For an instant, Surim wished she'd been as eager for his company as she was for the children's. He had no trouble in the romance department. Though none of the women he knew held the same appeal that Melissa held.

He was being pressured by several factions to take a wife, and have children to insure the dynasty. These days he seemed to be looking at every woman with the same question—could he live with her for the next fifty or so years? So far he hadn't found anyone.

Melissa slipped into the dining-room chair just as Surim and Max came in from the study. Once they were seated, a servant entered from the kitchen with a platter of meat. Melissa had rushed through her ablutions; her hair was still damp. But she had not kept the sheikh waiting for his meal.

She listened as Surim and Max discussed business, wondering what other activities the sheikh participated in. He had to take women out if he was looking for a wife. Did he discuss business with them? Or was it all romance?

She wondered what a date with him would be like, what they would talk about. Did he discuss the orphan children in his care with them? Or maybe he concentrated on wooing the woman, delaying any talk of family until he decided she was the one.

In the meantime, perhaps she should offer some suggestions to getting to know the children? She shook her head, hiding a wry smile. As if he'd listen to her. Who was she to advise the ruler of Qu'Arim? He had advisors galore. And a perfectly qualified nurse in residence. Though what the children needed was love and devotion and fun. And a chance to get to know Surim and establish new family routines and traditions.

"You're quiet tonight," Surim said, addressing her. "Too much activity today?"

Melissa looked up. "Oh, no. I enjoyed seeing the actual site of the new restaurant, and the plans you have for the resort. I'm sure it will be spectacular."

"Of course it will," Max said. "Surim doesn't do things by half measures."

"I thought to have a small gathering of friends and advisors before you leave. Most of them speak English, the ones who don't speak French," Surim said.

"I would like the opportunity to meet your friends here," Max said. "I already know most of your friends in England."

"And you, Melissa, would that please you?" Surim asked.

"I should be delighted to attend." She wondered if he would bring one of his potential wives with him, and she was disturbed to realize how much the thought bothered her.

When dinner finished, they moved to the drawing room. As they walked Surim and Max continued their discussion of the possibility of expanding Bella Lucia beyond this one overseas restaurant.

Passing through the wide entry hall, Melissa heard a noise. Neither of the men seemed to notice. Glancing up, she spotted Hamid peering between the railings of the balustrade. She looked at Surim and Max. They were too engrossed in their conversation to hear such a slight noise.

When they reached the living room, Melissa paused at the doorway.

"If you two will excuse me, I think I'll go on up."

Surim looked at her, frowning. "I apologize that our conversation centered on business. You must be tired of it after the long day we put in. We will change the topic."

"No, you two talk all you want. Max won't be here that long and I know you're friends from way back. I'll see you in the morning."

His dark eyes seemed to hold her gaze as he weighed her words. "Very well." With a slight inclination of his head, he turned back to Max.

Hurrying up the stairs, Melissa caught Hamid and Alaya as they tried to run down the hall.

"Hey, you two, stop right there." She kept her voice low, but knew the children heard her.

They stopped and looked back, nervously waiting as Melissa went to them.

"I thought we talked earlier about not spying," Melissa said in her sternest voice.

"We wanted to see you tonight," Alaya said.

"Do you know where my room is?"

Alaya nodded.

"In the future, wait there if you need to see me. Or leave me a note. But no more spying; it's wrong."

Alaya nodded. Hamid looked at his sister, then nodded solemnly as well.

"Now, what's up?" Melissa asked, smiling at the children.

"We wanted to see if you would read us a story," Hamid said. "Annis only reads in French and we don't understand."

"Or she speaks Arabic and we only know a few words that Mummy and Daddy taught us," Alaya said.

"You will need to learn the language if you're staying here," Melissa said. She started walking to the stairs leading to the third floor. "Maybe we'll ask Annis to start Arabic lessons in the morning. Tonight, I'm happy to read you a story. Is Nadia already in bed?"

"Yes. She was sleeping when we came down," Alaya said. "I wish we didn't have to stay here. Everything's so different from home."

"You'll get used to things in time, then it will be like having two homes. The one you had in England, and your new one here. Do you have friends back at home?" Melissa asked.

Alaya nodded.

"Have you written to them about your new place?"

The little girl shook her head.

"That would be fun for them to receive a letter from you telling them all about this house, your uncle and Annis. I bet none of them have ever been to Qu'Arim. Maybe you could get some photos to include in the letter." Melissa smiled as the enthusiasm started to show on Alaya's face. "This house is fantastic. Just a photo of the front would look like a museum or something."

"I'd like to write to Sally and Marta. You think they'd write back to me?" she asked wistfully.

"I'm sure of it. First thing tomorrow, I'll have Annis make sure you have paper and pencil. You write as much as you wish and then we'll get your uncle to post it," Melissa said.

"I should be delighted," Surim said behind them.

CHAPTER THREE

MELISSA turned around, surprised. "I thought you and Max were in the living room."

"He had a call to make before it got too late in London. I thought I heard voices, so came to investigate." He looked at Alaya. "If you wish me to post a letter, I'm happy to do so."

"Thank you, Uncle Surim," she said shyly, moving closer to Melissa.

"Uncle? We're cousins," he explained.

"Easier for them if you're Uncle Surim and your new bride will be their new aunt." Speaking softly, Melissa leaned closer. "They don't want a replacement for their parents just yet."

He raised an eyebrow. "My new bride," he said evenly.

Melissa swallowed. Was that some secret? She shouldn't have said that.

"I heard you were looking for a wife," she said, feeling embarrassed, as if she'd been caught gossiping behind his back.

His face was impassive. "That is the plan."

Heat turning her face bright red, Melissa was thankful when Hamid interrupted. "Melissa is going to read us a story," he said firmly. "Come on, Melissa."

"You have a way with the children," Surim said. "Don't let them pester you."

She glanced sharply at him. "They aren't pestering me, for

heaven's sake. They just want some adult attention. You should be reading them their stories. Annis's English is limited. She only reads French stories; they don't understand those."

"She speaks English," he said, his brow creasing.

"And stop frowning, it scares them," she said.

He looked at her in astonishment.

Melissa almost cringed. She needed to watch her tongue or she'd be asked to leave so fast her head would swim. This was a sheikh, not some bumbling idiot.

"Sorry, but I do think you should try smiling more." She bit her lip and looked at Alaya.

Surim stooped down until he was at a level with Hamid. "Should I read to you?" he asked gently.

Melissa was the astonished one. She'd never heard such gentleness in Surim's voice, nor expected him to do something so kind to a little boy.

Hamid seemed undecided. "Can you both read to us?"

Surim smiled and nodded, glancing up at Melissa.

Melissa was struck dumb. When he smiled his entire face changed. He looked younger. And much more appealing. A flutter of nerves centered in her stomach. He would have no trouble wooing some woman to become his wife if he smiled at her once a day.

Rising to his full height, he continued looking at Melissa, a hint of amusement in those dark eyes. "You have a way with children; do you have any of your own?"

"Of course not, I'm not married."

"Neither am I, but I seem to have acquired three."

Melissa wanted to point out he planned to ship them off to some school, but she kept quiet, conscious of the presence of the two children. Maybe if Surim spent some more time with them, he'd find he couldn't send them away.

"Come on, then, let's read these children to sleep," he said.

It was oddly intimate, Melissa thought, to be with Surim

tucking the children in bed. Almost as if they were the children's parents. Surim had dismissed Annis when she'd rushed out to see to the children. Melissa glanced across the bed to watch as he patted Hamid on his small shoulders. She thought it was the first time for the man.

"Sleep through the night, little one," Surim said, almost as an order.

Melissa hid a smile. He might be trying, but his manner needed polishing.

She selected two books, and handed one to Surim. "Want to start?" she asked.

"Ladies first. Besides, if they fall asleep on your watch, I don't have to read."

She laughed. "Very well."

His strategy worked. Before Melissa finished the book she'd selected, both children were fast asleep.

"Tomorrow night, you can read the first book," Melissa whispered as they left the bedroom.

"I would never be able to put as much enthusiasm into reading. Nor come up with different voices for the different characters. You have a talent for working with children."

"I should, it's my job."

"What do you mean?"

"I'm a nanny by profession."

He paused at the top of the stairs. "I thought you were a translator."

"Max very kindly found me some work between jobs—at my mother's insistence, I'm sure. She recently married Max's father, you know."

Surim nodded.

"Anyway, I finished my last job before Christmas and my next one doesn't start until February, so I'm helping out at Bella Lucia. They obviously knew I had no experience in anything except childcare, so Max found this job for me. I speak French and Italian and a smattering of German. I needed it when I lived in Switzerland."

"Where is your next job?"

"In Boston, Massachusetts, in the United States."

"I'm familiar with Boston," he said dryly. "Quite a change from Switzerland."

"And from what I've been doing. Until now, I worked at a childcare facility at one of the resorts in Switzerland. You know, come for a week and let us take care of your children so you can enjoy all the amenities. It was great fun, but now I want to try working for a family. When the McDonalds asked me, I jumped at the chance. It's what I was trained for." She had no intention of letting anyone know part of the reason for her desire for change was a love affair gone bad. So far she'd kept that secret.

"Perhaps you can offer me some insights into these children before you leave," Surim said, continuing down the stairs.

Melissa walked beside him, wondering how much she had to offer in the few days remaining. Still, if she could get them all comfortable around each other, that would go a long way.

"Perhaps," she said at last.

When they reached the door to her bedroom, he paused. She reached to open it. Surim stopped her, turning her to face him.

"Thank you for your help. The children seemed happier tonight than they have since they arrived."

To her surprise, he kissed her. His lips touched hers lightly, then he stood back. "Don't tell Max I'm taking advantage of his new stepsister. He'd have my head."

He turned and walked down the hall.

Melissa blinked, still not sure of what had happened. Her lips still felt the brief warmth of Surim's. Her head was spinning. And the way her heart pounded, she couldn't have imagined it.

Yet how astonishing.

In a haze, she entered her bedroom.

* * *

Surim continued down the hall, wondering what had come over him. He had dated some beautiful, sophisticated women. Enjoyed their company, their sparkling repartee. But he'd never kissed them on such short provocation. Melissa was kissable. He'd wanted to kiss her since he saw her laughing on the beach that afternoon.

She was nothing like the women he usually dated. His advisors and ministers would have a fit if they knew of his interest. Not that a kiss to thank her for her help with the children would endanger the country.

Was that all it was? A thank-you kiss? He was not a man to give embraces so freely.

Yet when he'd seen Melissa going up the stairs with his wards, he'd wanted to join them. Alaya and Hamid seemed quiet and awkward around him, but they blossomed around Melissa. He almost felt he could blossom around her. Shed the duties of office and enjoy an hour or two with her without the constant pressure of duty.

Unlike Annis, she seemed to have a real rapport with children. They'd all looked so happy at the beach. Then Alaya and Hamid sought her out after dinner. To his knowledge none of the children had ever sought him out.

He remembered how small Hamid had felt when he'd tucked him in. His shoulders were so frail in Surim's stronger hands. What would the boy do when he grew up? Would he want to travel as his parents did, or be content to find work in Qu'Arim and make a life here?

For a moment the thought of influencing all three children in how they grew and what they became was daunting. Yet he knew he had to marry soon and beget heirs for his own family, and for a future ruler of Qu'Arim. How effective he proved as a father would influence the lives of his own children.

And where would he find a woman to become the mother of those children? He had been enjoying the company of women for years, yet had never found a special woman to invite to share his life. He had given up on the elusive love that westerners believed in. A suitable union with a woman from a fine family would produce the heirs he needed. As long as they were compatible.

He knew women sought him out because of his wealth and power. Somehow he couldn't see Melissa being impressed by either. In fact, she didn't seem impressed by him at all. No one in recent memory had scolded him as she had.

He almost smiled when he remembered her fussing at him. She was a champion of those children. For a moment he wondered what it would be like to have her champion him.

He returned to the salon and his friend Max. Another complication—if Max found out Surim was kissing his newly acquired stepsister. Better to keep his distance. Melissa was only visiting for a week. Then she'd return to London and he'd resume his quest for a wife.

On Tuesday, Melissa and Max were the only two at breakfast again.

"Surim keeps early hours," she murmured as she took some eggs and bacon. She liked saying his name. Far from being daunted by the sheikh, after that brief kiss last night, Melissa was becoming more fascinated. He'd insisted that first day that she call him by name. Now she looked for ways to use it.

Max sipped his hot coffee and looked up from the paper he was reading. "He's putting in long hours because we're here. I saw him before he left; he said the small reception he's planning will be Thursday night. We'll fly home on Friday."

"Everything going all right?" she asked, sitting at the table.

Max nodded, his face serious. "Surim has done all the preliminary work as we discussed. Today I want to spend time with the contractor, reviewing the specs, and trying to convey to him the ambience I'm looking for, what a Bella Lucia Restaurant means beyond the fixtures."

Melissa's services were dispensed with around two o'clock. She was driven back to Surim's home where she went up to change and go find the children.

Annis was happy to have her take them for a walk. Once the three children were ready, they trooped down the stairs, chattering happily. Alaya confided she'd written her friends, Hamid talked about swimming and Nadia babbled quietly to herself, smiling up at Melissa from time to time.

They walked through the garden and to the beach. The afternoon was perfect and Melissa wished Surim had taken some time to spend with the children in such a carefree manner. If he could just get to know them, she knew he'd fall in love with them. She was halfway in love with them herself.

But Surim didn't join them for the afternoon, nor for dinner. Learning the men would return late, Melissa elected to eat with Annis and the children. After they were in bed, she went for a walk by herself in the gardens.

The paths were illuminated and she enjoyed the quiet of the evening, the air warm even after sunset. She sat on one of the benches for a long time, soaking in the atmosphere, enjoying the fragrant flowers. She found it so amazing to be enjoying this garden in January. How wonderful to have such a residence. It seemed to her Surim wasn't home enough to enjoy it.

Wednesday was a repeat of the previous day. Melissa regretted not seeing Surim, but she needed to keep this visit in perspective. She was not here to be entertained, but to help Max where she could. And when he didn't need her services, she loved spending time with the children.

Still, she wished Surim would make a few moments in the day to see the children. She'd half a mind to speak to him about it. Or was that just an excuse to see him again?

Thursday was the last day they'd work at the site. Max had booked their flight for early Friday morning. Melissa walked through the resort one last time, wondering if she'd get to come back some day when it was completed and see the final result. She knew from the drawings and plans it would be spectacular. Perhaps one day she'd return and take a tour.

The reception Surim had promised was to be held in the large ballroom on the left side of the main entryway of his house. Melissa had brought a suitable dress, but requested time to look for another that afternoon to take advantage of some of the boutiques she'd seen on the main thoroughfare. The limo had been put at her disposal. She stopped on the way back from the new hotel site at a boutique she'd seen each day and found the perfect new gown for the evening. It was floor-length dark blue silk and fit as if it had been made for her. Her black heels would have to do, as she didn't have time to find a shoe store.

After a quick snack in her room, Melissa dressed for the evening. She hoped she looked suitable enough to be entertained by a sheikh. A bit nervous, she was about to go downstairs when there was a knock on her door.

Alaya, Hamid and Nadia stood in the hall grinning at her.

"Oh, you look beautiful. Mummy used to get dressed up to go to parties," Alaya said sadly. "Annis said we could come to see you before we went to bed. I wish you were reading our story tonight."

"Oh, honey, I do, too. But your uncle has put on this party and I don't want to disappoint him, either. Besides, you can read to the other two. That would be good practice for your reading, and give your brother and sister happy memories."

"I guess. Will we see you tomorrow before you go?"

"I'll come up to say goodbye," Melissa promised, already feeling sad to have to bid farewell to these special children. "You'll have to write to me to make sure I keep up with what you are doing. And get your uncle to take photos so I can see how fast you grow."

"I don't want you to go," Hamid said.

"I know. But I'll write to you from England, and then from America. Won't that be fun?"

He shrugged, not looking at all convinced.

"Is anything wrong?" Surim asked, coming down the hall.

The children jumped and moved closer together.

"Not at all, they just came to see me before the party," Melissa said.

She looked up and almost stared. She loved the way Surim looked in his tuxedo; his broad shoulders filled out the suit to perfection. The white ruffled shirt made him seem all the more masculine and exciting. His tanned skin was a startling contrast to the pristine white.

His dark eyes sought hers and held her gaze for a long moment. Her heart fluttered and she became suddenly self-conscious. She'd thought she'd become used to gorgeous men when seeing Valentine family members. None could hold a candle to Surim.

"You look nice, too, Uncle Surim," Alaya said shyly.

Melissa narrowed her eyes sharply, hoping that overture would be returned in the manner meant.

"Thank you, Alaya. It's always nice to have a compliment from a lovely young woman," he said gravely.

Melissa wanted to applaud.

"Nicely said. Now, children, scoot up to bed. I'll see you in the morning," she said.

They each gave her a hug and then walked wide around their uncle and broke into a run for the stairs.

"You intimidate them," Melissa said, falling into step with him as they walked downstairs. The first guests would be arriving momentarily.

"I know little about children," he said.

"Spend time with them. Laugh with them and show them you care. You're their closest relative, right?"

"Their grandmother also lives in Qu'Arim. She is in frail health, however, so cannot care for them."

"Do they see her often?"

"No. They haven't seen her since the funeral."

He stopped at the top of the stairs. Lifting her hand, he kissed the back softly. "You look beautiful tonight."

"Thank you. And thank you for having the reception. I look forward to meeting others from your country."

"I've neglected you during your visit. You should have seen more of Qu'Arim."

"We were here for business," she said, wondering if he realized he still held her hand. "Perhaps I'll come another time and be able to see more."

"Perhaps." He let her hand go and escorted her down the stairs.

Melissa tried to quell the riotous sensations that flooded through her at his touch. It was a good thing they were leaving in the morning. She was infatuated with the man; staying any longer would put her heart at serious risk!

They reached the foyer just as the first guests arrived. Melissa excused herself from the sheikh and went into the reception room. She smiled when she thought about the children coming to see her dressed up. In the few days she'd known them, she'd grown so fond of them. Her heart ached at their loss, and the fact their guardian seemed so remote. They needed to be hugged, laughed with, and convinced they were cherished.

Melissa could relate because of her own father's death. She remembered how she'd felt when she'd finally realized she would never see her father again. All these years, and she still felt the loss. She couldn't imagine losing her mother as well.

The opulent drawing room began to fill. Melissa stood on the sidelines, watching the elegantly dressed women and splendidly attired men enter, talking, laughing softly. It was a wonderful gathering. She wondered whom among them Surim counted as close friends. Did he do what her friends did—go clubbing, or skiing? Was he a water buff, living so close to the Gulf? Or did he prefer more challenging activities like mountain climbing? Did he ever go into the desert and watch the stars from places far from man-made lights? She wished she knew more about her enigmatic host. For a moment she was lost in a daydream of Surim taking her to a quiet, secluded spot to share his thoughts and dreams with her.

"Madam?" A stately gentleman stood next to her.

"Yes?" Melissa smiled. He appeared to be in his late seventies, but still had a luxurious head of thick gray hair. His skin looked like burnished teak.

"His Excellency said you are from England. I am to make myself available to you for anything you may require," he said with a slight bow. "I am Asid ibn Tarvor at your service. I spent many years in England. I am especially fond of your Lake District."

"As am I," Melissa said with a smile. "How nice to meet you."

"Have you been long in Qu'Arim?"

"No, only a few days, and I've been working with the sheikh, though I have managed a few afternoons at the beach. What I've seen of the country is amazing."

Asid took her around, introducing her to others. After a brief exchange each time, they'd move on to the next group until Melissa felt she'd met everyone there.

They stopped near a small alcove.

"Have you visited one of our pearl farms?" Asid asked.

Melissa shook her head. Just then she caught a glimpse of Surim escorting a lovely woman whose dark hair was elaborately coiffed and who wore a beautiful golden gown that enhanced her voluptuous figure.

Asid noticed her glance and smiled. "Ah, Delleah. She is lovely, do you not think? It is time Surim took a wife."

Melissa nodded politely at the comment. Was this the woman he would marry? Or was he still looking?

She hoped the latter; she'd hate to think he was promised

to someone and kissed her! But, if Delleah was the woman Surim chose, she would make a beautiful wife. They were a stunning couple.

"I see Asid found you," Surim said as he and the woman at his side stopped in front of Melissa.

"Indeed, it was most kind of you to think about me. I would have been fine on my own, but Asid and I have had a most delightful discussion." She smiled politely at the woman at his side.

"May I present Delleah bin Attulla. Delleah, a friend from England, Melissa Fox. She is proving invaluable in the work we are doing at the new resort."

"Hardly that," Melissa said, greeting the woman.

Delleah's flashing dark eyes and pout did not bode well for an instant friendship. She shook Melissa's hand rapidly, then tucked her own into the crook of Surim's arm. "I'm sure Surim appreciates your working with the Englishman to facilitate the building of his pet project." She smiled at him. "Do let's move on—I want to talk to the ambassador."

Surim inclined his head slightly, then turned to escort her to a small group nearby.

"Beautiful woman," Asid said. "She will make him a fine wife and give him many sons."

"Always with boys," Melissa grumbled, feeling a tad jealous as she watched them walk away. She knew there could never be anything between her and Surim, but earlier he'd kissed her hand and told her she was beautiful.

Good grief, girl, she told herself, get a grip! She should be soaking up every moment of this fabulous gathering and not pining over something that could not be.

"Ah, but Surim needs sons to carry on the ruling of our country. He was an only child. What would we do if he dies before he had an heir?"

"Elect someone new," she said.

Hearing the intake of breath at her comment, she looked at Asid and smiled ruefully. "Sorry, western thinking. Let's hope Surim lives many more years and has a dozen sons."

"Perhaps that would be excessive," Asid murmured, his eyes twinkling.

Melissa laughed. "Tell me about your favorite spot in the Lake District," she said.

Asid proved to be entertaining, and Melissa enjoyed their conversation. She was very aware of Surim whenever she spotted him across the room, however, and once stopped mid-sentence to stare when he laughed at something someone had said. It was the first time she'd heard him laugh. His face softened a fraction, lost that austere façade she was used to seeing. And made her heart flip over. She turned so she couldn't see him.

"Would you care to walk in the garden? It grows warm in here," Asid said.

"I should love to. I've been in it a couple of times at night. The lighting makes it easy to walk through and the cooler night air is wonderful to enjoy."

Once away from the crowd, it grew quiet.

"You leave for England in the morning, I believe Surim told me," Asid said as they strolled among the flowers.

"That's right," Melissa said. "I shall be sorry to return to rain and cold after the wonderful climate here. But duty calls."

"You work with Max Valentine, I believe."

"Only temporarily. I'm filling in until my new job starts in February. I'll be going to America then."

"The women in our country are not so well traveled as in England."

Just then a wail sounded from the upper floor.

She turned, searching the windows, seeing a light go on on the top floor.

"Hamid," she said quietly. "Excuse me, Asid. I think I'll go see if I can help. Thanks for your company. I enjoyed myself tremendously. But a little boy needs me."

Without waiting for him to respond, Melissa turned and fled to the house, only slowing her pace to a rapid walk through the gathering of guests, then almost running up the stairs.

The closer she approached the nursery, the louder the screams sounded. She burst into Hamid's bedroom to see Annis standing beside the bed, shaking his shoulder in an attempt to awaken him, speaking in Arabic. Alaya bumped into Melissa, peering into the room.

"He woke me," she complained.

Melissa went to the bed, gently moved Annis aside and sat on the mattress, gathering the little boy into her arms.

"There, there, sweetie, it's all right. Wake up. You're having a nightmare, but you're all right. Wake up, Hamid," she crooned as she rocked him back and forth.

He pushed back a little and quieted down, then snuggled against Melissa. Soon his crying eased.

"Mummy?" he said bewildered.

"No, sweetie, it's Melissa. You're at your cousin Surim's house, remember?"

"I want Mummy," he wailed.

"Shh. Your sister is here and I'm here. You're fine."

"What is going on?" Surim asked from the doorway. Delleah stood beside him, looking around the room, and then at the children.

Annis spoke rapidly in Arabic. Delleah listened avidly.

"Enough," Surim said in English.

"The sooner you send them off to boarding school, the better, Surim," Delleah said.

Hamid stopped crying and looked at Surim.

Alaya turned, stunned. "You're sending us away?" she asked.

Melissa could have slapped Delleah. How cruel of her to make that comment, especially in English. She looked at Surim.

He couldn't send them from this safe haven. They'd lost their home, their parents—he couldn't split them up so they lost each other as well.

"Surim," she began, not sure what she would say, but something to plead for the children.

"I said enough!"

Surim turned to Delleah and spoke to her in Arabic. "I told you that in confidence. Is this how you treat such information?"

She looked stricken. It was well he knew this before their relationship moved any further. Trust was important to him. No matter what Delleah's agenda, and he had a strong suspicion what that was, it did not excuse such a lapse.

"I misspoke. I apologize," she said.

"If you will excuse me, I will deal with my cousins. You may return to the reception. Do not tell anyone of what went on here. Can I trust you this time?" He knew Annis listened, but didn't care. She would be discreet. And his anger was growing that Delleah would deliberately try to force his hand by speaking in English in front of the children.

He was equally aware of Hamid and Alaya drawing closer to Melissa. She held the little boy on her lap now, soothing him. All three stared at him as if he were a stranger.

"As you wish, Surim," Delleah said in a subdued voice. She turned and left without another word.

"What happened?" he asked Annis.

"The boy was screaming, I came in to waken him, but he was sound asleep, screaming. Ayyeee, it was terrible. Then miss came in and spoke to him in English and woke him up."

"You speak English; why didn't you talk to him in that language?"

"My English is not so good. And when I get upset, I forget it," she said, her eyes downcast.

Surim felt his frustration ratchet up another notch. Annis had been his cousin Mara's nanny when she was growing up. And he knew how well Mara had spoken English even before she'd moved to live in England. He had expected her mother to provide the best person for her grandchildren. Maybe three children were too much. Annis had had only Mara when she was growing up. And she'd been much younger.

"You may leave, Annis," he said. "We'll handle this."

Annis bowed slightly and scurried from the room.

He faced Melissa and the children. Only Nadia was missing. He hoped she'd slept through the whole thing.

Melissa spoke in French. "Please reassure these children you are not sending them away. They lost one home already; they can't lose another this soon. Plus, you'll never find a boarding school that would take all three together. Please do not separate them; they need each other as they recover from the loss of their parents."

"And what do you suggest I do instead?" he replied in the same language.

"I don't know. Get someone who speaks English to help them in this transition time."

He stared at her for a long moment. The answer to the situation lay with her. "Very well, I'll let them stay if you stay to care for them."

"What?"

The children looked at her. Melissa knew her voice had gone up several decibels, but the suggestion was preposterous.

"I can't stay here. I have a job waiting in America. I'm starting in a few weeks."

"Stay and help the children adjust," he suggested. "If you're serious about their needing help in the transition. It will also give you time to see more of my country. You would not have total care of them; we have Annis. But you could help them adjust."

Melissa tried to think. It was mid-January. She had a few weeks before she was due in Boston. She could stay until then.

How long would it take for the children to feel more at home? Could they find another English-speaking woman to help with the transition?

What would Max say? She'd committed to working with him until it was time to leave for America. It had been a fill-in job, she knew, but she'd made a commitment.

"Melissa, are we going to be sent away?" Alaya asked.

"No," Melissa said, one look at the children and her mind instantly made up. This was more important. Max would understand—she hoped.

She looked at Surim. "I'll stay."

CHAPTER FOUR

MELISSA couldn't believe she'd just committed to staying in Qu'Arim. She was scheduled to return to London in the morning with Max. She still had all her packing to do for her move to America. She'd never in her wildest imagination thought about remaining in Qu'Arim for another two or three weeks.

Max was another problem. She would be leaving him in the lurch if she didn't return. But her mind was made up. Second thoughts weren't going to change it. She couldn't let these sweet children be shuffled off to a boarding school.

"After the children are settled in bed, join me in the study. We'll discuss your stay, and then return to the reception," Surim said formally. With a slight bow, he left.

Alaya watched until he'd gone, then flung her arms around Melissa's neck. "Thank you! We'd love to have you look after us!"

"You're going to be our new mummy?" Hamid asked.

"No, darling, just a temporary visitor." For right now, it looked as if she was staying.

"Let's get some warmed milk with cinnamon and after you drink that you'll be ready to go back to bed with no more nightmares," she said to Hamid.

"Really?" The little boy's lower lip wobbled. "I get so scared. I think a truck is going to crash into me."

"It won't happen, sweetie. The milk will chase away the

nightmares and you'll sleep as good as Nadia," Melissa said, hoping he wouldn't have another this night.

Half an hour later Melissa went back downstairs. The noise level from the voices and the quartet playing in the background rose as she came closer to the ground floor. She looked around, trying to figure out where Surim's study would be located. She knew little about the house except for the third floor and the living room and dining room.

There was an open door down the hall from the reception room, a light shining out. She went toward it.

"Hold a moment, please," a voice called behind her.

Melissa turned. It was Delleah. The woman seemed to glide along as she walked. Her dress was lovely, but her expression was definitely not.

"I'm looking for His Excellency. He asked me to join him in his study," Melissa said. Surely Delleah would know the layout of the house.

"For what purpose?" Delleah asked.

Melissa raised her eyebrows in surprise. "I think that is between us."

Delleah glanced up the stairs. "About those children?"

"It's a private matter," Melissa said, getting annoyed with the woman. If she were so close to Surim, let him answer her questions.

"Private? I thought you just met His Excellency."

"We met on Sunday when Max Valentine and I arrived. If you'll excuse me." Melissa tried to break away without appearing too rude.

"The sooner he gets rid of those children, the better it will be. He is too busy to be encumbered with orphans," Delleah said.

That struck Melissa's hot button. "Their being alone in the world is all the more reason he should pay them attention," she said, quietly but fiercely. "They have recently lost their mother and father. He is their cousin and a link to their parents and he should lavish attention on them until they've recovered from the initial devastation of all they've been through."

Delleah waved a dismissive hand. "A suitable school will do wonders."

"Were you sent away to school?" Melissa asked. What was it with these people that they were so quick to send away the children?

"I was not so fortunate. But many of our children are sent to fine schools. It is not a horrible choice, but enriching," Delleah said. "I plan to send my children to France for schooling. They will get a more cosmopolitan education there then here."

"At age five and two children don't need to be cosmopolitan. Excuse me, I need to find Surim."

"Surim? You know him so well you call him by name?" Delleah clearly didn't like the situation.

Melissa wished she could take back the words. He'd asked her to call him by his name as a friend of Max's. Maybe in public he would wish for more formality. Something she should check on.

"I'll show you the study," Delleah said, walking past Melissa and heading down the hall toward the open door.

Melissa followed her, wondering what the woman was up to. She didn't seem the friendliest person she'd met. And she definitely wasn't Melissa's idea of a good mother. What would her children be like? If she had them with Surim, they'd be gorgeous, Melissa knew that much. But out of sight most of the time?

"Surim, we miss you," Delleah said when she stopped in the doorway. "When your business is finished with the Englishwoman, do rejoin us."

Surim rose from behind a desk, his expression neutral, and crossed to the door. "I would not neglect my guests except for matters of utmost importance. I'll be there shortly. Melissa, please come in. Delleah, if you'll excuse us."

He shut the door behind Melissa, almost in Delleah's face.

"Come and sit," Surim invited, motioning to the comfortable chairs near the windows. The faint illumination from the gardens cast a warm light on the shrubs and flowers visible through the tall windows.

Melissa sat and waited, her nerves on edge.

"I will speak to Max, if you like," Surim offered, sitting in the chair near hers.

"I'll tell him. As soon as we finalize arrangements. I can still do the translations from here, if he wishes, and if you will permit. I hate to leave a job in the middle of it," she said, hoping it would be agreeable with both men. Even if she had to do it after the children were in bed at night, she'd be able to keep up. Most of the plans had been finalized this week, so Melissa didn't expect a lot of translations in the next few weeks.

"I have committed to a new post in mid-February, however," she said.

"Cancel it," Surim ordered.

Melissa blinked. "No, I am quite looking forward to it. Besides, that gives me almost a month to get the children settled."

He leaned back and steepled his hands, resting his chin on his fingertips. "Annis was the children's mother's nurse. She's a generation removed now, but longs to raise these children. I hope working together you two can make a difference with the children."

"I'll do my best."

"And if they are not settled by the time your next commitment comes?"

"I'm sure you could find someone. Who wouldn't wish to work here? The accommodations are lovely. I think women will be falling all over themselves for the assignment."

"Yet you are not," he commented.

"I have a position lined up." For a second Melissa wondered if she should reconsider. Granted, she'd told the McDonalds she'd be there when their current nanny married, but Qu'Arim was nothing like Boston. If she extended her stay, she'd have the tropical setting to enjoy all year instead of living in months of winter each year. She already knew these children. She remembered the McDonald children; they'd stayed for two weeks. But they didn't need her as much as the three upstairs did.

Not that Surim had offered her the nanny's position. That stayed with Annis. She would stay to help out Max's friend, then head for Boston.

He studied her for a moment. Melissa pushed away her doubts. She could help for a short time. Though she knew if she wanted a shot at getting any concessions, now was the time, before he took her for granted.

"There are a couple of conditions to my staying," she said slowly, testing his reaction.

Surim continued to stare at her. She wished she knew what he was thinking.

Lowering his hands, he inclined his head slightly. "And those are?" No telling his thoughts from his voice.

"More involvement from you, for starters," she said audaciously. It was so important for him to spend time getting to know these children. Nannies were employees after all. And she was a stranger. Much as she loved working with children, they weren't her family or Annis's. These children were Surim's now.

That seemed to surprise him. "I lead a very busy life."

She nodded. "I'm sure, but you are in charge of that life. Carve out some time to spend with your children."

"They are not—"

Melissa raised a hand, knowing if she survived this interview, it would be a miracle. But she didn't care. She was fighting for those precious children upstairs.

"They are not your biological children, granted, but they are now your kids. You are their guardian, which makes you their parental figure. You'll have more influence on their lives than anyone else. I think it's important you get to know them, and let them get to know you."

"They are afraid of me," he said slowly.

"They don't know you. I think they're shy, scared and unhappy. And your announcement tonight about sending them away didn't help."

"It was not my announcement," he retorted.

Melissa waved her hand as if brushing the comment away. "And your other demands?"

"They don't get on well with Annis. Something should be worked out to make sure they can get along better before the children become too resentful. I think Annis is a bit over-whelmed—sad herself over the death of their mother. But they need to work together."

"Agreed. Suggestions?" he asked.

"I thought she could start teaching them Arabic. And have them teach her more English. Give them both a place, and help bridge the differences."

"Easily handled. Is that it?" he asked.

"One more thing. I think it's very important that they eat with you as family at least once or twice a week. Which will foster company manners, and get them used to their position in their society when they are older."

"A two-year-old at dinner? Will she dress?" The sarcasm was unmistakable.

Melissa held her ground. "I'll see about that. Maybe she should start at age three or four. But Hamid and Alaya are old enough. This is their culture, their history, their family. They will get their family values and traditions from you. It's important"

Surim nodded.

"And you would join us. Perhaps even get Annis to teach you some Arabic."

"I would like to, though I won't be here long enough to learn much. Still, it's a good idea; I can learn with them."

"Any other conditions?" he asked.

"No. Shall I get a uniform?"

He looked startled. "You are not an employee; you would remain my guest while you are here. I hope you'll have time to see more of Qu'Arim and enjoy yourself as well as help me out with the children."

"Oh." She hadn't expected that. She'd thought she'd be a sub-nanny or something. This changed things. For a moment the warmth of his kiss flashed through her mind. She was to remain a guest!

"Would that be a hardship?"

She smiled and shook her head. "Of course not; I had thought it a job."

"No. So, when I'm home, I will hope you will join me for meals. You can give me an update on their progress. And be the buffer between us on the nights they dine with us."

Melissa felt a surge of excitement. She would make the most of her weeks as a guest and see as much of the country as she could. Maybe Surim would take her—

He rose. "If that is all, I should return to my guests."

Melissa stood as well. She was a foolish woman if she thought this busy man would take time to show her the countryside. She admonished herself not to let her daydreams carry her away.

"I'll find Max and let him know I'm not returning home with him in the morning," she said, wondering if he would advise against her staying.

The sheikh escorted her back to the reception room. Delleah stood near the doorway, talking with friends and keeping her eyes on the door.

Melissa scarcely noticed as she entered and began to search for Max. She saw him near the opened French doors, in deep discussion with several men. Feeling a bit self-conscious, Melissa walked to the group, hoping to catch Max's eye and get him alone for a moment or two. She felt as if she were on a tilt-a-wheel: one moment she was a translator preparing to leave, now she was a guest of the sheikh's, staying for several weeks.

Max noticed her and excused himself from the group to join Melissa. "Something up?" he asked.

"Change in plans. The sheikh asked me to stay a little longer, to help with getting the children used to living here."

"What do you mean?"

She explained. Ending with, "Do you think I'm doing the right thing? And what about your translations? Could I do them from here and fax you the English?"

Max thought carefully before answering. "Melissa, you're the only one who can decide if it's the right thing. But you'll have a chance to see more of the country, unless I miss my guess. Surim's a wonderful host. But will you spend too much time with the children to do translations?"

"I don't think so. It's not as if I'm in charge of them. I'll do whatever is needed from here and fax you the results. That way there won't be any delays. It's been working that you got the faxed documents and I translated. Now, I'll just translate first. It's only for a few weeks. You know I start my new job in America in mid-February."

"Does Surim know?"

"I told him. If it looks as if the children aren't getting settled, he'll have plenty of time to find another qualified woman to help. It beats his other idea of shipping them off to some boarding school. Nadia is only two!"

"Well, if you're sure," Max said, concern creasing his forehead.

Melissa was anything but sure she was making a good decision. But the thought of the children wiped all doubts from her mind. She knew she could help get them acclimated to their new circumstances.

The party lost some of its luster for her as she began to catalog all the things she needed to do. Not sure she'd see Max in the morning before she left, she asked him to reassure her mother. She'd contact her in the morning. She found Asid ibn Tarvor to thank him for his courtesies and then left the reception to return to her room. It was late and she had things to think about. But her last thoughts, just before she drifted off to sleep, were of Surim.

Melissa awoke early the next morning, and quickly donned a skirt and blouse. She'd have to call her mother today to tell her the change in plans and to ask her to send some clothes. The outfits she'd brought were much more suitable to an office than spending time with children.

Once dressed, she quickly went upstairs. Hamid and Nadia were quietly playing in the nursery. The table was set for breakfast, but the food hadn't arrived. Nadia saw her first.

"Melissa!" She jumped up and ran to her. "Are you going to eat with us?"

Hamid rose and came over. "Are you really staying like you said last night?"

"I am to both. We'll have breakfast first, then plan our week. Where's Alaya?"

"She's still sleeping," Hamid said. "Shall I go and wake her up?"

Annis came into the room and looked surprised to see Melissa. "Did you come to see the children?" She looked around, noticing Alaya was absent.

"Actually, I came to have breakfast with them," Melissa said. Had no one told her of the change in plans?

"I will see the kitchen sends up more food," Annis said, clearly puzzled. "I hope we will not delay your departure."

"I think His Excellency needs to discuss things with you," Melissa said carefully, not wanting to offend Annis. "I'm staying for a few weeks to help with the children. I hope that together we can make the transition easier for them. It's hard losing their parents and then their home, and it will take a while before this feels like home for them."

"Are you really staying?" Alaya asked from the doorway. She was already dressed in shorts and a top and wore sandals. She smiled hopefully at Melissa.

"Just for a little while. I have to leave for America in February."

"We want you to stay forever," Hamid said enthusiastically.

Melissa smiled and tousled his hair. "I'll be here for a long visit. I shall love spending time with all three of you. You'll have to tell me all you know about Qu'Arim. Maybe we can go exploring." She loved seeing the children's delighted faces. "First, though, let's eat and then we'll make plans."

It was the middle of the school year at home, and Melissa suspected the children had had little schooling since their arrival. Not that she would have expected them to work over the Christmas holidays, but it was January, time to get back into a routine. She'd ask Annis what provisions had been made for their education. Nadia was far too young for lessons, except the fun kind that would teach her colors, shapes and numbers. Would the sheikh hire a governess or tutor? Once they knew enough Arabic, they could attend the local schools.

The three children were delighted with Melissa's company. Breakfast was enjoyable, and each ate everything on their plate. Annis did not remain, but left as soon as the meal had been served from the kitchen. Melissa hoped her feelings weren't hurt. She had to get her involved as she would be the one with them after Melissa left.

By four o'clock, the younger children were up from naps. Alaya had read a good portion of a new book while they slept. Now it was time for fun. Melissa had them get ready to go for a short swim. She wanted to assess the abilities of the children and get them into the fresh air and sunshine. They'd been patient all day

while she and Annis had discussed their care and education.
Melissa hoped the swim would be reward enough.

"For you, Miss Fox." One of the liveried servants brought
an envelope on a small silver tray.

Feeling like the lady of the manor, Melissa took it and
opened it.

'Max safely on his way. I am tied up and will be unable to
be home for dinner.' It was signed 'Surim'.

She studied the bold script for a long moment, feeling a
free-fall sensation in her stomach. She was disappointed. She'd
hoped to see him today. That was obviously out of the question.

Still she stared at the note. She'd been very careful not to
call him by name since Delleah had noticed. Not wishing to
presume on his relationship with her new stepbrother, she'd
kept their brief contact formal.

Now he signed the note with his name. Could she continue
to call him Surim? Or keep the more formal title?

With a sigh, she folded the paper and put it in her pocket.
Nothing she had to decide today.

By the time the children were in bed that night, Melissa was
tired enough to go to bed herself. Thinking a quick walk in the
gardens would refresh her, she slipped out from the opened
French doors in the living room.

The day had gone well. Annis had been happy to learn
Melissa was staying for a few weeks with the sole goal of
helping the children adjust. She had been pleased when Melissa
had asked her to teach them all Arabic.

"Enough for the children to be able to communicate on a basic
level. Reading and writing can wait for school, though I suspect
Hamid and Nadia will find it easier if they start school knowing
basics. Alaya is already reading English and writing composi-
tions. I expect learning Arabic will be more difficult for her."

"Do they wish to learn?" Annis asked, clearly puzzled.

"This will be their home, won't it? They need to speak the language. Who better to teach them? I understand you were the children's mother's nanny. They would so love to hear about her when she was growing up. You can practice Arabic with them when telling them of her childhood."

"We do not speak of her," Annis had said.

"Why ever not?"

Annis seemed to hesitate, frowning. "So not to remind the children of their loss."

"It would be good for the children to hear as much about their parents as they can, to keep them alive in their memory and so they'll know others remember them fondly. With love," explained Melissa gently. "I hope to arrange a visit with their grandmother to see pictures of their mother when she was younger."

Annis nodded. "There were many. I have some myself. Mara was such a special child."

"Then share that memory with her children. You'll find they will respond positively."

By the time she relaxed in the twilight, Melissa felt better than she had all day. This temporary stay would work out perfectly. She loved working with the children. She just hoped Surim would find time in his schedule to spend with them. He wouldn't be able to help falling in love with them.

"I see you have found a favorite spot of mine," a voice said.

Startled, Melissa smiled when Surim stepped from the darkness into the subdued light from the garden path. "I love your gardens. You know the English—we are always growing flowers. This garden is beautiful."

"I do not claim credit," he said, sitting beside her on the bench. "I have excellent gardeners who take care of that. The fragrances are a delight to the senses, as are the colors and designs of the plants."

"A haven," she murmured, acutely aware of him so close.

Now her heart was starting to race. She had better become immune to his charm or she was in serious trouble.

"Exactly." He was silent for a moment. "I have another."

"Another what?"

"Haven. It's in the desert, isolated, wild, beautiful. A small oasis deep in the interior. From time to time I go there to remember where our people came from. The hectic modern life is inevitable, but we were a nomadic people, calling the desert home. I like to return to remember."

"I bet it's beautiful."

"Some find it so. Others find it stark and unappealing."

Melissa sighed, imagining the scene. "I should love to see some of the desert. Your capital is as modern as London. And doesn't feel much different, except for the signs in Arabic. But to visit the desert, that would be quite different."

He smiled. She caught her breath and looked away before she did something idiotic.

"Perhaps we'll find time before you leave."

"I should enjoy that," she said primly, belying the joy that flared at the prospect. Then she turned to face him.

"Do you normally return home from work so late?" she asked. She knew running a country was a bit different from a job in banking, but these hours seemed a bit excessive.

"Tonight was another business dinner, with much negotiations and posturing. The ancient protocols are wearing."

"You're the man in charge—change them," she said flippantly. Being near him upset her sense of balance. She could stare at the man for hours, and probably find something new at each second. Like the few gray strands at his temples. He was too young to be going gray. Probably the stress of his position.

"How were the children?" he asked. "Run you ragged yet?"

"After one day? Hardly. They have lots of energy; the secret is to channel it and let it run. We made progress, I think. They like the beach. And Annis was a bit more relaxed around them today."

"Now they are in bed."

"Of course, and have been for more than a couple of hours. I need to check on them. Care to join me?"

He rose and nodded. As the light shone on his face Melissa saw the fatigue. It was not her place to make personal comments, but she thought he could use a good night's sleep. She hoped Hamid wouldn't disrupt that tonight.

Annis was still sitting in the nursery, crocheting. She rose when Surim entered, but he motioned her to resume her seat.

"All is well?" he asked in Arabic.

"They sleep. After the running around they did today, I expect they won't wake until morning," she replied. With a glance at Melissa, she continued, "Miss wishes for me to teach them Arabic."

"A good idea. Even if they don't remain here all their lives, they are from this country; it is appropriate that they learn our language and our customs. You would do well to teach them."

"She wishes to learn as well," Annis added.

"Is that a problem?"

"No. Will she be staying long?"

"I have hopes she will stay until the children are settled. She has other commitments in February. Do you think she is helping?"

"Yes. They were easier to deal with today. Maybe she could stay longer?"

"It is too early to say, but I also hope she will stay longer." He turned to look at Melissa, knowing she'd have something to say to his plans if she knew of them.

Melissa had crossed to the doorway to Hamid's room, pausing for a moment before entering. Surim followed in time to see her cover the little boy with a light blanket.

Hamid stirred. "Mummy?" he said, half asleep.

"No, darling. Mummy is in heaven. It's Melissa. You're safe. You'll always be safe here." She patted his arm gently. Hamid snuggled down and went back to sleep.

When she turned, she saw Surim.

"He's afraid, that's why he has nightmares. He misses his parents, but the nightmares are of a truck smashing into him."

"As the truck did his parents," Surim said, his face in shadow.

Melissa nodded. "As he imagines it. I think he will gradually get over this stage. But it may take a while."

"So we can expect more screams in the night," Surim said.

"Not expect, but maybe not be surprised by them," she said. "But I'm hoping with a regime of lessons and outdoor activities, they'll all be so tired at night, they'll sleep through. They are so fortunate to be here where the weather is conducive to playing outside. At home it's cold and rainy."

"We get our share of rain. But rarely does it get cold. If you need anything for the children, ask Annis. She'll get it for you."

"Tomorrow, you'll spend some time with them?"

Surim glanced at Hamid. He couldn't remember being that young. What did a grown man talk to a small child about?

"I have a meeting at ten."

"On Saturday? At least have breakfast with them," Melissa suggested. "We can eat at eight, and finish in plenty of time."

Surim nodded. "I'll see about breakfast. You will be there as well."

"Of course. If you have no time tomorrow, how about Sunday? You could come to the beach with us. The children love the water and playing on the sand. There are a lot of activities that include all three, despite the difference in their ages."

Surim mentally sorted through the things he'd planned for Sunday. Discarding them, he agreed. It was worth it, he decided a moment later, when Melissa gave him a delighted smile. He knew he stared longer than necessary, but her expressions fascinated him. Her smile was open and joyful. He suspected she didn't have a clue how to dissemble or hide her feelings. She was different from most of the women he knew. Maybe he'd take the time to get to know her better and find a way to get her to stay.

CHAPTER FIVE

PROMPTLY at eight the next morning Melissa arrived at the nursery. The children were already dressed and playing a game of keep away, with little Nadia the one in the middle. They greeted Melissa and ran over to her. Nadia lifted her arms to be picked up. Melissa scooped her up, hugged her and then held her as she greeted the other children.

"We're so hungry. Once you arrived, Annis said we could eat," Alaya said.

The table had been set for four, but there was ample room to add place settings. Melissa called to Annis.

"Good morning," the older woman said as she entered. She looked at the children, then back at Melissa. "Is there something wrong?"

"We'll need another place setting at the table," Melissa said. "Do we have the utensils here, or do we need to call down to the kitchen?"

"There are additional settings in the cupboard," Annis indicated. "But why? I will take a tray in my room. You eat with the children."

"His Excellency will be joining us."

"Who?" Hamid asked.

"Your uncle Surim," Melissa said. She put Nadia down and went to the cupboard.

There was whispering behind her. She gathered what she needed and turned to see the three children aligned together, a mutinous look on their respective faces.

"We don't want him here," Alaya said.

"He doesn't like us, so we don't like him," Hamid added.

"Nonsense," Melissa said, returning to the table and quickly setting an additional place. "You all just need to get to know one another."

"He wants to send us away," Alaya said.

"Can we come live with you?" Hamid asked.

"Oh, sweetie, I don't have a place of my own. Besides, I'm sure that would never be allowed. Let's do our best to get to know him. He may surprise you." Melissa hoped so. From what she'd seen thus far, Surim was much more suited in the seat of power than in the nursery. She hoped she'd be surprised.

He arrived a few minutes later. Formally greeting each child, he turned to her and raised an eyebrow, as if asking if she was happy with his presence.

"Good morning. We're glad you could join us," Melissa said. She couldn't help being slightly amused at his expression. Honestly, what would it take to get him to relax?

"No, we're not," Hamid muttered, scowling.

Surim's eyes met hers in amusement as he heard Hamid's comment. "So we eat? I do have a meeting at ten I can't be late to."

"We'll be finished long before then," she assured him.

They sat at the table, Surim at one end, Melissa at the other, with Alaya next to her and Nadia beyond. Hamid sat on the other side. Almost like a family, Melissa thought as she began to serve the English breakfast the kitchen supplied to the children. She gave a heaping portion to Surim, smaller portions to the children. The milk had been poured. The carafe of hot coffee was near Surim's place. Melissa wondered for a moment if he would pour his own, or did he expect her to jump up to serve him?

To her relief, he poured a cup and offered her the carafe. She declined, preferring tea.

"So what are your plans for the day?" Surim asked her.

"Children, what are we doing today?" Melissa asked, hoping to involve them in the conversation, wishing Surim had asked them, not her.

Silence met her question; all three looked at her with entreaty in their eyes.

"Nadia?" she prompted.

"Going to the beach," she said quietly.

"Right." Melissa smiled, wishing something would break the silence. "And what's your favorite part of the beach, Hamid?"

He stared at his plate. "Swimming," he said.

Exasperated, Melissa glanced at Surim. He was calmly eating. She couldn't give a guess to his feelings; his expression was totally impassive.

"Alaya, did you finish your letters to your friends? Maybe Uncle Surim could post them on his way into work today?"

"Why does he have to work on Saturday?" Alaya asked Melissa.

"Ask him, why don't you?"

The child hesitated, then turned to face Surim. "Why do you work on Saturday? My father didn't. He spent Saturdays with Mummy and us. I thought unless you work in a shop or something, Saturdays and Sundays were for family."

"Some things don't wait. There will be other Saturdays when we can spend the day together. What would you like to do if I didn't have to work?"

Alaya shrugged. "Nothing special. Going to the beach is nice. Especially in January." She turned back to Melissa. "I told my friends that in the letter. They'll be so envious."

"I worked in Switzerland before coming here. And there's lots of snow there now. I much prefer warmer climates!" Melissa said, smiling at the girl.

"I'd rather be home," Hamid muttered.

"This is your home, now," Surim said.

"No, it's not. And you want to send us away," Hamid replied, glaring at Surim.

"I want to go home," Nadia said. She pushed away her plate and knocked her milk glass, sending a cascade of white liquid off the table and right into Surim's lap.

For a stunned moment, no one moved. All three children looked at Surim in horror. Nadia's eyes filled with tears.

"I sorry." She began to cry.

"No sense crying over spilt milk," Melissa said calmly, jumping up to go to the child. She handed Surim another napkin and swept Nadia up into her arms. "Don't cry, sweetie, we all know it was an accident. No harm done."

She glanced at Surim. His suit definitely needed a cleaning before he could wear it in public. How he reacted to this mishap would give her the best clue as to how he was going to deal with the children. She hoped he wouldn't get angry over the two-year-old's accident.

He didn't. Slowly he rose, blotting the liquid from the trousers.

"It appears I need to change before I leave for my meeting." With that, he turned and left.

Nadia hugged Melissa. "It accident," she said.

"Of course it was, sweetie. Uncle Surim knows that. He wasn't even mad."

"Yes, he was," Hamid said. "Now he'll send us away for sure. What if we can't all go to the same school?"

For a moment Melissa thought he was going to start crying as well.

"He's not sending you away. I'm here to make sure that doesn't happen. His inviting me to stay doesn't sound like someone sending you away. Now finish eating or you won't have enough energy to play at the beach.

She resettled the children and the meal passed without further mishap.

Once finished, she asked Annis to watch them for a moment and dashed down the stairs, hoping to find Surim before he left.

When she reached the ground floor, she looked around. No sign of him, but she didn't expect him to be hanging around the foyer. She walked down the hall to the study. The door was open and he was standing by his desk, putting folders into his briefcase.

"Do you have a moment?" Melissa asked.

He turned and nodded. "But only a minute. I need to leave soon."

"I know. I wanted to apologize for the mishap this morning. She's only two."

"Am I such an ogre I can't recognize a child's accident?"

"I'm not saying you are, but you have to admit you don't have a lot of experience around children."

"Perhaps it would be better to wait until they are older before taking our meals together," he said, turning back to the briefcase.

Melissa stepped into the room. She was beginning to get a bit annoyed with the refrain.

"It's never too early for children to be part of a family, especially at meals. They were nervous. They'll do better when they get used to you."

"They don't like me," he said calmly. "I heard them from the hall."

For a stunned moment Melissa wondered if their careless comments had actually hurt Surim. She dismissed it. He was an adult; he knew children said things in the heat of the moment. But for a moment she wanted to reach out and reassure him.

"They don't *know* you," she said. "Remember back when you were little. You wanted to be grown up and do things with adults. But it was hard."

"I do not remember back when I was two," he said.

"Then use your imagination!"

He closed his case and looked at her.

"They are well cared for, have everything they could need."

"No, they don't. They need love. They need someone who is interested in them, in what they are doing, what they think, what they are learning."

"You're there for that."

"Not for long! They need family."

Surim took a moment to consider her passionate statement. She hardly knew the children upstairs, yet she was definitely their advocate. He liked the way she flared up in their defense. Her eyes sparkled, color flooded her cheeks. She had passion and determination. For a moment he was struck with how beautiful she looked. Would she flare in passion for the right man? What would Melissa look like in bed?

He looked away, not liking his thoughts. Too often over the last few days he'd caught himself thinking about his guest. She was leaving in a few weeks. Maybe asking her to stay had been a mistake.

For a moment, he tried to imagine being two and having just lost his parents. He'd been spared that. His parents hadn't died until he was seventeen. Not that they had spent much time with him. He'd gone off to school in England at age nine. He'd been lonely and homesick, but had hidden the fact from the world. Outwardly, he'd projected an image of self-sufficiency. Internally, he'd been a small boy longing for home and parents. Remembering would help him empathize with the children.

"I don't know how to make them feel wanted," he said slowly. He knew how to run his country, after years of trial and error; years of frustration and triumphs. But he didn't know how to relate to a two-year-old girl. He wasn't someone used to failure. Somehow, he had to learn to relate to them.

And focus on them. Not on the temporary guest who would be leaving in February.

Melissa nodded. "The only suggestion I can make is to spend more time with them. Today would have been good going to the beach. Can you join us later? Nadia naps after lunch, while the others play quietly. But we could go back after that."

The last thing Surim had expected when he'd awoken this morning was to cancel plans to take an excursion to the beach. He didn't have time to rearrange his entire schedule to deal with three children.

Yet they were Mara's children. And if he didn't get to know them now, then when?

"If I can arrange it, I'll join you." He'd have to call Delleah and cancel their plans for dinner. Not that it would be a hardship. He knew she had hopes of marriage, but after the way she'd betrayed his confidence he'd had second thoughts.

She had seemed suitable. Yet there were many suitable women available. It would be best to make haste slowly, as his teacher in England had often said.

"One more thing before you go. Can we arrange a time to take them to see their grandmother? I think that would help with the transition. I know you said she's in frail health, but a short visit would be all right, wouldn't it?" she asked.

"I will call and make arrangements."

"That would be perfect. I'll coach them on manners and hope she doesn't offer milk and biscuits in the drawing room," Melissa said, teasing.

He looked away before he forgot she was a guest in his home and reached out to kiss her. Her mouth was eminently kissable.

"She does speak English, doesn't she?" Melissa asked.

"Yes, quite well. She visited the children in England. Since the death of her daughter, however, she's been prostrate with grief and has not made an effort to see them. I will make sure she does so."

"Maybe I had better not tell them until you confirm. I don't want to raise hopes to have them dashed down."

Surim nodded. "I will have my secretary call once we've confirmed the visit. Now, if you would excuse me, I do have to get to that meeting." he said. But even as he spoke, for the first time since he could remember, he didn't want to deal with affairs of state. Maybe he should arrange that trip to the oasis with Melissa. Yet he hesitated. How involved with the English guest did he wish to become? He had not shared his desert retreat with anyone.

She nodded and turned to leave. Surim followed her to the foyer. Melissa intrigued him. She was the only woman he knew that didn't flirt. At least not with him. She was more concerned for three children she scarcely knew.

Was his interest in her merely because of that? Perhaps he was getting spoiled with the attention normally received and was annoyed she also didn't seem to fall in line.

Wouldn't Max laugh if he knew his thoughts?

Once in the car a few moments later, Surim reviewed his schedule for the next few days. With some juggling of appointments, some more delegation of duties, he might be able to free up a few days to spend with his guest. She was doing him a favor in helping with the children. The least he could do was make sure she saw more of the country—and didn't spend her entire visit with the under-ten set.

It was shortly after four when Surim strode onto the beach. The meetings had ended shortly after one, but he'd spent the rest of the afternoon trying to rearrange his schedule. He paused a moment watching the scene. Alaya was splashing in the water, laughing. From this distance he could see back across the years to when he and Mara had played in the sea. They'd been fearless—diving, swimming, racing. How she'd loved the water.

Hamid was building another sandcastle. This one was almost as tall as he was. Surim suspected he'd had some help from Melissa. But the moment she was occupied with Nadia. He wasn't sure what they were doing, but it looked as if they were making building blocks from wet sand. Too small to be for Hamid's castle. Perhaps they planned one of their own.

Melissa noticed him first. Her look of delight jolted something inside him. For a moment, Surim wanted to simply bask in the bright smile she gave so frequently. She was wearing shorts and her legs looked golden against the sand. Her laughter rang out and he soaked it in. He trusted her in a way he didn't often trust. Was it because Max vouched for her? Or her own innate sense of fair play that appealed to him?

She must have told Nadia he had arrived because the little girl looked over. Gravely she rose and started toward him.

He walked to meet her, noticing the other children had seen him as well.

"Hi, Uncle Surim," Nadia said simply, raising her arms to be picked up.

He lifted her, surprised at how little she weighed. "Are you enjoying yourself at the beach?" he asked. What did one say to a two-year-old?

"Yes. Me and Lissa are making cakes. Do you want one?"

Use your imagination, Melissa had told him. He smiled at the little girl. "I'd very much love to try one of your cakes."

"Only pretend, don't really put in your mouth," she said.

"I can do that." He'd reached the castle. "Good job, Hamid," he said, studying the structure. It was surprisingly complex for so young a child.

Hamid smiled, not meeting Surim's eyes, but he could tell the boy was pleased with the praise.

"Alaya, not so far out," Melissa called. Surim turned to look at the child in the water just as Alaya turned and swam back toward shore.

"She swims well, like her mother," Surim said joining Melissa.

"And she wants to swim farther out in the deeper water, but I can't watch her closely and the other two as well. If she gets in trouble, I don't want her so far out it would take long to rescue her."

"I will swim with her. Her mother and I loved to race to the buoy."

Melissa looked at the marker bobbing in the water some distance away.

"That far?" she asked doubtfully.

"We were a little older, but not much. Mara loved the water."

"So do her children." Melissa smiled at him holding the toddler. "I see you and Nadia have made up."

"Nothing to make up. It was an accident."

"Your suit was ruined."

"Milk-stained only. A competent cleaner will get it back to normal. And if not, it's only a suit. I have plenty."

"Want me to take her?" Melissa held out her arms for Nadia, but the little girl threw her arms around Surim's neck.

"No, we have cake," she said.

"I said I'd try one, but it's only pretend, I can't eat it," Surim said.

Melissa nodded. "Very good, Nadia. I've been telling her that all day. I think she believes the sand is sugar. It does look like it, though, so white and fine."

While Surim sat with Nadia and played they were eating cake, Melissa glanced around. Hamid was settled, Alaya not too distant.

"Melissa, come and swim," Alaya called. She stood waist-deep in the blue water, beckoning.

"Why don't you go swim with her now?" Melissa suggested. "Tell her about racing with her mother."

Surim nodded. "Do you want to go swimming too?" he asked Nadia.

The little girl nodded.

"I'll take her for a short swim, then bring her right back and go with Alaya," he said. In only a moment he'd set the toddler down to remove his shirt and shorts.

Melissa caught her breath at the sight of his bare chest. It was the warm color of teak, solid and muscular. She was surprised at how fit he was. Business suits hid all that. And a good thing, she thought, forcing her gaze away. She clenched her hands into fists, feeling the grit of the sand. Better than giving into temptation to trace the contours of those muscles. Feel the warmth of his skin.

Get a grip, she admonished. If Surim ever caught a hint of her attraction, he'd send her packing so fast her head would spin. Then what of the children?

Of course, leaving might be the best thing. She knew she would be a total idiot to fall for him. The sooner he established a relationship with these children, the better.

"Are you all right?" he asked.

Melissa nodded, scrambling to her feet. "I'll see if Hamid wishes to go swimming now," she said, refusing to let her eyes feast on that tanned expanse before her. She'd seen men swimming before, for heaven's sake. Ignore him, she told her roiling senses.

The remainder of the afternoon passed swiftly. Melissa kept a prudent distance from her host. The children were cautious in their approach to Surim, but by the end of the swimming race Alaya was laughing and seemed comfortable around her much older cousin.

Surim excused himself as they headed back for the house, claiming a prior engagement. Melissa was just as glad not to test the children's manners at dinner; they were too tired after their exertions to behave without being cranky.

Melissa was also glad to escape the presence of Surim for personal reasons. She was stunned at the attraction that grew the longer she was around him. She'd be leaving soon. And even if she wasn't, she would never succumb to the cliché of falling for the dashing man. Sheikh Surim Al-Thani could look at whomever he wanted for his bride. The last person he'd consider falling for was a children's nanny.

Besides, after thinking herself in love with Paul Hemrich, and having that end disastrously, the last thing she needed was to fall for a man so far from her realm. She'd gotten over the heartache of Paul during the last few months. But she was still feeling a bit bruised and had no wish to repeat that experience!

Once the children were in bed, Melissa retired to her room. She'd write to her mother and to some friends in Switzerland, and forget about Paul. And Surim.

However, Melissa found it was easy to forget the young German banker she'd found so fascinating, but a different matter to refrain from thinking about her host. Recalling the beautiful, sultry beauty she'd met at the reception, Melissa knew she didn't stand a chance, even if their circumstances had been different.

Sighing softly, she resumed her letters, trying to keep focused on them.

Try as she might, however, her letters related a lot about Surim, from working with him on the restaurant project, to his difficulty associating with the children, to the attempts he was making at forging family ties.

Throwing down her pen a little later, she rose and stretched. She'd reread the pages in the morning and then ask to have them posted. In the meantime, she herself was tired from the day in the sunshine. Was Surim still out at his prior engagement? Was it dinner with the beautiful Delleah? Would he be asking her to marry him at that very moment?

Frowning, Melissa hoped not. Delleah didn't seem to like the children. How would that work to have her become their stepmother?

Before going to bed, she'd love a hot cup of tea. Wondering if she could just zip into the kitchen and make herself a pot without bothering anyone, she left her room and headed for the dining room. From there she'd be able to locate the kitchen, she hoped.

She'd barely stepped foot on the ground floor before one of Surim's servants stepped out of the shadows.

"Do you wish something?" he asked in French.

"Some tea, please," she replied.

"I'm happy to get it for you. Please wait in the drawing room." He vanished into the darkened hallway.

"So much for a midnight kitchen raid," she murmured, walking into the still-lighted formal drawing room. It was decorated with exotic heavy furnishings, some pieces quite old. She loved the richness of the colors of the fabrics, the deep maroons, peacock-blues and iridescent greens. Brass tacks outlined several chair arms. On the walls were magnificent paintings, huge landscapes of the desert and some of the beautiful blue Persian Gulf. There were displays of pearls in one cabinet. She crossed the room to study them. Maybe she could get a tour at one of the pearl farms before she left Qu'Arim.

The display was fabulous. She wished she knew more about pearls. The color variation was amazing, from snowy white to deep cream even to one which was a dark, shimmering gray. A couple were the size of her thumb, but most were much smaller. Perfect spheres, they were displayed on satin that captured their sheen and enhanced the color.

"Beautiful, aren't they?" Surim asked from the doorway.

Melissa turned, surprised. "Oh, yes, they are. I wondered if I might be able to see the divers one day before I leave."

"I'm sure a visit can be arranged to one of the beds, but the pearl season is summer, not winter, so there would be little to see. You're up late."

"I'm waiting for a cup of tea. I thought I might just dash down to get it for myself, but one of your servants met me in the hall and asked me to wait here while he went for it. I didn't mean to cause any trouble."

"It is our pleasure to look after our guests," Surim said. "The more welcomed we make you feel, the longer you will stay."

She smiled wistfully. "It would be lovely to do so. I'll hate leaving this warm climate for snow and ice. But I've already accepted and it wouldn't be fair to the McDonalds to back out at the last minute. I know their children. They're counting on me. Besides, I can't stay on indefinitely. That would be taking hospitality too far."

"It would be my pleasure."

Melissa shook her head. "Thank you for asking, but I have to stand by my commitment."

He studied her for a moment, then inclined his head slightly. "The offer remains open should you change your mind."

The servant entered carrying a tray with a teapot and two cups. He placed them on the table in front of the sofa and bowed before leaving.

"Enough for two?" Surim asked.

"So it seems. Would you like some?"

"I should be delighted to join you."

He waited until she sat on the sofa, then took a seat on the chair next to it. Melissa poured the fragrant beverage into two cups, handing him one. His fingertips brushed hers when he took the cup.

"I may have some more documents for you to translate for Max tomorrow. I'll have them brought to the house," Surim said. "We discussed further enhancements tonight at dinner and I want to make sure they meet Max's approval. He's very protective of this new venture."

"Oh, I thought—" Melissa started, then quickly took a sip of tea.

"Thought what?" Surim asked.

"That your engagement tonight was personal."

"A date?" he asked calmly.

She nodded.

"It was a meeting with the contractor. The changes need to be incorporated early, so there was no time for delay. As I said, I consider you a guest in my house. I would include you in social events."

Melissa looked surprised. "I understood you are looking for a wife. I'd hardly expect to be included when you and a date are having dinner."

"Ah, but we don't need privacy if I have dinner with someone. In Qu'Arim we don't view marriage the same as you do in England. Here it is primarily an alliance between two families."

"Arranged marriages?"

"For the most part. Parents arrange the marriage settlement. Powerful families are allied with other powerful families, or the arrangements supplement areas of weakness within different families. Maybe one is strong in commerce while another is strong in transportation, a perfect mix."

"What about love?"

"One always hopes affection will grow from the union," Surim said.

"So no one marries for love? What about the children's parents?"

"As it happens, they had known each other as children and had fallen in love. Their parents settled the terms of the marriage, but for them it was the best of both our customs and western custom."

"So you're not looking for love in a match?" Melissa thought that sounded rather cold. She couldn't imagine being married and not being passionately in love with her husband.

Surim sipped his tea, regarding her over the rim of the cup. Setting it back on the saucer and placing both on the table, he sat back in the chair. "It's a western belief. I shall find a suitable woman."

"Sounds sad to me. Where would be the joy?" Melissa asked.

"I would choose someone who had similar interests; we would be compatible in that regard. And find happiness in children."

"You have three children—so far it doesn't look as if they're bringing you a lot of happiness," she commented dryly. If she hadn't stepped in, they would be on their way to a boarding school hundreds of miles away.

"You are correct. I will admit to being baffled by them. It seems effortless for you to get along with them."

"Training, practice and a genuine liking for them makes it easy," Melissa said, wondering how far she could go in expounding the need for more involvement with Alaya, Hamid and Nadia. "The best time to bond would be now when they are so lost from the death of their parents. And I do understand other commitments. Most of the parents for whom I watch their children are very busy. But the entire reason for having children is for family, don't you think?"

"These children are not mine."

"They are your family. You are talking about getting married and having a family, so this is your practice run." Melissa almost held her breath at her boldness. Would he get angry?

"I had a tutor when I was young, before I went to school in England," Surim said slowly.

"But you must have family memories. Special days spent with your mother and father. Holidays spent together. Birthdays."

He shook his head. "My father was too busy dealing with the various factions in the country. It was a difficult time in our history. My mother was sickly and didn't spend much time with me. They died together, returning from a visit to the Red Sea."

"You spent time with Mara. That was family." Maybe the man had no idea of how a proper family was to behave. The thought astonished her. Yet, if he'd had a lonely childhood, not been around children since, he probably didn't have a clue. For a moment, she felt sorry for the powerful man seated near her. Her own childhood had been happy and she had wonderful memories of the many things she and her mother had done together. How deplorable of his family to not insure every child had similar memories.

"Indeed. And in her memory, I am doing what I can for her children."

Melissa put her saucer back on the tray and rose. "Thank you for sharing the tea. I'm going to bed now."

He rose instantly. "I'll walk up with you. It is growing late and I have an early appointment in the morning."

They walked up the stairs and Surim escorted her to her bedroom door.

"Good night," she said.

"I regret I cannot fulfill your expectations as guardian for these children," he said.

"Of course you can. If you wish to."

"You believe that?"

"Absolutely. In no time, you'll wonder how you ever had a life before kids." She grinned at him.

"Sounds like a double-edged sword," he said, studying her expression.

Melissa laughed. "It can be. Let us know which evening we can all have dinner together. And any time you can spare to spend with them will help."

He leaned a bit closer and Melissa caught her breath. Was he going to kiss her?

"Good night, Melissa," Surim said and covered her lips with his.

For a split second she didn't move, then she stepped closer, reveling in the touch of his mouth against hers. When his arms enveloped her she slid her own around his powerful form, clinging as the embrace filled her with sensual delight. She had never felt so feminine and powerful as when kissing Surim.

His tongue brushed against her lips and she opened to him, letting him deepen the kiss. Conscious thought fled, right and wrong and danger disappeared. There was only this moment and this man.

A moment later he was gone, walking down the hall without a backward look.

Melissa stared after him long after he entered his bedroom and closed the door.

CHAPTER SIX

THE next afternoon Melissa sat down with the construction company's papers while Alaya read her book and Hamid and Nadia napped. The changes were minor, but she knew Max would want to be kept current on everything. It didn't take long to complete the translations. When she was finished, she headed downstairs to find someone to send them back to Surim's office for facsimile transmission to England. She felt better about leaving Max, knowing she was able to continue helping from Qu'Arim.

When the children were awake, she took them to the garden to play. She loved the beach, but wanted to make sure they had a variety of activities.

They had just finished dinner when the servant Melissa was getting used to seeing appeared in the nursery. He spoke rapidly to Annis, then turned to Melissa and spoke in French. "There is a telephone call for you. Please come with me."

"I'll be right back," she told the children and rose.

He led her to the study where a phone receiver was lying on the desk. Melissa picked it up, wondering if Max had a question on her translations.

"This is Melissa," she said.

"Hi, honey, how are you?" It was her mother.

"Mum, why are you calling? Is everything all right?"

"Fine here, dear. But I have some bad news for you. The

McDonalds called here a few minutes ago to cancel your contract. They're sending you extra money as a severance fee and hope you'll understand. Apparently their current nanny's plans for marriage fell through and she wants to remain with the children. And this after you gave up your job in Switzerland. What will you do?"

Melissa sat down in the chair. She'd been counting on that job.

Surim's words echoed in her mind—he'd offered her a position of some sort. She wasn't clear on what he expected.

She no longer had the Boston assignment; she could take one with him—if she dared. She couldn't imagine working with Surim, getting closer to him as they integrated the children into his household. Especially when he married and brought a suitable wife into the mix.

Maybe she could stay for just a little longer. She was already quite fond of the children. It would be easier for them to make the transition to the family with a familiar face. She spoke their language, though they had all started Arabic lessons this week.

"I might have the chance to remain here," she said slowly. This was something that would definitely take some thinking about. Right now she was a guest; if she went to work for Surim, her status would change instantly.

"A job? Or to continue the visit?"

"A job. I'll have to consider it. So I won't be home soon."

"Max and Robert were talking last night at dinner about the new restaurant in Qu'Arim. We're planning to fly out for the opening. I would love that. Do you think you'd work for the restaurant?"

"I'm not sure. But I do plan to come see the resort when it's completed. The setting is beautiful, and I expect the entire resort will be first class plus. Max is making sure the restaurant is perfect and it can only enhance their reputation," said Melissa. "Anyway, that's enough about the restaurant. How are things going?"

She and her mother chatted for another few minutes before

hanging up. She sat in the chair feeling torn. She had liked the McDonalds and their children. Had looked forward to caring for an infant as well.

If only she could segregate her feelings for her new boss, she might just have the chance of a place here.

The next few days went by without Melissa or the children seeing Surim. Annis related that he had asked after the children one night after they had gone to bed.

Fortunately for the household, Hamid's nightmares seemed a thing of the past. The little boy played hard all day, then slept soundly. Alaya was blossoming and wasn't sad as often as she'd been at first. Melissa hoped they were starting to feel as if they belonged.

Between Melissa and Annis, the children were prompted for good manners and encouraged in proper etiquette at each meal. Annis was also teaching them all basic words in Arabic. Sometimes they tried to hold a conversation, but no one knew enough words to make complete sentences. Hamid learned quickly. Nadia didn't even try. Alaya complained, but her accent was the best.

After breakfast on Thursday, Melissa received a summons to the study.

She entered a few moments later. Surim glanced up from a paper he was reading. "That was fast." He rose and indicated a chair.

"We just finished breakfast. You could have joined us."

"I shall make a note of that. This afternoon I plan to take the children to see Tante Tazil, their grandmother. I wish you to accompany us."

"That would be great. I know they would love to see her." She hadn't seen him since his kiss the other evening. She longed to ask what he'd been doing. Or even why he'd kissed her. Involuntarily, her gaze was drawn to his lips.

"That remains to be seen. She is quite depressed. I do hope seeing them will cheer her up, not bring unhappy memories. I heard their laughter the other evening. They are changing."

"You need to—"

"Spend more time with them," he finished for her. "I know. I am arranging my schedule to accommodate that. But some things can't be changed. Are you settling in all right?"

"Yes, thank you."

He leaned back in his chair and steepled his fingers. "I hear you had a phone call the other afternoon."

"Yes, from my mother."

"She is well, I trust."

Melissa smiled. "Of course. And looking forward to the opening of the Bella Lucia here in Qu'Arim. Robert has promised they will attend the event."

"I look forward to meeting her. Was there anything else?"

"Like?" she asked warily. He knew her job had been canceled; she'd bet a bundle on it.

"Like have you given more thought to my offer of a permanent job here?"

"In light of my other one being canceled, do you mean?" she asked. Max, he had to have told Surim.

"I heard that. I am surprised you didn't tell me sooner."

"I'm still debating if I wish to take advantage of your offer."

"I would raise the salary higher."

"I don't need it higher than the going rate," she said. Was that the way all businessmen thought? Throw more money at a situation to solve a problem?

"Shall we discuss concessions again?" he asked.

She looked at him sharply. Was he teasing? His face looked grave, but she suspected a lurking amusement in his eyes.

"Such as?"

"I have no idea. You had a list when I asked you to stay initially."

"And you are not fulfilling your part. What part of spending time with those children do you not get? A few hours one afternoon isn't enough to last all week."

"Dinner tonight."

"What?"

"We'll all have dinner tonight." She saw a glint of amusement in his eyes. "That will add to my score card."

Melissa frowned. "This isn't a game."

His dark eyes lost their amused expression. "No, I realize that. Shall we leave around one?"

"You realize Nadia usually naps at that time. Forgoing that could make her cranky."

"Ah. What would be a better time?"

"Three."

"Then I'll see you at three."

Melissa rose and headed for the door.

"And I hope to have your answer at that time, as well," he said.

She paused. "Exactly what would be my duties?" she asked.

He looked thoughtful for a moment. "About what they are now?"

"Hardly worth paying me for," she replied. "I think I had better return home soon. But I'll stay a little longer."

"The offer stands," he said, once again picking up the paper and scanning the report.

Surim didn't look up as Melissa left. He had been surprised when Max had mentioned on the phone yesterday that Melissa's job in the United States had been canceled. She had said nothing to him. Did she not wish to continue being with the children? Now that she was settling in, he could see the difference she made. Annis still gave a lot of the daily care, and he would not let her go. But the children blossomed with Melissa.

And he found her conversation refreshing. He placed the paper on the desk and leaned back, remembering her list of demands when he had first enlisted her help. He could just imagine an additional list if she stayed full-time.

What would it be like to have her give him a report each day on how the children progressed? She'd have her own unique slant on things. She reminded him of some of the girls he'd known when he'd lived in the UK. Bold, outspoken, confident in their own self-worth. Most of the younger women of his country were shy and quiet and never voiced an opinion until they knew what was expected. Then it mostly mirrored his own.

Not that he wanted anyone to argue with him, but sometimes it was refreshing that she had no agenda. She said what she thought. Would that change if she became dependent on him for her livelihood? He hoped not.

For a moment he thought about the other evening. He'd have to hold onto his emotions and not give way to impulse as he had with that kiss. It would be totally unsuitable in an employer-employee relationship.

He needed her. He hadn't a clue how to relate to those children. The three weeks in his care prior to Melissa's arrival proved that.

His thoughts turned to his need for a wife. Would he find a suitable bride soon? If so, within a year he could have his own son or daughter to raise. It was hard to picture, but he knew for the stability of his small country he needed to proceed and with haste. He was already in his late thirties. He hoped to live a long life, and not die before his son was an adult and trained to take over the reins of government.

For a moment Surim remembered his resentment and anger when his father had died. He had still been in school, had planned to study medicine. His father's brother could have assumed the leadership position, had he not been killed in one of the armed skirmishes two months prior to Surim's father's death.

Instead, Surim had been summoned home and plunged into politics with a vengeance. For years he'd had private tutors to educate him to college levels; all the while he'd been learning how to rule a fractious country. His ministers had helped, good strong men his father had chosen.

Surim gazed out the window, lost in thought. Some days he still wished he had become a doctor. There was a great need for medically trained people in the world, and he wanted to make a difference.

He had, but in a totally different manner than he'd dreamed of as a boy.

Ah, well, the dreams of childhood were not necessarily meant to be fulfilled. He turned back to the endless paperwork and began to review an updated report from the construction firm building the resort. This project was important. Not only to forge new ties with European countries, but to bring another source of cash to their economy. He didn't want Qu'Arim to be a one-industry nation. He had until three o'clock to get through some of the work that waited. Then he could take time with Melissa without guilt. He looked forward to it.

Melissa made sure the children were ready prior to three. It was a bit tight with Nadia waking only a few moments before the hour. Still, all were washed, brushed and in clean clothes at the appointed hour.

They went down the stairs, Hamid chattering a mile a minute. Such a difference from when she'd first arrived.

Melissa wore one of the suits she'd brought for her business dealings. She hoped the boxes of clothes her mother had sent would arrive soon.

The four of them arrived in the foyer just as Surim came from his office. He looked wonderful in his dark suit and pristine white shirt. Melissa had to force her attention back to Alaya as she jumped up and down with excitement. She'd much rather just eat Surim up with her eyes!

"Are we really going to see Grandmama? I haven't seen her

since the funeral; she was wearing all black and crying. I was crying, too, because I wanted my mummy and daddy. But now we're here. It will be fun, won't it?" she asked anxiously.

"She misses your mother, as you all do," Melissa said gently, brushing back the hair flying around with the child's jumping and feeling a little surprised Alaya had attended the funeral. "She'll be happy to see you. And you'll have happier memories after today. I know seeing her upset at the funeral must have upset you. Children need adults to be strong. But your mum was her only daughter and she was sad. Today she'll be happier for seeing you and your brother and sister." Melissa remembered Surim had mentioned the woman was suffering deep depression at the loss of her only child. She hoped the children's visit brought her spirits up.

"She's not going to die, is she?" Hamid asked.

Surim paused and looked at Melissa.

"Not any time soon. So tell me what you plan to say to your grandmother," Melissa said.

The three children recited, 'Hello, Grandmother,' in Arabic.

"Well done," Surim said. He looked at Melissa. "And you?"

"I'm happy to make your acquaintance," she said in perfect Arabic.

"I'm impressed."

"Annis is teaching us," Melissa said, pleased at his compliment.

The drive was short, lasting less than ten minutes. The house was impressive, with ornate plaster around the windows and handsomely carved doors.

Surim had called and talked with Tante Tazil that morning. She had still sounded as if the act of talking were more than she could do, but had said she'd be happy to see the children. He hoped the visit helped all of them, and didn't cause any problems with the children.

They were ushered into a sunroom. The sky was cloudless

and the room was filled with sunshine, flowering plants and light furnishings.

Melissa held Nadia's hand, and the other two children crowded around her, warily watching the older woman as they approached where she sat in one of the chairs.

She seemed older than Melissa had expected. Yet maybe the death of her daughter had aged her.

Surim beckoned them closer, clearly introducing Melissa. She spoke her phrase in Arabic and the older woman looked surprised. She replied rapidly and Melissa was totally lost.

Surim said something and the woman nodded, switching to French. "I thank you for taking care of my grandchildren. I am unable to manage at this time."

"They are delightful." Melissa urged them closer and murmured in their ears.

"Hello, Grandmother," they chorused.

She held out her arms and they ran to hug her. Tears spilled from her eyes. "My precious ones," she whispered in English. "I am happy to see you all."

In only a few moments she sat back, dabbed at her eyes, and smiled at the children. "I will have cakes and biscuits brought up."

She looked at Melissa. "If you like, I will ask for tea. I know the English like tea."

"Actually, Tante, I thought to show Melissa your gardens while you and the children visit," Surim said. "Melissa enjoys flowers, and your garden is beautiful."

"Grown a bit wild lately, I think," she said sadly, then gazed at the children. "But a good idea. You can report back on the work needed. Come, children, tell me all you've been doing since you arrived."

Surim led Melissa to the garden. It was quite tiny in comparison to his. Obviously a bit out of hand, as well.

"Tante Tazil is her own gardener, and I think has neglected things in her sadness," he said. "Do you recognize the flowers?"

"Yes, I think I see old favorites everywhere," Melissa said.

"Are you an avid gardener?"

"No, my mother likes to work with dirt, but not me. Though I do love flowers, as you said. This is a pretty setting, but I like your garden better."

"What do you like to do in your free time?" Surim asked.

She looked at him, wondering if he ever had any free time. "I loved to ski in the winter in Switzerland. I like reading and exploring. I read about a place, then visit and explore as much as I can. The advantage of living in Switzerland was being so centralized in Europe. I had planned to do the same thing from Boston."

"Until your plans were changed."

She nodded.

"So you like it here?"

"Of course. But that doesn't mean I want to work for you," she said without thought.

"Oh?"

She glanced at him uneasily. "I like visiting," she said. Let him make what he would out of that.

They joined the others in the sunroom a short time later. Melissa thought the children's grandmother looked much happier than she had when they had arrived.

"You must leave so soon?"

"We've been here long enough," Surim said. "We will return again next week if you like. And you are always welcome to visit at my house; you know that."

"Maybe I shall." Tante Tazil turned her attention to Melissa. "Would you mind taking the children into the garden for a moment? I wish to speak to His Excellency alone."

Surim watched as Melissa nodded and herded the children outside. He could guess what the older woman wished to talk about.

"I understand you are looking for a wife, Surim," she said, confirming his suspicions.

Surim nodded warily. "Even sequestered as you, Tante, you seem to know what is going on."

"You can't keep a secret; did you think you could? It is on the mind of everyone—whom shall you choose? I know a young woman who would be suitable. She was friends with Mara when they were young."

Surim involuntarily glanced through the window at Melissa. She was talking with Alaya and holding Nadia. For a moment, he could envision her holding a child of his. How would such an unsuitable match be perceived by his country?

"Surim?" Tante Tazil said sharply. She followed his gaze and frowned. "I do hope the children won't become too attached to the Englishwoman. The woman I'm thinking about has studied in Paris, so has a worldly cosmopolitan outlook that should appeal to you. Yasine bin Shora. I shall invite you both to dinner this week."

"I shall look forward to meeting her," Surim said. For a moment he considered telling his aunt he had prior engagements at dinner—eating with the children. But he didn't think she'd approve.

Surim called Melissa back in, and Tazil smiled at each of the children as they hugged her goodbye.

"Next week if I'm feeling better, you can come again."

"Do feel free to come visit at my house any time you wish, Tante Tazil," Surim said, giving her a kiss on her cheek. "Just let Melissa know so she can make sure the children are there."

"The sooner you find a wife, the better. You should not have waited so long," his aunt chided him.

Surim felt the restrictions of his position close in on him. Usually he didn't mind the challenges of leadership. But the pressure from his ministers, and now family, were daunting. He understood the need for an heir to insure a smooth transition of power when he died. But he didn't like the constant pressure to find a woman right away.

As he settled in the limousine he watched Melissa. She was a beautiful woman. Good things came in small packages—wasn't that an old English saying? Her eyes sparkled as she listened to Hamid. Nadia remained close, seeming a bit listless. Alaya sat next to him.

"Did you have a good time?" he asked.

"She's very old, isn't she?" Alaya said.

"No. But she is very sad because of your mother's death. Being around you and the others will help her get her energy back and then you won't think she's so old."

"I wish Melissa would stay forever. Can't you make her?"

Surim shook his head. "I can't force her to remain. But I will do my best to see if she can stay with us until you and the others are all grown up."

"I should like that!"

So would I, Surim thought, a bit startled at the knowledge. He looked at Melissa again, wanting her to smile at him as she did so easily for Hamid.

When they reached the house, Surim asked Melissa to remain while the children ran up to the nursery.

"Dinner will not be private and I wish to discuss your remaining here for the foreseeable future," he said. He led the way to the living room, shutting the doors behind them. "Do sit down," he invited, waiting for her to sit on the sofa before joining her. The fragrance of her perfume filled the air. Light and sweet. Not a bit cloying like Delleah's was sometimes.

"I can't stay beyond a few weeks," she said.

"So tell me the stumbling points and I'll see what I can address."

She remained silent, thinking. Her eyes roamed around the room, settling nowhere, and not looking at him.

"You like the children," he said to break the silence.

"Yes."

"Is it me you have a problem with?"

She shook her head. Then hesitated. "No, no problem I can't deal with."

Ah, there was something. His curiosity rose. "And that would be?"

"Nothing I can't deal with. I guess I just need time to think about staying. You're getting married; don't you think your future wife should have some say in who watches the children? Especially when you have your own children. She may not wish me to be part of your household."

"That won't be any time soon. If you prefer, we can arrange a six-month period."

"What if I don't suit?" she asked.

"I can't imagine that. But either party has the right to terminate before six months. And either way, I'll give you a severance package equal to six months' pay, to give you time to find another position that suits you."

"That's more generous than I need," she protested.

"But what I propose."

"Let me think about it." She rose and headed for the stairs, pausing at the doorway to look back at him. "I appreciate the offer. I'm just not sure I can do it." And she was absolutely certain she couldn't tell him the reason.

As Melissa went upstairs she admitted her attraction to Surim was growing stronger daily. She had no business even holding out hope she'd remain. Her best plan would be to stay another week, then get back to England where she'd be safe.

Maybe if she could focus on the children and virtually ignore Surim, she'd have a chance. Just because he set her heart racing every time she saw him was no reason to let him occupy her every waking moment.

He was seeking a wife. Melissa hoped he would find someone special. He deserved a wife who loved him, who wanted to make his life easier, and share the ups and downs. She wished he'd look her way. Not that she stood a chance. She wasn't even from Qu'Arim, and she could just imagine what people would think of their leader marrying a foreigner. For a split second, however, she remembered another leader who had given up a throne for the woman he loved. Love was the difference.

Melissa took a few moments to freshen up, then headed for the nursery. Tonight was dinner with Surim in the main dining room. Only Alaya and Hamid were participating. Nadia was too young. Annis would see she got her dinner as usual.

"Ready?" she asked when she arrived.

"Do we have to?" Alaya asked. "Uncle Surim will want us to have perfect manners and I want to eat and then play."

"Me, too," Hamid piped up.

"We can play another evening. Tonight we are dining with your uncle."

The long table in the dining room had been set. Melissa was pleased to note everyone was clustered near the head, rather than spaced out. It wasn't going to be a cozy dinner, but at least she would be near the children and Surim. No shouting needed.

"Remember all I taught you?" Melissa asked as she and the children went to the seats on either side of the table.

"Yes, sit quietly. Speak when spoken to," Alaya said.

"Use our napkins!" Hamid shouted, then laughed.

Melissa relaxed. She hoped the meal would be enjoyable and not stressful. She planned to do her best to make it so.

The conversation centered on the afternoon's visit to the children's grandmother. Melissa was pleased with the way Alaya and Hamid were behaving.

The entire meal went much better than breakfast a few days earlier had gone. Still, Melissa was tired from the stress by the time the children were excused. She rose to take them upstairs, but Surim shook his head.

"They know the way; they've explored the house on many occasions. Annis will put them to bed. Stay."

Alaya gave Melissa a hug and then Hamid, not to be outdone, came round the table to give her a hug.

"Will you read me a story before I go to sleep?" he asked.

"I'll be up in a little while. If you fall asleep before I get there, I'll read you two tomorrow, how's that?" Melissa asked, tousling the boy's hair. She was coming to love these precious children.

"I want a story, too," Alaya said, leaning against Melissa.

"Same deal. Now bid your uncle good night and scoot upstairs."

Hamid approached Surim slowly. When Surim pushed back his chair and beckoned, Hamid went to give him a hug. Alaya followed.

"Good night," they called and raced from the room.

Surim looked at Melissa. "Pass or fail?" he asked.

She laughed. "This wasn't a test. It was a family dinner. And I think it went well, but what I think doesn't matter as much as what you think."

"Surprisingly, I enjoyed it," he said.

"Why the surprise? They're super children."

"It is not the custom in my family to have children at the meals until they are almost adults."

"Who made that rule?" Melissa asked before she thought. "Oops, of course your customs are important, but it is nice to have the children share in family activities. How do you grow close if you don't?"

"Shall we have coffee in the salon? These chairs are not made for endless hours." Surim rose and escorted Melissa to the informal salon. The French doors were opened to the gardens. Faint illumination came from the lighting outside. The lamps had been lit in the salon.

She sat on the sofa and watched as he paced to the doors and paused.

"One reason my father sent me to school in England was to expand my knowledge of other societies. He had gone to school in France. His brother in Italy. So it was England's turn."

Melissa watched him. Where was this leading?

Surim turned and looked at her. "But boarding school is different from family life. I went home a few times with Max, who enjoyed a very different family life from my own."

Melissa's own family had been comprised of only her mother and herself after her father's death. They'd done many things together, from sharing meals and shopping trips to planning holidays together. All memories Melissa would cherish forever.

"The upshot is I'm not familiar with the English way of doing things."

"And you're not sure you want that for the children?"

"Actually, I think it might be a good way to make them initially feel safe and secure. I know Mara and Anwar spent a lot of time with the children. They loved living in England."

But you aren't sure how to go on, Melissa surmised. "So you do what English families do: have meals together, spend time in the evenings doing things as a family. Which usually means activities that can include the youngest child. Don't relegate them solely to the nursery."

Surim looked around the salon. "I will have the room made childproof."

"Or at least put the most valuable items away for a while. Children need to learn boundaries."

"I want them to feel free to roam everywhere. I didn't have that freedom when I was younger. I remember coming home at seventeen, suddenly in charge of the house. There were actually rooms I had never been inside."

Melissa was astonished. More so that he was revealing such personal items to her. What put him in such a revealing mood?

"Excellency, there is a phone call for you." One of the servants stood at the doorway, holding a portable phone.

"I'm busy," Surim said shortly.

"I wouldn't intrude except it is Madame ibn Horock and you are usually available for her."

"Tante Tazil," Surim said and crossed the room. "Excuse me a moment, Melissa; I do take her calls."

Melissa didn't know whether to leave or remain, but when he took the phone and stepped into the foyer she remained where she was. In only moments another man entered carrying a large tray with fragrant coffee and some small cakes. He placed the tray on the coffee table and said something to her in Arabic.

"Do you speak French?" she asked.

He replied in that language and indicated he would bring anything else needed.

"This looks perfect, thank you," she said and leaned forward to pour the coffee into the delicate cups. They were lovely, and seemed too delicate for Surim's strong hands.

Surim strode back into the room a few moments later. He sat on the chair near the sofa and Melissa handed him a cup of coffee.

"You take it black," she said.

"You noticed?"

"At your aunt's. Is she all right? Seeing the children wasn't too much for her, was it?" she asked.

"She is fine. In fact, she feels she's getting back to normal. That call was to arrange a dinner for me to meet a friend of Mara's Tante Tazil is convinced would make the perfect wife."

"How nice," Melissa said, taking a sip of her coffee and not looking at the man. She wished he had not taken the call, or at least not shared it with her. What would it be like to marry Surim? To live forever in this lovely home by the Persian Gulf?

The thoughts brought a flood of heat to her cheeks and she firmly pushed the idea away. There was no possibility he'd look at her.

Besides, if there wasn't a strong love bond in a marriage, she didn't want it. She'd thought she'd loved Paul, but now that she had had time to look back she realized she'd been in love with the idea of being in love. Paul had been dynamic and exciting and for a few brief months she'd felt like Cinderella at the ball. But there had been no lasting ties forged. Paul was about good times and fast living. She liked that, but she also liked evenings at home, doing little but relaxing. Paul had found those stifling.

She also put a high regard on fidelity, which Paul discounted as old-fashioned and out of vogue. Would he have felt the same if she'd been the one cheating? Probably, because he really hadn't loved her. He hadn't cared enough.

"You're very quiet," Surim said.

She looked up into his dark eyes, her heart catching. "I was just thinking about marriage, and how differently we view it."

"The western view is based on love," he said. "Yet your divorce rate is high, and, from what I saw when I lived there, not every union has an abundance of love."

"You're right. But for those who do, it's a special tie. My mother and father loved each other. She was a widow for twenty years before marrying Max's father last spring. She adores him and he her. I'm glad she didn't settle."

"Do you see an arranged marriage as settling?" Surim asked.

"No, I think that's even worse. What if you two don't suit? Will you have enough time in the courtship to get to know someone? Know whether or not you'll tolerate each other enough to live together for fifty or more years?" Melissa suddenly realized what she was saying—and to whom.

"Not that it's any of my business," she quickly added.

He smiled at her. "The interesting thing about you, Melissa, is that you don't treat me any differently than I imagine you treat your friends at home."

"We're hardly friends," she said, feeling uncomfortable.

"Maybe we could be," he suggested.

"I'm here for the children." And any overture of friendship would only go to making her fantasies more real. She needed to nip that attraction in the bud. If she wanted to succeed, she needed to remember the wide gulf between his position and hers. She had even less in common with him than she had with Paul.

But as she'd realized earlier, her growing feelings for Surim were stronger than anything she'd ever felt before. And where did that leave her?

CHAPTER SEVEN

OVER the next week Melissa and the children settled into a comfortable routine. They did Arabic lessons in the morning with Annis, and some catch-up lessons in English. They played outside in the afternoons. Twice it rained, so they spent time exploring the large house that was their new home.

Each evening, if Surim was home, he had them join him in the dining room for dinner—even little Nadia.

Melissa was pleased with the way the family was growing. Surim wasn't always home, and she tried not to worry about whom he was meeting and how the great marriage stakes were progressing.

The evenings he was home, he insisted she spend time with him in the salon after the children went to bed—ostensibly to review what they had done during the day. But while the conversation started with the children each night, it soon ranged to current events, to books they'd both read and talk of the new resort.

Melissa was emboldened to speak her mind when talking with Surim, as he seemed to like what she had to say, even when he didn't agree with her. Some evenings there were lively discussions when they opposed each other on a particular topic.

Always feeling revived and refreshed after spending an evening with Surim, Melissa wondered how he was faring in finding a wife. She hated the nights he was away, worried each morning he'd greet the children with news of his engagement.

He had not kissed her again. She knew she should be grateful not to get her emotions clouded over by the physical attraction she felt. Yet she wished he'd touch her, kiss her, hold her again. She'd never felt like that before, and was afraid no other man would make her feel exactly like that.

Yet she was being selfish. The children would benefit by having a new mother. It would make their family stronger, just as Surim had said. But until he announced an engagement, it would hurt no one if he stole a kiss or two.

Tonight he'd eaten with the children, but instead of leaving after the meal he sat in one of the large chairs brought up to the nursery.

"I thought tomorrow we would go shopping," he said.

"Shopping?" Melissa sat in the chair opposite his, cuddling Nadia in her lap. The child was looking at a picture book, pretending to be reading.

"Hamid, for one, needs some new clothes. And a haircut wouldn't go amiss either," Surim said. "I have arranged my schedule to have several hours free in the late morning. That way Nadia will be home in time for her nap."

He never forgot anything, she mused. And he was trying. The children seemed to be much more relaxed around him, but Surim himself needed to unbend a little more for her satisfaction. He didn't romp with them, or get silly. Was he too lost in protocol to bother?

"That would be wonderful. Would we shop the souks?" she asked.

Surim frowned, then shrugged. "If that's what you wish. I thought one of the stores on Amir Street, but we can see what the souks have."

"It'll be a good chance to practice our Arabic," she said.

"Indeed," agreed Surim. "How is your Arabic progressing?"

"Slowly coming," she replied in that tongue. "I do not have tenses in verbs. I can talk simple sentences. I can ask for food, the directions to the police station and a bathroom." She laughed, switching back to English. "I have a long way to go if I want to become fluent."

"And the children?"

"Hamid is fastest; he and Annis actually converse for several minutes. Alaya is getting the hang of it. Nadia can make simple sentences, but loses interest quickly. Once we know more, we can spend time each day speaking Arabic, which will help her adjust. It's a bit confusing, but there are bilingual children the world over. It's really easier to learn young."

"Tomorrow you can try your skills at the souks."

Melissa smiled. "That'll for sure brand me a tourist, then they'll raise the prices."

Surim was always amused by Melissa's practice of economy. Had she no idea how much money he had at his disposal? The children in their own rights had enough income to live comfortably even if they never worked. But she looked for bargains, and seemed more conservative of his spending than he.

"I believe I can talk them down to a reasonable level," he said.

"They won't recognize you, will they?" she asked.

"I have no idea. I haven't visited the souks since I was a teenager."

She gave it some thought. He'd love to know what she was worried about now.

"Maybe the children and I should go alone," she said a moment later.

"I assure you I can manage at the souks."

"But won't the crowds be dangerous or something?"

"I doubt most of the people will recognize me, or expect me to be shopping for rock-bottom prices."

She smiled at that, and Surim was again struck by how

lovely she was. Her green eyes fascinated him. Sometimes they were as clear as glass, other times they reminded him of mossy stream beds, deep and mysterious.

Alaya came and climbed into his lap, snuggling up against him. For a moment Surim savored the feeling her trust gave him. She was warming up the fastest, because of his stories of their mother.

"Tell me another story about Mummy," she said.

"How about when she was eight years old and fell down the stairs?" he began, recounting the story with some embellishments to make Mara look heroic. He and his cousin had been close growing up—at least during the summer months when he'd been home from boarding school. His love for England had filled her head and when she'd had the chance to move there, she'd jumped at it. She'd loved the freedom and excitement of London and had often talked to him over the last few years about her experiences.

She had raised her children more British than Qu'Arimian. He didn't begrudge her her happiness, especially in light of her early death.

He watched Melissa as he talked about his cousin. What kind of mother would she make? From what he'd observed over the last few days, she'd be very involved with her children.

At least she wouldn't be a doormat or yes-woman as the last couple of women he'd been seeing had proved. Yasine, the woman his Tante Tazil had introduced to him, had seemed the perfect match at the beginning. She was beautiful with dark eyes and long dark hair. Her manners were perfect. Her ability to make conversation on any topic would stand her in good stead in official functions.

But she didn't appear to have a thought of her own. Either she parroted what her father said, or waited for Surim to express his opinion and then concurred. Nice to a degree, but he found he liked a more stimulating discourse. And talking with Melissa was guaranteed to give him that.

In fact, he was in danger of letting his pursuit of a wife

dwindle, looking forward more to spending the evenings with the children and their guest.

One of his aides had commented on the fact that time was passing and had asked if he'd found a suitable bride. The ministers wanted the succession assured. It was not fair to the country to leave it in chaos if he should die suddenly.

Yet he hesitated. Maybe he'd absorbed more of western philosophy than he'd expected. He was not looking for love in a mate, but he did want someone compatible. Someone he could see himself spending fifty years with.

Melissa had planted that thought and now he couldn't shake it.

She looked up then and smiled at the picture of Alaya sitting on his lap. The little girl was thrilled to learn more about her mother. Even Hamid had left the train set he was building to sit near Surim's chair, enraptured with the tale. Who would have thought twenty-some years later Mara's breaking her ankle would make such an enthralling tale?

"You're good at that," Melissa said when he finished.

"Telling about the past?"

"And making it fascinating. Did Mara really do all those things?"

"She was an amazing young girl. So, now, off to bed. I see Annis at the doorway," Surim said, rising. He gave each child a hug, wishing again his cousin had lived.

"If you have time, perhaps you would join me in the study," he said to Melissa.

They needed to discuss plans for the next day. And he had another question to ask. One that would likely surprise her.

She joined him a short time later, having read the children a short story.

"Tomorrow, I have to leave early. The limo will come for you at ten, swing by and pick me up and we'll head to the souks. Practice your Arabic."

"Great, but please don't throw me to the wolves. They'll see I'm British from a mile away so you'll need to do the bargaining. I think the children will be thrilled."

"The children or you?"

She laughed. "Okay, I confess, I've been dying to go since I arrived. How perfect to have a translator with me."

"My services don't come cheap," he said, finding the perfect lead into what he wanted to ask.

"Oh?" Her merry smile brought one from him.

"I have an invitation to a reception at the British Consulate Saturday. I thought you might like to attend with me."

Melissa's eyes widened in surprise. "Well, if that's OK… Yes, I should love to. What time?"

"It begins at eight. Apparently the Consulate General is being replaced and his successor will be presented. He has already called on my office and I think he's brighter than the one leaving. You'll enjoy meeting him."

"Wait," she said suddenly. "Shouldn't you be taking one of your prospects?"

"Prospects?"

"Prospective wife. Over the last week, your evenings have been spent more and more with the children, leaving little courting time. Maybe you should ask someone else."

"I ask whom I wish and for this event it is you." How dared she second-guess him? Or tell him who to invite? She was as bad as his aides.

"Yes, Your Excellency." She gave a mock curtsey, which should have annoyed him, but almost made him laugh. "So what shall I say to the new Consulate?"

"Easy. You can tell him how much you love living here and never wish to leave."

She paused for a moment. Surim wondered what he had said to cause that odd look on her face. Then she smiled. "That's fair enough. Especially after I have a chance to go shopping and see more of Qu'Arim. You realize I've been here several weeks and have only raced through town, and seen the resort site a few times?"

"How remiss. I shall take a day or two off and take you to the desert, as we once spoke of in the gardens. How would you like that?"

"I should love it. When?"

"After the reception. We'll leave the children with Annis and fly to somewhere special."

"Your secret oasis?"

He nodded.

Melissa smiled brightly. "I'd be thrilled."

Surim wasn't sure he was doing the wise thing. Once she was there, he'd forever picture her when he visited. Still, he'd like to share that part of himself with her. He had a feeling Melissa would truly love it, just as she'd said.

He wanted Melissa to like Qu'Arim. To stay to keep the children happy.

"Saturday I thought we'd explore one of the pearl farms, and then attend the reception. The children shall spend the day with Annis."

"Oh, but—"

"No buts; it is decided."

Surim needed to work on his autocratic manner, Melissa thought wryly, then looked at him. He was the leader of an important country. He'd had the role thrust on him when he should have still been enjoying being a teenager. If he was a bit over-bearing, it was excusable. But if she was staying for long, they would surely clash more than once.

"Tomorrow the limo will arrive at ten," Surim repeated in dismissal.

"Thank you, that would be lovely." Melissa rose and headed for the door. "I'll see you then."

He looked at her with his dark eyes and her heart flipped over. Did he have any idea what he could do to a woman's equilibrium? She bid him good night and hurried off to her bedroom. Saturday he wanted to spend the day with her. And the evening. Without the children. She could hardly wait.

Reaching her room, she closed the door and did a little dance of excitement. She was going to see a pearl farm, and be escorted to a Consulate reception by the world's sexiest man. And then see his desert oasis. Just the two of them.

Would he kiss her?

Would she kiss him?

Stopping dead, she shook her head. That would only lead to disaster. He was doing all this merely as a courtesy to Max. A sheikh certainly didn't take out a nanny! Unless—for a moment she wondered if he was showing her all the advantages to living in Qu'Arim so she'd stay. Was it a bribe to get his way? Maybe she should give him her answer one way or the other and see what happened.

Surim drew a folder close, prepared to do a little work before retiring. Salid, one of his trusted aides, entered through the opened door, a sheaf of papers in hand.

"I have the reports on Yasine bin Shora and her family, Excellency. There is no subversive activity that we could find."

Surim held out his hand for the report. It was unfortunate that the ministry insisted on a background check for any woman he showed an interest in. He knew it was for the future good of the country, but it felt invasive and in bad taste.

He had not read the one for Delleah and her family; he would not read this one.

In fact, though he knew the importance of getting married, he was losing interest in the entire process.

He'd much rather spend time with Melissa. Wouldn't that interest the ministers?

"Thanks, Salid. Get to bed. I will not be working tomorrow. You may take the day off as well. Spend it with your family."

The aide looked surprised. "Thank you, sir. I shall."

Surim contemplated the outing tomorrow. It had been a long time since he'd taken a day off for pure foolish pleasure. Maybe he was working too hard, as Max had suggested.

His pet project was the new resort. He was constantly battling those who opposed it; those who wished to keep foreigners out. They didn't realize how much money would pour into the country with a lively tourist trade. Schools would be a primary benefit. And health care for the nomads who still roamed the desert. The proof would come, but until then it was an uphill fight.

He planned to discuss the possibility of tourists viewing the pearl farm Saturday, combining business with pleasure. Melissa would be a good source to learn what would appeal and what wouldn't.

Melissa awoke with anticipation. She'd wanted to visit the souks since she'd first learned she was coming to Qu'Arim. The exotic open-air markets had long fascinated her. She'd visited open-air markets in Spain and Germany, but couldn't wait to see what the local one had to offer.

She reviewed her clothes, wishing the box of things her mother had shipped would arrive. If it didn't get here soon, she might be leaving before it arrived. She had one sundress that she could wear without the jacket, making it a bit more informal. Other than that, she had little to wear. Maybe she'd find some clothes for herself as well as for the children.

For Saturday night, she wondered if she'd have time to find another dress and not have to wear the blue gown she'd worn to the reception Surim had given. She still had her dress from home, but would love something special.

But at the same time, she had to keep her feet on the ground.

She could not start daydreaming about being the woman of his choice. He'd said the reception was at the British Consulate and he'd invited her to mingle with some of her countrymen. He was being kind. She would not read anything more into it than that.

By the time Melissa arrived at the nursery, the children were halfway through their breakfast; Surim was nowhere to be seen.

Annis greeted her and for several stilted moments Melissa practiced her Arabic. The older woman never laughed, but her eyes twinkled quite a bit with Melissa's attempts.

"His Excellency told me to remind you he would be sending a car at ten to transport you and the children to the souks." Annis frowned. "It is crowded with unsavory persons there. Why would he take you to the souks?"

"I asked. I think it will be great fun."

"Is easier at the boutiques, I think."

Melissa smiled and shook her head. "This will be an adventure, for me and the children," she replied.

Promptly at ten she shepherded the children downstairs to the waiting limousine.

Hamid had a thousand questions about the vehicle. Ascertaining the driver spoke limited English, Melissa prevailed upon him to allow Hamid to ride in the front seat, securely belted, and answer all his questions.

She and the girls sat in regal splendor in the back.

"There's even a television," Alaya said, flicking on the unit. The program was in Arabic. She watched for a moment, then flicked it off. "I miss our telly. All of these are in Arabic."

"Oh, come on, Alaya, we have much better things to do than watch TV." Melissa smiled. "Do you remember your lessons in deportment at a souk?"

"Don't seem interested; don't touch anything. And always smile and say thank you if we buy something. It's the same as Mummy used to say."

"Good, you want to act as your mum wanted."

Alaya rummaged in the small purse she carried and fished out a photo. "This is the last picture I have. It's sort of small." She handed it to Melissa.

The young couple looked happy, smiling into the camera. Their dark good looks had been passed to their children. Melissa's heart ached at their deaths. How sad for all that the children would grow up without their parents.

She couldn't imagine growing up without her mother. Granted, now her life took her far away from the small flat they'd shared off Fleet Street, but she'd had the strong grounding of her mother's love as she'd grown, and they were only a phone call away these days.

With her mother's recent marriage, Melissa felt as if a big step had been taken away from her. Her mother loved her dearly, she knew that, but Melissa was no longer the sole light in her mother's world.

Melissa wondered if she'd ever find love, marry and raise a family. She loved working with children. Couldn't imagine not having kids of her own. But the man would have to be very special.

The limousine slid to a stop. The driver jumped out and ran around to open the passenger door with a flourish. Surim stepped into the vehicle.

Instantly Melissa felt as if the air had been compressed. Her heart fluttered again and she wanted to fling herself into his arms.

Shocked, she scooted as far from where he sat as she could. Had thinking about her mother's romance addled her brains? Surim Al-Thani was her host! Nothing more.

But he was a man. She threw a quick glance at him as he engaged Nadia and Alaya in conversation. A gorgeous man, with dark eyes and lashes so long she was envious. His suit was filled out perfectly. She had seen him at the beach, and now dressed for business. He'd looked fabulous in the tux when he'd held the reception in Max's honor. Did the man ever appear the slightest bit ragged?

He looked at her, capturing her gaze with his. She wanted to look away, but couldn't.

"Are you looking forward to shopping?" he asked.

"Very much so. Will there be pearls in some of the stalls?"

"Undoubtedly. But wait until we go to the pearl farm to purchase any. The prices will be lowest there."

The limousine stopped near the edge of the vast open-air market. They exited the car, and Melissa noticed a black sedan pulled in right behind them, two familiar men in suits climbing out.

"Your friends accompany us, I see," she said.

"They are here to make sure there are no incidents. The souks can get crowded and the children are small."

"Is there danger?" Melissa asked. She had never considered such a thing. Yet Surim was a very wealthy man. Even if he had few enemies, some unscrupulous crook could try to kidnap the children for ransom.

"Only from them getting lost. We pride ourselves on having one of the lowest crime rates in the world. Come, you are safe here."

CHAPTER EIGHT

THE souks were all Melissa had ever imagined. The open-air stalls seemed to go on forever. There were clear dividing lines between each one, with large banners hanging from the canopies, all with beautiful Arabic script, of course. She was just learning to speak the language; would she ever learn to read it?

As she walked down the crowded path she noticed several shops had placards proclaiming they spoke French or Italian or German or English. She could hear the chatter of a number of languages. Dress consisted of formal Arab robes, carefree tourist attire, and even conservative business suits.

There was a buzz of excitement in the air and everyone seemed to be enjoying the day. People bargained for prices, some quite demonstratively, others quietly. The shopkeepers seemed to enjoy the process as much as their customers.

Mounds of spices were first as they plunged into the crowded aisle, heaps of fragrant ginger, nutmeg, and other exotic seasonings. Then several booths of fresh fruit and, beyond, fish caught that morning.

"Is this like a food market? I thought there'd be clothes and things," she asked Surim after a moment.

"You can buy anything here. Come this way," Surim said as he wove his way through the throngs of people examining the merchandise. In another couple of minutes they were in a completely different area, with luxurious rugs displayed, olive wood and acacia carvings for sale. She saw bolts of fabric at one stall.

"This one will make up any item of clothing you wish; just pick out the material and let them take your measurements," he said, stopping to converse with the merchant.

Melissa kept tight hold of Nadia's hand. She made sure she had Alaya and Hamid in sight at all times. She didn't want to dampen the children's enthusiasm with too many restrictions. Still, this kind of shopping was quite different from what they were used to.

The variety of wares was amazing. From ornate furnishings to strands of gold necklaces. Pearls large and small; some set in fancy jewelry, some lying in shallow boxes for people to choose from. There was even a toy stall that had puzzles and sturdy wooden toys.

Nadia and Hamid loved that place best, spending long minutes trying out different ones.

"Shall I buy them each one toy?" Surim asked quietly in her ear. Melissa turned, bumping into him, he was so close. Yet where else would he go as the other shoppers crowded the wide aisles, jostling each other as they moved to close in on the best bargains? She stared at him, his face inches from her. For a moment the souks seemed to fade; there was just herself and Surim. She dragged her gaze away.

"It would be very nice, I think," she said. Surim leaned closer still to hear her and she could smell his aftershave. Its tangy scent started butterflies in her stomach, and she wished she could step away. Or step closer.

Drawing on her reserves, she smiled and eased back a few scant inches. "Nadia seems especially enchanted with that puzzle. I think it's perfect for a toddler. And Hamid likes the wooden trucks. He would be able to play with those at the beach as well." She hardly knew what she was saying. Every cell in her body seemed attuned to him.

"And Alaya—is she too old for toys?" he asked, the look in his eye suggesting he knew what she was thinking.

"No, but I think she was taken with some of the material at the place we passed a few moments ago. Maybe a sundress?"

"And you?"

"I'm having such fun. Haven't seen anything I must have, however. But I wouldn't mind a dress or two myself to tide me over until the clothes my mother is sending arrive. And there will be pearls to see on Saturday."

"A lovely strand to go to the reception that evening, perhaps?"

"I doubt I can afford a strand. But maybe a pair of earrings."

Surim said nothing, but narrowed his eyes slightly. Inclining his head once, he reached out to take her arm and pull her gently out of the way of some boisterous tourists.

"We'll buy the toys. One of the guards has located a stall with children's clothing. We will find what we need there."

The fascination held as they followed the guard and found several places to buy casual clothing for the children. Each was measured and an assortment of ready-made clothes was quickly held up for their choice. Selecting four outfits for each child, Melissa helped Nadia and Alaya, and kept an eye on Surim's assisting Hamid.

Just as they were ready to leave, Melissa spotted a lovely rich green silk. It would make a beautiful evening gown. And she wanted something grand for the embassy reception on Saturday.

"Wait a second, can you?" Not waiting for Surim's answer she turned to the shopkeeper and negotiated a price. Her measurements were taken and the fabric held up to the light. It shimmered with rich color, reflecting the sun.

"It will look beautiful on you," he said when she joined him a few moments later at the edge of the booth.

"I hope so. It was too lovely to pass up. And he said he would have it done and delivered to your house Saturday morning. Amazing."

There were definitely perks to this arrangement, Melissa thought, pleased with her purchase. She glanced at her watch, surprised to find it was already after noon. The shopping had flown by.

"Time to eat?" Surim asked.

"Something light would be good. Then I need to get them home."

"So Nadia can take her nap," he said, leaning close to better communicate.

Each time he did, Melissa felt an increased spark of awareness. She could get in over her head. She had to remember he was looking for a wife, not a relationship with a visiting nanny. He was leagues out of her realm. The brush of air that touched her cheeks as he spoke sent another message. She longed to lean closer. By turning her head slightly, she'd be able to touch his mouth with hers.

The thought sent flames of excitement licking through her veins, but she prudently turned her face and stepped away. Only to have Surim move closer, protecting her from being jostled by a group of rough teens laughing and shoving each other.

One of the men stepped closer to Surim and spoke rapidly. Surim shook his head.

"Are you all right?" he asked her softly.

"Fine." She smiled reassuringly at Nadia and glanced at Hamid and Alaya. For a moment she lost sight of Alaya and panicked, but before she could even voice her concern the child appeared at the far end of the stall, staring at another dress.

"If it gets more crowded, we should leave," Surim said, glancing around.

"I think we have enough outfits to carry them through several weeks. Where will we get Hamid's haircut?"

"I know a place. If you are ready, we will wind our way through the mob." Surim reached for her hand. Surely to keep her close. But his touch, as always, sent sparks of electricity coursing through her. She tried to concentrate on the children, but it was harder by the moment.

Melissa noticed the souks appeared more crowded than when they had first arrived. She admonished the older children to stay close, still grasping Nadia's small hand.

At one point Surim released her and reached for Nadia. "Let me take Nadia and you hold onto Hamid and Alaya."

Nadia smiled and looked around when Surim picked her up.

"Probably better for her to see things," Melissa said, beckoning the others. "She is so short she only had a view of knees."

Surim nodded, smiling at the little girl. He still looked a bit awkward holding her, but Melissa was pleased he'd volunteered. She'd bring them all together no matter what!

Hamid was not the quiet, docile child she'd hoped for at the barber shop. Once he realized he was the only one getting a haircut, he rebelled.

"Don't want to," he said, planting his feet and refusing to move beyond the doorway.

"You need a haircut," Melissa said, stooping down to be at his level. "Look at all the other men; they have short hair. Yours is getting scruffy, like a puppy. You don't want to look like a scruffy puppy, do you?"

Surim didn't wait for an answer, but lifted the boy and looked him in the eye.

"It is inappropriate to cause a scene in a public place. Do you understand?" His voice was firm, but not unkind.

Hamid stared at him wide-eyed and slowly nodded.

Melissa watched, knowing Surim would not severely discipline the child, glad he'd made it more of a question than command.

He set Hamid back on his feet and reached for his hand, and the two continued into the shop. The two girls had remained in the limousine with the driver. Knowing she was no longer needed, Melissa returned to the vehicle and got inside with the girls.

"Is Hamid going to be a long time?" Alaya asked, looking

up from working the puzzle they'd bought for Nadia. The two girls were on the floor of the limo putting it together. Nadia smiled as she hummed softly to herself as she tried to fit the large pieces in the wooden holder.

"Not long. Uncle Surim is with him. We'll go for lunch when they are finished, then back home for Nadia's nap. Did you like the souks?"

"They were different from shopping at home." Alaya abandoned the puzzle and moved to sit beside Melissa. "I was glad Uncle Surim was with us," she said.

"Me, too," Melissa said. She had enjoyed the excursion. She watched the entrance to the shop, waiting for him to appear with Hamid. They would have a quick lunch and then she'd take the children home while he returned to work.

Tomorrow, however, Surim would spend the entire day with her alone. She could hardly wait.

By the time they returned to the house, the children were getting rambunctious. Surim had found a restaurant that easily accommodated young children, so lunch had passed without incident. But on the ride back, Nadia had wanted to be held and had been cranky. Hamid had been in high spirits and had wanted to hurry home so he could play with his new toy. Alaya had been a bit annoyed with her siblings and had complained constantly to Melissa about the other two.

Melissa soon got them sorted out when they reached home. Nadia went straight to bed. Hamid played with his new trucks and Alaya drifted to her room, wanting to read one of her many books.

Annis asked after the expedition and Melissa relayed the highlights, then left to take a little time for herself. She walked out into the garden and headed for her favorite bench. She couldn't believe it was already February and so warm. The balmy air caressed her cheeks as she leaned back on the wooden bench to savor the peace and quiet. She was used to groups of children from the resort, but generally she'd had one age group at a time with activities suited to keep them occupied. It was more challenging to deal with three different ages and interests.

She loved caring for these children. Actually, she realized she loved them, full stop. She couldn't imagine now hard it was going to be to leave.

Or should she stay?

That might prove to be even harder. She was falling for Surim. Not that she'd ever tell anyone. But could she stay near him, seeing him every day, longing for his kisses and caresses once he was married to someone else?

Saturday dawned fair and clear. Melissa dressed in anticipation of the day she and Surim would share. She was delighted to be seeing where pearls were harvested. The fact that Surim was taking her was an added bonus. Or the highlight of the tour. One day out of time might be all she had. She'd cherish every moment!

She tried to put things in perspective. Due to her relationship to Max, Surim didn't relegate her to the nursery. She still had the guest room on the second floor. She ate most of her dinners with him. She had the run of the house, though she spent most of her time with the children.

Over the weeks she'd been in residence, she'd grown to know a lot about her employer from what he told her and from what she pieced together from the way he behaved around others. And the bits of information dropped as he compared his childhood with theirs.

She knew she shouldn't feel sorry for one of the most powerful men in the Persian Gulf area, but she did. Just a little. He hadn't had a close family. There apparently were few happy memories of his time with his parents. His best recollections always were about being at Eton. He remained friends with several boys from school. In fact, from what she could glean, he was closer to those men who still lived in England than anyone in Qu'Arim.

He also felt a strong duty to marry and produce children for the stability of his country. Yet she felt his reluctance. And anyone looking would see he was doing nothing toward that goal—instead he was spending his time with her.

It was almost nine-thirty by the time they left. Instead of the expected limo, Surim drove his own car again, as he had on her first visit to the resort site.

"How is the building coming?" she asked as they merged into traffic and began their day.

"On target so far. There have been minor mishaps, but nothing has delayed the process significantly."

"And when does it open?"

"We hope next autumn. We have a two-week window built in the construction schedule to accommodate any delays, but if anything goes beyond that we'll likely have to postpone the grand opening. Which I do not plan to do. We already have guests booked."

"Even before it's built? What are you showing for rooms and amenities?"

"We have artist renditions of the rooms, the front of the hotel, the lobby. Those have been incorporated into brochures and distributed to travel agencies around the world."

"Max is excited about opening a Bella Lucia outside of the UK,' commented Melissa. "Will he be coming back to check on things before the opening? I haven't talked with him in a while, not since the last set of translations."

"He'll fly in once more, but I shall handle things from this end. Some of the London office staff will arrive a month prior to opening to train local people to handle the day-to-day operations."

Soon, Surim turned onto the highway that flanked the sea.

The Gulf stretched out to the horizon, deep blue and calm. The breeze from the Gulf kept it from being too hot.

"It's beautiful!" Melissa exclaimed, gazing at the water. "I can't believe it's February and so warm. My mother said it was freezing in London."

"Perhaps we'll have time for a swim when we return home," he said.

"I should love that. I still can't get over being able to swim in the sea year-round."

Sometimes Surim wondered if Melissa liked him, or the location of his home. She never seemed to flirt. Did she realize how enticing she was when she challenged him? Her eyes sparkled and her laughter was infectious. Her kisses had him wanting more. Yet she never overstepped any boundaries. Was he so conceited he thought all women were after him?

He almost laughed. The only women who wanted an alliance with him were ones looking for a free ride with a wealthy man. He didn't want to believe that of Melissa.

The first pearling enterprise they came to belonged to the de Loache family, an old French family who had lived in Qu'Arim for more than a hundred years. One of their early ancestors had discovered a bed of oysters producing lovely pearls, acquired the land and launched a business renowned throughout the world.

Surim knew the owner and had arranged to have him give the tour personally. Not only for Melissa, but so Surim could discuss including tours on a regular basis as a tourist attraction exclusively from the new resort.

Claude de Loache was waiting by the long, low building when Surim drove up.

"Our host," Surim told Melissa.

In only moments, introductions had been made and Claude began to explain the different steps in pearling. Melissa was fascinated. Her attention was totally on what Claude relayed.

She asked intelligent questions and seemed to grasp all the facts quickly.

When Claude offered to take them out in one of the boats to actually see some of the oysters, she was delighted.

"If it's all right with Surim," she said.

Claude raised an eyebrow and glanced at Surim. "We bow to your wishes," he said.

Surim gave him a look. They'd known each other for many years. "It would be more than we expected, but I should like to as well."

Claude explained how they kept the oysters in beds in the sea, able to bring them up on huge flat beds using cranes. They were checked periodically to make sure everything was all right. Storms could wreak havoc, so they were especially concerned after a big one.

He had some of the men on the boat connect to the wire bed and haul it up. Dozens of oysters lay on the huge tray, water streaming off them as they were pulled from the depths. Claude reached over and took one, opening it and moving the soft foot aside. A small pearl gleamed in the sunshine.

"Too small to harvest, but doing well," he said, showing it to Melissa and Surim.

"How long before it is big enough to harvest?" she asked as he carefully replaced it on the big metal device and signaled the winch man to lower it back to the sea.

"A couple of years, probably. We have different sections of the seafloor marked for different durations. It takes a long time to make a truly beautiful pearl. We make sure no diseases sweep through, or predators. We have a continuous rotation of oysters; some are just planted, others are a year or two old and some are ready for harvesting come summer."

Surim suggested Claude consider giving tours. He suspected there would be many visitors as excited about the process as Melissa.

"Am I that transparent?" she asked, laughing. "I love every bit of information I've learned. Surim said there might be pearls to see—already harvested ones, I guess I mean."

"Indeed. In our showroom we have a large selection, some already made into jewelry, others loose to be chosen by discriminating buyers for their own particular designs."

The showroom was at the far end of the long building they'd parked beside.

Surim took her hand when helping her from the boat and seemed to forget he held it as they walked to the display area.

Melissa had no such luck forgetting. She was acutely aware of every inch of his palm against hers, of his strong fingers wrapped around her. Her arm actually seemed to tingle as they walked up the graveled path, listening to Claude explaining how he would have to change things to handle tours. Surim offered the incentive of additional buyers at the showroom. Sales meant a lot to the pearl farmer.

The showroom was elegant with thick carpeting beneath her feet and display cases and tables scattered around the large room. One wall had rows of necklaces and bracelets. Another had brooches, earrings and dinner rings.

The tables held corrugated trays with rows of loose pearls, sorted by size and color.

"This is amazing," Melissa said, transfixed by the displays.

Surim released her hand, placing it at the small of her back and urging her inside. "Wander around and see what you like. I'll talk with Claude. Take your time."

Melissa was fascinated by the wide variety of colors and sizes. One of the women at a table was sorting. She glanced up and smiled, saying something.

"I don't speak Arabic; do you speak French?" Melissa asked in that language.

The woman did. Melissa asked her what she was doing and was soon involved in learning how pearls were sorted, what made a gem-quality pearl and some of the ancient folklore about pearls.

When Melissa looked up some time later, Claude had left and Surim was leaning against the wall near the door, watching her.

"Am I taking too long?" Melissa asked, realizing how long she'd been talking with the woman.

"Not at all. I'm making mental notes about what tourists find interesting. I forget that not everyone would know about the pearl industry. And how enthralling it could be to visitors."

She smiled uncertainly.

"Did you see any you liked?"

"They are all lovely." She began to walk around the perimeter, studying the jewelry on display. Surim watched for signs of avarice, but saw none. She seemed to enjoy the pearls for their beauty, not to own them.

She finished her tour and spoke again to the woman sorting. Then she rejoined him.

"I'm ready to leave if you are."

"I thought you might buy something."

"Not today."

"Maybe I should buy you something," he suggested. Pearls against her skin would be beautiful.

"No, thank you," she said primly.

"A memento of our day together, nothing else."

"I don't think so," she said, heading for the door.

He caught her arm, stopping her.

"I can afford them, Melissa. Take them as a gift."

"I don't want you buying me pearls, Surim, and I'm not sure I want to splurge for them myself. Honestly, where would I wear pearls?"

"How about tonight? You're going to a formal reception tonight." His fingers registered the softness of her skin. She would feel like that all over, he knew. Before he got sidetracked, he let her go.

"I'll manage with the necklace I already have. It goes perfectly with the new dress."

Surim merely nodded. "Time to leave, I think." He conversed with the woman at the table in Arabic, who looked at Melissa and then at Surim and smiled. Melissa smiled back.

"What did you tell her?" she asked as they stepped out of the showroom.

"I thanked her for letting us see the lovely pearls."

When they left the pearl farm, Surim asked if she wished to see another.

"Not today. This one was perfect. I need time to absorb all the facts I've learned. Weren't they beautiful?"

He glanced at her again as he turned onto the main highway. "They are beautiful, made more so by the women who wear them."

"Tell me how long you've known M. de Loache. You sound like longtime friends, though he's a lot older, isn't he?"

"I've known Claude for many years. When I first assumed the leadership of the country, he was one of the first men to offer help however he could provide it. I would return the favor now, in increasing his business through tourism."

"Tell me about the early days. It couldn't have been easy to be a teenager taking on the leadership of an entire country. You hadn't even finished school, had you?"

Surim was silent, remembering how difficult it had been. He had not been groomed from infancy for the role, which would have made more sense. His father had not expected to die young and had felt there was time enough later to train his son. In the meantime, with factions warring within the country, he'd had other matters to attend to.

"It was difficult to deal with," was all Surim said.

"Did you ever finish school?" she asked.

"Did you think I was a dropout?"

She grinned. "Hardly, with your knowledge. But how did you go to school and run a country?"

"In the first place, most of the actual running of the country in the early days was done by the ministers. My father had chosen them well. They were good men; several remain in their positions even today. I was more a titular figurehead. So I had tutors galore. I finished basic education and then continued until I earned the equivalent of a college degree."

"Through tutors?" she asked.

"I was privileged enough to have professors from the university prepare a curriculum for me that I could follow from home. They would lecture, exam, and grade based on that."

"But no interaction with other students?"

"Very limited. When I wasn't studying calculus or world history, I was learning how to negotiate peace settlements between the warring factions in this country, and how to expand our national revenue through oil exports. There wasn't time to hang out with other students."

"Sounds lonely," she murmured.

He shrugged. "It was the way it was."

Surim didn't think often of those days. He hadn't had much choice and had gone along with the way things had turned out. He could imagine how Melissa would have handled things. She'd have found him a home, insisted he have time to grow at a normal pace and not be plunged into world affairs at the age of seventeen.

He, however, considered himself lucky the men his father had worked with had been loyal. There could have been anarchy at the time and that would have been disastrous for Qu'Arim.

CHAPTER NINE

SURIM drove to a restaurant he sometimes visited situated literally on the water. It was a floating facility anchored a short boat ride from the shore. The seafood was excellent and the ambience he knew would appeal to Melissa. She had such a sensuous feel for things. He knew she loved the flowers in the garden, not only their look and scents, but also touch. He'd seen her on more than one occasion plucking a flower and brushing it against her cheeks.

The way she pointed things out to the children in the garden, or at the shore, or even yesterday in the souks, supported her love for the natural world and her fascination with life in general.

When he reached the parking lot, she looked around with interest.

"Are we taking another boat ride?" she asked.

"To the restaurant there." He pointed to the floating structure several hundred yards from shore. From the smile that instantly appeared, he knew she approved.

"This is fantastic," she said a short time later when they were seated at one of the open windows and had placed their orders. The structure bobbed gently on the surface of the sea. The air circulating was fresh and warm. The smells coming from the kitchen were mouthwatering.

"I thought you'd like it," he murmured, watching her as she took in the quiet ambience of the place.

She smiled at him, just like the smiles she gave to Hamid and Alaya. "Surim, I have to say I'm having the time of my life today. Thank you for showing me part of your country. It's amazing."

"I'm happy to do it."

She let her smile fade slightly. "I feel guilty taking time away from your courting, though."

He was startled. "I assure you I have things well in hand." He had seen Yasine several times, and, while she sometimes bored him, he knew she'd make a suitable wife. In due time, he'd introduce her to the children and see the mutual reaction. If it went well, perhaps he'd propose within the month. But there was no rush.

Today was for himself and Melissa. It had been a long time since he'd seen Qu'Arim with fresh eyes and he was enjoying the novelty.

"Tell me about Eton. Did you ever find anything to like about England?"

"Initially, I did not. But I grew to enjoy my time in England."

"Because of Max and other friends, I bet. Didn't you miss your home?"

Surim nodded once. He had missed Qu'Arim. He had disliked the cold, wet climate of England. He had missed the familiar palm trees and native flowers. And swimming in the Gulf. He had loved his summers at home. He and Mara had been the best of friends. But he had also understood duty. His family's duty had been set long before he'd been born.

The waiter brought their lunch. Melissa tasted the fish in a light sauce and pronounced it perfect.

"It almost melts in my mouth, it's so delicate," she said.

"I am pleased you are pleased," he said.

She laughed. "Are you always so formal? Even around the children you don't seem relaxed and into playing with them. Loosen up a bit, and remember back when you were a child. I bet you were a terror. I've heard some of the stories of Max at Eton; could you have been far behind?"

Surim ate his fish, refusing to reminisce about the wilder days of his youth. They had vanished when a light plane had crashed, killing his father and mother. He could never recapture them.

"This is hardly the setting to be frivolous," he said, glancing around.

She followed suit and sobered up. "Of course, Excellency. I would expect you only to forget your role in private."

She ate her meal, gazing out over the water and virtually ignoring him. Surim felt annoyed that he'd ruined what had been a fun time. She had withdrawn and was totally polite if he asked her anything. But her spontaneity had vanished.

Melissa's enjoyment had dimmed with his comment about not being frivolous. That was what she was; she could see it. But she loved to laugh and enjoy situations. Not be formal and polite and follow protocol all the time. Much as she might fancy capturing the love of the man, she wouldn't wish to live her life like that. She embraced new experiences, always excited to learn more and see more.

This restaurant was perfect. She had never eaten on a floating one before and wished she could come another time. She was charmed that Surim had sought such a special treat for her. After the pearl farm and lunch, Melissa was sure the day couldn't get better. He hadn't said anything about the afternoon, except to suggest they might go swimming. For a moment she imagined the two of them on that beautiful stretch of beach. She'd love to be free to swim, float and generally enjoy the outing without any cares. Would he still be considering his duty?

"What are you thinking about?" he asked as he finished his meal.

She looked embarrassed. She should have kept up the conversation, not gone off in some daydream.

"Actually I was wondering if we were still going to the

beach later. I haven't had a proper swim myself since I've been here because I'm usually watching the children."

"We will go by the resort and then head for home. If we are very quiet, we can slip in, change and be gone before they know we're there."

She'd suspected he'd been more carefree before the responsibilities of his office pressed down. This sounded like fun.

"You're on. You really think we can do that?"

Surim smiled slyly. "I know a secret way into the house."

Melissa was enchanted. "A secret passage! Where is it?"

"I cannot tell you; you'll have to trust me."

She opened her mouth to protest, then closed it. "I do." She laughed, feeling lighthearted once again. And crashing head over heels for a man who put duty before all else. Was it her destiny to fall for unsuitable men?

After they ate, Surim drove them to the resort site. "I like to check on it each day," he said.

The outside walls had been framed. The floor joists for the second and third stories were in place, ladders leaning against them to allow workers easy access. Only a handful of workers were there. It was Saturday, and she knew Qu'Arim followed normal work weeks of Monday through Friday.

"I can see the shape better now," she said, looking from the car. "It's going to be beautiful, isn't it? I love the arched windows and the airy feeling of the high ceilings. Like at your house, right?"

"Similar. We want to incorporate our distinctive architecture to enhance the visitors' feeling of being in a different place than they normally go. We are extending the feeling to the entire layout, emphasizing the Arabian mystique and minimizing the western style that they see all over Europe."

"It will be fabulous."

"Max and his family will be here for the grand opening. You'll have to join us all for the event," Surim said.

They walked to the restaurant. The outer walls with their soaring windows facing the Gulf were completed. Inside they were plastering and incorporating mosaic tiles on the floors and part way up the two side walls. The designs were geometric and quite intricate. Surim led her toward the back where the kitchen had been laid out. None of the appliances were yet in place, but electrical wiring had been pulled and plumbing put in.

"It'll be much like the one I saw in Mayfair. Are you following their design?" she asked.

"It's Max's design that we're following. Come, let's see how far they have come on the lobby."

They explored for another half hour, remaining on the ground floor. Surim voted against their using ladders to see the upper levels. "Time enough when the stairs are in," he said.

Melissa complied, but she knew if he'd been on his own, without her, he would not have hesitated to climb up and see the progress. They walked out of the lobby and she looked around.

"Even before the landscaping is put in, it's gorgeous." There were several palm trees that had been worked around. And the view of the blue water stretching out before them was enough to satisfy even the most demanding tourist. "This is going to be a wonderful place for people to visit," she said.

"I hope so. It's been a dream of mine for a long time. I'm glad to see it come to fruition. If you have seen enough, we'll return home."

Home, a place to live and love. Melissa smiled and headed back for the car, knowing for however long she was to live in Qu'Arim, his house was truly home.

Surim drove the car to the back of the villa, into a multi-bay garage. He helped Melissa from the vehicle, and put one finger to his lips.

"Shh, now," he admonished.

She almost laughed. She had never seen a playful side to the man before and found it enchanting.

He took her hand and went to the side of the garage, peering around the edge of the building. Satisfied they were alone, he hurried across the stretch of lawn to the side of the house. Here he stayed close to the wall, slipping behind some shrubbery at one point. There was a small door.

"It's really a secret entrance," she whispered.

"Not so secret; the staff use it," he said.

"Don't tell me that. To me it's a secret way known only to a few. Where does it go?"

"Into a hallway that goes between the servants' quarters and the reception room. Come, quietly now. I hope we don't run into the children exploring."

"You know they do that?"

"Of course." He eased open the door and slipped inside, tugging her behind him. The illumination was dim when the door closed behind them, but Surim knew where he was going. He walked quietly toward the front of the house, entering the reception room in only a moment.

"Now's the tricky part. Here's the plan. We get to our rooms, change and meet back here in less than ten minutes. Can you do that?"

Melissa stifled a giggle, her eyes bright with laughter. "Aye, sir, no problem, unless the kids are out and about."

"That's why we have to be fast."

He eased the door to the main foyer open a crack and peeped through it.

Melissa almost held her breath. Was there someone out there? Finally Surim flung the door wide open and began to walk quickly across to the stairs. She almost had to run to keep up with his longer stride.

In her room, she let the laughter out as she hurried to find her bathing suit and cover-up. She hadn't had that much fun in a long time. She changed swiftly and grabbed a clean towel from her en suite bath. She slipped into sandals and headed for the door before she noticed the empty wrapping paper on the bed. She went to the closet. Her new dress was hanging there. Glad it had arrived as promised, she could hardly wait for evening.

Just then she heard what sounded like a thundering herd of elephants. Oh, no, it was the children.

She went to the door to listen. They seemed to be running toward the stairs to the nursery. Maybe Annis had taken them for a walk and they were now returning. She waited a moment after the last sound, then opened her door an inch. Peering into the hall, she saw it was deserted.

Quickly she closed her door behind her and lightly ran down the stairs. In less than a minute she was in the reception room, trying to catch her breath and not laugh aloud.

Surim followed a moment later. His eyes sparkled and there was definitely an air of relaxation about the man Melissa didn't remember seeing. She was so glad he'd asked her out for the day. It was her best day off ever!

They reached the white sand beach in only a few moments, slipping from the secret door and crossing the gardens in a circuitous route designed to foil anyone trying to follow them.

"I feel like a spy in a novel," Melissa said when they reached the beach. "I almost expect our escape submarine to be waiting just off shore." She looked toward the buoy. "I think I see the periscope!"

"And where will it take us?"

"Good question. I can't imagine any place more perfect than this one," she said, walking on the hot sand. She couldn't wait to plunge into the water and swim to her heart's content without having to worry about children on the shore.

She shed her cover-up near the water's edge and ran into the warm sea. She began swimming toward the buoy, not in a race but just to enjoy the sensation. In a moment Surim came up on her right.

"Did you want to race?" he asked.

"No, I'll leave that to you and Alaya. I'm just going to enjoy myself." She kept steadily heading for the marker. He kept pace beside her. When they reached it, she treaded water while Surim dove deep. A moment later he resurfaced and dove again. Then he brought up a lovely shell, which he handed to her.

"It's not a pearl, but another gift from the sea," he said gravely.

"It's lovely." She'd treasure it forever, more than a pearl or other jewelry she could get, because it came from Surim. The perfect shell was faintly pink on the inside, with even white ridges on the outside. It fit in the palm of her hand.

"The shells out here are more intact. Once a storm washes them to the shore, they get broken or chipped," he said.

They paddled around the deep water for a while until Melissa began to get tired. She swam back to shore slowly, savoring the feel of the water caressing her skin, the sun warm on her back.

She spread out her towel and lay down to let the sun dry the water clinging to her skin. Surim was still swimming. It was peaceful without the children. Not that she didn't enjoy every minute with them.

"You will burn if you stay long in the sun," Surim said.

She opened her eyes a slit and looked at him. When had he come out of the water to lie down beside her? Had she dozed off?

His fingertips brushed against her shoulder. "You are already getting pink."

"The bane of my life." She sighed and sat up. Fumbling for her cover-up, she tried to ignore the sensations that tingled down her arm from his touch. Impossible. She could only hope she looked unaffected.

"Your skin is beautiful; you do not wish to mar it."

Her breath caught and she couldn't speak. Closing her eyes, Melissa savored the sound of his voice, deep and rich. She wished they had the chance to explore the attraction she felt around him. But their worlds were too distant. He was getting married soon, and one day she'd return to England.

"I have to get back," she said, opening her eyes and gathering her things. "I want to have a nice hot bath and take my time getting ready for tonight." It was a lame excuse, but the only thing she could think up. Who in the world would take four hours to get ready?

He held out his hand to help her up and she placed hers in his. He brought her to her feet effortlessly. The warm expanse of chest in front of her tantalized. She wished she dared brush her fingertips across that skin, feel the heat and texture. She looked and her gaze locked with his. She felt as if she'd been touched, though there was still a good ten inches between them. His dark eyes hid mysteries she'd love to explore. His lips were sculpted and hers began to ache with longing to touch them again, to feel their warmth against her skin. Her breathing became erratic.

She had to get away or do something so foolish she'd be sent away instantly.

"Thank you for a wonderful day," she said, then turned and walked as fast as she could back to the house.

Thankfully, Surim didn't catch up.

Surim stood on the beach and watched her hurry away. For a moment he considered going after her. But didn't move. The sensations that swirled around them startled him. He knew better than to attribute them to anything but sex. Melissa was so sexy it made him ache. But she was also a guest in his house. One, moreover, who had personal ties to a longtime friend. He would do nothing to dishonor her or that relationship.

He'd wanted to kiss her but had been afraid a single kiss wouldn't be enough. He needed his emotions under better control before unleashing the desire that flared whenever he thought about her. He'd love to kiss her until she moaned with pleasure. Touch that soft skin all over. Make love to her far into the night.

Turning with an oath, he plunged back into the sea. Swimming to the buoy and beyond would cool the ardor.

Tonight he'd make sure she had a good time at the British Consulate, and then tomorrow take care to keep his distance.

He had a wife to find.

The thought was even more depressing than usual.

When it was time to leave that evening, Surim made a trip to the nursery. It felt strange to stop off before leaving, but he hadn't seen the children all day, and he wanted to check in on them before they went to bed.

"Excellency," Annis said when he entered.

Hamid and Alaya were playing a board game. Nadia was lying on the large chair, holding her blanket close.

"I came to see the children. They have been no problem today?"

"They have been easy to manage, though missing Melissa. I spent part of the morning reviewing what they've learned in Arabic."

"Very good."

He went to the small table where Alaya and Hamid played. "Good game?"

"She's beating me," Hamid complained.

"You won last time," Alaya commented, smiling up at Surim. "But I am the better player, probably because I'm older, right, Uncle Surim?"

"Most likely. But it isn't so much who wins, or how often, as how much fun you two have when playing."

"Well said." Melissa spoke from the doorway.

"Melissa!" The two jumped up from the table and ran to her.

Surim couldn't take his eyes off her. The long dress fitted her perfectly, subtly accentuating every curve, and the deep green of the silk brought out the sparkling green of her eyes and made her creamy skin, now tinged with gold after days out in the sun, look luminous. Quite simply, she looked incredible.

"Oh, you look so beautiful," Alaya said.

"Are you going out tonight?" Hamid asked. "I thought you'd spend it with us. I missed you today."

"I missed all of you today. Tomorrow we'll have a great time together, but tonight I'm going out with Uncle Surim. To a reception at the British Consulate."

Nadia struggled up from the chair and walked to Surim, forcing his attention from Melissa. "I'm tired," she said, holding up her arms to be picked up.

He scooped her up and looked at her. "Did you take a nap today?"

She nodded.

"Did you play hard?"

She nodded again.

"Then you have a right to be tired. Annis can put you to bed now if you want."

He looked at Annis, who came to take the toddler.

"She usually stays up until seven-thirty, but I can put her down now. I think she has a touch of sunburn from playing in the garden today," Annis said.

Melissa came over, her gown whispering softly as she moved, and brushed the back of her fingers against her rosy cheeks. "She does feel warm. Were they long in the sun?" she said in French.

Annis shook her head.

"Good night, baby girl. I'll see you in the morning."

Nadia snuggled against Annis's neck and closed her eyes. Surim was surprised. He knew Nadia was not as fond of Annis as she was of Melissa. Tonight she seemed listless. Maybe she had played too much trying to keep up with her older siblings.

After giving the other children a hug and kiss goodbye, Melissa was ready to leave. Surim bade them goodnight and ushered her from the room.

"I didn't expect to find you there," she said as they descended the stairs together. "But I was glad."

"As you point out on many occasions, they are my responsibilities."

"They're more than that. They're your family."

"Before we go," he said at the foot of the stairs, "I have something for you."

He withdrew the pearl necklace from his pocket and dangled it from his fingers.

"Oh, Surim, no." She gazed at the strand, a frown on her face. "I told you not to buy me any."

"Humor me, Melissa. Take this as a token from the children. A reminder of Qu'Arim wherever you may go in life."

"I can't."

"Yes." He unfastened the strand and encircled her neck, hooking it at the back. "They go perfectly with your dress. You look very beautiful tonight."

"Thank you." She brushed her fingertips over the pearls. "They feel cool."

"They will warm with your skin." He studied her with the pearls. Their color was perfect against her skin. They gleamed in the light.

"Take off the other necklace; I don't want to wear both. And thank you. Thank you very much," she said at last, turning to present her back so he could unfasten the gold chain.

"Where's the nearest mirror?" she asked.

"In the salon."

Surim watched her walk to the mirror and look at the new necklace. He was satisfied with her radiant smile.

The British Consulate glittered with lights and music as they entered. Surim received preferential treatment and Melissa as his escort accompanied him. They bypassed those waiting in the receiving line to meet the new Consulate and were swept to the front of the line, stepping in behind an elderly lady and her escort.

Melissa was thrilled to meet George Farmingham, the representative of England to Qu'Arim—especially when he asked her to promise him a few moments later in the evening as he'd like a fellow countryman's opinion of the country.

"So will you rave about our country?" Surim asked quietly in her ear when they moved on.

She smiled up at him. "What do you think?"

They entered the large reception hall. Surim nodded to acquaintances and exchanged greetings with others.

"Your Excellency," a soft voice said to his left.

Melissa peeped around him to see a petite young woman a few years older than she smiling diffidently at Surim. She wore a beautiful teal-blue gown, and her hair was shot through with pearls, their pale white color like sparkling moon drops in her dark hair. Melissa felt a spurt of jealousy when Surim smiled at her.

"Yasine, I did not know you were to be here."

"My father was invited and my mother was indisposed, so I came with him." She looked at Melissa, her friendly expression remaining. "We have not met, I believe."

"Yasine, this is my friend from England, Melissa Fox. Melissa, Yasine bin Shora. She was a friend of Mara's."

"How do you do?" Melissa said. Her heart sank. This was one of the women Surim had referred to as a candidate for his wife. She was truly beautiful and seemed sweet as well.

"I visited Mara in England several times over the years. I miss her dreadfully," she said, her smile fading as she thought about her friend.

"Melissa is helping with Mara's children. You must come some day and visit with them."

"I should love to," Yasine said. "I have not seen Nadia since she was a baby. Has she grown as pretty as Alaya?"

"Yes," Surim said.

"We have not spoken much about the children. How are you coping with instant fatherhood?" Yasine asked.

Melissa listened, glad Yasine was bowing to convention and speaking English at the Consulate. She and Surim could have had this conversation in Arabic. It was interesting she mentioned their not speaking about the children. Had they had numerous conversations recently? Yasine must have been the reason for Surim's late nights earlier in the week.

"With Melissa's help, I'm beginning to get to know them better. Children are a mystery to me."

Yasine laughed. Melissa had to admit the woman had charm and looks. She'd make a perfect match to Surim's own handsome features. And she seemed genuinely interested in the children.

"I suspect you are of the mind that children should be handled by the women in the household," Yasine said. "Yet my father was very involved with me and my brothers when we were young. I think we have a close relationship because of it."

One that Surim had lacked with his own father, Melissa thought. Yet neither of her companions voiced that thought. Had he shared that with Yasine? Melissa wondered. For a moment the special bond she thought between them faded. Any confidences he'd shared had to do with the children, not some regard for her. How foolish could one woman be?

A waiter circulated carrying a tray with beverages. She took one, sipping the cold liquid, wishing she could melt away into the crowd and see if there were any other British citizens present she could talk to.

Before she could say anything, however, the new Consulate came over.

"Ah, there you are, Your Excellency, Miss Fox. I believe I have met everyone invited here tonight and I am following up on talking with Miss Fox."

She was amazed he had remembered her name.

"Sir," she said, wondering what someone called a Consulate. Was there a special title?

"Do you mind if I steal her away for a short time?" George Farmingham asked after being introduced to Yasine.

"I brought her to circulate and see if she would find others from England here. Melissa is staying at my home and will be in our country for some time. I hope she finds friends," Surim said.

"Excellent, come with me, my dear, and we'll see what compatriots we can locate."

Melissa left with the friendly older man, ignoring the pang she felt leaving Surim with Yasine. But it was nothing to what might be in store, so she'd best get used to it.

Soon she had met a dozen UK expatriates living in Qu'Arim and loving it. One couple invited her over to visit on her next free day. A young man working in the tourist industry commented on the resort and she told him a bit about Bella Lucia going in, and the progress of the site. He asked if she'd be able to get hold of an invitation for him to see it before it opened.

George Farmingham seemed pleased to meet so many British citizens and suggested keeping in touch.

Melissa and the others had begun throwing out suggestions for a monthly get-together when she recognized one of Surim's aides approach him to speak to him. Surim looked over at her a moment later and immediately headed her way.

"Excuse me, Mr Farmingham. I need Melissa," he said when he reached their group.

"Of course. Do join us when you can, my dear," the man said, turning back to continue his conversation with the others.

"What is it?" Melissa asked.

"We have to leave. I just got word from Annis that Nadia is very ill."

CHAPTER TEN

"WHAT? What happened?" Melissa asked as she swiftly followed Surim to the entrance where the limo was already waiting.

He delayed answering until they were in the car and speeding away.

"Annis said she is vomiting and her fever has spiked to one hundred and three and she has diarrhea. I suspect her warmth from earlier wasn't from sunburn but from fever."

"Oh, dear. Poor baby." Melissa lapsed into silence, reviewing all her experience with sick children, and her training. Dehydration was a worry with Nadia's symptoms, especially since she was so little. What could be wrong with her? Were the others sick as well? She longed to hold the child close and comfort her. Couldn't the car go any faster?

Despite the minutes seeming to crawl by, they reached Surim's home in short order. Scarcely had the car stopped before Melissa was out and running into the house and up the stairs. Surim was right beside her.

She burst into the nursery to find Annis holding Nadia, rocking her. The little girl was pink with heat and listlessly lying against Annis's shoulder. She roused slightly when she saw Melissa and called her name.

"Sweetie, I'm here. I came as soon as I heard." She

scooped her up and held her close, resting her cheek against Nadia's forehead.

"Oh, Surim, she's burning up. I think we should take her to hospital and have a doctor look at her."

"I also," Annis said. "This is more than just an upset tummy."

"Come, we'll go straight away," he said, turning, his arm around Melissa's shoulders as if to lend support.

"Wait, where's her blanket? She'll want something familiar," Melissa said.

"Here." Annis brought it from the rocker. She patted the toddler's back and said something in Arabic.

"I hope that was a blessing," Melissa said as they hurried down the stairs. She had to move more slowly than she wished due to her long dress and high-heeled shoes while holding the child.

"It was. Do you want me to carry her?"

"It might be easier," Melissa said at the bottom of the stairs to the nursery. But when she went to hand her to Surim, Nadia clung and began to cry.

"Okay, baby, there, there, you're fine. You stay right here with me," she said, hugging her again, giving Surim a quick shake of her head.

"Just don't fall," he said, holding her elbow as they descended the main stairs.

In only moments they were heading for the inner city and one of the best hospitals in Qu'Arim.

It didn't take the doctors long to diagnose Nadia's illness.

"Meningitis? Where would she have got meningitis?" Melissa asked, stunned.

Surim looked at her. "Did you take her someplace recently? Was she exposed to crowds?"

"Except for the souks and the restaurant Friday, we haven't been anywhere since I arrived, except the beach and grounds. Oh, Surim, she's so little to be this sick."

He reached out and captured her hand with his, squeezing slightly and drawing her closer as he spoke with the doctor. The little girl was gravely ill. They immediately put her on an IV for fluids and medication. She was being taken to Intensive Care.

"I want to go with her," Melissa said at one point, not understanding a word the doctor was saying, but determined not to leave Nadia alone where she'd be frightened.

Surim spoke to the doctor and the man nodded.

"We can stay with her. She'll have a private room and full-time nurse. Do you want to go home first and change?"

"No, I want to be with her right now. Is she awake?"

"He says she is asleep and will be in her room in a couple of minutes."

The doctor spoke at length again and Surim nodded. The doctor bowed slightly and left.

"What was that last bit? More bad news?"

"Bacterial meningitis is highly contagious. You and I need shots, as does anyone in the household who has been around Nadia. I am having a doctor go to the house to inoculate everyone. Let's hope Alaya and Hamid don't come down with this. Once we have our shots, we'll be permitted to go to her room."

In less than twenty minutes Melissa and Surim entered the private room. A nurse looked up at their arrival and Surim spoke rapidly in Arabic. Melissa scarcely noticed; she rushed to the bed.

Nadia looked so tiny in the hospital crib. There was an IV drip into her left arm, the needle taped into place. She opened her eyes when Melissa arrived and held out her arms.

Wrapping her in the blanket, Melissa eased her from the crib, Surim helping to keep the tube untangled. She sat on the chair and cuddled Nadia close.

"There, sweetie, we're here. You're going to be fine."

She held her for several minutes and gradually Nadia grew quiet and sleepy.

"This place needs a rocking chair," she said, rocking back and forth with the toddler.

"I shall see to it," Surim said, hovering over the two of them.

"She's going to be all right, isn't she?" Melissa asked in French. She knew meningitis was especially deadly with the old and the young. She didn't want to even think about Nadia not recovering. But if she had to hear bad news, she didn't want Nadia to also hear it.

"It will be some hours before the doctor knows for sure," Surim said. He dragged another chair over and reached out to caress Nadia's cheek. "I didn't realize how tiny she is. When she's running around, she's so full of energy. Then, suddenly, this."

"It did come on fast, but I think that's expected for this disease. So there's someone else in this city who has this illness. Do you have a public health system to warn citizens? What about the other children?"

"It is taken care of. Now we have to concentrate on getting this child well."

Surim admired Melissa's composure. He could do no less, but the fear that grew inside was hard to contain. He brushed the child's soft cheek and felt the heat. She seemed smaller than her two years. And so precious. When had he fallen in love with Mara's children? He knew he'd never be the same if something happened to her.

Yet he felt totally powerless to do anything. He hated the feeling. He had the entire country at his disposal, yet the doctor said all was being done that could be. Nature and the antibiotics they were giving her would have to take their course.

He wanted guarantees. He wanted to know this child would survive, thrive and grow into a beautiful woman as her mother had been.

"How do parents stand it?" he murmured.

"What?" Melissa turned to look at him. She was so close. Her beautiful face was drawn with worry. Her eyes haunted.

He wanted to comfort her, but lacked the words.

"Deal with sickness with their children. I feel so helpless."

"Me, too. I guess it's just part of life. But it's hard, isn't it? This is my first experience with a serious illness, though I had training for it. At a resort, children are rarely sick, except for tummy aches for overindulging." She bit her lip, looking back at Nadia. "She's been through a lot for two years of life. I'm hoping she's strong enough to beat this."

"She is. She has to be!"

Melissa gave a soft smile and reached out to grasp his hand. "From your lips to God's ear," she said.

The hours dragged by slowly. At one point Surim persuaded Melissa to replace the sleeping child in the crib to give her arms a rest.

He asked the nurse to bring in a rocking chair. He called his aide and made sure he had things covered. Surim also instructed him to have the inoculation, and then make sure everyone at the house complied. He also told him to bring a change of clothing for both of them.

He called Annis to speak with her, telling her what Nadia had, and warning her to downplay the severity with the other children. He did not want them upset any more than necessary.

Melissa's eyes were gritty with lack of sleep. But she was afraid to doze off for fear Nadia would need her. She felt fearful the child would not respond to the medication. Or there would be lasting problems caused by the disease. How could she have left her tonight for a party when Nadia had needed her? She rose again and leaned over the crib, rearranging the light covers, hoping the child would wake up feeling better.

Surim came back into the hospital room.

"Any change?" he asked.

Melissa shook her head. She straightened and looked at him, wanting more than he could give.

"The doctor said there wouldn't be for a while; I was hopeful, however. They are doing all they can," he said, looking at the little girl.

"You say that often enough and I'll believe it," she said crossly. "Why can't they cure her instantly?"

"That's what I want as well."

"Surim, what if she doesn't get better?" Melissa asked on a whisper. "I couldn't bear that."

He reached out and pulled her into his arms. "She will get well, Melissa. I won't accept anything else."

Startled, Melissa gave a choked gurgle of laughter at the thought of Surim ordering the disease away. The laughter quickly dissolved into tears. She was so afraid for Nadia.

Surim's embrace tightened, trying to give her courage and hope by his presence. She relished the steady beat of his heart, the strength of his arms. She couldn't imagine spending this watch alone. What if the child had been in a boarding school, thousands of miles away from anyone who cared.

"Melissa?"

"She's so little."

"She'll be fine; we have to hold onto that thought."

She nodded, brushing her tears and looking up at him.

He brushed another lonely tear away from her cheek, then leaned closer and kissed her.

His lips against hers broke something loose inside. She wrapped her arms around his neck and kissed him back, pouring out the feelings she kept hidden. She loved this man. She knew they would never share a future together, but for tonight, being together in this hospital room, sharing the vigil, was enough. She'd draw from his strength and go on once Nadia was out of danger.

He ended the kiss far too soon for her. But only a second

later a nurse entered carrying a rocking chair. Had he heard her footsteps in the hall?

Melissa stepped away quickly. She could not bear to have adverse gossip circulate because of his comforting gesture. And that was all it was, for comfort. She appreciated his efforts. At least, for a few startling moments, it had taken her mind off Nadia's illness.

Once the nurse had checked the baby and left, Surim turned to Melissa.

"I'm glad you're here with me for this. I just wish she'd wake up and be fit again."

"Me, too," she said, leaning against him as he encircled her shoulders and the two of them watched the sick little girl.

Nadia, however, was slow to respond to the drugs. The next day passed with nurses and doctors watching her closely. Melissa changed into comfortable clothes brought from home. She rarely left the toddler's side, holding her when she was awake, watching her closely while she slept.

Surim was there longer than she'd expected. He left for a couple of hours in the afternoon, returning in time to spell her for a meal. He insisted she go outside and walk around the building if nothing else.

"I don't want you dropping from exhaustion. Then where would we be?" he asked.

"What about you?"

"I had exercise, and checked on the other children. They are worried about you and Nadia."

"Me?"

"In light of their parents' deaths, any prolonged absence is suspect," he explained.

"Of course. But I can't leave Nadia."

"Tonight, once she's asleep, I think it best if we both return home for an hour or two to reassure Hamid especially. I'd hate for him to have nightmares again."

"I don't want to leave her."

"You will do her no service if you get ill yourself. And the other children want to see you."

Melissa took a breath. He was right. And she worried about the others. She wanted to make sure they weren't coming down with meningitis too. "Very well." And maybe Nadia would be on the road to recovery by the time she saw Alaya and Hamid.

The two older children rushed to greet Melissa and Surim when they arrived home. They had been sitting on the stairs waiting for them.

"I thought you'd gone away," Hamid said, hugging Melissa.

"No, sweetie, just staying at the hospital with Nadia."

"Is she going to die?" Alaya asked.

"No." Melissa refused to consider that.

"Can we see her?"

"When she's well again, we'll bring her home and you'll all be together again," Melissa promised, hoping that would be sometime very soon.

"And how do you two feel?" Surim asked.

"I'm fine. Annis said my appetite is like a camel," Hamid boasted.

Melissa laughed. "I'm so glad to hear that. And you, Alaya?"

"I miss Nadia. When is she coming home?"

"We don't know that yet. But she's getting the best care at the hospital."

Alaya didn't look convinced.

"Come into the salon and we'll tell you all we know," Surim suggested, holding out his hand to Hamid.

The four of them soon settled on the sofa, the two children between the two adults.

"Mummy and Daddy went to hospital before they died," Hamid said gravely.

"Yes, but most of the time staying in a hospital gets people well. Nadia will get better and be home before you know it," Surim said gently.

"I know it now and she's not home," Alaya said. "Can we go see her?"

"Not just yet. When she's better, we'll see if that will be permitted."

Melissa was so tired she wanted to lie down and go to sleep for a week. But she knew they had to reassure these children and then she had to go back to the hospital. She was still too worried about Nadia to leave her for long. The toddler was not yet out of danger. And Melissa was afraid she'd wake up and not see a familiar face by her bed.

After spending time with the children, and putting them to bed, Surim took Melissa back to the hospital.

"I'm sure they will be fine. Annis will watch them carefully," he said in response to her worry about Alaya and Hamid.

"Physically, sure. But you saw how much reassurance they needed. I feel so torn."

"I don't think they'll stop worrying about Nadia until she's home."

"Which I do hope will be soon."

Melissa felt his warm, strong hand briefly squeeze hers, and she closed her eyes. He was trying to comfort her. Just as she was certain he'd meant to do when he'd kissed her at the hospital. Only she hadn't reacted as if it was comfort. Desire had spiked. Yearning for more than a brief embrace had flared. She had fallen in love with the man and he hadn't a clue. He was planning to marry a *suitable* woman from his own culture and Melissa was destined to be on the outside forever.

Only, she wasn't sure she could do that anymore. His kisses had unlocked something wild and demanding. She wanted more, and if she couldn't have it she wasn't strong enough to stay and watch him marry another woman and bring her to the lovely house by the sea. She couldn't bear to take care of his children when she suddenly wanted to have his children herself.

A darling little boy with dark eyes like his father. And, hopefully, a girl with long black hair, who would wrap Surim around her little finger just as Nadia had done.

Yet could she bear to leave Alaya, Hamid and Nadia? She loved those children. She'd had no idea working for a family would be so vastly different from her childcare position at the resort. There she'd made friends with children, but none had stayed beyond two weeks. She remembered different ones fondly, but none with the love she had for Surim's wards.

"We're here," Surim said a moment later.

Melissa blinked and looked around. He had parked in the car park next to the hospital. The journey had flown by.

"Are you sure you should be here tonight? You could stay home. I'll call if there is any change," he said, but Melissa shook her head.

"I need to be with her. She's so tiny. What if she awoke and we weren't there?"

"I'll be here. It's not as if she'd awake to strangers."

"You're staying?"

"Of course. Nadia is my own. I'm as worried about her as you are."

He reached out a hand and cradled her jaw and cheek. "But I'm also worried about you." He brushed his thumb beneath her eye. "You look so tired."

Her heart rate increased exponentially at his touch, at his words. Try as she might to remain rational, hope blossomed. "I am, and I'm worried. But I couldn't sleep at home. I need to be with her," she said firmly.

For a moment he gazed into her eyes, before leaning over and brushing his lips against hers.

"Then let's go see how our girl is doing."

Nadia was still sleeping. According to the nurse, she had not stirred while they'd been gone.

Surim checked on her while Melissa watched, seeing the difference in him from when she'd first arrived. When she left, she'd go knowing the children had made a place for themselves with Surim. He wouldn't send them away to a school. They had gradually formed a strong bond of love. Melissa wanted to be thankful for that, but she felt the happiness she'd known these last weeks slipping away. She didn't want to leave, but she couldn't stay.

About ten-thirty Nadia woke up. She was fretful, but sipped some juice and the nurse was pleased with that. Another round of tests followed. It was almost midnight by the time Melissa sat in the rocking chair and held the child. She still ran a high fever, but was kept hydrated by the IV. She was listless, which was so unlike her. Melissa rocked her gently, wishing she could send good health through osmosis.

Yasine tapped quietly on the open door. She was dressed as if for a party in a silk suit and pearls. She rushed into the room to Surim, who rose as she reached him.

"Oh, Surim, I just found out when I was at a dinner party tonight and had my driver come immediately." She looked at Nadia, cuddled with Melissa. "How is she? What distressing news."

"She is still quite sick." He escorted Yasine from the room. "Meningitis can be contagious; you should not be in the room."

Melissa didn't hear any more, except the low murmur of voices in the hall. She rested her head against Nadia's and continued rocking. She appreciated the woman's instant response. She would undoubtedly make a good mother for the children.

When Nadia fell asleep some time later, Melissa put her back in the crib. Surim still had not returned. Had he escorted Yasine home? She paced the room trying to work out the kinks from sitting so long in the rocking chair. When she went to the window, all she saw was darkness. The grounds of the hospital were not lit up this late. Still she gazed out into the night. The stars were bright in the sky. She wished she were in the garden at Surim's home. Enjoying the peaceful night—and with no worries.

"Melissa?" He had entered without her hearing him.

She turned.

"You need to get some rest," he said, crossing the room to her side. His hands came to her shoulders to massage away some of the tension.

She looked at the little girl in the crib, rather than look into Surim's eyes. He couldn't see her feelings, could he? She'd be mortified if he suspected. But every fiber of her being longed to sink in against him, absorb some of his strength.

When his hands moved up to her neck and then threaded in her hair, she almost moaned with pleasure. He tilted her head slightly and she looked into his dear familiar eyes, her heart catching.

He narrowed his own gaze and stared into her eyes. "I want to kiss you again."

A sweet smile came involuntarily. "I should like that above all things," she said simply. She was too tired to dissemble tonight. She already knew she had to leave. What would one more kiss hurt?

It didn't hurt at all; it was glorious. His mouth moved against hers, gently at first, then with more passion. Opening her lips, he deepened the kiss, bringing her fully against him as his hand slipped from her head to her back, pulling her against him. She angled her head slightly to better kiss him back.

Endless waves of enchantment swept through her. She wanted more yet would have to settle for this. Sadly, she gently withdrew from the kiss. She would treasure these memories her whole life, but she was realistic enough to know when to stop.

He rested his forehead against hers, his eyes dark and dangerous.

"I was not ready to stop," he said softly.

She smiled sadly. "Me either."

"Then why?"

She pulled away and went to the crib. "Surim, you are looking for a wife. Anything between us keeps you from that goal."

"I'm not married yet."

"No, but you will be. And I can't stay. I need to return to England."

"Stay with me, raise my children."

To see him for the next eighteen or twenty years? Watch him with his own children, and his cousin's? Have to see him with Yasine and know she wanted him for herself? She absolutely could not do that!

"The children have responded so well to your care. Hamid hasn't had a nightmare in weeks. They are learning Arabic and doing well with their English schooling. And they've even accepted me. You can't leave," he said urgently.

She was torn. The sincerity in his tone convinced her he wanted her to stay. But things were too difficult. She could not do it. Slowly she shook her head.

He was silent for a long moment, then in a calm voice he said, "Then you must be my wife, Melissa. I choose you to marry me."

CHAPTER ELEVEN

MELISSA looked at him in shock. Surim wanted to marry her? For a blinding second her heart swelled in joy. Then reality took hold. He didn't love her. He didn't believe in love. He was worried she'd leave and he'd have to find someone else to help Annis with the children. Had that been the reasons for his kisses, his taking her out? To keep her happy enough to stay and make the children's lives easier?

"I can't marry you," she said, stepping away, feeling sick at the thoughts that crowded her mind. If anyone had told her earlier that she'd refuse an offer of marriage from Surim, she'd have thought them crazy. But now, with no word of love, with no reason except he didn't like the idea of her leaving the children, how could she even think of accepting?

"It would be the perfect solution," he said reasonably. "The children love you. They've had enough disruption in their lives without another. You like Qu'Arim, at least the parts you've seen. And we get along fine."

"Oh, right, that's a great recommendation for a lifelong commitment to live together. I'm sorry, Surim, but my answer is no. And I think it best if I leave as soon as Nadia is well."

"No, I want you to stay!"

"This makes it awkward," she said, trying to remain steadfast in her resolve, but weakening by the moment. To be married to the man she loved, without being loved in return, would mean nothing but heartbreak.

"I know you like the children. Would being married to me be so difficult?" he asked, ducking his head so his eyes were on a level with hers.

She shook her head. "Surim, we aren't suited. We're from different backgrounds—oh, wow, is that an understatement."

He captured her shoulders, turning her to face him. "I was also raised in England, for the most part. More of my formative years were spent there than here. I have a job—it just happens to encompass leading a country—so you can say I work for my living. You know I need to marry to produce heirs. Don't you long for children of your own? You are so good with them, I'd think you'd like to have a houseful."

She stared into his warm brown eyes and yearned to have a little boy who would have those same eyes.

"You don't believe in love," she blurted out.

"We have discussed that issue before. Look at the longevity of marriages in my country. They function well without love. And affection grows. We would have a wonderful life together."

Pictures of the two of them at formal dinners and receptions flashed into her mind. Then with children, Melissa always taking care of them and after him to spend more time at home, to share in their lives before they were grown and gone. Or sitting alone in the salon waiting for him to return late at night and having a few words before bed.

Where was the vision of confidences shared, of plans made, of family time? Or couple time? She couldn't imagine it.

"I want more than affection," she said finally. "I want to be loved and cherished. I want to be more than a mother to a houseful of children. I want to be a partner and confidante and lover. I want it all. I don't want only a part of it."

Maybe she should think it over longer, consider all the ramifications. But her instincts were good and she knew she needed more in a marriage than what Surim offered, much as she longed to say yes.

"Thank you for the honor you offered me," she said, dropping her gaze lest she be swayed. "I appreciate it more than you know."

"But the answer remains no," he said softly.

She nodded.

He brushed a kiss on her cheek and released her, turning.

"If you have things in hand here, I'll return home and check up on the other children. I'll be back early in the morning," he said, already walking toward the door. He paused and looked at her.

"If anything changes with Nadia, have them call me immediately."

"I will." She held her breath until he left, then let the tears flood her eyes.

Was she a total idiot, refusing an offer of marriage from the man she loved? Giving away her chance to stay with children she loved? To have little ones of her own.

Confused, hurt and lonely, Melissa returned to the rocking chair. She had a lot of thinking to do. She knew much of Surim's background. He had not had love as a child. His parents didn't sound as if they had been in love. He had nothing to show him the way. Could she? Dared she take a chance? It was her life on the line. And potential happiness. Or potential heartbreak.

Surim drove through the dark streets. He felt curiously numb. He'd asked Melissa to marry him after seeing Yasine tonight. The young woman had expressed her concern for Nadia, but she didn't even know her. She was showing him how compassionate she would be should she be chosen as his wife.

His aides kept him informed about the gossip around certain circles. He'd known Delleah wanted to marry him. Had Mara not died and left him guardian of her children, maybe he and Delleah would have made a match. She was beautiful.

As was Yasine.

As was Melissa.

He was stunned she'd refused him. He thought he caught a glimpse of emotion sometimes when they were together. He knew he wanted to spend time with her every day. He loved talking with Melissa on any topic. She was bright, articulate, had definite opinions. And she could make him laugh. Sometimes she did it deliberately, he knew. But other times he laughed for the pure joy of being with her. And when they kissed…

The road to his house came up, but he passed by heading for the sea.

She liked living here. The one certainty he had about Melissa was she wasn't a person to play games. If she liked something, she showed it. If not, she was clear on that as well.

When he reached the road that ran along the Gulf, he turned toward the restaurant he'd taken her to for lunch only two days ago. It seemed a lifetime ago. Nadia's sudden illness had changed everything. Put things into perspective, he'd thought. Melissa would make a perfect mother. She loved those children. Her refusal had to mean she didn't care enough about him to stay.

Which hurt.

Surim was surprised to realize that was the emotion that filled him. He wanted her and she didn't want him.

The story of his life, it seemed. He should be used to it by now. But he had thought she was different.

Reaching the restaurant's car park, he pulled in and cut the engine. The silence was broken only by the soft soughing of the wavelets as they splashed against the shore. The night was dark, stars littered the sky. But Surim saw nothing, gazing out into the darkness, feeling the night reflect how he felt. Dark and silent.

Dawn was breaking when he started the engine again. He'd

thought long and hard about the situation, but could find no resolution. If Melissa had her way, she'd be gone soon and he and the children would be left alone.

Unless he took drastic steps.

He reached home in record time. After a quick shower and change of clothes, he was ready for the day. Heading for his office, he placed a call to Max.

"Hello?" a rough voice answered the phone.

"Max? Surim here."

"Do you know what time it is? It's in the middle of the night. What's wrong?"

"Sorry, forgot the time change. I need to talk with you."

"Now? Is it an emergency? Did something happen to the restaurant? Don't tell me the thing burned up. I thought we were on schedule for the opening."

"It's not about the restaurant."

"Then what the hell do you need to talk to me about at two o'clock in the morning?"

"Melissa."

"What? Is something wrong with her? She's all right, isn't she?"

"She's fine. I need some advice, actually."

"About?"

Surim wasn't sure he wanted to confess the next part, but he needed Max's input.

"I asked her to marry me and she said no."

There was silence on the line for a long moment. Then, "You asked her to marry you? Why?"

"She's blended in perfectly here. She's terrific with the children. Thanks to her demands, I've come to know those kids and love them. I can't imagine not having them as part of my life now. I know we wouldn't have come to this without her."

Surim took a breath, waiting to hear what Max would have

to say. If he laughed or made some sarcastic comment, Surim would take the next plane to London to settle with his friend.

But Max didn't say anything for a few seconds.

"Is that it?" Max asked.

"She'd be perfect."

"Surim, she's a woman. What's in it for her?"

"She'd be my wife; isn't that enough?"

"Nice, if that's what she wants. From the little I've seen of Melissa, and I don't know her that well, material things don't seem to figure high in her scheme of life. She values relationships. How do you feel about that?"

"I want her."

"Yeah, she's a looker all right. But more than that?"

"What more?"

"I know men aren't big on expressing emotions; my sisters tell me that all the time. But isn't there something missing from your big declaration? Something like love?"

"That's a western myth. In Qu'Arim we arrange marriages. And they are highly successful. We have a very low rate of divorce."

"Quote her that, why don't you?"

"I have."

Max laughed. "God, Surim, you're a piece of work. I'd have liked to have been there to hear her response."

"I have to marry to assure the succession. Why not to someone I want?"

"And Melissa is that someone?"

"Yes."

"Tell her."

"I did, and she refused me. Max, you're English, you'd have a better handle on what I should do to convince her to marry me. I would have no difficulties if she was from here."

"Tell me all the reasons you think this marriage would work," Max said.

Surim listed the aspects of being with Melissa that he liked. He talked about the evenings they'd spent together, the delight he felt around her.

"So now tell me what it would be like to have her gone from your life," Max said some time later.

After a moment, Surim shook his head. "I cannot."

"Why not?"

"Because I can't imagine her not being a part of my life."

When the doctor arrived, Melissa had been up all night. Nadia had wakened a short time earlier and eaten all the breakfast the nurse had brought. Her temperature was back to normal and her eyes looked bright again. She smiled at Melissa and was restless, wanting to get down.

The doctor examined her and smiled.

"She is better," he said.

Melissa knew that. Nadia had awakened with her normal zest for activity and running around, and it was hard to keep her in the bed or hold her.

"So she can go home today?" Melissa asked.

"One more day, just to make sure. But I'm certain she is on the road to full recovery. Children this young get sick suddenly, but recover almost as quickly."

Melissa was so happy to see the little girl look like her normal self again. She could hardly wait for Surim to hear the good news. She asked the nurse to contact him.

"So, little one, you're going to be fine," Melissa said to Nadia when the doctor and his entourage left. "Soon we'll be back home." Melissa stopped suddenly. They'd return home, but she had plans to make. Who would take care of these lovely children? Would Annis be enough now? They'd had too many changes in a short time.

By mid-afternoon, Melissa realized Surim wasn't coming to the hospital. She'd had the nurse phone him again, and taken the receiver to speak to him directly. She wanted some of the books Nadia liked. And maybe a couple of toys to counter her restlessness now that she was feeling better.

He was not there, but the person answering rang her through to Annis who promised to send the requested items.

"How are the other children doing?" Melissa asked.

"They went with Surim today. They were all overjoyed with the good news," Annis said. "As was I."

For a little while Melissa thought Surim might be bringing the others to visit Nadia, but when one of the servants arrived with her books and toys Melissa gave up on that idea.

Where would Surim have taken the children?

By the time Nadia went to sleep that evening, Melissa was ready to drop. The nurse urged her to get some rest, reminding her that the next day Nadia was to be released and Melissa could scarcely care for her at home if she was too exhausted to even stay awake.

She reluctantly agreed. Before long the limousine had been summoned and Melissa sat in solitary splendor in the back, dozing on the ride to Surim's home.

When she arrived, the lights were on, but upon entering she found the house was silent.

She went upstairs, wanting to check on Alaya and Hamid.

Miracle of miracles, they were both asleep, and it wasn't even nine o'clock.

Going to her room, Melissa quickly showered and crawled into bed. She hadn't seen Surim today and already missed him with an aching that wouldn't go away. Was this how she would spend the next week and months and years without him?

The next morning when Melissa rose, the sun was shining as brightly as almost every other morning she'd been in Qu'Arim. She dressed, anxious to see Alaya and Hamid, and then go to the hospital to get Nadia. She went up to the nursery, surprised to see Surim already at the table with the children.

"You got the message about Nadia, according to Annis," she said, entering the room, trying to quell the sheer delight seeing him brought.

"I did. We will all go to get her at nine. I have already spoken with her physician this morning," Surim said. "Before we go, however, I wish to speak to you in the study downstairs. After we eat."

"Sure." Melissa greeted the children and soon sat down to eat her breakfast, wondering what Surim would have to say. Was he arranging a flight home for her right away so not to hinder her departure? Or would he try again to talk her into staying? It proved awkward to be with him after refusing his proposal. Her heart fluttered with apprehension. Either way, she was on tenterhooks until their meeting.

He escorted her down the two flights of stairs, not saying a word. They walked into the study and he closed the door. Without another word, he pulled her into his arms and kissed her.

She clung with abandonment, returning each caress and touch, running her fingers through his thick hair, holding on tightly for the exquisite sensations that threatened to explode. She'd missed him so much last night. Yearned to see him.

"I'm so relieved Nadia is getting better," he said a moment later, resting his forehead against hers. "Thank you for your devotion, Melissa. I've hired a nurse to watch her for a few days, just to make sure she's all right."

"Annis and I could have managed."

"I know. But there is no need. We will bring her home, then, before you leave, I want to show you something. The oasis I told you about."

Her heart dropped. Was this his gesture of farewell?

Swallowing the lump in her throat, she smiled. "I should love to see the oasis. But shouldn't I stay with Nadia?"

"As I said, she'll be safe with the nurse and Annis. We will wait another day and then fly to the interior."

Melissa held onto her smile, hoping it reached her eyes and that the sadness she felt wasn't evident. She wanted to run to her room and shut the door and pretend everything was as it had been a week ago.

Surim established the nurse in charge of the sick room. The little girl made rapid recovery. He went to see her that evening, reading to her and staying until after she fell asleep. Watching her sleep, he was filled with love. How wise of Melissa to make sure he and the children got to know each other. He couldn't imagine his life without them now. Any more than he could imagine it without Melissa. But if he didn't change her mind, that was exactly what he faced.

Early Wednesday morning, Surim escorted Melissa to a private airport near the capital's huge commercial airport.

"We're taking a private plane?" she asked when he parked near the small terminal.

"I have a plane I keep here. It'll take us to Wadi Serene."

"Wadi Sarene?"

"The name of the oasis."

"It has an airport?" Melissa pictured the place in the middle of the desert, alone and isolated. How far off was her imagination if it had an airport?

"No, we'll land in a nearby town, and then drive to the oasis."

When they walked to the plane, Melissa realized Surim was the pilot. She was fascinated by this side of him and watched avidly as he did the preflight check, burning every moment into memory. The flight itself was different from the big jets she was used to. They could see the city, and watch as it gradually gave way to less-populated areas until they were flying over golden sands. Here and there were settlements, mostly surrounding oil derricks. Surim pointed out the sights and gave her a running history of his country as they flew west. Soon even those scattered settlements were left behind and only the timeless desert unfolded beneath them.

Some time later Surim pointed out the small group of buildings in the distance. Slowly they drew closer as he descended. The airport was a packed dirt runway with a bright orange air sock indicating the wind direction. He brought the plane down in a soft landing and taxied to the small building that served as the terminal.

"That was fabulous!" she exclaimed as she stepped from the small plane. "I was able to see so much of Qu'Arim."

"From a distance. Come, the Jeep there is mine."

"Kept ready in case you drop by?" she asked as she walked beside him to the car.

"No, I called ahead to arrange things. It should be packed with food and supplies for tonight and tomorrow."

It was almost sunset before they reached the oasis. A small stand of palm trees rose from the desert. When they drew closer, Melissa saw the huge tent near the trees, and even heard the bubbling of the spring.

A breeze blew, cooling the air, highlighting the silence of the expanse. In every direction she looked, Melissa only saw empty desert. She and Surim were alone.

"It's beautiful," she said softly, drinking in the serenity and peace.

"I like it." He pulled the Jeep near the tent and stopped.

The canvas structure was unlike any Melissa had seen before. It had to be at least twenty feet long, with flaps tied back as if unveiling a masterpiece. She got out and headed for the opening, pausing a moment in the archway, then stepping in. She felt like Alice.

The interior was unexpected. Thick Persian carpets covered the sand. Chairs and a table were to one side, already set for a meal. A bowl of fruit spilling over. A divan with plump pillows sat in the back. A low brass table before it. Hanging panels of rich tapestries divided the sleeping areas from the main part. Brass lamps glowed, illuminating the space, though the sunlight still seeped in through the opening.

Turning, she smiled in enchantment. "This is the most fantastic thing I've ever seen," she whispered.

Surim came to stand beside her, looking around his tent as if through her eyes.

"The tent reminds me of our roots. The interior of how far we've come."

"Thank you for bringing me. I shall never forget it."

He gazed into her eyes. "I'm hoping you'll come again. I've never brought anyone else here, Melissa. It's my special place. I never thought I'd share it. But I wanted you to see it, hopefully to like it. It's somewhere we can escape to when life gets too complicated.

"Marry me, Melissa. Spend your days and nights with me. Grow old with me."

"Surim." How could she continue to refuse? Yet how could she settle? Wasn't that a mistake?

"After careful consideration and consultation, I have to admit I had not fully thought through my proposal at the hospital. Now I have and can say with all assurance that I love you."

"What? Impossible!" She stared at him, astonished. That was the last thing she'd expected him to say.

His eyes danced in amusement at her response. "Why so?"

"You don't believe in love."

"*Didn't.* I've had it pointed out to me clearly that the tangle of emotions I feel for you are all combined in one called love."

"Who pointed it out?"

"Max."

"You talked to Max Valentine about me?"

Surim kissed her gently, then passionately. It was some time before Melissa could speak again. But once she could, she narrowed her eyes as she looked up at him.

"So you think you love me?"

"I do," he said.

"Since when?"

"I believe since the night you started making demands in exchange for agreeing to stay."

"That first week?"

"You have fascinated me from the beginning. Then enticed me. Then beguiled me."

"I don't know what to say."

"Try, Yes, Surim, I will marry you."

"It's about the children, isn't it?"

"No. This is about you and me. The children will grow up and move out. I want you with me as long as I live. I love you, Melissa. Say you love me."

She was silent, trying to believe, feeling the warmth of his words fill her, the honesty of his tone reaching her. Her heart felt as if it would burst with happiness.

"Oh, Surim, if you're sure you love me, I'll marry you in a heartbeat. I love you beyond anything!"

The gleam in his eyes shone as he caught her in his embrace and kissed her again.

"Affection grows in marriage," he said, "but I didn't expect to feel such strong passion before."

"Love explodes," she said, hugging him hard. "Are you sure? I've loved you for weeks, but hid it because you were going to marry some suitable woman approved by the Qu'Arim ministers."

"You are now in Qu'Arim and I'm marrying you and no one else. And we'll get the ministers to celebrate the marriage. What more could we want?"

"I'm not so suitable."

"If I say you are most suitable, who is going to argue with me?" he countered.

Melissa laughed joyfully. She didn't know of anyone who would argue with the sheikh of Qu'Arim. Certainly not her—at least on this subject.

He took a deep breath and held her close. "I want you, Melissa. I want you in my bed every night, you and me and nothing in between. I want to make love to you until we are both too old to remember what it means. I want you at breakfast, chiding me about neglecting the children. I want you at dinner, making sure the children practice good manners. And in the evening when it's just you and me reviewing our day, I want to see you in pearls, and laughing with me, and looking at me with the love in your eyes that you give so freely to the children."

Her heart began to pound.

"I want you with all the passion in my soul. I never thought I'd care for anyone the way I do you. I've come to love those children, but it doesn't hold a candle to what I feel for you. When Max asked me to envision my life without you, I could not do it. You have become a part of me. I can promise you I'll love you and be faithful forever. I'll do all in my power to keep you happy throughout all our life together."

"Oh, Surim," she whispered. The man who had lacked so much in his life was promising to make hers wondrous beyond belief. "I thought you wanted me for the children."

"I want to have children with you—a little girl with her mother's green eyes. Or a little boy to grow in the ways of our culture to assume a leadership role some day. Or become a doctor if he'd prefer."

"What?"

He smiled. "I'll explain another time. I do want children, Melissa, but only with you. And once they are grown, it'll be you and me for the rest of our lives. I couldn't imagine spending those years without you. I love you; how can I prove it?"

"You have no need to prove anything. I believe you. And I love you too." She had tears in her eyes at his impassioned declaration. Her heart was overflowing. He'd brought her, and only her, to his special place, this magical oasis. He'd proposed to her as she'd never dreamed of being asked. Her heart was so full she could hardly stand it.

"So, what do you think about our life together?" he asked, gently brushing an escaping tear from her cheek.

"I want all that as well," she replied simply, glowing with love for him and the future he painted. 'As long as you love me forever."

"Forever and a day," he said, kissing her to show her just how much.

* * * * *

THE VALENTINE BRIDE

LIZ FIELDING

Liz Fielding was born with itchy feet. She made it to Zambia before her twenty-first birthday and, gathering her own special hero and a couple of children on the way, lived in Botswana, Kenya and Bahrain – with pauses for sightseeing pretty much everywhere in between. She finally came to a full stop in a tiny Welsh village cradled by misty hills and these days mostly leaves her pen to do the travelling. When she's not sorting out the lives and loves of her characters, she potters in the garden, reads her favourite authors and spends a lot of time wondering 'What if...?' For news of upcoming books – and to sign up for her occasional newsletter – visit Liz's website at www.lizfielding.com.

This book is for my daughter, Amy;
the joy of my life, my dearest friend, she
fills my head with stories and never fails to
make me laugh.

CHAPTER ONE

'I'VE printed out the PR schedule for this week's lead-up to the re-launch. The *City Lights* tie-in—' Louise Valentine broke off as her cell phone began to burble. 'I'll have to take this,' she said, excusing herself from the Nash Group executives gathered around the conference table for her briefing. 'I'm expecting a call from the editor…'

But as she flipped open the phone the caller ID warned her that it wasn't editor of the country's major 'scene' magazine.

It was Max.

For a moment she couldn't think, couldn't move, but then he'd always had that effect on her. Reducing her to a quivering wreck with a look that suggested it was a toss up whether he kissed her or strangled her. Since kissing her wasn't an option, she'd made a point of keeping her distance other than at family gatherings. Even then, by mutual consent, they'd chosen opposite ends of the room.

Unfortunately that was no longer a choice for either of them, but clearly Max was as unhappy about that as she was. He had certainly taken his time about making a moment in his busy schedule to talk to her about taking on marketing and publicity for the Bella Lucia restaurant group now that he was in charge.

Well, too bad. Her schedule was busy, too. She wasn't sitting around waiting for the phone to ring. On the contrary, the phone never stopped ringing. She was in demand, a success in her own right.

She hadn't looked back since the day he'd fired her from the family business, leaving her in no doubt that, far from being an asset to Bella Lucia, as far as he was concerned she was nothing but a liability.

Okay, she'd be kidding herself if she didn't admit that there had been moments in the last couple of weeks when she'd found herself doodling ideas on her jotter, daydreaming about what she'd do if she did take on PR and marketing of the Bella Lucia restaurants; the fact that it would mean working with Max never failed to tip the dream over the edge into nightmare territory.

Even now he was only calling her because he'd had his arm twisted; she knew he'd have refused point blank to consider it if the suggestion had come from anyone but Jack. Max's half-brother might not have wanted to stick around and run the company himself, but as he was a major investor his suggestions carried the kind of weight that not even Max could ignore.

So far Max hadn't been able to find the time to pick up the phone and ask her if she was interested in the job, forget actually getting to the point of sitting down and talking the future through with her. Hadn't done one thing to make her feel she was needed, that her ideas would be welcome, let alone valued. Well, why would he? She wasn't a genuine Valentine—

'Louise?'

She glanced up, realised that everyone was waiting. She snapped the phone shut, turned it off, tried to recall where she'd been in her briefing. *City Lights*…

'As you know, *City Lights* ran the offer for a limited number of complimentary tickets to the opening of your London flagship restaurant in today's issue. Free food, live music and the opportunity to mingle with celebrities; a chance to live the aspirational lifestyle for a night.' She looked up. 'You'll be gratified to learn that the response was so great that it crashed the *City Lights* systems, a story that was reported in the later editions of the London evening papers and will run in the diary columns of tomorrow's dailies.'

'Well done, Louise,' Oliver Nash said. 'With luck the tickets will be changing hands on eBay for hard cash by this time tomorrow.'

'If they are,' she replied, matter-of-factly, 'luck will have had nothing to do with it.'

* * *

Max heard the voicemail prompt click in, then Louise's cool, businesslike voice suggesting he leave a message, assuring him that she would return his call as soon as possible.

That would be about as likely as a cold day in hell, he thought, ignoring the invitation and tossing the phone onto his desk. Why would Louise bother to call him back? Why would she waste one moment of her time doing what he wanted? It had been years but she'd never forgotten, or forgiven him for firing her.

As if he'd had any choice.

One of them had had to go and Bella Lucia was his future, the one fixed point in his life. Even when his father had been changing wives faster than most men changed cars. When his mother had been more interested in her career, her lovers.

Everyone knew that Louise was just filling in time at the Chelsea restaurant until she fulfilled her mother's ambition for her by marrying a title so that she could spend the rest of her life swanning around a country estate, decorating the pages of *Country Life*, while a nanny raised her kids...

Not that the problem had been all her fault.

The truth was that he'd never been able to think straight around Louise and it had been ten times worse since she'd returned from a summer spent in Italy with a full set of curves, blonde curls that looked as if they had been tousled by some dark-eyed Latin and eyes that seemed to mock him.

If she hadn't been his cousin...

But she was. Family. Which meant that after college she'd joined the company, working in *his* restaurant, a situation about as restful as ploughing a minefield; you just never knew when the next explosion was going to happen.

The effect on the staff had been bad enough, but when a particularly disruptive outburst had involved a group of diners he'd had no choice but to fire her on the spot. No choice...

He could cheerfully throttle Jack for putting him in this position.

All the time he'd been in Qu'Arim, setting up the new restaurant, he'd been doing his best to convince himself that his half-brother didn't know what he was talking about.

Obviously he was right about the need to bring in some heavyweight PR muscle. It was a different world from the dreary post-war era; when his grandfather had opened his first restaurant, people had flocked to eat good Italian food served in warm and welcoming surroundings. Under the control of his father and uncle, they'd grown complacent. They'd been living off reputation, history, for too long. The business had stagnated. The restaurant in Qu'Arim was just the beginning of a new era of global expansion, but to make it work they needed someone who could update the image, get them reviewed, talked about; re-define them not just as a London, but a worldwide 'A-list' restaurant group.

Except that it wasn't 'they' any more.

The future of the company was in his hands and his alone. *He* needed someone. And his brother had made it clear that he didn't just need someone with Louise's talent to take up the challenge.

He needed Louise.

Of course, Jack, having dropped that little bombshell, had waltzed off back to New York leaving him to convince Louise to drop everything and come and work for him.

Yes, well. Having driven her away in the first place, he had to be the one to convince her to return. Whatever it took. Because it seemed to him that just at this moment Louise needed him, just a little, too, whether she'd admit it or not.

He wasn't fooling himself that it would be easy. Louise might have been a useless *maître d'*, more interested in flirting with the customers than doing her job, but since then she'd carved out a brilliant career for herself in marketing and PR. Her client list included one of the most successful restaurant chains in the country. She knew everyone in the business. Everyone in the media. And her mother's high society family gave her an in with the social elite. She *was* 'A' list.

She was also bright enough to know that Bella Lucia needed her a lot more than she needed Bella Lucia.

That he needed her a lot more than she needed him.

If the situation were reversed, if he were in her shoes, he knew he wouldn't listen to one word she had to say until she was on her knees, begging.

He hoped, for his knees' sake, that she wasn't inclined to carry a grudge that far.

Fat chance, he thought, checking the time.

If he shifted himself, he should catch her leaving the office. It wouldn't be so easy for her to ignore him face to face.

'You are a wonder, Louise.' Oliver Nash had waited while she locked up, walked her down to the street and now continued to hold her hand long after it had ceased to be the kind of handshake that concluded a successful meeting. 'Are you going to let me take you to dinner somewhere special? So that I can thank you properly?'

'You'll get my account at the end of the month, Oliver. Prompt payment is all the thanks I need.'

'One of these days you'll make my day and say yes.'

She laughed. 'One of these days I'll say yes, you old fraud, and scare you half to death. Go home to your lovely wife.'

'You know me too well,' he said, then as he bent to kiss her cheek she saw Max leaning against his muscular sports car, watching them.

'Dumped your toy boy for a sugar-daddy, Lou?' he asked.

Louise was thankful that the shadows were deep enough to disguise the flush that had darkened her cheeks. Even now he only had to look at her, speak to her, be in the same room, to send a shiver of something dark, something dangerous, rippling through her body. To disturb the even tenor of her life.

Not that there had been much that was even about it in the last few months.

Oliver, his hand still firmly holding hers, raised a brow a fraction of an inch and, since there was no way to avoid making introductions, she said, 'Oliver, I don't believe you know my...' She caught herself. She was still readjusting to her new identity. Still forgot... 'I don't believe you know Max Valentine. Max, Oliver Nash is a valued client; the chairman of the Nash Group.'

'Fast food?' Max replied.

'Fast profit,' Oliver replied, more amused than annoyed at being the butt of a younger man's jealousy. 'How's business in the slow food sector?'

The exchange, unpleasant though it was, had given her time to recover, put up the barriers with a distant smile, and she stepped in before it deteriorated further.

'I'll see you tomorrow, Oliver,' she said.

'You'll be all right?' He looked up as a thin, icy rain began to fall, then at Max. 'I'd be happy to give you a lift.'

'Louise and I have business to discuss, Nash,' Max intervened, his hand at her elbow, before she could be tempted to let Oliver chauffeur her as far as the nearest underground station in his Rolls. 'Family business.'

His hand was barely touching her. Max never touched her if he could help it, not since that summer before she'd gone away to Italy; after that everything had changed.

They had changed. Become unsettlingly aware of each other in a way that, for cousins, wasn't quite…decent.

Except that now she knew they weren't cousins. That she'd been adopted…

Carefully lifting her arm away, she said, 'Office hours are from ten until six, Max—'

'It's nearly eight.'

He didn't look at his watch and she wondered exactly how long he'd been waiting for her to emerge from her office. Her PA had left a little after six—she had a life—and it must have been before then, or how would he have known she was still on the premises?

She refused to feel guilty about that. Or rise to his bait. She didn't have to explain herself to him. To anybody.

'For valued clients,' she said, 'office hours are infinitely expandable.'

'Infinitely?'

She ignored the innuendo. What she did, whom she did it with, was nothing to do with him.

'If you want to discuss business,' she advised, 'I suggest you call my secretary tomorrow and make an appointment. I may have an hour to spare some time next week.'

She turned to Oliver, said, 'Thanks for the offer, but I won't take you out of your way.' She kissed his cheek. 'I'll see you tomorrow at the photo-shoot.'

Neither she nor Max spoke until the Rolls had pulled away from the kerb. Then she turned to him, said, 'Aren't you missing something, Max?'

'A PR consultant?' he offered.

She shook her head. 'I was referring to your usual accessory blonde. I imagine they have names, but it's so hard to keep up.'

She gained a certain amount of pleasure in seeing him clamp down hard, forced for once to hold his tongue, keep his temper in check. Taking unfair advantage of his predicament, she looked up and down the nearly empty street as if his latest airhead might have wandered off to do some window-shopping.

'Maybe it's a little cold for such delicate creatures to be out,' she added, even as she mentally slapped her wrist for goading him when he couldn't retaliate. But she owed him for that toy boy/sugar-daddy remark. 'No, I've just remembered. At the Christmas party you were flirting with Maddie, but she left with Jack, didn't she? The brother who inherited your father's good manners.'

'According to Jack,' he said, 'the only blonde I need at the moment is you.'

'Really?' She tutted. 'Then you're really going to have to try harder, aren't you?'

And, having done with Max, she raised her hand to summon a cruising taxi. He beat her to the door, opened it, climbed in after her.

'Excuse me but this is my taxi. You have a car,' she reminded him.

'We have to talk.'

'You have to talk. I don't have to listen.'

He didn't wait for an answer but gave the driver her address.

'Hijacking my taxi isn't going to get you what you want,' she said.

'What will?' he asked, sitting back in the far corner of the cab, as far from her as he could get.

That didn't please her either.

'Nothing. I have a thriving business, more clients than I can handle. Why would I be interested in leaving that to work for Bella Lucia? More to the point, why would I spare one minute of my time to listen to you?'

'You're family, Lou. That should be enough.'

'Family? Haven't you been paying attention, Max? That was all just a pretty fiction invented by the Valentines. Your parents, the people who pretended to be my parents. If you're looking for a family connection you've come to the wrong person.'

'Don't be ridiculous. Of course you're family—'

She arched a brow. 'If you've come to demand my loyalty, you're going to have to try a little harder.'

'Not demand—'

She cut him off before he could perjure himself.

'As I recall, being "family"…' she made those irritating little quote marks with her fingers; irritating Max when she had the upper hand was so satisfying '…wasn't enough the last time I was on the payroll. It certainly didn't save me from the humiliation of being sacked in front of an entire restaurant full of diners. I'm sorry, Max, but I don't see the attraction of working for you. I may be blonde, but I'm not dumb.'

'That was a long time ago, Lou.'

'Yes, it was, but what's changed, hmm? You're still treating me like some stupid girl who doesn't know her left from her right. Insulting me in front of an important client. Ignoring my wishes. Well, I've got news for you: I'm not a girl, I'm a fully grown woman and I've built up a successful business from nothing, just the way William Valentine did. You should try it some time, then you might have a little more respect.'

She swallowed. Wished she hadn't said that. Bella Lucia was Max's life. He worked harder than anyone to make it a success. If it had gone down in the recent financial crisis, no one would have been hit harder, or deserved it less.

It was always the same. The minute she was with him, she lost her head, stopped behaving like a rational woman.

She leaned forward, rapped sharply on the driver's window. 'Pull over, please.'

The cabbie pulled into the kerb, but Max didn't move. 'This won't go away, Lou.'

Probably not, but she was tired, she had another long day ahead of her tomorrow, and while a row with Max was always exhilarating she discovered that she wasn't enjoying this one.

'You want me to get down on my knees and beg, is that it?' he pressed.

That was almost too tempting, but Max, on his knees, would not be a supplicant. He would simply be demonstrating—at least in his own eyes—that he was bigger than she was. That he could forgive and forget. That in clinging to her grudge, she hadn't been able to move on. As he knelt at her feet his eyes would still be telling her that he was the winner.

'All I want,' she said, carefully, slowly, 'is for you to listen to what I'm saying. I'm saying goodnight, Max.'

For a moment she thought he was going to protest, force the issue, but then without another word he opened the door and stepped out of the cab, handing the driver a note to cover her fare home—still trying to keep control—and, shrugging his collar up against the rain, he began to walk back to his car.

Louise, left in the cab, was shaking, hating Max for putting her through that, hating herself for caring.

'Is that it?' The driver, having clearly heard everything, turned around. 'Do you want me to drive on? You're not going to change your mind and want me to go after him? Once I turn the corner I'll be locked in the one-way system and there'll be no way back.'

Max could do nothing but walk away. Acknowledge that, having behaved like a moron, he'd got no more than he deserved. What made it worse was that he wasn't like that; at least not with anyone else. He made an exception for Louise.

She never failed to bring out the worst in him.

He only had to look at her and he reverted from civilised man into some kind of Neanderthal.

Maybe she was right, he thought, hunching his shoulders against the icy rain that matched his mood. Nothing had changed. They hadn't been able to work together all those years ago and time had done nothing to mellow either of them.

He'd made the offer but she wasn't interested.

He stopped, blew out a long breath that smoked in the cold air. If someone had made him an offer like that, he wouldn't have been impressed either.

He'd wasted a perfectly good opportunity. He'd planned to ask her to join him for a drink, a meal maybe, and when he'd turned up just after six he'd thought he'd timed it just right. It had begun to unravel from the minute he'd arrived when her assistant, who had already had her coat on, had told him that Lou was in a meeting that was likely to go on for a while, but he could wait if he wanted to.

Sitting around in the outer office waiting for her attention wasn't what he'd had in mind and he should have left then, but, having wound himself up to see her, he'd chosen to wait in his car.

How long could she be?

Too long.

He'd had time to dwell on the memory of the Christmas party. Another failure. He'd known how bruised she must be feeling. Discovering that you were adopted at her age must be like having the solid ground beneath your feet turn to quicksand.

He'd planned to talk to her, let her know that he was there for her, but then she'd turned up in that outrageous outfit with some underage muscle-bound jerk on her arm.

On one level he'd known that it was just her way of showing the older generation, her parents, his father, just how angry she was with all of them for lying to her and he didn't blame her for that.

On a more primitive level...

He shook his head. He should have made more of an effort, he knew. Called her, found time for her, given her a chance to sound off and get it out of her system. He'd been busy, they'd both been busy, but how long did a phone call take?

Not that she'd needed him; the Australian might have been on the young side, but he'd had shoulders wide enough for half a dozen women to weep onto at once.

He'd just got to the stage of telling himself if he'd been there for her she wouldn't have needed to reach for a stranger when she'd walked out of the building with Oliver Nash, at which point he'd offered a classic demonstration of how to make a fool of yourself without really trying.

Only Louise could do that to him.

He flipped open his cell phone, called Louise's number. *This is not personal*, he told himself. *This is not for me, it's for Bella Lucia.*

If he could just stop thinking of her as a difficult, disturbing nuisance, start treating her as the talented professional she undoubtedly was, start listening instead of jumping in with both feet…

This time when the voicemail prompted him to leave a message, he said, 'Louise, I know you're busy.' He paused. Whatever it took… 'When you have a moment I'd be grateful if you could spare me an hour to talk about the future, about Bella Lucia—'

'Max…' Lou's voice cut in. He stared at the phone, frowned. Could you override voicemail and take the call?

'Max!'

He spun around.

Louise was caught in the light from the store windows, raindrops glistening in her hair, on the shoulders of her long black coat.

She'd ditched the cab, come after him, and for a moment he couldn't find the breath to speak.

'Louise…I was just leaving a message.'

'I heard you.' She was almost smiling, he thought. 'You were so polite. You must be really desperate.' Then, when he didn't move, she spread her hands and glanced up at the sky, said, 'So? Are we going to stand out here in the rain, or did you have a plan?'

'A drink? Dinner?' he said, scarcely able to believe his luck. She'd come back. 'I know this really good Italian restaurant in the King's Road.'

'Dinner,' she said, 'but somewhere neutral. Not Bella Lucia.'

He clamped his jaw shut, suspecting that she was trying to provoke him. Hoping he'd give her another excuse to turn her back on him.

'Anywhere,' he said. 'You decide.'

The restaurant she chose was close to her office and she was greeted with warmth by the staff. This, rather than Bella Lucia, was clearly the restaurant she used to meet with her clients, with the media people she was wooing.

His failure.

They were shown to their table, served quickly and efficiently, left to themselves and, much as it pained him to admit it, on this occasion she'd made the right choice. If they'd gone to one of his restaurants, his attention would have been constantly distracted by what was happening around them. His ears tuned to the reactions of fellow diners, listening out for problems instead of to her.

He'd seen his father act that way. The business had always been more important to him than anything. Anyone.

He'd tried to emulate him in business, if not in his personal life.

Tonight he needed to focus his full attention on Louise, put his whole heart into getting her on board.

It wasn't difficult. At seventeen, when she'd returned from Italy a newly minted woman, she'd been stunning. The years since had only added layers of character, style, polish and it was easy to see why a man of any age would want to worship at her feet. He couldn't afford to join them.

'How was your trip to Australia?' he asked. 'Melbourne, wasn't it? Did you enjoy it? What's it like?'

'Is that code for would it make a suitable venue for a Bella Lucia restaurant?'

She was warning him to back off, he realised, telling him that her other, newly discovered, family was nothing to do with him. He wanted to dispute that. She was a Valentine and all her family were important. This was not the time, however.

'Are you suggesting that I have a one-track mind?' he asked.

She took a sip of water. Said nothing.

Obviously she was.

'So?' he pressed, turning her question to his own advantage. Getting her to open up about Bella Lucia. 'Melbourne? What do you think?'

'I think you're leaping to the conclusion that I give a damn about Bella Lucia.'

'It's fed, sheltered and kept the designer clothes on your back for two-thirds of your life,' he reminded her. 'Paid for the apartment that Uncle John gave you when you decided it was time to leave home. I think you might give the tiniest damn, don't you?'

It was cruel. She blushed, swallowed, but he'd got her. She might be angry, bitter, but she knew what she owed to John and Ivy Valentine. She might not want to play happy families at the moment, but she wasn't a fool, she must know she couldn't walk away from them that easily and if she needed reminding, he'd be happy to oblige.

But while he'd hooked her, she wasn't happy about it.

'How do you plan a marketing campaign?' he asked, bowing to her expertise, using flattery to reel her in. 'Where do you start?'

For a moment she resisted, toyed with the linguine she'd ordered. He didn't leap in, try to push her.

'The first thing is to establish the brand,' she said, at last.

'Brand?' He frowned. 'We're not one of Nash's fast-food outlets.'

She dismissed his remark with an impatient gesture. 'Don't be so narrow in your thinking, Max.' Then, 'What do you think brings someone through the door of a Bella Lucia restaurant?'

'It depends which someone. Which restaurant. They're each unique. Individual in style, atmosphere. A man who met his colleagues for a business lunch at Berkeley Square would probably choose to take his wife for dinner in Knightsbridge, might have a coming-of-age celebration for one of his children in Chelsea.'

'Who would he take to Qu'Arim?'

He thought about it. Thought who he'd take there, then shook his head to clear the image he had of Louise there. With him.

'A woman he was in love with,' he said. Then, 'The oasis is the very essence of romance.'

'A very over-used word.' She regarded him for a moment, then said, 'If it was a fabric, what would it be?'

'A fabric?'

'Cotton?' she offered. 'No? Cashmere? Tweed? Velvet? Linen? Silk?' She ticked them off on her fingers.

'Silk,' he said. 'With a touch of cashmere.'

'And if it was a time of day?'

'Night,' he said, before she could list the options. 'Black with a sliver of moon, stars close enough to touch.'

'Every man a desert sheikh, every woman his captive slave? That's not romance, Max, that's a sexual fantasy.'

'Is that bad?'

'Probably not,' she admitted, a touch ruefully. 'It's not very PC to say this but sex sells.' Then, more to herself than him, 'I wonder what a woman's response would be.'

His smile was slow, thoughtful. 'I'll take you there. Then you can tell me.'

'I'm the one conducting a market survey,' she said, swiftly evading the elephant trap she'd so carelessly dug for herself. 'Tell me more.'

He needed no prompting to describe the setting of the resort, the undiluted luxury. 'We're very fortunate, Lou. Surim could have had his pick of international restaurateurs.'

'The old school tie is still worth something, then.'

'If you're going to save someone from a beating, it might as well be a future head of state,' he agreed.

Louise shook her head. 'Sorry. I didn't mean to be quite that cynical. I know you're good friends. Do you still play polo in his team?'

'Not recently. It's tough finding time to keep match fit.'

'You need to get out from behind the desk, Max. All work and no play—'

'Says the lady who's just worked a ten-hour day.'

'Twelve, actually.' She pulled a face, shrugged. 'I was at the office at eight. But it's only while I'm working on the HOTfood relaunch.' Then, quickly, moving on before he could say anything about pots and kettles, 'Okay, tell me about the food at the new restaurant. Mediterranean? Arabic? What is there beyond tabbouleh, hummus, the mezza?'

He smiled at her ignorance. 'Arab cuisine was once the most sophisticated in the entire world, Louise, embraced by the mediaeval courts of Europe.'

'Really? I like that. Tell me more.'

As she pushed him for details, forcing him to reach beyond the basics, Max actually began to relax, feel that this was, after all, going to be possible.

'I meant it when I said I'd take you there. I'd like you to see it for yourself.'

'And after Qu'Arim, what then?' she asked, not picking up on his invitation, but not refusing it, either. 'How far and how fast are you planning to take this?'

'How big is the world? The Americas, Asia, Europe.'

'Europe? Have you considered Meridia?'

'Obviously it's on the list.'

'I suggest you put it at the top. Bella Lucia catered for the coro-

nation, and now that your sister is Queen I'd have a bidding war from
the gossip mags to cover the opening of a new restaurant there.'

'We don't display our clientele for the media, Lou. We give
them privacy.'

'Okay, I could use that as an angle. Pictures of the interior pre-
opening offering a glimpse of something most people will never
see. Mystery, privacy, the unattainable. A glimpse of lace is always
more intriguing than total nudity.'

Max found himself staring at the cashmere sweater Louise was
wearing. It was some complicated wrap-around thing that crossed
over her breasts, offering no more than a suggestion of cleavage,
a promise of hidden delights. She didn't have to explain the allure
of the unattainable to him. He'd lived with it for as long as he
could remember.

CHAPTER TWO

'THAT rather depends on who's wearing the lace,' Max said abruptly. 'And what she looks like when she's shed it.'

Louise raised an eyebrow. What was eating *him*?

'You've spent more time in Meridia than I have,' he went on, before she could ask. 'What are the options for us there?'

She shrugged, let it go. 'What are the limits of your imagination? Somewhere really sumptuous high up in the old part of the capital, near the castle. Or maybe something completely different. A place where families could sit outside and eat in the summer. Maybe somewhere with a dock, since everybody seems to have a boat.'

Seeing it in her mind's eye, she was suddenly seized with enthusiasm, her thoughts running faster than she could say them.

'A lakeside pavilion, perhaps. Something...'

'Something what?' Max prompted.

'Um... Something simple, uncluttered, informal,' she said, suddenly realising that she was using her hands to describe her thoughts. She'd always done that. Her mother used to say it was her Italian ancestry coming out. Nonsense, of course. There was no Italian connection; John Valentine had been born before his father had ever met Lucia. But then her entire history had been founded on lies...

'How soon can you wind up your business and join us, Louise?' he asked, cutting into the black thoughts that threatened to engulf her.

Bringing her back to earth.

'Excuse me?' Her tone was deceptively mild. Her assistant

would have winced. But for a few minutes there she'd let herself imagine a different future, forget reality, but Max never let her down. Already he was assuming he'd won, but then he was a man programmed never to lose.

'Why on earth would I give up a business I've built from scratch to come and work for you?'

Max smiled. 'It's a bit late to start pretending you're not interested, Lou.'

'I…' In her enthusiasm she'd leaned into the table and suddenly realised just how close they were. Close enough for her to drown in dangerously deep blue eyes that had been mesmerising her for as long as she could remember. Close enough to catch the warm, male scent of his skin. To feel the tug of something she'd been resisting since she was old enough to understand that it was wrong.

She sat back, putting enough distance between them to feel, if not safe, then in control. 'My interest is purely professional, Max.'

There had been a time she would have died of happiness to have Max wanting her, needing her, but there was no way she'd give up her independence and crawl back under the shelter of the Valentine umbrella. Not now. She didn't need them. Didn't need him.

'Apart from anything else, I'm considering branching out myself,' she said, 'opening an office in Melbourne, using that as my base in Australia.'

He looked as if she'd hit him with a club.

She might have enjoyed that more if she hadn't been swept away, just for a moment, thinking what might have been. If anyone but Max were involved.

'You have a life, a family here,' he protested.

'You think so? Now Dad's skeletons have climbed out of the closet I find myself excess to requirements.'

Max looked as if he was going to deny it, but they'd both seen just how far John Valentine would go for sons he'd only just discovered existed. Even when one of them had nearly ruined the company, he'd still been sheltered, cared for. Loved.

'Have you told your parents? That you're considering moving to Australia?'

Louise swallowed. 'Not yet.'

'You're hurting, I understand that, but don't cut yourself off from your family, Louise.'

Family, family… He was always going on about the precious family; as a boy he'd spent more time with hers than with his own…

'I take it the toy boy is part of the plan,' he said, an edge to his voice that could have cut glass.

Relieved to be out of the quicksand of family relationships, she managed an arch, 'Are you, by any chance, referring to Cal Jameson?'

'If he's the one who was all over you at the Christmas party, then yes, that's who I mean.'

'He wasn't all over me,' she declared.

So much for her vow to keep her cool. With Max, that was only ever going to be a temporary measure.

'Oh, please. You arrived at the Christmas party dressed like some centrefold Santa—'

'I always come as Santa!'

With the long-running friction between her father and Uncle Robert—Max's father—the family Christmas party was a mine-field of tension at the best of times and she'd taken to turning up in a Santa suit bearing a sack filled with clever little presents matched to each member of the family. Her contribution to peace on earth in the Valentine family; bath oil on troubled waters.

This year, though, there had been two new family members; the sons that John Valentine hadn't known existed until a few months ago. Her only reason for pouring oil would have been to set fire to it so she'd abandoned the traditional 'ho, ho, ho' Santa outfit in favour of a red suede miniskirt with matching boots, a white angora crop top and a mistletoe navel ring—one that lit up and flashed in the dark.

Her cheeks heated at the memory. With the twenty-twenty vision of hindsight it was obvious that inviting Cal to kiss her under the mistletoe—purely to wind up a scowling Max—had been a mistake.

She should have anticipated that he'd ask, 'How far under…'

'I have family in Australia,' she said, quickly, before Max made the kind of remark guaranteed to provoke her beyond reason. 'A married sister.'

'You barely know her,' he pointed out, infuriatingly reasonable.

'And already I like her a lot better than I like you. Nothing has changed, Max!' She stood up, desperate to escape, desperate for air. 'I don't need this.'

He was on his feet, blocking her exit before she could take a step. 'You need it,' he said. 'You need it like breathing. Admit it. You're lit up with excitement at the thought of coming back.' She shook her head, but he repeated the words. 'Lit up like the Christmas tree in Trafalgar Square.'

'No!'

'You're a Valentine, Lou. Bella Lucia is in your blood.'

She almost gasped at his lack of understanding. Where had he been the last few months? Had he any idea…?

No. Of course not. Max didn't do 'feeling'. He was so utterly focussed on Bella Lucia, so absorbed by it, that he didn't need normal human emotion.

Well, she would just have to explain it to him. In words of one syllable…

'Is that what you really think?' she demanded.

'It's what I know. It's what I see—'

'Shall I tell you what I'll be doing tomorrow?' she demanded, not interested in what he could see. The question was purely rhetorical; she was going to tell him whether he wanted to know or not. 'I'm going to be taking afternoon tea in the restaurant on the top floor of the National Portrait Gallery. Minimalist elegance, smoked salmon sandwiches and great views should conversation prove difficult.'

'Why should it prove difficult?' Then, barely able to conceal his satisfaction, 'You're kissing off the Australian?'

'What? No…' She swiped at the air in front of her face, pushing his interruption away, pushing him away, the pervasive power of his presence. 'Cal isn't…'

'What?'

'Cal isn't any of your business,' she snapped. 'I'm meeting my mother, tomorrow.' Then, just to be sure he understood, 'Not your aunt, Max. Not Ivy Valentine.' Not the woman who, all her life, she'd been told was her mother. 'I'm meeting Patricia Simpson Harcourt, the total stranger who, it seems, actually gave birth to me. The woman who'll be able to tell me who my father was, what he looked like, because the only thing I do know about him is that he wasn't John Valentine.'

'Louise—'

'You do see, don't you?' she asked, cutting short his attempt to interrupt, to tell her that it didn't matter. Because it did. 'You do see how wrong you are? Valentine blood does not flow through my veins. Not one drop of it. The only liquid connecting me to the Valentine family is the ink on the adoption certificate.'

'Please, Lou.' He caught her hand, refusing to let her pass him. Escape. 'Don't do anything hasty. Bella Lucia needs you.' Then, almost as if it hurt him to say the words, he finally said what she'd always wanted to hear. 'I need you.'

His words brought her up short. She might mock his dedication, but Max had always been the one everyone else depended on. The one that everyone else turned to in a crisis. For him to admit that he needed anyone had to be a first. For him to admit that he needed her…

'Y-you sacked me,' she said, more to remind herself what he'd done than jog his memory. It had been a scene neither of them was likely to forget. 'In front of the entire restaurant. You didn't care that I was family then—'

'That was the problem, Lou,' he cut in. Then, more gently, 'That was always the problem.'

'I-I don't understand.'

'Don't you?'

Of course she did. As a girl she'd worshipped him. She should have grown up, got over it. It hadn't worked out like that. Quite the contrary. Even now he had the power to reduce her to a gibbering idiot, a mass of exposed hormones. All it took was the touch of his hand to turn her to jelly. If she didn't get out of here now…

'Don't you?' he insisted. 'Are you really that stupid?'

'Thanks for that, Max,' she said, snatching away her hand. For a moment she'd thought that maybe, just maybe, they could make a fresh start but she'd been fooling herself. 'You've just reminded me why I'd rather starve than work for you.'

As Louise strode towards the door a waiter held out her coat.

She didn't pause to let him help her into it, but grabbed it and as he leapt to open the door walked out into the cold rain.

She glanced up and down the street, hoping to spot a cruising cab, but there wasn't a sign of one and, without stopping to put on her coat, she began to walk.

'Not one drop…'

Max was rooted to the spot for long seconds as her words echoed in his head, as the reality of what that meant sank in.

'Shall I bring the bill, sir?'

The waiter's voice jerked him out of the moment of revelation and he realised that he was letting Louise walk away, that if he didn't do something to stop her right now he'd have lost her, or, worse, that she wouldn't stop walking until she was out of all their lives. Not just lost to him, but to the family who loved her.

Not bothering to reply, he tossed a credit card on the table and headed for the door.

The same waiter, apparently anticipating his reaction, was holding his coat out and the door open so that nothing should impede him.

Louise was walking swiftly along the street, the high heels of her boots ringing against the wet pavement, her coat trailing from her hand. The fact that she was oblivious to the rain now coming down in torrents, soaking her hair, soaking her through to the skin, gave him hope.

She was upset, angry. If she didn't care, she would be neither.

'Louise!' His voice echoed along the empty street, but she neither slowed nor quickened her pace, made no sign that she'd heard him. 'Wait!'

A cab turned the corner and, ignoring him, she raised a hand to hail it, forcing him to sprint along the pavement to head her off.

'Here's a point for you,' he said breathlessly as he leaned against the door, blocking her escape.

She didn't protest, just turned away as another cab appeared, but he reached out, caught her hand before she could summon it.

'Here's a point for you,' he repeated more gently as with his free hand he picked a strand of wet hair from her cheek and tucked it behind her ear. Held it there. 'You were adopted.'

'Hallelujah,' she said, but she didn't move, didn't toss her head to dislodge his hand. 'For once in your life you were listening.'

Her words were spiky but her voice was ragged, hurting.

She was looking up at him, her eyes leaden in the street lighting, her lashes clumped together by the rain pouring down her cheeks. Or maybe it was tears and for a moment the impulse to kiss her almost overwhelmed him.

Not now...

He'd paid heed to the warning voice in his head all his adult life. Kept his distance even when the only thing in his head had been to stop her anger with his mouth, knowing that she wanted it, too; was goading him, tormenting him, tempting him to do something about the primal response that arc'd between them whenever they were in the same room; urging him to self-destruct. Now there was no impediment, no barrier, only hard-won self-restraint, some instinct warning him that this was not the moment.

'I was listening,' he told her, his voice cool, even though every other part of him was burning hot.

'So?'

So kissing her suddenly seemed the most important thing in the entire world.

This is about the restaurant, not you!

He ignored the voice of common sense. This was important...

'So you're not my cousin, Louise.'

'Give the man a coconut—'

Her skin felt like wet silk beneath his fingers. Her mouth was full and dark and suddenly all the wasted 'touch not' years crowded in on him, urging him to taste it, taste her.

'And if we're not cousins,' he continued, a little shakily, 'we don't have a problem, do we?'

Not now, idiot! Bella Lucia is more important than scratching a ten year itch.

But...

You'll blow the whole deal if you kiss her, because it wouldn't stop at a kiss. She'd come along for the ride, she wouldn't be able to help herself, but what then? She'd never forgive you...

But she'd come...

'We don't?' she asked, a tiny frown creasing the centre of her forehead. She drew in a breath as if to pursue it further, then shook her head, clearly thinking better of it. 'You're taking me for granted, Max,' she said.

'No...'

He denied it, but without sufficient conviction to stop her.

'Yes! You believe that all you have to do is turn up, snap your fingers and I'll fall in line. I have a career, a successful business, a life of my own—'

'I know,' he said. 'I know. You owe me nothing. But think of Bella Lucia. Think of your father...'

She jerked free of his touch then and he knew that in clumsily mentioning her father, he'd made things worse rather than better. She could have no idea how he'd felt as he'd watched her with her parents. Proper parents who always put her first. Doted on her...

She was hurting too much to listen to him tell her how lucky she was. How lucky she'd been all her life. Right now, he suspected, there was nothing he could say that would help. Maybe he would, after all, have been better served by less thought, more action but he'd missed the moment, allowed her to climb back on her high horse.

'Enough,' he said, letting it go. 'You're wet through.' He took her coat, wrapped it around her shoulders. 'You need to go home, get warm.' He opened the cab door, saw her safely in and this time resisted the temptation to join her, but instead, on an impulse, said, 'Would you like some company tomorrow?'

'Tomorrow?'

Louise couldn't think straight. They weren't cousins. Well, she'd understood that. In theory. She just hadn't thought through what that meant. Hadn't anticipated exactly how she'd feel in that dangerous moment when, for a heartbeat, she'd been sure Max had been about to kiss her. Finally. At last...

'When you meet this woman who says she's your mother,' he prompted, bringing her back to earth.

'She *is* my mother.'

'Is she? Really? More so than Ivy? I'm sorry, but it's hard for me to get my head around that.'

'Really?' She heard the sarcasm fuelled by frustration, disappointment, dripping from her voice. Why hadn't he kissed her? What else could he have meant when he'd said they 'didn't have a problem'? 'Well, if you find it hard, why don't you try putting yourself in my shoes?'

'Don't be so defensive, Lou.'

'Defensive?' He thought she was being defensive? 'You think I should be sweet, biddable, good little Louise and not make a fuss, hmm?'

'Sweet? Biddable?' He shook his head, might have been fighting a smile; his face was shadowed and it was hard to tell. 'Sorry, sweetheart, I know that you've managed to fool the older generation with that myth since you were old enough to work out that a smile would bring you more than a scowl, but you've always managed to keep that side of yourself well hidden around me,' he said. Seeing her sarcasm and raising it to scorn.

About to respond in kind, tell him that if she did, it was his fault, she clamped her mouth shut. The truth was that he brought out the very worst in her, that even now, angry as she was, all she wanted was to drag him into the cab with her and be very, very bad indeed.

She took a slow breath. She was losing control. Again. She'd got away with it once this evening; she wasn't going to risk it twice.

She'd always known she would do what he wanted, that despite everything she owed the family who'd raised her that kind of loyalty, but she hated the fact that it was Max who was doing the arm-twisting. She'd do it, but on her own terms.

Set her own price.

Not money…

And an idea slipped into her mind and lodged there.

She shook her head, forced herself to look at him. 'I don't need anyone to hold my hand, Max.'

'You have no idea how you'll feel. I won't intrude, but if you knew that there was a friend nearby. Someone you could talk to…'

'You?' she enquired, coolly, rescuing him as he ran out of platitudes. 'Can you really spare the time? With all those restaurants to run,' she reminded him.

'I'll make time.'

Her only response was to raise one eyebrow. It was not original, but he got the point.

'I promise.'

'Oh, right. So tell me, Max, would that be like the time you promised to escort me to my school prom?' She didn't wait for Max to come up with some plausible excuse for leaving her all dressed up, without a date, for the biggest night of her young life. Her father wouldn't let her out that late with anyone else. Not that she'd wanted anyone else. 'At the very moment when all the phones in the world apparently stopped working,' she added.

'You know what happened,' he protested. 'Dad was short-handed in the restaurant.' And he was the one thrown back on the defensive, dragging fingers through his thick, cropped hair in a gesture that was achingly familiar. 'Before I knew it, it was gone ten and there was no way I could get there in time. You know what it's like—'

'Yes, Max, I know.' She knew only too well what his promises were worth. 'It was like the time you promised to pick me up and take me to the airport.'

He frowned.

'No? Well, you didn't remember then, either, but don't worry, it's not one of those once-in-a-lifetime, never-to-be-repeated experiences; there's always another plane.' She suspected she was hurting herself more than him by dredging up all the times when, caught up in work, he'd let her down. But for once he was forced to listen and she persisted. 'And as for the time you left me stranded—'

'I'll be there, Louise,' he said, cutting her off. 'I'll be there,' he repeated, but gently.

Gently, she thought, he might just destroy her. She couldn't allow him to be gentle.

'If nothing more important comes up.'

But she was safe. Something always did. She knew that once he was working Max forgot everything, everyone else. That he always put the success of the restaurants, his responsibility towards the staff, before his personal life. Maybe that was the reason for the constant stream of girlfriends. It didn't, as she could testify, do much for a girl's self-esteem to be stood up for a restaurant.

'I won't hold my breath.'

Not waiting for more protestations of sincerity, she reached forward and pulled the door shut, gave the driver her address and huddled down beneath her coat, her teeth chattering as reaction set in.

Max watched as the taxi pulled away, disappeared into the murk of a wet January night, hard pressed to decide whether he was angrier with Louise for being so unreasonable, so prickly, or himself for not doing better. Not that there was anything he could do about it now.

What he could do, must do, was return to the restaurant and make his excuses for their abrupt departure. And give his card to the waiter who'd impressed him with his quick thinking, tell him to call if he ever needed a job.

Even as he did it, he knew that if she could see him Louise would curl her lip, give him the look that said, 'See? Business first, last and always…'

Maybe she had a point, but tomorrow she was guaranteed his undivided attention. Even if the roof fell in at all three London restaurants at the same time he would be there for her and not only because he would do anything to get her on board.

He'd be there because she was in grave danger of cutting all family ties, walking away. Her anger, her sense of betrayal, was clouding her judgement. But then she'd never been without two loving parents. Never, in her whole life, known what it was like to feel alone. Never would, if he had anything to do with it.

At least with him she'd never been afraid to show her feelings. Quite the opposite. And he smiled. For once, that might be a good thing.

Taking his own advice, he thawed out under a hot shower, running through the ideas Louise had tossed out over dinner. He'd just seen expansion as more of the same, but she'd seen the danger of turning Bella Lucia into an upmarket chain, with the expectation that each one would offer the same menu, the same experience, no matter where in the world you happened to be.

That wasn't what they did. Each of their London restaurants

was different in atmosphere, style, clientele. They had to carry that across the globe. Use that individuality as their 'brand'.

Already questions were piling up, ideas he wanted to bounce off her; he wanted to be able to pick up the phone now and carry on where they'd left off before he'd blown it all with one careless phrase. What was it she'd said? That she'd rather starve than work for him?

Despite the frustration, he grinned.

Starve? He didn't think so. Bella Lucia had been part of her life since she was old enough to lift a spoon; she'd have come back like a shot if Jack had stayed to run the company.

She didn't have a problem with the business. She had a problem with him.

So what would it take to get her to swallow that bitter pill? What would tempt her to work for him? Keep her from leaving the country and starting up again on the other side of the world?

There had to be a way. There was always a way. For anyone else it would simply be a question of money; how much would it take? But this was more than a job for Louise, just as it was more than a job for him.

For him it had become his life.

What could he offer her that she wouldn't be able to turn down?

And the same internal voice that had warned him so violently against kissing her was now taunting him, saying, *If you'd kissed her she'd be all yours…*

What did you wear to meet your birth mother for the first time? Something sweet and girly? The kind of clothes that a mother would want to see her daughter wearing? The kind of clothes that Ivy had bought for her. Pretty clothes. Good girl clothes. Hair bands, pie-crust frill blouses, modest skirts, an embarrassingly modest sugar-pink prom dress that had made her look exactly her age, rather than all grown up. A dress she'd modified so that the minute she reached the safety of the hotel she was going to replace the ghastly sweetheart bodice with a black strapless top that would knock Max for six.

She'd never been quite the Little-Miss-Perfect that her mother had believed her to be. Even at sixteen, she'd wanted Max to look at her, to hold her, to desire her. Her deepest longings, darkest thoughts, had always involved him.

How bad was that?

She'd been exhausted when she'd finally fallen into bed, but her sleep had been disturbed by a continuous flow of ideas for Bella Lucia. She should be totally focussed on the final run-up to the HOTfood launch at the end of week, but her sleeping mind had moved on; it was only when she'd tried to interest Max—always too busy to listen—that she'd been jerked awake, shivering.

She had to forget him, forget Bella Lucia, she told herself as she flipped through the classics that were the mainstay of her wardrobe these days. Elegant dresses for the evening, designer suits.

She'd temporarily abandoned them when she was in Australia; staying with Jodie she'd gone beach-girl casual, not just in her clothes, but in her attitude to life. Well, that hadn't lasted long before she'd been summoned home when her father had found a great big hole in the tax fund account. Already it seemed like a lifetime away.

Then her hand brushed against her shock-the-family red suede miniskirt.

It had worked, too.

Her mother had definitely not approved but she hadn't said a word. Just tightened her lips and forced a smile. Even welcomed Cal to the family party.

Max, of course, as always, had curled his lip and kept his distance.

She could never decide whether that was better or worse than his insults. On this occasion he'd quickly turned to flirting with Maddie, ignoring both her and her outrageous Christmas outfit.

From the way he'd reacted last night, however, it was obvious that he'd taken in every detail. And despite everything she smiled as her fingers lingered against the softness of the leather; no question, he'd noticed.

'Pitiful,' she muttered, pushing the skirt away, trying to push away the memory. Disgusted with herself for behaving so badly.

Certain that Max's perfect recall would be missing when it came to his promise to turn up this afternoon.

He'd have a million more important things to do than hang

around an art gallery in the unlikely event that she might need one
of his broad shoulders to cry on.

As if.

Not that she cared. It mattered not one jot to her whether he
turned up or not. Any more than it mattered which suit, which
shoes, she wore today.

She didn't need anyone. Not the mother who'd given her
away, not the mother who'd lied to her and definitely not the man
whose promises were about as reliable as the forecast of sun on
a public holiday.

She blinked back the tears and, catching sight of herself in the
mirror, pulled a face.

Oh, for goodness' sake! Who did she think she was kidding?
Today of all days she had to look fabulous and twenty minutes later
she was on her way to the office wearing a head-turning dark
plum suit with a nipped-in waist, a silk camisole a shade or two
lighter and ultra high-heeled suede peep-toe shoes that had cost a
mint, but exactly matched her suit.

The luscious matching silk underwear she wore purely for her
own pleasure.

'You're cutting it fine, Lou.' Gemma, her PA, held out her coat,
pointedly. 'There's a taxi waiting for you.'

'Thanks. If Oliver calls back about—'

'I'll handle it. Go.'

'But you'll need…'

'Go!'

'Okay! I'm gone…'

She'd thought the day would drag, but in truth it had flown by
with barely a moment in which to draw breath. Cramming in a last-
minute meeting had left her with no time to clock-watch, ponder
the coming meeting, how it would be to come face to face with
the woman who'd given birth to her before surrendering her to a
stranger. Suddenly that didn't seem such a great thing. Excitement,
anticipation churned with fear in her stomach and she wanted time
to slow down. Wanted to put this off…

Wanted someone to hold her hand.

Would he be there? Max…

The clock on the tower of St Martin's-in-the-Fields had already nudged past four as she paid off the taxi and walked through the door of the National Portrait Gallery.

She didn't linger, didn't look around to see if Max had, for once, kept his word. She wanted it too much. Better not to know, to be able to pretend he was there in the shadows watching over her. And if, by some miracle he was there, she wouldn't want him to know how much it mattered. How scared she was. So, looking neither to left nor right, she headed straight for the lift, punched the button for the top floor where the restaurant provided a rooftop view of Trafalgar Square, distant Westminster, the Eye…

She'd heard all about her mother from Jodie, of course, although she suspected that her half-sister had glossed over the bad bits—and there were always difficulties in the mother/ daughter relationship—wanting her to be able to make up her own mind. Knew what to expect. In theory.

She'd seen photographs.

She'd always thought she looked like Ivy Valentine; everyone, even the few members of the family who'd known the truth, had always said how much like Ivy she was—perpetuating the lie.

Once she'd seen a photograph of Patricia Simpson, however, she'd seen the lie for what it was. Here, in the shape of the eyes, the way her hair curved across her forehead, something about the chin, was a genetic imprint that unmistakably linked them and she'd never doubted for a moment that she was looking at her birth mother.

She stepped from the lift, hesitated. Took a moment to steady her breathing, slow her heart-rate, just as she did before a big presentation. Putting on a show…

Then she walked into the restaurant.

She'd imagined looking around, hunting her mother out, but there was no missing her. She might be in her early fifties, but she was still a head-turner.

Her red hair, no doubt kept that way with chemical assistance these days, slid sensuously across her cheek. Her long, finely muscled dancer's legs were crossed to advantage, showing off high insteps, exquisite shoes.

She was sitting by the window, but she wasn't looking at the view. Instead she was chatting to a man sitting at a nearby table, chin propped on her hand, her throaty laugh reaching across the room. He couldn't take his eyes off her and neither could Louise.

Seeing the reality was like the difference between an old black and white movie and Technicolor.

For a moment she couldn't breathe. Couldn't move.

A waiter hovered to seat her, but she ignored him. The rest of the room disappeared. There was only her mother and, as if somehow sensing her presence, Patricia Simpson Harcourt looked up and their eyes connected.

CHAPTER THREE

LOUISE had tried to imagine this moment. Picture it in her mind. What would she say? Would they shake hands? Hug?

Her mother stood up in what appeared to be slow motion and Louise began to walk towards her, barely conscious of a floor that felt like marshmallow beneath her feet.

Neither of them said a word, they just reached for each other, clung to each other for what seemed like an age, until gradually the sounds of the restaurant, other people talking, the clink of a spoon, began to impinge on the small bubble of silence and they parted, Patricia holding her at arm's length.

'Well, look at you!' she finally said. 'You're so beautiful.' Then, with a grin, 'And you have such great taste in shoes!'

Louise shook her head. Shoes? 'It's obvious where I got it from…' she began, hesitated, her tongue tripping over the word she'd been rehearsing, but there was no way she could call this glamorous woman "Mother", or "Mum". 'I don't know what to call you,' she said.

There was only the briefest hesitation before she replied, 'Patsy, darling. Call me Patsy.' She turned away quickly, smiled and nodded at a hovering waiter. 'I've already ordered,' she said, sitting down. Then, head slightly to one side, 'Louise? It suits you. I was going to call you…'

'What?'

'Nothing. Pure indulgence.' Then, 'Zoë. I was going to call you Zoë.'

'I'd have liked that.'

'Yes, well, it wasn't meant to be.'

Louise waited. She wanted to ask the big question. *Why?* Instead she said, 'I only found out that I was adopted a few months ago. If I'd known, I'd have looked for you before.'

'Things happen for a reason. Ten years ago I was not the person I am now; I might have been bad for you.' She smiled. 'The earth turns, things change. Now is the right time for us to get to know one another.'

'Maybe…' But it wasn't her mother she was thinking about. What had happened had been out of her control. With Max things were different. It was her decision.

Everything would be so different this time…

Without warning her body seemed to tingle with anticipation, excitement.

'Louise?'

She gave a little shiver. 'Sorry?'

'I said that there's no point in dwelling on what might have been.' Then, looking at her more closely, 'Are you all right? This must all have come as something of a shock to you.'

'No. I'm fine.' *…we don't have a problem…* 'Can I ask you about my father?'

'Oh, well… There's not a lot to tell.'

'His name?' she prompted.

'Jimmy. Jimmy Masters.' She gave a little sigh. 'He rode a motorbike, wore a leather jacket, smouldered like a cut-price James Dean. He was totally irresistible. Not that I tried very hard,' she confessed, with a rueful smile. 'To resist him. He took off, never to be seen again, the minute I told him he was going to be a daddy.' She shook her head. 'I didn't want to give you up, Louise. It was hard, I had no idea how hard it would be, but everyone said you'd have a better life with a good family.' She leaned forward and took her hand. 'I've only got to look at you to know that I made the right decision.'

She did? That wasn't quite what Louise had wanted to hear. She wanted regret, remorse. Instead, beneath that bright, confident smile, Louise realised, Patsy needed to be reassured, to be told that she'd done the right thing.

Just like everyone else, her birth mother wanted her to understand, absolve her from her guilt...

'I've had a lovely life,' Louise said.

It was true, she had.

She'd been cherished, loved, given everything she'd ever wanted. Everything except the truth. The companionship of a sister she hadn't known existed...

They'd all known. Her grandparents, Max's parents. And they'd all lied. The bitterness was as strong, as tangible as the aloes her nanny had painted on her fingernails to stop her from biting them.

But she couldn't get past the fact that she'd had a blessed life. That she owed them for that. She'd always intended to help with Bella Lucia—once Max could bring himself to ask nicely. She would repay them with her time, her skill and then she would be free to do whatever she wanted. Be whoever she wanted to be. The only thing she wasn't prepared to do was give up the business she'd worked so hard to build, give up her independence.

It more important than ever now.

Her rock.

And, in a heartbeat, she understood a little of what Bella Lucia meant to Max. It had been the one fixed point in his life. When his parents had packed him off to boarding school to get him out of their hair, when Aunt Georgina had disappeared for months on end on some painting expedition with her latest lover, when his father had been drooling over his latest wife, Bella Lucia had been his rock...

While she had two mothers who cared about her, who had ever been there for him? They'd been so close once... Because of what her family had done, their lies, he'd lost that, too.

Without warning tears stung against her lids, not for herself this time, but for Max and to distract her she picked up her bag, opened it, said, 'I've brought you some photographs. If you'd like them?'

And suddenly they were both blinking and laughing as she produced a little wallet filled with her firsts: first steps, first birthday, first day at school in a blazer a size too big with her hat set just so, so that the badge showed...

'Oh, please, put them away and look at them later, or we'll both end up with panda-eyes,' Louise said, torn between laughter and tears. 'I want to hear about you, Patsy. Jodie told me you've just got married again. Tell me about Derek.'

She lit up. 'Every woman should have a man like Derek Harcourt in her life.' As she poured the tea the blaze of diamonds on her left hand caught the lights. 'He really cares about me. Keeps me on the straight and narrow with my diet—I'm a diabetic, did you know?' she said, pulling a face.

'Jodie told me.'

'You'll need to keep an eye on your own health. It's hereditary.'

'I'll take care.' Then, 'Tell me about your honeymoon trip. You went on a cruise?'

'It was heaven…' Once she was off, the conversation never lagged.

They talked about Jodie, Australia, Louise's business. About everything but the Valentine family. It was like talking to someone she'd known all her life. But eventually the conversation came back around to her.

'I have my Derek and Jodie has her Heath. What about you, sweetie?' Patsy asked. 'They say everything happens in threes. Is there anyone special in your life?'

In that split second before she spoke, Louise remembered the way that Max had looked at her. The way she'd felt…

'No,' she said, quickly, but even as the word left her mouth a little voice was saying, *No problem. No impediment. Nothing to stop you…*

Her mother raised one perfectly groomed brow and Louise distracted her with tales about old boyfriends. The ones she might have married if they'd asked.

'Just as well they didn't ask,' she said, laughing. 'It would have been a total disaster.'

She didn't tell her about the one she'd convinced herself was everything she was looking for in a husband: the one who'd told her to stop fooling herself before he'd walked away.

'I hate to say goodbye,' Patsy said as, finally, they walked towards the lift. Then, when she didn't immediately respond, 'You *do* want to see me again?'

Louise, momentarily distracted by the back view of Max, apparently absorbed in a painting, said, 'Yes, yes, of course I do.'

He'd come.

He'd actually turned up, had waited in case she needed him.

'I, um, want to meet Derek, too.'

The lift arrived and Patsy stepped in, holding the door. Louise forced herself not to glance back and stepped in beside her, arranged dinner for the next week, then hugged her mother goodbye on the pavement before seeing her into a taxi.

'You're sure I can't give you a lift?' she asked, from the back of the cab.

'No. I'm fine. I'll give you a call about next week.'

She waited, waved as she drove off. Then turned and walked back into the gallery, took the lift back up to the top floor.

When the doors opened, she saw that Max had not moved and she didn't know whether she was irritated by his certainty that she'd come back, or warmed by the fact that he'd waited for her. There were no clear cut lines with him.

'I thought it was best to stay put,' he said, as she held the door and he stopped pretending, joined her in the lift, 'or we might have been chasing one another around the houses for the next ten minutes.'

'Only if I came back,' she pointed out, trying not to smile, but without much success.

'True.' He seemed to be finding it easy enough to keep a straight face. Then, 'You're very like her.'

'Yes. It's strange. All my life people have been telling me I'm like my… Like Ivy Valentine…'

'She's still your mother, Lou. She was the one who raised you. And you are like her. Okay, some of it's superficial, chance. Your colouring, height. But it's not just that. You hold your head the way she does, you use the same gestures. You have her class.'

'You don't think Patsy has class?'

'Patsy?'

'It's a bit late in the day to start calling her Mum, don't you think?' She shrugged, as if it didn't matter. 'She asked me to call her that.'

'It suits her,' he said, taking her arm as they headed for the door.

She stiffened momentarily, then forced herself to relax. If she pulled away, he'd think that what he said, did, mattered to her.

'What's that supposed to mean?' she asked, once they were outside, but keeping her voice light.

He held up his hands in mock surrender. 'She's classy.'

'Not quite the same thing.'

'What can I say? She's a real head-turner, Lou.' Then, with a wry grin, 'Don't let her near my father. He has a fatal weakness for that chorus-girl-fallen-on-good-times look.'

'Your father has a fatal weakness for women full-stop.'

'Life has never been dull,' he agreed, and it was Louise who found herself reaching out to him, tucking her arm through his as they walked away from the square. 'I don't think you understand how lucky you've been. How much I envied you the sheer ordinariness of your family.'

'Ordinariness?'

'It's what boys yearn for. Parents who don't attract attention.'

'Oh, dear. Bad luck,' she said, laughing. 'How is Aunt Georgina? Where is she?'

'In Mexico, painting up a storm. Apparently the light is magical. She's living with someone called Jose who's half her age.' He looked at her. 'Ring Ivy, Louise. Don't abandon something precious to chase rainbows.'

She shook her head. Unwilling to admit that he was right. But Max had been no more than a toddler when his parents had split up. Since then there had been a succession of stepmothers, half-siblings, step-siblings from his father. Drama and lovers from his mother. No one, she thought, had ever put Max first. It was scarcely any wonder that he had given all his heart, his loyalty to the business. Bella Lucia had never hurt him.

She looked up, but not far; in her high heels her eyes were nearly on a level with his.

'I will call her,' she promised.

'When?'

'Soon.' Then, because all that hurt too much to think about, 'Chorus girl fallen on good times?'

'The glamour, the clothes, the diamonds in those rings…'

'So what you're saying is that she's a classy "broad" rather than a product of the finishing school, debutante system? Now I'm afraid to ask what I owe to nature as opposed to nurture.'

It was the height of the rush-hour and Max, sensing approaching quicksand, used the excuse of looking around for a cruising cab to avoid her direct gaze.

'Well?' she demanded.

'I thought you didn't want to know.'

'Oh, please…'

'It's not something I could put into words,' he said.

How could you possibly quantify the smoke and mirrors of sex appeal? Pin it down, list the components. Item: hair, the colour of ripe wheat rippling in the wind. Item: two eyes, blue-grey, unless she was angry, when they were like storm clouds threaded with lightning. Item: one mouth…

He found himself staring at her mouth. Parted slightly, as if she were on the point of saying something outrageous. On the point of laughing. Dark, rich, enticing. The colour of the small sweet plums he picked in his Italian grandmother's family home on rare and treasured holidays, when he'd been taken along to keep his half-brother Jack from getting into mischief. To give his father time to spend with wife number three…

'Do you think there's any chance we'll find a taxi at this time of day?' he asked, abruptly.

She lifted a hand and, as if by magic, a black cab materialised alongside them.

'Where are we going?' she asked as he opened the door.

We? That was promising.

'Mayfair. My office,' he said, taking advantage of the opportunity she'd given him. 'I'm going to make you an offer you can't refuse.'

'Oh, this should be good,' she said, climbing in without argument.

Something of a first, that, but he was too busy enjoying the view to comment on it. Item: one pair of finely boned ankles that drew the eye upwards in an appreciation of her long legs…

Pulling himself together, he told the driver to take them to Berkeley Square, the home of the Mayfair Bella Lucia and the company offices, and then climbed in beside her.

She was glowing, he thought. Happy. A transformation from her arrival at the gallery. She hadn't seen him, but he'd arrived before her, seen how tense she'd looked. The meeting with her mother had gone well. Maybe that was a good thing. Patsy lived in London…

'What do you think it will take?' she asked, breaking into his thoughts.

'Sorry?'

'I'm interested in what you believe you'll have to offer, before I can't refuse?'

'If I told you that, you'd know more than I do.'

'No, Max. I already know what it'll take. You're the one who has to find the perfect combination.' She was smiling, but her face offered no clues. 'I hope you've got nothing else planned for the rest of the evening.'

He tried to forget the mountain of paperwork on his desk as he said, 'I cleared my diary. I've got as long as it takes.'

To say that her expression changed would have been an exaggeration, but for a split second he thought he'd found the key. Then, she glanced out of the window, as if the passing traffic was of more interest than anything he had to offer. Then, 'Try, Max.'

'Try?' he repeated, confused. She wanted him to open negotiations here, in the back of a taxi?

'To put it into words. What I owe to Patsy.' She turned to face him. 'What I owe to nature.'

He had the uncomfortable feeling that she was playing with him. That she knew exactly what she wanted and that when she was ready she would tell him; in the meantime she was enjoying making him sweat a little.

'Sorry, Lou,' he said. 'I have an aversion to having my face slapped.'

'I would never slap your face, Max.' Her lashes swept down as she did her best to hide a satisfied little smile, demonstrating beyond any doubt that sex appeal was so much more than the sum of its parts. Describing it was like trying to catch mist. Or trying to explain a smile when the difference between the mechanics— some magic movement of muscles that lifted the mouth and went all the way up to the eyes—and the combined effect were so utterly indescribable…

'You were quite prepared to throw a fully loaded vase at my head,' he reminded her.

'That was a long time ago, Max. And I didn't actually hit you.'

'Only because your aim was so lousy. As it was you wrecked the table behind me. Dinner and dry-cleaning bills on the house, for eight.'

'I'm surprised you didn't deduct the cost from my wages when you fired me.'

'My mistake. Dad took the damage out of mine.'

She shook her head, biting on her lower lip to stop herself from laughing. He couldn't take his eyes off it. He wanted to tell her to stop, pull her lip free, kiss it, bite it…

'I'm sorry.'

'Believe me, it was worth every penny to get you out of my hair.'

'Careful, Max…'

'You were a terrible *maître d'*, Louise. Be honest. I did you a favour.'

She smiled. 'Yes, I suppose you did.' Then, 'I can't even remember what you said that made me so mad.'

'Everything I said made you mad.'

'True.' Suddenly sobered, she said, 'So why are you so anxious to have me come and work for you?'

Because he was crazy, he thought.

They didn't have a problem? Who did he think he was kidding? Working with Louise was going to try his self-control to the limits.

He took a slow breath.

'I want you to work *with* me, Lou, not *for* me. I respect your skill, your judgement, but we both know that I could buy that out in the marketplace. What makes you special, unique, is that you've spent a lifetime breathing in the very essence of Bella Lucia. You're a Valentine to your fingertips, Louise; the fact that you're adopted doesn't alter any of that.'

'It alters how I feel.'

'I understand that and, for what it's worth, I think Ivy and John were wrong not to tell you the truth, but it doesn't change who or what you are. Jack wants you on board, Louise, and he's right.'

'He's been chasing you? Wants to know why you haven't signed me up yet? Well, that would explain your sudden enthusiasm.'

'He wanted to know the situation before he took off last week.'

'Took off? Where's he gone?'

'He was planning to meet up with Maddie in Florence at the weekend. To propose to her.'

'You're kidding!' Then, when he shook his head, 'Oh, but that's so romantic!' Then, apparently recalling the way he'd flirted with Maddie at the Christmas party, she said, 'Are you okay with that?'

He found her concern unexpectedly touching. 'More than okay,' he assured her. 'I was only winding Jack up at Christmas. It's what brothers do.' His first reaction when Jack had tossed Louise in his lap had been to assume that it was tit for tat.

'You must have really put the wind up him if he was driven to marriage,' she said.

'Bearing in mind our father's poor example, I think you can be sure that he wouldn't have married her unless he loved her, Lou.'

Or was he speaking for himself?

'No. Of course not. I'm sorry.'

Sorry? Louise apologising to him? That had to be a first. Things were looking up.

She laughed.

'What?'

She shook her head. 'Weddings to the left of us, weddings to the right of us and not one of them held at a family restaurant.' She tutted. 'You know what you need, Max? Some heavyweight marketing muscle.'

'I'm only interested in the best, Louise so why don't we stop pussyfooting around, wasting time when we could be planning for the future?' The thought of an entire evening with her teasing him, drawing out concessions one by one, exacting repayment for every time he'd let her down, every humiliation, was enough to bring him out in a cold sweat. 'Why don't you tell me what it's going to cost me? Your bottom line.'

'You don't want to haggle?'

Definitely teasing.

'You want to see me suffer, is that it? If I call it total surrender, will that satisfy your injured pride?'

Her smile was as enigmatic as anything the Mona Lisa could offer. 'Total surrender might be acceptable,' she told him.

'You've got it. So, what's your price?'

'Nothing.'

He stared at her, shocked out of teasing. That was it? A cold refusal?

'Nothing?' Then, when she didn't deny it, 'You mean that this has all been some kind of elaborate wind-up? That you're not even going to consider my proposal?'

'As a proposal it lacked certain elements.'

'Money? You know what you're worth, Louise. We're not going to quibble over a consultancy fee.'

She shook her head. 'No fee.'

Outside the taxi the world moved on, busy, noisy. Commuters crossing *en masse* at the lights, the heavy diesel engine of a bus in the next lane, a distant siren. Inside it was still, silent, as if the world were holding its breath.

'No fee?' he repeated.

'I'll do what you want, Max. I'll give you—give the family— my time. It won't cost you a penny.'

He didn't fall for it. Nothing came without some cost.

'You can't work without being paid, Louise.'

'It's not going to be for ever. I'll give you my time until…until the fourteenth. Valentine's Day. The diamond anniversary of the founding of Bella Lucia.'

'Three weeks. Is that all?'

'It's all I can spare. My reward is my freedom, Max. I owe the family and I'll do this for them. Then the slate will be wiped clean.'

'No…'

He didn't like the sound of that. He didn't want her for just a few weeks. Didn't want to be treated like a client, even if he was getting her time for free. Having fought the idea for so long, he discovered that he wanted more, a lot more from her than that.

'You're wrong. You can't just walk away, replace one family with another. You can't wipe away a lifetime of memories, of care—'

'It's the best deal you're ever likely to get,' she said, cutting him short before he could add, '…of love…'

'Even so. I can't accept it.'

'You don't have a choice,' she said. 'You asked for my bottom line; that's it.'

'There's always a choice,' he said, determined that she shouldn't back him into a corner, use Bella Lucia as a salve to her conscience, so that she could walk away without a backward glance. Something that he knew she'd come to regret.

Forget Bella Lucia.

This was more important and, if he did nothing else, he had to stop her from throwing away something so precious.

'That's my offer, Max. Take it or leave it.'

'There must be something that you want, that I can offer you,' he said, assailed by a gut-deep certainty that he must get her to accept something from them—from him. Make it more than a one-way transaction. For her sake as much as his. 'Not money,' he said, quickly, 'if that's the way you want it, but a token.'

'A token? Anything?'

Her eyes were leaden in the subdued light of the cab, impossible to read what she was thinking. That had changed. There had been a time when every thought had been written across her face, as easy to read as a book.

He was going into this blind.

'Anything,' he said.

'You insist?'

He nodded once.

'Then my fee for working with you on the expansion of the Bella Lucia restaurant group, Max, is a kiss.'

CHAPTER FOUR

MAX heard the words, struggled to make sense of them.

'A kiss?' What the hell…? What kind of a kiss? 'Just one?'

'Just one,' Louise replied.

Even in his head words failed him.

He was being choked by a collar and tie that were suddenly too tight. He fought the urge to loosen them. This was a game. He might not have been able to read her mind, but she'd clearly been reading his.

And now she was asking for the very thing he'd been resisting with every fibre of his being. Teasing him. Raising the stakes…

She was so *hot* in that sexy little suit, those high heels. Her hair curled in soft wisps around her face that seemed to direct his gaze directly to a mouth that was pure temptation and, given the fact that he'd been fighting the urge to kiss her, and more, for as long as he could remember, his sudden reluctance to comply with her simple request was hard to explain. Except that a kiss fallen into in the heat of desire, or passion or even simple lust, was one thing. But this cool, dispassionate proposition was something else.

It couldn't be that easy…

'Now?' he asked, doing his best to match her composure.

'You're in a hurry to seal the contract?'

Not just teasing but taunting him…

Or was that disappointment at his obvious lack of enthusiasm?

'It's your call,' he said, a touch hoarsely.

'Okay.'

Was that 'okay' now? Or 'okay' she'd leave it up to him?

She waited, offering no help, not coming an inch to meet him halfway.

Oh, hell…

Feeling very much like a teenager faced with his first real kiss, unsure quite what was expected of him, what 'a kiss' in this context entailed, heartily wishing he hadn't leapt in, said the first word that came into his head. "*Now…?*"

But she was waiting, eyes wide open, while he hovered on the brink of insanity, torn between an urgent need to go for the straight-to-hell moment he'd been fighting all his life and the suspicion that she was somehow testing him, making certain that they could work together, that he could control himself. That she could control herself.

As he hesitated between heaven and hell the taxi swung around the corner, throwing her off balance, so that instead of kissing her he had an armful of her when they came to a halt in front of the restaurant.

An armful of the softest, sexiest woman a man could imagine only in his wildest dreams. Delivering on those dreams—or were they nightmares?—that had haunted him, souring every other relationship, until he'd finally stopped trying to find someone who could drive her from his thoughts and done what he'd always done, thrown himself heart and soul into work, turning to the one thing in his life that had always been there, never let him down.

Bella Lucia.

She didn't move and it was all he could do not to deliver with the kind of kiss that she would regret calling down on her head. Not some polite token that would torment his soul, surely her intention, but a kiss that would mark her as his with the kind of pledge that would seal their alliance for eternity.

The driver leaned back and opened the door when they didn't move and he realised with relief that there was someone waiting to grab the cab. That time had run out.

'Bad…' His voice caught in his throat. 'Bad timing…' he said.

'Maybe,' she said, so softly that she was almost inaudible. Then, before he could do or say anything, she extricated herself from his arms, climbed out onto the pavement, walked towards the restaurant without looking back.

'You all right, guv?' the driver asked as, hands shaking, he handed over the fare.

'Fine,' he said, abruptly. There was nothing wrong with him that a long, cold shower wouldn't fix. 'We should have been wearing seat belts. Keep the change.'

The discreet façade of the Berkeley Square Bella Lucia fronted one of London's most exclusive, most luxurious restaurants, a place where financiers, politicians, the world's deal brokers came to meet, eat and talk, confident of their privacy in the gentlemen's club atmosphere.

Louise regarded it with every appearance of composure, even though she was trembling, holding herself together through sheer will power despite the sudden urge to bolt.

Performance nerves, that was all.

She knew how to use the adrenalin rush to see her through big presentations, major launches. When it came to business she had no trouble keeping her feelings under wraps and she could do it now. Except that hadn't been about business.

She didn't know what it had been about except that Max had been pushing her and as always she'd responded with a reckless disregard for the consequences.

She turned as he joined her, smiled distantly, still performing as he wordlessly held the door. She walked ahead of him through the panelled, ground floor entrance, across the small bar with its comfortable leather chairs where the staff were already preparing for the evening, into the restaurant, aware all the time of the heat of his arm, not quite touching, at her back. Still feeling the pressure where he'd caught her, held her.

'I've always loved this moment,' she said, calling on every reserve of control to act as if nothing had happened. Using the excuse to stop, rest her hands lightly on the back of a chair as her legs began to wobble dangerously. Looking around. Anywhere but at him.

'Pure theatre,' Max agreed, without having to ask what she meant. He knew.

Behind the scenes, in the kitchen, the food was being prepared, the front of house staff were assembling. Out here the tables were laid with snowy white cloths, polished silver, glasses, fresh flowers. Not just theatre, she thought, but the grandest of opera, everything was ready, waiting for the audience to appear, for the conductor to raise his baton and the evening to begin.

Until a few months ago that had been her father. This restaurant, the smaller private dining rooms on the floor above, the offices on the top floor, had been the heart from which he'd run the Bella Lucia empire.

'He nearly lost it,' she said, more to herself than Max, using anger to drive off the intensity of that moment in the taxi. She was angry, she realised, because of all of them Max would have been the one who lost most. Perhaps everything... 'All for the sake of a son he hadn't known existed until a few months ago.'

'He'd have done the same for you, Louise.'

Would he?

When Daniel and Dominic had turned up, twin images of John Valentine, saying 'Hi, Dad...' they'd been received like prodigal sons by John, while her reward for thirty-something years of dutiful daughterhood had been the shocking revelation that she was not actually Ivy and John's daughter at all, but had been adopted at birth.

She'd suddenly felt invisible, excluded.

Blood was thicker...

'He wouldn't have had to,' she said, keeping her voice even, matter-of-fact.

Easy for you to say, the still small voice of her conscience reminded her. John Valentine would have given you anything. Has given you everything...

Which was why she was here now. Paying her dues.

'Forget the past, Louise,' Max said, catching her hand, holding it, forcing her to look at him. 'Bella Lucia is still here. We're still here. It's the future that matters.' His hand tightened around hers as if he could somehow transmit his excitement to her by direct contact. 'Expanding. The new restaurant in Qu'Arim is just the beginning. I'm going to launch the third generation of Bella Lucia onto a world stage. Close your eyes, stick a pin in a map and ten years from now we'll be there. Don't you want to be a part of that?'

No! Yes…

All her life, ever since she was a little girl, she'd longed to be here, centre stage. Back then her dream had been to be at her father's side, but Max—older, male, the first-born Valentine grandson—had always been ahead of her.

Now he needed her he was using family ties to draw her back into the business, but it would always be his empire. She would always come second. Second to her father was the way of the world, she could have lived with that; second to Max was never going to be enough.

Why did it have to be him?

Because it was his life, she thought, answering her own question. He loved it. He was like his father in that, if in nothing else.

The staff had always trusted him, turned to him. Even now he was doing this as much for them as for himself. They were, she realised, his family. Which was why she'd do her best to help him put Bella Lucia on the world map.

She'd do it for him, for her father, for the Valentine family that she'd always thought she was a part of. And for herself, too, so that she could walk away with a clear conscience. All debts paid. But she would walk away…

'Lou?' He was pressing her to commit. To say the word.

'Yes,' she said, as matter-of-factly as if he'd asked her if she wanted a drink.

Her answer was always going to be, had to be, yes.

For now. Until the fourteenth of February. Valentine's Day.

'What's the matter? You don't look convinced?' She let loose a smile that was trying to break out. 'You did say that you wouldn't take no for an answer.'

For once Max seemed lost for words, a predicament so rare that she'd have to be a saint not to take some pleasure from the situation. The truth was that all day she'd been on pins, nervous about meeting her mother for the first time, nerves that had been made worse by the background tension: her cast-iron certainty that Max was simply going through the motions to convince Jack that he had done all he could to bring her on board. That he didn't really want her.

But the meeting with her mother had gone better than she could ever have imagined and then, when she'd seen Max waiting for her at the gallery, that for once he'd kept his promise, made time for her...

She didn't, in her heart of hearts, believe that anything other than desperation would have driven him to make such a gesture, but he had made it, demonstrating beyond words that she was the one in the driving seat. That he needed her, that the family was relying on her. Taking her seriously for once.

How could she not say 'yes'?

'For the moment my time is completely booked up with the relaunch of HOTfood, but once that's out of the way—'

'When?' he demanded, impatiently. 'When can you start?'

'After the party on Friday.' She looked up at him. 'After that I'll be all yours.'

It was only when she wanted to tuck a loose strand of hair behind her ear that she realised Max was still holding her hand, and as she looked up at him she found herself remembering years before when, on a family trip to the beach, he'd reached out to her when she couldn't keep up with him and Jack as they'd scrambled over the rocks.

How he'd stopped, come back to hold out a hand to her. How safe she'd felt.

Remembering how safe she'd always felt. How lucky she'd been...

'You haven't got a fistful of clients hammering on your door?' he asked, abruptly abandoning her hand to straighten a fork on the table.

'What? Oh, yes. Well, actually, no...' She tucked back her hair, said, 'I haven't taken on any new jobs since my return from Australia. I didn't want to tie myself down.'

He frowned. 'You were really serious about leaving?'

Was she?

In truth she hadn't known. It was as if she'd been poised between her old life and the possibility of something new, waiting for some small sign to set her on the right path.

What she'd got, in the shape of Max Valentine, was a three-lane motorway direction sign saying 'BELLA LUCIA'...

His question suggested that as far as he was concerned it was a momentary whim to be brushed aside now she was back in the fold and, deciding that it was wiser to leave him with that impression, she lifted her shoulders in a wordless shrug.

He let it go, said, 'I didn't ask if you were free this evening.'

'No, you didn't.'

'Are you?'

There were two possible answers to that question.

One… She could tell him that she had to work and then waste the evening pointlessly stressing over the last minute details of the HOTfood party even though she knew there was nothing left to do, or…

Two… 'No, Max. I'm not free. I'm having a working supper with the new head of the Valentine empire. Unless you've got something more interesting planned?'

His response was a sudden smile that involved every part of his face, deepening the creases that bracketed his mouth, lighting up his eyes in a way that almost impossibly intensified the blue. The kind that took time, that she hadn't seen in years.

'I can't think of anything more interesting than that,' he said and she was forced to bludgeon down the heart leap, the foolish warmth at his admission that being with her would be a pleasure rather than a pain.

'Interesting' was what he'd actually said.

In some cultures 'interesting' was a curse…

'If that's your measure of interesting, Max,' she replied, 'you need to put some serious thought into getting a life.'

He looked as if he was about to say something. He clearly thought better of it, because instead he shrugged, said, 'This *is* my life.'

He'd got that right, anyway. The restaurants, the people who worked for them; he'd strived for success not just for himself, the family, but because he knew that it was the men and women who worked for them who would suffer most if things went wrong.

He'd only fired her, she realised, because her volatility when she was around him threatened that success…

'Come on, let's get started,' he said, ignoring the lift in favour of the stairs. 'I've been thinking about some of your ideas.'

'Which ones?' she asked, taking them rather more sedately in her high heels and narrow skirt.

'All of them, but especially Meridia. I really think you're on to something so I sent Emma an email and asked her to look out for likely locations.'

'Your sister doesn't work for you any more, Max,' she reminded him. 'In fact I imagine being Queen of Meridia doesn't leave her with too much spare time to spend running errands for you.'

'You think?'

He stopped without warning, turned and, a step below him, she was suddenly cheek-to-chest close. Without thinking she swayed back to avoid touching him, just as she always had, just as he always had, but now he put out a hand to grab her, steady her as she took a step back. Save her from a fall. Keep her close.

'If we're not cousins,' he'd said, 'we don't have a problem…'

Not for him, maybe, but it was as if that moment when he'd come close to kissing her had intensified her response to him. Even through her coat, the sleeve of her suit, his hand was applying heat to a square of skin just above her elbow that spread like wildfire to every part of her body.

Just the simple act of breathing became suddenly more difficult. *Yes…*

The word whispered through her mind, silken temptation.

This was what you wanted. Max at your feet. Max in your bed…

'Yes,' she said. Then, when he waited for her to elaborate. 'I do think.'

'Well, never mind,' he said, with a tormenting smile that she knew only too well, 'I've got you for that now.'

Got her? To run his errands? Was that what he thought? Not even close…

'You think?' she enquired, throwing his words back at him as the heat intensified to a dangerous calm. She knew this feeling, recognised this, welcomed it even; the motorway sign was flashing an urgent warning 'SLOW — ACCIDENT AHEAD' but, just as she always had, she ignored it.

'What are you looking for?' Max asked as she cast about her before fixing her gaze on the vast arrangement of flowers on the half landing where the staircase split into two and curved away on either side.

She blinked, collected herself, swallowed.

What was she thinking? She was grown up, an in-demand consultant, not some stupid girl with a crush.

Get a grip. He was just teasing.

There had been a time when his teasing had made her insides curl up in a paroxysm of pleasure that this godlike figure had noticed her.

A lifetime ago.

Then there had come a time when it had just made her mad.

Now...

'A vase,' she said. 'If you think I'm interested in running your errands, Max, you obviously need a large dose of cold water.'

For a moment he just stood there and she knew, just knew, that it was going to be a rerun of the last time they'd worked together; he said something dumb, she responded like an outraged cat, spitting and arching her back, then he blew up.

And she felt nothing but regret.

'Since your aim is as bad as your timing,' he said, after a monumental pause that had probably been no more than a heartbeat but which had seemed to stretch for a hundred years, 'maybe we should take the cold shower as read.'

Her timing?

'My timing is off? I like that! You were the one who couldn't wait. One kiss, a token, how hard could that be?'

No! No... Do not remind him of that foolishness...

'My mistake. Just tell me when and we'll seal the contract.'

Tell him it was a joke. That you didn't mean it...

Now!

But her gaze was riveted to his mouth, her own lips burning with a lifetime of unrequited longing, of denial, and with her breath caught in her throat she was unable to speak.

'Your call,' he prompted, clearly in no hurry.

It was enough to break the spell. With extreme care, she said, 'Thanks. I'll let you know.'

'Any time,' he said, then turned away before she could respond, taking the rest of the stairs in a couple of strides.

By the time she'd caught up with him on the top floor where the offices were situated she'd recovered her composure, had reminded herself that this was supposed to be a working supper. Posted a mental note to keep a curb on her tongue.

It would probably get easier with practice.

In the meantime, Meridia.

'Are you—we—doing the catering for this big gala dinner and ball Emma is throwing to launch her "Queen's Charity"?' she asked, focussing on business.

'I'm signing the contract on Monday. Do you want to come?'

'To the ball?'

Was he asking her…?

'I imagine Emma will want you there.' Then, as she hesitated, 'She adores you, Louise.' Oh, right, just more propaganda on behalf of the family.

'Of course I'll go,' she said. 'Who in their right mind would give up a chance to buy a new dress?'

Most people would have taken her response at face value. The look Max gave her suggested that he was not so easily fooled.

'All right, Max. I'll be there for her.'

Just for Emma.

After a moment he nodded, accepting that she was sincere. It was frightening how easily he could read her.

'Good. But I was asking if you want to come with me to Meridia on Monday.'

'Oh, I see.'

It was unnerving how much she'd wanted him to be asking her to the ball as his partner. Still sixteen and waiting for her prom night Prince Charming. Still yearning to feel his arms around her. Instead she got a business meeting…

'Well, it would be useful.' Then, forcing herself to keep to the point, 'Actually, since we're doing the catering I'd like to discuss the possibility of a behind-the-scenes-in-the-palace-kitchens feature with the royal PR people. The work involved in putting on a royal gala ball. If you're serious about moving into Meridia—'

'I'm serious. You're right; it's the obvious place to start.'

'Then the "Queen's Charity" tie-in would be exactly the moment to announce the fact.'

'Hold on. It's a little premature to be thinking that far ahead.'

'It's never too soon for thought, Max. You have to take advantage of media at the moment when they want something from you.' She saw his doubt. 'It's not until June and the feature wouldn't appear until the week of the gala. You can drop the news into an interview I'll set up for you to talk about that. That's if you're serious—'

'I told you I'm serious!'

'Good,' she said. 'Good. Then we need to make the most of the moment, ride on the coat tails of the publicity that will generate. Whatever happens, the royal connection will add lustre to the outside-event catering side of the business.'

He still looked doubtful. 'Do you really think Sebastian will allow photographers, journalists, to roam loose in the palace? Isn't there a danger that we'll be perceived as using our royal connection for commercial gain? I'm concerned it will hurt Emma.'

'Just the kitchens, a glimpse of the food we'll be serving—we can photograph that here. Some behind-the-scenes pictures of the banqueting room being made ready would be good, but since that's already part of the tour visitors can take it's hardly likely to prove a problem.' He didn't look convinced. 'Sebastian will want publicity for the charity and it's the charity I'll focus on. Obviously the copyright of the photographs would be invested in that. The major lifestyle magazines will pay huge money for a royal feature like this.'

'You've been giving this a lot of thought.'

'This is PR 101, Max. Sebastian's a modern monarch. He knows he's going to have to sell his country to tourists, industrialists, bankers. Put together royalty and romance with fabulous food and you have an unbeatable combination. Add a charming young queen launching a charity to help the world's poor and Meridia is the winner.'

He glanced at his watch. 'Five minutes. You've come up with all that in five minutes?'

'That's just the thinking. I still have to make the connections, set up the deal. Do the work.' She managed a smile. 'I'm going to need every minute of that three weeks.' Then, before he could press her for more, 'We'll all be winners, Max. And besides, I won't have to persuade Sebastian,' she added. 'That is one job I'm happy to leave in the capable hands of your little sister. She owes me.'

'For transforming her from a rather plain duckling into a stunning swan?'

'Emma isn't plain,' she said, scolding him. 'Far from it. She just needed a little help with her confidence; all I did was bring out the inner princess.' Then, unable to resist fishing for a compliment from him, 'You noticed how lovely she looked?'

'When Sebastian introduced her as his future queen at his coronation the entire world noticed. You did a great job.'

'She was such a beautiful bride,' she said, unable to resist a little sigh of satisfaction, not just because her efforts had been so amply rewarded, but that Max had been generous enough to credit her with the transformation.

'It's what you do, isn't it?' he said. 'Make people take notice. Create an image.'

'More than an image, Max. My job is to create a feeling, an "I want" response, to choreograph a reflection in words and pictures that reinforce the desire so that when anyone thinks of the ultimate in a rare, luxurious dining experience, anywhere in the world, the first name that comes to mind is Bella Lucia.'

'Can you really do that?'

'I'll give it my best shot.' Then, feeling a little self-conscious at having made a pitch to someone she'd known all her life, she turned away, indicated his laptop. 'Can I borrow that to go online, do a little research?'

'Now?'

She stopped, looked at him. 'Is that your stock answer, Max?' Then, quickly, 'Yes, now.'

'I thought…'

'What? That we were just going to have another cosy supper?' Hadn't he learned from what had happened yesterday? 'When I say I'm having a working supper, I mean *working*. Since you appear to be more interested in the supper, I'll leave you to organise that.'

'Thanks,' he said, drily. 'Actually, I have got a pile of work to catch up with so I'll need the laptop, but you could use the machine in your father's old office,' he said, leading the way. 'You'll probably want to upgrade it. Have the whole office redecorated if you like. Buy some new furniture.'

'Why would I want to do that?' she asked, walking through the door, touching her father's desk, slipping into his huge leather chair, remembering the times she'd begged to stay with him when her mother had dropped in after shopping, for coffee, lunch.

How she'd climbed onto his lap, drawing pictures while he'd worked, nibbling on the little savoury treats he'd had sent up for her from the kitchen. Both of them getting a ticking off from her mother for spoiling her appetite…

'For three weeks,' she added, pushing the memory away. Except, of course, they both knew he wanted more than that. 'I've got state-of-the-art equipment in my own office,' she said.

And suddenly she had his full attention.

'I thought…'

She knew what he thought. That she'd move in here while she worked on the Bella Lucia account and in one bound he'd have her back in the family fold.

'Just so you know, so that there are no misunderstandings, Max, what you're getting from me is a marketing plan. An image. Some publicity. Some ideas. You're not getting my business, my life or anything else.'

Not for a kiss.

Max watched as she switched on the computer, absently tucking a strand of hair behind her ear as the machine booted up, concentrating on the screen as she logged onto the internet. For a moment he thought that she'd forgotten him, but then she glanced up as if surprised to still see him there, before her attention was reclaimed by the computer and she turned back to the screen.

He returned to his own office, sat at his desk, trying to work out whether he'd got what he wanted, or whether it was Louise who was calling all the shots. True, she was working with him, but very much on her own terms, in her own office. That wasn't what he'd envisaged. What he'd wanted.

What did he want?

His plans were huge and he'd never doubted his ability to put them into action; he'd got that drive from his father. He'd been less than thrilled with Jack when he'd suggested he needed Louise. But it had been impossible to avoid the fact that the world had felt a very lonely place as he'd stepped up to take sole responsibility for Bella Lucia, all the people who worked for him relying on him to make the money that paid their mortgages, for their children's shoes.

Knowing that they were going to be in this together, made the whole thing so much more... What? He sifted through the words that offered themselves. Satisfying. Pleasing. Enjoyable... No, more than that. And as the right word dropped into his mind he grinned.

Fun.

It had stopped feeling like the weight of the world on his shoulders and had started to feel like an adventure.

And there was still the kiss to look forward to, he thought, smiling as he reached for the stack of paperwork.

He was deeply absorbed in the quotations for a redecoration of one of the Mayfair dining rooms when Martin, a waiter who'd been with them for years, arrived with a tray and began to lay the small dining table in the corner of his office. He glanced at his watch, saw that it was nearly nine.

'I hadn't realised it was so late.'

'Miss Valentine rang through to the kitchen to see if you'd ordered anything. I offered to bring up a menu, but she just asked for the mushroom risotto.'

'For both of us?'

'I could ask Chef for something else if you'd prefer?' Martin said, catching his initial irritation at not being consulted, but unable to feel the almost instant follow-up of something much nearer pleasure that she already felt sufficiently at ease, at home, to call down and order food.

Maybe, he thought, that was the way to do it. If he stopped pushing so hard, she'd relax, come back in from the cold without even noticing she was doing it.

'The risotto will be fine, Martin. Did she choose a wine?'

'No, sir.'

'Ask Georges for a bottle of Krug, will you?'

'Krug?' the waiter repeated. It wasn't something he'd want to make a mistake about.

'A small celebration. Miss Valentine is going to be working with us for a few weeks.'

'I'm delighted to hear it, sir.'

A few minutes later, having asked Martin to give him ten minutes before he brought up the food, he walked through to the other office, bearing two glasses of champagne.

'Supper's on its way up,' he said. Absorbed in what she was doing, Louise raised a hand to indicate that she'd heard him and carried on working. He set down the glasses and joined her behind the desk interested to see what she was doing. 'Is that Meridia?' he asked, leaning over her shoulder to look at an aerial photograph of a small island, surmounted by an equally small castle.

'I downloaded Google Earth so that I could take a close look at the capital, refresh my memory of the layout. And then I remembered this,' she said, using the mouse to fly them in over the island, before moving lower, taking him on an aerial tour around the castle. 'Do you see?'

'Very pretty. So?'

'It's a fishing lodge that belongs to some distant cousin of Sebastian's. Emma told me about it. He's a bit of a black sheep, apparently; *persona non grata* in the country. It's got a natural harbour, a small beach…'

'So?'

She turned and looked up at him, clearly expecting a response. 'So, it would make a perfect setting for a Bella Lucia restaurant,' she said, her eyes sparkling with an infectious enthusiasm that sent a charge of recognition skipping through him. She was, he thought, as excited by all this as he was.

'I can certainly see the attraction, but unless the man is looking for a tenant…'

'Well, he can't use it himself. I called Emma to run the idea past her and ask if there was any possibility of us looking at the place when we're there on Monday. It's all fixed.'

He frowned. 'Oh, come on, it can't be that easy...' Then, 'You're serious?'

'Of course. I don't have time to mess about. Oh, and I've arranged for us to meet with the director of the State Tourism Office, too.'

'You seem to have organised everything.' He straightened, no longer smiling. 'Are you sure you need me to come with you?'

'I'm sorry, Max?' she said, instantly catching the change in his mood.

She said it not as if she were truly sorry, or actually thought she might have overstepped some unseen line, but as if he were the one in the wrong.

'The words "bull" and "china shop" leap to mind. There's a fine difference between being keen,' he said, 'and rushing in without taking time to consider all the options.'

'I've suggested a location that I've already seen, I've arranged a viewing—using my personal contact with a queen, no less,' she pointed out, 'and I've organised a meeting with a man who would be useful in setting up a joint venture with a local hotelier, since— and correct me if I'm wrong—I assume you don't have any plans to move into the hotel business, too.' She paused for half a beat, then said, 'What have you done in the last couple of hours?'

'Cleared a mountain of paperwork I should have been attending to this afternoon instead of hanging around the Portrait Gallery waiting for you,' he said. 'This company doesn't run itself, you know.'

'Nobody asked you,' she reminded him. 'I didn't need you. You were the one who insisted, wanted to show how much you care about me—'

'I do, Louise. We all do.'

'Please! What you want is for me to play happy families, come and work for you, and now you think you've got all that, it's as you were. Well, if this is going to be the kind of "working together"...' and she did that really irritating quotes thing again, presumably with the precise intention of irritating him '...where I'm supposed to stand on the sidelines making suggestions while you make all the decisions, sorry, but I'm not interested.'

'This is going to be a working relationship, Lou,' he said,

holding onto his own temper by the skin of his teeth, 'where we discuss things, then we decide what to do, then we take action.'

'If I'd waited for you to order supper, we'd have starved,' she said, already beyond reason, but then her reaction to criticism had always been to overreact. The simplest thing had sent her overboard. A suggestion that her skirt was too short. A reprimand for flirting with the customers…

She was incapable of backing down, admitting a mistake.

'Dammit, Louise,' he said, 'you haven't changed one bit—'

'Dammit, Max, neither have you!' She was on her feet, in his face. 'You're still the same arrogant, overbearing, despotic, pig-headed idiot you always were!'

CHAPTER FIVE

LOUISE was outraged. He'd said this was what he'd wanted her for, but when she used her initiative, got on with the job, he couldn't handle it.

'Forget it, Max,' she said, reaching for her bag. 'This is never—'

'Don't!' He grabbed her by the shoulders before she could pick it up, spinning her around to face him. 'Don't say another word!'

'Never,' she repeated, blazing her defiance at him. 'Going—'

'Lou!' he warned.

'To—'

His mouth descended on hers with the impact of fire on ice, stopping her words, stopping her breath, stopping her heart.

For an instant the world was an explosion of hissing, sizzling reaction on the surface while inside she remained frozen with shock. Then his arms were around her, pulling her close and she was clinging to him as her lips, her bones, her brain were overwhelmed by the heat and began, very slowly, to melt.

This was it.

This was the moment she'd yearned for, struggled against all her adult life. To know this, feel this.

To taste Max on her lips, feel the silk of his tongue stopping her angry words, showing her that she wasn't alone. That he was suffering too...

Her arms wound themselves around his neck, her fingers made free with hair that she'd longed to touch, knowing in some dark corner of her mind that she'd wantonly engineered this, forced this moment.

She'd wanted this ever since that moment at the Valentine's Day party when, sixteen years old and full of herself, she'd grabbed his hand, insisting on teaching him the steps of the newest dance. And then, as the music had changed to something slower, she'd seen something shift in the way he was looking at her, seen his eyes darken and felt something new, something dangerous stir, respond, deep inside her, wanting a lot more.

She'd known, as he pulled away, that everything had changed between them. That a touch was no longer innocent. That even to look was an invitation that damned them both.

Young, angry, stupid, she'd pushed him and pushed him to take what she could see he wanted, what she wanted, even while she'd known it was forbidden, could never happen, until that final eruption when he'd sacked her, humiliated her, driven her so far away that there had been no way back.

She understood now that he'd been protecting himself, protecting both of them, in the only way he knew how.

But the day her father had told her she was adopted, all that had changed.

We don't have a problem...

He'd said it, but even then he'd held back, as if unable to overcome years of keeping the dark, unspoken need under tight control. Now, though, with his body hard against hers there could be no more pretence, no ignoring the truth between them. That she felt alive, wicked but alive as she never had before; knew that this was what she wanted, this was the token she'd demanded in return for coming back. Not just a kiss but his total surrender so that she could finally be free of the crippling desire for Max Valentine that had ruined every relationship she'd ever had.

Even as she clung to him he pulled back a little to look at her, his eyes dark, intense, yet giving nothing away, the habit of concealment too strong...

'You were saying?' he murmured, cool, self-possessed.

'I was?' Her body might be in flames, but she would match his cool... 'I don't recall,' she said, reclaiming her arms, understanding that, for now at least, the kiss was over.

Her composure would follow in its own good time.

His response was a slow, wide, seductive smile. 'Then I believe, we have a contract, Louise,' he said.

'You think?' she asked as he stepped back, picked up the glasses he'd brought with him. 'I don't believe I mentioned where exactly I wanted it. The kiss.'

She took the glass he was offering her before he actually spilled the contents, then continued, quite casually, 'You do know you're taking quite a risk giving me this? Track record would suggest that I'm as likely to toss it over you as drink it.'

'Maybe if I told you that it's Krug?' he offered.

'You think that would stop me?'

He managed a wry smile. 'On the contrary. I imagine it would add to your pleasure.'

Pleasure? There was no pleasure in it. In the past, when she'd thrown things, all she'd wanted was for him to stop saying things that made her angry, stop him criticising her, making her hate him.

'On the other hand, you do tend to respond in the heat of the moment. If you were going to throw it, you'd have done it already instead of talking about it.'

'True.' And besides, his way of putting a stop to a fight was so much more…interesting. 'If I've leapt in with both feet, Max, I'm sorry. I'm used to working on my own, not having to answer to anyone except the client.'

'I am the client.'

'So you are. My mistake.' She looked up, met his gaze directly then, with the smallest of shrugs, 'I may have got a little carried away in my excitement.' And he could take that any way he liked. 'Tomorrow I'll print out a note to stick on my computer—"TALK TO MAX".'

'Whilst I treasure the rarity of an apology from you, I suspect I'm the one who should be grovelling. This is what Jack wanted you on board for. Your quickness. Your vision. You weren't stepping on my toes, Louise. On the contrary, you were giving me a lift.' Then, 'Not that I'm trying to dissuade you from talking to me.'

Anything but, Max thought.

He'd kissed her because it had seemed the only way to stop her saying words that would have ended everything, to exert the control that was slipping away from him. He'd lost that the moment she'd begun to kiss him back. He was still numb with the shock of it; the only thing on his mind her scent, faint, seductive, making him want to pull her back into his arms, bury his face in her skin…

He was walking and talking as if nothing had happened, but inside he was in turmoil, only able to think of kissing her again, this time not for himself but for her.

Kissing her throat, her breasts, every inch of her until she was whimpering with pleasure, with need, so that they could finish what he'd started. Begin anew…

But he could never do that again. Next time it really would have to be her call, and she'd made it clear enough that she would call, that they had unfinished business. He could only hope that she wouldn't wait too long.

Even while he was sending urgent signals to his feet to step back, put a safe distance between them, she flipped her hair behind her ear out of the way in a give-away gesture that suddenly seemed as familiar to him as drawing breath.

She'd always done that, he realised, even when she was a little kid. When she was unsure of herself, out of her depth. Then, when she'd done it, she'd always looked at him for reassurance. Now she looked away.

'It might be a good idea to schedule a regular daily meeting,' she said, 'just to keep one another in the picture about what we're doing?'

Poised, composed, but now he knew it was all just an act. A very good one, to be sure, but it was no more than an ice glaze that hid a totally vulnerable core.

Beneath that apparent self-assurance her heart would be pounding, her mouth dry, her knees weak. He knew because that was the way he was feeling…

'What time would suit you best—morning or evening?' she prompted.

'The evening,' he said, without having to think about it. The evening offered all kinds of possibilities. A chat could become a drink, could become dinner, and after that anything was possible. 'Seven?' he suggested.

'Six-thirty would be better.' She waited, he had no choice but to nod. 'I'll slot half an hour into my diary.'

Not what he'd had in mind at all. But it was a start.

Her mouth lifted in a wry smile. 'Just listen to us, Max. Being so-o-o polite to each other. Who would have believed it possible?'

He forced a grin in response. 'Better make the most of it, Lou—it can't possibly last.'

'No.' For a moment they just looked at one another. 'But then who would want it to?' And he knew without doubt that she would call him on that kiss and when she did he'd better be ready to deliver everything she wanted.

The very thought almost fried his brains.

'You do realise that this job is going to take chunks out of any pretence at a personal life?' he said, making an effort to change the subject, but failing dismally.

'Is that why you can't keep a girl, Max?' she asked.

There was a time when that kind of remark would have brought him to the boil, hearing only the words, the implied criticism. Now all he heard was genuine concern.

'Relationships need time, hard work. You have to work at them if you want them to last.'

'No one has ever been that important to you?'

'Apparently not.' Then, because talking about his failures held no appeal, 'What happened to the Honourable James the gossip columnists had you all but down the aisle with a year or so back?'

'That was nearly three years ago.'

She reached for her hair again. Looked away. *No… Look at me…*

'As always,' she said, 'they mistook a light-hearted flirtation for something more important.'

About to suggest that it had looked a lot more than a light-hearted flirtation, he took pity on her. Whatever had gone wrong it was clearly still too raw to talk about and he was torn between a need to hit James Cadogan, and to wrap his arms around her and make it go away.

Since neither of the above was anything like a good idea, he settled for, 'There's a lot to be said for light-hearted flirtation when everyone knows the score.'

'My sentiments exactly, but then PR isn't exactly a nine-to-five job, either,' she said. 'In fact this is the only evening I've got free for the rest of the week.'

'Then it's a good thing I made an effort this afternoon.' And because he didn't want to remind her of all the times he hadn't made an effort, let her down, he raised his glass and said, 'A toast? To Bella Lucia. The future.'

By way of reply she lifted her glass, clinked it against his, said, *'Salute,* Max!'

Before he could reply, Martin tapped on the open office door. 'Your food is ready, Miss Valentine.'

'Thank you, Martin.' She made to move, then, when he didn't follow, 'Max? Risotto won't keep.'

But food was the last thing on his mind. She hadn't responded to his toast to the future of Bella Lucia, but had replied with the Italian equivalent of 'cheers'.

Louise was exhausted. Her feet ached; her head was pounding from music so loud she couldn't hear herself think. She'd spent the week not only orchestrating media involvement in the HOTfood launch, but clearing her desk of all the niggling little jobs that had to be done, leaving her free to concentrate on Bella Lucia. Free to fly to Meridia with Max after the weekend.

Max.

Their working supper had ended as soon as they'd eaten. She'd made the excuse of an early start. He'd found her a taxi but it had taken all her powers of reasoning to dissuade him from escorting her home. By then she'd been desperate to get away from him, to clear her head, afraid that if he saw her to her door she'd drag him inside, tear his clothes off, tear her clothes off.

Distance didn't help.

Not even the coldest of showers could shift the memory of that kiss from her head. It was as if the lid had been lifted on desires she'd kept damped down for years and she'd got to the point where she was almost afraid to close her eyes, risk sleep, because when she slept she had no way of keeping them under control.

At least the week was over. Having spent what seemed like an endless evening at the HOTfood launch party the last thing she needed was to arrive home in the early hours of Saturday morning to find Cal Jameson camped out on her doorstep.

'All the hotels full?' she asked, irritably, as she fitted her key in the lock. Stupid question. Since his brother was now married to her half-sister, Cal apparently considered himself family. And family were put on earth to provide free food and accommodation whenever you were in town. Which, since Cal was in the travel business, was often.

Which was what you got when you took advantage of the innocent. She should never have fallen on his neck in gratitude when he'd obeyed her sister's orders and turned up at Christmas, blond, wide-shouldered and to die for in a perfectly cut dinner jacket, thus saving her from the embarrassment of arriving at the family party without a date.

Max always had some stunning eye-candy in tow and it was a matter of honour that she should match him, point-for-point, with the desirability of escort. Cal had delivered on appearance and that was all she'd asked for. She'd been away so much last year, had had so many other things on her mind, that she'd left it too late to round up a gallant willing to brave the Valentine family *en masse*.

When she'd seen that Max was on his own she'd felt a momentary pang of regret, but then he'd started flirting with Maddie, while she... She sighed. No use regretting what couldn't be changed.

'I left a message on your machine to say I had a stopover,' Cal said as he followed her upstairs like an eager puppy, totally oblivious to her lack of enthusiasm.

Maybe, she thought, she should send him over to Max, since he was so hot on the subject of family.

'When?' she asked.

'Just before I left Dubai. Don't ask me what time it was. I've crossed so many time zones in the last twenty-four hours I don't know what day it is.'

She didn't bother to enlighten him, but opened the door to her apartment, dropped the keys on the table, kicked off her shoes and tossed her coat over a chair. The red light on her answering machine was flashing, giving credence to his story. She ignored it.

'It wouldn't have made any difference what time you called. I haven't been home since six-thirty—'

'Jeez, Lou, what kind of bloke do you think I am?' She found the energy to raise an eyebrow. 'No, honestly,' he protested, 'it was earlier than that. You might have had a hot date or something.'

'It was the or something,' she assured him. 'When I said six-thirty, Cal, I meant six-thirty this morning.'

'You went to work dressed like that?'

He didn't wait for her denial, but whistled appreciatively at the clinging ankle-length dress she was wearing, chosen solely because it didn't wrinkle, even when it had spent all day rolled up in the bag she used to carry the essentials when she had to change on the job.

'You're welcome to stay,' she said, because he was family, sort of, 'but whatever you want, I'm afraid you're going to have to fend for yourself. I'm going to bed.'

'I'll take that,' he said, grinning broadly.

She finally cracked and laughed.

'No, really,' he assured her. 'I'm happy to share. I can see you're too tired to make up the spare bed.'

'In your dreams, Cal.'

'I've brought you a comfort package from Jodie,' he said, fishing out a padded envelope from his backpack.

'Jodie? How is she?' She missed her sister so much. Would phone her in the morning. 'And Heath?'

'Good.' Then, 'Double chocolate Tim Tams?' he said, waving the package temptingly in her direction.

'Really?' But no, she was not going to encourage him. 'Sorry, I've found a local supply.'

'You're kidding? Who'd have thought the Poms were that bright? What about DVDs of the latest episodes of *Beach Street*? I'll bet you can't get those two for the price of one at your local supermarket. Jodie tells me that you're an addict.'

While it was true that she had become…engaged…by one of the Aussie soaps while she was staying with her sister, she wasn't prepared to admit it.

'It's the spare room or nothing. If you want the bed made, you're going to have to do it yourself.'

'Fair enough,' he said, grinning. Totally unashamed. 'You can't blame a bloke for trying.'

Wrong bloke, she thought.

'You know the way, Cal. Don't disturb me before noon unless the building is on fire.'

An insistent ring on the doorbell dragged her from a dream in which Max had been kissing her. He'd started at her toes and it was just getting interesting… No, that was an understatement. It was already interesting. It was just getting…

'All right, all right…' she muttered as the doorbell rang again, pulling on a wrap, staggering to the door to press the intercom.

'Yes?'

'Louise, it's Max.'

'Max?' She felt herself blush from the toes up.

'Didn't you get my message?' he asked, while she was still trying to get her brain around the fact that he was here, at her door, when her subconscious was telling her that he was in her bed…

'What message?' Then, rubbing her hands over her face in an attempt to wake herself properly, 'No, don't tell me, just come up.' She buzzed him up, blinking the sleep out of her eyes as she checked the time. Eleven-thirty?

She was half an hour short of dream time, but on the other hand she did have the reality.

She yawned, eased her aching limbs, filled the kettle, switched it on. 'I'm in the kitchen,' she said, when she heard the door.

'Ah.'

She turned and was for a moment transfixed.

She couldn't remember the last time she'd seen Max in anything but a dark suit, or dinner jacket. Wearing a pair of washed-out jeans, an open-neck shirt, soft leather bomber jacket, he looked so much more like the boy she'd once worshipped.

They'd been such friends, had always had such fun until her hormones had got in the way.

She'd missed that so much. Missed him.

Her life, she realised, had never been quite so joyful, quite so sunny, since she'd fallen in lust with him and, too young to hide her feelings, had destroyed something truly special. She ached for that lost innocence. Ached for his friendship…

She swallowed. 'Ah?' she repeated.

He grinned. 'The answer is clearly no. You didn't get my message.'

'Er, no.' She glanced at the answering machine, its red light winking. Frowned as something nudged at her memory.

'Did I get you up?'

'What?' Then, realising how she must look—not so much Saturday casual, as Saturday slob in an old Chinese silk dressing gown hanging open over the baggy T-shirt she favoured for sleepwear, no make-up and her hair standing on end—she belatedly pulled the wrap around her for decency's sake and tied the belt. Ran a hand self-consciously over her hair in an attempt to smooth it down.

'I had a late night,' she said, unhooking a couple of mugs from the rack. 'It's Saturday, for goodness' sake!'

What she did in her own time was none of his business.

Unlike what she did in her dreams…

'Don't be so defensive, Lou. You've had a long week. How did the launch go last night?'

'Defensive?' Yes, defensive. When had that become her default mode when dealing with Max? She shook her head. 'Sorry. Why don't you just tell me what you said?' she suggested.

'Something along the lines of "Why don't we have lunch at the Chelsea restaurant tomorrow to discuss how we're going to handle the Meridia trip? I know you're busy so don't worry about calling back unless the answer's no…"'

He opened his hands, inviting her response.

Thoughtful, fun…

'Ah,' she said.

'Maybe we could make that brunch? If we have it here you wouldn't have to get dressed.'

Brunch in bed…

No, no, no…

'Um, maybe,' she said, brushing at her cheek as if she could somehow rub away a rerun of the blush. 'I don't know what I've got in. I've been too busy to shop.'

'Eggs?' he suggested, apparently oblivious to her heightened colour, more interested in the egg basket hanging from the overhead rail. 'Why don't I whip up something while you take your time and wake up?' he suggested, apparently catching on to the fact that she wasn't quite with it.

One of the perks of coming from a family in the restaurant business; everyone had to put in some time in the kitchens and the men didn't think it beneath them to cook.

She found herself smiling. Really smiling. 'That would be nice,' she said. And realised that she meant it.

'Scrambled do you? Coffee?'

'That sounds good,' she said, then, afraid that she was grinning like an idiot, she ducked away, reached for the basket, then yelped as pain shot through her scalp as Max had the same idea.

'Oh, damn! Hold on, your hair is caught in my cuff. Don't move,' he said, unnecessarily, as he lowered his wrist to unravel it, making things worse.

'Don't pull!'

'Sorry. Here…' He lifted his arm, leaned into her, pinning her against the table with the weight of his body as he eased the tension on her hair.

Off balance and held fast, her face pressed into his shoulder, she had no option but to keep still while he tried to work it free, forced to breathe in the scent of leather, freshly laundered linen, something else—nothing that had come from a bottle. Something indefinably male. Memorably Max.

'What's taking you so long?' she mumbled into his shoulder, in danger of drowning in Max-scented air.

'What?' Then, 'Hang on, I've nearly got it…' And then she was free, except that his arm was round her now. And he hadn't moved. 'Okay?' he asked, looking down at her.

Your call, her inner temptress murmured. *Go for it.*

'What?' She shook her head. 'No, I'm very far from okay,' she snapped, pulling free and gasping in sufficient fresh air to wash out the scent of him, rubbing her hands over her arms as if to free herself of the memory of his touch. Then, nursing her tender scalp. 'What kind of idiot are you?'

'The idiot who offered to make you breakfast? As opposed to the idiot with half a yard of hair flapping about in the kitchen.'

'Half a yard of…' Words failed her, but not for long. 'This isn't one of your restaurant kitchens, Max—'

'*Our* restaurant kitchens.'

She'd started off angry with herself, but this miserable attempt to wrong-foot her just made her mad at him.

'This is *my* kitchen, *my* space. I don't have to tie back my hair and put it in a net. When I'm here I don't have to do anything I don't want to.'

For a moment their eyes were locked in a combat of wills, the air crackling between them. Despite all the resolutions she'd made that week to be good, to be *mature*, if she'd had anything to hand other than the egg basket she'd have crowned him with it. Fortunately for him, she knew from experience just how much she hated cleaning up raw egg.

Maybe Max saw her dilemma, remembered the time she'd flung first and thought later, because without warning he began to laugh.

For a moment Louise couldn't decide whether she was outraged or wanted to join him, but while she was thinking about it her mouth took off on its own and a hiccup of laughter escaped before she could slap a hand over her mouth to keep it in.

'Just remember that I'm not some wet-behind-the-ears sous chef you can order around,' she finally managed.

'No?'

Without warning Max was not laughing, but reaching out for her, pulling her close, wrapping his arms around her, enfolding her in his warmth. Not taking his eyes off her as the heat of his athletic body began to seep into her bones.

'No…'

'I won't forget,' he said, mistaking her intuitive denial of her body's response to him for agreement. Then, his voice soft as velvet tearing, echoed her own thought. 'You have my word…'

'Lou!' The front door slammed shut, making her jump. 'Lou, are you up?'

Cal?

Oh, hell, Cal!

'Time to wake up and smell the sausages, gorgeous!'

She'd known, at the back of her mind, that there was something. If Max had just given her a moment to wake up, properly, five seconds to think straight instead of stunning her brain cells with an overload of pheromones...

It was hard to say who moved first, only that Max was no longer holding her, that somehow she was by the kitchen door, putting as much distance as she could between the two of them before her unwelcome visitor burst in with all the unrestrained enthusiasm of a Labrador pup.

She didn't even know why. They weren't doing anything wrong...

'Damn, Lou,' Cal said, his back to Max as he tossed the keys on the counter, dumped a bag of groceries alongside them without ever taking his eyes off her. 'You looked like sex on a stick last night, but given the choice I'd take you rumpled every time.'

She tried to speak. Make it clear that he would never be given the choice. All that emerged was a croak.

'Shocked into silence by the fact that I've been shopping, eh?' he said, with a grin. 'Needs must,' he said, 'and, let's face it, you didn't have anything in your fridge that a real bloke could eat for breakfast.'

'I wasn't expecting any kind of bloke,' she finally managed, looking anywhere but at Max, knowing what he must be thinking would be written all over his face. And who could blame him? She was the one who'd let him think that she and Cal were more than...than they were. 'Real or otherwise,' she added, helplessly.

'I know, but as always the welcome was as warm as the bed. In fact, my scrumptious, why don't you toddle off back there while I cook you up a CJ special...?'

Max didn't exactly clear his throat. It was more a low growl, alerting Cal to the fact that she was not alone.

He turned, glanced at Max, then at her, and with a careless shrug said, 'Or maybe not.' He turned back to the shopping, began to unpack it. 'No problem. Plenty for three...'

'Thanks for the offer, but I don't do threesomes,' Max replied and, with a nod in her direction, 'You should have told me you had other plans.'

'Max…' she protested. Too late. He wasn't listening. For an answer. An explanation. For anything.

'I'll see you on Monday morning, Louise. Check-in is at six-fifteen. I'll pick you up at five-thirty.' And with that he walked out of the kitchen, without so much as a glance at either of them, closing the front door very quietly behind him as he left.

She remembered that quiet anger.

It was nothing like the flashpoint moments when he'd shouted at her, she'd shouted back; up and down and over in a moment. Well, until that last time, anyway. But that white-lipped quiet when he was too angry to speak, that was something else. She'd seen it when his father's last marriage had broken up, when his brother Jack had given up trying to please their father and walked out of the family home, the business, the country. Losing Jack had been another huge blow for him. The two of them had been so close, but when he'd left Jack had cut himself off from everyone…

Did he think that was happening again? That history was re-peating itself with her? Understanding began to filter through the layers of her sleep-fogged brain…

'He seemed a little tense,' Cal said, distracting her.

'He's got a lot on his mind.'

'Oh, right. Just as long as I didn't ruin a special moment.'

She glared at him. Then, because it wasn't his fault, but hers, she said, 'No, Cal. You're all right. Max just wanted to talk about work.'

'On a Saturday?' He grinned. 'Bit keen, isn't he?'

'Keen?' As she laughed she remembered laughing with Max. How good it had felt. 'Describing Max as "keen" about the business is like suggesting Rip van Winkle took a nap.'

'He needs to relax. Take things easy.' Then, 'So… Breakfast?' He reached up and unhooked a frying-pan from the overhead rack.

How ironic that Cal, a man normally so idle that he looked pained if he had to pull the ring on his own beer can, had today of all days decided to do something to justify his keep.

On second thoughts it was far more likely that hunger had driven him to action. That and genuine fear that if he'd woken her, she'd leave him sitting on the pavement next time he turned up unannounced; that he'd have to find a hotel and actually pay for accommodation.

In fact, now she actually looked at him, she realised that his offer of breakfast in bed had been all talk. Far from leaping into action, he was holding the frying-pan in the helpless manner of a man who was making a gesture, assuming that like any sensible woman she'd quickly relieve him of the burden; anything rather than let him loose in her immaculate kitchen.

'Not right now, thanks, Cal,' she said. 'But you go right ahead.'

She ignored his crestfallen expression and instead helped herself from the carton of orange juice he'd so thoughtfully provided. She carried it through to the living room and, in an effort to wipe out the memory of Max's expression as he'd walked out, put one of the *Beach Street* DVDs that Jodie had sent her into the machine. Then she broke open a packet of Tim Tams—if ever a moment called for chocolate—and told herself that she'd go after him later. He'd be easy to find. He'd be in his office, or one of the restaurants. Funnelling his anger, converting it into action, making it work for Bella Lucia.

Not that he had any reason to be angry. She had the sole right to anger in this scenario. How could he think her so shallow, so *easy*?

She'd never bed-hopped. Had discovered the very first time that it was not the way to drive him from her mind. On the contrary. It had only made the longing more desperate. As the chocolate hit her anger began to melt into something dangerously close to regret and, without warning, tears threatened.

'Are you sure I can't fix you a fried-egg sandwich?' Cal called from the kitchen, hopefully. Or was that desperation in his voice?

'I'll pass,' she assured him, then, as the familiar theme tune swept her back to the warmth of Melbourne, instead of letting go and indulging herself, she found herself wondering why, when Cal was a freeloading pain in the backside without a scruple to his name, she wasn't ever tempted to decorate him with the contents of her egg basket.

Actually, it didn't take a genius to come up with the answer; she wasn't roused to fury by Cal for the simple reason that nothing he did actually mattered to her.

CHAPTER SIX

LOUISE'S attempts to distract herself with *Beach Street* were a dismal failure. Tensed for the sound of the doorbell, waiting for the phone to ring, she was unable to concentrate.

Neither obliged.

Why would they? Max had told her what time he'd pick her up. What else was there to say?

An apology for acting like a jerk, perhaps? Something along the lines of 'It's none of my business who you have staying in your apartment...'

It wasn't any of his business.

Liar!

The little voice that had taken up residence in her head turned up the volume, refusing to be ignored and infuriatingly, she knew that it was right.

The way she'd responded to his kiss, her very bold—

No, she was done with fooling herself; if she was reduced to a blush just thinking about it she'd been a lot more than bold.

The way she'd responded to his kiss, her *brazen* assertion that she considered it no more than a down payment, made it his business.

When Cal had walked into her apartment as if he'd owned it, owned her, Max had had every right to be mad.

Which was the second time she'd been forced to admit, to herself if not to him, that he was right and she was wrong.

Not good.

Okay. Forget the apology, but he'd said he wanted to discuss their trip to Meridia. He might be mad at her, but he still needed to do that. When he'd calmed down he'd call her and she'd be able to tell him that he'd got it totally wrong, that she and Cal were not an item, never had been, never would be, so he could stop behaving like an idiot and get back here.

The thought briefly prompted a smile. Then reality brought her back to earth.

Apart from the fact that Max didn't like anyone telling him he was wrong—which was, of course, what made it such a pleasing proposition—there was the small detail of what would happen next.

Would they pick up where they'd left off? With his arms around her and an expression in his eyes that promised her a world of trouble?

And your problem with that is…?

She swallowed, nervously.

Yes?

'No problem, okay!'

At her outburst, Cal appeared from the kitchen. She glared at him, daring him to comment; he held up his hands in mute surrender and beat a hasty retreat.

No problem, she repeated, but this time silently, in her head. It was time to admit, at least to herself, that she wanted Max to finally lose it, make the kind of passionate, no-holds-barred love to her that he had done in her wicked imagination a thousand times.

Then, surely, she would be able to wipe him from her mind. Get over it. Forget him.

But not right now.

In the past it had always been Max in control of their relationship. Max doing the right thing. Max behaving well…

Just this once she needed to be the one in the driving seat, the one making things happen. If she ran after him, begged him to listen, no matter what happened afterwards, he would still be dictating events.

Abandoning the television, telling herself firmly that whatever he'd wanted to talk about would have to wait until Monday, that she wasn't hanging around the phone waiting for him to climb down off his high horse and get down to work, she went to take a shower. A very cool one. Then she went to her office to finalise the HOTfood account.

Work had always been an escape from her feelings. They had that in common. He'd been right about that, too. He had done her a favour by firing her from the restaurant.

If she hadn't been so angry with Max, so desperate to prove herself, she doubted she'd ever have made such a success of her business. She'd have simply drifted from job to job until she'd settled for marriage, children, domesticity.

She'd come close. But Max was always there. An unfulfilled ache…

She turned on all the lights, reached for the file, and she was doing fine until the cell phone on her desk began to ring.

She made a grab for it, then forced herself to let it ring three times, to take a calming breath, before she looked at the caller ID.

It wasn't Max, but her mother.

The one who'd brought her up. Held her hand when she was nervous. Cuddled her when she was sad. Bathed her knees when she grazed them trying to keep up with Max…

Lied to her.

She wanted to leave it, do what she'd been doing for weeks and let the voicemail pick up, unable to cope with the stilted awkwardness of a conversation where neither of them knew quite what to say, but found she couldn't do it.

'Hello, Mum.'

'Darling? You were so long I thought I was going to get that horrible voicemail thing again.'

'Sorry. I did mean to call you back.'

'I know you're busy.'

'Yes,' she said, hating that her mother felt she had to make excuses for her. 'How are you? How is…?' She closed her eyes, stumbling at the first hurdle, unable to bring herself to say the word. She'd always been Daddy's little girl but the minute he'd discovered he had sons he'd brushed her aside. Second class…

'Good,' her mother said, quickly filling the too obvious silence. 'Daddy's a lot better. Walking the dog, eating plenty of fruit and fish, keeping the stress levels down. Even finding time to play a little golf now he's retired. The heart man is very pleased with him.'

'That's good.'

'Oh, it won't last. He's bored out of his mind, fretting about the business. Whether Max is coping.'

'Coping? You're joking. He's in his element. Full of plans—'

'You've seen him?' Then, not waiting for an answer, as if that too was some information she had no right to, 'I know how capable he is. He shouldn't have had to wait so long for his chance. But Uncle Robert wouldn't retire unless your father did, and you know your father…'

Her mother pulled up again realising, perhaps, that was the one person she didn't know.

'He's fretting, Louise. The restaurant was his life. Maybe if you could come over, go for a walk with him, reassure him…'

No, no…

'That's why I was ringing. Is there any chance of you coming to lunch tomorrow?'

'I don't—'

'No one else, just us,' she said, offering swift reassurance that the prodigal sons wouldn't be there.

How much more painful all this must be for her mother, Louise thought. To have her own inadequacies as a woman so cruelly exposed, to be eclipsed by the sons of a woman who'd taken money from William Valentine to 'disappear'.

'It's been so long since it was just the three of us.'

But it never had been just the three of them. She had another mother and father, John Valentine had sons…

So many lies.

She couldn't… 'I'm just so busy at the moment. I'm in the office now.'

'You work too hard, Louise.'

'I love what I do, but this is different. I'm going to be working for *Bella Lucia* from Monday and I've got a lot to clear up before then.'

'Max managed to persuade you?' Her mother sounded surprised, which was understandable, given their history. 'Well, that's good news. Daddy will be delighted.'

Her mother's obvious relief that she'd be close, held within the family circle, at least for a while, set up her nerves like a nail on a chalkboard. Was that the real reason why Max wanted her? Not for her talent, but to please her parents? Was that part of the deal he'd made with Jack?

Did it matter? She was in control. She'd do a job that would bring kudos to her own consultancy. Gain an international reputation. It wasn't only Max who could go global.

'We're flying to Meridia at the crack of dawn on Monday,' she said, without comment. Pleasing 'daddy' wasn't any part of *her* plan. 'I'm sorry, but I really will have to give lunch a miss.'

'I understand. Another time. Will you be seeing Emma?' she asked, changing the subject, unwilling to hang up.

'I expect so.'

'Well, give her my love. And make sure you wrap up well. Have you got a really warm coat? The kind of thing you wear in London won't do. It'll be much colder in the mountains.' Then, maybe realising that she was behaving like a fussy mother, she let it go. 'Louise, have you met…?'

This time it was her mother who stumbled, unable to say the word.

'Patsy Simpson?' Lou filled in for her. 'Yes, we had tea together this week.'

You had time for that, that busy little voice whispered in her ear. In the busiest week of your life you still found time for tea with Patsy…

'Oh.'

The sound was small, agonised, as if a knife had just gone in, taking her mother's breath away. Louise knew exactly how she felt. It was the way she'd felt when her father had told her she'd been adopted. Still felt…

'Was it…a success?' Ivy finally managed. 'Will you be seeing her again?'

'We're having dinner next week. I'm meeting her new husband. Max is coming with me…'

Unless he'd changed his mind. Without warning, Louise's throat seized as her eyes filled with tears…

'Louise?'

'I'm sorry, Mum, really, I have to go.'

'Yes, of course. If there's anything…' She caught herself. 'Well, you know.'

Yes. She knew. But it was as if an invisible barrier had been erected between them; where there had been spontaneity, warmth, there was now just this horrible awkward *politeness*.

Her fault.

Ring Ivy. Don't cut yourself off…

Max's words echoed in the empty space where her family had once been. And not just his words. He'd betrayed to her feelings that she'd never suspected, an envy of the warmth of a family life he'd never experienced.

It was for him that she picked up the phone again, rang the familiar number. 'Mum?'

'Louise…'

'I will come. Soon. I promise…'

Max stared at his cell phone, flicking through the names in its memory; the modern equivalent of a little black book. It was Saturday evening and he didn't have a date. Hadn't had a date since before Christmas. Longer. He tried to recall the last time he'd taken a woman out for the evening and discovered that it had been before his grandfather, the patriarchal William Valentine, had died the previous summer, precipitating the events that had thrown the *Bella Lucia* empire into such confusion.

He'd warned Louise that this business was hard on personal lives and he should know. But he was no longer involved in the day to day management of the restaurants. He was now responsible for the entire business and he had to think global, which, conversely, meant that his evenings—should he wish them to be—were suddenly his own.

He glanced again at the phone. There was only one person he wanted to phone but she was otherwise engaged with her dumb blond Australian, and, giving up, he tossed it onto the chair beside him, staring out unseeing over a Thames that reflected the gun-metal grey of the winter sky.

It was as if his memory had been overwritten and the only face in his brain's database belonged to Louise.

Louise, her blue-grey eyes dancing, hair the colour of a wheat-field in summer, silk beneath his fingertips…

Louise, lips parted as if she were about to say something out-rageous…

Louise, eyes more black than grey, lips soft and yielding under his own…

He turned abruptly from the window as the phone began to ring. Picked it up.

Not Louise but his mother.

'Georgie?'

'Max! Darling! How are you?'

'Fine.' He fought down the surge of feelings, of hope that for once she was calling him just for a chat. Like a real mother. 'You?' he asked.

'Well, actually, darling, I'm in a little bit of bother…'

Left with the choice of calling Max and putting him straight, spending what was left of the afternoon working, or going home and playing handmaid to her unwanted guest, Louise decided on none of the above and went shopping, instead.

She found a beautiful coat in a bright, cheering red cashmere that came nearly to her ankles. Utterly gorgeous and warm enough to please a dozen mothers, she told herself as she opened her bag to take out her wallet. Then discovered that she was holding her cell phone.

Call him…

She shook her head, fighting off the memory of that moment in the kitchen when Max had held her, looked at her as if the only thing he'd wanted was to make her dream a reality. Before she could do anything she'd regret, she pushed her phone to the bottom of her bag out of harm's way, found her wallet and paid for her coat.

Then she went in search of a hat, boots—no point in doing half a job—and threw in a scarf and lined gloves for good measure.

Then she undid all that good work by splurging on some gossamer silk underwear that had a tog value on the minus side of the scale.

Her subconscious did no more than raise its eloquent eyebrows. They said, 'So, who did you buy those for?'

She ignored it.

Thermal underwear was taking sensible too far.

Cal did his best to interest her in going clubbing that evening, but she pleaded pressure of work. Instead she phoned Jodie, spending an hour telling her about meeting their mother and catching up with her news, then made a cup of cocoa, and, determined on a early night, went to bed with nothing for company but a couple of books she'd found about Meridia.

She hadn't been to the gym all week and after yet another dream-filled night—this time spent chasing something unnamed, unseen that she was glad to wake from—she went and worked up a good sweat before going home and finishing off the Tim Tams for breakfast.

After that she spent the rest of the day at her office with her cell phone switched off and by the time she got home Cal had gone, leaving the flat a tip. Presumably the wilting flowers were his idea of thanks for her hospitality. She tossed them in the bin and got out the vacuum cleaner, glad to have something to keep her occupied. Stop her from dwelling on the fact that none of the messages on her machine had been from Max.

When the doorbell rang on the dot of five-thirty on Monday morning, Louise flipped the switch and said, 'I'll be right down.'

She slipped into her new coat, set the black velvet beret at a jaunty angle on her head, picked up her roomy shoulder bag and went downstairs.

Max was waiting in the car with the engine running.

'Got everything?' he asked as she slid in beside him, clipped her seat belt into place.

So much for Miss Business Efficiency of whatever year you cared to mention.

What was the point when she didn't even get a 'good morning'?

'Everything important,' she replied and ticking them off on her fingers, 'Hairspray, lipstick, emergency nail repair kit...' She looked across at him, suddenly wanting not to make him angry, but to make him laugh. 'Safety pins...'

If he was tempted to smile, he did a manful job of hiding it and, too late to do any good, she wished she'd kept a rein on her temper, or at least her tongue.

A first, that.

They made the airport in what must have been some kind of record, for silence as well as speed, on roads that were relatively clear so early in the morning. Although half an hour had never felt so long.

Things didn't improve when they reached the terminal building. Max just leaned across her, took an envelope out of the glove compartment and handed it to her.

'You handle the check-in while I go and park.'

Unmistakably an order and considering it was combined with the silent treatment her immediate reaction was to tell him to stuff Meridia, stuff Bella Lucia and to go run his own errands. But even as she opened her mouth she found herself recalling her earlier regret and—another first—kept her peace.

'Right. Well, I'll be—'

'I'll find you, Louise,' he said, cutting her short. Then, 'Will you please move, before I get a parking ticket?'

She manfully resisted the temptation to drop his passport and the tickets in the nearest bin and take a taxi home, but he was un-appreciative of her restraint and once they were boarded, closed his eyes, suggesting that even silence was a strain. That he couldn't bear to look at her.

Because he thought that she was involved with Cal? Nothing else had changed since the evening they'd spent talking about the business over supper, not touching, keeping their distance after that searing kiss.

Which meant what, exactly?

That he was jealous?

She glanced at him as if some clue might be found in his posture. In the give-away tension around his closed eyes as she watched him.

'Are you together?' The stewardess, breakfast tray in hand, joined her in regarding Max, unsure whether or not to disturb him.

'Never met him before in my life,' Louise replied, turning away and smiling up at the woman.

'Oh. Right. I don't suppose he said anything about breakfast, then?' The woman sounded harassed. No doubt someone had already given her a hard time for trying to do her job, something Max would never do. He knew the stresses and was always con-siderate of anyone in the service industry.

Unless it was her, of course.

He'd always made an exception in her case.

And recalling her revelatory thoughts about Cal, she asked herself, So why would he bother? Unless he cared?

The stewardess was still waiting.

'Breakfast? Oh, wait, he did say something about looking forward to it.' Feeling a desperate urge to smile, she instead raised her eyebrows, inviting the woman to agree that he was clearly crazy. 'I guess he didn't have time to eat before he left for the airport.'

That finally did raise a smile—or maybe it was a grimace—and Max opened his eyes, straightened in his seat.

'Now would be a very good time to use one of those safety pins, Louise,' he said. 'To fasten your lips together.'

Max regretted the words the minute they left his mouth. He'd spent most of the weekend reminding himself that it was always a mistake to mix business with pleasure, but when she'd swept out of the front door in that dramatic scarlet coat, sexy little hat, common sense had taken a hike. Even so, he'd thought he'd covered himself with the most innocuous of remarks.

"*Got everything?*" What was there to take offence at in that?

And now he'd done it again. This time with intent.

Apparently they couldn't be together for more than a minute without one of them lighting the blue touch-paper. This time he was the guilty party and there was an apparently endless moment while he waited for the explosion. He was ready for it, wanted it, he realised in a moment of searing self-revelation. At least when they were fighting he knew he had her total attention. That she wasn't thinking about anyone but him.

It didn't happen.

Instead of taking the tray from the still hovering stewardess and tipping it in his lap, she leaned forward, picked up her bag and, from a miniature sewing kit, extracted a clip of tiny gold safety pins.

She unhooked one, turned and offered it to him. 'Go ahead, Max.'

In the clear bright light of thirty thousand feet, her eyes were a pure translucent silver and for a moment he couldn't think, speak, move.

'Whenever you're ready,' she prompted. And pushed out her lips, inviting him to get on with it.

It was all he could do to stop the brief expletive slipping from his own lips.

'It's a bit small,' was the best he could manage. 'The pin,' he added, quickly, in case she thought he was referring to her mouth.

Too late, he realised that there was no safe answer as she lifted one brow and said, 'So, I have a big mouth.'

Pushing him, inviting him to do his worst…

He felt a surge of relief. This was better. 'Too big for this pin,' he said, closing his hand around hers. Happy to oblige.

They were six miles above the earth. Where could she go?

'Sorry about that,' she said.

Her mouth was innocent of a smile but without warning a dimple appeared in her left cheek and he felt a surge of warmth, knowing—because he knew her as no one else did—that it was there.

'I'm rarely called to pin up anything bigger than a shoestring strap, or a broken zip at a photo-shoot.' The dimple deepened as if she were having serious trouble keeping the smile at bay. 'I'll make a note to pack something larger in future.'

'Good plan,' he said, taking the pin, letting go of her hand. Touching her was firing up the kind of heat that no shower was cold enough to suppress. 'In the meantime I'll hang onto this one, just in case.'

'In case of what?'

'Just "in case"', he said, dropping it into his ticket pocket. 'Who knows when one will encounter a shoestring-strapped damsel in distress?'

Then, because this elegant, perfectly groomed version of Louise was so different from the way she'd looked on Saturday, warm, tousled and sleepy from the bed she'd shared with Cal Jameson—when for a moment he'd looked into her eyes and seen himself reflected there, as if he were the centre of her soul—he turned away, unable to bear it.

'I'll pass on the food, thanks,' he said to the stewardess. 'Just leave me the juice.'

'Me, too,' Louise said. Then, turning to him, 'Do you want to run through what we're doing today, Max?'

Not as much as he'd hoped, but work had always served him well enough in the past.

'Why not?' And he watched as she produced a folder, opened

it, handed him a copy of the papers. Within minutes he was absorbed in the ideas she'd managed to throw together over the weekend. 'Impressive,' he said. 'Considering the distractions.'

For some reason that made her smile.

'I spoke to my mother, too. Ivy…'

'You called her?'

'She called me. She wanted me to go to lunch yesterday.'

'Perhaps there was something in the stars.' She frowned, not understanding. 'My mother called me, as well. She wanted me to bail her out of jail.'

He hadn't meant to tell her. He'd never told anyone. Not his father, not Jack. She was his mother. His cross.

'Max…' Louise laid her hand over his. 'I'm so sorry. Is she in desperate trouble?'

'Nothing that money won't sort out. Unpaid bills. It just took a bit of sorting out.'

'I would have helped.'

'I didn't need any help,' he said. He didn't need anyone. 'I've done it all before.'

'It's a shame we didn't make it to the fishing lodge,' Louise said as they returned to the chauffeur-driven car Sebastian had thoughtfully laid on for them.

The day had just ebbed away. Lunch with Emma and Sebastian had been unexpected. Wonderful, but even an informal, private lunch with the king and his new queen was not exactly an eat-and-run deal. Then the meeting with a leading hotelier had been long on formality, short on substance, and who could know that the Director of Tourism thought he had to 'sell' them Meridia? Organise a tour of the city, with stops at all the historic sites. It would have been unpardonably rude to tell him they were already 'sold', but it had left them too short of time to get out to the island in daylight.

Now they barely had time to make their check-in at the airport and, although Max had said nothing, it was as clear as day what he was thinking. That the wasted time was entirely down to her.

'I should have listened to you, Max, instead of trying to cram everything in. We're going to have to make another trip to look at it.'

'That won't be necessary.'

She stopped, stared after him. He'd didn't even want to look? Was rejecting it sight unseen. Had he just been stringing her along, making some crappy pay back point about leaping before they'd looked…?

'You've decided against it?' she demanded, already regretting jumping in to take the blame.

Realising that she wasn't keeping pace with him, he turned to face her.

'No, Louise. On the contrary. I want to see it very much, but I thought it likely that we'd need more time so I've arranged for us to stay over until tomorrow.'

'Oh.' She should have felt happy that he was, after all, enthusiastic about the project, but instead she felt oddly flattened. Excluded. Was that how he'd felt when she'd gone ahead and made arrangements without talking to him first? 'You didn't think to mention it?' she asked as she joined him and they moved on.

'I did, but at the time you were otherwise occupied.' It was true— Emma had claimed her attention over lunch, wanting to talk about the coming ball. Ask her advice… 'Is it a problem?' Max asked, standing back so that she could step into the rear of the car, then joining her. 'We could always stop somewhere to buy a toothbrush.'

'Not necessary.'

She glanced at him, then quickly looked away.

They'd been sitting shoulder-to-shoulder close for most of the day, but clearly regretting letting slip his problems with his mother—showing a chink in his armour—he'd kept his distance mentally, put up some kind of invisible wall between them. Maybe it had simply been a business thing, a protection against the simmering undercurrent that was always there, just beneath the surface.

Now they were on their own for the first time since they'd landed, she was doubly conscious of his nearness, not as a business colleague, but as a man.

'I never travel without one,' she said, aware that he had looked at her, querying her response. 'A toothbrush.' The 'everything' she hadn't got around to listing for him was her emergency pack consisting of spare underwear, a clean T-shirt and a toothbrush; having been held up by delays on more than one occasion, she never travelled without it.

'Nor do I.' Then, 'I'm sorry if I've interfered with your plans for the evening. Did you have something special arranged?'

'On a Monday? After a full day travelling? Are you crazy?' Then realising what he meant, she added, coolly, provocatively, 'Just an early night.' And felt a curious mixture of feelings as his jaw tightened. A giddy heart lift that he cared enough to feel jealousy at the thought of Cal Jameson in her bed. Regret that, despite the changes in their relationship, the fact that he'd felt able to open up a little to her about his own problems—and whoever would have believed Max Valentine had problems?—they were both still caught up in a loop, unable to break the habit of striking first, thinking later. 'So?' she prompted. 'Where are we staying?'

'At the lodge,' he replied, equally cool. Equally provocative. 'We'll have all night to make ourselves familiar with the interior, consider the possibilities and, if we're still interested, all day tomorrow to look around the island.' He paused briefly. 'I trust the arrangements I've made meet with your approval.'

She frowned. Did he really think she'd object? Or was it that he was still so angry with her that he felt he had to score points?

After the incident with the safety pin they'd both been on their best behaviour, managing an entire day without rubbing each other up the wrong way. Now, with no one around to see, they were, apparently, to return to sniping terms.

Well, not her. Not any more. 'They do, Max,' she said, very quietly. 'I should have thought of it myself.'

'You've been fully occupied with your own affairs, no doubt.'

'It has been quite a week,' she agreed, even though she was certain he wasn't referring to the HOTfood re-launch, but holding to her determination not to be roused. 'Twelve-hour days as standard. But as of five-thirty this morning, I'm all yours.'

'I think not.'

It was probably fortunate that the car pulled alongside the jetty at that moment, that they were fully occupied transferring themselves to a launch that was waiting to ferry them across to the island. It was hard work being this good when she wasn't getting any help.

But the journey gave them a fairy-tale view of the city from the lake, the floodlit ancient castle, layer upon layer of lights descending and then reflected back in the ripples. They stood in the bows and watched its retreat before turning to each other.

'That's a good start,' Max said.

'Magical. I'm glad we had a chance to see it at night.' Then as the boat slowed she turned to see the approach to the island, the fishing lodge. Equally magical. 'Come on, let's see if the arrival lives up to the journey.'

It did. A liveried footman was waiting at the jetty to lead them up a broad flight of stone steps that opened out onto a wide terrace, through a pair of huge, two-storey height doors. Once inside a vast entrance hall, the footman bowed them into the hands of a butler, before disappearing.

'Good evening, Sir. Madam.' He took their coats, passing them on to a hovering maid, and already Louise's mind was working overtime.

They could keep all this, she thought. Sell it as a chance to be treated like royalty…

'I'll show you to your room,' he said, leading the way up a wide wooden staircase that opened up onto a magnificent first-floor gallery with rooms on three sides. The lodge might have been small by castle standards, but not by any other measure.

He opened a door, crossed the room. 'Your dressing room and bathroom are here, Madam.' Then, turning to Max, 'What time do you wish dinner to be served, sir?'

'Not too late. It's been a long day,' Max said. 'Seven-thirty?'

'Certainly. A fire has been lit in the drawing room. Please ring and ask for anything you want.'

And with that the man was gone, leaving them both in a vast room dominated by an ornately draped and very high four-poster bed. At its foot, on a low chest, stood their bags.

Side by side.

CHAPTER SEVEN

THERE was a long moment of silence, then Louise cleared her throat and said, 'I think there must have been a slight misunderstanding. The butler must have assumed we were husband and wife, rather than...

She stopped. It was hard to break the habit of a lifetime. Max was not family. And sharing a room with him, a bed with him, was her darkest dream...

'I'll go and sort it out,' he said.

'No.' The word escaped her before she could corral it, keep it safely locked up.

Maybe.

Maybe she didn't try as hard as she might have done.

This felt like fate saying, '*Now...*'

'No?' he repeated, his face expressionless, giving nothing away. For a moment, when he'd taken the pin from her, kept it, anything had seemed possible. Since then he'd kept all interaction on a strictly business level, kept his distance, not just physically, but emotionally.

'I'm desperate for a cup of tea,' she said, losing her nerve. 'Let me freshen up and then we can both go.'

'I thought you might want a little privacy in order to phone your Antipodean friend,' he said, stiffly. 'Explain that you won't be home tonight.'

'I don't have to explain myself to anyone, Max, least of all Cal Jameson.' Or him, for that matter, but it was time to put an end to this. Set the record straight. 'And after the state he and some girl he brought home with him on Saturday night left my flat in, he's very far from being my friend. In fact the next time I find him on my doorstep at two in the morning, I'll be very tempted to leave him there.'

'Girl?' Max repeated, homing in on the one important word, going to the heart of what she was telling him.

'He must have picked her up when he went clubbing. They woke me coming in at some unearthly hour...' Then, all innocence, 'Oh, please. You didn't think *I* was sleeping with him, did you?'

'You implied as much—'

'No, Max,' she said cutting him off, dropping the pretence. 'You implied it. In front of a valued client, what's more. *You* implied I was sleeping with him, too, I seem to recall, which might have been funny if it hadn't been so insulting.'

'*He* certainly implied as much.'

'Cal? Or Oliver Nash?'

His mouth tightened. 'You know who I mean.'

'Well, yes. Apart from the fact that he's married, Oliver is far too much a gentleman to have done anything of the sort.'

'Not too married, or too much of a gentleman, to be above asking you out to dinner.'

'Too much of a gentleman to have boosted his ego by implying I was sleeping with him.' Then, furious with him for being so dense. 'The man's an incorrigible flirt, Max, but it doesn't mean anything.'

'It might have meant nothing to you, but I can assure you that given half an inch of encouragement, he'd have been in like Flynn.'

Jealous, jealous, her heart sang...

'He didn't have any encouragement because I never mix business with pleasure,' she said, firmly. 'As for Cal, he's like a big overgrown puppy. He understands the word no, but believes that if he ignores it, I'll forget I said it.' Then, because it was suddenly vital that he was absolutely clear. 'The most intimate exchange between us was that kiss under the mistletoe at the family party. In full view of everyone.'

'But you went home with him.'

'Yes, well...' She turned away, feeling hideously exposed, but knowing that she had to clear the air between them if they were going to work together. If they were ever going to finish what they'd started. 'Taking Cal home wasn't my idea of fun, but Jodie found the idea of sharing her honeymoon with her brother-in-law less than enthralling and, since she'd sent him gift-wrapped as my date for the evening, I returned the favour by letting him stay in my spare room.' She looked back at him, willing him to understand, cut her some slack. 'It's what sisters do, Max. They help each other out. You'd have done the same for Jack, wouldn't you?'

'Taken home a good-looking woman who fancied the pants off me to give Jack some space with Maddie? I could see how that might work,' he said.

'Oh, forget it!' She grabbed her bag, headed for the bathroom.

'No.' He raked long fingers through his hair, ruffling it in a way that she found unbearably sexy. 'I'm sorry. Tell me.'

An apology from Max now? They were coming along…

'There's nothing to tell, Max. That's the point. Except that Cal now treats my flat like his own personal hotel, turning up unannounced whenever he's passing through.'

'I'm sorry, Lou.' Another apology? 'I should have called you, offered to take you to the Christmas party.'

No, this wasn't an apology. It was something far more significant…

Afraid he'd see, read the unbearable yearning in her eyes, she turned quickly away with, 'Oh, right. Like I'd have said yes.'

She didn't wait for his response, but scooted into the bathroom, not coming out until she'd combed her hair, freshened her lipstick. Wiped the need from her face.

'I'll see you downstairs,' she said, when she emerged, heading for the door before he could say any more. Not looking at him, because to look at him was—as it had always been—to invite disaster.

She rang the bell, explained about the rooms, asked for tea, and by the time Max joined her the footman had returned with a tray laden with tea things, accompanied by a maid with a three-tiered tray containing tiny sandwiches, cakes, pastries.

'You know, I don't think we need a hotelier,' Louise said as she handed Max a cup of tea. 'I think we just need to keep these people on to run the place.'

'I doubt they'd want to trade the quiet life they have at present for the long hours and hard work of the commercial world.'

'I was…' Joking. 'Never mind.' She shook her head, putting down her own cup. 'I'm going to take a look around.'

Without waiting for him, she walked out into the magnificent entrance hall with its marble tiled floor, grand staircase, open hearth in which a fire had been lit since their arrival.

'This would make a perfect wedding venue,' Max said, joining her. Then, taking the lead, opening the door to a richly decorated banqueting room, 'It's not quite the way I imagined it would be.'

'You pictured stone walls running with damp, cold enough to freeze your marrow?'

'No, but a fishing lodge does suggest a certain rustic finish.'

'Yes, well, maybe we were being a little too literal in our use of the word. According to Emma, "going fishing" turns out to have been something of a euphemism within the royal family for meeting the mistress. This place might look mediaeval, but it was actually built as a *folie d'amour* by some goaty minor royal in the late nineteenth century. It's practically new by Meridian standards.'

'You weren't just discussing ball dresses when you disappeared for girl talk, then?'

She gave him a withering look. 'It belongs to a branch of the family who spent money like water and lived a hedonistic lifestyle. The owner of this place is what used to be known as a "remittance man". He's paid a pension by the old king to stay away. Sebastian takes care of the running costs, pays the staff just to keep them in work. Nothing would please him more than to see it put to good use.' Then, as if as an afterthought, 'He is also extremely keen to expand the tourist industry.'

'I know.'

'You do?'

'We discussed all this at length when he rang me last week.'

'He rang you?'

'He wanted me to know, if I was serious, that local laws mean

I would have to have a Meridian partner, which isn't a problem. As you already pointed out, we'll need someone to run the residential side of the property.' He looked around. 'He also wanted me to know that it will have to be preserved as it is.'

'And no doubt Bella Lucia will be responsible for conserving it?'

'That would be the deal.' He looked up at the gilded ceiling. 'It's a good one, too. We couldn't hope to find anything like this; certainly couldn't build it.' Then, 'The only thing he didn't tell me was how beautiful it is.'

'Maybe he thought you knew.' She gazed about her. 'So, was that one of the things you planned to discuss with me on Saturday?'

He smiled. 'You'll never know, will you? Shall we continue the tour?'

They found a library, a billiard room with a number of rather splendid stuffed fish mounted in glass cases—possibly the origin of the 'fishing' euphemism—a charming morning room and a vast, heated conservatory.

'Oh, yes,' Max said, turning slowly to take it all in.

'You like it?' Louise asked, only then realising just how important it was to her to have got it right. Demonstrated her worth.

'This would make a perfect informal restaurant, spilling out onto the terrace in summer. We'd have the formal dining room for weddings, functions, parties and there are a couple of smaller rooms for other private parties.'

'It would suit those small, high-level business conferences, too,' she pointed out. 'There are what? Ten, twelve bedrooms? A honeymoon suite for bridal parties...'

'It has everything. And it will be completely different from all our other restaurants, too. Meridia's Bella Lucia will be unique, total luxury.'

'You already have a name for it?'

'It names itself. And about the staff, I was wondering if they'd be prepared to stay on and train the new people?'

She smiled. 'We could ask them.'

He nodded. 'Maybe you'd like to talk to them tomorrow. While I'm inspecting the kitchens, cellar and the utilities. The public rooms will need very little work. I don't think we'll find anywhere else that we can take over so easily.' He turned, touched her arm. 'It's a great start. Thank you, Louise.'

'You're welcome,' she said, tucking a loose strand of hair behind her ear. Looking at the ceiling, desperate not to show him how pleased she was.

He didn't let go, didn't stop looking at her.

'Louise…'

She waited, certain he was going to say something important, not about business, but about them. But after a moment he shook his head, let her go.

'I'd better take a shower before dinner,' she said, needing to escape, catch her breath. 'I'll see you down here just before seven-thirty.'

She managed to walk from the room, but then bolted up the stairs, shutting the door behind her and leaning against it. Afraid he'd follow her. Afraid he wouldn't…

The maid who was waiting for her kept her face carefully expressionless as she said, 'Shall I draw you a bath, Miss Valentine?'

She took a breath, pulled herself together. A shower. She should take a cold shower…

She shivered at the thought. Rejected it.

'Thank you…?'

'Maria, miss.'

'Thank you, Maria. That would be wonderful.'

'Since you don't have any luggage, miss, Her Royal Highness said you might like to choose a dress from the wardrobe.'

The girl opened up a huge walk-in closet lined with racks of dresses, shoes and everything that went with them.

'Oh, my goodness…' She walked along the racks looking at the elegant vintage gowns, touching the delicate fabrics. Black, beaded silk, sapphire lace, slipper silk in all colours… 'These are beautiful. Who owned them?'

The maid shrugged. 'I've no idea, miss. The count used to have parties here. In the old days.'

Louise picked out an art deco sliver of pearl-grey silk, held it against her.

'They shouldn't be here. They should be in a museum.' Then,

'No...' She'd seen gowns in museums. Dead things. Bits of cloth that looked nothing without a living, breathing person inside them.

'Yes, miss?' Louise shook her head. 'I'll run your bath.'

'Thank you,' she said, then picked up the phone, called Emma.

'Hi, Lou! What do you think of our little castle?'

'It's absolutely beautiful, Emma, perfect, but, tell me, did you know there are dozens of fabulous vintage gowns, shoes, everything here?'

'The mistress's wardrobe? I've heard about it.'

'My dear, you should see it! Have you any idea just how hot vintage clothes are right now? You were looking for something special for your ball—well, I think this could be it. A fashion show—I'm sure you could round up some celebrities for that. Then they could be auctioned off—it's been done before. The press will be salivating, it will bring in all the Hollywood divas and your charity will raise a mint...'

'Louise! You are a genius. I don't suppose I could talk you into organising it for me?'

'Oh, please! Try and stop me!'

'There's just one condition.'

'Anything.'

'You'll be doing this for charity so you won't get a fee, but I want you to have something.'

'No, I'll do it for...' for the family, that was what she'd been going to say '...for you.'

'You've already done so much for me, Lou. Now it's my turn to repay the favour. My condition is that you wear one of those dresses tonight.'

'But... But suppose I spill red wine down it?'

'Drink white if it worries you, but that's the deal.'

'You know, Emma, since you got to be Queen, you have become *so* bossy!' She smiled. 'Thank you.'

Max, having been shown, with profound apologies for an error that had been no one's fault but his own, to another room, found a footman laying out a slightly old-fashioned dinner jacket and dress shirt. His initial response was to say thanks, but no, thanks, but it occurred to him that they would have found something for Louise, too, and she wouldn't hurt their feelings by rejecting it.

He was the only one she didn't care about hurting. Telling him one thing with her eyes, another with everything she did, said. If she ever found out the truth…

He went downstairs at seven-fifteen so that she wouldn't be left on her own, took the whisky the butler poured for him, but, too restless to sit in the drawing room, he paced the hall, his head full of the new restaurant, which of a number of world-class chefs he might tempt to take charge of the kitchen, the start-up costs…

All it took to distract him was a whisper of silk and he turned, looked up.

Louise, her hair twisted up and held in place with some kind of exotic jewelled clip, her hand trailing lightly on the banister rail, draped in a slender silk gown whose soft folds displayed every curve of her body, clung to her long thighs as she moved, was slowly descending the stairs.

For a moment he was transfixed.

He'd seen her dressed for an occasion countless times before; looking like a queen for some other man. But this time she'd dressed for no one but him…

Regaining the use of his limbs, he crossed to meet her and instead of the usual sarcastic remark—gauged to provoke a response guaranteed to leave them both despising the other—he said the first thing that came into his mind.

'You look absolutely stunning, Louise.'

'Thank you,' she said as she reached the bottom step. 'I didn't intend my entrance to be quite such a Hollywood performance, but the dress is a little long and the footwear…' she hitched up her skirt an inch or two to display a matching high-heeled sandal '…is a little on the large side. The stairs required extreme care.'

'I enjoyed every moment of it,' he assured her, then as a clock began to chime the half-hour the butler appeared to announce that dinner was served.

Max extended his arm. 'May I escort you in to dinner, Miss Valentine?'

She smiled, laid her arm along his. 'Thank you, Mr Valentine.'

Dinner was served to them in a small dining room that they had missed on their exploration. Richly decorated on the most intimate scale.

It was a room plainly made for lovers, yet despite their surroundings, the wonderful food, fine wines, exquisite clothes, he felt himself retreat a little, become more distant, determined to keep the conversation firmly fixed on the safe subject of business. He laid out his ideas, she offered marketing, PR strategies.

Neither of them wanted coffee, and when they moved to the drawing room so that the staff could clear away Louise didn't settle, refused a nightcap. His overwhelming reaction was relief. The entire day had been a strain and he needed to escape from this brittle concord before he did, or said, something to shatter it.

'I'm ready for bed, Max.'

'It's been a long day. We'll take it easy tomorrow, just potter around. Take a load of photographs. Come on, I'll see you to your room.'

'I'm not helpless,' she said as he took her arm, shivering a little at the unexpected contact.

'Not helpless, but at the mercy of those shoes. I'm not prepared to risk my most valuable asset taking a tumble and breaking her neck.'

She glanced at him, as if surprised, although why she would be when he'd made it plain that he'd do anything to get her to join him, but she said nothing until they reached her door.

Instead of opening it, ducking quickly inside, as he'd expected her to, she turned to face him, said, 'You never did tell me what you wanted to talk to me about on Saturday, Max.'

'To be honest I was rather hoping we could both forget Saturday.'

'All of it?'

Not the moment when he'd seen her standing in her kitchen, hair tousled, flushed from bed. Her wrap hanging open, her lovely legs bare. Not the moment when she'd looked up at him as if he were the only man she'd ever wanted...

'Maybe just the last bit, where I behaved like a moron.'

'I don't want to forget that part, Max,' she said, her voice so soft that he had to bend his head to catch the words. 'You wouldn't have reacted that way if…'

She hesitated as if to say the words would be to expose them both so he said them for her.

'If I hadn't wanted to throttle Cal Jameson. If I hadn't wanted you for myself.'

Now…

The voice in Louise's head was so loud that she was certain Max must hear it too. But he didn't move.

'This room,' she managed. 'It wasn't a mistake, was it?'

Max shook his head and, emboldened by a tiny sigh that escaped her, said, 'It wasn't a spur-of-the-moment decision. I realised we'd need more time and when I spoke to Sebastian, I asked if we could stay here. He gave me the number so that I could make my own arrangements with the staff; the butler misunderstood and I didn't correct his mistake. I thought, hoped that this might be somewhere private, neutral ground where we could continue our discussion about exactly where you wanted me to kiss you.' He looked up, met her gaze head-on. 'A place where we could conclude all contractual obligations to your complete satisfaction.'

She came close to smiling. 'In an icy, rustic stone lodge?'

'You wouldn't have felt the cold,' he assured her.

'No?'

She shivered, despite the heating, but still he didn't touch her, even though her body was doing everything but scream at him to go for it, even though she could feel that his hand, still supporting her elbow, was not quite steady…

He was giving her total control. Her call…

She opened the bedroom door and led him inside, turning to face him as the door closed behind them

'Show me,' she said, her voice scarcely strong enough to reach him and, lifting her hand, she touched a fingertip to her cheek. 'Kiss me here.'

His eyes seemed to take on a new intensity and for a moment she was afraid that she'd unleashed a passion that he wouldn't be able to hold in check but when, after a pause that seemed to last a lifetime, his lips touched her cheek she felt no more than a whisper of warmth. Enough to send a flash of heat through her and for a moment she swayed towards him, dangerously close to flinging herself on him. If he made one move...

But he didn't. He was leaving her to set the pace, take it where she dared.

If she had the courage.

Responding to his unspoken challenge, she moved her hand, touched her chin.

'Here,' she said, on a breath.

His eyes, darker than pitch, warned her that she was playing a dangerous game. Did he think she didn't know that?

This was their time. Now. It would be brief, glorious but brief, like a New Year's Eve rocket, and afterwards, when it had burnt out, she would be free of him.

They would both be free...

'Here,' she said, raising the stakes, touching her lower lip, anticipating the same exhilarating, no-holds-barred kiss with which he'd stopped her walking away. Would use this time to carry them both over the threshold of restraint and beyond thought.

But he did no more than touch her lower lip, tasting it with his tongue. It was all she could do to remain on her feet; her only compensation was knowing how hard this must be for him. To hold back, wait. It would have been difficult to say which of them was trembling more, but he was forcing her to make all the moves, insisting that she be the one to tip it over the edge from a teasing game into a dark and passionate reality.

'Now, Max,' she said. Unfastening her dress, she let it fall in a shimmering puddle of silk at her feet, leaving her naked but for the scrap of silk and lace at her hips, lace-topped hold-ups, high-heeled sandals.

His response was to pull loose his tie, remove his jacket and toss it aside, finally turning the key in the lock without ever taking his eyes off her.

She'd thought she'd die with the sheer force of desire his first kiss brought bubbling to the surface, but now every cell in her body seemed to sigh, melt as his mouth kissed a slow seductive trail over her breasts and down across the soft curve of her stomach.

In that moment she felt like a conqueror, a queen receiving tribute from a vanquished king whom she'd made her slave.

But then he hooked his thumbs under the ties of her silk panties removing the last barrier between them, using his mouth until 'now' became not a command, not permission to touch, but a whimpering entreaty, a plea for his hands, his body, for all he had to give, and she knew that she'd made a mistake.

As he finally took pity on her, responded to her 'Max...please...' lifting her acquiesent body in his arms, carrying her to the great four-poster, she discovered that, far from being the one in control, she was the conquered.

Louise woke in a series of gentle waves. First there was a boneless, almost out-of-body consciousness in which she was dimly aware that it was morning, but felt no pressure to do anything about it. Then came a gradual awareness of a soft pillow beneath her cheek, limbs heavy with the delicious languor of utter contentment.

She nestled down into the pillow, unwilling to relinquish her dreams.

Something warm tickled her shoulder.

She twitched away, burrowed deeper.

It happened again and this time she reached to pull up the sheet, tuck it in, but instead of the sheet her hand encountered warm skin over hard bone.

Her face still buried in the pillow, she flattened her hand over a nose that wasn't quite straight, a mouth blowing soft, warm breath against her palm.

Not a dream, she thought, as finally awake she recalled where she was, who she was with. Every word, every touch, every little whimper as she begged him to love her. Every fierce sound she'd wrung from him in return...

She turned her head, opened her eyes.

Propped on an elbow, he'd clearly been watching her, waiting for her to wake. The fact that he'd grown impatient sent a ripple of delight coursing through her veins and she slid her fingers through his hair, fantasy fulfilled; she had never seen his short, thick, perfectly groomed hair without wanting to do that. Disturb the outer perfection, shatter his control. She'd done that, she thought, in a moment that was pure victory. Then she rolled over onto her back, drawing him to her.

She'd wanted to be free of him, of the dark primal need for him that had destroyed every other relationship. But there was no hurry. She had until the fourteenth to put together her PR and marketing plan. All the time in the world.

'Did anyone ever tell you, Max,' she said, 'that when you wake a woman from her dreams, you have to replace them with something more…substantial?'

'First you have to tell me your dreams, my sweet,' he said, his smile slow and lazy, his eyes smoky-soft in the early-morning light. 'Tell me all your dreams, your wildest fantasies, and I promise you that I'll do whatever it takes to make them come true.'

'You promise?' The word sent a tiny shiver of apprehension sweeping through her. She dismissed it, said, 'Have we got that long?'

CHAPTER EIGHT

'WELL, that's a give-away smile. Who is he?'

Louise, lost in her thoughts, hadn't realised she was smiling and abruptly straightened her face. 'He?'

'Oh, come on.' Gemma, her PA, was grinning fit to bust herself. 'Only a nomination for an award, or a new man in your life, could put a smile that wide on your face. Since it isn't the award season…' She held out her hands, palms up, in a gesture that said 'case proved'. 'So, come on. Give.' Then, slapping her forehead, 'No, don't tell me—'

'If you insist,' Louise replied, more than willing to change the subject. 'Did Max send over the artist's impressions of the Qu'Arim restaurant? He said he'd have them here by lunchtime.'

Was her voice quite steady as she said his name? Should saying 'Max' be quite such a secret pleasure when she was supposed to be clearing him from her system?

'You've used your royal connections to hook yourself a Meridian prince,' Gemma continued as if she hadn't been interrupted. '*That's* the reason you stayed over for an extra day.'

'Just call me Princess Louise,' she agreed. 'The drawings?'

'Hmm, not a prince. You didn't blush.'

'I'm a PR consultant, Gem. I do not blush.'

'If you say so.' Then, 'You can't have any secrets from your PA, Lou. It's not allowed. If I don't know what you're up to,' she said, sitting down and propping her elbows on the desk, 'I won't be able to fend off questions from the press when they get wind of it.'

'Don't worry about it. In the unlikely event that the press should show any interest in who I'm dating you have my full permission to tell them everything you know.'

'Unlikely? Are you kidding? You dropped off the gossip planet when you split with James. As far as the diary hacks are concerned, you owe them three years' worth of copy.' Then, her chin in her hands, 'So, you are dating?'

'No, Gemma.'

'Sorry, not convinced. A girl doesn't get that kind of glow without some serious attention from a man who lights up her soul.'

Max did not light up her soul. She wasn't that kind of fool. Every other part of her, maybe…

'I've been taking vitamins,' she said.

'What kind? I want some.' Then, 'Really not dating?'

'You mean the institution where a man asks a woman out, takes her out to a concert or for a meal or whatever he believes is the fastest way between her sheets?'

Gemma nodded expectantly.

'No. I'm not doing that.'

It was true.

Dating was part of the getting-to-know-you ritual in which a couple circled around each other, tested each other against their own lives to see if they were a fit. Or, failing that, whether the sexual attraction was powerful enough to counteract common sense…at least for the time being.

With Max it wasn't like that.

They didn't have to play that game. They'd known each other all their lives. Why waste time sitting opposite one another in a fancy restaurant where the whole world could see them making small talk and leap to its own conclusions, when they could be sharing supper in bed? Why waste time providing gossip for the tabloid diary writers?

Besides, the secrecy added a certain piquancy, an extra level of excitement to their affair.

'You're smiling again,' Gemma said.

'I can't think why when I'm still waiting for those drawings.'

'They haven't arrived yet.' Then, turning her head as someone came into the outer office, 'Correction, the boss has brought them himself.'

'Max?'

Louise saw the exact moment when Gemma realised the truth. Not that she said anything. She didn't have to. She looked at Max standing in the doorway, holding not just the large envelope containing drawings of the Qu'Arim restaurant, but a spray of dusky pink roses, glanced back at Louise and then pointedly removed herself from the office, closing the door behind her.

'Were all the couriers busy?' Louise asked as he dropped the roses on her desk.

'The message I'm delivering is far too personal to entrust with a spotty youth on a motorcycle.'

His hands braced on the arms of her chair, he bent to kiss her, taking his time about it.

The thrill, the tiny shock of delight, was still as new, as startling as the first kiss they'd shared. It made her feel like a giddy eighteen-year-old. And as old and knowing as time.

He pulled back an inch. 'Besides, I'm on my way to talk to the accountants.'

'And you decided to take the long way round?'

He grinned, propped himself on the desk. 'Not because I need the exercise.'

'Oh, please, I'm not complaining,' she said, laughing. 'But I fear that we've just been rumbled.'

'Rumbled?' He glanced at the closed door. 'Gemma?'

'I think the flowers might have been the give-away.'

'A gift from a grateful employer.' Then, 'What, Oliver Nash never sent you flowers?' he asked, glancing at the vast arrangement that had been delivered to the office, a personal thank-you for the HOTfood launch.

'He sends Flowers,' she said, emphasising the capital F with a broad gesture that suggested vast quantities of hothouse blooms. 'And they are delivered by messenger. He doesn't drop by with a bunch of roses from the flower seller on the corner.'

'His mistake.' He grinned, looked at the roses. 'Although I

didn't set out with flowers in mind, I have to admit. It was just when I saw these they reminded me of you.'

'You needed reminding?'

She picked them up, ruffled the velvety petals beneath her fingers and then, aware that he was waiting for her to ask in what way exactly they had reminded him of her she looked up, inviting him to elaborate.

'Reminded me specifically of the moment when you dropped your dress at your feet. They're exactly the colour of the incredibly small amount of underwear you were wearing, wanton hussy that you are—'

'Sh!' she said, her face turning the same colour as the roses.

'A wanton hussy who blushes like a schoolgirl.'

'I don't!'

He didn't argue, just reached out, hand closed, and rubbed her hot cheek with the back of his fingers.

'Is it such a big deal, Lou? Gemma knowing? People saw us dining with Patsy and Derek last week.'

'No one we knew.'

'Maybe not. But the *maître d'* recognised me and when one Valentine eats in a restaurant that's not his own, it's gossip. When two of us do it, it's news. You're not exactly low profile, Lou, and Patsy didn't opt for discretion in her choice of restaurants. She wanted to show you off.'

Louise groaned. 'I know. Half the staff at that place are probably Diary stringers for the redtops, but I couldn't bear to disappoint her when she was so excited.'

'No, of course you couldn't.'

'From now on we'll have to be more discreet.'

'Will we?'

'Please, Max,' she said, imploring him to understand.

'You have a problem being seen out with me?' He shook his head. He was still smiling, but not right up to his eyes. 'And I thought the reason we stayed in was because you couldn't get enough of my body.'

'Well,' she said, desperate to tease him back to a smile, 'there's an upside to everything,'

'But?'

'But nothing. I don't care about other people, Max, only Dad. He's just getting over his heart attack…'

'And you think if he knew that I was sleeping with his little princess the shock would kill him?'

'I'm not… I'm not prepared to take the risk, are you?' she said, flaring up briefly at his lack of sympathy. Then, silently begging him to understand. This affair was too hot to sustain itself for long; it would burn itself out in its own heat soon enough… 'You know how he feels about your father.'

'Bitter. Chip on his shoulder a mile high.' Max was not with her on this one. 'But I'm not my father. Besides, don't you think he should have got over that at his age?'

'Try to understand, Max. Your father was the son of an adored second wife while my father saw his own mother abandoned, without support, dying of pneumonia.'

'The country was at war, Louise. Life was hard for everyone.' Then, 'It's not just that, though, is it?'

She shook her head. 'No. Your father had everything. Not just two loving parents, but looks, charisma, women falling at his feet.'

'Children of his own?'

'Sons,' she said, the word like a knife to her heart. But even as she said the word she finally understood why her father had wanted to keep the fact that she was adopted a secret. No, not so much a secret as sweeping it under the carpet. Pretending it wasn't so. Because even in this, most basic of human functions, he'd been eclipsed by his younger, more glamorous half brother…

He'd never been able to forgive his father for being there for Robert. Caring more about Robert. Never able to forgive Robert for having everything.

Was she falling into the same mistake? Unable to forgive, to move on?

He didn't deserve that from her.

'He's finally caught up in the son stakes,' Max reminded her.

She shook her head.

'But even in that he was deprived, don't you see? He didn't know they existed until last year. He blamed William Valentine for that, too.'

He shrugged. 'To be honest I have more sympathy with your mother. Have you been to see her recently?'

She shook her head.

'She needs you, Lou. No matter how much you enjoy Patsy's company, Ivy's your mother too.'

'You think she'd understand…this? Us? Approve?'

'Like Patsy, you mean?'

Maybe that was why she'd enjoyed the evening with Patsy so much. She hadn't judged them. They hadn't had to hide their feelings from her.

'As my mother, Max. As John Valentine's wife.'

'The reason Patsy isn't bothered, Lou, is because she hasn't been involved. There's no history.'

'That's not true!'

'For Ivy, you're her whole life. Talk to her, Louise.'

'Not about us,' she said, not wanting to go there. Determined to keep him with her on this one thing. 'This isn't…'

'Isn't what?'

She shook her head. 'Serious,' she said, opting for the easy answer.

'Not serious?' There was a momentary pause. 'Are you telling me that you're just playing with me? That all you want is my body?'

'Absolutely,' she said, grabbing at this chance to turn it into a joke.

'Is that right?' He let the past go and, with an imperceptible contraction of the lines fanning out from the corners of his eyes, began a slow, seductive smile that made her forget all about her mother, her father, instead jolting her into one-hundred-per-cent awareness of him. 'Are you sure it isn't because being with me makes you feel just the tiniest bit…wicked?'

'Only "the tiniest bit"?' she managed, through a throat apparently stuffed with cobwebs. 'I was hoping for much better than that.'

His answer was to open his hand, cup her head, lean forward and kiss her, long and deep, his tongue a silky invader that ransacked her mouth, turning her limbs to water.

'Better?' he asked, when he'd done and she lay back, limp in her chair.

'Much better,' she said, smiling like an idiot in a way that would have confirmed all Gemma's darkest suspicions.

Blissfully better.

Her plan had been to gorge on a glut of Max Valentine so that she would lose her appetite for his kisses, his love, but the truth was that they were addictive; the more she had, the more she wanted.

With him she held nothing back. There was no reserve. He turned her on like a searchlight.

'So,' she said, her voice pure vamp, 'do you want to make out on my desk?'

He kissed her once more, but briefly, before straightening. 'While I'd love to stay and play, sweetheart, I've got an appointment that won't keep,' he said, backing towards the door, grinning. 'But hold that thought until our evening meeting. I'll see you on my desk at six-thirty…'

'You're walking out on me?' Okay, so she hadn't actually meant it. Well, probably hadn't meant it. But no way was she letting him get away with that…

'It isn't easy,' he assured her, but he kept on walking.

She let him reach the door before she said, 'So you don't want to check that the underwear really does match the roses, then?'

He lost the grin. 'You're wearing it?'

'There's only one way to find out.'

When he'd gone, Gemma appeared in the doorway. 'Max was in a hurry.'

'He was late for an appointment with the accountant.'

Believing her had been his first mistake; coming back to check for himself had been his second.

Two out of three wasn't bad.

She'd felt the need to test her power, make it as hard as humanly possible for him to leave, but he'd eventually managed to tear himself away. Late, it was true, but still not here. Not that she should be surprised. Max had always taken his responsibilities seriously. Put Bella Lucia before anything—anyone—else. It was, now she understood him a little better, easier to see why.

'So?' Gemma picked up the roses. 'Do these go in water or the bin?' She sniffed them, pulled a face. 'They've got no scent,' she said, as if that settled it.

'Max didn't buy them for the scent.' And her smile returned as she remembered exactly why he'd bought them. For the moment he was finding more than enough time for pleasure. 'Put them in water, Gem. I'll have them on my desk.'

Next time he called in, he'd see them there and he'd remember, too.

She caught herself. Next time? She shook her head as if to clear it. Enjoy the moment, she reminded herself. Enjoy each time he broke stride, found precious time to be with her.

Then she smiled. She might not have been able to do more than delay him but she'd done a very satisfactory job of distracting him. The image she'd planted in his head, her scent, the taste of her, would be with him all the time he was with the accountant, discussing the costs for fitting out and launching Bella Lucia in Meridia.

When Gemma returned with the vase, she lingered, fussing with the flowers until Louise put down her pen, sat back and said, 'Okay. You've obviously got something on your mind. Out with it.'

'It's nothing.' Then, finally, she looked at her. 'Just… You will be careful, Lou?'

'Careful? Is this where I get the "safe sex" lecture?'

'Well, if you think you need a refresher course, but to be honest I was more concerned about your heart. Max Valentine is not exactly Mr Commitment, is he?'

'That's not fair!' Louise responded without thinking. Defending him. Who, in all his life, had ever been one hundred per cent committed to him? Put him first?

Then, as Gemma's eyebrows hit the ceiling and she realised that she'd overdone it, she tried to limit the damage.

'I'm not looking for commitment,' she said. And it was true, she wasn't. Hadn't been… 'This thing between Max and me…'

How to explain it to Gemma? Impossible when she wasn't entirely sure what it was herself. It had all seemed so simple…

'This "thing"?' Gemma prompted, making quote marks that suggested scepticism, if not downright sarcasm.

No, it *was* simple.

'It's not serious. Really,' she stressed when her PA, who knew her far too well to be easily fooled, did not look convinced. 'It's just unfinished business, that's all. Something that's been simmering away since we were adolescents. It should have happened a long time ago. Would have if we'd known the truth, that I was adopted. That there was no impediment to a relationship.'

'So all that snapping and snarling at one another was no more than repressed lust and now, what, you're just getting it—getting him—out of your system?'

'You see? Easy,' she said, with more conviction than she actually felt. It had been so heart-stoppingly special to look up, see him there. 'It's no more than a bit of fun,' she insisted.

Gemma was looking at her a little oddly and even as she said the words she knew, deep down, that it had gone way beyond that.

But it was a temporary madness. It had to be. She'd given herself until the fourteenth. On that day all debts would be paid and by then Max Valentine would be out of her system, as Gemma had so neatly put it.

'So why be coy?' her PA persisted. 'It's not as if either of you are involved with anyone else. Max is apparently wedded to his job and it's been nearly three years since you split up with—'

Louise stopped her with an impatient gesture. She didn't want to think about James, let alone talk about him.

'Dad's had enough shocks lately, don't you think? You know the history.'

She'd spilled it all to Gemma, needing someone completely neutral to talk to after her father had blurted out that she was adopted. It was Gemma who'd held the tissues, poured the brandy, found out how to trace her real mother.

'I can see that your dad wouldn't be exactly thrilled by the idea of you and Max as an item,' Gemma admitted, 'but neither of you are kids…'

'No. We're not. I told you, it's no more than a…' Louise made a vague gesture, unable to say the words again.

'A bit of fun,' Gemma said, obligingly filling in the blanks for her.

'So,' she said. 'You must see why we're not broadcasting it.'

'And Max feels that way too?'

Her PA was nothing if not persistent. 'You were the one who pointed out his commitment problem.'

'So I did.' Then, brightly, 'And actually I do understand, boss.

If I was having "a bit of fun" with a man who put an urgent appointment with his accountant ahead of some hot lunchtime sex, I wouldn't want anyone to know, either.'

'Gemma!'

'No, honestly, your secret is safe with me,' she said, grinning wickedly, 'although next time you might try—'

'Enough!'

'Only trying to help,' she said, turning to go. Then, turning back, 'Just do yourself a favour, Lou, and remember that while Max Valentine is undoubtedly having fun—' She held up her hands '—okay, okay, you're *both* having fun,' she went on quickly before Louise could interrupt. 'But when it's all over, when he's got you out of *his* system, he'll be able to walk away without a backward glance.'

Once she would have believed that, before he'd opened up to her about his mother, his childhood. Not just that painfully cryptic moment on the plane but in the quiet moments of intimacy he'd somehow been able to respond to her queries about how things had gone with a frankness that had shown her a new side of his character. She knew that the charming, untouchable, totally in control Max Valentine had a vulnerability that she suspected no one else had ever seen.

But she was vulnerable, too, hiding inside her own shell, and with an archness she was far from feeling she said, 'Are you suggesting that I won't?'

'All I'm saying, Louise, is that it's taken you three years to get over James Cadogan. I very much doubt that you're a woman who can do detached "fun".'

'Gem—'

'It's okay, lecture over,' Gemma said, backing off. 'I'm going to get a sandwich. Can I bring anything for you?'

'Please,' she said, relieved to be moving into safer territory. 'Salmon,' she said. 'And a blueberry yoghurt.'

'Anything else?'

A chance to do things again, perhaps. Max had been casual enough about her need for secrecy, but he didn't like it. It wasn't as if they were doing anything wrong, anything they need be ashamed of. They were together and, no matter how temporary their affair was intended to be, in some deep, hidden recess of her soul, she knew she wanted the world to know, to see what they had.

'Lou?'

She shook her head. 'Nothing.' Nothing anyone could give her.

'I've got confirmation of an article in a heavyweight international financial journal today, Max. The package I put together of the Qu'Arim restaurant sold it to them.'

'Mmm?'

He was engrossed in a booking list and only gave Louise half his attention.

She reached over and removed the sheet of paper he was working on and when he looked up, she kissed him. Only when he was kissing her back did she pull away. 'It's half past six, Max. My time.'

He leaned back, squeezed the space between his eyes. Smiled at her. 'You look good enough to eat.'

'That is not out of the question. First, business.'

'A financial journal?' he said, just to demonstrate that he'd been listening. 'Why would they be interested in us?'

'The first new Bella Lucia in twenty-five years may only be of passing interest to the kind of people who make their global deals over lunch at the Mayfair restaurant,' she began. 'Something to note for the next time they're in Qu'Arim—'

'Only of passing interest?'

Question the interest quotient of his precious restaurants and suddenly she had his attention.

'So what's the big deal?' he asked.

'The big deal is not a single restaurant, but that it's the first in a new era of expansion. This magazine is read by people who know us, trust us, show it by coming here to make their deals in the discreet atmosphere of the Mayfair restaurant. They can smooth our path overseas, Max. They'll come to us with partnership proposals, finance.' Then, when he didn't immediately congratulate her for being brilliant, 'Tell me if you think I'm stepping on your toes again, Max.' Then, more concerned at how tired he looked than that he wasn't interested in what she had to say, 'If you're really too busy to spare me half an hour this evening?'

'No, no…' He dragged his fingers through hair that already bore the evidence of previous abuse. 'Really. Tell me about it.'

'I'll make an appointment for you to meet with their features writer,' she continued. 'In the meantime they want pictures, not just of you but of Dad and your father, too. I've organised that for tomorrow. Here. The Mayfair restaurant will be familiar—'

'For goodness sake, Lou, we've only just managed to shoehorn the pair of them out to pasture. Give them an inch—'

'Relax. You'll be front and centre, but the features writer will want some background on William Valentine, personal memories. How he built his empire from scratch after the war, when there was still rationing.' She smiled. 'They like men who can overcome apparently insurmountable obstacles to make things happen. And three generations of Valentines make us look solid.'

'We are solid.'

'I know, but trust me on this, Max. It'll look good.'

'Yes, of course it will. Sorry.' Then, 'You've spoken to your father?'

'No, I was busy. Gemma organised it all.'

'Lou…' He got up, put his arms around her, pulled her close. 'You can't go on punishing them like this. They love you.'

'They lied to me.'

'They were afraid.'

'They were?' She pulled back. Looked up at him. 'Why?'

'They were afraid that you wouldn't love them as much if they weren't your own parents.'

'But that's…' She was going to say that it was ridiculous. But he'd had stepmothers who'd had children of their own. For whom he was just a tiresome add-on. How had that felt? 'You're right,' she said. 'I just need a little more time.'

'Don't leave it too long.' Then, gesturing at the paperwork on his desk, taking the crumpled paper from her own hand, 'Let me get this straight and we'll go and have a drink.' He pulled a face as he returned to his chair. 'I'll need a drink.'

'What are you doing?' she asked, looking over his shoulder and felt a sharp chill. 'Oh, you're working on Valentine's Day.'

Huge tips from goofily happy men and a fabulous party afterwards to celebrate the anniversary of the opening of the Chelsea restaurant on Valentine's Day in nineteen forty-six. It was a magic occasion. And this year was their diamond jubilee, so they were pulling out all the stops.

'It's next week,' he said, looking up at her as if he wanted to say something. Thinking better of it.

He didn't have to say it. They both knew that the fourteenth was her own self-imposed deadline.

'How are we doing?' she asked.

'Booked to the rafters. All that stuff about us in last week's *City Lights* seems to have made everyone crazy to celebrate with us.'

'It's word association, Max.' He looked up. 'The juxtaposition of diamonds and Valentine's Day. It was an easy sell.' Then, 'Maybe you should insist that all the men are going to be packing the real thing before we accept their bookings.' Max frowned. 'We don't want any of our female diners to go home disappointed.'

'You're talking about engagement rings?'

'Well, obviously.'

'Wouldn't that rather spoil the surprise?'

'If an unmarried woman gets taken out to dinner at Bella Lucia on Valentine's Day, the only surprise will be if there isn't a ring hidden in the dessert. What could be described as a dumb-male, tears-before-bedtime scenario.'

He laughed. 'Right.' Then, sitting back, easing his neck. 'Would you believe that I've never had a Valentine's Day date?'

'No.'

'It's true. There's never been a Valentine's Day when I haven't had to work. From the day I turned eighteen and was old enough to serve a drink, it was the one night I had to turn up and pitch in.'

'Well, that's one way of avoiding matrimony,' she agreed, dropping a kiss on his forehead. 'You're clearly too busy to talk marketing and PR tonight. Let's give it a miss.'

'No…' He reached out, caught her hand. 'You could stay and help. It is all your fault that we're overwhelmed.'

'Thanks, but I'll pass on that one.'

'You could just stay and let me look at you.'

'Tempting, but once you get drawn into the nitty-gritty of how much chocolate, how much champagne you're going to need, you'll forget I'm here.'

For a moment she thought he might protest. Thought he might abandon planning the biggest night of their year and take her for that drink he'd offered. Instead he dragged his fingers through his hair, and, his attention already back on the complex planning required to ensure that everything ran smoothly, he said, 'You're right. I'll see you later.'

No. She should say no. Begin to ease away now while she still could…

'If I'm asleep…' she said, putting a spare set of keys on his desk and instead of taking a step back, keeping their relationship at a level where just sleeping together was enough, she said, 'Don't wake me.'

Max picked up the keys, watched her gather her things, smile back at him as she headed for the door, hating to see her go. She brightened his day, had changed his life in ways he couldn't begin to understand. It gave him a new kind of strength, and yet it frightened the life out of him, too. He'd surrendered something to her, lost the one thing that had kept him together even during the blackest times. Control.

'Louise…' She paused, turned back. 'About the Valentine's party…'

He'd been doing his best not to think about the huge party the family threw each year, after the restaurants closed—a celebration, a thank-you to all the staff. All day, as he'd been working on the plans for that evening, he'd remembered their deal, that she planned to draw a line under her involvement on that day…

'What about it?' she asked.

'You will be there?'

She hesitated. He almost thought her shoulders sagged a little. Then she nodded.

'Sure, Max,' she said. 'I might even dance with you.'

'Uncle Robert!' Louise dropped her briefcase on Max's desk, kissed his father, bestowed the kind of brief, distant smile on Max that she'd always used around her family. His eyebrows rose a touch, he held her gaze for a moment longer than felt right, but then just nodded. Let it be. And that felt wrong, too. This was all wrong. She should go to him, kiss him…

'How's Aunt Bev?' she asked, turning to Max's father.

'Good. She sends her love,' he said. 'Your father isn't with you?'

'He's making his own way here.' She glanced at her watch. 'The photographer isn't due for another fifteen minutes…' She turned as the door opened behind her.

Her father had lost weight since his heart attack. Had been taking exercise, watching his diet. He looked fitter than he had done in a long time, she thought.

Fitter and angrier.

He was carrying a folded newspaper and, ignoring her, he walked up to Max and slapped it against his chest.

'Do you want to tell me what's going on?'

'John…'

John Valentine silenced his brother with a look. 'He's a man. Let him speak for himself. Well?' he demanded.

Max had caught the paper before it fell and, without answering, looked at it. Said one brief word.

'"Kissing Cousins?"' John Valentine demanded as Max offered the paper to Louise so that she could see for herself.

It was just a single paragraph in the diary column of the *London Courier*.

Headed, Kissing Cousins? it said:

We are delighted to learn that our favourite PR consultant, Louise Valentine, is back in the family fold. Relations have been somewhat strained, apparently, since the disclosure that Louise was adopted. All is now peace and harmony, however, and she's putting her talents to good use, working with her cousin Max Valentine to promote the family's exclusive Bella Lucia restaurants.

Louise, who was once a regular girl-about-town and closely linked with the Hon James Cadogan—soon to be married to former model Charlotte Berkeley—has, in recent years, devoted all her energies to building her own business. Max, rarely without a beauty on his arm and frequently seen playing in the Sultan of Qu'Arim's polo team, has also dropped out of the social scene to concentrate on ambitious expansion plans overseas.

The couple, who were recently spotted dining together with Louise's birth mother, the lively Patsy Simpson Harcourt and her new husband, are said to be inseparable, although they're keeping their romance low-key at the moment. We wish them both well.

'Said?' she demanded. 'Who said? No one...'

Louise barely stopped herself from letting slip her own version of Max's expletive, but it was too late. She'd already confirmed her father's worst fears.

'Well, I don't have to ask if it's true. I've only got to look at you.'

'Daddy...' The childish word slipped out, maybe because that was exactly how she felt. Like a child who'd disappointed her father.

'I'm not blaming you, Louise.'

Blaming her!

'I realise you've been knocked for six by everything that's happened and he's clearly taken advantage of you when you're in a vulnerable—'

'Would someone mind telling me what the hell is going on?' Robert demanded.

Louise handed the paper to her uncle without a word, but he didn't get a chance to read for himself before his brother rounded on him.

'What's going on?' John demanded. He took a step closer. 'What's going on? You have to ask? He's your son,' he said, pointing at Max, 'and the apple doesn't fall very far from the tree. Ask him what's going on!'

'Dad! Please.' Louise reached for her father's arm, concerned for him. 'Did you travel into town on your own?'

'Of course I travelled on my own. I've been commuting between Richmond and Mayfair all my working life. I don't need a minder to hold my hand.'

'You haven't been well. Maybe I should call Mum...'

But before she could reach her cell phone, he took the hand

she'd laid on his arm and tucked it firmly against him, pulling her close, as if to protect her.

'Like father, like son,' he said, still looking at his brother. 'Max will play with Louise's feelings, destroy her. William Valentine all over again. You're just like your father, Robert—'

'William Valentine was your father, too.'

'Just like your father,' John Valentine repeated. 'And your son is just like you. You can't be trusted around a decent woman, any of you.'

'Well, I don't know about that,' Robert drawled. 'I'll admit to having had more than my fair share of wives, but I'm not a hypocrite. At least I married the mothers of my children, all of them, and while I may not have been the best father in the world, I never lied to them. They knew who their parents were.'

John released Louise and lunged at his brother, grabbing him by the lapels of his jacket, holding him as if he wanted to shake him.

'Dad!'

Max and Louise said the word in unison. Neither of them took the slightest notice, but as Louise leapt in to separate them Max caught her, held her back.

'Leave them,' he said as she tried to shake him off. 'It's time they settled it.'

'Well, what are you waiting for, big brother?' Robert sneered, provocatively, before she could answer. 'Go on, hit me. Heaven alone knows you've wanted to do it for long enough. Why don't you relax that stiff upper lip for once in your life and take a swing at me?'

CHAPTER NINE

FOR a moment nothing happened. Then, as his brother shuddered, eased the vice-like grip on his jacket, Robert said, 'Let it go, John. Let it go.'

'How can I? Our father stole my sons from me! Bought off their mother, kept me in ignorance to save a scandal.'

'He acted from the best of motives. You'd just married Ivy. He was so proud…' Robert shook his head. 'He was always so proud of you. You were the good son, the one who made a good marriage, brought honour to his house with your rich, well-connected bride—'

'I married for love.'

'The rest was just a bonus?'

For a moment Louise thought her father would take up his brother's invitation and hit him.

'No!' she cried.

For a moment John seemed beyond hearing, but then he almost visibly pulled himself together and taking a step back from the brink, released his grip on his brother's jacket. 'Ivy…' His face softened. 'In my marriage, I've been the most fortunate of men.'

'Ivy has been the most fortunate of women, John.' For a moment Robert's devil-may-care features were haunted by something very like regret, then, brushing it aside, he said, 'Dad didn't want anything to spoil that for you. Your boys never went without. He didn't abandon them, the way he abandoned you.'

'But I did,' John replied. 'I did…'

As Louise let out a small sound that echoed her father's anguish

Max drew her close and she didn't hesitate as she turned her face into his shoulder, knowing that his only concern was for her.

'I didn't know…' her father said.

'Blame their mother for that if you must blame someone,' Robert told him, unmoved. 'She didn't want you in her life. Made the decision not to tell you about the twins. Face it, John, if her singing career hadn't flopped, if she hadn't decided that marriage to you was the soft option, no one would ever have known about your boys.'

'She was in trouble. She had a right to my help. He should have told me, Robert. He got it wrong,' John said, finally letting go. 'But then he didn't ever really know me. He didn't want to. You were his joy. The one with a true flair for the business he loved, while I was just a glorified accountant. The truth is, I made him feel guilty.'

Robert didn't dispute it and Louise saw her father's shoulders sag a little. Felt an ache for the boy he'd been, the man he'd become. Family, but always just a little bit on the outside. Like Max, she thought. And like Max, needing to be in control of everything, refusing to allow anything to deflect them, disturb the even tenor of their lives. And it was Max, regarding his father, his uncle, with something like despair, whom she turned to, reached out to.

'And because he didn't learn from his own mistakes,' she heard her father say, 'I've been put through the same wringer.'

'I'm not excusing him—'

John and Robert Valentine, still fighting a sixty-year-old battle, did not even notice them as Max took her hand, held it, drew her closer, put his arm around her.

'No?' John glared at him. 'It sounds very much like it.'

'Well, maybe. You're right about a lot of things. He was uncomfortable with you and I can understand why you resented me. But what happened in the past, to you, to your mother, was not my fault.'

'You had it so easy. You were so spoiled…'

'Maybe that's why I'm not the man you are, John.'

John didn't appear to hear him. 'My mother suffered so much. I sat and watched her die and I couldn't do anything.'

'It was a terrible thing for a boy to go through.'

For a moment Louise thought Robert was going to put his arm around his brother in a gesture of comfort.

'Yes…' she whispered, urging him to do it, for the two men to forgive each other so that they could move on. In response, Max pulled her a little closer.

Forgiveness.

John and Robert weren't the only ones who needed to find that in their hearts. As she felt all the hurt, that terrible sense of betrayal fell away from her. Her father loved her. Why else would he be angry with Max? Nothing else mattered… She had to tell him that so that they could all move on.

Robert clearly thought better of such an unrestrained gesture, but put his hand on his brother's shoulder. 'A terrible thing,' he repeated. 'But it wasn't anyone's fault that your mother died, John. Everyone was short of food. There was no penicillin. Even if he'd been there, instead of away fighting, Dad couldn't have done anything to save her. You must know that.'

'He shouldn't have stopped loving her.' Her father looked desperate.

'People can't help their feelings, John.' And he looked across at Max, as if he, too, was asking for something, some understanding.

'She was his wife!' He shook off his brother's hand. 'What would you know about fidelity?' And he took a step back, turned to her. 'Don't you see, Louise?' he said, pointing at Max. 'It's what Valentine men do. William, Robert with an endless succession of wives, Max with his string of girlfriends.' Then, letting his hand fall, 'And me, too.' The fire went out of him. 'Robert's right. I'm no different.'

'No, Dad…' she said, hating to see him in so much pain. To see him blaming himself. If she'd been there, hadn't been so wrapped up in her own hurt…

He brushed her protest aside. 'I had an affair, moved on and never looked back, never gave the girl another thought in forty years. Had twin boys who never knew their father…'

'It wasn't like that. You didn't know—'

'I should have known. It's something in us, Louise. The Valentine gene. Max has got his arm around you now, but it won't last. He'll stop loving you. He might not mean to hurt you, but he won't be able to help himself.'

'No!'

No more secrets. No more lies. Especially not to herself. She didn't know what the future held for Max and her; all she knew was that hidden away their relationship didn't stand a chance. 'You're better than that.' Then, in a gesture that no one could mistake, she took Max's hand in hers and, standing at his side, said, 'You're better than that, Daddy. And so is Max. Tell him, Uncle Robert. Tell him!'

'Louise is right, John. He's not like me,' Robert said. 'Max, Jack, the girls, I don't know how it happened when I was such a screw-up as a father, but they've all turned out better than me.'

But John couldn't let it go.

'No…' He shook his head as if to deny what was before him. 'I've seen you hurting, Lou. When you and James split up I thought my heart would break, too. I know you've never got over it.'

'No, it wasn't—'

'You're my little girl and your pain is my pain.' A sigh escaped him. 'I've loved you since the moment we brought you home, loved you more than any words can say, but I should have tried, should have told you. Daniel and Dominic are special, very special to me, but you are my most precious daughter. No blood tie could be stronger.' He reached out, covered her hand, the one holding onto Max, with his own. 'No one could ever replace you.'

'I know, Dad.' She looked at Max, smiled at him. He knew the pain of family breakdown, but he understood the true value of family, too. She'd have lost that but for him. In every way that mattered, John Valentine was her father.

She kissed Max, just to show him that nothing, no one, could keep them apart, and then she stepped forward, put her arms around her father, gave him the hug she should have found it in her heart to give him months ago, when he'd been hurting, when he'd needed her most. 'You don't have to tell me,' she said, her eyes full of tears. 'I understand.'

She'd been so afraid that Max was trying to drag her back, keep her from her new family, but she'd been wrong. She'd thought he'd been trying to control her when all he'd wanted was to show her that she didn't have to choose, that she could have both; made certain that she didn't throw away the family, the life, she had. One could, it seemed, never have too much family as far as Max was concerned.

'I may have forgotten for a little while,' she said, 'but I've always known. I'm sorry I haven't been a better daughter. So sorry…'

'No, no. Hush… It's all right. I understood. Just, tell your mother…' He looked at her. 'We both need to tell your mother how much we love her. This has been so hard on her.'

As he said the word—love—she couldn't stop herself from looking at Max and she knew that she'd been fooling herself. There was no way she was ever going to get Max Valentine out of her system. He wasn't just 'unfinished business'. He was part of her. Without him she could never be whole.

It wasn't some *coup de foudre*, a blinding realisation that she was in love with him, but rather an acknowledgement of the fact that she'd been in love with him all her life and, although the words were for her father, she looked at Max as she said, 'Promise me that you won't blame Max for what has happened between us. He didn't take advantage of me. I was the one who wanted this,' she said. 'Wanted him. I always did. Even before I understood the feelings.' She was laying her heart bare to him. Trusting him. 'It may not last. There are no guarantees, but at last we're able to know one another in ways that we once thought impossible. That's more than I ever hoped for.'

'Impossible?' As her father realised what she was saying, he groaned. 'Because you believed you were blood relations?' He shook his head. 'Then that's my fault, too…'

'Don't! The past is gone. Now, today, is all that matters. Tomorrow, next week, who knows? Only that the future is ours and, whether we make or break it, it's our joint responsibility. It takes two to build a partnership.'

'But only one to break it.' For a moment her father continued to glare at Max. Then, with the slightest shrug, he said, 'Heaven help you if you do anything to hurt her.'

'No one can say what the future will bring, Uncle John, but maybe you should trust Louise to make her own decisions. Believe me, she's more than capable of taking care of herself. I've just had a grandstand demonstration of where she learned that fly-off-the-handle temper.'

Robert Valentine laughed. 'He's got you there, John.'

'I haven't got a quick temper,' Louise declared, roundly, then, recalling her father's recent heart scare, she said, 'Dad! Are you okay?'

'Okay? Of course I'm okay. Why shouldn't I be…?' And then he too recalled that he was supposed to be taking it easy, not getting excited, and clapped his heart to his chest. 'It's okay,' he said, grinning as he saw their concerned faces. 'It's still beating.' Then, 'But, um, better not tell your mother about that little outburst, eh? She'll only make a fuss.'

Louise flung her arms around her father's neck. 'Idiot,' she murmured in his ear. 'I do love you.'

He hugged her back, said, 'Then do something for me.'

Give up Max? Please, no, don't ask that. Not now…

'I know how much I've hurt you, Louise. I'm only just beginning to see how much my foolish pride, my need for secrecy, has cost you, but I'm to blame, not your mother. Stop punishing her. Live the day God has given you.' Then, standing back to look at her, 'If this last few months have taught me anything, it's that.'

'I'm learning,' she said, glancing at Max. Mouthed a silent 'thank you' to him. He gave the slightest shake of the head, as if it was nothing to do with him, but she knew better.

The fact that they were here today was because he'd pursued her, refused to take no for an answer.

It was because of him that she was no longer alone and it was his hand she reached for as she said, 'I'll call Mum, talk to her, I promise. Today.'

Satisfied, and having given Max a look that told him in no uncertain terms that, whatever Louise had said, he'd be held responsible for any pain, John turned to his brother.

'How do you feel on that subject?'

Robert, who'd been brushing down his jacket, smoothing his rumpled lapels, looked up. 'What subject is that?'

'Living the day. Life being a one-time offer.'

'I wouldn't gamble on getting a second crack at it,' he agreed.

'Then I'd suggest it's time we stopped fighting past battles and made the most of what we have while we can enjoy it.'

Putting the word to the deed, he extended his hand, every inch the Englishman in the manner in which he formally declared an end to hostilities.

Robert, as much his father's son as John, took it, held it. Then, his Italian mother's genes rushing to the fore, he threw his arms around his brother and was still hugging him when the restaurant rang up to tell them that the photographer had arrived.

Max couldn't take his eyes off Louise as she talked to the photographer, made sure that she got exactly what she wanted. Totally professional. Once she turned and saw him watching her, flicked a strand of hair behind her ear, smiled right back.

It was the look of a supremely confident woman and as she turned to her father, settled his tie, laughed at something he said to her, he felt as if he'd lost her.

Not physically. She'd made her feelings public. But she'd stepped back inside the charmed circle, to a place where he couldn't follow.

After the photographer had gone and their respective parents put the word to the deed by staying to have lunch together, Louise and Max were left alone in the office.

'I ought to go,' she said.

She felt churned up, oddly vulnerable, her nerve endings exposed by so much raw emotion. It wasn't just John and Robert Valentine making their peace after so long, or even her own accord with her father; she now realised that while she'd laid her heart on the line, Max had said nothing. She needed to think about that. What it meant.

'I've got a pile of stuff waiting at the office and time is running out.'

'Nothing that won't keep for an hour.' Taking her hesitation for agreement, he said, 'We could both do with a little fresh air after this morning's melodrama. As the boss I'm taking an executive decision to go for a walk in the park.'

'You're not my boss, Max,' Louise said, matching his flippancy as she took her long scarlet coat from the stand. 'You're a charity case.'

'I think we need to talk about that,' he said, not rising to this provocation. 'The kiss covered until the fourteenth and you've done a great job. Now we have to discuss the future. What kind of retainer it's going to take to keep you as Bella Lucia's PR consultant.'

She glanced up at him as he took her coat, held it out for her. Nothing in his face gave her a clue whether that was all he wanted from her.

'I'm very expensive.'

'I'm sure, between us, we can hammer out some kind of financial package.'

'No discounts for family,' she said, her heart slipping into her boots as she let him ease her into her coat. 'The "kiss" deal was a one-time offer.' Like life, she thought, but when he didn't answer this echo of her father's words rang hollow in her ears.

'You should have brought some bread for the ducks,' she said as fifteen minutes later they skirted the lake in St James's Park. When, despite his apparent desire to talk, the silence had stretched to breaking-point.

'The greedy little beggars are too fat to fly as it is and, besides, I want your undivided attention.'

'We couldn't talk somewhere warm?' she asked.

'I want to ask you something. It's important. I don't want any ringing telephones, any distractions.'

She frowned. 'What? What is it?'

'I want to know what really happened between you and the Honourable James Cadogan.'

'James?' It was clear that Max had something on his mind, but that was the last thing she'd expected. 'He's ancient history,' she said, but uneasily.

'And yet the man's name crops up whenever you're mentioned. The *Courier* mentioned him today. And your father seemed to think I was catching you on the rebound, too. Taking advantage of your broken heart.'

'Oh, please.' If that was his problem, well, no problem… 'The *Courier* was simply rehashing the last piece of gossip they had on file, and as for Dad, well, reading it just reminded him what a failure as a daughter I am. Robert's daughter married a king, while I messed up my relationship with a simple "honourable", a man who, I might add, my father thought would make the perfect son-in-law.'

'I don't think he was alone in that. I remember thinking at the time that if I heard his name connected to one more string of glowing adjectives I'd punch a hole in the wall.'

She managed a smile. 'I used to feel the same way when you were dating Sophie Blakiston. Whatever happened to her?'

'I didn't turn up once too often and she married an earl.'

'You don't learn, do you?'

'I didn't have much of an example in my old man.'

'No, it's not that. It isn't other women that tempt you away. You just love Bella Lucia more.'

'Now you're just trying to change the subject.'

Maybe, but he hadn't denied it.

'Of course I am,' she replied. 'No one likes to talk about their mistakes.'

'And what about James Cadogan? Was he a mistake?'

Louise, wanting him to let it go, said, 'Yes.' Then realising that this wasn't any better, 'No.' Then just shook her head.

'So why did you two break up?' Max persisted. 'Whatever happened then changed you. After Cadogan there's no one. It's like your personal life entered an ice age.'

'Stop trying to make it out to be such a big deal, Max. It came to a natural end. That's all.'

'No more than a light-hearted flirtation? That's odd, because, according to my mother, your mother was already drawing up the guest list for the wedding, choosing stationery for the invitations, talking designers for the dress—'

'Pure fantasy,' she said, but was unable to meet his steady gaze, couldn't bear the silence that told her plainer than words that Max was not convinced. She stopped, turned to face him. 'All right! It wasn't just fantasy. It was much more than that. Satisfied!'

He took her arm, continued walking. Waited.

'I was nearly thirty. Way past time for a girl to be married and producing babies, according to my mother, and, as she was quick to tell me, no one better was ever likely to come along. Not exactly the fairy tale, but no girl past the age of sixteen believes in those.'

Not if her Prince Charming of choice had a barbed-wire fence around him hung with warning notices saying 'do not touch'.

'So you were settling for the best you could get?'

'That's not fair to James. He *was* any girl's ideal husband. My mother was out of her mind with happiness; even my father approved.'

'The man must have been a saint,' he said, a touch acerbically. Then, 'Or was it because in the fullness of time he'd have made Daddy's little girl Lady Cadogan?'

'Now you're just being nasty. James was a lovely man. Any father would have been delighted with him as a son-in-law. Any woman would have been lucky—'

'Methinks the lady doth protest too much.'

She shook her head, shivered.

An ice age...

Max stopped, removed the scarf he was wearing, wrapped it around her neck, but didn't let go of the ends, holding her within the circle of his arms and instantly she felt warmer.

No ice there...

'So what went wrong?' he asked.

'Me,' she said. 'I told you.'

He frowned.

'What? You don't believe that? You don't believe Little Miss Perfect capable of dumping the best prospect for matrimonial bliss ever likely to come her way?'

'You're mistaking me for someone else, Lou. I never thought you were Little Miss Perfect.' His eyes creased in one of those rare smiles that made his eyes seem impossibly blue. A smile that assured her he knew her far better than that. 'Daddy's Little Princess is another matter.'

She laughed. He was the one person who'd always been able to make her laugh. Before life, hormones, got in the way. How she'd missed that.

'Was I that bad?'

'Appalling,' he said, but with a smile. 'All frills, curls, and ponies. Once Jack and I lured you away on adventures, you weren't too bad. For a girl.'

'Thank you. I know you meant that as a compliment.'

'I knew you'd understand.' Then, releasing the scarf, he led the way to a bench that overlooked the lake and, with his arm around her waist, drew her close to keep her warm.

'So, Princess, tell me about Prince Charming.'

'I hoped you'd forgotten.'

'That bad?'

No more secrets…

'James did nothing wrong.' She sighed. 'He took all the flak from both families when it fell apart, but it was my fault, Max. All my fault.'

'Tell me,' he said.

She glanced at him. He raised his brows, an invitation to spill it all out. Get it off her chest.

'Trust me, Lou.'

'You won't sell my secrets to the *Courier* diary correspondent?' she said, in an attempt to make a joke of it.

'Trust me,' he repeated. No smile. No sexy little twitch of his eyebrows. He was in deadly earnest, now. Asking her to bare her soul to him. Expose her heart. Leave herself without anywhere to hide.

To put her heart where her mouth had been half an hour earlier and demonstrate that she trusted him not to hurt her.

Maybe to prove that she wouldn't hurt him. That was an unexpected thought. She'd never seen Max as vulnerable in that way. His family had hurt him, but he'd never appeared deeply touched by any of his own romances…

No more secrets…

'It wasn't that I didn't try,' she said, looking across the lake, afraid to see the panic in his eyes as he realised what she was telling him. 'I wanted it to work. James really was perfect. Not just because there was a title in the offing, that the family owned half the county. He was really nice. Good. Kind. And he loved me.'

She turned to Max then, because she had to see his reaction. Had to know…

'We were going to announce our engagement on my birthday.

Major party. Crates of champagne on order. My mother was ecstatic; my father was strutting around as if he owned the entire world.'

'So?'

'I tried, Max. I did all the right things, said all the right things and I thought it was going to work but in the end he said… James said…'

She felt trapped, laid bare in a way that simple nakedness could never expose her, but Max took her hand, held it, gave her his strength.

No more secrets, but it was so hard…

'He said that he loved me, wanted me to be his wife. He said he knew that I didn't feel those things as strongly as him, but that he'd accepted that. That he accepted that in a relationship there was always one person who loved more—'

'He must have had it bad,' he said, but not without sympathy.

'But not, apparently, fatally. He said that he could accept all that, but he was beginning to suspect that there was someone else.'

He turned to her. 'He thought you were cheating on him?' he said, with a deadly calm.

'No! No. He said… He said that when he was holding me it felt as if I was looking over his shoulder, scanning the horizon, waiting for someone just out of sight to ride to my rescue. He wanted me to talk about it. Reassure him, I suppose.'

'But you couldn't?'

'No. He was wrong, Max.' She stared at their hands, locked together. 'He was wrong to accept less than my whole heart under any circumstances, but I was wrong, too. I should never have let it go so far. I hurt him and I deeply regret that. A partnership should be an equal passion, don't you think?'

'I would hope for that.'

'Would you accept less?' she asked.

'If there was no other choice, if only one person will do, then there must be the temptation to accept what's on offer, hope for more in time,' he said, frowning. 'But it's not a deal I could live with. Not the kind of foundation for the kind of marriage I'd consider. The kind that will last a lifetime.'

'That was the point. He didn't have to work at loving me while I …'

While she had been settling for second best.

When she realised that Max was waiting for her to finish the sentence, she shook her head. 'Whatever I was doing, he deserved better than I was giving him.'

'Tell me about the other man. The one out of sight.'

She looked away, but he caught her chin, forced her to face him. And she didn't have to say the words. He knew.

'That's why there's been no one else?' he persisted.

'What would have been the point?'

'What indeed?' He got up, pulled her to her feet, tucked her arm firmly beneath his and continued walking.

That was it? She'd just performed open heart surgery on herself and he shrugged it off as nothing. She glanced at him. He wasn't looking at her, but straight ahead, and all she had was his chiselled profile against the cold blue of the sky.

'So, this affair we're having is your way of getting me out of your hair, is it?' he asked.

'That's a rather cold way of putting it.'

'But I'm right? I get you and your talent until the fourteenth. After that, you're going to move on?'

'That was the plan,' she admitted, miserably.

'And is it working?'

She lifted her shoulders in the smallest of shrugs. 'Not yet.'

'No. I had much the same outcome in mind, but the truth is there's nothing cold about what's between us, Louise. There never has been. It's always been fire, never ice. So the question we have to ask ourselves, you and I, is where do we go from here?'

'I'm rather enjoying "here",' she said.

She wasn't so certain about Max.

'Isn't that the point? We aren't "here" any more, are we? No more secret affair. Everyone knows about us now. That already takes us somewhere else.'

'It must have been Patsy, don't you think?' she said, unable to give him a direct answer. She didn't know where they were going. Only that he was right. With exposure, the mutual admission that they were both on an escape mission, came a change of direction.

One that she wanted.

Watching her father and uncle reach out for each other had

shown her the futility, the waste of hiding one's feelings. If what she and Max had was to grow, it needed light, air…

'She must have been the one who spilled the beans to the *Courier*,' she prompted, a little desperately, when he didn't answer.

'I imagine so. She had us pegged from the minute she saw us together and she does have something of a runaway mouth.' Then, 'Are you angry with her?'

'Why would I be angry? We left your father and mine having lunch together, taking a trip down memory lane and laughing about it. That's something I thought I'd never see.' And she smiled, because that was wonderful. 'Without her, it might never have happened.' Then, 'Without you, Max.'

He looked at her. 'Me? What did I do?'

'You refused to let me go.'

He didn't come back with some major declaration, merely said, 'So, now we've been outed, I guess you're going to expect a little more by way of entertainment than supper in bed?'

On the point of saying that she couldn't think of any more entertaining way of spending her evenings with him, she thought better of it. It was time to move on, be open.

'Infinitely more,' she said. Then, 'Are you going to be free tomorrow evening?'

'What's happening?'

'Several things. I've got a late meeting so I'll have to forgo our six-thirty debriefing, but I do happen to have a couple of tickets for the Royal Opera House charity gala. A client sent them to me. I was going to give them away but maybe it's time to take our relationship on its first real public outing.' Then, when he didn't immediately respond, 'I'm asking you out on a date, Max. If you don't say yes within the next thirty seconds I might just die of embarrassment.'

'What time do you want me to pick you up?'

She'd expected more reaction. Didn't he realise just how big a deal this was for her? Was she being a complete fool? About to ask him, she decided she didn't want to know and let it go.

'I'll have to meet you at the theatre. No later than seven-fifteen,' she warned. 'It's a royal performance so we'll all have to be seated before the Queen arrives.'

'Seven-fifteen.' He nodded. 'So, what would you like to do this evening?'

'I'm going to see my mother, remember?' Weirdly she felt only relief. 'Want to come?' she teased.

'Scared what she'll say about us? Want some protection?' he replied, picking up the beat.

'No!' Then, 'Well, maybe, just a bit.'

'She'll be so glad to see you, Lou, she wouldn't care if you'd dyed your hair green. Give her my love.'

'I will. But more importantly,' she said, 'I'll give her mine.' She hailed a passing cab, then lifted herself up on her toes, kissed his cold cheek. 'I'll see you tomorrow. Seven-fifteen.'

Max watched her go, a mixture of feeling churning around inside him. He'd had to know what the deal was with James. If she was really bouncing back, using the undeniable sexual charge between them, using him to wipe the other man from her mind.

Now he knew the truth. And it terrified the life out of him.

The world seemed like a freshly minted place and the evening positively sparkled as Louise stepped out of the taxi outside the theatre. She had spent the previous evening with her parents, talking about her adoption, about how putting off telling her the truth had gradually, without anyone actually making a decision, become a permanent situation. Because it hadn't seemed to matter. She was their daughter. Why complicate things?

It had seemed that simple.

But now together, they had faced up to the mistakes of the past and, as a family, were looking forward to a brighter happier future, she thought, smiling as she paid her fare, looked around, certain that Max would be there waiting for her. Or maybe he was already inside, a drink waiting…

Or then again, maybe not, she thought, after she'd fought her way through the crush to the bar and realised he wasn't there.

She glanced at her watch. It was okay. He had another five minutes. She bought a programme, glanced through it, conscious of being alone in a crowd in which everyone else had someone to talk to.

An announcement asked people to take their seats.

She went back outside. Took out her cellphone, checked for messages. Nothing.

She could ring him, but, actually, what was the point?

On the stroke of half past, she dropped the programme in the nearest litter bin and hailed a taxi.

Gemma put her head around the door. 'Have you got your mobile turned off, Lou? Max says he's been trying to get you since last night.'

'That can't be right. Max apparently doesn't know my mobile number.'

'Louise…'

'I'll say one thing for you, Max, you're consistent,' she said, not looking up from her desk. She heard the office door close as Gemma left them in private. 'And I'm dumb. You've been standing me up since I was sixteen. A smart woman would have got the message by now. A decent man would have learned not to make dates he didn't intend to keep.'

She made a careful note on the file in front of her, waited for the excuse. She knew it would be good. He'd had a lot of practice.

'The Chelsea kitchen flooded.'

Yes, that was good, and no doubt true, since all she had to do was pick up a phone and check for herself.

And she wasn't unreasonable. It was a crisis. They happened. All he'd had to do was call her. She wouldn't have been happy, but she'd have understood.

When he didn't continue, didn't offer an apology, she finally looked up. A mistake.

Until now, she'd been protected from her feelings, had believed that to love him in this way was wrong. Inside that shell she'd been able to keep up the pretence that she loathed him. It wasn't just a dress that she'd let fall at her feet, it had been the armour plating with which she'd protected herself. There was more than one way of being naked…

'You want me to use that in the marketing campaign?' she prompted, attempting to regain that lost ground.

'You're angry.'

'Only with myself,' she said, with a dismissive gesture. Before she could resume reading the report in front of her, he caught her hand.

'Please, sweetheart, try to understand.'

She swallowed. His hand was cool, strong, but then he *was* strong. He'd always been the first one to leap in to take care of problems. Always been there when a broad pair of shoulders was needed. She'd seen him taking care of the staff, concerned about their welfare. Knew he'd paid for private treatment for Martin's wife. She couldn't fault his commitment, his kindness. She just wanted a little of that for herself.

'It was lucky I was there. No one seemed to know where to find the cockstop.'

He sounded so sincere, so *reasonable*. But it wasn't reasonable. It was an excuse.

He was the one who'd challenged her over the secrecy of their relationship, implied that she was running scared. But she wasn't the one with the problem. It was him. All night she'd been going over it. Remembering how, when she'd been alone in defending him, declaring herself, he'd been silent. The only time he'd spoken up was for his precious family. Desperate to hold it together, even though, for him, it had always been falling apart…

He never let the business down. Only her. How many times did it have to happen before she got it through her thick skull.

'Bad management, Max.'

That got to him. Hit him where it hurt…

'Walking away to keep a date with you would have made that better? How? The staff carried on, working up to their ankles in water—'

'Bonuses all round for them, no doubt—'

'They earned it! We rely on them every night of the year. They have to be able to rely on me, too!'

Of course they did. She knew that. She even understood. But deep down, she knew it was more than that.

'Then you did what was most important to you. You have nothing to reproach yourself for,' she said.

'Of course I reproach myself. I let you down but it was long past curtain-up before I'd got everything under control. Then I had to go home and get changed.'

On the point of telling him to close the door on the way out, she hesitated. 'Changed?'

His smile was wry. 'I had a clean shirt in the restaurant, but I needed shoes, socks, trousers…'

Without warning she had a mental picture of him, wading into the situation, not caring about his dinner jacket, dress shirt. About her, waiting for him at the theatre. All he would see was the people who worked for him, whom he knew, cared about, struggling to cope, to carry on as if nothing had happened. How could you not love a man like that?

How could you live with him?

Because this was the reality of a relationship with Max.

'I came to the theatre to meet you.' He reached for her hand. 'Waited until everyone had gone.'

'Am I supposed to apologise for not being there?'

He shook his head. 'I'd tried calling you. When you didn't answer, I assumed you'd decided to stay at the theatre. But then, when I came to the flat, you didn't answer your bell, either. And you'd put the deadlock up on the door.'

'You call *before* you stand someone up. Not to apologise afterwards.' Then, relenting, because she couldn't help herself, 'All you had to do was ring me. Two minutes…'

'I was up to my elbows in freezing water.' He took her other hand. 'If I promise that in future I'll let all the restaurants flood to the ceiling while I call you to tell you I'll be late, will you forgive me?'

'You couldn't make that promise. Not with your hand on your heart, Max,' she said as with a sinking heart she realised the truth. That her father had been partly right about him.

Max wasn't like his father—he wouldn't cheat on her with another woman. Bella Lucia was her only rival for his love. It was always there for him…

'And if you did, I wouldn't believe you.'

He had the grace not to argue. Instead he said, 'Will you give me another chance?'

'Last night was important, Max. It was special. A new start.'

Max felt her hands slipping from his grasp. Saw real pain dull her lovely eyes. Knowing that he'd done that to her wrenched at him, tore at something buried so deep that he could not admit it, even to himself. And remembering how he'd challenged her about keeping their relationship a secret, he felt shame.

The secrecy had suited him just fine.

Louise wasn't just any woman. If the family knew about them, he'd have to stand up, say the words. Mean them. The way she had, yesterday. He'd listened to her defend him, praise him, tell the world how she felt about him and, like the fool, he'd stood there like a dummy, unable to respond.

Then afterwards, she'd walked with him, told him about James, torn out her heart and placed it, bleeding in his hands. And even though he knew, he understood, he hadn't been able to respond. All he'd done was grudgingly accept her invitation and then let her down.

He'd used Bella Lucia to wreck every relationship he'd ever had before it became too demanding. To drive women who cared for him away. It was an inbuilt flaw, a consequence of his childhood, he knew. A self-fulfilling expectation of abandonment.

This time it was different. No matter what he had to do, from now on Louise would always come first.

He gripped her fingers, refused to let her break contact. 'Give me another chance, Louise.'

'How many do you need?' She sounded brittle, edgy.

'Just one. Truly. Give me one more chance and I'll never let you down again.'

She didn't answer. She didn't believe him.

For a moment he felt like a drowning man. Sinking. Without hope. And then he understood. Like her, he had to strip his feelings bare...

'I want you in my life, Louise.' Not enough. 'I need you.' There was a flicker of something. Like a light coming on... More than that. Like a fire... 'And when I asked you if you would be at the Valentine party, what I really wanted to say was, will you be my date?'

'Your date?'

'My first and only Valentine.' Then, as she smiled. 'Say yes, and I promise you that there will be no tears before bedtime.'

'Tears...?'

'Say the word, Louise, and I promise that on the night I'll be bearing the essential diamond. I love you, Louise.'

Louise's breath caught in her throat. He was really saying he loved her? Was asking her to marry him? For a split second she felt like Cinderella must have done when she tried on the glass slipper.

Then reality crashed in.

'Max…' she warned.

'That's the wrong word.'

'No…'

'Now you're just playing hard to get.' From supplicant to the Max she knew in one easy bound.

She shook her head. 'It's too soon. We need time to get to know one another.'

'We've known one another all our lives, Louise. It's the sex we're catching up on.'

Was it? Really? Could he change, just like that? Unlikely… 'It's madness,' she said.

'Oh, well, thanks.'

'You see?' Another minute and they'd be hurling insults… 'You ask me to marry you…' She paused. 'At least I assume that's what you're doing, although a more ham-fisted, ungracious effort would be impossible to imagine, and already I want to throw something at you.'

And without warning he was smiling. 'Well, that's promising. I've missed our spats.'

'Unbelievable!'

'I swear it's true. I've especially missed them since making up became so much fun.'

'Stop it!'

'You want me to woo you, is that it? Do a PR job on myself. Sell you on the idea?'

'If you had the slightest clue about how to do that,' she informed him, 'you wouldn't need me.'

'Not for your marketing skills, no.' He was grinning… How dared he be grinning? 'Since we're being brutally honest here, you should know that I'd be happy to keep you around just for your highly imaginative taste in underwear.'

It wasn't a blush searing her cheeks. It was the combination of the winter sunshine striking in through the window and the central heating turned up too high...

'You're not doing a good job of selling me on the idea of marriage, Max.'

'You're not making it easy.'

Louise didn't want to be 'sold'. Or to make it easy for him. He was right, they were having fun, but he was still Max Valentine. The same man who'd left her high and dry more times than a girl with any kind of a life should be able to recall.

Hearing the last bell calling the audience to their seats, being the only person left in the theatre foyer was still painfully fresh.

He'd promised it was the last time, but could he change? When it came to a choice between *Bella Lucia* and her, would he ever put her first?

'There's no such thing as an easy sell,' she told him. 'You need to do your market research.'

'Is that right? For that I need your co-operation. Dinner at my place? Nine o'clock.'

She should say no...

And yet... And yet... When he'd held onto her hands, she'd seen something in his face, something more than the light banter. And when he'd said he loved her, she'd known he was telling the truth.

'Nine o'clock? You're sure you can manage that?'

He crossed his heart. 'You can depend on it.'

Max's apartment was in an ultra modern development overlooking the marina in Chelsea. He had acres of blond-wood open-plan floor-space, a space-age kitchen and simple, minimalist furniture that enveloped her as she sank onto the soft leather sofa.

'Hungry?' he asked.

'Not desperately. My mother came up to town and took me out to lunch.'

'Then we'll leave it for a while. Everything okay? With your mother?'

'Hugs, tears. She wanted to know about us.'

'What did you tell her?'

She grinned. 'As little as I could get away with. She's like Dad. Suspects it will all end in tears.'

'And you?' He handed her a glass of white wine. 'What do you think?'

'I think they're probably right,' she said, taking a sip. Then, 'But I'm here to be sold.'

'Right. Well, round one involves a questionnaire.'

'Oh?'

'The kind of thing that you do,' he said. 'Branding?'

She nodded. 'You need to know what I feel about you so that you can build on your pluses. And round two?'

'That rather depends on how round one goes.'

'Right,' she said, setting her drink on the table, kicking off her boots, tucking a cushion at her back and stretching out on the sofa. 'I'm sitting comfortably. You can begin.'

He lifted her legs, sat down beside her and dropped them across his lap. 'Okay,' he said, absently stroking her feet. 'First question. What three words would you use to describe me?'

'Arrogant,' she said. 'Workaholic. Hot.'

'Arrogant?'

'You don't get to comment on the answers. You collate them, study them, act on the information they give you.'

'Arrogant?' he repeated.

'You don't object to "workaholic" or "hot"?'

'Workaholic is the bad one?'

'I'm not here to do the work for you, Max. You have to study all the results. Ask yourself what's important. What you have to change to get the outcome you want.'

'I see.'

'Two out of three isn't bad,' she said.

'Only if they're the right two.'

'True.' He was, it seemed, learning. 'Shall we move on? I said I wasn't desperately hungry but I will want to eat tonight.'

'If I was a country which one would I be?'

'Switzerland.'

He frowned. 'Why's that?'

'I refer you to the answer I gave earlier.' Then, 'You're like a Swiss clock; you never stop.'

'I could wind down a little.' She refused to be drawn into a discussion of every answer. That wasn't how it worked. 'A landscape?' he continued.

'Birmingham, Stoke…something industrial.'

'No need to hammer the point. I get the picture. I work too hard.'

'We both work hard, Max. The difference is that you put work first.'

'People rely on me.'

'Delegate.'

'I'm trying, Lou.'

'What would you do if someone phoned from Mayfair, right now, and said the restaurant was on fire?'

'Tell them to call the fire brigade?'

'Liar.' Then, because maybe she was learning something from this, too, 'I'd expect you to go, Max. I'd want to be with you.'

For a moment he seemed lost for words. As if the idea of dealing with a crisis together hadn't occurred to him.

'If I was a time of day?' he said, moving on.

'Six-thirty.'

He smiled at that and she knew he'd got it. Understood that the time she associated with him was that moment when she walked into his office at the end of the day and he stopped whatever he was doing, they had a drink and just talked. Even when he'd been working on the Valentine party, and she'd left him to get on with it, because she knew how important it was. It worked both ways.

'Remember that one, Max,' she said. 'That one's important.'

'A smell?'

Uh-oh, she'd been doing so well until then. In control. Now, without warning, she was plunged into the scent of warm skin, sharp, clean sweat, newly washed hair.

'Shampoo,' she said, quickly.

'And if I was a shampoo, which would it be?'

'Mine.' Her turn to smile. Well, she'd written the questionnaire, she'd known which question was coming next.

'And finally, a car?'

'Anything expensive, fast and reliable.'

'Reliable?'

Never lets you down, she thought. No wonder he'd picked up on that one. What on earth had she been thinking?

'Scratch "reliable",' she said. 'Make that durable.' Then, because he gave her a sharp look that suggested he hadn't missed the subtle difference, 'It goes with the Swiss clock.'

CHAPTER TEN

'MAX…'

Max had stopped stroking her feet and Louise realised that her words had hit home. Maybe there was hope for him and, curling herself up onto her knees, she reached out to him and, playfully ruffling her fingers through his hair, she said, 'Why don't we move on to part two?'

'Part two?' He looked at her. 'Is there any point? You've made it very clear that you think I'm just a work-obsessed—'

She put her fingers over his mouth. 'I told you, Max, the skill is in interpretation. You have to look at *all* the results. It's just as dangerous to concentrate on the words that sting, as it is to grab for the words that confirm what you want to hear. Only then can you act to change things.'

He regarded her with the suspicion of a smile. 'You think?'

'I think,' she assured him. 'Trust me, Max. I'm the expert and it's not over until it's over.'

He shook his head. 'Maybe another time…'

'No.' She didn't want him to think he'd failed. She wanted him to understand what she wanted, needed. That she needed him…

'Part two,' she said, firmly.

'I don't…'

'But I do.' And since she knew what came next, she prompted, 'Which three words would you use to describe your feelings of anticipation about using the Max Valentine product?' she prompted.

'I'm a product?'

'For the purposes of market research. Work with me on this.'

He shrugged, took a breath and, looking straight ahead, as if dreading her answers, he obediently repeated, 'What three words would you use to describe your feelings of anticipation about using the Max Valentine product?'

'Urgency,' she offered. 'Excitement. Impatience…'

He glanced at her, the beginning of a smile tugging at his lips. 'Impatience?'

Suiting the deed to the word, Louise locked her arms around his neck and swung herself over to sit astride his lap.

'Which three words,' she said as she began to unbutton his shirt, 'would you use to describe your feelings during the use of this product?'

'Which three words…' he began. She leaned into him, stopping the words with her mouth, and when she'd got his full attention and he was kissing her back she moved on to trail her lips over his throat, across his chest. Then, as she began to unfasten his belt…

'Desire. Passion. Heat…'

It was much later when, her eyes closed, her voice dreamy, soft with fulfilment, she said, 'Which three words would you use to describe how you feel after using this product…?'

'Shattered,' Max said, before she could answer her own question. 'Sated.' He kissed her. 'Complete.'

'Good answers,' she murmured.

'You give good questions,' Max said, touching her face, stroking back her hair. 'I loved your version of part two.' Then, 'Can we try mine now?'

She opened her eyes. 'You had a different version?'

'My part two consisted of me going down on one knee and asking you to marry me. When I failed part one—'

'This isn't an exam,' she said, quickly, cutting him off. She was still sure that it was too soon. He hadn't failed, but she was certain that he needed time to think about this. Or maybe she was the one fooling herself. Maybe she was the one who needed time… 'There are no right or wrong answers.'

'I know. It's all in the interpretation, but it's pretty clear that you think I'm work obsessed. That I put the restaurant before everything else.'

'I don't care about everything else. My problem is that you put the restaurant before me. You always have.'

On the point of denying it, he nodded. 'You're right. I should have called you last night.'

'No. You should have been there. Last night was important to me. Important for us. I think that scared you.'

'No!' Then, 'Maybe, just a bit, but there was a crisis. I didn't spend time considering options, I just did what needed to be done. You know how it gets.'

She knew. And, despite everything, she did understand. But she wasn't letting him off the hook on this one. He needed to understand her point of view.

'That was the manager's job. You shouldn't have even been there, Max. Your role is to look at the bigger picture now. You have to trust your staff to deal with the day to day problems.' She shook her head. 'Failing that, you take time to make a call. Look, I know how it is. I've waited tables at functions when staff haven't turned in for a PR do but my mother taught me to use a phone when I was very small. To call home when I was going to be late. To call someone when you can't make a date.'

'I'm from a broken home,' he said.

'That's it, Max.' They'd got to the heart of the problem. Finally. 'You want the whole-heart relationship, but you're afraid of the commitment. Afraid of being hurt.'

'You're right.' He closed his eyes. 'You think I never put you before work, but let me tell you that I've spent all day thinking about us. Thinking about me. How I am. I won't ever do that to you again. I promise.'

'Promises and pie crusts,' she said. 'Made to be broken.'

'Not this time. You have my word.' Then, 'You do believe me?'

'I believe that you mean it now. Tomorrow... The day after...'

'No. You have to believe. It's more than that. I can't lose you.' He reached for her, wrapped his arms around her. 'Not now I've found you. I want us to be together always. I want you to be my wife, Louise.'

A lump rose to her throat, so that she couldn't speak. It was like all the Christmases, birthdays, Valentine's Days, rolled into one. Every dream coming true.

And still she hesitated.

She knew that at that moment Max would have promised her anything. Deep down inside her, though, there was still that small nagging doubt. That he meant everything he said, she was certain. Whether he still understood what that meant, she wasn't totally certain. Wasn't convinced that it was a risk she should take.

But then she'd learned from experience that safety wasn't enough, either. James had been a safe bet, 'a banker', the kind of husband any woman would be fortunate to have.

Max, on the other hand, was always going to be a gamble. But when life without him meant putting her heart into permanent cold storage...

'Why don't you save it until the fourteenth, Max?'

'The fourteenth?'

'Valentine's Day. We have a date, or have you forgotten already?'

'Actually, I don't remember you saying yes to that.'

'I didn't. I'm saying it now. Turn up with the ring in your pocket, do your stuff then and we'll make an announcement.' Her flippant tone gave nothing away of the tangle of emotions in her heart.

'You want me to go down on one knee in front of everyone?'

'Would you do that for me?'

He hesitated for barely a second. 'Anything.'

'I'm the only one you have to convince, Max,' she said, then leaned across and kissed him. 'Make it a solitaire. Not too big. I don't want it to look as if it came out of a Christmas cracker. Now, can we eat?'

Everyone worked on Valentine's Day. Even John and Robert were pressed into service at the Mayfair restaurant, working together, a pair of world-class experts in smoothing out wrinkles, keeping diners whose tables were delayed from getting fractious.

Max was at the Knightsbridge restaurant. Lavish, contemporary, it was a favourite with the social elite as well as the aristocracy of the theatre.

Louise was playing hostess at the Chelsea restaurant, a popular haunt with the livelier celebrities who arrived trailing a crowd of paparazzi. She knew them all and would be at her best there, Max knew, and, as the original restaurant, it was traditionally where they held the huge after-hours party where everyone, all the staff, all the family, gathered to celebrate the year.

This year, as their diamond anniversary, was extra special in more ways than one. Max patted his jacket where the ring he was going to give Louise—a solitaire, a single carat, he wanted her to know that he'd been listening—was tucked into his ticket pocket, along with the safety pin she'd given him.

When he'd emptied his pockets on his return from Meridia, it had been there among his change and keys. Such a small thing and yet it had signalled a change in their relationship: a move from war to peace. A symbol, a link that somehow held them together, and since the night when he'd told her he loved her, asked her to marry him, he'd taken to carrying it with him.

He hoped to get away some time in the evening. He'd arranged for a bottle of Krug to be waiting in the tiny office and, with the door firmly closed, he'd make a proper job of his proposal. He'd seen the flicker of uncertainty in her eyes. A momentary shadow of doubt. He had to convince her, once and for all, that without her Bella Lucia meant nothing to him. It was true. He'd looked into the abyss, the dark emptiness of life without her, and he knew it was true. She would always come first.

He glanced at his watch. Ten o'clock. A quick look around. Everything was humming. No problems. He could slip away now, be back before…

'Mr Valentine—' He turned at the hushed urgency in the *maître d*'s voice '—we've got a bit of a problem.'

No. Not tonight…

'I'm just leaving, Jane. See Stephanie.' Nothing, no one, would stop him from putting Louise first tonight.

'It's not…please…'

She looked as if she might faint. 'Steady, now. What is it? What's the matter?'

'Table five. Charles Prideaux. The actor?' she added, in case he didn't know. 'He's not well.'

'What's the matter with him?'

She pulled herself together. 'He's clammy, no colour, complaining of indigestion.'

'Classic indications of a heart attack. Call an ambulance,' he said, turning away.

'No! He won't allow it. He doesn't want to attract attention. He seems more concerned about his wife finding out he's here with some young actress when he was supposed to be at a business meeting than whether he's about to die.'

'The two may not be mutually exclusive.' But not in one of his restaurants. 'Where is he?'

'One of the other diners found him in difficulties in the loo and called a waiter. We've put him in the office.'

Who's with him?'

'No one. He wouldn't let me get anyone else even though I'm not a first aider. He said I could only get you.'

'Hell, he shouldn't be left alone.' Whether he liked it or not, Max was involved. 'OK, Jane, it's not your fault—you've done well, considering the circumstances. I'll take it from here. Can he walk?'

'With help.'

He looked at his watch. It would take half an hour, no more. 'Get him back to him now and take him out through the rear. I'll drive him to the nearest A and E.'

Louise took a tray of coffee out to the paparazzi wanting to be the first with photos of newly acquired diamonds. It was cold out there and, despite their bad press, she understood they were just doing a job like everyone else. And their presence meant the restaurant was a favourite with A-list celebrities.

If she hoped to catch a sight of an eager Max arriving early she wasn't admitting it, not even to herself.

So far the day had gone well.

Among a very impressive, but ultimately clichéd, number of red roses, it was the elegant basket of lilies of the valley that had been delivered to her desk from a fashionable florist—sweetly scented, pure as a child's promise—that stood out.

There was no name on the card—unlike the roses, which had been mostly from party organisers, people who wanted to be in her good books and used the play on her name as an excuse to remind her of their existence. There were just four words.

"For my first Valentine."

Gemma had been seriously impressed and it took a lot to impress her.

'Any scoops, Louise?' Glad of the distraction, she turned to the photographer. 'Anything we can phone in to the news desk?'

Several sets of tantrums, a lot of tears—not all of them from the women—but nothing unusual on an occasion so invested with emotion.

'You know the secrets of the dining table are sacrosanct, Pete.'

'What about you?' he asked, changing tack. 'Rumour has it that Max was seen coming out of Garrard's earlier in the week.'

Garrard's? A visit to the royal jeweller's suggested he'd taken her words to heart, but she kept the cool smile in place, said, 'Now you're just fishing.'

'And I think I just got a nibble.' He grinned. 'You didn't deny it, you just changed the subject. As good as an admission from someone in PR.'

'Louise!' She turned as one of the waitresses put her head around the door. 'You're wanted.'

Max...

'Table three. He says he wants to thank you for introducing him to the girl he's with. At some party? They've just got engaged.'

'Oh, right. I'm coming,' she said, throwing a quick glance in the direction of Sloane Square. Stupid. He hadn't said he'd be early; it was just that she'd seen the champagne, was aware of an undercurrent of excitement, of furtive glances in her direction.

Max would be here. He'd promised.

He was busy. They were all busy, but he wouldn't let her down. Wouldn't let Bella Lucia down. This was BL's party as much as theirs...

* * *

Max hadn't banked on being saddled with the girlfriend.

'I have to go with him,' she said. 'He might die.'

There was no time to argue and he bundled her in, making the hospital in record time, but that wasn't the end of it.

'Call my wife,' Prideaux begged. 'Tell her where I am.' Then, 'Make sure Gina gets home safely.'

The words said one thing, his eyes said another, sending out a desperate plea to get the girl out of the way before his wife turned up.

Easier said than done. Gina was having hysterics and convinced her lover was about to die, was vowing never to leave his side.

It took him and two nurses to prise her from Charles Prideaux's side, get her out of the treatment room. At which point she flung herself, sobbing, into his arms.

As he comforted her, absently reassured her, he stared at the clock, ticking remorselessly round to eleven. Louise wouldn't expect him before half past.

There was time.

It took patience, endless tact, to get Gina calmed down, to explain that the hospital had called Charles's wife, that she would have to leave.

When he thought that she'd finally got it, that he could put her in a taxi and go to Louise, she sat down in the waiting room in the manner of a woman who was not to be shifted.

'Let her come. She needs to know about us. That Charles is going to leave her.'

He didn't care about her. Or Charles Prideaux.

He did care about some innocent woman who'd walk into this. He knew what that was like. He'd seen it happen three times. Seen the fallout. The agony. And not just for the women involved, but for the children.

'Gina, this isn't the moment. Charles isn't in any state to cope with this kind of emotional upheaval. He needs to be calm right now if he's going to make any kind of recovery.'

The tears started again, but she didn't resist as he steered her through the main doors. 'Where do you live?' he asked.

'Battersea.'

He took a deep breath. 'I'll take you home.'

'It's okay, Max. You've done enough. I'll get a taxi.'

He would have liked nothing better, but he didn't trust her. She was an actress looking for an easy route to stardom. Why else would she be out with a married man twice her age? There was no doubt in his mind that the minute he left her, she'd be back inside, waiting for Mrs Prideaux to arrive. Act out her big scene. She'd quite possibly call the tabloids to make sure she got maximum publicity, too.

'Charles asked me to make sure you get home safely, Gina,' he said. 'And that's what I'm going to do.'

She swore, then. Proving he'd been right. Ignoring her rage, he opened the car door and after a moment she got in.

He took a breath. A result. Now all he had to do was call Louise, put her in the picture. Even as he reached for his cell phone he realised he didn't have it with him. They were forbidden in the restaurant and he always made a habit of putting his away in the office.

Half an hour. He'd be there.

Max hadn't come.

She had watched the staff from the Chelsea restaurant arrive, but he wasn't with them. She'd waited for someone to pass on a message, some explanation of the hold-up. She had imagined car accidents, every kind of disaster.

Even his father had been concerned. Max was, after all, the host this year. This was his party. His celebration. His role to thank everyone for their hard work.

She'd heard Robert ask Stephanie, her half-brother Daniel's wife and the Knightbridge restaurant's manager, where he was. But she'd shaken her head.

'He left at about ten. Everything was running smoothly. I assumed he was coming here.'

Louise was standing outside in the small courtyard in front of the restaurant where, in the summer, people liked to eat alfresco. It was empty now, too cold to tempt anyone outside. She stood listening to his cell phone ring. The voicemail click in, his familiar voice asking her to leave a message, that he would get back to her.

He wouldn't.

He'd tried. She understood that. Knew that if he'd ever loved anyone, he'd loved her. But it hadn't been enough. He still couldn't break free, make that leap to commitment. Maybe it had been wrong of her to expect it. He was who he was. The result of his upbringing, just as she was. Nurture over nature. She'd gone into this with her eyes open, expecting, wanting, no more than a brief, exciting affair.

She'd had that.

And it had been exciting. Wonderful. And it was over.

She turned as the door opened behind her. Her parents were leaving.

'Louise?' her mother said. 'What are you doing out here on your own?'

'I just needed some air. Are you leaving?'

'It's been a long evening. I don't want your father overdoing things.'

'I suspect he's made of sterner stuff than you give him credit for,' Louise said, with a smile she dredged up from the soles of her designer shoes.

'Any sign of Max?' her father asked, glancing at the phone in her hand.

She snapped it shut. 'No.' Then she shivered despite the warmth of her coat. 'To be honest I'm about done here.'

Done with Max. Done with Bella Lucia. Done with the icy damp of a London winter.

'Do you want a lift home?'

'It'll take you out of your way.'

'No problem.' He ushered her into the back seat next to her mother, then, having given the driver her address, climbed in next to her.

Neither of them mentioned Max again. Instead as they headed towards Kensington her mother chatted brightly about a holiday they were planning, doing their best to distract her so that she didn't have to do more than drop in the occasional "umm". Pretty much all her aching throat could manage.

'Louise?' Her mother took her hand, stopped her before she left the car. 'Are you going to be all right?'

'Fine,' she said, pulling herself together, pasting on a smile, hugging them both, fiercely. 'Fine. I'll call you tomorrow.'

The red light on her answering machine was winking at her as she let herself in. She switched it on and it informed her that she had 'one new message'.

'Lou? It's Cal. I'll be in London tomorrow—' She switched it off. He might be, but she wouldn't.

'Have you seen Louise?'

He knew he was in trouble.

It had taken hours to get rid of Gina. She'd had him driving round in circles, taking out her anger, her disappointment, on him. He would have appealed to her better nature, assuming that she had one, but he doubted that a plea to smooth his own path to married bliss would have moved her to pity.

He'd gritted his teeth, telling himself that Louise would have heard what had happened, understand why he had been held up. That he hadn't stood her up for Bella Lucia.

The party seemed to be in its final stages. Slow music, couples wrapped in each other's arms. His father was sitting in the bar, a glass of malt in his hand. Wife number four, Bev, was vainly trying to get him to leave.

'Lost her, have you? Careless that. But you're a Valentine. We're made that way.'

'She's gone, Max,' Bev told him. 'I put my head out of the door for some fresh air and saw her leaving with John and Ivy.'

'Uh-oh. You are in serious trouble,' his father said, pointing at him with the glass, which was clearly not his first.

'More serious than you know.'

'You were supposed to make a speech, too. Or had you forgotten that? Thanks for all the hard work. Great year. Expansion…'

And the rest. The extra bit about Louise Valentine making him the happiest man alive.

He'd got that wrong, too.

Again.

If he hadn't bottled out of the gala, tonight wouldn't have been such a huge, make-or-break deal.

He hadn't been putting nearly enough effort into making her the happiest woman...

It was very late when he pulled up in front of Louise's apartment, but he couldn't let her go to sleep believing that he'd let her down. He had to explain. And when he looked up he could see that there were lights on. Despite his relief that she was still awake, he suspected that was not a good sign. It was the same intuition that warned him not to use the key she'd given him, but ring the bell.

'Yes?'

'I need to talk to you, Louise. To explain.'

He'd anticipated resistance, but she buzzed him up without comment. She was still wearing her evening clothes. A dark red figure skimming dress that was slit to the thigh.

'You look lovely,' he said, moving to kiss her.

'Thank you,' she said, turning away before he could touch her.

He'd expected a rocket. Missiles. Fire.

Her cold politeness was much, much worse. He prayed that she was simply thinking of her neighbours...

'Look, I'm sorry I didn't get to the party before you left.' She waited, her back to him, very still. 'I had to take a guest to the hospital. Charles Prideaux, the actor.'

'Really? I hope he gave you his autograph.'

'Surely someone told you?'

'No one knew where you were.' She spun round to face him. 'Forget me for a moment, Max. That we had a date. That you were going to turn up with the ring and we were going to announce our engagement. You let down your staff, too.'

'Lou...' He hadn't anticipated this kind of reaction. Louise, calm, was a whole new experience and he didn't know how to get through to her. 'I had to take the man's girlfriend home. Before his wife arrived. She was difficult.'

'That was not your problem, Max.'

'Yes, dammit, it was. She was going to stay and make a scene. Confront his wife.'

'And you thought it was your duty to protect the man from the fallout of his infidelity?'

'Protect his wife.'

'Of course. My mistake.'

'You do understand, then?'

'Yes, Max. I understand.'

She didn't sound as if she did. If she'd understood, she'd have put her arms around him and held him and made the whole hideous episode go away.

Louise looked at him, confused, a little angry, and thought her heart might just break.

When she'd heard the car draw up outside, had looked out and seen it was Max, her first thought had been to ignore him. She'd used the deadlock on the door so he couldn't get in. Then he'd rung the doorbell, taking her by surprise, and she'd known that wouldn't do.

She owed herself more than that. She needed to face him. Put an end to this once and for all. She'd buzzed him up and then slipped out of her wrap and back into her dress. Stepped into shoes that brought her nearly to his height. Full body armour.

She'd wanted him to see that after tonight there was nothing he could do or say that could provoke her into anger, or reduce her to tears. But even then, some little part of her heart had hoped that he'd find a way to touch her. Bring her back to life.

But she couldn't allow it.

Tonight he'd not only stood her up, but he'd stood up Bella Lucia to save some sham of marriage. Still trying, in his head, to protect his mother from his father's infidelity. To save himself from the fallout.

And he had no idea what he'd done. He thought he could brush it aside, that all he had to do was turn up, explain and everything would be all right.

'Is that it?' she asked.

'You want me to go?'

He sounded surprised.

'You've apologised, explained. What else did you have in mind?'

'Don't be like this, Louise. It was a genuine emergency.'

'You should have called an ambulance.'

'Believe me, I wish I had.' Then, 'I have the ring…' He reached into his ticket pocket, produced a perfect diamond solitaire.

'So it's true. You did find time to visit Garrard's?' She took the ring from him before he did anything as hideous as taking her hand and placing it on her finger.

He frowned. 'How did you know that?'

'One of the photographers outside the restaurant said you'd been seen there.' She moved it so that the diamond flashed fire, burning her with its brilliance. 'Be prepared to read about it in the *Courier's* Diary column tomorrow.'

She took one last look at it, then handed it back.

'You don't like it?'

'It's quite lovely, Max.' But too late. 'Unfortunately if you married me you'd be committing bigamy. You're already married to Bella Lucia.'

'That's ridiculous!'

'Is it? Really?' She considered trying to explain. That she wasn't turning him down just for herself, but for him, too. That forcing him to put her first was hurting him as much as always coming a poor second was hurting her. They were bad for each other. But it was too late. She was too tired. And he wouldn't believe her anyway. Better to keep it simple… 'You did understand what I said on the last occasion you stood me up? You do recall asking for one last chance?'

'Yes, but…'

'But?' She shook her head. 'Don't bother to answer that, Max. There is no "us".'

'If you'd been there…' he said, a little desperately. Then, angry at being backed into a corner, 'I don't know what you expect—'

'I expect nothing from a man who would put business before life.' Her throat was beginning to ache. The words were becoming harder. 'Of a man who is incapable of doing anything else.'

It was why she hadn't leapt in with an eager 'yes' the instant he'd asked her to marry him, she understood that now. Some inner sense of self-preservation had come to her rescue. The small, still voice of common sense telling her that, no matter what he said, he could never change. That she would always be waiting for him to turn up. To a party, their marriage, the rest of their lives.

If she'd made a promise to him nothing short of an act of God would have stopped her from delivering on it, but there was no point in telling him that. All that remained now was pride. The need to walk away with her head high.

'What we had was great while it lasted, Max, but if we're honest it was just sex. Steamy, memorable sex, but nothing more than the gratification of old desires.' The casually dismissive words seemed to be coming from someone else. 'Curiosity satisfied, ghosts laid,' she said. 'Now, we can both move on.'

'No! I don't want to move on. I love you!'

'Need, desire…'

Love was something else. Something more. It was because she loved him that she couldn't stay with him. Knowing that each time he let her down he'd feel more guilt…

Another minute, she begged, enough strength for just one more minute…

She hadn't needed a ring, or even for him to say the words. The words meant nothing. 'I love you' was in what you did, the way you treated someone.

This was how James must have felt, she realised. Maybe she deserved this numbing blow to her heart that, for the moment, left her beyond feeling. She should be grateful for that reprieve, however short. The pain would come soon enough, but it was a familiar heartache. She'd lived with it before. Through all the years when he was out of reach. She could live with it again. For the moment all she asked was the strength to finish it without falling apart and she crossed to the door, opened it, a silent invitation to leave.

For a long moment Max didn't move. He just looked at her with the bewildered expression of a child who'd been shouted at and didn't know why.

He just didn't get it. Never would…

'Please…' she said.

It sounded too much like a plea, too weak and in two strides he was beside her. For a moment she thought he was going to seize her, kiss her as he had before when she'd been on the point of walking away. But this time he just stood there, looking at her as if he was imprinting her image on his brain. Or maybe that was her, taking one last look…

'I'll see you tomorrow?' he asked, finally. 'At six-thirty?'

Business as usual? Was he serious?

It was too much…

'You will be there?' he pressed when she didn't answer.

She shook her head, but he didn't take it as a refusal, only as an admission that she didn't know.

'You're exhausted,' he said. 'We'll talk about this tomorrow.' And then he walked through the door she was not so much holding open as clinging to, down the stairs, out of her apartment. Out of her life.

It was all she could do not to call him back but she hung onto her sanity just long enough to hear the street door close. To close and lock her own front door.

It was only when she heard his car start, pull away from the kerb, that all the bottled up emotion shattered and she picked up her answering machine and hurled it at the wall, where it broke in a dozen pieces, along with her heart.

CHAPTER ELEVEN

MAX left because she'd given him no other option. Louise had somehow managed to blank herself off from him, put herself some place far beyond the flare-up of temper that would have worked for him. He could have used her passion to break her down, bring her into his arms, but she'd put up a wall of ice to keep him out.

That in her own living room at close to two o'clock in the morning, she'd been wearing high heels, a dress he knew she'd have discarded for the comfort of her wrap the minute she'd got home, told him that it was deliberate. That she was playing a part.

The fact that she was still awake, clearly hadn't even thought about bed, bothered him more. She hadn't removed her make-up, and her hair was pinned up in that sexy way that suggested all it would take was one pin to bring it all tumbling down in his hands.

It all suggested that sleep had been the last thing on her mind. That she had more important things to do...

He pulled over, turned in his seat to look back. Her light was still on and for a moment he was tempted to go back, do anything, promise anything...

No.

She'd made it clear that she thought his promises were meaningless, and she was right. He'd been making promises to her all his life and then letting her down.

He needed to think about that. Really think about it before he could go back, attempt to change her mind, convince her that he wanted to be with her for the rest of his life. He had to ask himself not what he wanted, but what Louise wanted from their relationship. And why he wasn't giving it to her.

She'd told him all he needed to know, but, convinced that the proposal was nothing more than formality, he hadn't bothered to use the information. Analyse it. Hadn't listened to what she'd been telling him.

What three words would you use to describe yourself...?

Driven. Dumb. Dumped.

Louise went back to her packing. Concentrating on folding, packing. It took a while. She'd need suits as well as holiday clothes for this trip.

The last time she'd gone to Melbourne, she'd been running away from one family, searching for a new one. This time was different. This time she was reclaiming her life from a crippling obsession that had held her in its thrall since childhood hero-worship of Max had changed into something out of reach. Ultimately destructive.

She should have had a husband, children of her own by now, but there was no going back.

She didn't have a family of her own and it seemed unlikely that she ever would have. But she did have a thriving business and a talented assistant whom she was ready to make a partner.

Gemma could bring in a junior, continue to run the London office. She, in the meantime, would concentrate on expanding her own business. Stop scanning the horizon for something, someone, who would never be there.

Her phone began to ring. It was the airline confirming her seat on the evening flight out of London Heathrow.

That was something her contact at the diary page of the *Courier* would be interested in, she thought. An unmistakable message that even Max would understand.

And a kindness. In his anger, he'd blame her. She didn't want him to feel guilty. He was how he was. He couldn't help it.

She'd call Gemma first thing, catch her before she left for the office and brief her about everything that had to be done. She'd better call Patsy, too, in case there was anything she wanted to send to Jodie. Then she'd spend the day with her parents out at Richmond Hill before going straight on to the airport.

Max...

He'd asked her if she planned keeping their six-thirty date. Well, it was just business, so it didn't matter if it was Gemma who delivered the completed marketing plan which was, even now, sitting on her desk waiting to be delivered.

At six-thirty, she'd be unfastening her seat belt. Settling in for the long flight east.

She replaced the receiver, then bent to pick up the pieces of broken answering machine that were spread all over the carpet.

Under one of the larger pieces, she found a tiny gold safety pin. She looked at it for a moment, sitting back on her heels, wondering how on earth it could have got there. Even if she'd dropped it, and she couldn't imagine how since the only pins she had were kept in the carryall she used for work or travelling, her cleaner had been in yesterday morning and she wouldn't have missed it.

She reached out a finger and touched it, remembering the moment when she'd given one exactly like it to Max. How he'd taken it. Put it in his ticket pocket, next to his heart.

It had been a special moment. A moment when anything might have happened. When it *had* happened.

No regrets.

She'd got what she'd wanted. If it hadn't worked out quite the way she'd expected, if she hadn't managed to get Max out of her system, she still had more than she'd ever dreamed possible. She'd dared to risk everything and, even if she didn't have Max, she had somehow reclaimed her life. No more deep freeze...

She picked up the pin, placed it on the table beside the broken bits of answering machine, then frowned as she remembered the moment Max had pulled that damned ring out of the same pocket.

No. It couldn't be. He'd been wearing a dinner jacket tonight.

For it to be the same pin, he'd have had to move it from suit to suit along with the rest of the contents of his pockets that he carried with him, always.

'It doesn't mean anything,' she whispered. 'It's just habit…'

But even as she said the words a tear welled up, fell. Soaked into the carpet.

Max hadn't slept. He'd spent the night thinking. About Louise. About himself. About the bleakness of a future in which she wasn't there at the start and end of every day.

Shining a light into every corner of their relationship, exposing feelings that he'd always refused to acknowledge, finally understanding a pattern of behaviour that had ended in that scene last night.

Searching for some way to show her that, despite everything he'd done, he was serious. That she was more important to him than a hundred restaurants. That he loved her…

He woke, groggy, just before ten, still in the armchair, an idea, half formed, struggling to the surface. He showered, shaved. Resisted the urge to go straight to her office and tell her what he was going to do.

Six-thirty. That was their time.

It would give him time to put his plan into action so that she'd understand that it wasn't some empty promise.

She had to understand.

It was his secretary, bringing in the mail, who looked doubtful. She listened to him telling the company lawyer to set the wheels in motion, insisting that it be done in time for his daily meeting with Louise, then, when he rang off, said, 'Are you expecting Louise this evening?'

'Has she called to say she can't make it?'

'No, but…'

'But what?'

She went and fetched the early edition of the *Courier*, folded it back at the diary page.

In between a torn heart, one enclosing a photograph of Louise, one of himself, was the headline:

"NO DIAMONDS FOR THESE VALENTINES…

Expectations were high of an announcement that Max Valentine had popped the question to his latest squeeze,

Louise Valentine, at the Bella Lucia Diamond Jubilee party last night. Max, who has been working with Louise on the expansion of the restaurant group, with new premises in Qu'Arim and Meridia already well in hand, was spotted recently in the Queen's jewellers, Garrard's, investing heavily in a girl's best friend.

Max, however, wasn't at the party and I have it on good authority that London's favourite PR consultant has already booked her business class ticket and is at this very moment packing her bags, preparing to hotfoot it to Australia, eager to expand her own expire.

He didn't stop to question the veracity of this statement. It rang too horribly true. Instead he raced to her apartment, grabbed the front door as someone was leaving and raced upstairs, hammered on the door to her apartment.

It was opened by Cal Jameson.

'Max,' he said. 'Louise said to expect you.'

'She's here?' Relief flooded through him. 'I have to see her, tell her…'

'She was leaving as I arrived,' Cal said. 'Gave me a key, told me to make myself at home. I'm staying for a week this time—'

'Where is she?' he demanded, cutting him short. He wasn't interested in Cal Jameson's plans. Only in finding Louise.

'I couldn't say *exactly*. Somewhere between here and Melbourne. That's in Australia,' the younger man added helpfully.

'She's gone? Already?' Max clawed back his hair. 'She can't have. What about work? Her parents?'

'Damm it, Max. You've got it bad. You need a drink—'

'I don't want a drink. I just want—'

'Louise. I know, mate. I know. You'd better come in.'

Louise gripped the arms of the seat, hating the moment of take-off. Hating the moment when the huge jet banked over London. Letting out a sigh of relief as the ping of the seat-belt warning light went off.

A stewardess offered her a drink, but she shook her head. No alcohol, minimum food, lots of water. And sleep. She needed sleep. At least the unexpected upgrade from club to first class gave her all the stretch room she needed.

She even had an empty seat beside her.

No one to disturb her while she laid out her plans for expansion into Australia, she congratulated herself. No one to disturb her, ever again.

It couldn't be more perfect, she told herself as she bent to retrieve her laptop at her feet.

Then someone took the seat beside her.

She glanced sideways at her new companion, nodding distantly, not making eye contact — the last thing she wanted was a chatty travelling companion—then did the fastest double take in history.

'Max!' His name was expelled on what felt like the last breath in her body. Then, 'What are you doing here?'

'It's six-thirty,' he said. 'We always meet at this time of day.'

'But Gemma was going to—'

'Stand in for you? While I'm sure she's a perfectly capable young woman, that wasn't the deal we made. And as I'm sure you'll recall, Louise, I paid in advance.'

She gasped. 'I can't believe you just said that.'

'Of course you can. You can believe anything of me. The fact that you'd get on an aircraft and run away to the other side of the world to avoid me proves it.' He opened his briefcase, took out a thick envelope. 'Not that I don't appreciate it,' he said. 'It has given me an opportunity to demonstrate just how serious I am when I tell you that I'll never stand you up again.'

'I'm not running away!' she said, fiercely. 'This has nothing to do with you, Max. This is about me. I've spent my whole life wanting something just out of reach. It's time to grow up, move on, live the life I've got, not the one I dreamed…'

She applied the brake to her mouth, but not soon enough.

'Not the life you dreamed of?' he asked, gently.

'Not all dreams are good dreams, Max.'

'No. And not all mistakes are bad.' He leaned back, closed his eyes momentarily. 'Not that last night was a mistake. I did what I thought was the right thing, Louise. I can't change who I am.'

'I know. I understand…'

'It was all the other times that I got it wrong. But maybe not entirely wrong.'

Louise swallowed. 'No?'

Oh, that hurt. For the last sixteen sleep-deprived hours, she'd been too numb for the pain to bite, but suddenly, hearing Max say that one word brought her whole body to agonising life and she had to bite back the cry of pain.

'No,' he repeated, then rolled his head to look at her. 'How else would I have known how it would feel to lose you? How much it would hurt?'

No, no, no… 'Please, Max, don't do this.'

'I have to. I have to explain. If, when I've done, you don't want me here, I'll move to another seat. Go away. Never bother you again.'

That wasn't what she wanted to hear, either, but she took in a deep breath, let it out. Nodded.

'I spent most of the night thinking about us. About how, all my life, I've been pushing you away. Not just the surface stuff, avoiding each other, making sarcastic comments about the boys, the men who trailed after you like puppies. Deeper than that.'

'I didn't know there was anything deeper,' Louise said. Then shook her head. It was so easy to fall into the habits of a lifetime. Dangerous. Sniping led to anger and anger led to passion. And after passion there was only pain…

'I thought about the night I was supposed to take you to your school prom,' Max said, not rising to it. 'We were short-staffed, I didn't lie about that, but if I'd said to Dad that I had to go, reminded him that Uncle John had asked me to be your escort, he'd have found someone to cover.'

'You were more interested in the business even then, Max.'

'No. The truth is that your father had drafted me in as a safe pair of hands, someone he could rely on not to forget himself with "his little princess", was the way he put it. I knew just how you'd look. Sweet, innocent, in a demure frock but with that look in your eyes that said everything. A look I'd have to resist or burn in hell.'

'You were so wrong about that.'

'Wrong?'

'Anything but sweet and innocent. I had a killer dress stashed away in my bag and I had designs on you. You were right to run scared.'

'Really?' A ghost of a smile lit up eyes that were grey with tiredness. 'Uncle John nearly scalped me for standing you up. What he'd have done if he'd even suspected…'

'It didn't happen.' She found an answering smile from somewhere. 'I suppose I should thank you for saving me from myself.'

'I haven't finished, yet. There was the time you were flying to Italy. A year older, you were learning to hide your feelings, but I didn't want you to go. I knew those Italian men would be all over you. That they could have what I wanted.' He dragged his hand over his face. 'When you came back, I could see…'

'What could you see, Max?'

'One look was all it took. One look and I knew that you'd taken that step away from me. I thought something inside me had died.'

'Only thought?'

'When you dropped that slinky dress at your feet,' he said, with a grin, 'I realised it had only been wounded.'

'His name was Roberto,' she told him, by way of punishment. 'Six-foot two, short dark hair, blue eyes.' She shook her head, realising, too late, that she wasn't punishing him, but herself. 'I knew by then that I couldn't have you. Mustn't want you. He was the nearest I could get.' Then, desperate to put that behind her, 'This is ancient history, Max.'

'But don't you see, Lou? It established a pattern. Last week's kitchen flood was just the latest in a long line of similar excuses.'

'But we were together.'

'Were we? Hiding away as if we were ashamed of our feelings?' She waited. 'This was different, Louise. You'd asked me out on a date and it wasn't like dinner with Patsy and Derek—something that could be brushed off as a family thing. It would have been just the two of us at a gala where we'd be recognised by half the audience. You were ready to make that statement, say to the world we're a couple, while my sub-conscious was still programmed to sabotage anything that seemed like a relationship. That was anything more than sex.'

'Is that supposed to be some kind of excuse?'

'Yes. No… I'm just trying to explain that this is what I've been doing all my life. Running away from you. Unable to commit to anyone else. Telling myself that love is fool's gold, no more than a meaningless convention to lend the lustre of respectability to baser desires. A lesson I learned at my father's knee.'

'So?'

'So last night wasn't like that. I was frantic. I couldn't leave that stupid girl. I didn't have my cell phone to call you. But I was sure someone would have told you what happened. I only learned today that Jane, the one person who knew the whole story, had been too shaken up by the incident to come to the party.'

'Oh.'

'Last night I tried to help someone in trouble. You need to know that I'll always do that, even when it isn't convenient. Even when it's downright inconvenient. Just as you need to know that I will always put you before Bella Lucia. I meant what I said the other night. I love you.'

He produced the ring from his pocket, held it in the palm of his hand. 'You can stop looking at the horizon, Lou. I'm here. This is yours. Along with my heart.'

When she didn't take it, he closed his hand around it, took a document from the envelope, tucked the ring inside.

'Maybe this will convince you I'm serious.'

'What is this?'

'A partnership in Bella Lucia.'

'A partnership?' For a moment she didn't know whether to laugh or cry. Did he really think that would make a difference?

'An equal partnership. Take it, Louise, be my partner in every-thing, or I'm going to quit the business.'

What? 'You can't do that, Max. It's your life.'

'No, you are my life. And without you…' she waited '…what would be the point?'

Her words. What she'd said to him. When he'd asked her why she'd stopped dating. What would have been the point?

'What, my love? You think I don't know? You think I haven't been there? One woman in my arms and another so deeply ingrained in every cell that nothing I do can drive out the thought of her?'

She searched his face, saw the truth. That he had reached deep, found something within himself. Surrendered himself in a way that she'd never thought possible.

Not that he wouldn't get distracted, drawn towards some new scheme and forget everything else for a moment. But it would be the normal distractions that everyone lived with. He would never be running from her again.

'What would you do?' she asked. 'If I said no?'

'Become a beach bum,' he said. 'Take up surfing. Cal Jameson promised to give me lessons.'

'Cal?'

'He was the one who found out what plane you were on. Organised the upgrade so that I could sit beside you.'

'You mean it wasn't just luck? That you paid…' She frowned. 'So where were you? Why did you wait until we'd taken off?'

'Our date was for six-thirty. It was the one time I knew you'd be thinking of me.'

'Oh.'

'And I wanted to be sure you couldn't walk away. And once I'd shown the stewardess the ring, she let me stay in club class until after take-off.' He picked it up, held it between his thumb and finger. 'Will you marry me, Louise?'

'A beach bum?' she said. Then, laughing, 'You are such a liar, Max Valentine.' But she held out her left hand, allowed him to slip the ring onto her finger. Kiss her.

'Shall we get married in Queensland?' he asked.

'I'm not going to Queensland. I'm going to Melbourne to open my Australian office,' she reminded him.

'Yes, I saw your little goodbye note in the *Courier*, but I'm going to Queensland. I've been given a lead on a fabulous new resort opening up there. Rainforest. The barrier reef. A marina…'

'Sounds wonderful.'

'So come and give me your opinion. Then I'll help you set up your own empire if that's still what you want.'

'Mmm. Maybe I should think about that. As a partner in Bella Lucia, I'm going to have other responsibilities.'

'As my wife, the mother of my children and a partner in Bella Lucia, you may have a point.'

'As my husband and the father of my children, you're going to be pretty busy yourself.'

'So, we have a deal?'

'No, we have a partnership, but forget the quiet wedding, Max. This time you have to turn up and face the music, a full dress occasion with a dozen bridesmaids, emotional family members and enough rose petals to scent all of Richmond Hill. She grinned. 'Do you think you can manage that?'

'Wild horses wouldn't keep me away.'

'Well, just in case you need reminding,' she said, unfastening a tiny gold pin from under the collar of her jacket, transferring it to his, 'you'd better have this. Don't lose it again.'

Louise was driven to her wedding in a ribbon-bedecked open carriage drawn by two white horses, her father at her side.

At the church gate, she was met with a barrage of photographers eager to get pictures of the high-society guests, of the bride herself. Inside the church porch, Jodie, who'd flown over for the wedding to be her matron of honour, was waiting to straighten her veil and train.

She had the bright nosegay of tiny bridesmaids, the daughters of Bella Lucia staff, each wearing a dress a different shade of pink from palest rose to darkest fuchsia, as well as two distinctly unimpressed page boys, firmly in hand and they all fell in behind the bride and her father without a fuss.

'The groom did manage to turn up, then?' John Valentine asked the verger.

'Oh, very eager, sir. First to arrive. I always think that's a good sign.'

'Hmmph. Well, yes, I'm sure you're right.'

Louise smiled behind her veil. She hadn't doubted Max, not for one moment. It wasn't that he never missed a date, but these days he never failed to phone and let her know if he was having a problem. If he'd be late.

'Ready?' the verger asked.

'Ready,' Louise assured him. 'And just as eager as the groom.'

A signal was given and as the first notes of the Wedding March reached them she leaned against her father just for a moment and said, 'You have been the best father a girl could ever have. Thank you.'

For once lost for words, he just squeezed her hand in reply, tucked it beneath his arm before setting off with her up the aisle.

The church was full, not just with their parents, but crammed with Valentines from all over the world. Rachel, Luc and their baby, Rebecca, Mitch and their children, Emma, Queen of Meridia, with her king, Melissa, who had eyes for no one but her sultan, thanks, it appeared, to a little help from Max, Jack with Maddie, Beverley. Daniel and Stephanie, and Dominic with his wife and children. Patsy and Derek were there somewhere, too, but Louise saw only one man. Not even his best friend, Sheikh Surum Al-Thani of Qu'Arim, in all his robes, standing at Max's side, could eclipse the joy shining from the vivid blue eyes of the man she had loved all her life. From this day forward they were to be together for always. Partners. Lovers. Friends. Husband and wife.

As she reached him he smiled, took her hand, raised it to his lips and a soft sigh rippled through the church. Then they turned to face the vicar and the service began.

'Dearly beloved…'

Only when the vicar asked, 'Who giveth this Woman to be married to this Man?' was there the slightest hiccup in the service. Instead of simply putting her hand into Max's, her father said, quite distinctly, 'Me. I do…'

Afterwards, in the vestry as they signed the register her mother scolded him, but he was unrepentant. 'I just wanted Max to know,' he said. 'I wanted everyone to know that I'm happy.' He turned to his brother, put his hand on his shoulder. 'Really happy. It's a wonderful day.'

Max and Louise stood at the head of the receiving line, to greet their guests as they arrived for the reception. The guest list of family and friends read like an international Who's Who. They had come from Australia, America, France, Meridia, Qu'Arim. Old family from Italy mingled with Ivy's aristocratic relations.

And there was Patsy.

She came in last with her new husband and Louise kissed them both, then turned to her mother and said, 'Mum, may I introduce Patsy Simpson Harcourt and her husband Derek. Patsy, this is my mother.'

For a moment both women seemed frozen, then Ivy Valentine stepped forward, put her arms around Patsy and said, 'Thank you. Thank you, Patsy, for giving me the most wonderful daughter any woman could ever ask for.'

Louise might have cried, but at that moment Jack tapped a spoon against a champagne glass and said, 'We're going to have the best afternoon and evening of our lives here, but before we get started I want us all to raise a glass in memory of William Valentine, who opened the first Bella Lucia restaurant sixty years ago and without whom we wouldn't be here today.'

A murmur of assent ran around the room.

'With Max and Louise now in charge the future is assured, so a toast to William Valentine and the great family he founded, to Bella Lucia. And to the next sixty years.'

'Sixty years?' Max looked adoringly at his bride. 'Are you game for that, my Valentine?'

'To be honest, I'm not into these short-term relationships,' she said, with an impish smile. 'But ask me again in sixty years. I'll give you my answer then.'

* * * * *

Beauty and the Reclusive Prince
by
Raye Morgan

"ENOUGH!"

Isabella Casali's cry was snatched right out of her mouth by the gust of wind that tore at her thick dark hair and slapped it back against her face. What a night she'd picked to go sneaking onto royal property. The moon had been riding a crest of silky clouds when she'd started out from the village. Now the sky had turned black and the moon was playing hide and seek, taking away her light just when she'd stepped on forbidden territory. Where had this sudden storm come from, anyway?

"Bad luck," she whispered to herself, squinting against another gust of wind. "I've got reams of it."

She knew she ought to turn and head for home, but she couldn't go back without finding what she'd come for—not after all she'd done to work up the nerve to come in the first place.

The grounds of the local prince's palazzo were famously said to be the stomping grounds for all sorts of supernatural creatures. She'd discounted it before, thought it was nothing but old wives' tales. But now that she'd come here and seen for herself, she was beginning to get the shivers just like everyone else. Every gust of wind, every snapping twig, every moan from the trees made her jump and turn to see what was behind her.

"You'd better hope the prince doesn't catch you."

Those words had made her smile when Susa, her restaurant's vintage pastry chef, had uttered them like an aging Cassandra just before Isabella had left for this adventure. Susa often had wise advice, but this time Isabella was sure she was off the beam. What had Susa said again?

"They say he patrols the grounds himself, looking for young women who stray into his woods…"

"Oh, Susa, please," she'd scoffed. "They've said the same thing about every prince who's lived in that old moldy castle for the last hundred years. The royal Rossi family has never been a very friendly bunch, from what I've heard. When you don't get out and mix with the citizens, you're bound to get a bad reputation."

She'd chuckled at the time, completely unconcerned, even though the royal grounds were the last place she wanted to venture onto anyway. Given a choice, she would have stayed home with a good book.

"But it's mostly because they're such a mystery," she continued, thinking it over. "I'll bet they're very nice people once you get to know them."

Susa raised her eyebrows and looked superior. "We'll see how nice you think he is when he has you locked up in his dungeon."

"Susa!" Isabella was reluctant enough to go on this mission without the older woman raising more reasons why she should just stay home.

"Besides, Papa has been sneaking in there to collect the *Monta Rosa Basil* we need for years and, as far as I know, he's never seen a royal person there yet. I don't believe a word of it."

Her father, Luca Casali, had discovered the almost magical properties of this fine herb years before and it had transformed his cuisine from average Italian fare into something so special people came from miles around just to get a bowl of exquisitely cooked pasta topped with the steaming tomato-based sauce Luca had come up with.

The special recipe and the herb were a closely held family secret. Only a few knew that the delicious flavor came from a plant that could be found only on a hillside located on the estate of the royal Rossi family in Monta Correnti.

For years, her father had gone once a month to collect the herb. Now he was ill and could no longer make the trip. It was up to Isabella to take up the mantle as herb-gatherer, reluctant as she might be. She'd decided she might have less risk of being caught at it if she went at night. She was a little nervous, but fairly confident. After all, her father had never had a problem. She told herself calmly that she would do just fine.

But that was before the storm came up, and the moon disappeared, and the wind began to whip at her. Right now, every scary rumor seemed highly plausible and she was definitely looking over her shoulder for marauding royalty.

Earlier, when the sun was still shining, she'd thought it might be interesting to meet the prince.

"What's he like, really?" she'd asked Susa. "When he's not enticing young women into his bedroom, at any rate."

Susa shrugged. "I don't know much about him. Only that his young wife died years ago and he's been sort of a recluse ever since."

"Oh." Isabella thought she'd heard something about that a long time ago, but she didn't remember any details. "How sad."

"They say she died under mysterious circumstances," the woman added ominously.

"Are there any other kind in your world?" Isabella shot back.

Susa gave her a superior look and turned away, but at the same time Isabella was remembering what Noni Braccini, the restaurant cook who had taught her most of what she knew about Italian cooking when she was a young girl, used to say.

"Nothing good could happen in a place like that." She would point a wrinkled finger toward where the old, crumbling palazzo stood and mutter, "Bats."

Isabella would look at her, nonplussed. "Bats?"

She would nod wisely. "Bats. You don't want bats in your hair."

Isabella would find herself smoothing down her own wild tresses and agreeing quickly, with a shudder. "No, no, indeed. I don't want bats in my hair."

And that was about all she knew about the prince in the castle. Of course, there was the fact that the essential herb grew on a hillside on castle grounds.

Noni had died long since, but Susa was still around to give dire warnings, and she'd said matter-of-factly as Isabella was going out the door, "When I was a girl, it was common knowledge that the Rossi prince was a vampire."

"What?" Isabella had laughed aloud at that one. "Susa, that's crazy!"

"He was the grandfather of this one." The older woman had shrugged. "We'll see, won't we?"

Isabella had laughed all the way to her car, but she wasn't laughing now. It wasn't just what Susa had said in warning. There were plenty of other old stories swirling in her head. Her childhood had been full of them—tales told in the dark at girlfriend sleepovers, stories of blackbeards who captured women and held them within the castle walls—vampires who roamed the night looking for beautiful victims with virgin throats—seducers with dark, glittering eyes, who lured innocent girls into their sumptuous bedrooms. Suddenly they all seemed too plausible. She was half regretting that she'd come to this frightening place at all, and half angry with herself for being such a wimp.

"Come on," she muttered to herself encouragingly. "Just a bit further and we'll get this done."

After all, how bad could it be? Even if she did run into the prince, he couldn't possibly be as wicked as Susa had painted him. In fact, she remembered seeing him once, years ago, when she was a teenager. She'd been visiting a hot springs resort area a few hours from the village and someone had pointed him out. She'd thought him incredibly handsome at the time—and incredibly arrogant-looking.

"The old royalty are all like that," her friend had said. "They think they're better than the rest of us. It's best to stay out of their way."

And she had, all these years. Now she was rambling around on royal grounds. The quicker she got this over with, the better.

Just a little further and she would find the hillside where the special basil grew, pick enough to fill the canvas bag she'd brought along, and head for home. Of course, it would help if she could see more than three feet in front of her with this stupid flashlight that kept blinking off.

"Oh!"

Her foot slipped and she almost tumbled down the hill. At least the problem with the flashlight was solved. It *did* tumble down the hill, and over a ledge, and into the river. Even above the noise of the wind, she could hear the splash.

Isabella wasn't one to swear, but she was working up to it tonight. What a disaster. What had she been thinking when she'd decided to come here all alone in the middle of the night? She'd known she was just asking for trouble.

"I just wasn't made for this cloak-and-dagger stuff," she muttered to herself as she tried to climb higher on the hill. All she wanted was to find the herbs and get out of here. She hated doing this. She dreaded getting caught by guards…or the prince. Or attacked by vampires—whichever came first.

The wind slashed through the tops of the trees, howling like a banshee. Lightning flashed, and in that same moment she looked up and saw a figure all in black atop a huge horse, racing down on her.

Time stopped. Fear clutched at her heart like a vise. This was too much. The dark, the wind, the sight of danger crashing toward her—had she taken a wrong turn somewhere? Suddenly, everything was upside down and she was terrified. Without a pause, she screamed at the top of her lungs. The sounds echoed through the valley, louder and louder, as lightning cracked and thunder rolled.

That lifetime of scary stories had set her up to think the worst. Every story flashed through her soul in an instant. She was shaking now, panic taking over, and she turned to run.

She heard him shout. Her heart was in her throat. She was dashing off blindly, startled as a cornered deer, and she heard him coming up behind her. The hoofbeats sounded like thunder striking stone, and his shout was angry.

She was in big trouble. He was going to catch her. She couldn't let that happen! She had to run faster…faster…

She couldn't run fast enough and she couldn't get her breath. Her foot slipped, wrenching her balance out from under her. She started to slide down the steep hill. Crying out, she reached to catch herself on a bush, but it pulled right out of the ground. Suddenly, she was tumbling toward the river.

She hit the water with a splash that sent a spray in all directions. She gasped as the icy water took her in. Now she was going to drown!

But she barely had time to reach for the surface before the strong arms of the man in black had caught hold of her and she was pulled instantly from the racing water.

He had her. Stunned by the cold, shocked by what was happening, she couldn't find her bearings. Disoriented in the moment, she realized dimly that she was being carried toward the horse, but she was a bystander, watching helplessly, as though from afar. For now, it seemed there was nothing she could do to resist.

Later, she was mortified as she remembered this scene. How could she have succumbed so quickly to the overwhelming sense of his strength like that? She'd just suffered a shock, of course, and that had pretty much knocked her silly, but still... As she remembered just how much the feel of his strong, muscular arms seemed to paralyze her reactions, she could do nothing but groan aloud in frustration. How could she have been such a ninny?

But in the moment, she was spellbound. The moon came out from behind the clouds, turning the landscape silver. Trying to look up at his face, all she could see was his strong chin, and the smooth, tight cords of his sculptured neck. And still, she couldn't seem to make a move.

Special thanks and acknowledgement are given to Raye Morgan for her contribution to The Brides of Bella Rosa series.

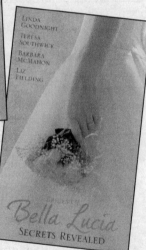

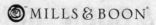

millsandboon.co.uk Community

Join Us!

The Community is the perfect place to meet and chat to kindred spirits who love books and reading as much as you do, but it's also the place to:

- **Get the inside scoop from authors about their latest books**
- **Learn how to write a romance book with advice from our editors**
- **Help us to continue publishing the best in women's fiction**
- **Share your thoughts on the books we publish**
- **Befriend other users**

Forums: Interact with each other as well as authors, editors and a whole host of other users worldwide.

Blogs: Every registered community member has their own blog to tell the world what they're up to and what's on their mind.

Book Challenge: We're aiming to read 5,000 books and have joined forces with The Reading Agency in our inaugural Book Challenge.

Profile Page: Showcase yourself and keep a record of your recent community activity.

Social Networking: We've added buttons at the end of every post to share via digg, Facebook, Google, Yahoo, technorati and de.licio.us.

www.millsandboon.co.uk

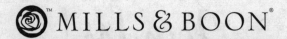